The Healer's Girl

Ande Li

808 ROOM 808 PRESS

Publishing Imprint for authors Maurice X. Alvarez & Ande Li

Copyright © 2017 by Ande Li at Room 808 Press

ISBN-13: 978-0-9834104-1-6
ISBN-13: 978-0-9834104-2-3

Source: Digital copy

Acknowledgements

Many thanks to my beloved family and friends, especially my ever-supportive husband and occasional co-writer/muse/therapist M.X.A.
Much gratitude and affection are also owed to my dear friends, who read for me and helped me tell 'Fleece's story in her truest voice.

Prologue

My days grow longer, but they feel shorter, and there are too few remaining. They feel numbered, as the humyn would say. It is clear that there will be no rest for me until I am reduced to ashes. She will not stop until I am dead, therefore, I must endure. Even if I am gone, I wonder whether it will be enough for her, or whether she will try to slaughter the last of us. I imagine that she would try, given the opportunity. Perhaps I would, too, if I were in her place.

Years ago, I would have never thought it possible, but I fear that my years of isolation have undermined our chances for survival. Malya and her allies have grown stronger, while I have weakened. Left unchecked, her power will be greater than mine, too soon, and that cannot be allowed. Perhaps a few more years will be all that I shall last, but a few more years are all that I need. This apprentice must not be allowed to surpass her mistress, regardless of the cost.

Today was an awful, black day for my Moonteyre. Never have I felt more at home than in this little elfyn village, and in return for their hospitality, I have brought these gracious people more suffering than I have spared. There have been so many pains to heal, so much to do, that I have neither the hours nor the strength to do it all. Even with all those that I helped today, I am bereft and frustrated by my limitations as a Healer. If I were to go, perhaps their ills would leave with me, but I cannot risk that I would only be abandoning them to a fate of extermination.

My sweet Rija died this morning from a hemorrhage. I was away with other patients when I was told the news of the sudden change in her condition, and I was too late in getting back. It happened in a matter of minutes. I feared the worst, but not all is lost. Before she died, Rija gave birth to Winter's second daughter. While he is mourning deeply, Winter remains strong for his girls. He was relieved that his second-born is beautiful and healthy, and he does not seem disappointed that his second child is also a girl. For that, I am truly heartened.

The infant has a crown of black curls, just as Winter and Frost had when they were born, so chances are that she, too, will shed the dark locks in time. I'm told that she screamed mightily as she emerged, with her eyes open wide and bright and furious, as though she already realized that something was wrong in her world. On first impression, they look like Winter's charcoal black eyes, but in the light they are as clear and as blue

1

as the night sky, just like our Rija's. As new and innocent as she is, the child has her mother's piercing stare, and I almost cannot stand to meet her eyes. It is my nerves, I know, to read so much into an infant's unfocused gaze, yet I already know her to be more than she appears.

Little Frost shows none of the jealousy that we had feared and, in fact, seems very fond of her baby sister. It is good that she does not equate her sister's birth with her mother's death. I should wonder about whether Frost is even aware of what has happened today, but I am inclined to believe that she knows more than she lets on. She is surprisingly mature for her five years.

Sadly, I cannot say the same for the rest of Winter's family. I fear that his siblings will shun the baby as they do him and Frost. When the two brothers came to see the child, their envy was plain in their eyes; they resent their niece's beauty and keen alertness, making disparaging remarks about how humyn she looks, and how garish her colors are. Winter himself did not bother answering his brothers' unkind words. He knows that his child is beautiful and healthy, and that is all he cares and wants to know.

I was not as gracious to Winter's kin. For once, I did not stay quiet. I had witnessed their appalling behavior too many times before: all the years of Winter's youth, when he and Rija were wed, when Frost was born, even when he built his home. Their father would be disgusted, if he were still alive, to see his sons behaving so callously towards their newly-widowed brother. I told them this, and many other things, maybe a bit too much. How priceless was the pallor in their faces! I will keep the image in a cherished place in the back of my mind, to dust off whenever I feel less than charitable towards them, which is more often than I would admit to Winter. They behaved themselves for the rest of their shortened visit. They respect me, as they should, but they also fear me, which pleases me more.

It is still too soon to tell how Rija's passing will affect the family she leaves behind. It has certainly reminded Winter of his own mortality. Earlier, while we sat together in the kitchen, he noted his baby's full head of hair, wondering when her true colors would come in. Then, in the next breath, he turned to me and asked if I would look after this daughter of his when he dies. Frost, he said, he knew would be fine, but this one would never truly know a mother's love.

What possessed him to say such a rueful thing? I know that he did not say it to be cruel, but his words stung me nonetheless. They served to remind me that, had I been more watchful with Rija, I might have saved her.

I answered him that yes, of course, I would watch over the girl. It did not occur to me to reply otherwise. I asked him what name he planned, desperate to change the topic.

Rija had been considering "Snow," he said, while he had been jokingly contemplating "Lambswool." They were taking the chance that the child would inherit Winter's white locks, and he was thinking of keeping one of the names in memory of Rija.

And if her hair stayed black, I asked him.

Winter grinned his wonderful, wistful smile. "Then she will be ironically named."

Chapter 1: Delicate Flowers

When my father died, he took a piece of my world with him. What remained behind was colder, less sweet, and irrevocably dimmed, and so was I.

He died in the late spring of 995, on the day I completed my fifteenth year. Winter was the only parent I had ever known, and during the year that followed his passing, my sister Frost and I grieved and recovered together. People were respectful, as Frost's beauty and grace evoked charity and sympathy from all. By contrast, I was considered unremarkable, even homely, by elfyn standards. However, I had the good fortune of being Frost's little sister so I, too, benefited from the kindness of others.

In the months that followed Winter's passing, I also had the Healer to counsel me. She had been fond of my father, for all the years that she knew him, and her affection had naturally extended to Frost and me. Occasionally, the Healer made brief stops to our house, to sit for tea or to sample from our herb garden, with her apprentice-of-the-moment in tow, and while they did not understand the history of our relationship, they did not dare to question her atypical cordiality. The Healer's apprentices never remained long in service, either by her choice or theirs. Of the dozens that I knew, a few stayed as long as months, and there was one who lasted less than a day. However, she never lacked for applicants, as she was the most renown healer in the Dark Lands, and even a brief stint with her was highly coveted.

Imagine my surprise, then, when on my sixteenth birthday and the anniversary of Winter's death, Healer Clyara asked if I wanted her to be my *keeron*, my mistress. Naturally, I accepted her offer. With a glint in her golden eyes, she promised me that it would change my life.

Exactly one week after that, Glory arrived at the Healer's doorstep. I didn't know who she was, but I sensed at once that she was unique, and that her visit was a harbinger of the change that Clyara had promised.

I had been dusting the top bookshelves, while the Healer was in her kitchen picking through her basket of fresh herbs. It was already dark outside, but I was in no hurry to return home, as I liked the studious clutter of Clyara's cottage. The air was laden with odors from the greens and the books, mixed with the Healer's own exotic scent. Her favored perfume was evocative of enduring substances like minerals and spices, rather than the transitory lushness of fruit or flowers, as was the fashion.

A knock sounded, the door creaked open, and I turned to greet our unexpected visitor.

I guessed it was a girl, from what showed of the slender build. The rest of her was hidden under a bark-brown woolen cloak and hood, despite the balmy spring weather. She was taller than my mistress, which was an exceptional trait. She closed the door quietly behind her and asked, "Is Clyara home?"

Hardly anyone called the Healer by name. Even the Elders of Moonteyre only ever called her "Healer," so the informality struck me. "Yes, she is. Is she expecting you?" I stood frozen in place, unsure yet of whether to call my mistress.

Thankfully, the Healer saved me from my dilemma and emerged from the kitchen. She seemed to recognize our visitor, but her reaction was difficult to read from her neutral expression. At last, the Healer said, "How did you find your way here?"

"I asked for you and was directed here," she said simply. "Am I not welcome?"

"Of course, you're welcome, always," my mistress said, more warmly. "I am just … surprised. Please, come in."

"Thank you, *Keeron*," the girl replied, her voice young and light in pitch. "I will not inconvenience you more than necessary." She lowered her hood to take off her cloak, and I nearly dropped my dust rag.

Whereas Clyara was tan, with dark eyes and straight, dark amber hair, the stranger was pink-skinned, with burnished citrine curls. The girl finally looked at me and smiled with an expression that resembled wonder. The color of her eyes was difficult to discern in the dim sitting room, but they were startlingly pale. I had never seen anyone like her before in my life.

Humyn. She's humyn. The folktales and legends told to me by my father often contained accounts of the strange, elusive beings from the fabled Fringe and the ancient Realm, creatures who sometimes ventured into the dense woods around our Dark Lands. These humyn had fair hair and eyes like this girl's. I couldn't see her ears, whether they were as small and rounded as chicken eggs, as described in the storybooks.

"Mind your manners, and don't gawp, Snowfleece," my mistress whispered, pushing the stranger's cloak into my hands. "Perhaps you could hang this up and make some tea for us, please." She stopped and looked at our guest sternly. "Glory, you know better than to hide your wound from me."

The girl straightened, and her hand went to her side immediately, and I saw a stain of red soaking through her dark clothes. "It's nothing, Clyara. A couple of bandages will take care of it."

5

"Snowfleece, put some extra water to boil," Clyara amended her order, and pointed to the one carved armchair in the room that wasn't occupied by bottles or books. "Sit, Glory, and tell me what happened."

In the kitchen, I set the kettle on the fire, hung the cloak and rushed back to listen at the kitchen door. It was frustratingly difficult to hear anything, and what words I did hear made no sense, if they were in the elfyn tongue at all. All became quiet, and I strained to hear.

"You may as well listen in here," Clyara's voice rang. "This concerns you, too."

I snatched a stack of towels and Clyara's basket of supplies and reentered reluctantly, chagrinned at being caught eavesdropping. Clyara was focused on her patient's left side, exposed to show a fresh red gash. Inured by past experiences of accompanying the Healer on her rounds, I was hardly moved anymore by the sight of a bloody laceration. I set the towels and basket next to Clyara and waited. I made an effort not to stare at the humyn.

Our guest smiled at me. "This is not the introduction I imagined in my head. My name is Glory, and it is a pleasure to meet you. Snowfleece, is it?"

"Are you humyn?" I blurted.

She wobbled her head, as if uncertain. "Humyn. Yes, I suppose you could call me that. My mother certainly was. She was your *keeron's* apprentice, many years ago."

"So, there are others like you?"

Glory laughed, her voice girlish without sounding frivolous. "Of course, there are others, many others, across the river, in the forest … everywhere but here, it seems. You're surprised?"

"I have told her nothing, yet," my mistress said, keeping a cloth pressed against the wound to staunch the blood. "She's only been with me a week, officially. Find me the fresh *rijkil*, Snowfleece."

"Only," Glory said, sobering. "Unfortunately, word has already reached Mother that young Zephyr is no longer serving you, so she is very interested in learning about your new apprentice."

I raked through Clyara's latest harvest gingerly, careful not to bruise the tender foliage and delicate blooms that she had picked that day. I found morels, foxgloves, wild sage… The *rijkil* was near the bottom, still warm from the late afternoon sun. Clyara had nipped the blossom underneath its sepals, so as to minimize the trauma for the plant. I cradled the dark blue bloom in my palm, careful not to disturb its tender, slender petals spiraling from its crimson heart like an indigo flame. The *rijkil* is one of the most delicate of flowers in the pine forests, and it was a rare find even then, before the days of the Expansion, and I marveled at it until Clyara plucked it from my hand.

She unceremoniously pulverized the dainty blossom between her palms and laid her blue-stained hands on Glory's side, making our patient wince with pain. "My apologies, my dear. This will only take a moment."

"As I was saying, our allies are minding the borders as well as they can," Glory said, between gritted teeth, "but even they can't keep all of my mother's spies out, not when she has the Imperial Guard at her disposal. Augus has effectively given her the throne."

"That was inevitable," Clyara said, "as are the leaks in intelligence. Our friends have already done more than enough, and I am indebted to them." She gave Glory a reassuring glance. "I still have tricks for managing the rest, not to worry."

"What does your mother want?" I interjected, passing a jar of salve to Clyara.

"She wants too much," Clyara answered for her. "The kettle is whistling, Snowfleece. Please tend to it," she nudged.

By the time I prepared the tray of tea and biscuits and returned to the receiving room, Clyara had finished her work, and Glory was sound asleep in her chair, her clothes neatly rearranged over her bandaged side. Clyara said a few blessing words under her breath and took a cloth that I had rinsed with scalding water, while I poured some tea for her.

"Thank you, 'Fleece," Clyara said, wiping her stained hands clean. "White tea and currant biscuits. You know my routine, already. Am I that predictable?"

I did not answer right away. Da had always taught me to be polite in the Healer's presence, and I could almost imagine him looking over my shoulder to make sure that I remembered my place. "I presumed that our guest may want some refreshment."

"She may want some when she wakes," she said, taking the cup from my hand and glancing at my expression. "What's that scowl about?"

"It's just that you called me 'Fleece."

"Doesn't everyone call you that?"

"Everyone else, yes," I said. With my hands free, I began to rub the etchings on the silver locket that I wore around my neck. I didn't enjoy having my hands idle, and touching the locket that once belonged to my father helped me feel close to him. "But you and my father always called me by my full name."

"What do you prefer?" she asked.

"I suppose 'Fleece is fine," I said, brushing back my heavy, tar-black curls. "The 'snow' part of my name doesn't seem to fit."

"There's still time," she said. She leaned against her desk and nodded to our sleeping patient. "So, do you believe that she is humyn?"

"Isn't that what she said?" Her pale yellow hair and pink skin were very convincing, not to mention her glass-green eyes, now shut in deep slumber.

"Do you always believe what others say?"

"Not always," I admitted. When my father died suddenly, there was gossip that he was killed by a jealous husband, or savaged by a pack of rabid wolves, although his body was found without any physical wounds. When the Healer's previous assistant left abruptly with his family, several weeks ago, theories had circulated that the Zephyrs had gone west towards the Lost Realm and perished, as no one had heard from them since then. "So much of it is rubbish. There's a rumor that I could be humyn, too."

Clyara shrugged and took another sip. "There's a theory that all of us are, to some extent. From where do you think our ancestors came, if not the Lost Realm, descended from the ancient humyn race?"

Remembering my history lessons, I was ready with the answer. "The books say the elfyn came from the north, and before that, they had crossed the Northern Sea from the far eastern continent that crumbled into the ocean. The ones that remained behind were lost. The scholar books don't mention humyn."

"So, you're quicker to believe what you read, than what you hear," she said.

It did sound odd, the way Clyara said it. Eager to switch the topic, I asked, "Why is Glory here? What does her mother want?"

Clyara returned to the tray to refill her cup and fill one for me. "Glory came to warn me, and also to get away from her mother, Ma-ly-a," she pronounced stiffly. "As for Malya, she just wants me dead."

"What?" I said, flabbergasted. "Why would anyone want to hurt you?"

"Because I tried to kill her first," Clyara said matter-of-factly. "Not at first, of course. It took a long while for us to reach that point in our relationship. Years before your parents were even born, Malya sought me out to become my student. I was impressed by her dedication and maturity, but over time, I realized that she was mad for knowledge and power," she said. "She was becoming too unstable for me to manage, and she was too dangerous to leave alone, so I did what I thought was best and tried to destroy her before she could turn on me."

It was inconceivable to me that the Healer would have wanted to harm anyone, and just as surprising to me was her calmness. "You're not a killer."

The Healer returned to Glory's side to check her bandage. "It was a long time ago," she said, "and I would certainly prefer a peaceful life for us all, but the feeling is not mutual. I imagine that Malya is furious about Glory's flight and betrayal, if she's sending assassins after her to silence her." She gestured to the soiled cloth that I had collected from the floor.

"Oh, be careful not to touch the orange stain, that's from a poisoned blade. A few hours more, and Glory would have been delirious, or unconscious."

I looked at Glory's innocently pretty face and was appalled that anyone would want to hurt her. I wondered what kind of life Glory was fleeing. "What kind of danger exists in the power to heal?" I asked, although I suspected I knew the answer. "Malya didn't just learn healing from you, did she?"

"Smart girl," Clyara smiled. "No, she learned many things from me. Some call what we do magic, sorcery, divine arts, what have you ... but, if abused, any kind of power can be dangerous, even the power to heal."

Clyara took my cup and the stained cloth and turned me towards the door. "It's late, 'Fleece, and I've kept you far longer than I intended. Tomorrow morning, when we've rested, we'll decide what to do next."

"I'm not tired," I said. I wanted to stay, to speak again with Glory when she awoke, and learn more about her.

"You're dismissed for the night, Apprentice." Her voice was soft, but the tone was unshakably firm. I knew better than to challenge my mistress further, especially so soon in my apprenticeship. "Go home and rest."

I arose earlier than the sun, unable to sleep with thoughts about Clyara, and about the humyn. Glory, I reminded myself. Her name is Glory. It was too early to go to the cottage, but I was too restless to stay in bed. I knocked on my sister's bedroom door and waited a beat. "Are you awake?"

"By Ajle, 'Fleece, it's still dark outside," Frost replied. Still, when she opened the door, she was dressed for the day, but her eyes were half-closed and her white locks half-combed. "How long did you stay at the Healer's last night? I didn't hear you —"

"Come to the river with me," I said, tugging her sleeve. "I want to see something."

Moonteyre was still dark, and the mountains in our backyard, bordering the eastern edge of town, the Ajlekyrn — Heaven's Fortress — were still cloaked in the late-night fog. Its highest peak, Ajlekuun — Heaven's Door — was hidden altogether. I led Frost west, past the outskirts of town and down to the jagged eastern bank of the Yirae River. I peered across to the distant opposite shore, where the skyward-spiraling evergreens seemed diminutive.

"What are you looking for?" Frost yawned. She tucked an errant silver curl behind her ear and followed my line of sight.

"Remember when Da used to take us across to the west bank?" While the traffic up and down the Yirae River was regular, the western bank was too rocky and treacherous for practically anyone except for thrill-seekers and intrepid lovers to venture too close, especially given the long hours required for the journey. Aside from the Healer, who went to gather herbs and mushrooms there, it seemed that only my father ever found it worthwhile to venture into the brooding evergreen forest, but after Glory's comments the night before, I had to wonder if there was more to see.

"He said he preferred the quiet on that side," Frost said. "More animals to hunt and trap there, too."

I nodded. "It helped that we weren't squeamish about handling little animals like other girls."

"You were practically the son he never had," Frost quipped. "What is this about?"

I looked at Frost squarely. "I met a humyn last night."

"You've finally lost your mind."

"Maybe. She said she was humyn. She came to the Healer's last night, and she said there are more of them in the woods, across the river. What if they're real?"

Frost took a breath, as if to speak, but she shook her head. "Let's suppose they are real. Why hasn't anyone seen them before?"

"Maybe they're hiding from us, for some reason."

"Maybe the Healer and this girl were just teasing you." Frost gestured over her shoulder at the village behind us. "Moonteyre has farmers and craftsmen. We're not threatening enough for anyone to want to hide from us."

I recalled Clyara's remarks about her former apprentice Malya but also considered the possibility that Frost was right, as she usually was. I was grateful for Frost's perspective, and I decided to start my eighth day of apprenticeship free of expectations about meeting any more humyn. As the sun lit the highest branches of the Ancient, Moonteyre's oldest and tallest oak tree and its village center, I parted ways with Frost and promised I would come home sooner that night.

At Clyara's cottage, the doors were locked and the windows were open, so I hitched my skirt and climbed inside through the kitchen window. The kitchen was immaculately neat, the cottage still and silent, and I realized that Glory was already gone.

I entered the receiving room from the kitchen and stopped short. My mistress was seated in her oak armchair, contemplating a bulky, hard-bound volume that rested on her lap. She glanced up at me, and gestured me to the seat across from her, which she had already cleared in anticipation of my arrival. "Good morning, 'Fleece," she said. "Prompt, as always. I did not think the locks would deter you much."

"Good morning, *Keeron*." I took the empty seat and forced my hands to remain still on my lap, instead of grasping my locket. "Why are your doors still locked?"

"We should have privacy this morning," she said. "Glory passes along her regrets that she was unable to say good-bye in person."

"She didn't go back to her mother, did she, *Keeron*?"

"Certainly not. I accompanied her to a place where she will be safe. Drink," she said, and passed to me a cup that was standing atop a stack of books beside her. "You know, the title of *keeron* irks me. It's so stiff."

I took a sip and found it pleasantly chilled. "Should I continue calling you 'Healer', then?"

"In the presence of others, you may," she said. "When we are alone, I would prefer that you call me 'Clyara.' It is the name given to me by my mother, and not something I hear often enough. I've missed the sound of it," she said, idly leafing through the pages of the tome on her lap. "Finish your drink, my dear."

Why was she so insistent about it? I peered into the cup and saw only water, so rather than prolong the effort, I lifted the cup to my lips and drained it in a single swallow. I had expected to taste something, even just minerals from the well, but the water left nothing on my tongue. It was bland, like boiled water, and I felt foolish for my brief suspicion. I placed the cup on the floor next to me, and nearly fell out of my seat.

My limbs and spine sagged bonelessly, failing to support me, and it was only by luck that I was able to find purchase and push myself back into the chair. My head felt too heavy for my neck and flopped sideways onto a pillow that I could swear wasn't there a second before. I focused my eyes upward and saw Clyara standing over me, stroking my brow. My face felt hot and cold at once, and my eyelids slowly dropped…

My eyes snapped open, and I sat up with an effort. I was in Clyara's patient bed, and it was still early, based on the morning sunlight streaming through the curtains. My tongue felt thick and heavy, and I hardly felt my throat when I swallowed. I didn't feel strong enough to stand, and my head was pounding, but I breathed deeply and savored the fresh air. The condition felt like a hangover, but far more wretched and debilitating.

Clyara was nowhere to be seen, and I wanted desperately to speak with her, to ask her what was happening to me. I saw the open window through the gauzy curtains and thought briefly about calling out for help, but I reconsidered the impulse. My mistress had done this to me for a reason, perhaps to test my worth. In seeking help, I would have disgraced myself, showing everyone that I could not handle the stresses of being Clyara's apprentice.

I lay back down, as another wave of dizziness passed over me. There was another, more menacing possibility. Perhaps Clyara had thought better of her decision to have me as her apprentice and poisoned me. As I lay with my head against the cool pillow, I dismissed that idea. If she wanted me dead, I would've been. I wouldn't have been lying on her patient bed tediously theorizing about the possibility. *I'm not going to die.*

11

That's good.

"No, you're not going to die." Clyara was leaning against the doorjamb, her hands folded.

I craned my neck back to look at her. "Ever?" I joked.

"That remains to be seen," she said. She crossed the room and opened the curtain slightly, to let in more sunlight. Her hair glistened in the light, but her eyes reflected nothing. "How do you feel?"

"Like I've drunken a half-bottle of ramsblood muddled with a big stalk of numb cane," I said, relieved that I wasn't drooling as I spoke.

"Good," she said, coming back to my side. She perched on the edge of the bed and showed me the cover of the book she held. It was the same hard-bound tome that was sitting on her lap earlier that morning. "Read the name," she said, and held my hand against the cover.

"'Practical Geology: A Scholar's Guide to Mineral and Metallurgic Lore,'" I said, noting the gold-leaf lettering and the brown fabric binding, frayed at the corners and edges.

My fingertips tingled, as though I had grasped a chunk of ice, and I pulled my hand away from the book. Intrigued, I eased myself upright, as Clyara opened the front cover.

It wasn't a book anymore, but a box, and nestled in the metal-lined compartment was a black silk pouch. Clyara set the book aside and opened the pouch. "Remove one," she said. "Don't think, just take the first one that comes to you." It was dark inside the small bag, and in my imagination, it might have contained puffs of down, or rusty tacks, or enraged fire ants.

I trust you, Clyara. I braced myself and reached into the pocket, and I felt the cool, hard brush of polished stones across the back of my hand. Aware of Clyara watching me, I felt around and retrieved one from the collection. It was about the dimensions of my thumbnail and was perfectly smooth and spherical, translucent and amber in hue. She closed the pouch, which she set back inside the book, and rose to replace the tome on her shelf, tapping the spine one last time. "Remember where they are, 'Fleece. One day, you will be responsible for those stones, and they must be kept safe."

"I promise," I said, intrigued by the marble nestled in my palm, like a ball of honey turned to glass. "What are they?"

"You'll see," she said, perched on the edge of the bed again. "Show me the stone you chose." I held it up for her to see. It glimmered beneficently. "Good choice," she said. "Now, swallow it."

I looked at Clyara doubtfully, but she answered me with a nod. This was another trial, I was sure of it. I popped the ball into my mouth, towards the back of my throat, but it lodged there and would not budge. My first instinct was to spit it back out, but I knew that it was the wrong thing to do. My anesthetized tongue and throat were still assaulted by intense heat and bitterness, and I realized that I had to swallow the stone quickly.

I deluded myself with thoughts of honeyed tea and mint and forced myself to push the ball down my throat, all the time conscious that Clyara was watching me. The burning in my mouth and throat faded, eventually, and I relaxed, but Clyara continued to observe. I took a couple of deep breaths to ease a dull ache in my chest that would not subside. It amplified into a searing, ripping pain that spread throughout my body; was the cursed thing trying to burrow out of my chest? What if Clyara's last apprentice hadn't decided to leave, but had perished just like this!

What have you done to me? I thought, meeting her eyes. I opened my mouth to speak, but my voice would not come. *What is this thing inside me?*

I was consumed by the pain, yet unable to scream or plead. Clyara grasped my shoulders and eased me back into bed. *Shhh. It is easier if you do not struggle. Sleep, if it lets you.* She acted untroubled by my condition and seemed curious about my reaction, as if I were the subject of an experiment. She tucked the covers around me and touched my cheek. *Welcome to your new world, Snowfleece of Moonteyre.*

Chapter 2: Minor Adjustments

With my eyes shut, I was aware of my own soft bed under me, and the warm cover of my blanket over me. I stilled the sound of my breathing and heard footsteps approaching. *Humyn? Killer gems? What could that kind of dream suggest?* I coughed once and regretted it, as my throat was excruciatingly raw and dry.

Relax, 'Fleece, came Clyara's voice. *And good morning.*

Why are you whispering? I opened my eyes and blinked several times before my eyes adjusted to the light, and several more times before my vision was clear. It was Frost who sat at the edge of my bed, but I sensed that Clyara was not far. Frost lay her hand on top of mine, and I felt my own on top of the coverlet. Her silver hair was loosely plaited, and she was still in her dressing gown.

I held onto her hand tightly. "By Ajle, I'm so glad to see you. What a nightmare!" I pulled myself up to sit, then felt my head swimming and slid back under the cover.

"Slowly," Frost said, sweeping back my hair. "You've been asleep for a while." She looked over her shoulder and nodded to Clyara, who appeared in the doorway. "The Healer's been here since dawn, waiting for you to wake up. I'll give you two a moment to catch up."

Clyara waited until Frost started down the stairs before she spoke. "How is your head?"

"It's been better," I said with an effort, getting up more gradually. "I'm just a little dizzy. What a dream I had! Everything seemed so real. There was this humyn girl—"

"Glory?" Clyara smiled.

I froze. "It wasn't a dream. And this pebble I swallowed yesterday?" The pain in my throat was less, but the tightness remained in my chest.

"A mage's gem," she said. "It was three days ago."

"Three days!" I cried. "What's in that thing?"

"It holds a store of magical energy. It is nothing to be concerned about, really. Your body and the gem need time to adjust to one another, that is all, and the numbing draught helped to relax you, to ease the transition. That you awoke at all is a very promising sign. It was a good match."

"So you said." I was deep in something that I struggled to comprehend. What had Clyara called it? Magic, sorcery, divine arts ... Was this part of the requirement to become a Healer like Clyara? What did she mean by my "new world"?

"Things will become clearer, over time," she said, perhaps seeing the questions in my expression. "As soon as you are up to it, you can return to work," she said, placing her cool hand on my forehead. "No fever, but you'll feel sore and weak a while longer."

I closed my eyes and took a deep breath. My room was filled with a mixture of scents: rose and jasmine, the warm minerals and spice from Clyara's perfume, and something new … linen, leather, and forest notes of cypress and sandalwood. "I remember being in your patient bed. How did I get back here?"

"I asked a friend to bring you home," Clyara said. "Why do you ask?"

I took another breath. "Someone's been in here that I don't know."

"Yes, that is true," Clyara nodded. "Your senses are stronger already, good. I'll expect to see you later, after you've had a chance to speak with Frost. I think she has some news for you."

After Clyara left, I took a moment to change into fresh clothes and met my sister downstairs. I noticed the start of a line near Frost's right eye that only appeared when she smiled. "Has it been quiet without me?" I asked.

"I've barely noticed," she said with a wink, setting a glass of water and a dish of berries and lemon bread in front of me. "You know, I'm going to be married in a few months, you could at least help me with planning instead of pretending to faint for no good reason," she joked.

I looked at her askance over the top of the glass, as I took a tentative sip. "None of the wedding details will meet your exacting standards, regardless, so I consider the unconsciousness a welcome respite."

"What did happen, 'Fleece? Are you all right, really?"

I nodded. "Clyara gave me something that changed me, physically. I don't know all the particulars, yet, but I feel different."

Frost took a seat across from me. "Is it dangerous?" she asked.

"I don't know," I repeated. Seeing her brows knit with worry, I made an effort to smile. "We've known the Healer our entire lives. She wouldn't do anything to hurt me." I felt less sure about that than I had a week ago, but I remained positive, for Frost's sake. "She said you had some news to share?"

"Oh, that," Frost said, and her expression grew even more serious. "A message arrived from our uncles yesterday."

"And?"

"They said they don't feel it's fair to displace you from the only home you've known," she started. "But if we insist, they'll decide which of them is best suited to take you in. Also, they don't think it would be in your best interest to move in with them now, especially with all the preparations going on for the arrival of Rose's baby."

I shrugged. "But we knew that would be their answer all along. They know we would not beg for their charity. You didn't tell them about my becoming the Healer's assistant, did you?"

"Of course, not," she scoffed. "They would just try to claim credit for it, somehow. So, since they declined to take you in, I took the liberty of asking Tracker when he stopped by last night."

I straightened. "Ask him what?" She didn't mean…

"Whether he would mind if you stayed with us, and he says he wouldn't," Frost said. "Don't look at me like that. You're my sister, and Tracker would no sooner turn you out than me. Eat something, 'Fleece. We can discuss this later. You haven't had anything to eat or drink in three days. That's a new record for you."

I ran to Clyara's after breakfast, feeling more energized than I had in months and eager to see what Clyara had planned for me. I had my skirt hitched around my knees as I blazed through the village square, and I wasn't entirely unaware of disapproving glances, but I didn't particularly care anymore. I would never be as beautiful as Frost, as a swamp duck could never be a swan, but we were both equally Winter's daughters. My uncles' message, meant to shun and belittle, was liberating in a way that I couldn't have imagined, and I was almost giddy with laughter by the time I reached Clyara's cottage.

She was tending to her drying herbs behind her home, her hair and skin honey-gold in the morning sunlight. She acknowledged me with a nod and continued her quiet conversation with her guest, an elderly gentleman with a greying beard and unfashionably long hair. He looked unfamiliar to me, but Clyara apparently knew him well, as evidenced by her warm smile, and the fact that he was carrying her basket.

I stumbled over a rock, but thankfully, neither of them seemed to notice. I straightened my skirt and my posture and executed my best curtsy. It seemed fitting, given the genteel manner of Clyara's mature visitor. "Good morning, *Keeron*. Good morning, Sir."

"Good morning, Apprentice," the man greeted, bowing his head to me. "You appear to have recovered quickly." Despite his age, his figure was strong and well-defined, and he moved with an almost feline grace.

As I approached, I caught the smell of sandalwood. Was he the friend that Clyara had asked to take me home? I suddenly became self-conscious about being carried by this man, of being so physically close to him without any knowledge of it, and my face warmed. He was tall for an elfyn man, at least a head taller than Clyara and me, but my awareness of him went deeper than his corporality.

Clyara cleared her throat, and I snapped out of my reverie. I found myself still staring at the man, my eyes focused on the deep creases by his dark amber eyes, and I said without thinking: "I apologize, if my bedroom was a mess. I don't often entertain there."

Why in Ajle did I just say that to him! I yelled in my head.

Clyara pretended not to hear, but the man held my gaze and smiled. "No apologies necessary. I don't make a habit of visiting young ladies in their bedchambers, either." He returned his attention to Clyara, as well as her basket. "Let me not keep you from your duties, Healer. I am at your service, always." With that, he gave a slight bow and disappeared around the front of the house.

Once I was sure that Clyara and I were alone, I asked, "He is the friend you mentioned, isn't he? The one who took me home?"

"Wouldn't it be awkward, if it turned out that he was not?" she teased. "Let us go inside and out of the sun. You look flushed."

Four days later, almost exactly a week after I had swallowed my gem, Clyara found me in her study, doubled over in agony.

I was unable to walk, or even stand up, for much of the day. In the meanwhile, the sharp, slicing pain coursed through my body, visiting each of my extremities, and my head, my gut, and so forth, multiple times but in no particular order. Clyara imparted some words of advice and encouragement, and I tried to listen attentively, but really, all I wanted was to be left alone. And perhaps a carafe of Clyara's numbing draught. I remained in Clyara's guest bedroom, rather than stagger all the way home and up the stairs to my room. The hours passed uncomfortably until the torture finally subsided.

From the quiet chirp of crickets and the scratching of field mice outside the window, I knew that it was dusk when I was finally myself again. The sound of lively chatter and children's laughter meant it was not yet late. The air smelled damp and sweet with freshly fallen rain, tinged with the faded scent of my jasmine perfume and fresh fruit and bread from the kitchen. When I opened my eyes, I was unprepared for the vividness of the colors and shapes that surrounded me. How could a candle be so bright! I shut my eyes and started again, more slowly.

I saw the room through squinted eyes. Next to the ivory beeswax candle on the cherry wood nightstand was a green-tinted glass filled with pale orange nectar that glistened like starlight, with its fragrant little bubbles of pulp. I was content just to stare into the glass for a good while before I emptied it. For the first time, I noticed the fine detailing on all the simple furnishings in Clyara's guest chamber, from the delicate marquetry on the headboard, to the flecks of dust coating the top of the armoire. From the bed, I noticed the soft fraying on the sun-faded ribbon that adorned a straw bonnet that hung on the back of the door, and the etchings on my locket that dangled from the armoire doorknob.

Clyara rapped softly on the door. I recognized her footsteps approaching before I heard her voice. "Are you awake?"

"Yes." I sat upright in bed, as the door opened.

"Congratulations on surviving your adjustment." Clyara watched me from the doorway. "You only cursed me twice."

"I remember that," I cringed, getting to my feet. "I was still listening to you, really. Everything is very vivid now, just as you had said, and the aches are gone. The magestone must be done with its calibration."

She nodded. "Your gem needed to read your body for a few days first, to understand its limitations, before it knew how to augment it. And this morning, it was finally ready to finish its work. You're recovering right on schedule."

"Why didn't you warn me earlier that something like this would happen?" I asked, trying not to sound like I was complaining. "I felt like I was going to die." *Again*, I wanted to add. What other surprises did Clyara have for me?

She led me out to the kitchen. "It's not easy to predict. The process could take one day, or seven, as it did with you. I didn't want you to dread waking every morning, wondering if that was the day for your adjustment."

"That makes sense," I mumbled. As usual, I took Clyara's word. I didn't know enough to question her, nor did I see a reason to, despite all that had happened to me over the past few days. She may not have been entirely forthcoming, but nor was she malicious or unkind.

I took my time walking home. I was abashed at how I had never noticed the rustling of waving grass and clover along the paths, the soft clack of pebbles underfoot, nor appreciated the bright clang of utensils from the metalsmith's cart or the heady, sweet and savory aromas of the baker's offerings. In fact, everywhere I turned, there were sounds, smells and colors that I had never noticed before, much less appreciated.

The front of my home, with my sister's flowerbeds, dazzled with a kaleidoscope of color and scent. The creeping clover borders were verdantly fragrant with recent rain. Droplets clinging to the violet alyssum florets and feathery pink dianthus reflected the orange and gold hues of the setting sun, made the petals glow even more brightly. I felt the slope and pressure of each stone in the walkway, where Da had set them five summers before. I turned the hammered brass knob on the front door, feeling through it the vibrations of the door creaking open. Inside, in the evening cool, Frost's rose perfume wafted to me.

"I'm home," I announced, closing the door behind me, marveling at the home where I had spent my entire life. It was familiar, yet new.

"In here," Frost's voice came from the kitchen.

I wandered down the hall in a daze, studying the shelves that lined the walls, and noticing how some were tilted just a bit, and when did that little spider make its home in our alcove? Rounding the corner to the pantry, I noticed a tiny crack forming in one of the floorboards.

Frost was pouring a cup of tea for me. She was puzzled about why I was staring, but there was no way I could make her understand how pretty she was. Her soft, snowy ringlets fell about her shoulders like garlands of gossamer and cream, and within the indigo of her irises shimmered flecks of sapphire and aquamarine. She handed me my cup, and I clearly heard her thoughts, as though she had spoken them aloud: *She has a lot on her mind. She'll tell me when she's ready.*

Autumn was when Moonteyre was in its full splendor. We gathered with the neighboring villages to celebrate the harvest season together, sharing the finest fruits of our collective labor. The valley vineyards yielded an exceptional crop of wine grapes that year, 996, and the Red Lake artisans expressed newfound inspiration with the designs of their maroon clay figurines and pottery. With the entire valley awash in hues of gold, red and purple, Moonteyre was a breathtaking sight from the soaring heights of the black granite Ajlekyrn. It was only fitting for our "Heaven's Fortress" that the vista be that ethereal and divine.

In the middle of it all was Clyara, our celebrated Healer. She was singular in calling Moonteyre her home, as healers elsewhere in the Dark Lands were characteristically nomadic and transient figures. Clyara did not like to leave her cottage unattended for long periods of time, so most patients came to her, and usually scheduled beforehand, as not to disturb her. She also did not like to leave me unsupervised for more than a few hours, as though some mishap would occur, if she didn't keep constant watch.

There really wasn't anything that I could do to get into trouble. Part of my apprenticeship was learning herb and mineral lore, until I knew every plant and type of stone in the forest on sight and smell. Some flowers, for example, like the sunflower orchid, soothed and relaxed the flesh before healing magic was applied, but only the golden bloom, and not the caustic leaves and roots. Other plants, like *rijkil*, served to agitate the body into natural regeneration. Some plants were best in their pure state, while others were meant for salves and tinctures, and some were better when fresh-picked, while others became more potent once dried and powdered.

Also, scheduled for the first harvest full moon in 996, was Frost's wedding. I abided by Frost's request to not wear a dress that was grey or black, a first since our father's death. This particular dress was rose, pale green, and ivory, richly embellished with ribbons, and to this day, I believe Frost chose it for me out of sisterly mischief, as I had never before nor since worn such a fluffy, fanciful combination of colors.

The afternoon before the ceremony, I made my annual pilgrimage into the Ajlekyrn mountains, to my parents' graves, to make my offerings and to keep them apprised of current events. Of course, I didn't truly believe that they could hear me, or make use of the food I brought. I just needed to be with them. Their tombs stood half-way up the mountain, facing the western exposure of the Ajlekuun, one of the highest of the range.

I cleared the weeds from my parents' graves and brushed out the dirt and moss that had obscured the engraving of the headstone. My mother's gravestone read: *Rija, Aelora* or translated: "Rija, Beloved." My father's read, very simply: "Winter." For the people who knew and admired him, nothing else was necessary. I arranged the loaves of bread and apples on top of the altar stones, laid out a small blanket and knelt between them.

"Frost is getting married tonight. Before her twenty-second birthday, just like you said, Da. It's only been two years since they met, I know, but they're in love, and that's the most important thing, isn't it? You'd both be so proud of her. She's never been happier or felt as sure of anything.

"We finished the marriage sash just this morning; you know how hard it is to get everyone to agree about how it should look. Your sisters-in-law are the worst," I said, recalling how my uncles' wives had berated the finished sash. "They resent not being invited to take part in the ceremony, and I think your brothers still feel that Frost dishonored them by not asking for their approval to marry." I took a deep breath to rest my strident voice, and to ease my animosity towards our kin.

I continued brightly, "I'm in the fifth month of my apprenticeship, and it's going well, I think. Clyara's taught me a little about healing, and I'm learning some physics and chemistry, and plenty of botany. I don't think even the senior teachers know some of these things, so Frost and I sometimes study together. Clyara says that knowledge of nature will help me even when my magic fails, that I'll never become a proper healer until I understand nature, just as I'll never be a mage of any worth unless I use my knowledge to help others."

I paused at the feel of a breeze, as it was full of odor and sound. Crisp, papery leaves rasped across the stones and weeds, near a chipmunk scavenging for acorns. It was picking its way closer to me through the leaf debris, having caught the aroma of the food I had brought. "Clyara has a point. This still feels so strange. I feel like a baby, discovering my senses all over again, and I can't tell anyone else. Most people would be terrified if they knew what the Healer and I can sense, especially in their thoughts. I'm not even sure how much to tell Frost."

As I stared at the engraving on my father's stone, his name evoked his image in my mind, and I felt myself missing him more than ever. It stung that my mother was a stranger to me, that I never had the opportunity to see her smile or feel her arms around me. What was there to say to her?

I had to return to Moonteyre before I was missed. As Frost's Attendant, it was my responsibility to oversee the details of her wedding. Frost's friends had entrusted the marriage sash and the rest of Frost's outfit to my care and had promised to return later in the day to help her get ready, which hopefully meant that she would not have to deal with our family by herself for any length of time.

Clyara intercepted me on my way home. Matching my brisk stride pace for pace, she said wryly, "You are just in time. Your elders have decided to call at your house, so I think I shall make an appearance, so that I may bask in their magnanimity and munificence."

As soon as we were in sight of the house, I heard the piercing voices of my aunts, airing our family's personal business to the community. My uncles were quieter, but their tones were still icy and sharp. I excused myself to Clyara and broke into a trot, intending to put a stop to the tirade before the whole town turned out to listen. Already, there were curious pedestrians slowing their pace, drawn by the sounds of bickering, and I had to weave my way past them.

Opening the door, I saw my aunts and uncles on one side of the room, with three of my four cousins either cowering near them or staring at the walls with disinterest, the exception being my youngest cousin Rose, who was watching and petting her pregnant belly as though she was still bewildered at how she had arrived at her condition. While she alone of my cousins shared Frost's white tresses, and was only a couple of years younger than my sister, she had none of Frost's intellect or self-awareness. Rose's own betrothed was nowhere in sight, a testament to his superb good sense.

Standing at the other end was Frost, alone but uncowed, with her arms crossed resolutely, her lips set tight and her dark eyes keenly narrowed. At my entrance, they all turned their gazes to me, and it was my Uncle Peer's wife, Aunt Ginger, who found her voice first.

"About time you came home, you stupid, lazy girl!" she began, in a voice as hard and brittle as glass. Likewise stood her hair, in stiff, elaborate brown curls like spun caramel. "Look at your hair: it's like a raven's nest! You're still unmanageable and wild, wandering off by yourself without a word to anyone when there's work to be done—"

"Don't you dare speak to her like that!" Frost raged, standing with me. "She's done more for me than all of you combined, which you would know if you ever cared to inquire." Her voice was surprisingly even, but her fingers gripped my sleeve tightly.

"It's no wonder she's turned out so poorly, considering that she has you as a role model," snipped my Aunt Daisy, soft and pale and rounded in shape like her namesake. "And you wonder why we won't have Snowfleece in our house!"

"Exactly," Aunt Ginger rejoined. "What an awful influence you would be on our dear Rose and her baby! Well-bred women never talk back to their elders, which you would know, if you had a proper mother."

"Proper mothers do not bully orphaned children," said Clyara, in a voice like a thunderclap, silencing the room. She had entered the house and shut the door without anyone's notice, but now she had everyone's full attention. It was not often that the Healer paid anyone a social visit. Clyara stood with her fingers knitted loosely in front of her, watching the room, impassively.

My uncles and aunts bent their heads and backs to the Healer immediately, and out of the corner of my eye, I saw Frost's lips twitch with satisfaction. Winter's brothers had always resented his closeness to the Healer but probably had not expected our family's ties to her to endure after his passing. My uncles were sweating with their agitation, and my aunts were tugging at my befuddled cousins to curtsy their reverence to the Healer. My four cousins, all privileged young women, were clearly unaccustomed with the practice of showing deference.

"Am I to understand that neither of you is prepared to receive your niece into your home," Clyara addressed our uncles, her voice softer now, but like a blade honing against a steel. "Even a year after your brother's death?" She added, soothingly, "I know, it is a hardship to provide for another child, and a young woman like Snowfleece would certainly disrupt the harmony of your families." She flashed a wink at Frost and me but remained deadpan for our relatives. "She's assertive, outspoken and independent."

Aunt Ginger and Aunt Daisy nodded, raising their chins ever so slightly, relieved that the Healer understood them. She did understand, of course, and with little measure of sympathy, but they were too self-absorbed to notice. "She's too bookish for her own good," Aunt Ginger said. "And she looks so little like us, she would never fit in," Aunt Daisy added.

Clyara nodded her head sagely. "You're quite right, you don't deserve to have her in your home." She turned her gaze to me, her eyes warm with impish affection. "I would like you to stay with me, Apprentice."

I was frozen in place, stunned by Clyara's sudden and absurdly generous offer, but I heard Aunt Daisy gasp, and possibly the muffled thud of Aunt Ginger fainting onto the rug. *Are you certain?*

"With your permission, of course, Frost," Clyara said over my shoulder. "It would be my pleasure to open my home to your sister."

My father's eldest brother Uncle Peer made a sound like a congested moose and managed, "Apprentice? Now, wait a moment. As their uncle…"

Clyara merely turned her eyes slightly towards him. "Your nieces have waited in vain for you to act, for more than a year. In doing nothing, you have forfeited your rights, so I will deal with Frost and Snowfleece directly from now on."

Clyara returned to the door. "I hope to see you relaxed and happy on your special day, dear Frost. If there is anything I can do to make things go more smoothly," she said with a furtive glance at our extended family, "please do not hesitate to ask."

After that, it was a simple matter to send our relatives on their way, and it was within Frost's rights as the head of the household to refuse my aunts entrance when they attempted to return later in the afternoon, "after her temper has cooled." They simply did not comprehend that it was not Frost's anger that prevented her from enjoying their company, but rather her very low tolerance for jealous negativity and small-minded arrogance.

When Frost's friends arrived shortly before dusk to help with the last of the preparations, I pulled her aside briefly and made her take a deep breath with me. "There is nothing that won't keep until tomorrow," I reminded. "Let yourself enjoy this time, these last precious hours of unmarried bliss."

"You're right, 'Fleece," she nodded. "This doesn't happen every day."

"Thank Ajle for that," I laughed, herding Frost back towards the other women to complete her transformation.

And what a metamorphosis it was! That night, Frost was a vision of otherworldly beauty, draped in brilliant white, the color of purity and new life. While she was always naturally pretty, little details enhanced her loveliness and made her exquisite. Her silver hair, adorned with iridescent autumn snowdrop sprays, was swept back from her neck and graceful bare shoulders, and with every step she took, the air around her was faintly scented by her rose perfume, complemented that night with orange blossoms. As if to bestow divine consent, the harvest moon loomed brightly and low in the cloudless sky, gilding Frost with its benign glow.

Tracker awaited his bride at the offering table, nervously picking at his pristine white garments. He was a handsome figure, with his tawny skin contrasting with the milk-white of his embroidered garments. As soon as he saw Frost coming to join him, his eyes never left her again. He was enthralled, as was everyone in attendance, but especially me. With my new senses, I absorbed every sight, sound and scent with such staggering clarity that I almost wept at her magnificence.

Frost and Tracker exchanged the vows they had written themselves and made the offerings to their ancestors together. I presented Frost's marriage sash to Tracker, and he tied it around her waist to signify his respect for her ties to her loved ones. They raised their glasses to one another: separate vessels, sharing the same wine, consumed together. Two beings, sharing a new life, as one.

It was done. Tracker and Frost were married, at last.

Chapter 3: Life Apart

Over the next few days, I moved into Clyara's guest room, which was small but comfortable. There was room for some personal items, but I remained fastidious and asked Frost to keep my belongings crated, just in case the arrangement did not last.

Once I was living under Clyara's roof, I became aware of how irregular and full her schedule actually was, but I adjusted to her pace. That meant waking and sleeping at odd hours in order to complete reading assignments on a variety of subjects, from astronomy to zoology, and performing exercises in and outside the house, that taxed my reflexes and concentration and seemed to have no relevance to my skills as healer's assistant. I could understand the importance of meditation and simple gymnastics for improving and maintaining my health, of course, but the necessity of knowing archery, knife-throwing and hand-to-hand combat was more dubious.

"Am I to be a warrior, as well as a healer?" I asked her, after one such arduous session. I picked myself off the ground, rubbing my sore and bruised arms, after Clyara had flung me into a bed of dry pine needles. We were spending our free afternoon in the forest on the western bank of the Yirae, far from the chaotic preparations for the Harvest Festival that night in Moonteyre.

"I wish for you a peaceful life," she said, picking a needle from my hair, "but you should know how to defend yourself."

"Defend myself from what?"

"From whatever or whomever would do you harm," she said. "Everything I teach you is important. Besides, the strength you command must be both physical and mental. There is no point in having the knowledge, or the power, to heal if your body is incapable of sustaining the punishment involved." As if to press the point, she gave my tender shoulder another vicious jab. "It is good that you recover quickly. You still have a lot to learn."

As I straightened, I took my eyes off her for a second. That was a mistake as, before I could see her act, Clyara yanked my arm, throwing me off balance, twisted my arm behind me and pinned me to the ground. She anchored her knee on my spine. "You need to keep your guard up, always."

I tried to wriggle out from under her, without success. This is humiliating! She's old enough to be my grandmother.

"Oh, I'm much older than that," she laughed, getting to her feet, and pulling me up with her. "You may as well speak your mind. Even if I could not read your mind, I can see it on your face."

"I can't fight you," I admitted. "You're my *keeron*, you're the Healer."

"Don't let that fact stop you," she replied. "Remember that I was once Malya's *keeron*, also, and I tried very hard to kill her. Don't ever underestimate my will. If I have to injure you to make my point, I shall."

That sobered me. "Did you train like this, as an apprentice?"

"I did not, but I wish I had," she said, leading the way back home. "I didn't bother with your predecessors," she said dourly. "Especially the last one, he was undisciplined and unfocused, and he wouldn't have endured any of it. Had I offered a magestone to Master Zephyr, it would have rejected him. The others before him were similar, except for Malya."

"You've gone through a lot of apprentices, then," I noted.

"Not really. I was in a cave for some years, and had no need of company. I only needed an assistant once I became a healer." She sounded annoyed, as if she found her role to be a nuisance. "Please understand, 'Fleece," she said, more gently, brushing some debris from my sleeve. "I do what I must to keep our people alive, but I would be much happier if I were obsolete. As would our people, despite what they think now."

"What about the other healers? Are they also like you?"

She smiled grimly. "Some, perhaps. We are solitary creatures, generally, not given to socializing and exchanging secrets."

The trip back to town was uneventful, as everyone was too busy getting ready for the Harvest Festival to give us more than a passing glance, but Frost ambushed me outside of Clyara's cottage and led me to my room, declaring: "'Fleece, the festival's starting soon, and you still need to change your dress and clean up." She was already dressed, head-to-toe in harvest shades of tangerine and scarlet.

"I'm not really in the mood," I protested.

"Even more reason to go," Clyara said, watching Frost sit me down on my bed. "You have the evening free, and I can't imagine a better way for you to spend it." A bowl of fresh wildflowers and my comb were on my night table. "I told Frost she was welcome to set up whatever she needed, while we were out."

"Thank you, Healer," Frost said, then picked a twig out of my hair and passed me a wet washcloth. "You have mud on your cheek, 'Fleece. By Ajle, at least I hope it's mud... Will you be going tonight, Healer?"

Clyara shook her head. "I still have work to do." With that, she left.

"Wait, what work? Hey!" I exclaimed, as Frost pulled just a little too hard on my tangled locks. Glancing down, I spied a drape of deep azure blue next to me on my bed. "That's your favorite dress."

"That *was* my favorite dress," Frost said, starting to plait my hair. "Tracker doesn't think it's appropriate for me anymore, since I'm a married woman," she said tartly. She plucked a blue cornflower from the bowl and wove it into my black braid deftly.

"You could wear a sack and still turn heads, but it's sweet of you to let Tracker win once in a while."

"What can I say? Marriage is all about compromise," she said.

Something about her tone struck me as wistful. "You are happy, aren't you?" I asked.

"Of course, I'm happy!" she said, tucking a marigold into my hair. "I was just remembering when I was little, when I used to listen to Mama and Da talk. It seemed like they never asked each other to give up anything."

"Da almost gave up his family to be with her," I said. Winter had been very frank with us, letting us know from an early age that our mother had been rejected initially by his family, and if not for the Healer's endorsement, they would have never been allowed to marry. Our mother had a modest upbringing near the Red Lake and no wealth or property, but our father had loved her unconditionally.

"It would've been no great loss," Frost said. "I still haven't responded to our uncles' invitation for a visit, and I don't plan to, unless it's accompanied by an apology. They've yet to acknowledge their behavior towards you on my wedding day."

"The chances of an apology are slim to none."

"I would wager the same, and I lose no sleep over it," she said, setting down the brush and tucking a last flower into my hair. "You are part of my life, and part of me, and anyone who refuses to accept that doesn't deserve my regard."

She said it with such stern resolve that I was briefly taken aback. My big sister had matured into a strong woman at some point during my childhood, and I was impressed. I could only imagine how formidable she would be someday, as a mother guarding her children. "All right."

She took a deep breath, and her bright smile returned. "Sorry. This is an evening of festivities, I shouldn't be so serious. Here, get changed, and I'll take the bowl back to the kitchen."

The sleeveless dress was nearly cobalt in color, which had complemented Frost's cream complexion and platinum hair perfectly. She had added a flourish of crocheted lace to the bodice years ago, but I noticed that the lace had since been removed. Once I wore it, I realized why Tracker had rejected it, and even Frost raised an eyebrow at me, as I adjusted the ties at my back.

"I don't recall the bodice being so low or snug on you," I said.

"It wasn't," she said. "The lace seemed excessive, so I took it off. I don't think you need the extra embellishment like I did."

27

I tugged at the front of the dress to try to cover my "embellishments" a little more. "I should change into a different dress."

"There's no time, and I took all your drab grey sacks back to the house to launder," Frost said innocently. At my scolding look, she said, "You're sixteen, for Ajle's sake. Dress and act like it, for once."

The festivities were already underway by the time we met Tracker at the fairgrounds, as revelers from nearby villages had arrived early, including those from the Red Lake and the neighboring North Woods. Frost hooked her arm with mine to keep me from bolting home, and I felt her stiffen when she noticed that Tracker had been joined by his new acquaintance, a young man from the North Woods named "Ohynn." Even Tracker seemed chagrinned to be in Ohynn's company, and I smelled the inebriation on the younger man before we were even close.

Before Tracker even completed our introduction, Ohynn took my hand as a non-verbal invitation to dance and pulled me away before I even uttered an acceptance.

Ramsblood was clearly Ohynn's drink of choice, and the cloying, sour odor permeated his skin and clothing, even at that early hour. As handsome as I thought he was, I was apparently not as eager an admirer as he was accustomed to having, in all senses of the word. He held me uncomfortably close to him, wrapping his arm around my waist as if to embrace me, and stared openly at my chest. When I began to push him away, he attempted to pull me closer towards him for an off-hand kiss. I twisted out of his embrace and left him standing alone.

Flustered and insulted, I felt it was best to leave before I could hurt him, so I charged through the crowd with my head down, but Ohynn's sharp, slightly slurred voice was inescapable: "If you were as friendly as your sister, maybe you could catch a man."

I looked up from the ground and happened to catch Frost's glower in Ohynn's direction. Many of the celebrants, in fact, had stopped and turned to see what had transpired, having only caught my dramatic exit.

I looked at him squarely and said: "Maybe if you were a man, I would make the effort."

The musicians, oblivious to the spectacle at the end of the floor opposite from them, started playing a bright, rhythmic tune. Ohynn was red-faced and standing unsteadily, but he had a look of determination about him, as if he would try to put me in my place. I welcomed the opportunity, standing my ground and balling my hands into fists at my sides. If I aimed just right, I could incapacitate Ohynn with a single shot. I was thinking to aim for the solar plexus.

I suddenly felt a hand grasp my wrist gently, and I looked over at Tracker. Seeking to defuse the situation, he half-dragged me back to the dance circle before Ohynn was even within paces. "I'm sorry, I didn't know he would do that," he said, glancing behind us. "He didn't hurt you, did he?"

"Just my virgin sensibilities," I quipped. "I've encountered worse."

"I'll straighten him out later, I promise."

I nodded. "I'd be happy to do it, if you'd prefer."

Tracker took my hands in his and spun me about for the start of the dance. "What a strange sense of humor you and your sister have. Half the time, I don't know whether you're serious or not."

I watched for some sign of temper, but there was only a glimmer of heat in his gentle eyes. My brother-in-law didn't think enough of his friend's rudeness to draw more attention to it, so I followed his lead. I whispered, "If he speaks out of turn again…"

"Or, if he lays an unwanted hand on anyone again, the first one to reach him gets to put him down for the night," he promised. I opened my mouth to protest, and he said, "We need him strong enough to work till the end of harvest. If he's still a loutish fool after that, anything goes. However, if he were hurt, wouldn't it be more work for the Healer?"

"Only if his body is found," I muttered.

The dance began with Tracker, but with the turns and exchanges, we wove away from each other, and he joined Frost at the opposite end of the floor. I curtsied to my faceless new partner and lifted my eyes to Clyara's elder gentleman friend. I had last seen him before my adjustment completed, months ago, and I laughed with my surprise. He bowed his head and smiled, with creases adorning his eyes and the edges of his lips, and he took my hands into his, whisking me back into the current of the dance.

We didn't try to speak over the music, but our eyes couldn't avoid contact. He half-smiled when the dance brought us close to Ohynn, who had already forgotten me and was busy with another girl, so I guessed that Clyara's friend had witnessed our brief confrontation. It was the perfect smile for him: sardonic, sheepish and rather sweet.

I confess that my feelings were clouded by the intimacy demanded of the dance, but from our limited earlier meeting, I had not expected the potent energy that I enjoyed in his touch, through our palms pressed together and his strong fingers on the small of my back, tugging playfully at the ties of my dress. He seemed ageless rather than ancient, the lines on his face becoming trophies of experience, rather than scars of wear. He was virile and masculine, and the perfect complement to everything that was feminine in me.

Our time was too brief, and still no words were exchanged. I returned to Tracker's hands, and Clyara's friend rejoined his much younger partner. I glanced in his direction more than once, each time feeling something akin to disappointment when he did not meet my eyes. The feeling was ridiculous and involuntary. Once the dance ended, I excused myself from Tracker's company and went to get something to drink. I needed a moment to sort out my emotions.

I closed my eyes and forced myself to take small sips and measured breaths, until my face no longer felt hot. I had felt attraction before, but never so suddenly, and never for anyone so much older. I was sixteen, and he was old enough to be … who knew how old he was? *What is wrong with me?*

I took a deeper breath and recognized the very faint scents of cedar and cypress in the air. They were rich, dense woods that evoked images of dark, ancient forests, alive with dangerous and powerful forces, but I was drawn into a sense of calm. Darkness meant anonymity and safety, and power meant control. I knew the scent, and I anticipated the voice.

It never came. Instead, I heard a small child's voice calling, "Healer Alessarc, can you come see my father, please?"

Healer Alessarc? I looked up in time to see Clyara's friend disappear into the throng, following a young boy. *He's a healer!*

"'Fleece, are you all right?" Frost touched my cheek, and her fingers came away wet.

I hadn't even noticed that my eyes were tearing. "It's nothing."

"Does 'nothing' have a name?" she asked.

I wiped my eyes and looked down at my empty cup. "Maybe it was something in my drink."

Frost looked down at my cup, disbelievingly. "Harvest punch?"

"Is that what I'm drinking?" My mouth was so dry that I barely tasted the sweetness of the juices. His presence was gone, and I breathed a sigh of relief. "His name is 'Alessarc,'" I mouthed silently, as though the sound of his name alone would summon him into our presence.

"Oh, him." Frost straightened and folded her arms. "What did he do?"

"You know who he is?" I said.

"Of course, I know who he is! I wouldn't let a strange man into your room without at least a perfunctory introduction," she said. "Clyara said he was a healer from Red Lake, and he brought you home from the Healer's house after your … magical procedure," she said, discreetly. "Did Alessarc say something to you?"

I shook my head. "What do you know about him?"

"Just that he seems a little old for you, but it could work." Frost took me by the hand to lead me back to the party. "Come on, let yourself be young and silly. The party's only begun, I'm sure it'll get better."

Off in the distance, we saw an unconscious Ohynn being carried off by a couple of the farmers and set aside like one of the decorative haybales. A third man was walking away, with torn cuffs and a broad, satisfied grin.

30

"Splendid," Frost said, beaming. "It's gotten better, already."

With the harvest season of 996 ending, the days of growth came to a gradual end, and winter fell upon the Dark Lands like a silver shroud. The Lands became still under the cover of snow and ice, peacefully hibernating, waiting for the thaw, like so many of its denizens.

Over the winter months, Clyara ventured to visit patients in the regions outside Moonteyre, particularly those who were too ill to come to us. She was less comfortable receiving praise than she was tending to the goriest, most devastating wounds, but she never lost her temper or composure under even the most trying circumstances. She would simply say "thank you" and "my pleasure" and keep her visits short, in preparation for the next appointment. I was an observer, nothing more, but I studied Clyara's technique exactly, for the inevitable day that I would succeed her. At Clyara's word, I would have gladly shared her burden, but I waited in vain.

Even through the winter, the Yirae was clear enough of ice for trading barges to travel back and forth along the eastern riverbank. Many of the younger, more adventurous elfyn even spoke of possibly traveling south after the thaw, to explore the unsettled, rockier slopes of the Ajlekyrn. Some of the others spoke of crossing not only the vast Yirae, but an even mightier river rumored to be far to the west, the waterway of the Lost Realm. Such notions never failed to alarm the Elders, who were quick to remind the upstarts that "no one has ever left the Dark Lands and returned to tell his tale. Even if our ancestors had come from the west at one time, they would not have fled their homes without reason."

As elfyn are not impetuous or overly intrepid as a whole, a few earnest pleas from the Elders were enough to quell most adventurous notions. Moreover, within the safety of the Dark Lands, the idea of anyone ever entering our borders was a fanciful one, at best. Perhaps if someone had asked me what I thought, I would have divulged what little I knew about the humyn, but I was considered odd enough already, and didn't need to add to my reputation of strangeness by volunteering wild, unsubstantiated theories.

Rather than expressing myself, I retreated further into my role as apprentice, and focused my efforts on my studies. By the start of the new year, I had also started to practice telepathy, from simple empathy to focused mind-reading, when I would attempt to pick thoughts from Clyara's mind. "Think of telepathy as another of your senses," she advised. "In time, it will become as effortless to you as sight or taste."

Next, came the spells. Clyara gave me a thick, leather-bound book from her bookshelf and passed it to me, and I could barely suppress my grin upon taking the tome in my hands. I was given two weeks to read it and understand it well enough to apply the knowledge.

Memorization was nothing new to me, and I had read the book thrice by the end of the following evening, leaving me more than ten days to understand what it was that I read. Spells were not so much about gestures and words as they were about thoughts and will, although the former helped me to properly structure and express the latter.

Until I became more adept, the "magical" words and syllables that comprised my spells also helped me to concentrate, to pace myself and time the release of the gem's power, which was crucial to preserving my energy and overall well-being. I found out quickly, that improper spellcasting could leave me weak and drained for hours afterwards, much like physical overexertion or severe heat exhaustion. Clyara told me of a young mage who was unconscious for two days after casting a spell above his capacity.

The spells contained in the tome were some of the essentials: levitation, light-casting, freezing and thawing, and my favorite: flight. As it had been with my physical training, these spells had no curative purpose, but I didn't mind. I was eager to learn everything I could about magic, in whatever form. Periodically, I felt a twinge in my chest, as though I was catching my breath after exercise. The pain would subside quickly, leaving me feeling a little different, refreshed and stronger for the effort. By the end of my allotted two weeks, the pains had ended, and I took my gem's dormancy as a sign that I was ready to practice what I had learned.

On a sunny winter morning, Clyara took me back into the pine forest to test me. "In your own words," she began, "how is magic different from natural ability?"

"Abilities stem from my body's own resources and are tied to my senses, aging and growth," I stated. "What we call magic is the manifestation of will, with my gem acting as the catalyst for my goal. My gem learns my intentions and makes them real, by drawing from resources around me and manipulating them."

Clyara nodded. "And why is the magestone necessary?"

"The magestone fuses with its host, releasing particles into the host's blood," I replied easily, "which travel throughout the body and strengthen the bond between gem and mage. Without these particulates, magic would not be possible."

"Simplistic, but good enough for a novice. Let us see, then, what you've absorbed." She picked a small, plump rosehip from a nearby bush and held it in the crease of her palm. "Lift it."

I focused my attention on the rosehip and recited the spell for levitating it, and I felt fairly stupid when the fruit remained inert. Clyara made no disparaging remark, nor an encouraging one. She merely waited for me to concede defeat, or to try again.

Defeat was not an option. I knew I possessed the power to lift at least a tiny morsel, I only needed to concentrate. I repeated my spell, setting aside my doubts about my own abilities and thinking more of the simplicity of the task. *Come on, get up!*

The rosehip shot into the air, ricocheted off an overhead tree limb, and struck my forehead, squarely and hard. As I cursed under my breath, rubbing my brow, Clyara commented: "Not bad, Snowfleece. Your control could use some work."

Clyara escalated my training quickly, and I soon learned that her threat months earlier, about hurting me to make her point, was absolutely sincere. Once the trees began to leaf out in the early spring, she especially liked to conduct our sessions deep in the western forest, far from the prying eyes of Moonteyre.

I don't want to die. My eyes reflected back at me in the trembling blade that tacked a strand of my hair into the tree trunk behind me. Clyara had thrown the knives directly at me, almost gleefully; perhaps I would have been unhurt if the blades struck me, but I didn't want to take the chance. I caught my breath and dropped to the ground as a dagger whipped past me. I thought I had avoided it, until I saw a thread of blood forming on my right shoulder.

"Your spells!" Clyara exclaimed, launching yet another dagger at my head. As soon as a knife was thrown, a new one materialized in her hand.

I concentrated on the gestures and the words to cast a magical shield, and what relief I felt when the blade bounced off of it! Especially since the blade was aimed right at my heart. The shield reverberated with each blow, and the constant barrage quickly wore through it; five seconds after I had cast the shield, one knife came within three inches of me.

I dashed deeper into the woods for someplace to hide. Finding no refuge on the ground, I sought one in the air. I whispered and gestured my spell to float into the branches and turn invisible. I held my breath and waited. Clyara walked beneath me, but she circled back. She gazed up into the trees. "I can't see you, but I can smell your perfume. It's too early in the spring for wild jasmine."

I canceled my levitation spell and dropped on top of her, startling her with my boldness and knocking her to the ground. I turned to run, but Clyara canceled my spell of invisibility, caught my ankle and pulled it out from under me, sending me tumbling into the soggy brush.

I resurfaced to find her laughing, her dress and cloak immaculate despite our melee. "Very good, 'Fleece, your best time by far." She offered her hand, and I let her pull me up.

I touched my chest when I felt the familiar sharp pain inside it. I took a couple of deep breaths, but the ache did not subside right away. "There it is again. What's happening to me?" With every breath that I took, my lungs felt crushed and heavy. "It's growing, isn't it?"

Clyara rested her fingertips on my breastbone for a moment. "You can control more energy, so your stone is expanding to accommodate you." At my look of consternation, she said, "It'll stop, in time. Eventually, you may even outgrow your stone, and if you wish, you can replace it with another, more powerful gem. The stronger one would then assimilate the weaker."

I walked alongside her, wondering how far off that day would be. "And I would get that gem from you?" I remembered the pouch of amber pebbles that she kept hidden in a false book in her cottage.

She paused before answering. "Yes, it's my duty as your mistress." She pulled a stem of winter cherries from overhead and offered me one, which I happily accepted. "I hope to be a better *keeron* than the one I had."

I nibbled on the sweet pale fruit. "You don't talk about him much."

"I never talk about him at all, if I can help it," she said. "When I met him, I was young and naïve, and Aron was the almighty Healer. I was so in love with him that I would've done anything for him. I knew that the only way to catch his eye was to be a mage myself, so I stole little glances at his books whenever I could and tried to practice what I learned.

"Naturally, without a gem, mine was a futile effort. I was so mortified, the day he saw me trying to cast a spell! He laughed so mercilessly, I thought I would die. But I caught his attention, and I became his apprentice." Her smile was bittersweet, as though the memories still stung. "That was over a hundred thirty years ago."

That alone was a revelation, as she looked like a woman of sixty, although I knew her to be older. She had never seemed to age in all the time that I had known her, yet she was a mage before my great-great-grandparents were even born. "I never knew any of that."

"No reason you should." She brushed a blade of grass from my shoulder and resumed the lead. "It was not an easy life. Aron didn't love me, and by the time I realized it, I had already been with him twenty years, and magic was all I knew." The forest seemed to still just to hear her. "I grew to love magic as he did, but I grew to loathe Aron, too. He knew that I hated him, but he did not see me as a threat. Eventually, I endured enough of his abuse and learned enough of his magic and one day..."

I waited for her to finish, but she was silent. "Yes?"

Evenly, as if she were speaking of the weather, she finished, "At the end of my fortieth year, I killed him and claimed his gem for myself." She turned around and looked at me. "He wanted me to give up something precious, and I refused. I took his life, before he could take mine."

"Is this what you fear from Malya, that she'll become powerful enough to take your magic from you?"

"All *keerons* fear this from their apprentices, to one degree or another," she said. "I was alone for decades before I decided to take an apprentice, and I had the spectacularly bad luck of choosing Malya as my first. For years afterwards, I could not bring myself to bestow a gem on another successor, but I sensed that you were different."

"But you still think that I would betray you," I said.

"Me? No, I have no worries about you," she replied. "But my gem, well… After residing in me for more than a hundred years, it is quite comfortable there, and it does what it can to convince me that I'm safer alone. All gems do that, really, even yours, but the more powerful it is, the stronger its influence. It explains our solitary lifestyle, I suppose."

How parasitic our magestones seemed. "They seem alive."

"In a sense, I suppose that is true."

"Did you know that when your *keeron* gave you your first stone, that it could control you like that?" I would've appreciated the information sooner, ideally before I took my gem, but I had only myself to blame, for not asking for details ahead of time. I had been so entranced by the promise of magic that I hadn't thought to ask about the risks or consequences.

"Aron told me nothing," she said. "I'm telling you now because this is your last chance to change your mind. If your power continues to grow at this rate, you won't be able to surrender the gem without crippling yourself," she cautioned. "The longer you wait, the stronger the bond will become between your body and your gem, until your life is tied to it."

I looked at her. *You knew this?* If she noticed my stare, she gave no indication. Perhaps it was knowledge that she felt was unnecessary at this point in my training. Like knowledge about the humyn.

"There is no shame in forfeiting the gem now," she said. "I wish some days that I had had the will to do it. You've learned enough to be a healer without magic, but if you want to stop, you must let me know soon."

No pressure. None at all.

As much as I disdained the idea of something inside me controlling my health and possibly my mind, some part of me found it to be a fair exchange: mild neurosis and the hosting of a parasite, albeit a non-living one, in return for power and status, for the benefit of the elfyn as a whole. I decided, after a couple of days of deliberation, that my magestone was a necessary evil.

I did not discuss the matter with Frost; it was a matter between my mistress and me. Clyara was relieved at my decision, from what I could read in her solemn smile, but she wasn't entirely surprised. She recognized that I craved the stability and respect that a healer's life promised. My choice to keep my magestone felt instinctively, intrinsically right.

Its presence was starting to feel natural, and I felt whole.

Chapter 4: Healers

I turned seventeen in the spring of 997, and my curls remained stubbornly tar-black, unlike Winter, Frost, and our cousin Rose, all of whom had completely white hair by the time they were twelve. I had neither beauty nor charm to distinguish me, and I had no use for either. Few outside of Moonteyre knew me as "Snowfleece", and even fewer bothered to call me by name. Most knew me simply as "the Healer's girl," which suited me fine. For the first time since my father's passing, I had a purpose, and I was happy for it.

As the other youths of my age were seeking apprenticeships and finishing their schooling, while doing their best to attract the attention of potential partners, I spent my free hours buried in Clyara's books, keeping myself too busy to think about relationships. Magic seemed a more realistic, practical and achievable goal than love.

I even managed to avoid having the Feast of Seventeen, that awful social debacle during which I would have displayed myself in some garishly frilly gown, for all the Dark Lands to scrutinize and judge like livestock. Frost knew better than to press the point, although she did mumble something about not having been spared in kind.

Despite my increased responsibilities and knowledge, Clyara refused to let me cast spells beyond her supervision. I was relegated to mixing tinctures and scheduling her appointments, as well as keeping order in her home. I abided by her wishes, until the day that I didn't.

It was late spring, not too long after my first anniversary as Clyara's apprentice. The Healer had gone to make her rounds with her patients and left me in the house with chores. I didn't mind staying in from the heavy downpour, or having some time for myself. I had finished cleaning the cupboards and counter in the kitchen when I heard a knock at the back door. Peering around the opening door, I saw Alessarc.

He met my eyes just as I recognized him, and he paused in the doorway. He looked about seventy years of age, unchanged from when I had last seen him at the Harvest Festival. I had tried to keep him out of my thoughts in the intervening months, if only to forget my embarrassment about his effect on me, but I felt the unease welling again, too quickly.

"Is your mistress home?" His gravelly baritone filled the room.

"No, but you're welcome to wait for her," I offered, suddenly feeling very small in his presence.

"Thank you, I'll return later," he said, turning away.

"No need to go back out in this rain," I said, pushing the door closed and out of his reach. "She should be back soon," I smiled awkwardly, anxiously twisting the dust rag around my knuckles. I had never spoken with Alessarc for any significant length of time, and I was at a loss. I wanted to be polite, but his dark golden eyes focused on me with such frank familiarity that I felt naked. I think I blushed. "Please make yourself at home, and I'll just get back to work," I managed.

He didn't sit, nor did he head towards the sitting room. "Can I help?"

"Help? No, thank you, I'll be … I mean … Would you like some tea?"

His lined brow creased further. "I make you nervous. I should go."

"If I'm nervous, it's only because I don't know anything about you," I confessed. "Aside from your name, and that's only because I overheard it. Not that I was eavesdropping, or anything like that." I bit down on my lip when I turned my back to him. Every sentence spilling forth from my lips was as ineloquent as the last. Perhaps, if I kept my mouth shut for a while, I could salvage what little remained of my dignity.

"There isn't much to tell." He seemed bemused by my behavior and volunteered, "I can make the tea for myself, if you'd like to get the door."

"What?" I had been so distracted by his presence that I hadn't even heard anything, but when I went to check, there was a quiet, urgent knock at the front door. A tiny girl came in, pale and shaking. She held one tiny hand to her knees, stained pink with the mixture of blood and rain. Lily was the four-year-old granddaughter of one of the Elders, and I was surprised to see her alone.

"My legs hurt," she said plaintively.

"Let's take a look at them, then," I said, pointing her to a chair. I wrapped a blanket around Lily's damp head and shoulders, then went to rummage around on Clyara's table for some clean cloths and a half-empty bottle of witch hazel tincture. "Tell me what happened."

"I slipped in the mud and scraped myself," she said.

"Is that what you're going to tell your parents?" She wasn't being entirely truthful, I could tell by the seriousness of the "scrapes". They were good-sized abrasions, across both knees. I knelt in front of the girl and cleaned her wounds gently, letting her grab my hair when the stinging of the injuries overwhelmed her. Out of the corner of my eye, I saw that Alessarc had taken position in the doorway to watch, out of the child's line of sight.

"I went to climb rocks in the quarry and slipped," she said at last.

"That'll be our secret, Lily," I said with a reassuring smile. "You're very smart and brave to come here all by yourself." Cleaning the cuts, I saw that they went deeper than they first appeared; the child needed more than bandages. I placed my hands on her legs and concentrated on the words of the healing spell.

"Your hair's very soft and pretty," she marveled, stroking my black curls. "It's not at all as prickly as a thornbush, like my mama said."

Alessarc laughed soundlessly, and I had to close my eyes to focus my attention. I had never attempted a healing before, but having watched and heard Clyara so often, I mouthed the words without having to think about them. When I opened my eyes, I saw that my tiny patient was smiling at me. I pressed my thumbs gently into her bare knees and asked, "How do they feel now?"

"Better," she said, wriggling free of the towel and blanket. "Much better!" She squealed happily at the sight of her whole, dimpled knees, gave me a tight hug before she ran to the door.

"Be more careful next time!" I called after her.

"I will!" Lily remembered her manners at the last moment, turned and curtsied. "Thank you, Healer! Bye!" And she was gone.

I did it! I remained kneeling, stunned and exhilarated by what had happened. I had healed, and I had defied Clyara, both in the same act. Only when I heard Alessarc in the kitchen taking the whistling kettle from the stove did I get to my feet. "Did you see what I did?" I said excitedly, as he reemerged.

"Yes, Apprentice, I did," he said staidly, passing me a freshly-rinsed, scalding towel. "Your bedside manner was excellent," he said.

"Thank you," I smiled, wiping my hands clean.

"The cloth is not for your hands," he said, glancing at my skirt.

I looked down and saw the fabric of my skirt stained crimson against my knees. The unexpected sight of my own blood was bewildering and jarring. Alessarc guided me to sit down where my patient had been moments before, but it took him kneeling in front of me and easing my skirt over my knees for me to realize what had happened. Clinically but tenderly, he took the cloth from my hands and wiped the blood from my fresh wounds.

"It's all part of what it means to 'pass the pain,'" he said, tending my injuries with a gentle touch. "I thought your mistress would've explained how healing works, when she taught you."

"I didn't know that it means to pass the pain to another, literally."

Alessarc stopped and looked at me. "She didn't teach you, did she."

"I learned from observation." I hastily covered my knees, seeing that my gem had finished mending them, but the stains on my clothes were glaring. Alessarc passed me the cloth and stood, and my eyes followed him. I asked, "Are you going to tell her about this?"

"That you did a healing, or that I didn't try to stop you?"

Neither sounded very good. I stood and said, "You didn't know beforehand. I'll tell her myself."

The door opened again, and Clyara entered without looking over. "Tell me what?" She looked bedraggled and tired, and she was busy drying off her wet clothes and hair with an air spell.

My confession seized in my throat, and Alessarc said, "Lily came by, and your apprentice helped me tend to her." He knocked the towel out of my hand, as if by accident, and stooped to retrieve it. I felt a wisp of air against my legs, and Alessarc stood, giving me a reassuring wink. I glanced down and saw that the bloodstains were gone from my skirt.

"I see," Clyara said. "But Lily came up to me at the Ancient and told me the 'black-haired Healer' helped her."

Alessarc shrugged. "It was easier to let her think that. After all, I'm a stranger to her. Besides, you haven't taught your apprentice healing, yet."

"That is true," Clyara said amiably. "Was that all, 'Fleece?"

I was looking down at the knee-shaped blood splotches on the sitting room rug. Casually, Alessarc swept his foot across the stains, and they disappeared. "Yes, that was it," I said, forcing myself to look at her.

"I came by to tell you, *keeron*," Alessarc said, "that I will be away for a while. I'll return before the end of summer, at the latest." He handed me the blood-stained towel and exchanged a meaningful glance with Clyara on his way to the door, and I recognized that they had a telepathic exchange, however brief. To me, he bowed his head and said, "A pleasure, as always, Apprentice," before he left us.

Clyara took a seat and pointed me to the other chair, and I knew I was in trouble. "He doesn't like to lie, especially to me."

"I didn't ask him to, honestly," I said.

"I know you wouldn't," she said, knitting her fingers thoughtfully. It was only then, as her bell-shaped sleeves fell to her elbows, that I noticed the bandages that she always wore on her arms and legs under her robes to hide the constant injury that her body suffered for her calling. "Did he teach you healing, or did you learn it on your own?"

"I taught myself, watching you. Are you upset with me for it?"

She took a heavy breath, so I knew that she was, at least a little. "I knew you would be a challenging apprentice. You're too clever and driven to be anything less, but we must be careful. Spells can weaken you too easily, especially healing."

"You've been taking the same risks," I noted. "I could help you."

"You are helping me, more than you realize," she said, gently. "And it's for that reason that I will not have you risking your well-being. No more healing spells for you, for now." She looked down at the sitting room rug. "You'll need to use some mineral tincture on the rug, still. It looks like Alessarc missed a few spots cleaning up after you."

By the summer of 997, my duties to Clyara had grown to occupy most of my waking hours. As we approached mid-summer, we also became increasingly aware of the impending "Healer's Day." For the elfyn, especially in Moonteyre, it was an important holiday, as it was the one day every third year that Clyara allowed herself to rest, and that the people of Moonteyre could show their gratitude to their treasured Healer.

Clyara's *keeron* Aron had decreed the feast day for his own sanity and convenience, during his time as a healer in the Dark Lands. It was the only way to discourage his fellow townsfolk from constantly showering him with homespun gifts and food. When Clyara came to Moonteyre as its Healer, she renewed the tradition for herself and in memory of Aron: her passion, her master, and ultimately, the victim of her unleashed power.

The feast of 997 was my first as an active participant, or at least as something more than a bystander. My role as Clyara's apprentice, as far as I understood it, was to oversee the preparations and to make the rounds on her behalf among our patients during her day of rest. Clyara was tight-lipped about her expectations of me, as usual, sealing herself in her cottage on the day. She was not expected to emerge until the feast started, later in the day.

I took Clyara's basket of supplies with me and spent the day tending to patients, concluding the afternoon by arranging to meet Frost on the east bank of the Yirae. The cool water was welcome against my skin in the mid-summer heat, but it was especially soothing after the stresses of the day. Across the river from where I stood was the pine forest where the humyn were rumored to dwell, and in the year that I had been Clyara's apprentice, I had never spotted one. Yet, I continued to look every time I visited the river.

"Long day, 'Fleece?" Frost greeted, as she came down to the water.

Without a word, I gave Frost a hug and did not release her until I felt sane again. After the day I had, I needed to think about something — anything — other than the frailty of living beings. I said, finally: "I tended two plow accidents, a leg fracture and a pitchfork in the arm. Plus, three burns and a knife injury at the fairgrounds. I don't know how Clyara does this every day."

"She's been doing it for a long time, that's how. You must be suffering in all those layers that you're wearing, on a hot day like this." Frost stroked my shoulder to comfort me and felt the hidden padding. "You wrapped yourself in bandages?"

"A healer's habit that I picked up, that's all," I said vaguely.

"Your arms are bleeding!" she gasped, noticing the stains on my wrappings where some water had soaked through. She stood back and noticed the coverings on my extremities, hidden by my dark clothes. "'Fleece, what did you do to yourself?"

"I healed," I said evenly, gripping the basket handle tightly. I had never divulged the self-cannibalistic nature of healing magic to Frost, but it only took my clever sister a moment to figure it out. "I'm fine, really. After the first couple of times, it didn't bother me that much, anymore."

"You transfer someone else's injuries to yourself." Frost shook her head in dismay. "You could get yourself killed doing this!"

"I won't," I assured. "This thing inside me, this magestone, mends me from within. As long as I pace myself, I won't suffer any lasting harm. Trust me, I know how to do this."

We were interrupted by the sound of howling. Not a single yowl, as from one of the village hounds, but a chorus of voices from the other side of the river. I didn't think Frost could hear it, given the distance and the rushing noises of the river, and it even took me a moment to decipher where it was, but her eyes were riveted on the opposite bank.

The howling deepened into snarling, and I could just make out the shapes of a dozen or so large wolves, who charged through the woods in tight formation, in pursuit of something invisible to me. One of the wolves, a pale-eyed, silver-coated animal, stopped and watched the others continue their chase, then looked across the water, directly at us. Its muzzle twitched briefly, then it lowered its eyes in the semblance of a bow. A voice sounded in my head, as clear as speech: *We serve, and we protect you.*

As quickly as she appeared, the silver wolf sped away to rejoin the others. Before I could say anything, Frost turned to me. "She spoke."

"You heard her, too?"

She nodded. "Inside my head. But how can that be? Wolves don't speak, do they?"

"Not that I'm aware." I was just as astonished about our encounter as Frost was, and I became uneasy at how still and silent the forest became. "We should start heading back."

I parted ways with Frost at the Ancient and returned to Clyara's cottage to report to the Healer on my rounds. I stroked my fingers along my sleeves, feeling the bandages over my tender skin where I had taken my patients' wounds and newly healed. I braced myself for a confrontation; I already knew what Clyara was going to say.

She met me inside the doorway, looking grave. "You've healed again, and repeatedly."

"There's only so much I can do with herbs and bandages," I said, setting Clyara's basket down and closing the door. "You have to trust me, and let me help."

She shook her head. "You cannot cast without supervision. It exposes you too much," she said. "Not just healing, but all spells. Every time you cast without me to shield you, you risk being found by those who hunt us.

41

Malya has not forgotten us, and she will not stop until she has destroyed us both."

"Then teach me how to shield myself." At her hesitation, I said: "I would rather have you guide me, than follow Malya's path and learn on my own."

"You have a point. I will consider it. Now, go change out of your bandages. No more healing for you tonight."

Clyara and I arrived at the fairgrounds promptly at dusk, and I spent a few minutes at her side, greeting Elders and former patients. I was glad that my magestone had mended my arms and shoulders without leaving any scars, as my dress had cap-like sleeves and an open neckline that hid nothing. It was made of pale, pearlescent pink muslin, and it happened to be the only dress in my armoire that was light enough for a summer evening. I had a suspicion that Clyara had let Frost into my room to clean out my wardrobe, again.

During a lull in the evening's activities, while the musicians had a drink to cool off, I saw an opportunity to make an early departure.

You're not going to abandon your well-wishers, I hope, I said.

I will stay for them. Clyara managed a smile. You've done enough for me today, 'Fleece. Get some rest, and we will discuss your new regimen in the morning. I've decided to intensify your training.

I was so elated by Clyara's decision that I almost gave her a hug, but I restrained myself, given the curious eyes all around us. Instead, I bowed my head to her and said, *Thank you, Clyara.*

You may not thank me at this time tomorrow. Go. Leave while you can.

Free for the night, I was looking forward to a solitary hike up the Ajlekuun, hoping to catch the sunset from the summit, if I was lucky. I redoubled my pace, weaving through the crowds, when I heard my name in conversation. I stopped and glanced over my shoulder and saw Ohynn, of all people, standing with a group of young men who were watching me.

I stifled a laugh and shook my head. "Not interested, sorry," I said under my breath.

"Not interested in what?" came a quiet voice next to me.

I teetered in my surprise, but Alessarc caught my arm. I laughed at my own clumsiness and regained my balance. "Good evening and welcome back, Healer Alessarc."

"Thank you." He looked relaxed and was dressed in a fitted linen tunic for the warm night. "Good evening, Apprentice. Leaving already?" *I'm jealous.*

I chuckled at the secret joke. "Yes, going far away where no one will find me. Come with me," I said, tugging his sleeve, as I resumed my path through the crowds to escape the din. *I need your advice on something.*

42

That sounds serious, he said. I released his wrinkled sleeve, and he offered his hand instead. His palm was warm but not soft, and it radiated an energy that flowed into my core. He took the lead and quickly found us a private, quiet corner behind a stand of pin oaks, not too far from the path. "So, how can I help you?"

I clutched my locket nervously. "I healed again today."

"Clyara told me," he said. "She's not angry with you, Apprentice, just concerned that you're rushing this. I know it's frustrating to wait. I remember how torturous and grueling it felt, when I was your age."

"She told me it was dangerous for me to cast without supervision."

"That is true. You have to trust your mistress; she will never lie to you. She may evade and inveigle, but we all do that." He stooped a little to meet my lowered eyes. "What else is bothering you?"

How does he read me so well? "In the past, I've seen her cast a different healing spell."

"And you want to know what it is," he deduced, and I nodded. "I won't teach it to you. It's a curse passed down from Aron."

"Then please explain to me what it does," I said. "Clyara casts it too quickly for me to hear it. She's used it to heal traumatic, horrific wounds, and I know she couldn't possibly absorb these injuries herself."

He sighed and said, after a pause, "It would be something that she uses as a last resort. Instead of transferring the injuries to herself, the spell transfers the injuries … well, away."

"Away where?" Then I realized: "To the humyn, to her enemies."

"Sometimes, yes," he said, looking around to check that we were truly alone. "To someone or something else of her choice, more or less."

I recalled some of the cases I had witnessed: flesh torn to the bone, severe hemorrhages, gangrenous infections … each one becoming a curse inflicted upon an unsuspecting victim. "That's despicable!" I hissed, stepping back from him. "Who is she to decide—"

"I'm not debating the ethics of the spell with you," he said evenly, with an effort. "You asked me to explain, so I did. Now you see why your life is in real danger, and why your mistress sees the need to protect you."

"But I don't know this spell!"

"That doesn't matter," he said, taking my shoulders to calm and still me. "You are Clyara's apprentice, so you are perceived to be a threat. Look, she didn't compose the wretched thing, and there are others who use the spell, more cruelly, so she does what she can to keep the elfyn safe."

"You're a healer. Do you use it?"

"It's not a healing spell," he said, begrudgingly. "But yes, I've had to use it on occasion, for defense."

Alessarc's hands felt warm on my bare arms, and I glanced at them.

His hands and arms were tanned, but they were supple and smooth, unlike his lined face and throat. "You hide your true age, for some reason."

"I'll be sixty-seven at the end of this year," he said, dropping his hands. "I was born in the year 930. I have records to prove it."

"You may be fifty years older than me, but your hands don't match your brow, Alessarc. I suspect that mages don't age the way normal people do," I said, remembering that Clyara was over one-hundred-fifty but looked a fraction of that. "It must be something in the way the magestones preserve their hosts." Even his physique, draped simply in airy linen, was trimmer and more defined than that of a typical older man.

"You can be very observant, sometimes. I can see why Clyara has her hands full with you," he said, with his infectious, mischievous grin. "I should retreat before you discover all my secrets, and before your mistress discovers that we've been conferring without her knowledge." He raised my hand to his lips and gave it a soft, gentle peck. "A pleasure, as always."

"Why do you do this, Alessarc?" I asked. At his inquiring look, I elaborated, "Why do you speak with me, if it might displease Clyara?"

"Because it pleases me," he said directly, then bowed his head. "Good night, Apprentice."

I watched him leave, and I wondered about his continued interest in my apprenticeship. I was partly to blame, as I found it too easy to converse with him. Apart from Frost and Clyara, he was the only one to whom I could speak plainly about the magic I learned. Moreover, Alessarc was the only grown male, apart from Tracker and my father, who seemed to view me as more than a potential conquest, at a time when I was starting to notice the unique charms and qualities of men.

My shoulders still felt warm from his touch, and my hand still tingled from his brief kiss. *Maybe I just like to be around him.*

Chapter 5: The Beginning and the End

Your father is dead, child.

A neighbor had come to the school to tell Frost and me that our father had died in an unfortunate accident. Winter was found lying on the ground behind the house, a short distance away from a ladder that remained propped against the wall, without a mark to indicate any deliberate harm. Frost and I saw his body, but we couldn't understand how he died from such a short fall.

I discovered the truth on the morning we buried him, when I stole a look under his shroud. His throat had been crushed like a roll of parchment, so brutally that his shattered bones jutted from his torn flesh. Why hadn't we seen that earlier? It was such a horrific sight that I had been dumbstruck, and I never told Frost what I had seen. It was one of the few secrets that I kept from her.

Keep her safe.

The images in my dream shifted backward, and I was celebrating my tenth birthday with my father and Frost. He took his silver locket off from around his neck and held it out to me, the polished silver almost glowing in the lamplight. I knew what was inside the locket; it was a tiny portrait of my mother, a chestnut-haired woman with dark eyes.

I was your age when I found it in the woods. I had it for years before your mother arrived from the North Woods. She said she spoke to me because it caught her attention. I had a picture of her put inside after we were married. It's yours now. She would've wanted you to have it.

I awoke from my dream to find Clyara sitting on the edge of my bed, tucking a slim, leather-bound volume inside her robes. "What time is it?" I asked groggily, and through the window I could see that the sun was far from rising. The etched silver of the locket hanging from my bedpost glinted in the light of the candle that Clyara had brought.

"Still early," she said brightly. She levitated the thin blanket off me, and the sudden rush of cool air against my half-covered skin was enough to snap me out of my fatigue. Only once I was on my feet did she let the cover settle back onto the cozy feather bed.

"Time to go," she said. She blew out the candle and took my wrist.

Suddenly, a swirl of air and light enveloped us, and I shut my eyes tight against the blinding windstorm. Another of Clyara's tests, perhaps?

45

Then, as quickly as it had come, it was gone. I opened my eyes a sliver and stumbled backwards in amazement.

Clyara and I were standing in the middle of the pine forest, and I was still in my thin linen shift and slippers.

"To start, perhaps you could show me what you've picked up without my help?" she suggested.

"Where do I begin?" I said, still clearing the drowsiness from my head. Chagrinned and exposed, I spilled it all. "There are these." I cast a small fire on a dry branch overhead and extinguished it. I crouched to touch the ground and sent a small tremor through the forest floor under us. I closed my eyes, willed myself to appear next to Clyara, and found myself by her side when I reopened my eyes. "There are a few more."

"I give you that much free time?" she remarked.

"Funny, it usually doesn't feel that way," I said.

"Well, that is a relief," she said. "Let's get you dressed. We can't have you accompanying me on visits in your nightgown."

Between patients, we spent the remaining daylight hours in the woods, refining what I knew, and for the first time in a long while, I felt like Clyara's apprentice again, and not an intrusive houseguest. She corrected my mistakes and was candid about her own past ones, and she taught me some things that I may have never learned on my own.

However, all that knowledge carried a price. Recognizing that I was no longer a true novice, Clyara didn't spare me her more dangerous assaults. I found myself dodging large spheres of fire, ice and lightning; I cast a spell to speed myself through an obstacle course of collapsing sinkholes that Clyara tossed under the needle-strewn forest floor, and "blinked" my way out of the ones that caught me anyway.

At the end, to avoid an irate brown bear that my mistress had summoned, I transformed myself into a wood mouse and hid in a fallen log, and I found that I couldn't change back. I was depleted, and I lay on my side panting and helpless, wondering what I had gotten myself into by taking up Clyara's challenge. She found me easily, and she lifted me gingerly out of the hollow of the trunk, cradling me in the cup of her palm. *Always leave yourself enough to revert.* As she picked my fallen clothes off the ground and sent the bear back on its way, she held my tiny form against her chest, and I felt myself lulled by the deafening resonance of her heart against me and the scent of her all around me.

My mistress was testing me, yes, but she would never endanger my life. She cared for me as if I were her own child, as much as she eschewed sentimentality. *There are always some who would take advantage of you, especially if they know what you are.*

The humyn. Will I need to know how to fight them? I asked.

There has been enough bloodshed. You need to know how to defend yourself, if you must, and be patient with those who attack out of fear.

I felt the air moving around us, and I knew that Clyara had returned us to the cottage. She set me in the middle of my mattress, and I opened my eyes to the expansive, hilly plain that was my bed. My door seemed as far away as the Ajlekyrn, and equally vast. Clyara loomed over me: as tall, as still and as silent as any of those regal mountains.

Sleep, you've had a long day, she said.

Will I be ready, some day? I asked, barely able to keep awake.

Ready for what, Snowfleece?

Ready to meet the one who killed my father.

Justice will come in time. Sleep, now.

You know who killed him? I asked. My eyes were no longer willing to open, and I felt myself stretch across the bed in my natural form, as Clyara pulled the blanket over me. I was so tired that I didn't even hear her answer to my question, if she gave one at all.

By the end of summer, Clyara and I had settled into a routine and rhythm in our daily existence that served us both well. Clyara was generous with her time and knowledge, and I enjoyed the challenges of learning how to harness my new power. If not for the dangerous nature of some of the spells she taught me, I would have considered my life an idyllic one.

Also, Frost shared with me the joyous news that she and Tracker were expecting their first child. They were converting my old bedroom into a nursery, and I couldn't be happier for their good fortune. I was excited to become an aunt for the first time, and looked forward to hearing mayhem and mirth in our family's house again, after years of quietude.

I had also begun to imagine a bright future as Clyara's successor, and the idea was no longer as daunting as it had seemed the year before, when everything had begun. However, the universe had other plans for me.

It was a clear, sunny day in early autumn. Clyara had given me the morning to myself, and I chose to spend it meditating in the oak forest north of Moonteyre. I found a patch far from civilization and lay down on the forest floor to gaze up into the verdant canopy high above. The sounds of the woods, from the rustling of the leaves to the melodic mimicry of the mockingbirds, lulled me into a state of peace. I perhaps even fell asleep.

Whatever the case, I stirred from my trance when the forest fell eerily silent; I had always found it to be ominous when the birds fell quiet during daylight.

Snowfleece, I need you home now.

There was a peculiar urgency in Clyara's call. Shielding myself first as my mistress had taught me, to avoid detection by anyone who would track me by my magic, I recited a spell of speed to quicken my passage back to Moonteyre. Reaching the outskirts of the village, I cast a spell of invisibility on myself to avoid being detained by well-intentioned passersby. From the terseness of Clyara's summons, I had expected the worst, but nothing looked out of place, and people were untroubled, so I relaxed but did not slow.

Once I caught sight of Clyara's cottage, I blinked inside and discovered that she had gone. She left a note for me on her sitting room table, weighed down by her earthenware teapot. I burned the note as she directed therein and proceeded to carry out her written instructions to the letter.

First item on the list. From Clyara's bookshelf, I pulled the bulky, hard-bound brown textbook and lay my hand on the cover as I had the first time. There was no writing visible on the cover, so I had to recall the name. "'Practical Geology: A Scholar's Guide to Mineral and Metal Lore,'" I said and felt the familiar icy tingle underneath my fingertips, as the gold letters reappeared. I retrieved the silk pouch of magestones stashed within and buttoned it into my skirt pocket, and replaced the book back on the shelf. *Next.*

I jumped at the unexpected knock at the door. I hesitated to open it, until I heard Frost calling me through it. She looked paler than usual, her eyes wide with anxiety. "What's the matter?" I asked her.

Frost came inside and shut the door behind her. "Some strangers have been going from home to home, asking about you and Clyara. They look affable enough, but something about them seems a little … off. I've been trying to avoid them, until I find out a little more about them."

My mind was still busy processing Clyara's list of instructions. "This is not a good time for visitors. Clyara's stepped out, and I'm to follow."

"Follow where?"

"I'm going … The less you know, the better, I think." I gave her a reassuring embrace. "Don't worry. I'll be back as soon as I can."

Before Frost could protest, I blinked out of the cottage and into the back yard. The sooner I finished my errands for Clyara, the sooner I could return to see to the matter of these "strangers."

Hurry, came Clyara's insistent call, leading me south. Her track was faint and becoming weaker. Without knowing exactly where she was, I couldn't teleport directly to her, so I had to follow her trail while I had one. As the sounds from the village dwindled, I was able to narrow my focus southward. Clyara was leading me somewhere into the woods between the valley and the Ajlekyrn.

Something inside me knew exactly where to go, where to turn, which rocks to climb, as if she led me by the hand. I found a hollow at the base of a boulder, and I placed the pouch of magestones inside it as Clyara had ordered. *Step two completed.* I took note of the landmarks and followed the Yirae River south, towards the mountains. I looked up along the sheer face, wondering how best to ascend to where Clyara was waiting.

Protect her, I heard, and this time, it was not Clyara's voice, but I recognized it. Frost and I had heard her voice the afternoon of the Healer's Feast, from the silver wolf across the river. Behind me, the snarls of wolves echoed in the forest, although the beasts themselves were hidden from me. There were other voices, too, that sounded like cries of anguish and pain, but there was nothing that was close enough for me to see. *Hurry,* the voice spurred me. *Your mistress needs you.*

I repointed my attention on the mountain ahead of me. It was going to take too long to climb, so I stilled my mind long enough to prepare my levitation spell, but I ascended too sharply. In my nervousness and impatience, my focus fell short, and I slammed into the cliff wall, abrading myself against the jagged granite before I reached the top.

I threw myself up over the edge, painfully rolling to a stop. I froze.

Even with her back to me, I couldn't mistake Clyara's adversary to be anyone but Malya. Her hair, like Glory's, was burnished and golden in the sun, and her form, from the little that her white robes revealed, was tall and lean like her daughter's. She made me think of a waterfall in its full majesty after a storm: glorious to behold, but overwhelming and deadly just the same. And she stood mere meters from me.

I did not dare make a sound. I scrambled silently to crouch behind a boulder and peeked, ready to sprint at a second's notice. From my vantage, I spotted Clyara fifty meters away, maybe more, and she was not alone. She was on her knees, her robes frayed and her slender body heaving with every difficult breath. Flanking her, as though they were guarding her, stood two gaunt figures in jewel-hued robes. They were more than gaunt, they were skeletal, and they were utterly still.

You've taken my child from me, keeron. I think that entitles me to yours. Malya whirled to face me, a glinting blur swirling in her wake towards me.

I raised my arms to shield myself, just in time, and my barrier was pummeled and shredded by the onslaught of steel and glass that Malya had shot at me. My shield would only hold for a few seconds more, so I willed myself to stay calm and focused on a spot a few meters away, just enough to get out of range, and I blinked.

Clyara took advantage of Malya's momentary distraction to send forth a wave of energy that threw Malya even further from me. Even as Clyara got to her feet, she looked fragile and unsteady, with the wind swirling dust, fire and smoke around her delicate figure. *Come closer to me, Snowfleece,* Clyara beckoned with a motion of her hand.

Malya rebounded quickly and watched me blink to my mistress's side, her green eyes boring into me. Clyara's two companions closed around me, and I cringed at the sight of them up close; they were desiccated corpses, with scraps of dry sinew clinging to their bleached bones. Their ragged, richly colored garments were styled like Clyara's silks—healer's robes.

Stay with them. The gemwraiths will protect you, Clyara said.

Seeing me safe in the company of her undead guards, Clyara returned her full attention to her adversary. She raised her hands and created an umbrella just as a storm of fire showered upon our heads. With a wave of her hands, she swept the smoldering debris from the ground and sent the wave of cinders back on the other sorceress.

Malya had magic that I had never seen before. She chanted spells that opened portals, summoning deadly creatures of all shapes and sizes, from swarms of hornets to a hulking stone giant.

Clyara let Malya exhaust herself with her efforts and destroyed most of the portals before Malya's minions were able to emerge. Clyara dispatched the others speedily, and still was able to get in the occasional shot at Malya. Clyara kept a shield around the two "gemwraiths" and me always, and glared at me whenever I tried to cast a spell. *Save your strength, my girl,* she warned. *You will need it—all of it.*

Sudden weakness and numbness overtook me. To my horror, my flesh was shriveling to a parchment-like state. Clyara whispered something under her breath and smiled to reassure me. Before my eyes, her fine features became withered and ashen, and her sacrifice restored my body to normal. I turned to Malya and saw her victorious sneer.

I couldn't just stand by and do nothing while Clyara guarded me with her life. I tried without success to dispel the shield that Clyara had cast around me. In my despair, I pounded my fists against the shield and pleaded with her to let me help her. *Why am I here, then?* Clyara merely shook her head and closed her eyes. She folded her hands together, as a hot white light enveloped her. Malya made her own gestures to an equivalent end.

They released their forces at each other, in unison, and the result was a deafening, blinding explosion that shook the earth and tossed them both to the ground. Clyara's shield crumbled apart around me, and I clung to the boulder that I fell against, with the gemwraiths shielding me like a bone cage. The boulder shifted under me, until the tremors stopped and the dust settled.

Malya lay twisted and prone on the ground, with her robes like cerements over her. Clyara knelt on the ground silently, her exhaustion clear on her face and in her uneven, labored breath. I ran to her side and knelt beside her, with the gemwraiths just a step behind me.

She grasped my hand feebly. "I can't see. Is she dead?"

"I— I don't know. She isn't moving." My concern was for my mistress only. "You'll be all right, Clyara, won't you," I implored, gripping her hand as she lay down. I was shaken by the trickle of blood from her lips and nose, signaling internal wounds. The gemwraiths stood in grim silence. "We must get her home, now!"

Clyara squeezed my hand. "There isn't time. You must be sure, and destroy us both." She squinted at her gemwraiths. "Spare me their fate."

"You're not going to die, Clyara. You can't."

I turned towards a bright flash about four hundred meters away and saw polished metal glistening in the sunlight, the armor and blades of at least two dozen figures clad in grey, charging from a portal towards us. Upon seeing Malya upon the ground, they began shouting something that I could not understand, but their outrage was palpable. I had only a few seconds, maybe a minute, to get Clyara away.

In the brief moment that my eyes had left her, Clyara had turned almost white, and only a faint flicker of her eyes told me that she was still alive, barely. "Don't fail me, my girl," Clyara reminded me. "Carry out my wishes, and be kind." Her light eyes turned to the sky, and closed.

The gemwraiths were tugging at my arms, and the advancing wave was closer now, but I was rooted to Clyara's side. I held her hand and felt her chest fall with her last breath. My eyes were too tired to tear, and my voice caught in my throat. *Goodbye, Clyara.* I touched my hand to her heart and felt its stillness under my palm. *My keeron and my friend.* My hand jerked back when her body started to move again. *She's not dead!* I thought to myself joyously, squeezing her hand.

Her hand stiffened, and her eyes began to open. The gemwraiths leaned closer, ready to receive her as one of their own. *Spare me their fate,* she had said. I dropped Clyara's dead hand and ignited her body with a pure blue fire before I could hesitate further. I was to make sure that there was nothing left of her corpse to animate. Her rapidly burning body became a mound of heavy, thick ash, with her thimble-sized, ice-transparent stone in the center of the smoldering black char where Clyara's heart used to be.

I looked up sharply at the sound of metal striking bone. One of the gemwraiths had stepped in front of me and suffered a shot fired by one of the attackers. The metal pellet was embedded in one of the wraith's bared ribs, cracking it, but it seemed to take no notice of the damage. Most of the hostile strangers were less than a hundred meters from us now. Humyn, if I had to guess, but I wasn't staying around to verify that.

Some of the humyn stopped their charge to attend to Malya, who was rising to her feet. *By Ajle, she's still alive.* As if she sensed me, Malya opened her eyes and reached her hand towards me, a smile forming on her lips.

I couldn't fight her, not now, but I wasn't about to leave Clyara's gem behind for her, either. I concentrated and erected a wall of flame and smoke to hide us from the approaching humyn, and reached for Clyara's magestone amidst her ashes. At the instant that I touched the clear white gem, the gemwraiths riveted on me with a ferocious new energy.

Oh, no.

I blinked out from between them and ran for my life.

Chapter 6: Into the Wilderness

Dodge the wraiths, avoid the humyn, save the gem. I gripped Clyara's magestone tightly in my fist and fled my pursuers, skimming over the rocky terrain. I cast a shield over my shoulder and stayed low to the ground, trying to avoid the flying ammunition. I could only run for so long before I would run out of land; already I saw the cliff edge close ahead of me. I turned my eyes up to Ajle and prayed for guidance, and the birds that soared overhead gave me an answer.

I ran towards the edge with renewed determination. *Damn, what if it falls out of my pocket?* I popped Clyara's white gem in my mouth and leapt off the rock ledge, launching myself into the air as far as I could. *Don't panic.* I began to fall, I saw the ground fast approaching, but I knew I had time to cast—

The wraiths leapt after me! They were risking their own destruction for the sake of Clyara's gem. Their bones closed around my body, and their weight pulled me head-first, down to the jagged rocks below.

I suppressed my panic, watching the ground race up to meet me, long enough to cast a spell to transform. Feathers sprouted from my shortening arms, and my shrinking body slipped out from my clothes and the bones that tightly clasped them.

The mountain currents carried me up, above the tangle of bones and cloth. The beak of my compact merlin form was just large enough to firmly hold Clyara's gem, with the weight of the stone barely hindering my flight. I was unable to get the distance I wanted, however, even with such a fast and agile body. At least, I was too small a target for the humyn to reach me with their projectiles, but I made myself invisible to avoid their attention, anyway.

The gemwraiths stopped their fall and untangled themselves from my garments. They apparently still possessed some residual power, as they soared through the air and closed in on me again, sensing me through my spells. I tried to cast a shield around myself, but the barrier was useless. A hand reached through it unhindered and grabbed hold of one of my claws, crushing my fragile bones. I fluttered and kicked madly to get away, only to have the other wraith start closing its hand around my head. Unless I gave up the gem, I was going to be torn in two.

I opened my beak and let the stone drop into the open air, but I wasn't planning on giving up just yet. The wraiths released me instantly and turned their attention to retrieving the gem that was slipping through their grasp like a raindrop through a fishing net.

I ignored the pain in my foot to reshape myself into something larger, faster and more powerful: a falcon. I folded my wings against my body for a stoop, and I dove after the gem alongside the less-aerodynamic gemwraiths. I flapped my wings to slow briefly, then shut my beak around the stone. On my ascent, a wraith hand struck me, sending a shock like lightning through me.

The force of the blow shoved me forward, and the stone lodged in my throat. I changed back into my natural form to avoid choking on the magestone and reflexively swallowed. *Ajle save me, what have I done!* Clyara's gem slid easily down my throat.

I forgot about the wraiths behind me; any amount of pain that they could possibly inflict was minuscule compared to the agony that overcame me. It was like the pain that I had felt the first time I had taken a gem, but now the pain was twenty-fold. The energy and power of Clyara's stone gripped me as it tore throughout my unprepared frame. I felt my old stone crack apart inside me as the new one took its place. My muscles tightened, my joints stiffened, and I plummeted towards the jagged rocks, paralyzed as I watched the ground speeding towards me. In my disturbed state, even that terrible fate of being broken on the rocks, was preferable to being ripped apart alive by the stone.

My life flashed before my eyes, and I remembered Frost, and my father. I remembered when I had taken my first gem; Clyara had spoken to me when I was unconscious, and the words reemerged from the back of my mind: *Be strong! It is only pain.*

But such pain! Still, the memory of her restored some sanity to me, and I blurted a spell to slow and stop my fall, only a few meters from the ground. The gem allowed me my spell, its energy coursing through me. I recited the spell like a mantra, willing myself to remain hovering over the sharp stones. Gingerly, I floated to the ground, my bare feet carefully stepping across the rough ground. I watched the pursuing wraiths descend and shut my eyes tight with overflowing tears when the shredding agony returned. I struggled to keep my footing, exposed in more than one way before the ghastly pair.

They did not approach, nor did they turn away. For the first time, they spoke to me, their voices papery and faint in my head: *We serve.*

They waited, as I picked up my clothes from the rocks and retreated to the wall, out of the humyn's line of sight high on the cliff. The wraiths followed me but remained at a respectful distance, leaving me to dress and think in peace. The gemwraiths had not attacked Clyara, but when she died, they immediately sought the gem for themselves. Clyara had alluded to becoming a gemwraith if her remains weren't destroyed, so it stood to reason that both of the gemwraiths had carried the same gem inside of them at some point and were still somehow bound to it. It should have been obvious: gem-wraith. Now that I had the gem, and had shown that I was strong enough to bear its power, at least for the moment, they were linked to me and would serve me as they had served my mistress.

They were mindless, cursed shells of once-living men, slaves to the gem and to me. They stood patiently before me, awaiting my orders, as though they had not just tried minutes earlier to rip me apart with their bare-boned hands. Even as they stood so placidly, I was still favoring the leg that one of them had broken in his fist.

"What do I do with you?" I wondered aloud, watching them. They would never find peace until they were freed, and I was so unnerved by their physical presence that I had no desire of their company, so I did what seemed best for all of us, not pausing long enough to think of the consequences.

"Rest now, and be at peace." I called a spell to mind, and as I recited the words to myself, the wraiths seemed to straighten and brace themselves. The disintegration spell took effect, and the wraiths bowed their heads and crumbled to dust without a struggle, leaving only their tattered silk robes behind.

Watching the dust being scattered by the breezes, I felt a slow burning on my skin and in my nostrils. I stepped back from the dust cloud, but it was too late; the ashes had already dissipated. I rubbed my eyes and face against my sleeve to clean off any residue, but there was little relief. To distract myself and get my bearings, I focused on the glow of the sun setting behind the forest. I peered up at the cliff from which I had dived but heard no sign of the humyn mob that had chased me. For the moment, at least, I was safe.

As I began to recite the blink spell to leave the area, the burning from the wraith dust crept into my mouth and throat, choking me and ruining my concentration. I coughed, to no avail. Every breath I took immersed me deeper in the invisible fire. My new gem churned with renewed vigor, as though it was celebrating my new debilitating pain. *What a treacherous little rock.*

I awoke face down in the silt, with the gentle waves of the Yirae River lapping at my ankles. My shattered foot had long healed, perfectly, as far as I could tell by the pre-dawn light. My face was stiff with dried, caked mud, and my nails were broken, but no longer bleeding. The tight skin under my torn fingernails stung, reminding me that I was still alive. I rose to my feet shakily, remembering the night in pieces. Aside from the crumbs of dirt in my nostrils, I breathed freely, and for that, I was glad.

I recalled moments when the gem tested my strength. It seemed to know when my situation was precarious enough that it could try to exploit my weakness. Such as when I was cleaning myself off by a fast-moving stream, the pain gripped my limbs suddenly. I lost my footing and had to fight the current to stay afloat; I didn't do too badly, considering that I hadn't gone swimming in such turbulent waters in years. I even managed somehow to survive the plummet through the churning falls themselves.

Once the moon had risen high enough to light my path, I had hiked back up the mountains and turned in the direction of Moonteyre under a spell of invisibility. Following the Yirae River, I encountered a make-shift camp along my trail. I heard voices speaking in a language that was mostly unfamiliar to me, but I felt the anxiety of the speakers. Again, the gem gripped me with a burst of pain centered on my heart, and I clenched my teeth tightly on a willow branch to keep from crying out. I slipped away into the darkness unnoticed and sought another route.

As the night wore on, I had looked for a more permanent shelter. I yearned for the comfort of home, but I was sure that in my present condition, I would only do more harm than good if I were to return. At the least, my return without Clyara would raise questions that I was not yet ready to answer. Frost seemed unbearably far away, and I briefly wondered when I would ever see her again. I made an effort not to think about Clyara, but the memory of her cremation weighed heavily in my mind.

So, there I was at dawn, alone on the bank of the Yirae River, still far south of home. Although the sun was coming up past the horizon, my exhaustion was yet to be relieved. I yearned for my bed, the warmth of my blankets, or even my scratchy woolen shift instead of my tattered dress. I curled up against a hollowed trunk by the riverbank and slept.

I awoke while the sun was high. Moonteyre was far away, and Frost was still waiting. Her face was dim in my mind, like distant memories of years past. Always, my thoughts remained in the present, on the gnawing, furious pain that churned inside my chest. Clyara's magestone would not be ignored, and it would not let me rest until I had let it express itself, and I was not ready to test myself just yet. I focused my attention instead on my surroundings.

For all the traveling and exploration that I had done as a child, visiting other elfyn and exploring the wilderness, I had never really spent much time in this part of the southern lands. Except for perhaps Clyara, I knew of no one who had ever ventured so far from Moonteyre, so the Yirae Falls were the perfect temporary haven for me, to hide and shelter me until I had the strength to return home. I traveled cautiously, moving among the shadows and generally keeping out of sight. By dusk, I had returned to the safety of the falls and found a shelf to hide myself from the cold night winds.

Now, without any other distractions, the voices and visions of home nagged me, memories evoked by the smells clinging to my hair and clothes. I tried not to lose myself in my memories of Moonteyre, but I yearned for an asylum. I curled into a tight ball, digging my nails into the flesh of my arms to distract from the maddening churning in my chest, from which there was no escape. The throbbing gem taunted me, threatening to tear my heart asunder and burst out onto the water-logged ground at my feet, but at the same time, it would not reject me. At least, not yet. I tried to focus on the water of the falls coursing overhead to divert my attention, without success.

I peered into the darkness around me, and I wondered if there might be someone watching, if someone else knew of the power inside me and coveted it. More creatures like the gemwraiths, or humyn, lurking in the shadows. I gauged everything for magic: the water, the ground, the trees, the air … I braced myself to strike out at the first opponent. The gem seemed to twist inside me like a worm, straining my sanity, but at the same time warming me and promising incredible power.

Vengeance. Remember vengeance, whispered the wind in my ear. *You may not be able to raise the dead, but you can find justice for them. Think of the one who killed Clyara. A humyn killed your father, you know that in your heart.*

More destruction to be had. It had to end somewhere, there had to be another way. I buried my head in my hands and cried. My heart ached, not simply because of Clyara's gem, or the fact that I had lost my mistress. *How could I have been so blind to what was coming?* With the havoc that Clyara and Malya had caused over the years, wasn't it just a matter of time before one or both of them would fall? Only, the elfyn were innocent; while they benefited from Clyara's magic, they had no inkling of her darker nature.

The more I tried to avoid thinking about it, the more I returned to my failure to stop Malya. I had stood by and watched her get to her feet, standing victorious. If the humyn who chased me truly were her followers, then who knew what kind of retribution they had in mind for me, now that my mistress was gone?

I had no direction, no guidance, no one to explain to me what to do or what my next steps were. I couldn't face the elfyn by myself, to explain to them that their Healer was dead, but I also couldn't imagine a life without Frost. Invariably, if I returned to Moonteyre, I would become the new Healer, but I was only seventeen, and I had yet only cast a handful of healing spells. I wasn't ready to become Healer, and I was unprepared to be the shield against Malya's wrath, should she turn her attention towards the elfyn again.

The gem continued to prod and taunt me, and I could do little to discourage it. It suddenly occurred to me that it could be restless, like a fussy infant. With my reticence to use my magic, I hadn't thought to tax the stone, but sooner or later, I would need to work with it. As my knowledge grew, so proportionally would my control over the cursed rock. Even as the thoughts entered my head, the gem twisted sharply inside me and tightened my chest, daring me to try to tame it.

In my rage and pain, I slapped my hands down against the ground and sent a tremor that carried up, into the walls of the cavern, and shook loose a torrent of rocks and mud upon my head. As I hid my head from the falling debris, I laughed; wouldn't it be pathetic if, after all that had happened, I had managed to kill myself so stupidly? A large chunk of rock fell a short distance from me, and I heard something like a panicked gasp from underneath it. *By Ajle, I've hit something!* I staggered to the fallen boulder and cast a spell of dim light in the cavern.

A fire serpent was pinned, its gold and orange scales glistening in the weak light. It was a juvenile, judging by its slender, coiled length and the markings on its cowl, which it spread with a frightened hiss. At least it was alive and unhurt, just trapped, as far as I could tell.

Carefully, as not to startle the tiny snake, I levitated the hefty boulder with an effort, and saw as it wriggled clear, that it had scraped itself against the sharp edges. It moved away from me quickly, wanting nothing to do with me.

"I'm sorry," I said, following the unfortunate animal at a safe distance. I came closer once I caught its attention, and I laid my hand on its back. It curled back and snapped at me, but missed, luckily for me. Its small fangs were big enough to hurt, and its venom would have blistered my skin as quickly as an adult's toxin. I paralyzed it for just a moment with my touch, and I pressed firmly against its wound with my other hand.

I didn't even think to recite the words aloud, I knew the spell so intimately. I felt the energy flowing from my heart through my blood, coursing through my arteries and fingers. *From the weakened to the blessed.* I pulled my hand away from the healed patch of new skin and fine, smooth scale, and I stepped back when the serpent started to recover from my paralysis spell.

The snakelet slipped into the darkness, and I chastised myself for my carelessness. Now that Clyara was gone, I had to be more responsible for my own actions. I walked back to my sheltering corner and felt a raw stinging in my side. Looking down, I saw the waist of my frayed dress stained with droplets of fresh blood where I had sustained my reptilian patient's wound.

Months ago, I would have been whimpering at such an ugly scratch. Now, I simply shook my head with annoyance. I leaned against the cave wall and waited. The pain of the wound started to fade, while the gem slowly churned. The blood on the dress dried to a stiff brown patch, long after my skin had healed. I prodded the flesh beneath the dried blood and felt no soreness.

In fact, I felt better than I had since I had awoken. The gem had been appeased. For now.

My tiredness kept me asleep until well into the morning, when I felt strong enough to emerge from the falls. I splashed myself with the cool fresh water and rinsed my dress of its recent stains. I picked some berries for my breakfast on my way up along the Yirae Falls, back towards Moonteyre. Ready or not, I needed to return home. I was sure that there were some who would feel that things were better without me, especially once the truth surfaced, but I was certain that Frost wanted me home, and I owed her an explanation for where I had been.

I thought to skirt around the campsite I had encountered the day before, but as I approached, I noticed that the camp had been abandoned, hastily. The fires had been extinguished, and there was no trace of the humyn who had camped there, but a couple of the tents remained standing, and a few utensils were left behind. I proceeded towards to Moonteyre, and it was almost noon when I reached the outskirts, with clouds rolling in overhead. I remained hidden among the townsfolk, unsure of the welcome I would receive, but clearly nothing traumatic had transpired here. The day looked like any other. The craftsmen were out selling their goods, and the children were playing in the square, under the careful watch of the elders sitting under the shady boughs of the Ancient.

I visited Clyara's cottage and saw that nothing was disturbed, much to my relief. I took my etched silver locket from the doorknob in my room and slipped it into my pocket without looking inside at the portrait of my mother. I didn't linger in the cottage, as the smells and sights only served to remind me that Clyara was indeed gone.

I found Frost behind the home we once shared, taking down the laundry from the line. I wanted to hug her, but remembered that I was still invisible to her. She stopped and looked around, her eyes passing me without notice. "Is that you, 'Fleece?" she asked in a low voice.

Yes, I replied shortly, surprised that she had sensed me.

"Where have you been?" she whispered, returning to her laundry lest someone was observing her.

Hiding, and thinking. Is anyone still asking about Clyara?

She shook her head. "They left and returned again briefly yesterday, but they haven't asked me anything." She picked off the last items and picked up the filled basket. "Let's talk inside."

I followed her into the house and canceled my invisibility once I was within the familiar walls. Frost gasped at seeing me so suddenly, and at my haggard state. Still, without hesitation, she wrapped her arms around me and smoothed down my curls, and her gentle, supportive embrace recharged me. "Thank Ajle that you're all right." She held tightly onto my hand, as if she feared that I would slip away again.

"Clyara is dead," I said emotionlessly.

Frost's expression darkened, and her grasp tightened further. She had questions, but she saw that I was not up to the task of answering. "Let me get you a change of clothes and something to eat," she said, leading me into the kitchen. She left me briefly to find fresh clothes for me, and I had the chance to look around the room. How tidy and cozy everything was. I tore a piece of bread from the loaf on the table and ate ravenously, keeping my eyes averted from the dirt caked under my chipped nails and grass hanging down from my overgrown bangs.

Frost returned with some clean clothes and a basin. "Finish eating, I'll draw some water for you." She filled the basin and warmed it with some water from a kettle on the stove, moving efficiently, but her mind was elsewhere. At last, she handed me a cloth and a bar of soap and asked: "Are you back to stay?"

"What a strange question. Where else would I go?" I rinsed myself off and changed into the warm, dry clothes, and felt immediately better.

"I don't know, 'Fleece," she said, peering at me. "You seem uncertain. What's wrong, aside from the obvious?" She took my hand and proceeded to trim my jagged fingernails with clippers, as she used to when we were children.

I did feel like a child again, entrusting Frost to keep some secret that I couldn't bring myself to share with our father. Frost would never judge me, never reprimand me, never betray me. "I can't be the Healer's successor."

Frost bowed her head thoughtfully. "I thought you might say that."

"So, you're not surprised. I have to tell the Elders."

She shook her head and switched to my other hand. "That's not a good idea. They'll want to know the details of Clyara's whereabouts, and I don't think you're ready to tell them, if you can't even tell me. Then, they would insist that you stay, and you wouldn't have the heart to deny them."

It seemed that Frost had been thinking while I was gone, too. "What would you suggest, then?"

"Just leave," she said frankly, "and do what you must. Moonteyre has managed without a Healer before, and it'll do so again."

"Abandon Moonteyre," I said.

"'Fleece, you obviously have another matter on your mind; don't tell me if you don't want to, but is it very important to you?" I nodded. "Does it affect us, our people?" I bobbed my head uncertainly, but eventually nodded. "Enough to keep you from us?"

"It's the reason that Clyara is gone."

Frost saw something in my expression that made her draw a breath between her teeth. "I can't let you risk your life, you know."

"You can't stop me," I said morosely.

"Not physically, no," she said, "but I could talk you out of it." She looked at me for a moment and seemed to sympathize with my conflict, even if she didn't quite understand it. She said finally: "I'll keep silent, just this once. And I won't tell anyone that I saw you."

I was thankful for that. I was tempted to stay, there in the comfort and safety of home, but it was a false security, after all. I was too aware that there had been a camp of humyn less than a day's distance away, and there could be others. I was slightly reassured that they hadn't attacked my people, but I was also cognizant that perhaps they had no reason to attack because I had been elsewhere. Until I was certain that Malya and her fellow humyn mages would not try to exterminate us, I could not stay and draw their notice. Forgetting or ignoring the humyn presence wouldn't change anything for me, and would only delay the inevitable first contact. Sooner or later, the elfyn and humyn would meet, with potentially disastrous results if the circumstances were bad, such as a war between their mages.

"I should go before it's dark," I said.

"So soon," she said. "I don't suppose you'll tell me where you're going." She looked at me closely. "Better that I don't know?"

I nodded. I was going to miss her, perhaps more than Clyara. She was my only family, my sole link to my history, and my remaining tie to the elfyn.

"I'll pack some things for you," she said, turning towards the bedroom. "You still have some clothes—"

"It'll be easier if I travel light," I said gently, catching her arm. "I need you to do something for me."

"Anything." She followed me to the door with her dark woolen cloak.

I pulled out my etched silver locket from my pocket and held it out to Frost by its black silk cord. "Keep this safe until I return."

Frost clenched her hand tightly around the trinket, and draped her cloak over my shoulders. "I'm glad to hear that you intend to come home. May the stars guide you," she said, embracing me one last time.

"May Ajle keep you safe," I returned. I locked my arms briefly around my sister, committing all the sensations of that moment to memory. I was going to need the solace of her strength to see me through the days ahead. I cast the spell of invisibility around myself, wiped the tears from my eyes and opened the front door.

One last thing, I said.

"Yes?"

Humyn do exist. Keep your eyes and mind open.

Frost said nothing, answering only with the slightest bob of her head. I kissed her cheek and walked from the house without looking back. I gazed at the slate grey sky and welcomed the prospect of rain.

I walked westward out of Moonteyre, against the direction of the cleansing storm. Without seeing her, I still sensed Frost in the back of my mind. A part of her wished me luck and success and another, more practical aspect, was preparing her for the worst: the possibility that she had seen me for the very last time. I quickened my pace, leaving everything behind, as quickly as my feet could manage.

First, I had to find out where Malya had gone. I decided that my first destination would be where the humyn dwelled. While the rain slowed to a stop, I rowed across the Yirae still under a veil of invisibility, to the dark pine forest where Glory had once said humyn could be found. Soon after passing into the forest, I heard faint voices in the distance, getting closer, and I changed my direction to avoid a confrontation. Hopefully, no one had noticed the ripples in the water when I came ashore.

I was leaving too many footprints in the damp soil, so I recited a spell to change form. I blended Frost's cloak and my dark clothes into my new shape, rather than discard them for the humyn to find. I took flight into the trees as a starling. I skimmed over the ground and through the trees easily, lighting at last upon a branch in the lower canopy.

The other birds in the tree knew that I did not belong, but they did not shun me. Other starlings chirped melodically to me, and I understood them after a quick spell, as clearly as if they spoke elfyn. *Good day.* Together, we watched a band of humyn pass through the underbrush where I'd just been standing, all garbed in the same shade of dull grey.

I heard the humyn's agitation in their voices, even if I did not understand their words, and I saw their exhaustion and frustration on their faces. They found some of my footprints, and they spread out to look for me, but it was no use. I had eluded them, if only by accident.

They will go soon, chirped a bird next to me. *They will tire by nightfall.*

Do they come often? I chirped back, surprised to be engaged in conversation.

Yes, answered another, older starling. Her iridescent feathers gleamed, even under our cloud cover. *They come to hunt you and the other like you.*

It took me a moment to get her meaning, that by "the other like you" she meant Clyara. *We did not hurt them,* I said.

We know that, she replied. *We have known the other like you for generations, and she has always been a friend to us, but the humyn feel differently.* The starling and the rest of her flock suddenly squawked their anxiety as a chorus and took flight.

Their retreat was so abrupt that I almost fell off the branch in my alarm. I clung tightly to the perch and fluttered to keep my balance. The other, larger birds in the tree stayed calm and watched the starlings' flight with mild interest. Some of the humyn looked up to see what had spooked the smaller birds, but they saw nothing out of the ordinary and returned to their ground search.

When the leaves and branches settled, the object of the other starlings' panic landed not too far from me. It was a larger bird, several times larger than me, with a handsome, proud profile: a mottled grey hawk. He stopped a moment to groom, tucking his head behind his wing. When he turned his head to look at me askance, his eyes were bright and piercing. *Brave little morsel.*

He wasn't addressing me in the starlings' whistles, but I understood him. I chirped aggressively in reply, *Do not even try.*

The hawk's crest feathers stood briefly on end, but they settled just as quickly. *You are not a starling. You are not a bird at all.*

I followed the hawk's sharp eyes down through the dense cover of branches. He was watching a rodent that scampered for cover just as a humyn stepped thoughtlessly next to it. *No, I am not,* I answered. I was wary of this predator socializing with prey, but I decided to be polite.

The hawk nodded sagely. *You are a mage?* I simply chirped the affirmative. *What are you doing up here? Are you running from home?*

I have no home, I said.

A blackbird on my left whistled and ruffled her feathers nervously. They were lustrous, with a sheen like onyx, and she towered over me on the end of the branch. *Poor starling. Where will you go? It will be nightfall soon.*

The hawk watched her intently, his expression fierce even while his wings were folded and relaxed. The grumbling of humyn around the trunk of our perch distracted us, and the hawk turned his imperious stare towards them. *Yes, we must find you a nest.*

A painful twinge shot through my body, and I shuddered; my feathers stood briefly. The transformation spell had drained me, and the day's travel had taken its toll. I still had enough energy in reserve to revert, but not for much more. I was much relieved to see the last of the humyn leave the area. *I will be fine.*

My appearance must have given away something, for the raptor cocked his head to one side with interest. *Come, young one, we must find you proper shelter, closer to the ground.*

I straightened on my perch and peered at my fierce new acquaintance, reasonably sure now that he was, also, more than he seemed. *Can a starling trust a hawk?*

As much as a hawk can trust a mage. Follow me. He took flight and circled, waiting for me to follow, and I did fly after him, with some reluctance. *Stay back for just a moment.* He landed on the forest floor some distance from me, and I waited for his signal in a nearby pine.

His transformation was beautiful to watch. With a graceful, almost liquid, fluidity, the hawk was enshrouded in a swirl of smoke and transformed into the shape of a tall, cloaked man. The voluminous black wrap and hood covered the man's figure and face, divulging nothing about him. He spoke aloud for the first time, in elfyn, in a soft, clear voice. "There's no one around; you can change back now, if you'd like."

It was hardly a shock to learn that the hawk was really a mage, however, trusting him was another matter. I thought briefly about eschewing good manners and taking flight again. I was suspicious, even afraid, as I knew absolutely nothing about him. Still, he hadn't betrayed me to the humyn, and he was offering me shelter.

He mistook my hesitation for inability. "Are you able?"

Yes, I telepathed, flying to the forest floor.

"Take your time." He turned his back to me and said, "If you can't get your clothes back, I can conjure something for you." Quietly, I changed back into my natural form and felt the fabric of my dress and cloak reform against my bare skin. I was heartened that he respected my space and my privacy; his back was still to me. He was waiting for my permission to turn around.

I smoothed down my skirt and took in my strange surroundings. I didn't recall ever being in this particular corner of the forest, even in Clyara's company; this was the furthest west I had ever been. I also took a moment to study my new acquaintance's silhouette. He was like Alessarc in his stature, but this man's bearing was prouder, more regal, as though he belonged in a more cultivated, grander setting. "I don't believe I know you."

"Then that is something we have in common," he said affably. "Are you a new student to the Arts?"

"Fairly new," I said. I had apprenticed with Clyara for barely a year, and had only studied magic for a portion of that. "How did you know to speak to me in elfyn?"

The hood turned slightly. "If you were humyn, your avian disguise would have been unnecessary. I commend you on your wisdom. This is a dangerous place for one so young and of little experience, humyn or elfyn. May I turn around now?"

"Yes, if you'd like," I said, bracing myself. I could tell by his tone that it was not in his habit to ask for consent.

He turned and dropped his hood. His black hair startled me, as I had expected to see streaks of grey — at least brown, something more elfyn —

and his features were young and smooth. A warm smile lit up his handsome, humyn face.

Chapter 7: The Den

Ask a dozen elfyn to describe the humyn of lore, and you'll no doubt hear the same generalities after a while: pale skin, pale eyes, and either very fair hair or very dark hair. Broad-shouldered and long-limbed, usually. The point is, the folkloric humyn did not share the same earthen hues and slight build of the elfyn, and certain traits distinguish them easily. Glory, for example, had looked clearly humyn, even to my uninitiated eyes.

Anyway, the man standing before me was humyn. I felt it, as much as I saw his ice-blue eyes and fair skin against his jet-black hair.

He, too, seemed surprised by me. "My, but you are elfyn."

My legs were unsteady, but I planted my heels. I hardly thought I looked elfyn, with my uncommon colors and height, and the way he continued to stare was unnerving, but I imagine I was equally stark with my gaze. *Steady, 'Fleece, don't show him any fear.*

He kept his distance, but he raised his hands in supplication. "Please, I don't mean to frighten you. I won't harm you, I swear."

I did not answer, but nor did I bolt.

"I'm sorry you distrust me," he said softly, "but I am trying to help. It's true that I'm humyn, but I have no love for my kind, as they spurn mages of any variety." He frowned with resignation. "You're certainly free to go if you want, but I can provide shelter for you for the night. You'd be safe."

I looked up and saw the sky filled with the rich lavender hue of imminent nightfall. My curiosity about this humyn was greater than my fear of him, and if he could be an ally, it would've been imprudent to refuse his offer. "Perhaps for the night."

"You won't regret it," he said, taking a couple of steps closer. He whispered a spell under his breath and touched my head, so that I could understand his words, although his language was different. "My name is Jaryme. You can tell me your name, only if you want to."

JA-re-mee, I repeated silently, stressing the first of the syllables as he did. "Snowfleece," I answered, assuaged by his respect for my mental privacy. "Thank you for your offer."

I walked a couple of meters behind him to keep him in sight and kept pace easily with his long strides. I did not volunteer information about myself, but neither did Jaryme speak about himself. As the forest darkened with the dusk, we quickened our steps. "We're near my camp," he said finally.

We came to a small empty clearing, and Jaryme motioned to me to remain behind him. He raised his hands dramatically, and a large black tent gradually materialized before us, taking up most of the clearing. There was a glimmer of light visible through the semi-translucent fabric of the tent.

It looked almost as large as a cottage, almost too big for only one. "Do you live among many others?"

"Presently, no. As I said, I avoid contact with humynkind, and I believe I would be shunned by the elfyn."

"Do the other humyn know you live out here?"

"You need not worry about hunters," he smiled grimly. "They're just as likely to kill me; the only good mage is a dead one, as far as they care. So, the short answer to your question is: no, they don't."

"Just making sure," I nodded. "Thank you for your hospitality … Jaryme. I'm very much at your mercy." Something about his stiff formality told me that he didn't trust me completely, yet he had taken me to his home. It was just as well; I was planning to keep my guard up, too, at least for a little while. Awkwardly, I said, "I hope I'm not putting you out."

Jaryme drew aside a flap of fabric and invited me to enter first. "Not at all. I seldom have the chance to play the host." Inside, a tall, single torch illuminated the tent with a soft, flameless white glow. A heavy drape hung from the ceiling to divide the tent into two sections. "Please help yourself to some food."

There was a bowl of fruit and bread, and a plate of sliced, dry-cured meat, sitting atop a wooden table against one of the walls. Above it hung a small rectangular mirror. I took a small cluster of grapes and took a nibble. It was the first food I had eaten since the last of Frost's bread earlier that day, so I devoured the grapes and reached for more.

I caught my reflection in the mirror, for the first time in days, and I was aghast at my own state. Despite rinsing off earlier that day, and a hasty grooming by Frost during my brief visit, my dark hair was tangled and soiled grey again, and my pale skin was just as marred with streaks of dirt. I must have looked frightful to Jaryme, yet he had welcomed me. I straightened my posture, picked a twig from my hair and took another cluster of grapes.

I noticed a ring on Jaryme's finger as he tore off a piece of bread. A luminous blue, transparent cabochon gem was set like a gleaming eye in the fine gold and black design. It was a sizeable stone and a bold setting, and it looked at home on Jaryme's large, fine hand. "It's an impressive ring."

"Thank you. It belonged to my mother's father." Jaryme finished his food quickly and went to his cot against the far wall of the tent. He pulled out a well-stocked trunk from under the cot and took out a blanket and pillows.

"How does your family feel about your isolation?" I asked.

"My parents died years ago," he said shortly.

"I'm sorry," I replied, at a loss for anything else to say.

"Oh, don't be sorry. It wasn't your fault, after all," he said lightly. He noticed my discomfort right away. "I apologize, I didn't mean to make you uneasy, Snowfleece." He brushed off the cot and disappeared behind the drape. "Your accent is very distinct. Are you from Moonteyre?"

I turned sharply. "That's not entirely a guess, is it."

"It's an educated guess, you might say. Everyone who lives in the Dark Lands knows of the great Healer Clyara, and it was common knowledge that she had recently taken a new apprentice from Moonteyre. Since I don't know of other elfyn mages with apprentices, I can only assume that you are the object of that hearsay. Does Clyara know you're this far from home?"

I pushed the more obvious answers to the back of my mind and merely answered, "I doubt it. She's been busy."

It was hard not to trust Jaryme, especially with his gentle manner and handsome smile. Yet, I found it impossible to trust him. There was something about him that made me vigilant, and I spoke very little. He attributed my quietness to tiredness and dimmed the torch, suggesting that we resume our conversation in the morning. He even brought me a comb and a basin of water to let me wash up before he retired to his section of the tent behind the drape.

I lay awake for some time, and I was sure Jaryme did, also. I thought only of Moonteyre and my family, and of when I would see them again. There were other thoughts that I consciously avoided, simply because of the presence of my enigmatic host at the other end of the tent. Still, the cot was the most comfortable bed I had had in days, and my eyes inevitably closed.

I awoke on my back, squinting at the brilliant sky. *Sky?* After squinting for a few seconds, I realized that I was seeing the sky through the sheer fabric of the tent roof. I stared at the rapidly passing wispy clouds and hoped that the fair weather would stay; I was planning some extensive traveling, although I wasn't entirely certain as to my destination.

I sat up in bed, rejuvenated. The night's rest had done wonders for me. As I looked out the tent flap, I realized from the intensity of sunlight that the hour was closer to afternoon than morning. I jumped out of bed and folded the linens. I was very grateful for Jaryme's kindness, but I wouldn't have thought of inconveniencing him for a second evening.

"Did you sleep well?" he asked, when I emerged from behind the drape. He spoke in elfyn to accommodate me, but I saw him casting another spell of translation for me. Cups of fresh water and new baskets of food waited on the table. My mouth watered just looking at them.

I glanced at Jaryme, but he was looking outside through one of the tent flaps. I plucked a warm roll from a basket and gulped it down, musing briefly about where the food could have come from, but too hungry to truly care. *He's a master mage, he can conjure all this easily*, I reasoned. "Yes, I slept very well, thank you," I answered.

"Good," he smiled, turning back to me. "What are your plans for today?" he asked indulgently.

"I should be moving on," I said casually. "Thank you again for your generosity." The water was sweet and cold. "I'm lucky to have met you." He looked at the floor with a shy grin. "No, really. And I'm ashamed to say that I still hardly know anything about you."

"What do you want to know?" he asked.

"Whatever you want to tell me." I would have been happy to find out anything about my mysterious patron. "Who you are, how long you've lived here."

"There isn't much to tell. I'm just a mage," he shrugged. "I've been coming here every year, for the past ten years, for a respite from living in the Realm."

"You come from the Realm?" I asked with genuine fascination. It was real! The Realm was a land known only to me in stories. It was the humyn domain, just as the Dark Lands was the elfyn. "What is it like there?"

"It's … different," he said. "Imagine long, straight paths paved with poured concrete and brick, where the only trees and plants you see are in pots, or encircled by mortar. The only animals you see are horses for the carriages, pets and livestock in cages, or vermin to be exterminated." He noted my bewildered and horrified expression. "It's hard, grey and dead. I can't accurately describe how bleak and terrible it is. It's nothing like here."

I listened raptly. "Are there many mages in the Realm?"

"Mages? No, it's not a land of magic," he said with a tinge of regret in his voice. "Humyn mages are very rare, and the ones that move about freely," he pointed to himself, "often come here to the Dark Lands to rest and recharge. It's worth the risk of encountering hunters to be here."

Speaking of humyn mages… "Have you ever heard of the mage Malya?"

His smile froze. "We've crossed paths before. The hunters like the ones we eluded yesterday, act on her orders, to recapture mages who have fled the Realm and force them into her service. Why do you ask?"

My heart was sinking; if I wanted to reach Malya, I was going to need a way to get to the Realm. "I had no idea that Malya had such influence.

She was just someone that my mistress had once mentioned," I said, avoiding his eyes. "That reminds me, I should probably be on my way before I'm missed."

"It's dangerous for you during the day," Jaryme cautioned. "The woods are still thick with the mage hunters. You would probably fetch a nice reward for them."

"Then, my presence here endangers you, too," I said diplomatically, unsettled more by his smile than his words. "I'll be all right on my own, really."

"I'm sure you would be, but there's no point in taking unnecessary risks. Wait till nightfall, at least, when the hunters have returned to their camps. I'll accompany you to anywhere you wish to go."

It was a generous offer, and one that seemed sensible enough. A few more hours wouldn't truly matter in the grander scheme, and would allow me more time to figure out what I needed to do. I took a cup of water from Jaryme's hands and drank deeply. With his careful attention to my needs, Jaryme could spoil me too easily.

"Pardon me for saying," he began, "but you still look exhausted. I would venture to guess that last night was the first full night of sleep you've had in days. Am I right? You should rest for a while longer, then, and get your strength back. I'll wake you when it's dusk."

I drained the cup of water and held the cool earthenware cup in my hands. I was more tired than I had realized, and I probably would have benefited from another nap. A nagging headache was starting. "Maybe you're right."

"I am right," Jaryme said. He took the cup from my hands and took it back to the table, and I returned to my side of the drape and lay down. "I'll be right here if you need anything," he called from his side.

A quiet thought, a distant whisper, crept into the back of my mind, as my eyes started to close. *Leave.* I glanced imperceptibly around the room for a possible source, but there was only Jaryme in the tent with me. He was standing by the window with his back to me, his mind apparently on other matters. A part of me still distrusted Jaryme. *Just talking to myself again.*

Leave now. The suggestion entered my mind unbidden, and I knew it wasn't my own. It was someone else, then, intruding on my thoughts. I forced my eyes closed and pulled the blanket up to my chin. Someone was anxious to get me to leave Jaryme's company, and I wasn't about to go without a good reason. For all I knew, it could have been Malya's hunters, trying to draw me into the woods, away from the safety of Jaryme's tent.

I kept my eyes shut and calmed myself, ignoring the growing urges that the tiny voice planted in my head. I tried to nap, but the voice kept me awake with its constant nagging. Eventually, I gave up trying to sleep. I sat up in bed and eased my eyes open.

The lighting in the tent had dimmed. I looked up through the clear top of the tent and saw an evening sky. *By Ajle, where did the time go?* I got to my feet, and the sounds of my shuffling drew Jaryme's attention.

"How did you sleep?" Jaryme asked, holding my chair for me as I took a seat at the table. "You looked so peaceful, I didn't have the heart to wake you."

I rubbed my temples and looked at the bowls of food queasily. The nagging suspicions in my head were becoming stronger, and they becoming harder to disregard. "I can't stay. Everyone is probably sick with worry."

"You're in no condition to travel," he said, holding my hand. As Jaryme beseeched me to stay, I felt my eyelids growing heavy. When I gave in to the desire to close my eyes, my head felt light and heavy at the same time. The warning voice was still at the back of my mind, but I was too exhausted to be bothered by it.

"I'm sure your mistress would prefer that you stay somewhere safe," he said softly. "Early in the morning, before the hunters are out, I'll go with you back across the river. If you'd like, I can even teach you some of my spells; I can't imagine that your mistress would mind."

I managed a grateful smile. Jaryme's offer sounded reasonable, and I had been able to trust him so far. I wasn't even sure myself where I wanted to go, yet, so I could at least use the night to plan my next moves. In any case, I was too tired to argue. It was just going to be for one more night, anyway.

WAKE UP! The voice boomed in my head again, this time like a clarion against my ear. I sprang upright in the cot, immersed in the blackness. By the light of the moon and stars, I saw shadows passing outside the tent. One was inside the tent with me, less than a few meters from the cot. *GET OUT!*

"Jaryme?" I called, casting flare lights to illuminate the tent.

A figure leapt from the darkness into the light and forced me back down on the cot, clamping my neck firmly to the pillow. The full weight of a body fell on top of me, pinning my legs and crushing my ribs. I gasped for air and stared into the featureless contours of my attacker's masked face and at the dark garments he wore. I tried to scream for help, but my cry was soundless. With a small telekinetic blast, I managed to knock over the table behind me, but it tumbled silently against the ground.

Enough of this. I slapped my hands to either side of my attacker's head and burst his mask and hair into flames, and he struggled, but he held onto me. I had to bite his hand, drawing his blood, to force him back. How many more of these hunters were there? Where was Jaryme, for Ajle's

71

sake? I could hear the keen sounds of scraping metal and the smell of smoke coming from outside.

"Stay inside!" Jaryme ordered from outside the tent, over the commotion.

GO, NOW! commanded the voice in my head, louder and more insistent now. As I bolted from my cot, another hunter slipped into the tent, training his peculiar weapon on me like a crossbow. I retreated into the shadows and ducked down. A sharp crackle split the air, filling it with a sulfurous odor, and small punctures riddled the tent, missing me by centimeters. *RUN!* I ignored the voice long enough to gesture a spell that shoved my attacker out the door and smashed him headlong into a tree. I paused by the tent flap, to make sure he wasn't coming back.

RUN!

I fled the tent, bolting out of the clearing and into the forest. I aimed generally for the north, but I didn't care particularly which direction I was traveling, as long as Jaryme's camp was far behind me. *Go north.*

I was safe, for the moment, as none of the hunters had managed to track me. I felt guilty for leaving Jaryme to fend for himself, but a part of me knew that he would be fine. I slowed when I came across another clearing in the forest, a few kilometers from Jaryme's camp. A small crowd of humyn was chattering around a small campfire, and I could hear some of their conversation as I crept past the camp. *Don't stop. Keep moving,* the voice in my head cautioned, but I needed to find out their intentions towards my people, so I ignored the warning and crept closer. I understood a little of the language from hearing Jaryme speak, and the rest from reading the thoughts of the speakers.

"I tell you, it's true! Emperor Augus is dead," one of them said. A ripple of disbelief went through the group, until another spoke.

"…No one's seen Malya since Augus's death. Some say she's grieving, others say she's sick. Either way, without an heir, Malya is Empress."

What are the chances that it's a different Malya? I wondered.

"She's a mage, idiot, she can't get sick," rebuffed another.

Someone else rejoined, "I heard that she's actually dead, but that her magic is keeping her intact. That's why nobody's seen her, cause her flesh is starting to rot away."

The rest of the group shared a great common utterance of disgust. I joined them in silence. *No, definitely the same Malya. Empress Malya,* I thought with dread. She couldn't be dead; I saw her stand after her battle with Clyara.

"I never liked Malya," muttered the first voice. "I always said there was something strange about the way Augus became Emperor so soon after she showed up. And there must be something about that daughter of hers, Glory, the way no one ever sees her."

"I hear she's dead, too. Whatever's the case, we're on our own for a while," another said. "Let's just hope those filthy elfyn don't come for us."

"Why do you say that, coward?" another sneered.

"Cause we don't have a mage, you fool, and we never caught theirs," he replied to a quieted audience. "And have you seen their villages? They're breeding like rats. We may have enough guns, but I still wouldn't want to get on their bad side; they would outnumber us two hundred to one."

Bad side? I never thought of the elfyn as having such a thing as a bad side. I stilled at the sound of rustling leaves and lowered myself to the ground. I cursed my own stupidity when I looked down at my clothes; I hadn't thought to make myself invisible. Maybe it still wasn't too late—

"Hands up," ordered a voice behind me. "Slowly."

I turned my head slightly and saw one of those metal crossbow-like implements pointed at me, albeit unsteadily. I raised my hands to my sides and rose from the ground, slowly. The humyn who had caught me was little older than me. "I can explain," I said, but my elfyn words meant nothing to him.

"Well done, boy," said another of the humyn, emerging from the clearing. "Goddess herself has delivered our enemy to us." By now, the others around the campfire had noticed our exchange, and once they recognized me, the hostility was open and swift, with weapons quickly drawn.

"No, we need to take her alive," ordered the senior humyn. As he and the others discussed how to take me into custody, I cast my spells: one to shield myself, and one to become invisible.

Neither was effective against the heavy rope net that enveloped me and forced me to ground. Peering through the web, I focused on a patch of unfamiliar land to teleport, and that was when I glimpsed the head of the sword pommel that hit me.

Crows and vultures. The mad, shrill cries of the birds were so close. *They must think I'm dead.* I had a splitting headache and pains all over. I wanted to massage my head, but my hands wouldn't move. I gasped as something hard and heavy struck my side. *Where am I again?* I cracked my eyes open and groaned. I was bound and gagged, on the floor inside a tent, with hunters gathered around me. It wasn't the caws of birds that I heard, but their jeering and angry taunts. It was for the best that I didn't understand their language. The metal bars of my cage couldn't keep out every stone that they casually hurled or the sticks they jabbed, but it at least kept me out of their literal grasp.

What a pathetic end. Unable to speak or gesture my spells, and without

73

any idea of where I was, I was stuck. For some reason, the humyn hadn't executed me. Not that I was disappointed, of course, but ... why?

Someone called from outside, and several of the hunters left the tent grudgingly. Almost immediately, a thick red-orange smoke filled the tent, and those who still stood in the tent quickly fell in unconscious heaps. I tried to pick my head up, even as the settling smoke was intoxicating me. A grey-cloaked figure walked out of the smoke and crouched before me, unaffected by the cloud around us. "Not a word, understand?" He was speaking elfyn! More impatiently, when I didn't respond: "Do you understand!"

I nodded quickly, peering at the man's almost-familiar face. *Jaryme?* They could have been brothers. He had the same flawless skin, coal-black hair and intensely blue eyes, but the features were more delicate, almost boyish. He ripped the lock off the cage door, as though the padlock were fashioned of paper instead of steel—he was a mage like Jaryme, too. With the door open, he then pulled a dagger from his cloak. I squeaked through my gag and backed into the bars of the cage.

"Not another sound, or I will leave you here to fend for yourself," he said gruffly, then muttered something under his breath, shaking his head. He reached into the cage and jerked me towards him by my arm, and before I could further complain, he turned me around and, with a single stroke, sliced through the ropes that bound me. "Get away from here, and don't come back," he whispered hoarsely. "You should listen to the voice inside your head. Whatever you decide, for the Goddess's sake, stay the hell away from Jaryme."

I turned back as I got my hands free, in time to see my rescuer draw his grey hood back over his head and vanish into the fading smoke. I shed my gag and the rest of my binds and crept out the back of the tent before the smoke entirely cleared, stepping carefully around my unconscious captors sprawled on the ground. As the first humyn awoke, I focused on an old pine in the distance and teleported into the woods, far out of their reach.

Feeling the last fading twinges of pain in my flesh where I had been jabbed and stoned, some small part of me wanted the satisfaction of dealing the pain back on my captors, but that would have been a waste of my energy. They must have been receiving their commands from someone, and my efforts were best concentrated on finding out whom. In the meantime, however, I needed to find shelter and recover my energy. All my sleeping at Jaryme's camp had left me oddly unrested. Perhaps his "brother" who had rescued me had the right idea in warning me away from him.

I took a chance on listening to the voice in my head and continued north, navigating by the stars and trees. From my days of wandering with

Clyara, the forests near the river were as familiar to me as the Ajlekyrn, and my only real concern was my endurance for the lengthy hike along the bank and against the flow of the Yirae River. My legs buckled more than once, but spells were out of the question, except to hide myself. I did not want to chance leaving an energy trail for others to track, nor did I want to expend more energy than absolutely necessary, not knowing how long I would be traveling.

North was good, strategically. There were denser wilderness areas further northeast of Moonteyre, where the Yirae joined with the sea, where I knew I could be alone for as long as I needed. I had never been there myself, but Clyara had mentioned having gone there to meditate when she was younger. The Black Oaks, she had called them. It was also where she had spent many of her years of isolation before her emergence as the almighty Healer. If they could hide her from Malya, perhaps they could hide me, too.

Before dawn, I had just reached the plains on the edge of the pine forest, farther north of Moonteyre and the Yirae than I had ever been. The night air was cooler than I was accustomed to, and I shivered even as I kept moving. A jarring image popped into my mind of my new, pristine white gem lying in a pile of my bones and ashes, and the vision encouraged me to redouble my efforts. Once every few minutes, I thought I was being watched, but there was nothing I could see or hear; clearly, my gem was stirring feelings of paranoia again. Besides, I kept myself invisible, so no one would have been able to see me on the plains.

Finally, the sensation of being observed was overwhelming, and I stopped short. I spun around, peering across the harsh, sparse terrain as far as I could in the dim early dawn light. I couldn't see anyone on the plains with me, but I was not alone, I was sure of it. A breeze brushed past me, and I caught the mingled odor of metal, leather and sweat, and the faint sound of shuffling feet. I spotted a massive outcropping ahead, and instinctively, I darted behind it for cover.

A wolf howl—keening and resonant—sounded close by, catching me off-guard with its proximity, as I didn't smell the animal at all. I pressed myself back against the rock wall, and heard a low snarl, from the direction I had come. The deep growl was followed by another, from another vantage nearby, then by sounds of footsteps, the scrape of metal and urgent voices. I shifted slightly, to get a better view, but I was nudged back against the wall by an invisible force. It was a gentle push, but an irresistible, persistent one.

I was in the presence of another, and I opened my mouth to speak, but I was stopped by a warm pressure against my lips, and a voice in my head: *Shh.* As much as the unexpected company startled me, I was more alarmed by the sudden din of voices from the other side of the outcrop, exclamations of ferocity and pain that were both humyn and animal. I moved the other way to try to see what was happening, and was stopped again. *Give them another minute.* Almost to the second, the yelling and snarling dwindled to silence, and the presence next to me became visible, in the form of a looming figure cloaked in darkness.

By Ajle, not another hooded man! Bristling at the memory of my recent encounters, I attempted to cast a spell to blink away, only to have him cancel it with a patient wave of his hand. *Great. Another mage, too.*

It is done, interjected another male voice, deeper and rougher. *There will be no more hunters today.*

"Thank you, Grey-Eye," answered the man beside me. Aloud, the voice was a smooth, soothing baritone, and it was the same voice that had visited me back in Jaryme's tent and accompanied me through the night. It was deeply, intimately familiar to me, as though I had heard it all my life, and I aborted a second spell attempt. Whoever this man was, he hadn't tried to hurt me, yet.

My attention was diverted by the approach of a large grey wolf with a smoke and silver pelt, jogging out from behind the rocks and brush. It stopped at a respectful distance and focused its reflective eyes on me: one amber, one grey. Its muzzle was clean, but its breath bore a tinge of blood.

"Thank you?" I said uncertainly.

The wolf's ears perked, and it bowed its head, but kept its mismatched eyes focused on me. *We are ever at your service, Protector.*

My jaw dropped. *You're telepathic!*

He averted his gaze slightly towards the man next to me. *She seems a little slow this morning. She must be tired.*

"Of course, she's tired, so mind your manners," the man chastised. "Come, let's get you some shelter and something to eat before you fall down."

"Wait, I don't even know who you are," I said. I stepped back from the stranger, suddenly aware of how close he stood, and he allowed me that.

"Friends," he said softly, moving behind a fold in the rock to lead the way into a hidden passage. With the wolf herding me, it was understood that I was to follow, and I let myself be led. I trailed the man a couple of steps, studying him while I could. He was broad-shouldered like Jaryme and my rescuer from the humyn camp, and similarly stood a full head taller than me. His open slate-colored cloak revealed his lean, lithe build, and simple, fitted clothes that flattered his trim physique, but his face was obscured.

We have followed you since you left the humyn camp, to keep you safe, Grey-Eye said.

"I thought it was just my imagination," I said.

You are not so oblivious, then. You were careless not to hide your tracks and scent.

I found Grey-Eye's frankness chastening, but refreshing. I accepted his thoughts as is, trusting that I had never known an animal to lie. Then again, I had never actually met a telepathic wolf. I had seen them and heard them, but had never engaged in conversation with one. "Were you the ones who called me away from Jaryme's camp?"

"Yes, I was," the man answered. He led us down a slope, then steps down into a cavern with high-arched tunnels, which soon assumed a labyrinthine complexity with turns and hidden edges. There was little light to illuminate our path, so I was forced to remain close, but surprisingly, I didn't mind his nearness.

"Do you often waylay weary travelers with your ... um, friends?"

You were thinking 'pets', and my pack belongs to no one, Grey-Eye said indignantly, and overtook us both to lead the way through the passage.

"And we didn't waylay you," the man replied, walking alongside me behind Grey-Eye through the stone maze. "We were watching over you."

He waved his hand, and the illusion of the stones around us dissolved, revealing a room formed of the surrounding boulders. With a snap of his fingers, torches on the cave walls ignited to illuminate the chamber with a warm, steady light. The torches were more for us than for Grey-Eye, who had already lain down underneath a wooden table at the opposite end of the sparse room and was sprawled between two chairs. In the brighter space, Grey-Eye's eponymous mismatched irises seemed to almost glow.

The man dropped his cowl and paced the room, as if to ensure that nothing was out of place. In the glow of the magical torchlight, my host's hair, eyes and skin took on various shades of bronze and gold—oddly elfyn colors for an otherwise humyn-looking man. His shoulder-length hair was tied back loosely with a strip of black cloth, and his handsome face was clean-shaven and unlined. He wasn't anyone that I recalled from Moonteyre, but I blurted: "Where have we met before?"

He finally turned around to face me squarely. "Depends on how you would define 'met'," he said. Without a glance around, he flicked his fingers, and the cavern brightened more. "That's better, don't you think, Apprentice?"

Seeing him directly, I recognized him, almost, but the way he addressed me was unmistakable.

"Alessarc?"

Chapter 8: Apprentice and Master

"'Sarc' will be fine."

He regarded me with the same sheepish half-smile that I recalled, and he gestured over his shoulder at the carved table next to him, where Grey-Eye lay underneath. "You look like you're about to collapse. Please have a seat?"

I slid into one of the upholstered chairs, my eyes fixed on him. I was still marveling at how young Alessarc appeared. From his hands, I had known that he was not the distinguished old gentleman that he pretended to be, but I didn't expect him to look only a few years older than Frost. "How do I know it's really you?"

"You'll just have to trust me, Apprentice," he said dryly, adding the mature gravel back into his voice for effect.

"Why did you disguise yourself as someone older?"

"It was a favor to your mistress," he said. In the confusion back in Jaryme's camp, I had forgotten Frost's cloak, and in the damp chill of the cavern, I regretted it. As if he sensed my thoughts, he shed his own cloak and wrapped it around my shoulders without pretense. With his broad shoulders filling his stark white shirt and dark waistcoat, he looked more imposing than before, especially standing over me. He touched my arm and said, "I know about Clyara."

"I'm sorry," I said in a whisper, unable to imagine the kind of loss Sarc must have felt. "I know you were close, and I wish..."

He pulled the other chair closer, sat next to me and took my hands in his. It was only when I saw my pale, bony hands in his large, tanned ones that I realized how frail and pathetic I must have looked. "It's not your apology to make," he said. "The important thing is that you are safe. Frost and the others are unhurt?"

I nodded. The memories of the past few days streamed through my mind with painful clarity. "They'll be lost without a healer. Only Frost knows that Clyara is gone." I squeezed my eyes shut, resting my eyes for the first time in hours, and felt a stabbing pain in my temples. "Oh, that doesn't help."

"Here," he said, passing me a small, paper-lined box containing what looked like balls of dirt rolled in fine mulch. That, and a large cup of tea. "I could give you a couple of pills, too, but I have a feeling you'll enjoy these more. They'll help alleviate the pressure in your head and make you feel better, more quickly than meditation, especially in your state."

I sipped from the cup of tea but peered into the box uncertainly. "What are they?" I had seen similar boxes in Clyara's cottage periodically but had never bothered to ask what they were.

"Chocolate," he said. "Dark chocolate truffles, to be exact."

Meaningless words. I took one to try, to be polite. It had an intensely sweet, rich aroma, and it smelled tannic, creamy and floral all at once. As I felt it melting between my fingers, I popped it into my mouth before it slipped from my grasp. The flavor was complex and sublime, sweet and bitter, unlike anything I had ever tasted before in my life.

Sarc let me savor the first truffle in silence and didn't venture to speak again until I reached for a second. "I was worried that you weren't hearing my messages."

I said you were just ignoring him, Grey-Eye rejoined, stretching out at my feet. The heat from his thick fur was heaven against my cold legs, and I contemplated curling up against him for his warmth.

"I was ignoring you," I admitted. "But as you must know, I was also otherwise detained." I wrapped my chilled hands around the earthenware cup, smelling the hot, fragrant drink before I took another sip. "How did you know where I was?"

Sarc seemed to collect his thoughts before answering. "When I learned that Clyara was gone, I knew you would be the next target, so we tried to locate you first. We didn't expect you to be intrepid enough to travel so far west." He conjured a bowl of biscuits and dried fruit and set it on the table, along with a carafe of tea. "Where were you trying to go?"

I took a chunk of dried fruit between my fingers and looked at it for a good while, thinking of how to answer his question. "I thought it would be best to stay away from the elfyn for a while. They may struggle without a healer for a time, but I don't want to take the chance of endangering them more by returning." Something about his thoughtful gaze reminded me of Clyara. I nibbled on the sweet, tender fruit and avoided his eyes. "I was also trying to find out what happened to Malya, but it doesn't seem like her followers are even organized very well."

"Why do you say that?" he asked, shifting in his seat.

"Well, the last group of hunters I encountered said something about not having a mage, but the group before that most certainly did." I drank the last of the tea and watched Sarc refill my cup from the carafe. "Then, this man saved me from the second group, and I thought: maybe, he was the mage working with the first, except that he wasn't trying to capture me. He set me free and directed me to come this way, in fact. I'm sorry, I'm not making much sense, am I?"

Not really, Grey-Eye yawned, *but go on, if it makes you feel better.*

Sarc passed me a freshly pressed handkerchief from his vest pocket.

"You have some blood on your lip there... Malya died in the duel, and she was returned to the Realm."

"That can't be. I saw her stand," I argued. "She looked directly at me." I wiped at my mouth and looked down at the hunter's dried blood on the handkerchief. "Unless ... if her body's intact, she would be a gemwraith," I said, recalling Clyara's skeletal escorts.

"And she still has her magestone."

"So, Malya can still use magic," I scowled. "This keeps getting better."

"Now, she's seen you and knows who you are," Sarc said, watching my face for some indication of panic or fear.

"Of course, she does," I sighed, recalling the last time I dealt with gemwraiths. I was able to dispatch my own wraiths, and even that was with difficulty. Malya was a wholly different scenario. Fulfilling Clyara's dying wish was going to be even harder than I had anticipated. "She wants me dead, too, I imagine."

"You were the apprentice of her adversary," he said. "And the heir to Clyara's magestone. You do have it, don't you?"

"Yes, I have it," I said quietly, shielding my mind.

"Did Aron and Set give you a hard time?" I peered at him for clarification. "Clyara's gemwraiths. She must have summoned them for your protection."

"She did," I nodded, recalling their caustic ash in my nostrils. "I had to run pretty fast to keep the stone out of their reach. I'm sorry, did you say 'Aron and Set'?"

"Clyara's predecessor, and the one before him," Sarc said, standing up from the table. "The former bearers of her magestone." Grey-Eye got up from under the table, too, and shook his brindled silver coat; he was so still, I'd almost forgotten that he was there. As Grey-Eye stretched, Sarc cleared the dishes from the table, too quickly for me to even read the spell from his lips. "We can continue this, after you've rested. You must be exhausted from your journey."

I let Sarc hold my chair for me, as I rose to my feet unsteadily. My legs trembled, too tired for any more walking. "If what you said is true, I have to keep moving, before more hunters come."

My legs folded suddenly, and I was lucky that Sarc was there to catch me. I braced myself against the table, but my limbs became dead weight, and Sarc scooped me up when he saw that I was unable to stand. "Wait for me outside," he said to Grey-Eye.

While I watched Grey-Eye lope from the chamber, I felt my eyes closing. I leaned my head heavily against Sarc's shoulder. "What did you do to me?"

"I think it's more about what you've done to yourself. You can rest back here for a while." He turned and nodded to the empty back wall. A

80

four-poster bed materialized: a sizable one, with a dark wood headboard and smooth ivory sheets. It smelled faintly of sandalwood and cedar. "We'll talk more after you've gotten some sleep."

He set me down on the edge of the bed, and turned down the covers. "Into bed you go, young lady," he said, holding his hand out to me. "You'll be safe, I give you my word."

"I don't have many options." I shed the cloak from around my shoulders and slung it over his outstretched arm and reached down to take off my slippers, but once again, my body felt too heavy, and I barely managed to stay upright after the shoes hit the floor. Sarc guided me under the covers without comment and tucked me under the blankets. He was gentlemanly in a way that reminded me of my father.

Sarc smoothed my hair back from my brow and remarked, "You're starting to show some silver. That wasn't there the last time I saw you?"

"Maybe it's finally my time," I said. "Might also be the stress of the past few days."

"Perhaps." He stood and bowed his head respectfully. "Hopefully, you will find peace tonight. Sleep well, Apprentice." He dimmed the torches with a glance and disappeared into the shadows. "We'll be outside if you need us."

"Thank you, Sarc," I called into the darkness. To hell with caution. If Malya wanted to kill me, I would be helpless to defend myself until I recovered my strength, anyway. In the meantime, I had Alessarc keeping watch over me. *Sarc. Whatever his name is*, I mused as I nestled deeply into the sandalwood-scented sheets. The bed was so soft, so comforting ...

I blinked to clear my eyes, but my vision was still blurred, and my lids were heavy. The dim torchlight didn't help. The gem pulsed stridently in my chest, but I felt no pain. I didn't rush to get up; I held up Sarc's handkerchief to study it. Three letters were darned into the corner: A.N.E. *Alessarc-something-something.* What did the other two letters represent? *I don't even know his full name...*

I sat up in bed and looked around the empty cavern. I heard Grey-Eye and Sarc out by the cavern entrance, and I carefully tapped into their telepathic conversation.

She's young, Sarc said. *She still has a lot to learn, and she'll need as much help as we can provide. First, we need to get her into hiding.*

She is not one to hide for long, the wolf said.

Her mistress made the decision for her, it's not up for debate.

I would not dare to debate Clyara's 'chosen one,' Grey-Eye quipped.

Don't start on that, again. This is not what I would've planned for her, either. Sarc paused. *But I must have her trust, at least for now. When she discovers the truth, well...*

81

Worry about that later, Grey-Eye advised. *We need to discuss a strategy for the queen. She is safe and undiscovered now, but she is also not self-aware. There are details that the prophecy does not mention.*

That will keep, also, Sarc assured. *The less she knows now, the better.*

The conversation stopped abruptly, and I climbed quietly out of the bed. As soon as I stood up, the bed and all its furnishings vanished without a trace, and the torch brightened to near-daylight intensity. I straightened my dress and smoothed back my hair.

"Good morning."

I turned and nearly stumbled, but Sarc caught my arm. I stepped back, as though I had been shocked, and I flushed with embarrassment at my own clumsiness and surprise. "How long have you been standing there?"

"Not long. How much did you hear of our exchange?" he asked plainly.

"Not much." No use denying that I'd been listening. I had to squint to see Sarc's face clearly, although he was only an arm's length away. Everything in the room was looking very dim. "You're not playing tricks with the light, are you?" Sarc shook his head. "No, you wouldn't do that," I muttered. "What is this truth that I need to discover? And where are you planning to take me?"

"That's not important now," he said, touching a cool hand to my head and lifting my chin to look into my eyes. He shed his cloak and wrapped it around my shivering shoulders. "Your pupils are dilated," he said. "How are you feeling?"

"It's nothing." I leaned against the cavern wall to balance myself, counting off the days in my head. This was only the fifth day since I took Clyara's magestone. This adjustment was earlier than the last.

"I'll be fine," I said, though I felt less sure. I remembered my last adjustment as just an afternoon of some cloudy vision, muscle cramps and minor balancing problems. *What's Clyara's magestone going to do with me?* I cried out, feeling the sharpness in my chest as though a knife ran through it. *I had to ask.* I pulled free of Sarc's steadying hands and leaned my head against the wall. What I really wanted to do was to curl into a ball and disappear from his sight. "I'm sorry I didn't tell you about taking Clyara's gem."

"I suspected as much. Gemwraiths are nearly impossible to handle otherwise." Sarc caught me before I slumped to the floor, and he eased me to the ground and propped me against the wall. "Grey-Eye, slight change of plans."

The wolf had slipped in without my notice. *I see.*

"The Protector took her *keeron's* stone."

"It was an accident!" I cried.

You win that bet, old man, Grey-Eye replied, ignoring me. He and Sarc shielded their minds from me while they conversed, and Grey-Eye left as quickly and as quietly as he had entered.

"What?" I snapped, feeling another stab. "Tell me what's going on."

"Not to worry," Sarc soothed. "Malya will be especially persistent in hunting you when she realizes that you're prone, so it's important that we move quickly."

"You said something about hiding me."

"That is the plan," Sarc said. "Can you stand up?"

Even as my eyes continued to weaken, I nodded dumbly and gripped his arm for balance, waiting for the pain in my chest to ebb. I consciously focused to see him, but he remained blurry around his golden edges, slowly becoming formless. All I saw around me were vague blooms of light and dark.

He was speaking, but his voice sounded thin and distant. "Good. Now, I will keep you out of Malya's reach, but I can't do that here." He wrapped his cloak closer around my shoulders.

"Where are we going?" His touch calmed me somehow, despite my predicament. He was speaking, but his voice was indiscernible. "What did you say?" I said aloud. Maybe. I barely heard myself.

I said there is a place prepared for you, he telepathed back. *It's not very comfortable, but it's safe.*

"Uncomfortable is better than death," I replied. The colors in front of my eyes slowly faded into blackness. I reached my hand out, and he squeezed it. Devoid of my vision and hearing, I especially appreciated the touch. I took a deep breath, still able to distinguish the aromas in the cavern: loamy earth, rich and pungent oil and tallow.

Stay there. He placed my hand gently at my side. *I'll be right back.*

The scent of sandalwood and cypress lingered in Sarc's wake, and I breathed it in for comfort. I closed my eyes and felt the first tears trickling from the edges. I had never felt so timorous, or so defenseless. I hadn't been so unaware of my surroundings since my first adjustment the prior year. Sarc had been there to help me, then, too. "Sarc! Are you still there?"

Of course, I'm here. Where would I go?

It was humiliating to be so weak, so dependent on another. "Sorry."

Don't be, he said. *Better that it happen today than yesterday.*

He was right about that. If I had met Jaryme a day later, who knew what the hunters would have done to me? "What are you doing, Sarc?"

Preparing a portal. I'll be with you in a moment.

I felt a breeze, something I hadn't felt since I had entered the cave. The breeze grew stronger, blowing through my hair and clothes. "Where did Grey-Eye go?"

I was startled by Sarc's sudden presence next to me. *He returned to his pack and will direct the others.* He lifted me to my feet and anchored his arm firmly around his cloak, around me. *Stay close to me, no matter what.*

I huddled into the folds of the cloak as we walked into the gust, my fingers locked in a painful grip on Sarc's sleeve. The wind blew hot and cold, pushing me back against Sarc's arm as he pulled me alongside him. The approach to the portal felt like it would take forever…

Then stillness. Sarc's arm dropped from around me. I stooped and felt the cool, lush grass that tickled my legs, but could not hear its soft rustle. I reached towards the direction from which we had come, but the portal had already gone. I would have liked to have seen it, or heard it, so up close. I had never seen Clyara use one, but she had told me about them.

We have to keep moving, Sarc cautioned. *A portal leaves a great deal of trace energy in its wake, and if the Empress's hunters find the cave, they'll be able to follow us here.*

The air felt cold and damp, so it seemed that it was still night, or early morning. My recovery was hours away, if my new adjustment was anything like my first. *It could be worse,* I thought to myself, deaf and blind. My remaining senses and Sarc's company made it more bearable. I smelled wet, minerally clay in the moist air, mixed with the smell of my own fresh perspiration. The area was familiar to me, not too far from home. "Are we near the Red Lake, by any chance?"

It's not too far from here. Why?

Not to be indelicate, but I have no idea how many hours, or days, this process will take, so I'd like to have a moment of privacy, if that's all right with you.

If it will make you feel better, of course, we can stop at the lake. It's about a kilometer away.

At the time, it was still an unfamiliar term. *'Ki-lom-eter'?*

I mean, it's close. He took my hand and stayed near. If my grimy state repulsed him, he was very good at hiding his distaste, even telepathically.

Couldn't you create the portal a little closer to our destination?

Not without the traces leading the hunters right to it. Likewise, we have to be careful with our spells. Careful, he warned, *there's a rock by your right—*

Foot, I finished, as I kicked into the stone, with the fabric of my slippers offering little protection. I bit down on my lip and hobbled next to Sarc, feeling the pain in my foot shooting up my leg. *I'll be fine in a moment, as soon as my gem is done testing my resilience.*

You're taking this well.

What options do I have? It's dangerous to interfere with the adjustment; I have to let it run its course. I managed to stand on my feet again and ignored the pain that lingered. *I've felt worse.*

Oh, stop. Now, you're being maudlin, he teased. To my shock, Sarc hoisted me into the air; in my panic, I locked my arms tightly around his neck, feeling his heartbeat and smelling the faint scents of woods through his clothes. Unnerved by our intimate contact, I tried to loosen my grip, but my own irrational fear of falling prevailed. *Relax, I'm not going to drop you.*

It's not that. Shouldn't I transform into something easier to carry?

No, you'll just confuse the gem, he said. *Just leave it to me.*

Thankfully, the lake was close. Sarc set me down near the lakebed, and I sighed with great relief that my foot was better, if still a little sore. Sarc led me to the water's edge and set me gently on my feet.

I'll respect your privacy, he said.

I have no choice but to trust you, I laughed in resignation. *You will point me in the right direction, won't you, if I walk towards the woods instead of the water?*

Of course. Here, I'll take your slippers and your dress. Take my hand, and follow the slope down into the water, slowly. That's it.

I never felt more vulnerable, wearing close to nothing and not even having my magic to protect myself, but there was a freedom in being unable to hide. Letting go of my insecurities, I luxuriated in the cool, sweet water. Feeling the fine silt of the Red Lake between my fingers, I regretted that I could only touch it and remember its familiar dark maroon hue. While the lake cleansed me, the bracing water distracted me from my self-doubts and pains of the adjustment, at least for a little while.

It's time to go, Sarc said at last. *Need a hand?*

No, just point me towards land and pass me my clothes, please. The air and water shifted against me, as Sarc nudged me in the right direction, then I felt my dress draped around my shoulders. I didn't bother reading Sarc's thoughts for whether he watched me dress, and I didn't particularly care. I doubted that there was anything I had that he hadn't seen before, and on someone much prettier, too. I tugged my slippers on and stopped to touch my ankle.

What's wrong? he asked, brushing his hand against mine.

I stood and grasped his hand, but I hardly felt it, as though I was touching him through layers of blankets. *I'm not sure, my arms are numb.* I barely felt the weight of Sarc's cloak on my shoulders, and I almost stumbled over another rock. *I think I'm losing the rest of my senses.* I took a deep breath and ran my tongue across my lip, but I could no longer smell nor taste the water of the lake. *All of them.*

It was only a matter of time. They'll return soon enough. I just felt Sarc squeeze my hand reassuringly, but only through our thoughts. He sensed my consternation of losing touch with the world, to become completely estranged from it. *You won't be alone. I'll stay as long as you have need of me.*

At the last, I lost my links to the tangible world. My mind was alert and frantic, but my body would not cooperate. I was becoming petrified, literally. I wanted to cry, but I couldn't even do that. I felt too stressed to sleep, so I remained awake and fretful, as though I was pacing in circles inside my head. There was only the little comfort in knowing that I would eventually recover.

The hours blended and stretched interminably, and all I had was Sarc. I held onto the reality of him with all that I had and still felt my ties to him unravel, until there was only our shared thoughts. It didn't help the situation that he spoke less and less to me with the passage of the day. Shut out from my body, I depended on him to anticipate and tend my needs.

I've built a fire for us, and I've given you some water, Sarc said.

I was able to drink it?

No, I poured it over your head, he joked. *Yes, you drank it, silly.*

I could be drowning and not know it. Where are we? Is it night yet?

Soon, the sky is darkening. As for where you are, I've set you down under an oak tree, propped between two roots. You look very much at peace.

That sounds nice. If only I felt as peaceful as I look. You must be as eager as I am, for this to be over.

Oh, I don't know. I don't often meet a beautiful girl who's unable to resist me, he jested. After a moment, he said, *What? No retort? Do you really think I would be so dishonorable and cowardly, as to take advantage of someone who's helpless to respond?*

It's not that. You called me beautiful.

That can't be the first time you've heard that, Keeronae.

It is, and … what did you call me again? The term "keeron" is used to address a master or mistress, but "keeronae" translates to "master of masters" and was not something I had heard before.

'Keeronae'? That's your title. You are the Highest Master, or will be. You may not feel that way now, but it's your fate.

The prophecy that you and Grey-Eye were discussing back at the cave?

Clyara didn't tell you very much about it, I gather. It is a long story.

And you will never have an audience more captive than me.

Chapter 9: Haven

In the spring of the year 900, on the night that his child was born, a humyn mage by the name of Junus Escan had a dream. Escan was already old, he had seen much of the world, but he had never experienced anything like his horrid vision. In his dream, Escan saw an age of much death and destruction, brought about by a faceless creature of madness and evil. The mage saw people that he had never seen before, but whom he seemed to know personally, each of them playing roles in the battle for the Realm, and the rest of the world beyond its borders. At the end of his dream, the Realm fell into despair, into an epoch of darkness and oppression.

Blessed—or cursed—with a perfect memory, Escan awoke from his dream with each detail etched into his mind. He was never to have the vision again, but he thought about it often, trying to make some sense of it. He told no one about his dream, not even his wife. She died never knowing what troubled her husband for so many years.

It was only decades later, when his daughter Malya returned to the Realm as a mage in her own right, that Escan realized his dream's portent. He feared for himself, but he feared more for the fate of the Realm he loved and served. Malya had returned from the Dark Lands with many of the elfyn mages' secrets, to have her vengeance on those whom she felt had wronged her.

That's the most depressing thing I've ever heard, Sarc.

There's more to it, you impatient girl, he said. *I was only pausing to gather my thoughts. It's been a while since the story's been told.*

After Aron's death, Clyara spent many years alone in the Dark Lands, before she decided to accept an apprentice, and she made her fateful decision in choosing Malya. After the realization of her folly and her subsequent failure to rectify her mistake, Clyara went into self-exile to hone her skills. She spent years seeking a way to defeat Malya, while hoping to keep the elfyn out of danger by keeping her distance from them.

During her years of seclusion, Clyara had had her own premonition about the struggle between darkness and light. She saw a different outcome; in her vision, the forces of light were eventually victorious, and the world flourished in an era of enlightenment and peace. Clyara foresaw her own death and the young apprentice who arose from her literal ashes to finish her work.

As part of her efforts to stem the coming tide of destruction, she ended her self-imposed isolation and returned to the Dark Lands. It was there that Escan finally found Clyara, after a considerable effort, and begged for her counsel, telling her all that he knew. Naturally, Clyara was displeased that her humyn counterpart had not sought her out before Malya came into her service, but Clyara believed that not all was lost. Clyara convinced Escan that their hopes lay in finding successors to their cause and told him of her own revelation.

They had some time to prepare, as the visions had foretold that Clyara's successor would not appear for many years still, so while the Realm and Dark Lands remained unaware, Clyara and Escan began their work. They knew that once the time came, events would unfold quickly.

She knew that her apprentice would never be ready in time, Sarc finished. Unfortunately, so did everyone else. While Clyara and Escan planned for the worst, Malya planned to exploit their weakness.

I knew very little about Clyara's apprentices before me. *She didn't seem to have very much luck choosing her apprentices.*

Luck was never part of it, my dear, Sarc confessed. You were the one that Clyara saw in her vision.

I don't understand, what about the others… Then I remembered the short tenures of those of Clyara's apprentices that I had known. *She waited for me.*

Fifty years can pass in a blur, if one keeps busy. The Realm and the Dark Lands did not suffer much for the wait.

What could possibly be so special about me?

It may have been something she saw in her vision. Clyara never said, but she was adamant about you. She made your guardians swear an oath to protect you, at any cost. Sarc paused. It makes us seem fanatical, doesn't it? But, we were still loyal to our people and our lands, and we kept them safe. It would have been pointless to wait for you, Keeronae, if there was nothing left to save when you arrived.

Keeronae. Master of masters. I felt a cold dread seep into my heart. *That doesn't make me feel much better, Sarc.* How many people were suffering as we spoke, while I was safe in Sarc's care … Safe? Why did I think that? Because he hadn't killed me, because he knew Clyara, because he hadn't handed me over to the humyn? Now that I was powerless to run, the doubts were emerging. It was possible that he was taking me to a "refuge", but wasn't it just as possible that he was delivering me to Malya?

Calmly, 'Fleece, I cautioned myself, shielding my thoughts. I was at his mercy, after all. *He could kill me right here, if he wanted to.* I felt him prodding at the edges of my mind, curious about what I was thinking. *I'm such a fool!*

My mental shield came crashing down, like a tower of blocks, and

Sarc was just outside of it. His adeptness astounded me. For just a moment, my mind was unguarded, vulnerable to any attack he wished, and I braced myself for a psychically painful assault.

Instead, Sarc withdrew and asked, *Was there something you wanted to say?*

There was no hiding from him. *I was just thinking how stupid I've been.*

I wouldn't call you stupid. A little ingenuous, perhaps. At my silence, he soothed, *Plus, your new gem must be playing on your suspicions and self-doubts like it used to with Clyara, so don't be so hard on yourself.*

I should be grateful that you have a forgiving nature. Is that why you were Clyara's 'chosen one'? What is that about?

Oh, that, he said. *Your mistress picked me to see you through your transition after she was gone. She interpreted her vision very literally, that you would rise from her ashes, so she suspected that the gem would someday be yours, and if so, you were going to need some support for your adjustment.*

She certainly got that part right. What else did she tell you about me? I asked casually, trying my best to hide my distress. My telepathy was starting to fade; in moments, I was going to be unable to project my thoughts to Sarc. I needed to know his intentions, for better or worse. A sense of peace and warmth passed through me; as much as I tried to cling to them, my doubts slipped away and faded like smoke, leaving only unconditional faith and utter calm. *Did you do something to soothe me, Sarc?*

Yes, because I don't have time to earn your trust in the usual ways, and I want you to rest easily. Your voice is getting faint, besides, and the sun has finally set.

I want to know more. I had so many questions, and I had run out of time.

I can't hear you anymore, Sarc informed. *But I hope you can still hear me. Your senses will return soon, sharper than ever, and all this will be an unpleasant memory. Tomorrow, everything will become clear.*

I believed him with all my heart, and I listened to his soothing voice as I started to doze. Whatever spell Sarc had cast to clear my mind and help me sleep, it convinced me that nothing could hurt me, and that everything would be better in the morning. However far away the morning was, and whatever awaited me then, I would be fine.

I awoke groggily. The fog of sleep lifted when I realized that a breeze had awoken me. I felt my body's every shiver with giddy delight, and I breathed in the cool night air in gulps, relishing its chill in my mouth and throat. I could move again, and I touched my arms and legs and with ecstatic joy, burying my face in my hair to smell the earthy residue of the Red Lake and feel its softness against my skin. *I'm alive! I'm alive!* I repeated to myself in a joyful delirium.

My heart was pounding, and the gem was dancing inside my chest. I could feel my blood coursing through me. I turned onto my stomach, and listened to the night with dawning disappointment. There was only silence. My hearing hadn't returned yet. I opened my eyes, and there was only an empty blackness to greet me; my vision hadn't yet returned, either.

Not yet, Keeronae, came Sarc's voice inside my head.

I flipped onto my back with my eyes wide open to where I knew the sky to be. I yearned to see the stars and clouds overhead, and to hear the calls of the nocturnal forest creatures. *Not much longer, I hope.*

My heart continued to race, and I felt my body hungrily absorbing every pulse of energy that my gem produced. My fingers and toes tingled and twitched with the sudden jolts of power that shuddered through me.

No, not much longer, he said.

Take my hand, please? I asked.

Sarc was there in the next second, his warm hand covering mine. *Go back to sleep.*

I closed my eyes and enjoyed my rediscovered senses, and Sarc's touch soothing me. Even that simple contact felt precious and luxurious after my hours in the void. I would be myself again soon, I just needed to be patient.

When I awoke again, I knew instantly that I was in a different place. The cool air felt and smelled different, and instead of hard ground underneath me, there was the cushion of a mattress. I sat up and swung my feet around, dragging Sarc's cloak off of me and feeling my slippers underfoot next to the bed. "*Hilafra,* I got up too fast," I groaned, then closed my eyes again, my head swimming.

My own voice echoed in my head worse than a shriek, and my eyes watered from the stinging brightness around me. *I heard. I saw!* I eased my eyes open, and the tears gushed forth to protect my light-sensitive eyes from the onslaught of the innumerable colors around me. For a second, I thought I was hallucinating, but it was all too clear, too real. *I can see it all!* With perfect clarity, I saw brilliant, glowing, jewel-like hues in the chamber, reflecting torchlight from sconces that filled the room.

I staggered to my feet and took in all of it. My bed stood within a library, or a study, with books and scrolls in every corner, lining shelves or arranged in stacks or piled on top of crates. Glorious, vivid tapestries peeked between the towering bookshelves, and even sprawled across the floor as plush rugs. With my sight returned and improved, I could discern every delicate stitch of iridescent thread. I touched everything in front of me, to assure myself that it was all real. "By Ajle, it's incredible," I murmured and heard my voice echo through the chamber.

I touched a book that topped a stack, a book of spells. As I brushed my fingers across the cover, I felt and heard the "zip" of my nails against the ribbed grain of its fabric binding. I opened the front cover, then tapped it to watch it close shut with a dull thump. It was like the sweetest music I had ever heard! Even the scent of the room, the perfume of old paper and lignin, was invigorating and inviting.

There were so many books, but then again, there was still so much that I wanted to learn. I darted through the chamber, seeing all that I could, fearful that this was a dream from which I was to soon wake. I crossed from this room into an adjoining one, which was spare in its decor except for a large rack of weapons against the wall. Most of the implements I knew only from descriptions in storybooks. There were books here, too, scattered by the entrance, as though they had spilled over from the main chamber. Most of the books there detailed martial techniques and strategy.

"What an amazing place—" I stopped and looked around, and sighed.

I returned to the bed where I had awoken, where Sarc's cloak lay in a heap near the footboard. There was little trace of him, only in the faint scent of him on my clothes. I picked up the cloak and breathed it in for comfort, and found underneath it a familiar black silk pouch weighing down a folded note, on top of a small wooden chest.

The small bag was a little dusty from its hiding place in the hollow of a boulder but seemed otherwise intact. I picked up the precious pouch of gems that Clyara had entrusted to me on her last day and wondered how it had gotten there, peering inside to see for myself that they were all present. How did Sarc know where I had hidden the gems? *Well, why wouldn't he know? He was Clyara's confidant well before I came into her service.* I lay the pouch of dormant gems back on the chest, and picked up the note.

The boldly-scrawled message had to be from Sarc, if I were to guess, for it read:

I am sorry to leave you, but I hope you understand that this is something you must do alone. As I had promised, I delivered you safely and remained until you no longer needed me. Your guardians will see to it that the Dark Lands remain safe until you are ready to return, and the door will open for you, when it is time to come home. Don't rush, as you only get one chance here. See you on the other side, S.
P.S. The wires hang in the back. Close your eyes when you push the button. Trust me on this.

I sank to the floor. *Alone.* There was also something else about these rooms that I realized then. "The door will open..." *What door?* There was no exit to be seen. No door, no window, no visible holes. I hadn't known what to expect from the refuge that Sarc had promised, but I knew this wasn't it. I had anticipated privacy, but I hadn't foreseen being hermetically sealed within stone walls by myself.

Perhaps this was a cruel joke, and I was actually secured in a prison, meant to contain me until Malya was ready for me. *Ready for me? Whom am I kidding?* Why would a prison have included a library and an armory at my disposal? To raise my hopes? I wasn't sure what terrified me more: being helpless, or being alone. *What if I died here? No one would ever know about it.*

I set my fears aside, refusing to panic. I read Sarc's note again, more carefully. Everything I needed to become "ready" was here, somewhere. The loneliness would pass eventually, and I would rejoin the humyn and the elfyn in time. The time was still to be determined, but how long could it possibly take? A few weeks, maybe, a few months, at most? Most importantly, in this sanctuary, I would prepare myself, and I would never be helpless again.

Where to start? I reached for the wooden chest in front of me, at the foot of the bed. Inside it was a delicate, bridle-like headpiece connected by wires to a sleek case made partially of the same golden metal, partially of materials that I couldn't even identify at the time. I fingered the pliable wires dangling off one side. "These must be the ones he says hang in the back," I mused, turning the helmet-like device around in my hands. I found the button that Sarc mentioned but did not push it.

I took a few deep breaths. *I trust you, Sarc.* I fitted the metalwork on my head and took one more breath, closed my eyes and pressed the button.

At once, the headpiece clamped tightly onto my head like a pair of hands, and while the sensation wasn't painful, it startled me enough that I snapped my eyes open in alarm. At the same time, words and images began to flash inside my mind, and my eyes crossed trying to make sense of the juxtaposition of the pictures in and out of my head, without much success. I shut my eyes again as Sarc had recommended and focused on the "inside" images for now.

Inside my head was a grid of pictures and words, the only one of which I understood was the word "Elfyn". Before I could think of what to do next, the grid changed into a lengthy alphabetized list, and I spotted the phrase "History (Realm)" among the topics. The device picked up on my mental selection and cleared the images from my head.

It flashed the words: "Your selection: History (Realm) will commence in 5 ... 4 ... 3..."

When the count reached zero, the words vanished, and my brain exploded.

My brain didn't literally explode, of course, but it certainly felt like it. Words, numbers and pictures assailed my mind relentlessly, cramming into my consciousness until I could think of little else, forcing my brain to keep up or else shrivel up in surrender and die. If not for my apprenticeship with Clyara, I am certain that I would have gone mad within moments.

As it was, the information came so quickly that there was no time to pore over details and wonder about their veracity. The device was there to give me the data, and it was my own responsibility to analyze and interpret it afterwards.

The images cleared from my mind finally, and the headpiece released its grip on my skull to signal that the lesson was over. I removed the gear from my head and found that I was stiff all over, and clammy with perspiration. I was mentally exhausted, naturally, but my body had endured its own stresses from the experience. Even my gem, rather than lying dormant with my physical inactivity, felt hot and restless in my chest.

I stared at the device in my hands. It was unlike anything I had ever seen, and I was sure that it had been created someplace far from the Dark Lands. If it had been crafted by humyn of the Realm, then their science or magic was far greater than that of the Dark Lands, and it would only be a matter of time before the elfyn were conquered or eradicated. Where had Sarc gotten such a thing? How much more was there to learn through its use?

With an effort, I set the device and headpiece back into the chest and climbed back onto the bed, sprawled on top of the mattress with my head still spinning with facts, figures and images of long-gone people and places. Of these things, I dreamed.

The main point I gathered from the very painful lesson was that the Realm was alive and thriving, despite elfyn legends to the contrary of the humyn civilization self-destructing and falling into obscurity. Out of the more than thousand years of Realm history force-fed to me, I learned some key points, as follows.

The Realm was formed out of common need, marked by a period of conflict and bloodshed. It was founded through the union of warring tribes, each of which contributed their various strengths to the welfare of the collective. The ten founding tribes, that endured and remained committed to the concept and reinforcement of their union, called their combined lands and peoples the Peaceful Realm.

A strong government was needed to keep the Realm in order, and a man was selected who had no particular allegiance, who could be trusted to be impartial and fair to all. His name was Jyrun Soless, and he became the first Father of the Realm. It was not until much later that the position evolved and grew to the level of imperial authority, but the year of his appointment became known as the first Year of the Emperors.

After Jyrun Soless came his eldest, a daughter named Kaylis. She ascended at the age of twenty-nine and was known for fortifying her border cities against attack by neighboring tribes not yet affiliated with the Realm, and for finally asserting her dominance in the region by managing to tattoo the leaders of each of the non-aligned tribes across their throats with the Realm insignia, in the indelible blue dye of the ironroot flower. Until they died, each tribal leader bore that reminder to never underestimate the reach of Mother Kaylis of the Realm.

Over time, the languages of the tribes blended into a universal language for the Realm, a "common" tongue, and standards of measurement were adopted for the convenience of trade. The humyn grew accustomed to living in close quarters, with many of the cities home to populations in the several thousands; by contrast, even the largest elfyn villages like Moonteyre never held more than two or three thousand at any point in their history.

For centuries after the formation of the Realm, the sea to the west remained largely unexplored, and the uncharted regions east of the Realm were cloaked in mystery, superstition and unexplained phenomena. Thus, the latter became known as the Dark Lands.

The device confirmed what Jaryme had told me, that the Realm was not a land of magic. There was no mention of mages or magestones, despite the detail about the Realm's more mundane aspects. Certain things, apparently, were better left unmentioned.

When I awoke, I remained in bed for a few moments to ruminate on what I had seen and dreamt, to try to see the possible truth in the words. Even if the history I had viewed turned out in the end to be nothing more than an elaborate myth, it made me think. Maybe the humyn weren't so different from what I knew of my own kind.

It was time to resume my studies. I examined the shelves and picked up a history book written in elfyn, about a city called Altaier. It was the seat of Jyrun and Kaylis Soless because of its strategic central location and the convenience of the river that passed through its heart. It was widely known as the cultural and technological hub of the Realm, where innovations like the printing press made information widely accessible, and the invention of gunpowder made the Realm a formidable military force.

Amazed and impressed by the accomplishments of the humyn, I became ashamed of my own deep-seated ambivalence towards them, but I also realized that getting over my bigotry would take some time. Perhaps in my solitude in the Haven, away from the well-meaning influences of others, I could unlearn so many so-called truths that I had heard as folklore and taken for granted since childhood.

If Malya had indeed become Empress of the Realm, then there was no telling what she would do, to the Realm and its peaceful neighbors, and the Dark Lands beyond them. Who was to say that Malya would stop with the Dark Lands? Perhaps, she wanted to rule the world. Or destroy it. If she had become a gemwraith, if what Sarc said was true, who knew what she was thinking now, if she was in fact still capable of thinking …

I closed the book in my lap and once more regretted my lapse. My mistress had asked me to destroy Malya, and I had failed her. Now, Malya was the ruler of the Realm, with an army of tens or hundreds of thousands at her disposal. *What a mess I've made of things.*

I'll fix it, somehow. It was too late to worry about what I should have done. All that mattered now was that I would not fail again. To ensure that, I needed to learn all I could about my enemies before I faced them.

I looked inside the front cover of the book and saw the message in elfyn: "By the patronage of Her Imperial Majesty Adeliaraine, in the year of the Emperors 970." *970?* For the elfyn, the present year was 997. It was certainly possible that we measured the passage of years as the humyn did, as the book didn't seem more than a few decades old, but how could that be? Did we really share a common history?

I returned to the chest and brought out the device again. I donned the headpiece, closed my eyes and pushed the button without much hesitation this time, and I found the topic I wanted quickly enough: anatomy.

The imagery was perhaps more graphic and detailed than that to which I was accustomed, but taken clinically, appropriate enough for academia. The illustrations depicted stereotypical humyn—complete with the tiny ears, big hands, pale hair and eyes—but I found with some surprise that their physiology was otherwise identical to what I already knew as elfyn.

I tugged at the headpiece when the lesson began to focus on soft tissue composition, and the device paused the lesson. What makes the humyn, humyn? Culture, language … what else? What had convinced me that Glory was humyn? Mainly, it was my own superstition, and the matter of Glory's atypical hues, but those elfyn with black or white hair seemed just as exotic.

By the time I finished the lesson, the better part of a day must have passed, and my mind was fuzzy. I closed my eyes and pondered what I had learned, and why the truth had been kept from the elfyn for so long. Our myth of isolation had been going on for centuries, too long for Clyara to be the only party responsible. And, even while the elfyn were convinced that there was nothing outside of the Dark Lands, why didn't anyone come from the Realm to set the history straight? Somebody knew the truth!

After I had rested my eyes, my mind was still buzzing with new concepts and old emotions. I found a stack of books on one shelf at my eye level, purposefully kept in plain sight, with a black cloth strip tied around them.

As I gathered the books into my arms, I could tell by just the crispness of the paper that they were recent additions to the library. I gingerly slipped off the knotted black muslin strip and recognized it as the same type that Sarc wore in his hair. What else could he have left for me? I opened the first volume and read the first handwritten date: "Spring, Year of Our Emperors 498."

Sarc's handwriting was clear and bold on the page, and the words were elfyn. I skimmed through the first volume and saw the same, evenly neat script throughout, even as the dates spanned decades. It took me a moment to realize that I was reading from a journal, a transcription from a secret history, before the evolution of humyn and elfyn.

Finally, I had an account dating back to the dawn of magic.

Chapter 10: Ancient Words

"My name is Iavan, and I am the Prime Advisor to the Twelfth Emperor of the Realm. I have just returned from my most recent foray into the Dark Lands, where I came across a most incredible find."

Thus began the first entry, dated from the spring of the year 498, when Lord Iavan's diplomatic travels led him to a mysterious case of gems. He did not explain the origin of the magestones, if he knew at all. He kept his journal mainly to record his experiments with the gems, including "the excruciating consumption" that he had attempted on a whim, after multiple attempts at dissecting and deconstructing had failed.

In short, Prime Advisor Iavan learned that the stone bestowed powers, and he used his new gifts to gradually grow his power in the Imperial Court until his influence rivaled that of his Imperial masters. Intrigued by his advisor's sudden talents, the Emperor dispatched agents who discovered Iavan's store of "magestones" and brought one back to him.

The Prime Advisor was astute enough to realize that his position was in jeopardy, once the Emperor learned how to harness the potential of the magestone in his possession. With his family, his remaining store of stones, and a small group of dissidents with their families, Iavan fled the Realm and found sanctuary in the wilderness of his beloved Dark Lands, in the uncharted regions. Whatever knowledge and resources the mage could not take with him, he demolished and burned.

After his exodus, members of the Imperial Court who followed him from the Realm informed him of what transpired. The Emperor, driven mad by the undisciplined use of his gem, began to imagine conspiracies fomenting in his court, and he swiftly targeted his perceived enemies. He managed to have several of his advisors executed, before the rest staged an uprising to unseat their monarch, and in the chaos of the insurgence, killed him.

The members of the Court knew nothing about magic and magestones, so they were horrified when the late Emperor rose from the dead. Luckily for them, their capable guards easily subdued and burned the wraith Emperor. His remains were scattered into the Inearan Channel, but the fate of the unlucky magestone was unknown.

The late Emperor's son took his throne as the Thirteenth Emperor of the Realm and applied the lessons he learned from observing his father's descent into madness. The new Emperor decreed that magic would no longer be allowed in his court, and instead he encouraged advancement through science: knowledge accessible to any, for the benefit of all.

The dissidents also struggled in their new homeland. They were met with initial suspicion by the brown-haired, tan-skinned people who were indigenous to the Dark Lands, but they were gradually integrated. Iavan weighed his options, and while he longed for the comforts of his Imperial home, he also understood that he could not return to the life he once had. If the magestones were ever to return to the Realm, and fall under the control of one Emperor or another, they could be used to create a formidable army. Even in the Dark Lands, Iavan guarded the gems and the rest of his knowledge from the curious eyes of his fellow expatriates, from even his own family.

The eventual passing of his loved ones marred his years of magical discovery and growth; Iavan witnessed the burials of his three children, each of whom had lived long enough to see their own grandchildren reach adulthood.

After the death of his youngest child, Iavan felt that it was time to pass his knowledge to another. He chose the most capable of his great-grandchildren, his daughter's only grandson, to be his apprentice. "Perhaps one day, the lands will merge," he wrote, "and magic can flow freely between them."

Iavan's great-grandson and successor left no journal. The second journal contained entries dated in the year of the Emperors 750, kept by a man who called himself Set. He was the predecessor of Clyara's master.

Set made passing references to several outsiders who came questing in the Dark Lands for the knowledge of magic, all of whom were turned away, or avoided until they gave up the search. He described the outsiders as "brutish, coarse and smelly," in contrast to the "refined grace and slender elegance" of the dwellers of the Dark Lands.

His prejudice seemed as much a result of his upbringing as his personal opinion. He described the banal, bland and deficient as "only humyn", while he proclaimed the beautiful, delicate and extraordinary as "elfyn," borrowing the term from folklore from centuries past. To further differentiate himself from the gem-users who had preceded him, Set coined the title for himself of "mage" for "one who practices magic".

By now, the "elfyn" had started to develop their own language, a marriage of the native tongue of the Dark Lands with that of the Realm. Set's journal reflected the evolving language, including more colorful references to nature and a more lyrical, flowery cadence, contrasting with the crisp precision of the Common language, the lingua franca of the long-forgotten Realm.

As the languages mixed, so did the people. Since the newly-evolved elfyn adapted well to their bucolic lives, few ever wandered outside the Dark Lands. The new generations of elfyn, who knew the Realm and humyn only through passed-down stories, created their own mythology, including a heaven called "Ajle", tales of great warriors and legends of a fallen humyn civilization.

Aron, Clyara's master, kept the third volume. His first entries were dated from the year 800, picking up where Set had left off. Aron's account began with his dramatic confession of killing his *keeron* Set, in self-defense. It seemed that Set had a vision the previous night that his apprentice Aron would someday, somehow, bring about the near-extinction of the elfyn, and Set decided to sacrifice his apprentice's life for the welfare of his people.

Aron described in full detail how Set looked in his transformation into a wraith, and how Set showed no glimmer of a soul in his dull, open eyes. To stop his *keeron*'s resurrection, Aron commanded all his physical strength to tear the gem from Set's chest, but the master's metamorphosis to wraith was complete. According to Aron's account, he swallowed the stone to keep it from the creature's possession and ordered the wraith to leave at once, and the creature acquiesced, never to be seen by Aron again.

Like Set before him, Aron felt that the elfyn were better off without the existence of the humyn to complicate their simple lives. Like Set, Aron oversaw the gradual revision of countless texts, to mold elfyn history into what he felt was best for his people. Like all the elfyn of his own age, Aron had lived his life without ever having seen anyone from outside the Dark Lands. He saw no harm in letting the elfyn believe that the humyn and their Realm were merely the products of superstition. In all the years after Lord Iavan's passing, no one else had ever emerged from the Realm; as far as Aron knew, the Realm had been gone for centuries.

When it came time for Aron to choose an apprentice, he decided upon an unassuming, slight-figured man who called himself Jyrun Uscari. The young man had followed Aron for weeks from a respectful distance, waiting outside the mage's door in all kinds of weather. With his mouse-brown hair and pale eyes, Uscari was an atypical specimen, but his sensibilities, his grooming, his manner … everything else about him was positively elfyn.

Jyrun Uscari served Aron very well for several years, but the *keeron* found that Uscari was becoming increasingly secretive. One day Aron awoke to find Uscari on his way to his room with a store of magestones and a collection of books. Uscari had been planning to one day take them back to the Realm, back to the humyn.

Shaken by the revelation that the humyn still existed, Aron

confiscated Uscari's every possession, including the robes he had given him. He spared Uscari's life in allowing him to keep his gem, but Aron banished his apprentice from the Dark Lands, vowing to destroy him if he ever set eyes on him again. After Uscari's exile, Aron found that a number of the stones had already been stolen. Uscari was never seen or heard from again.

Aron spent years devising the tools of his revenge, even as he struggled to rebuild his trust in others. He began to reshape his role in the community to be that of a healer, but with less than noble intentions. With the knowledge that the humyn civilization still survived, and that the treacherous Jyrun Uscari was among their numbers, Aron experimented with the magic that he knew, to create such spells that acted as plagues upon the humyn, and Uscari in particular.

Aron described his process of creating the so-called "healing spells", his concentrated efforts to steal the life and limbs from one to restore to another. Through his hatred for the humyn, he had created the role of a god for himself.

What helped him diffuse his anger and hatred was a young woman who had caught his eye, and in whom he sensed a great potential. In all the years since Iavan's first experiments with magic, there had never been a woman mage, but Aron decided to take the chance on this young woman named Clyara Soless. Unarguably, Clyara was beautiful, but Aron was more interested in how to use her skills for his needs. She seemed to be in love with him, which made her even easier for him to manipulate.

Sarc had transcribed three of the four volumes in his neat, bold script. The last of the four volumes, written by Clyara's own hand, was a slim, tan leather book that I remembered well from my years in her company. I opened the volume gingerly and touched the fine dark print with trembling fingers.

It was the year 860, and Clyara Soless was twenty years old. She had just begun her apprenticeship with Aron, the Healer of the Dark Lands.

Her journal entries were candid and full of self-deprecating humor, but very infrequent, jumping weeks and months at a time. They tracked her growing disillusionment with her master, at the same time that her power and love for magic grew. Aron, always formal and emotionally aloof with Clyara, became increasingly bitter and sharp-tongued, and he thought nothing of using Clyara's feelings against her, to keep her under his control. Certain of her loyalty to him, he taught her his "healing" spell and told her about her traitorous predecessor Jyrun Uscari.

When she could longer stomach the emotional and physical abuse she suffered from Aron, Clyara killed her *keeron* in 880. She saw the first gemwraith come for Aron's stone, and she watched Aron's metamorphosis into the second. While he was reanimating, she gouged Aron's magestone from his chest and swallowed it in hopes of claiming his power. She intended to destroy the wraiths, but she was too weak from her battle with Aron and wracked by the torturous side-effects of taking his gem. When they did not move against her, she realized their value as guards under her command. Their limited senses were extensions of her own, inextricably linked to her through the gem. During the days that followed, Clyara used her gemwraiths as her eyes and ears to get through the debilitating phase of the adjustment. When they had served their purpose, Clyara sent them into the mountains, to return whenever she wanted their services again.

Sifting through her *keeron*'s belongings, Clyara found a map of the Dark Lands among his books. Aron had built a sanctuary for himself, a place for meditation, a place to hide if Uscari's power ever grew to match his own. Clyara used the map to find "the Haven", as she called it, and there she discovered the books and journals that Aron had archived over the decades. She studied in the Haven whenever she had the chance, and she taught herself the archaic common tongue, by reading the tattered, centuries-old journals of the mages who came before her.

Through Aron's careful efforts, as well as her own, Clyara became a master mage in her own right, and she followed in Aron's tradition of healing. Just like her master, she felt no love for the humyn and sought only to help and strengthen elfynkind, at any cost. Clyara traveled through the Dark Lands as a wandering Healer, never settling in any one place long enough to let others see that she did not age as they did. In 920, when Clyara completed her eightieth year, she looked no more than thirty-five, but she was exhausted and decided that it was time for her to choose an apprentice.

Clyara selected Malya Escan, a willowy young woman with uncommonly light eyes and hair. Malya was twenty-five when she became Clyara's apprentice. Clyara confided to her journal that she was envious of young Malya's skill and drive, and that she felt it was unsafe for Malya to remain, both for the young woman and for the Dark Lands.

The record of Malya's apprenticeship with Clyara ended abruptly after the first year. From one page in the volume to the next was a decades-long gap. She did not write of her first, fateful meeting with Malya's father, Junus Escan. She did not write of his prophecy or her own premonitory dreams. She did not write of her change of heart regarding the humyn. She wrote nothing of her first meeting with my appointed guardian, Alessarc. Perhaps she was too busy to write, or perhaps she felt that the events were too trifling to detail.

Her next entry was dated in the year 970, ten years before I was born. Clyara was one-hundred-thirty years old, and already established as a respected Healer for twenty-five years; she had finally decided to stop wandering and settle into the quietly thriving town of Moonteyre.

Clyara reconfirmed her continuing conflict with her former apprentice, and her own self-loathing for living the lie of a healer's life. Clyara cast the "healing" spells as infrequently as she could, and she became an expert on medicinal herb lore to supplement her skills. Clyara could see no way out of her lifestyle without endangering her people. Just as she was casting these spells to help the elfyn, Malya and her allies was casting the same spells for the humyn.

Clyara tried her best to shield her elfyn from Malya and the other unnamed humyn who would hurt them; she also continued to hide from the elfyn the truth of what they were. With her magic to maintain her, Clyara outlived all the other elfyn in the Dark Lands, to become the eldest Elder and its resident historian. She alone among the elfyn knew what existed outside the Dark Lands, taking brief journeys when she could, and she stocked her Haven with many souvenirs from her visits to the lands west of the Yirae River.

Then came the summer of 980, and Clyara began her account of my life. She made an entry on the day of my birth, to express her sorrow at not being able to save my mother. She made a vow to my father to always watch over me. In hindsight, I could interpret that she already knew me for what I would become, but she stopped short of putting her thoughts to paper.

I was surprised to discover how closely Clyara had monitored my childhood. She had already started to notice my traits in which she saw potential, and she paid close attention to the way that others treated me and my responses in turn, especially after my father's death. If she already knew whom I was, and if she felt as threatened by my potential as she was by Malya's, then she was making a conscious effort to not write about her feelings.

She recounted the night of my adjustment with my first stone, remarking that she was confident about my recovery, and her concern with a visitor who came that night:

> Alessarc arrived this evening, in his usual guise and looking very much like his grandfather once did. It was bittersweet to see him that way, as it reminded me of what I had forsaken years ago. He looked well, but tired from his trip. I did not tell him about the circumstances around the departure of my last apprentice, young Zephyr, but I suspect he knew.
>
> I told him that I was glad that he was able to come on such short notice, and he answered that he had been expecting my call, as soon as he heard that I had returned Glory. He accompanied us to Winter's home, and Frost left us to our work, eventually. She was cautious, but she

trusts us. Bright young woman, not unlike the others of her mother's line.

My girl is not yet ready to know of other mages, but she needs a proper guardian, and this bonding needed to take place while Snowfleece is prone. Still, I will never forget Alessarc's pained expression when I reminded him of my request. "There must be another way," he said. "Give me something else: a lock of her hair, a clipping of her fingernail."

I convinced my dear Alessarc that he had to take a living piece of her into himself in order to bond with her. I cut her palm and gave her hand to him quickly, before he could change his mind. He was reluctant to taste her blood, but he did finally drink, deeply. Whatever he did not finish seeped back into her before her gem healed her wound.

He hated it. He felt as though he had raped her, taking something from her that she had not freely given. Had I not convinced him that her life depended on it, he would have never agreed to it. I assured him that she will understand. It was my decision, and I should be the one to suffer her scorn, but I will be long gone by the time she discovers her guardian's secret. Now that he has bonded with her, he will be able to call to Snowfleece and help her when she needs him most, and she will know to trust him despite herself.

Despite myself! Whether it had been done for my own good or not, I still felt desecrated, with the knowledge that a part of me was inside Sarc, and that he had used that bond to influence me. Was there anything of myself in my decisions, or had they all been carefully planned? And of my feelings for him from the start, how many of those had been true?

I closed the journal and stared at it for a good while. Despite her laxness for recording the details of her own life, Clyara had been fastidious about the details of mine. After her years of observing me, Clyara knew me well, better than I realized. She knew that I would forgive her almost anything, and that I would understand that I owed my life to her foresight.

Seeing a loose page inside the back cover of the journal, I pulled it free and managed a weak smile. Even in death, Clyara managed to surprise me — and still does, to this day. She had left me a beautifully detailed map of the Dark Lands and the Realm for the day that I would leave. She wrote in her graceful script at the bottom of the map: "Last chance to make it right, my girl. Don't disappoint me."

I hadn't yet failed Clyara; she knew from the beginning that I wouldn't be ready for Malya. She had prepared her Haven for my arrival, and she assigned a capable guardian to the task of seeing me there.

Coaxed into a forgiving mood and heartened by her confidence, I opened the journal again and finished reading through to her final entry:

Snowfleece must accomplish what I could not, bring an end to the strife. My path has denied me a child to raise as my own, so perhaps I have unwittingly claimed this girl as a daughter. I have expectations of her that I could not have possibly met when I was her age, but I have also given her the opportunity of a thousand lifetimes. She will pay for her gift with the understanding of her responsibility, and that will help her against my former pupil.

Malya knows her end is near, and as much as she will try to avoid her fate, she will ultimately fail. She knows of Snowfleece, but the knowledge is hers at the cost of her daughter's loyalty. Glory has seen Malya's deliberate malice, but I fear that the discovery came too late. I only hope that the refuge that I have chosen for Glory will hide her long enough. I did not want to abandon her, but it was necessary to protect Snowfleece.

About my apprentice, I have no concern. Her guardians will wait for her and watch over her until her time comes. Regardless of whether she uses Aron and Set, after I am gone, Alessarc will see to it that she reaches her Haven safely. He may not agree with my choices, but he will abide by them. I would not have chosen him, if I had any doubts, regardless of our ties.

As I close my journal, I shall leave it behind with the others that Alessarc has translated and transcribed, so that 'Fleece will one day read and understand. And, perhaps, forgive.

Chapter 11: Comforts of Home

What time is it? What day is it? When did I pass out?
While my head was cushioned on an edge of the feather mattress, it was nowhere near a pillow or even the headboard, which was an arm's length away. It wasn't the first time that I had barely made it to bed in my exhaustion, and certainly wasn't to be the last. *How long have I been sleeping?* I laughed aloud and looked at the ever-burning lamps all around me. Without the sun's help, and with every clock that I had ever conjured vanishing by the time I awoke, I could only make a guess about how much I slept.

I picked up the usual scrap of coal from next to my bed and added a scratch to the array decorating the scrap of parchment that I had pinned to the headboard. *Five hundred fifty-two days. More or less.* Between my erratic regimen of diet and exercise and whatever my magestone was doing, my body had reprogrammed itself altogether, so I couldn't even trust my own internal cycles and systems. I might have slept a few hours, or a few days.

At least I hadn't had the strange dreams that sometimes haunted me. Some were awful, some were splendid and sensual. Mostly, they were awful. The settings were usually in Moonteyre, and it was too painful to feel so close to home and yet so removed, so I tried to forget them all. Still, they reminded me that I would not be alone forever, and that my purpose was greater than just survival. If I wanted to get out, I needed to learn everything I could, and quickly.

What was I doing last night? I stood unsteadily and tossed Sarc's cloak back on the mattress. I kicked a hard crust of bread and sent it skittering and tumbling across the rugs and tiles into the next room, swept my overgrown white bangs back from my dusty face, and threw my tattered dress on over my head for warmth. I had found a storage chest with some clothes that fit me, but it didn't seem worth the effort to dress neatly when there was no one around to notice. I secured my greying hair into a knot with a ribbon and trudged into the other room.

The heavy text was face down on the floor where I had left it. *Oh, yes, I remember now.* I had been in the middle of practicing my spells when I decided that I had had enough and that I needed sleep. Thankfully, the purple spotted cow that I had conjured in my unfocused exhaustion had turned back to dust.

"Let's try this again," I muttered, rubbing the sleep from my eyes. I cast the spell once more, and this time got my thoughts straight and my timing more precise. The tiny grey and brown sparrow materialized from the floor and hopped closer, peering up at me hopefully. "Thank you," I said with a wave and a heartfelt sigh of relief. The conjured bird bobbed its head, pecked disinterestedly at the fallen bread and dissolved back into the stone tiles.

It was a small success, but an encouraging one. It felt like weeks that I had been trying to master conjuring by intuition and thought, without using hand gestures and reciting spells from a book. While the teaching device that Sarc had left for me was comprehensive in its range of scholarly topics, magic was not amongst them. My magical studies, therefore, remained a manual exercise.

To celebrate, I took a dry biscuit and transformed it into a slice of soft, sweet bread. While Sarc had left me with enough dry food and fresh water to last a few weeks, if not months through careful rationing, I had rushed to learn how to conjure my own nourishment, with my tolerance for bland, imperishable biscuits and desiccated fruit quickly wearing thin. The results were minimally appetizing at first, but I had gotten better. The food and drink didn't taste like sawdust anymore, or like something liberally sprinkled with sawdust.

After breakfast came language studies. I levitated a schoolbook from the floor and materialized a broom. "Bra-uum," I said with an effort, in the common language of the Realm. I had butchered the word, but I had to keep practicing. If my plan was to confront Malya on her own land, in her Realm, I had to at least know how to ask for directions in the local dialect.

I set the schoolbook in the air and swept the crumbs and assorted squalor off the floor, as the book hovered at my eye level. "'The big cat j-jumped out of the sm-mall bag,'" I read painstakingly, glancing at the crude line drawing beneath the sentence. "E gati utjo ba," I translated aloud into elfyn. Amazing how much a language can change in four hundred years.

As I cleaned, the book followed me. At last, I can speak like a nervous four-year-old, I thought gloomily. I returned the book to the shelf, along with the dozens of others that I had recently completed, supplementing what The Device had covered on subjects ranging from history and science to the physical disciplines of acrobatics and swordplay.

I drew a quarterstaff from the stand against the wall and practiced what I remembered from the lessons, judging my form by conjured mirrors. Without Clyara's critical eye to gauge me, however, I didn't think my exercises were enough to make me effective in combat, but the exertion helped relieve my restlessness. Besides, with the irregularity of my meals, I knew my strength was only a fraction of what it had been during my apprenticeship.

I swung the staff over my head, tensing and stretching each muscle in my arms and shoulders. The world was changing outside of the Haven, and I was helpless to intervene. Already a year had passed, and I was no closer to finding a way out. I growled my frustration and hurled the staff head-on towards the wall but detoured it at the last second to avoid the tapestry that hung there and smashed the staff into the ground instead. As I shuffled to retrieve the splintered pole, feeling no release from my tantrum, I glowered up at the tapestry's vivid depiction of Moonteyre from the heights of the Ajlekyrn during brilliant, fiery autumn.

I usually avoided the tapestry since the scenery was a constant reminder of the home I was missing, but now as I knelt inches away from its embroidered surface, I noticed a vertical seam on the stone wall beneath the drapery. I followed the line up to where it disappeared behind the tapestry and lifted the corner of the textile to look behind it.

Hilafra.

An interesting word: *hilafra*. Nowadays, it's spoken as a mild expletive, but it had an innocuous etymology as: "hole in my head." The term seemed appropriate as I gazed at the hairline split in the otherwise solid granite. It was as hard to see as a hole in my own head.

I touched my fingertips to the crack and jerked my hand back at the electric jolt that triggered. *Nothing is ever as easy as it looks, is it?* I lifted the drapery off the brackets and set it aside, to get an unobstructed view of the wall, and saw the message in glowing letters, set into the stone:

Opening scheduled: 1,244.12.41.26

The last numbers of the message appeared to be counting down: 26, 25, 24… As I stared at the numbers, it occurred to me that it could be a counter, but a thousand two hundred days would have meant three more years.

"*Hilafra*, I need to be here that much longer?" I said, sitting back on my heels. I had already been there for well over a year, and while I had learned a great deal, there was more to master. I was still far from proficient at casting spells by intuition as my mistress had often done, and I hadn't even managed to learn enough of the common tongue to engage in brief conversation.

Getting to my feet, I stared into the chamber at all the thousands of books, strewn throughout the Haven in an order of my own logic. "Did I really read them all?" I was familiar with most of the volumes, even the stacks of religious and philosophical texts. "I've been here for over five hundred days by myself, why not? What else would I be doing?" I said, half to myself, and half to the magestone.

Due at least in part to my extended isolation, I had begun to think of my magestone as a companion. It certainly gave the impression of a peevish and petulant personality, in the way it taunted and prodded me. On occasion, it also drew me to hidden nooks and crevices in the Haven that concealed additional maps and notes, mostly from Aron, who clearly was obsessed with keeping secrets and maintaining control, and the hoarding habits of a mad squirrel.

Regardless of whether he was Clyara's master, Aron seemed a twisted, bitter man who deserved no respect from me. It was because of him and his infernal "healing" that relations between the elfyn and the humyn had deteriorated so far. If only he hadn't created that spell... *Oh, forget it.* There was nothing that could be done to change the past, except to find a way to repair relations once I rejoined the living.

As I brushed back my overgrown locks, I studied my slender hand and thought about the gems' restorative powers, especially as they manifested in Clyara and Sarc. Provided that I didn't die fighting Malya, I was likely to live for at least another century. What would I do with a hundred years? I could experience everything that this world had to offer, many times over if I wished it. But I would do it alone, with no one to share all my years, no one to understand and empathize.

Not too different from my life now. I craved the outside, the natural sunlight; I missed the company of people, especially Frost. I thought of her a great deal, especially whenever I chanced to see a lock of my lightening hair, now more white than dark. I thought of the humyn mage Jaryme, who had befriended me and sheltered me from hunters. I thought of the gemwraith empress Malya and her daughter Glory, if she was even still alive.

I sank back onto the bed, suddenly overcome by a deep sadness. It was as though I had lost a part of my soul. My world was dead, and there was no purpose or reason in anything that was around me. I curled into myself and just cried, but I felt no emotional release from it. More than anything, I was astonished by my sudden melancholy. There was no reason for it. I mustered my composure, wiped my meaningless tears and sat up in bed again.

My solitude was taking its toll on me, that was it. I needed something to tether myself to reality before I lost my grasp of it. I grabbed the first thing I touched and held it tightly. Even with my eyes closed, I knew the texture of Sarc's cloak, and I took a deep breath of the cedar and sandalwood that remained infused in the wool. *Sarc waits for me.* Emotionally, I needed to believe it, even if, intellectually, I knew better. I just needed to hold on a little longer, long enough to focus on my sole task, which was to learn everything I could. Learn everything, and reclaim my freedom.

I smoothed the wall with a spell, etched the new mark into the wall and touched the engraved numbers. *One thousand forty days.* A little less than three years since my arrival, and a couple more years left, according to the counter on the wall. Out of habit, I called a few words out to the wall, to see if anything would trigger it to open: "Wall … open … exit … please?"

Nothing worked. Nothing ever worked.

I was anxious, but my calmer, more prudent conscience had always prevailed, convincing me that it was better to stay in the Haven, to use my resources while I had them. Once I left, I wouldn't be able to return for some time, if ever. According to Sarc's note, I only had one chance.

I pulled out a tunic and skirt from the open chest at the foot of the bed; the clothes were loose, but it felt nice to have something soft and unsoiled against my skin. Besides, the dress that I had worn on the day I arrived, was no longer part of my wardrobe, having long ago frayed to the point of becoming relegated to cleaning rag material.

I stood from the bed, snapped my fingers and caught a small plum in my hand. It tasted as sweet as the fruit from the finest orchard. Finishing that, I returned to the main chamber and picked up the half-finished astronomy text that I had left bookmarked on the shelf. I had been trying to learn the sky, for the purpose of navigating my way to the Realm.

"Let's see," I mumbled in the common tongue, scanning through the common words on the page. "If the Fates are that way," I said, pointing forward and sketching the constellation on the darkened ceiling in sprinkles of magical light, "then the Great Serpent is there, and the Silver River points west…" I set the book down and gazed up at the illusionary night sky that I had made. The stars, planets and galaxies swirling above me were fixed and ageless, unchanged, even from when our world was new. I returned the room to its usual brightness, humbled to know that nothing I did or was, would ever affect the path or fate of any of those celestial forms.

Stop. Buried deep inside my mind, I heard a tiny, nagging voice, growing louder by the second. It was a woman's voice, screaming. I dropped to the floor, gripping my sleeve where I felt a blade bite into my shoulder. I looked down and saw my blood-streaked dress, except that the dress wasn't mine, and the hand that I feebly lifted to shield myself was adorned with a simple silver band.

Frost! I was somehow feeling her pain, or some echo of it. The phantom blows wracked and shook me, until I could barely stand; I could only imagine what my sister was feeling. *Who's there? Who's doing this to you?*

'Fleece, stay away. Frost's weakening voice tormented me, as I shared her fading agony. She was fainting, slipping away, then she was gone.

"Cowards!" I screamed at her unseen torturers through my streaming tears. I didn't care if she was bait for a trap set for me: I couldn't let Frost suffer. My body still tingled, and my skin felt raw, galvanizing me for my immediate departure. I told myself that I was ready to leave. *I have to be.* If anything happened to Frost, nothing I did would matter anymore, anyway.

I summoned Sarc's cloak around myself and grabbed Clyara's map from the shelf. I returned to the seamed granite wall and tried again: "Ready ... Sarc ... Clyara ... damn it!" In desperation, I cast a spell to try to pry the seam open, without success. I even touched it again, and again received a shock. I forced my hand against the wall, enduring the shocks, hoping to ... what, exhaust the wall? I fell to my knees, feeling another wave of ripping pain tear through my body through my tie to Frost.

"Please," I pleaded with the impervious wall, "I need to go home."

"Password has been accepted," responded a soothing, disembodied male voice. Sarc's voice. The wall began to tremble, and the seam began to split.

I scrambled to my feet and glanced at the tapestry that I had set aside over a year ago, the one that used to cover the wall. It was a tapestry depicting Moonteyre, with its fields and mountains ... and with my father's house stitched at its center. "Sarc, you trickster." *Home. Hilafra, I'm dim.*

The seam widened into a doorway, and between the edges awaited the majestic black peaks of the plutonic Ajlekyrn. The afternoon sun's glow burst into the Haven like a wave, making everything in the cavern bright and golden, for the first time in years.

I stepped over the threshold and into the embrace of the warming light, feeling a surge of energy burst through me like another electrical tingle. It startled but did not hurt. Stunned for a second, I blinked to clear my vision and looked over my shoulder. There was only the stone face of the mountain, with no trace of an opening to be seen. My exit was unmarked, so my haven was still hidden and would hopefully remain undisturbed. I turned my back to the mountain and gazed down from the precipice, into the gorge.

I needed just a moment to orient myself. The last time I had seen the riverbed from that height, I had been fleeing for my life. The riverbed didn't seem so far away anymore. With a spell, I descended vertically from the mountain, so fast it felt like falling, with the bracing cool air rushing up over me like water. The surrounding forests looked fuller, more mature, and the trees had flourished since I'd seen them last. They were vibrant and verdant with lush summer growth. The hills were carpeted emerald, but they looked a little flatter where wind and rain had worn away the earth.

I glided across the rugged landscape, not bothering to traverse the rocky ground itself, following the afternoon sun westward towards home. Feeling the urgency of the moment, I was nonetheless struck by the late-day colors and sweet, heady smells of summer. My Dark Lands may have resembled what I recalled, but the novelty and the vividness of everything around me were overwhelming and jarring after the austerity of my recent cloistered existence.

Closer to Moonteyre, men and women came running from the fields with tools in hand, responding to the tolling of the town hall bell. It felt strange to be in the company of people again, after so long. "The marauders have returned!" someone called in common. "They're taking Elder Frost."

Over my dead body. I concentrated on Frost and teleported. I appeared too far, still, but I was within sight of her, along with a couple of shrieking children who were being carried off. A small army dressed in black, a group of villagers, and a pack of two dozen wolves were entangled in what looked like a three-way battle. Hesitant to cast a general spell without understanding the situation, I made myself invisible and joined the confusion.

The wolves did not need sight to sense my presence, and they cleared the way for me. Unobstructed, I followed the uniformed men who held my sister and crushed their throats from a distance until they fell limp to the ground. One of them clubbed her on the back of the head to subdue her, and I stumbled from the head-splitting pain; reflexively, I picked him up and tossed him to the wolves to dispatch. Until I reached Frost's side, I forcefully shoved aside anyone who unwittingly got in my way, friend or foe.

Seeing themselves outnumbered, the invaders retreated, taking their fallen allies with them. They attempted to take the squirming children, too, except that several of the wolves had caught up with the would-be captors and were clamping their powerful jaws on the children's clothes, tugging until the invaders had to relent and give up their captives. Once the children were in their midst, some of the wolves remained to form a close, guarding circle, while the rest joined the villagers' chase after the surviving members of the retreating invasion force.

I dispelled my invisibility and tended to Frost. She was still unconscious, with cuts and bruises on her body and head. I wrapped my arms tightly around her, shut my eyes and chanted my healing spell silently, repeatedly, like a mantra. *I'm so sorry, Frost.* I cried when her pain passed to my body; she never should've had to endure it for me. *I shouldn't have been gone so long.*

A crowd had gathered around us. The two children were kneeling on the ground with me, with faces far too grim for their youth. The boy was an older toddler with Tracker's brown hair and eyes and determined jaw, and the girl had dark eyes and tar-black hair, and looked just a little over a year old: old enough to walk and nearly ready to speak. The wolves stood close by, and one of the silver-coated males came to the fore.

Ever at your service, Protector, Grey-Eye addressed solemnly with a bow of the head, his mis-matched eyes lowered respectfully. He was one of the largest of the pack, and was clearly a respected member. The other wolves followed his lead and also bowed to me, eliciting whispers amongst the crowd.

"I'm honored, friends," I nodded to them. *It is good to see you again, Grey-Eye. Who were those invaders?*

Grey-Eye regarded Frost sympathetically. *The marauders come from the Realm of the Dead Mage Queen, to serve as her eyes and ears here. They come to wreak havoc, to try to draw you out prematurely. Your guardians will be displeased that you emerged too soon.*

"I couldn't stay idle," I said. "They are my responsibility."

They are our responsibility, he said stiffly. *This incident was unfortunate, but your family would have remained safe.*

Frost stirred, effectively ending our discussion.

"Snowfleece?" Her waking visage was one of confusion, softening to relief and joy at the sight of her children. She threw her arms around them and grabbed my hand tightly. "Rigel, Kaylis, are you all right?" Frost looked them over, making sure they were unhurt. The children were shaken and clung to their mother, but they did not cry. They looked at me but did not speak. "Children, don't be frightened. I've told you about your Aunt 'Fleece." She touched my face, happy and relieved to see me, but not surprised.

Rigel stood behind his mother suspiciously, and Kaylis gazed at me with wide black eyes before she launched herself at me, grabbing fistfuls of my hair for balance. *Kaylis, Mother of the Realm.* "My goodness, Frost!" I exclaimed, holding Kaylis's small, squirming body, with her teething spittle soaking into my bodice. "You've been busy."

"You've no idea," she said dryly. She got to her feet and took Kaylis from my arms, her eyes following me, as I got to my feet. "You've grown."

I had. I was at least a couple of centimeters taller than my sister, and taller than many of the elfyn standing around us.

"Well, what's everyone staring at?" she addressed in the common tongue to the crowd, circling her arm around my waist. "My sister has come home."

"She is no longer one of us," remarked a woman in the crowd.

"She was born in Moonteyre, same as me," Frost said. "Even Tracker would have agreed that she belongs here as much as any of us."

The mention of Tracker quieted the crowd. "As you say, Elder Frost," the woman said quietly. No one else questioned Frost further.

Frost bowed her head to the wolves. "I shall always be in your debt."

They lowered their heads to her, their ears and haunches relaxed in submission. As one, they turned and cantered back towards the woods, and the people were careful to leave a clear, wide path for them.

Some of the people were hobbling or clutching their wounded limbs, and their stoicism and resilience moved me; were these the same elfyn who had been so dependent on Clyara's healing magic only a few years ago? "Would they allow me to heal them?" I asked Frost in elfyn.

"It's a lot of injury and blood, amongst the lot of them," Frost cautioned.

"I would not offer, if I couldn't manage it."

"Wait here," she said, then walked towards a gathering of Elders, with Kaylis still clinging to her neck. As she spoke to them, they shook their heads vehemently in protest, until she finally said, loudly enough for anyone outside their circle to hear: "I would suggest that we let the wounded decide for themselves whether they wish to be healed. We'll be home if anyone needs us." She marched away from the Elders and rejoined Rigel and me.

"The idea didn't go over well?" I asked.

Frost shook her head. "They're afraid to invite trouble, that's all."

She and the children led me to a stone cottage not too far from where the crowd was milling. Like the other houses in the new Moonteyre, it was a small, plain structure. There was ivy covering the stone walls, and fragrant, thorny bushes of riotously pink roses all along the perimeter. Frost opened the door and let Rigel inside first. "It's not on the knoll anymore, and it's not as spacious as the old house..."

"It's beautiful," I said with a thorough gaze around. There was nothing for me to recognize in the details, but after spending the better part of the past three years in a cave, I could hardly comment on any home. "It must have taken some time to build. Even the stones for the walls..."

"They were salvaged from the old house, I insisted on that," she said. "Otherwise, I wanted it built as quickly as possible. Everyone was very kind and gracious after Tracker died, but I didn't want us to depend on the hospitality of others for too long."

"When did Tracker die?"

"Almost a year and a half ago."

"I'm very sorry," I whispered again. *If I had been ready to leave sooner, maybe...* "I wish I had been here. Maybe I could have done something or said something to help you."

Frost shut the door behind us and set Kaylis down. "Rigel, take your sister to your room to play while Aunt 'Fleece and I catch up." She watched them disappear around the back corner. "Don't blame yourself, 'Fleece," she said, laying her hand on my arm. "You helped me a great deal by lending me your strength, more than you realize."

"What do you mean?"

"On the morning I buried Tracker, I felt bereft and inconsolable, but I still needed to take care of Rigel, and my grief wasn't helping the pregnancy. I wished that you were here with us, and somehow, the thought of you was enough to give me the strength I needed."

I recounted the days and recalled my emotional episode in the Haven. Somehow, whether it was intentional or not, Frost had linked to me and managed to share her pain and mourning with me that day.

Frost led me to the kitchen and gestured for me to sit with her. "It has been an interesting few years since you left. A caravan came to Moonteyre soon after you left, to offer surrender. Their own land in the west was raided and razed, their crops were destroyed, and they thought that we were somehow responsible. It was their delegation that had come to seek out Clyara the day she vanished."

In the west. "They were humyn."

"Yes, just as you had told me," she said. "More importantly, they were desperate for our help. They were just settlers, trying to survive. We realized that the marauders who pillaged them would eventually make their way to this side of the river, so we allied ourselves with the humyn, which I don't believe the marauders expected us to do. These humyn learned to speak elfyn, and we learned to speak their 'common'. It wasn't long before we realized that we had more similarities than differences, and the children born into the combined families have been healthy and beautiful.

"It was hard for Tracker and some of the others to accept. He didn't believe in our two peoples mixing like that. He didn't even like the fact that I was learning to speak the new language. Then, one morning, while I was out with the children, he locked himself inside our house and set it ablaze…" She stopped to take a trembling breath. "He left a note in his shop that said that he would rather die than live in this 'impure' world."

I was aghast at the ugliness of the sentiment. "I can't even imagine Tracker thinking that way."

Frost shook her head. "I couldn't either, until I heard him for myself. He changed after the humyn arrived, after Clyara and you had gone." She glanced to the rear rooms. "But he loved Rigel more than anything. He was so excited that we were having a second child, and Rigel was just a baby learning to talk, but he followed his father everywhere. He's hardly spoken since Tracker died."

Now that Frost had mentioned it, I noticed that it was only Kaylis's squeaky babbles that came from the bedroom. I wanted to do something for my nephew but didn't know how to start.

The awkwardness of the moment was interrupted by a quiet knock on the door. Frost opened it and greeted the group gathered on her front step. "What can I do for you?" she addressed easily in common.

"With all respect, Elder Frost, we're here to speak with your sister," replied one of the young men.

"You're hurt," I said, joining Frost at the door. I could smell the fresh blood on him, and most of the visitors looked battle-weary. The Elders had given their blessing after all, or at least had agreed to turn a blind eye this once.

"Not as bad as some of the others," he replied.

"Show me," I said. Frost gave me a doubtful glance, and I touched her arm reassuringly. I walked to each in the procession, absorbing their wounds in turn. All limbs and digits were present, thank Ajle, and most of the injuries were minor overall, but after the tenth patient, I began to tire. I continued, enduring the pain and exhaustion with a smile, drawing strength from my memories of Clyara's devotion when my limbs started to waste away under my modest clothes. They bowed their heads in thanks, some of them calling me: *aylonse*—friend in blood and hardship.

I did my part, and I expected someone to ask whether I would stay to fight alongside them, but no one did. At the end, I was light-headed and considerably weakened, but I accepted my patients' gratitude with as much dignity and grace as I could muster and returned inside to where my sister waited. She shut the door behind me and looked at me with clear amazement.

"It's the least I could do," I managed to smile. "They risked themselves to defend Moonteyre, and you." And it was a pleasure to heal again, despite the pain. The satisfaction I felt was worth my soreness.

Frost winced at the dark patches on my tunic where I was bleeding through. "I'll be right back. Sit, relax, just don't stain the furniture," she joked.

I took a seat in one of the kitchen chairs. I closed my eyes and relaxed, letting my body heal gradually. With each injury that I had repaired, my gem was becoming more efficient with my own recovery. I had noticed it before, when I had revived Frost. I snapped my head up at a raw sensation on my shoulder.

Rigel snatched his pointed finger back from my blood-marred shoulder and gazed at me fearfully with huge, expressive eyes. Kaylis peered from behind her big brother.

"It's fine, you just startled me," I said gently. "I'm not hurt, anymore. See?" I pulled aside the collar of my shirt and let them see that the blood had stopped flowing, and that my flesh was whole again, my skin reknitting before their eyes. Rigel prodded my shoulder again and smiled wondrously. At first, I didn't mind, but when he didn't stop, I had to ease away gently. "That's enough for now. Aunt 'Fleece is still a little sore."

"Aunt 'Fleece is indulgent to a fault," Frost called from the other room.

"It's an aunt's prerogative to indulge her nephews and nieces."

"Then it's lucky that you only have one of each." Frost reappeared, carrying a tray full of food and a small pitcher of water. She gave Rigel and Kaylis each a wedge of apple and sighed when they decided to stay with us in the kitchen. "You're wasting away, Sister. It's about time you ate some normal food, and acted your age."

"And what might that be?" I asked half-seriously.

"Twenty years, and two months and ten days, yesterday."

From the calendar on the kitchen wall, I saw that I had been gone two years, ten months and nineteen days. *So much for spending five years in the Haven.* It was strange to see year 1000 in print, too. Frost followed my eyes and said, "It turns out that the elfyn and humyn calendars are the same. Curious, isn't it," she said wryly.

"You know it's not a coincidence," I said.

"We figured that out. Even more reason for us to combine our resources and learn more about each other's histories. We find out more every day."

"That's wonderful." My eyes drifted to a mirror on the sideboard, and I saw that the years had not been kind to me. I was gaunt and unkempt, but with an immaculately clean grey cloak. My skin had taken on a vellum-like pallor, having lacked exposure to the sun for so long, which made my dark eyes and brows seem even starker and more sunken. The effort exerted during the repeated healing didn't help. My head was completely covered in white, or more precisely, white layered with grime and dust. My silver locks had finally grown in, at last. My father had named me correctly, after all.

Even so, sitting between my cherubic, pink-cheeked nephew and niece, I was an unlikely part of Frost's wholesome world.

"You look fine," she remarked, noting my self-examination.

I smoothed down my dirt-strewn hair. "I look ghastly."

"Yes, you do, but I'm glad to see you anyway. Maybe you could use a hot bath and a change of clothes," she said. "And a haircut, and a nail trimming… Where have you been? Living in a cave?" The look in her eye told me that it wasn't just a lucky guess. "You look pretty clean, all things considered."

I laughed. "My cave had everything I needed to stay alive and well. I don't think Clyara would have willingly remained there, as long as she had, without installing some modern conveniences." I never quite figured out how the plumbing or disposal systems worked, but I was thankful that they functioned. "I would've liked to have contacted you, to let you know how I was."

She nodded. "Clyara's friend Alessarc came to visit a couple of days after you left, to tell me that you were unharmed, but that you would be away for a long while. He emptied Clyara's cottage and returned to me the few things that were yours. There's a young family living there now."

"I'm glad the cottage is being used." There was little chance that I would ever want to return there, with the bittersweet memories that it held for me. "It's good that he visited you. Everything happened so suddenly, and there was no time to tell you myself."

"It's fine, 'Fleece. I could still feel you close by. Besides, Alessarc provided the entertainment that afternoon with his visit," she said with a crooked smile.

I closed my eyes. *What did my guardian do?* "I can't even imagine."

"He introduced us to Grey-Eye and his pack," she laughed. "It took a while for the Elders to compose themselves. The children in town just thought it was delightful that we had so many giant puppies visiting." She touched my hand with soothing warmth. "I want to thank you. I know what you've been through for me. I felt your presence this afternoon, just as I felt it the day I buried Tracker, and when I gave birth to Rigel and Kaylis. You lent your strength to me, whether you meant to or not."

"I wish I could've done more for you," I said dully, at a loss for something more profound to say. I think Frost had a better understanding of our relationship than I did, even then. "I wish I could stay."

"Stay, then. You've only just arrived."

Rigel and Kaylis resumed their play around us, and I was tempted to linger. "I should go while I still have the will." I looked at Frost squarely. "I can't stay. You've seen for yourself what the marauders do, and you know they'll just keep coming. The sooner I go, the better."

"Go where? This is your home, this is where you belong."

"It's more than that. I have to stop these attacks at the source, face our enemies once and for all."

Frost looked at me sternly. "No one's asked you to be a martyr."

"I'm only a martyr, if I die. Seriously, Frost, you know as well as I do that I have to do this. There is no one else here who can."

She nodded, solemnly. "I know that you're old enough to decide what is right for yourself, but that doesn't mean I want you to get yourself killed."

"Thanks. Your confidence is touching."

She understood me well enough to know that my levity was a mask. I didn't want to go any more than she wanted me to leave, especially with no guarantees of a safe return. "Well, you'll just have to make the most of your time here, then," she said, squaring her shoulders. "You can start with that bath."

Chapter 12: Running with Wolves

When I was a young girl, I carried a patchwork satchel made of scraps from my father's work shirts. Filled to capacity, it was about the size and shape of a large pumpkin, and for several summers during my childhood, it had been my constant companion. It was light but practically indestructible. Sure enough, when our house burned down, there was little for Frost to salvage, but the satchel survived, as the chest of my belongings was below ground level, in the kitchen crawlspace next to the root cellar.

Frost packed some clothes for me, as well as some supplies and my old locket. Unfortunately, my mother's picture was lost in the fire, as well as the cord from which it hung in my sister's bedroom, but the metal locket itself stayed intact. It now dangled from a fine black gauze ribbon, not unlike the one that I wore in my hair, that Sarc had used to bind the stack of my predecessors' journals. I barely recalled reading them all; already, my time in the Haven felt long past.

When I was finally ready to leave, the sun was low in the sky, but still bright. People were milling about out of doors, far enough away to give us our privacy, but clearly curious about my return. Most of them recognized me, if not as Clyara's former apprentice, then as Frost's inconstant little sister. We reached the southern edge of Moonteyre unmolested, except for one or two passersby who wanted to speak to Elder Frost.

"Elder," I said with amusement at my sibling, who was then all of twenty-five years-old. "I guess you've been keeping busy, to get yourself a title."

Frost shrugged. "The title's perfunctory. I'm just a mediator, when I'm not teaching. People come to me with their grievances, and I help with their resolutions."

"I'm sure it's harder than you make it sound. The Elders have always been stingy about bestowing titles." I crouched to hug and kiss Kaylis and Rigel. "I'll be back sooner than you know," I said breezily. I froze the smile on my face for Frost. "I will be back. Really."

Her smile for me was tinged with sadness. She embraced me tightly and smoothed my damp, combed hair. I heard her clearly in my mind without even trying. *I know, 'Fleece. But I'll still miss you while you're gone.*

Maybe I'll come back to celebrate the end of the millennium, I promised myself.

"I'll hold you to that," she whispered against my ear.

I pulled away with a sense of astonishment. Could she hear my thoughts?

"If you don't come back, I'll have to go fetch you," she said. "You should go before it gets dark."

I nodded absently. It was just my overactive imagination, perhaps.

"Which way are you going? Into the Ajlekyrn?" she said, gazing towards the southern range.

"Briefly. There's something I have to do first, then I'll be heading towards the Realm," I smiled, pointing westward. "Want to come along?"

"The Realm! Are you sure?" She undoubtedly had heard personal accounts from the humyn folk who had fled there for the safety of the Dark Lands.

"Not entirely, but I have to try. It's the only way to have peace here."

"If you change your mind, you will always be welcome here." She squeezed my hand one last time. "May the stars guide you, 'Fleece."

"May Ajle keep you all safe, Frost."

I crossed the unmarked border of the newly expanded Moonteyre without another look back at her, or her beautiful children, or the place that I had once called home. It was hard enough to leave them behind, so soon after our reunion.

Once well past the limits of Moonteyre and beyond the watchful eyes of the town sentries, at the foothills of the Ajlekyrn, I closed my eyes and envisioned my father's grave. In an instant, I was there, bathed in the warm orange light of the setting sun, looking down at my parents' tombstones. At the sight of them, the familiar melancholy resurfaced after lying dormant for years, and I was fifteen again, tossing the first fistful of dirt into my father's fresh grave, haunted by the recent vision of his shattered throat.

I blinked away a tear and looked away from the tombs, up the mountain at similar structures. There were some new ones, carefully tended and undisturbed. At least the marauders hadn't come this way, or they hadn't resorted to graverobbing, yet.

My parents' graves had been lately weeded, by Frost's hand, no doubt. A recent marker stood not too far up the path from Winter's, a simple structure marked by an engraved slab that read, in elfyn and in common: "Beloved Husband and Father, Tracker of Moonteyre, 972-998."

I climbed the path to the foot of Tracker's grave and regarded the stone for a moment. "I know it was hard to see the world change," I said, "but you were a coward to leave the way you did. Your family deserved better." Lingering guilt gnawed at me. Maybe there was something more I could have done, something I could have said. Tracker and I were never close, but Frost was in love with him, and they had been happy together, for a time. "I will keep them safe. I swear it." Frost and her children deserved a life free from fear and violence.

I returned to my parents' graves and sat on the ground with my shoulder leaned against my father's marker. I was drained, physically and magically. "You've only been gone five years, Da. How can you be so hard to remember?" I saw only the letters on the stone, not the man behind it. Slowly, I traced the engraved characters, and the memory of Winter's face slowly returned; his kind smile, and his dark eyes and white hair that I now shared.

The cool evening wind tousled my drying hair, but Sarc's woolen cloak kept me from shivering. There was a part of me in Sarc that I could never get back, but it was that part that had saved my life. I stroked the soft grey fabric of the cloak, recalling Sarc's resolve and his welcome company. He had called me "*Keeronae*." He believed in me, just as Frost did when she hugged me good-bye.

"I met a man, Mother," I said. "He keeps to himself, like you did. He seems to be a gentleman, like Da was. There is a small matter of him drinking my blood once while I was unconscious, but that was Clyara's idea, anyway," I smiled. "I think you would have liked him."

I looked up the mountainside at the array of graves. Some of them probably belonged to unfortunate victims of "healing magic", who had died through no fault of their own. Even my father … no, his death was different. The way his throat was mangled had nothing to do with healing. His murder was unwarranted and without purpose. My mother's death, while also senseless and random, was at least untainted by deliberate malice. One day, I swore, I would find my father's butcher and exact justice.

I lay down between my parents' graves and watched the last glow of sunlight fade from the horizon. I was alone, exposed and prone, but I needed this one night with them, before I journeyed to the Realm to meet my destiny. I wanted to see Winter in my dreams one last time, and perhaps even my mother the way my mind imagined her.

I hid my hands under the cloak and found my locket. I felt the strange designs carved on the silver surface. "You know, neither of you ever left anything to explain what these etchings meant. Maybe I'll find out on my own someday."

I curled up under Sarc's cloak and closed my eyes. The time-faded, comforting aromas of fragrant woods, still infused in the woolen fabric, surrounded me. The memory of my guardian instilled hope in my mind, and I fell into sleep gladly.

I slept soundly, and the open night air restored me. After so much time in the Haven, the feel and smell of fresh, sweet air was a salve for my sullen mood, and my dreams were untroubled. In the morning, I meditated to refresh my mind and conjured some fruit and biscuits as offerings for Tracker, and my father and mother.

"I'm going west," I said, remaining so still that gradually the squirrels and birds scurried around me to investigate the fragrant, savory offerings. "I have to find the ones who are sending these invaders to our home, and I believe I'll find them west of the Yirae, further than we've ever traveled together, Da. Clyara also tasked me with finding and ending Malya, and to do that, I have to leave you all behind."

I avoided looking around at the graves that speckled the hills and focused on the gravestones before me, which were now overrun by quarreling sparrows and jays. I left them alone, as my parents wouldn't have minded the company, and Winter had always been in favor of leaving nature to its own devices. "I'm sure Frost told you about her new home. Did she tell you that she had asked to have the eaves extended, when she was building it? This way, the swallows have room to nest underneath, as they did in our house."

After I left my parents' grave, I skirted Moonteyre and continued southwest into the forest skirting the Ajlekyrn, with only a far glance at the land that raised me, and that was only to make sure that the peace hadn't been compromised by my return. It didn't appear to be. The farmers were hard at work harvesting the summer crops, and preparing the fallow fields for the last planting before the harvest.

The weather was warm and sunny, reminiscent of the early autumn day that was Clyara's last. The memories from the last time I was in that forest came back to me. I was seventeen again, racing through the forest, driven by the deluge of recollections, until it hurt to breathe. Clyara had called to me, during the last minutes of her life. She needed me, but I was to hide the gems first. No, the magestones could not fall into Malya's hands. It would be the ruin of us all, the end of the world. Just beyond those trees was the rock, and just inside it lay a silk bag containing precious magical gems. That was true, once. The silk pouch of magestones was now safe in the Haven, buried behind a mountain wall, but I wanted to see—

I stopped suddenly, snapped back to the present by the smell of newly turned soil. Someone had been there recently for the gems, within the last few days; rocks had been overturned, some were shattered, and trees were uprooted. The ground was pocked with holes, and torn scraps of black fabric littered the ground and snagged bushes. Even the boulder, where I had hidden the gems, had been moved.

I recognized the marauders' uniforms from the ragged black scraps. Malya's marauders. Even here in the forest, the "dead mage queen" was causing discord and fouling my home. I circled the desecrated space, feeling that something was amiss. The marauders hadn't found the stones here, yet they hadn't continued their search elsewhere in the forest? The fabric scraps were slightly weathered as if by the sun and wind, so they were most likely not the same group that had attacked Moonteyre the day before. Also, they were so meticulous about their search; it seemed strange that they would have left their clothing scraps behind.

My foot sank suddenly and deeply into a soft patch of earth, and I stepped back from the recently loosened soil. Curious about what was buried, I levitated the fluffy top layers of dirt, and I choked at the sight and stench of what I had unearthed. I hastily reburied the gruesome find, but the image was indelible in my mind: a mass grave, filled with the clothes, bones, remains of hair and flesh of at least a dozen marauders. From the contorted limbs and tortured visages on some of the death-bloated faces, it seemed that they had died awfully. Had Malya decided to punish her soldiers for their failure? Or was it someone else, preying on the hunters from the shadows?

Greetings, Protector. Grey-Eye telepathically announced his presence, as did the others, before their shadows appeared amidst the dense, old-growth oaks. One by one, the silver, grey and black wolves showed themselves, as to not startle me with their number. All counted, there were thirty-two of them, including six pups of various ages. Some I recognized from the skirmish the day before in Moonteyre, but if they had been injured in battle, they were stoic about their pains. They stayed a polite distance from me, though the younger pups seemed longingly curious. *Strange to find you in these woods, unless you have reconsidered returning to your haven?*

No, I said. *Now that the marauders know that I am out…*

I can assure you that news of your return has not left the forest, Grey-Eye said grimly, his nostrils slightly flared, as he smelled the air around me. *Is something else bothering you?*

I took a deep, calming breath. *I just didn't expect to find this,* I said, indicating the destruction all around. *And that … grave.*

Yes, Grey-Eye said imperiously, eyeing the patch of fresh soil. *My daughter's pack encountered that detail not long ago. Sun-Catcher does not suffer intrusion or vandalism well and is severe with transgressors.*

I can see that, I said, a little unnerved by his nonchalance. *Are your packs always so thorough?* I wondered how many other such makeshift burial sites were scattered throughout the forest.

Only if we have not fed in a while, he explained, watching his pack file past me, westward towards the Yirae riverbank. *Do not be alarmed, Protector. The hunters are not our regular prey, but their fatty flesh can sustain a pack for days. And we are careful to bury what is too large for the carrion feeders to use, large bones and the like,* he said pointedly.

I kept an open mind about the arrangement. It certainly wasn't for me

123

to question their ways. Most importantly for me, they were respectful of my family and their neighbors and were respected in return. *Do my people know what you do with the marauders?*

We do not eat our meals in the presence of your people. That would be unduly rude, he said. He herded me to walk alongside him, amidst the rest of the pack. *We are resting tonight by the channel. If you insist on not returning to your haven, then you are welcome to travel with us until you find your way.*

I changed form to travel with the pack, for anonymity and for speed. The ripe air of summer was even more lush and bracing to the senses when I was lupine, to compensate for my limited color vision. The pack ran tirelessly through the forest, even the pups, and with my satchel across my back, I was challenged to keep pace, especially in the heat. The strongest adults stayed on the perimeter of the group, guarding the pups and the elders from possible danger; I was allowed to run on the outside, but two or three adults always stayed close. While some dropped off and others rejoined, the group never numbered less than twenty-five, moving as a unit.

I thought wolves traveled in smaller family groups? I asked Grey-Eye.

The lesser wolves do, he said, without condescension. *But our lineage was bred to protect, so we grow and align ourselves as necessary. As the hunters grow in the size of their packs, so must we, if we are to keep the advantage.*

None of the members seemed dominant to the rest. *You don't assign an alpha or leader?*

No, that is a misconception, he replied, non-plussed. *Each of us has something of value to the pack. For example, Green-Claw over there*, he said, gesturing to an elderly silver female, *she is our herbalist.*

And what is your specialty, Grey-Eye?

Without a pause, he said, *I am the ambassador, when we must make contact with people. One of my skills is feigning domestication.* His pale eyes were icy. *It is not as easy as it sounds.*

We stopped at the east bank of the Yirae soon after noon. While the wolves refreshed themselves in the clear, sweet water, I reverted to my natural form. I watched the southerly, leftward flow, far from its sources in the Red Lake and the northern Ajlekyrn. Even in late summer, the flow was strong and steady, and I stood transfixed at the riverbank, admiring the power and grandeur of the Yirae. It was a view I had missed during my years away.

As I joined the others on the grass, some of the pups took a moment to satisfy their curiosity about me, sniffing my clothes and feet. One of the coal-coated pups licked my hand. *Magical humyn*, she said gleefully, and scampered back to her mother's side. Another pup wedged his muzzle under my elbow, and his littermate used the drape of my skirt as a tunnel.

The feel of their luxuriant, velvety fur and gentle claws was relaxing in a very primal way. I played with them absently, as I pulled Clyara's map from my satchel to trace our path.

We had traveled over sixty kilometers since the morning, and there was at least another two hundred kilometers of forest and mountains before the channel. That knowledge would've been useful, except that I couldn't quite remember what a kilometer was.

It is time to go. Grey-Eye nuzzled the pups away and back towards the adults. He studied the map over my shoulder and twitched his ear. *Cartography was never one of Clyara's talents. The land is much more mountainous, and the channel is much wider than that.*

I'm trying to make out the distance.

A kilometer is a little more than half a mile, he translated easily. *About three-fifths. Her scale is a little off.*

I looked back at the map and tried to fathom the vastness of the channel and its surrounding terrain: wider than Red Lake, and longer than the Yirae, a waterway to the sea! And the sea itself: a body of saltwater so huge that I would not see its shores, alive with creatures that I had only read about in Clyara's books or seen through The Device.

Grey-Eye loped off to join the pack. *Try to keep up.*

After the wade across the river, the pack's pace through the trees and valleys was dizzying. They were apparently accustomed to a frenetic lead, as even the youngest of them moved easily through the dense undergrowth. We passed quickly and quietly through the patches of primary forest, far from where I had first encountered Jaryme and the mage hunters. I remembered that night in the tent as though it had only been hours ago, not years. With the memory still so clear, the faster we left the forest, the easier for me.

Near dusk, Grey-Eye called for a brief rest as we came to the southern tip of the forest, and a couple of the young adults ventured ahead as scouts. Grey-Eye conferred with the other adults, almost like a council, before returning to my side.

I had changed back to humyn form to collect some valerian and creeping sage for jars that I had taken from Frost's pantry, and Green-Claw directed me to the patches with the most potent, compound-rich growth. *It's a habit I acquired from my mistress,* I said to Grey-Eye. *It must seem strange that I would go through the trouble when I can just use magic to heal.*

I would consider you a fool, if you took no precautions at all, he answered. *As such, I consider you a little too ambitious. It is still not too late to go back to the Haven.* I gave him a wilting glance. *Your guardians would tell you the same.*

I'm certain they would, but it's too late. As it is, I regret not having left sooner. I may have stopped Tracker from killing himself.

Most likely not, he said, wrinkling his nose at the pungent sage.

I paused. *What do you mean? What do you know about what happened?*

He stretched out on the grass next to me, as if realizing that my questions were just starting. *I know that during the autumn before his death, two of our strongest had to drag him out of the Yirae by force. He knew us, so his struggle was not for fear of us. He did not want to be rescued.*

How could you know – I stopped myself. *You're telepathic. Of course, you would know.*

Just as we knew that he could not be swayed, as much as your sister tried. Even your guardian came to speak with him, at my request, but your sister's mate refused to speak with him, claiming that he looked too humyn to be trusted. Some people cannot be saved, Protector, despite every effort.

Thank you, Grey-Eye. You have taken great care with my family, and my people.

He lowered his muzzle to his paw sheepishly. *You are welcome, but it is our privilege and duty to serve. Now, would you consider remaining with your people, until your guardians return for you?*

I laughed and laid my hand on Grey-Eye's massive paw, impressed by his persistence. *I don't even know when my guardians are returning, or if they even have such plans. No, I will not wait for them.*

As you wish, he said, rising to his haunches. *I will leave you to your own design.*

Thank you. I followed his gaze towards where his scouts had gone. The hair on his scruff rose, and his ears perked. *What's wrong?* Grey-Eye wasn't the only one of the wolves to notice that something was amiss. The adults in the pack tensed and growled, with their teeth bared, and they herded the pups and elders around me. As they gathered close, I packed the rest of my herbs and became one of them. That was when we heard sharp pops, followed immediately by one of the scouts' thin, distant cry, eerily like a scream, followed by the other, closer.

A rustle of the undergrowth announced the hunters' immediate presence. Before they even appeared, small explosions split the air, and several of the adults fell. I cast a dome shield around us all and watched the small band of marauders emerging from the trees, with their swords and guns drawn. Their black uniforms made them less visible against the forest shadows, but their gunpowder stench was strong enough to mark their position.

While the rest of the marauders moved into position around us, some of them stood back, aiming their rifles carefully. Another round of explosions jarred us, and our shield rattled like a windowpane under hail. The wolves, though shaken by the noise, clawed furiously at the shield to escape it, to engage the marauders in battle.

We wish to fight, Grey-Eye growled at me.

Wait a moment, I snapped back. *The marauders aren't going anywhere.*

They were, in fact, all outside the shield, trying futilely to beat it down with their swords and their bullets.

I lay my paw on one of the fallen wolves and felt her labored breath. Her pup was at hand, licking the mother's muzzle and the hole in her shoulder where she had been struck. I dislodged the small metal pellet in the open wound with a spell and focused my gaze on one of the hunters: *I pass the pain to you, unworthy and beyond Ajle's grace.* The wolf's wound sealed.

The targeted marauder, finding himself suddenly wounded, distracted the others with his surprised yell and retreated with his hand to his bleeding shoulder. *Now!* I dropped the shield, and the wolves were loose. I turned away from the carnage, but the dying humyn's screams were too much to ignore. In that moment, I saw the faces of the dead marauders at the bottom of a shallow pit: each was someone's son, or father or husband. But, humyn or not, they had threatened what I loved, and they deserved the same lack of mercy that they would have shown us.

One charged at me with his sword high. Before he even got within meters of me, he was taken down and ripped apart by a trio of my new friends. All around me, the humyn were outmatched and overwhelmed so quickly that it was all I could do to watch it happen. The hunters' firearms were useless once they had been discharged, and their swords were worthless once the wolves were stubbornly upon their limbs. Our attackers' dying screams sounded strangely bestial, and progressively, I stopped cringing at the sound.

For the moment, I was a wolf protected by my pack. The occasional humyn who were foolish enough to turn their attention to me were mauled before they ever got close. Even the older pups, following the examples of their elders, charged when the younger ones and I were threatened. I healed the wolves injured in the melee, only to watch them charge back into battle zealously.

The battle, such as it was, was mercifully short. Drained from the healing and the shape-shifting, I changed back into my normal form and lay flat on the grass. A few of the larger wolves dashed away in the direction of where the scouts had gone, to retrieve their remains. While the wolves feasted on the flesh of their slaughtered enemies, I stared up into the clear, dark blue sky and told myself that it had turned out for the best.

You do not approve? Grey-Eye approached, his long pink tongue wiping caked blood from his muzzle. *By consuming them, we gain their strength and honor them by speeding their return to the earth.* He circled me and stretched out the grass next to me in repose.

I know. It's just that—as disagreeable as it is, even to me—your supper and I are of the same species. This is a new experience for me.

Yet, you are not sorry to see them slain.

127

No, I'm not, I admitted. *If it comes to a matter of survival, I suppose I am a pragmatist. They attacked with the intent to kill, and we defended ourselves. It is as simple as that.*

Indeed. You were even willing to use the transferring magic to give our pains to the humyn, even though they are your own kind.

The wolves were relaxing, satiated and tired, and the pups were playing with the remains of the meal. One was rolling a stripped forearm with its paws, as with a stick. I closed my eyes at the scene.

Grey-Eye's mouth hung open in a slack-jawed smile when he read my expression. *It is perhaps not all that simple, Protector. We are proud to serve the true queen, as we have done for generations, and we accept that death is a part of our duty. Whenever the marauders come —whether it is for you and your family, for your gems, or for the queen —we ensure that they do not leave, at the cost of our lives, if necessary.*

It's a daunting task, I remarked. *There's a lot of land to guard.*

There are over … a thousand miles from the source to the mouth, he said. *Shared among the twelve packs, it is manageable, and we grew in number over the mild winter.*

This queen of yours, what does she know of what you do? I asked.

As much as she does of your role, he answered enigmatically with his lolling grin. *Which is to say, not a great deal. We all perform our functions because it is necessary, not for honor or recognition.*

What else can you tell me about the queen? I was intrigued about her, and what my role was as her "Protector."

There is nothing to tell, he said. *You will know her when the time is right.* He refused to say any more, and he was too adept with his telepathy for me to peek into his thoughts. The rest of the pack was equally unreadable, as much as I tried. Grey-Eye suggested that I nap, to recover my strength, and I was too tired to argue.

As I lay half-awake, I watched the wolves' customary grave-digging ritual for their enemies and fallen compatriots. With most of the adults digging the pits, it was quick work. They left some scraps for the carrion birds that had gathered, and dragged the rest of the remains into the pits, careful to keep the wolves and humyn bodies separate. They retained some of the marauders' personal effects for their own amusement and study. The pups, especially, were fascinated with some of the metal compasses and timepieces, enthralled by their movements and sounds. A couple of them were batting a decapitated skull across the blood-streaked grass before an adult confiscated it and returned it to the pit with the rest of the humyn remains.

While the pups frolicked, the adults circled the grave of their fallen, with their grieving whimpers and howls so solemn and despairing that all I could do was sit idly and ache for their loss. Grey-Eye looked over at me, his pale eyes hooded, and his ears low against his head. *When did you last allow yourself to grieve, Protector?*

Apart from helping Frost through her mourning, I could not remember. *I've had neither the time nor the tears to spare.*

I have been told that time must be made for emotions, or they will abandon you out of spite, he said. *Tears keep the heart from becoming dry and brittle.*

That sounds terribly sentimental, coming from you, Grey-Eye.

He seemed to smile, wanly. *Not my words or my viewpoint, but an interesting perspective, nonetheless.*

Whose words, then? My guardian Alessarc's?

He slowed and let the others pass him within the circle. *They were told to me by your mistress Clyara.*

I bowed my head in shame and felt the first tears burning my cheeks. Once they started, they welled quickly. *I never mourned her properly.*

He nodded his head towards the circle. *Come, then. It is never too late to honor the dead.*

When I awoke, it was night, with the stars and luminous moon lighting the clearing. The burial mound for the fallen wolves was covered and marked with a circle of stones and two weapons crossed on top. The one for the humyn was filled but was otherwise unmarked. Next to me on the ground was a large, weighted burlap pouch. The wolves had gone, except for Grey-Eye, who was watching a large barn owl launch itself from one of the mounds with something gripped in its talons. Once the owl had disappeared into the shadowy sky, Grey-Eye returned to my side.

The others have returned to the den. We did not think it necessary to wake you. As I started to get up, he said: *That is a gift from my pack.*

I lifted the pouch, noting the hefty clink of coins. *I don't think I need this much.*

You don't know how much you will need, he said, getting to his feet and taking a deep stretch. *They will only litter the land, as we have no use for them.* Next to the burial mound, he gestured to the crossed weapons with his paw. *You are welcome to take the weapons, too.* On the pommel of the sword hilt was fine print and a design that resembled the Imperial insignia that I had seen repeatedly in the books in the Haven.

I picked up the other weapon: a weighty, roughhewn rifle. As much as I disdained its purpose, I was fascinated by its construction, having seen pictures of it only. Powder and pellets were poured into the open end, and a fuse was lit at the closed end to expel the pellets. It was a crude weapon, but requiring less skill than a bow and more portable than a cannon. The abrasive odor of the residual powder clung to my fingers, as I turned the primitive firearm in my hands. *There's a number here on the grip … '998'?*

Grey-Eye said, *Most of the weapons we find bear markings like that. The year of construction, we surmise. We have only seen such weapons recently. The steel is poor, brittle with carbon, not nearly as refined as the old swords.*

It's made to kill, not to be passed down as an heirloom. Just the same, I don't think I'll need it. I replaced the harquebus back on the mound and glanced at Grey-Eye. He seemed tired. *You haven't slept since this morning?*

He shook his head. *I will sleep once you are safely on your way.*

I need to reach the Realm, so that would mean traveling through the Fringe, I said, recalling the area on Clyara's map delineating the border between the Dark Lands and the Realm. *Is there a best route there?*

Yes, and I will take you, if that is where you wish to go.

Grey-Eye did not seem as adamant anymore about my returning to my haven, so I accepted his offer while it stood. *I would be honored to have your company, but don't you think I can make it to the Realm on my own?*

He bowed his head sheepishly. *Stay close.*

Chapter 13: Unexpected Company

Grey-Eye led an ambitious path westward through the night woods, as though he was challenging me to prove him wrong about my unpreparedness. Either he did not anticipate marauders along our path, or he was unconcerned. He did not slow for me, nor did he turn to check my pace. Gradually, just before the hours of dawn, the woods thinned, with the faint outline of foothills visible in the distance.

Further and further we went from Moonteyre, as my thoughts returned to it. I thought about Rigel, and how profoundly his father's loss had affected him. I thought of little Kaylis, and how she was too young to know her father, but how someday, she would still miss having him in her life. The same way I didn't know my mother, but I still missed seeing her picture in Da's locket.

We haven't come across any of the old humyn settlements, I noted, once we were in the heart of the valley.

There were few settlements in these isolated areas, and any that existed have long since been abandoned and reclaimed by the land. My children's packs patrol here regularly, so we should not encounter intruders. Grey-Eye slowed to sniff at the grass. *The queen's home is near.*

The queen lives here? In the middle of nowhere?

She did, once, long before my time. Then the evil came for her, and she fled into the Dark Lands, and she's remained hidden there since. The Fringe Dwellers keep her home as it was left, in remembrance of her passage. Knowing my next question, he continued: *The Fringe Dwellers are our allies on this side of the Channel. Their ancestors have held the borderlands since before the first mages came from the Realm, and they are the only humyn who have not retreated from the marauders' advance. However, they are too few in number to keep the marauders out entirely.*

We stopped. *We've reached the homestead, Protector.*

We stood at the edge of the open field, with the mountains of the Fringe, in the distance, tinged pink by the dawn sun. Pyramids of stones, larger single boulders, and patches of golden wheat and wild grain, marbled the plain. In my haste to wade through the waist-high grass, I nearly stepped on the spiked end of a fallen rake.

Be careful with what you touch, Protector, Grey-Eye cautioned belatedly. *Except for the addition of the graves, everything is as it was left. I have been told that energy radiates from the land here like nowhere else.*

I walked ahead. In the middle of the field, the tumbled ruins of a house were strewn with broken fixtures and utensils. As still as the land looked, I was uneasy and distracted by visions. With each step, images of carefree play in the warm afternoon sun interposed with the darker, bleaker images of what still remained. One moment, I saw a cloth doll in my tiny, dimpled hands and a jovial old woman dressed in a modest gown, watching from afar. In the next, I saw a weather-worn, sun-blanched scrap from the same nurse's dress jutting from underneath one of the stone mounds.

I lifted the edge of a fallen blanket and saw a small, dirty rag doll there, partially protected from the elements, in the shape of a black-haired girl. The fabric body was stained and discolored with age, and I picked it up.

The visions came in a rush, flooding my senses. I was a young girl, hiding under a shaking table, clutching the doll tightly against me for courage. My house was falling apart all around me, and my guardians were helpless to intervene. I buried my face against the strong, double-coated neck of the large white wolf-dog panting next to me. Argos would have joined the others outside, had my fingers not been clenched on his collar.

My nurse was calling for me. She raised the hem of the tablecloth and found me cowering. She held out her small, plump hand, and I grabbed it. I screamed as a wall came down behind me, and my nurse rushed me out of the house ahead of her. Outside the house, my other wolf-dogs were baying and whining, and Argos was with them.

Go with your guardians. Run, Aelora, and don't look back.

My nurse gave me a final shove out the door before the house crumpled. I didn't have time to look back, as my metallic servants—my steel golems—crowded protectively around me, guiding me. One of my golems stepped quickly in front of me, and I shielded myself behind it as the rubble smashed into it. I dropped the doll at my feet—

I became the old woman, clinging to my charge's doll for strength; I knew I would never see her again. My hip was broken in my fall, crushed under the bricks and stones, but I tried my best to ignore the pain and managed to avoid chunks of the ceiling that came crashing down over my head. The remainder of the roof ripped away, just as I made it out into the open. The walls crumbled behind me, as I dragged myself out into the green fields of wheat. I needed to see for myself that my little princess had made it to safety.

The sky was filled with a shower of boulders, pummeling the ground and everything in their path. I struggled to sit and craned my neck to look for my princess and her dogs, but they were nowhere to be seen. *Goddess watch over Aelora.* I fell again, this time out of exhaustion, and I whispered a prayer of thanks. A shadow fell over me, and I knew that death had arrived at last. The sorceress was casting a spell, and I looked defiantly into the face of the golden-haired witch, into her cold green eyes. *Malya, you will pay for this treason —*

The doll fell from my shaking hands, onto the patch of grass where I was kneeling. The cloak around me couldn't keep me from shivering, but Grey-Eye's calm helped. I knew the memories, as well as though they were my own. I had seen the demolition of this place through the eyes of Aelora and her nurse. This princess, the one that the wolves called "the queen," was long gone, taking with her the secrets of why Malya had come to kill her. I was seeing ghosts, remnants from another time.

Gradually, the visions faded, and Grey-Eye pulled the blanket back over the old doll, hiding it from my sight. *All the mages who pass through here have visions,* he said. *The land has a way of amplifying one's abilities, but some mages are more sensitive to the energy than others.*

I got back to my feet and wrapped the cloak tighter around myself. *Her name is 'Aelora.'*

It means 'treasured' in your elfyn language, does it not?

I nodded. *I didn't expect for her to have an elfyn name.*

Her parents were well-read, I am told, he said. *This is a dead place now, filled only with ghosts. There is no need for you to linger here, and still much more awaits you beyond our borders.*

He spoke with a sense of finality. Maybe it was how the morning light illuminated him, but for the first time, he looked weary. *You're not coming with me, are you, Grey-Eye.*

He shook his head. *My questing days are long behind me, Protector. I have duties to my pack now, and I think you will do fine on your own from here.* Coming from Grey-Eye, that was a great compliment. *You will be safe traveling through the Fringe, if you remain respectful and vigilant. When you reach the Realm, seek out one named 'Slither,' if your guardians do not find you first.*

I'll remember that, thank you.

It has been an honor to escort you, Protector. He bowed his head to me with lowered eyes.

I crouched and stroked his massive jaw, feeling the heat of his smooth silver fur underneath my hand. *Thank you, Grey-Eye. The honor was mine. May the stars guide you home with haste … aylonse.*

He seemed to smile at my elfyn farewell and title. *And may Ajle keep you safe, whichever path you take.* He disappeared into the tall grass without another look back.

For a while after he was gone, I remained still to listen to the rustle of the grass and distant birds. While I missed Grey-Eye's company, I also enjoyed the quiet. As is with all such good things, my solitude would not last, and I relished it while I could.

The mountains of the Fringe turned from rose to crimson to violet to indigo with the passage of the day. They seemed deceptively close, and as the sun approached its zenith, I was still kilometers from the foothills. I wasn't even walking; I was soaring across the plains in the guise of a hawk, with the wind at my back. The snow-streaked peaks were an early clue to their awesome dimensions. My own beloved Ajlekyrn seemed dainty by comparison.

I was actually in the legendary Fringe! Only two days before, I had been meditating in a cave that felt like a world away, with barely a concept of what the Fringe was. Now, the mountains loomed before me in all their glory. It was like a most vivid dream come to brilliant life. That I was floating across the prairie added to the surreal, fantastic quality of it all.

By dusk, I had come a considerable distance from the ruins of Aelora's home, but I was earthbound. Having barely eaten all day, my energy, magical or otherwise, was nearly spent. With the last of my energy, I reached the foothills of the mountains at last. I curled up against the cool granite and slept uneasily, dreaming of people and creatures long gone.

The teasing, musical laughter of children accompanied the visions of Rigel and Kaylis playing catch with the wolves. With an impish smile, Rigel turned to me with the leather ball cradled in his arms and threw it to me. When I looked down at what I had caught, Malya's eyes opened and stared up at me from her laughing, decapitated head.

I awoke with a start, and I snapped my eyes open. The last thing I expected to see were eyes staring back at me. I jumped back, as did the girl who had been watching me. The older woman also watched me with interest but did not come as close. Both of them wore thick, black braids, and layers of linen against their dark, flawless skin. Both of them continued to stare at me with their nut-brown eyes. At a glance, they looked like sisters.

Fringe Dwellers? They certainly resembled Iavan's description of the people he had encountered when he fled the Realm, all those centuries ago. They also looked nothing like any marauder that I had seen before. With my heart pounding, I slowly stood with Sarc's cloak around me and my satchel over my shoulder. "G-greetings," I ventured in the common tongue. They smiled and nodded in unison. "I'm sorry, am I tris-trespassing?" I asked.

The women looked at one another, then shook their heads. "The Fringe belongs to no one," the elder replied, slowly for my benefit. "You're welcome to stay as long as you'd like. We were merely concerned about your wellbeing, as you chose to sleep in the open."

I didn't know that I had had a choice. "I'm fine. Thank you."

"You are not of the Fringe," she continued her inquiry.

"No, I'm not. I'm on my way to the Realm."

The mention of the Realm sparked a clear interest. The younger spoke: "You don't speak like a child of the Realm."

"I'm from the Dark Lands, but I have business in the Realm."

"Do you serve the Empress Malya?" the younger asked.

I stiffened a little at the question. "No," I replied more harshly than I intended.

Instantly, the women vanished. *They were mages?* I wondered for a moment if they had even been there at all, but they seemed too real to be an illusion. *How did they even find me here, and where did they go? Hilafra, what if they're servants of Malya, and they've gone to tell her I'm here!* With that alarming thought, I became fully awake and scrambled to my feet. It was best to keep moving, in case other surprise visitors decided to make an appearance. I floated up the side of the mountain to peer over to the other side.

It was a small village in a lush, emerald-hued valley, a generous scattering of stone huts with thatched straw roofs. Many of the people looked like the women who had visited me, dark-haired and dark-skinned, but there were others who were varied shades lighter and darker. Like the women who had visited me, the others in the village dressed in thin, simple robes. *Dwellers of the Fringe.* Steam and smoke rose from a bonfire in a near clearing, while a sheltered well stood alone at the northern border of the settlement, to my right.

I considered avoiding the valley altogether, to just teleport to the opposite mountain, but I would have been lax in my duty if I just passed it over. I had a responsibility to my family, the wolves, and the rest of the Dark Lands to verify whether these mages were allies, or followers of Malya. With luck, I would perhaps even learn something about the dead mage herself. Learning from my past mistakes, I cast an aura of silence and a spell of invisibility over myself, and taking a deep, fortifying breath, I descended into the valley.

I floated along the outskirts, careful not to even leave footprints on the ground, and keeping well out of others' paths. Outside one of the huts, I passed a barrel-chested man with a thick black beard who was sharpening a large knife against a stone. Rooting by his feet were piglets, unbound and free-roaming like most of the livestock in the village.

I circled the man, noting the fine workmanship of the various items he used. The handle of his knife was intricately carved, and the blade itself was perfectly straight and gleaming. The colorful, bold designs on the bowls and dishes reminded me of the styles of elfyn artisans.

The door of one of the huts flapped open, and a young woman

emerged: the younger of the pair from the mountain. "Father," she called, and the bearded man looked up from his grinding. "You have to come see this!" she said, beaming, before dashing back inside. The man set down his tools, humming quietly to himself, and strolled into the hut. Curious, I followed him inside, and my mouth fell open.

In front of a stone bench stood a gleaming metal figure, in the semblance of a woman, legs just slightly apart in a combative stance. The open, unblinking eyes were polished metal like the rest of it, unmarked by pupils or irises. Runes etched into its gleaming metal skin marked it as a golem, just like the ones I had seen in my vision at the homestead ruins, but it otherwise resembled a finely crafted statue.

The man stood before the golem without concern. It stood a couple of centimeters taller than me, towering over the girl but was still dwarfed by the father. "When did she awake?"

"I don't know, but isn't it exciting?" the girl said. "She was like that when I came in just now. Do you think she's been summoned?"

The man straightened and stroked his coarse beard. "It's possible. Have you told your mother?"

The girl shook her head. "I think she knows. She's the one who sent me to look in on her." She tugged her father's sleeve. "Maybe we should just leave the door open, in case she needs to go."

"That's a fine idea, Rija," the man smiled, opening the door for her.

Rija. I turned my head at the sound of my mother's name, but the pair had gone. I turned my attention back to examining the golem and noticed that it had moved.

Its unblinking gaze was fixed on me! It bowed stiffly from the waist and from somewhere in its lifeless skull came a low, hoarse and emotionless voice, that said in common: "I await your command, Mistress."

A golem capable of speech! Incredible, but... "I think you've mistaken me for someone else," I whispered, then realized that I was still cocooned in silence, but it tilted its head as though listening intently.

It continued to stare, unaffected by my invisibility and ignoring my cues for quiet. "You are the Mistress. You carry the beacon."

What do I have that could possibly— I stopped rubbing the locket hanging from around my neck and looked down at the designs that had always puzzled me. "This?"

"Yes," it answered flatly, its rough voice becoming smoother with use.

"Really." *My own golem. That's ... different.* Regrettably, the locket had been with me too long for me to sense anything from it about its original owner. From its condition, the golem's age was difficult to discern; it could have been old enough to have waited decades for its master or mistress's return. Its presence was a mystery, and none of my concern. "Go back to sleep, golem. I don't need a servant."

"I am to follow and protect you, wherever you choose to go, Mistress."

Great, another guardian. I didn't need the company, as interesting and eye-catching an accessory as she could be. "Look, I didn't mean to reawaken you. There must be some way to put you back to sleep, until your real mistress comes for you."

"No, Mistress, I shall serve you until I am destroyed."

If I had activated it with my presence, perhaps I could deactivate it by leaving, quickly. As I went silently to the door, the golem followed immediately. I stopped just beyond the door, to spot a place on the mountain where I could teleport, when the young woman Rija approached. Like the golem, she looked at me as if she saw me plainly.

"If you've come for the golem, no one will stop you," she said. "No one will hurt you here. Everyone is welcome in the Fringe."

As I contemplated her invitation, the golem asked: "Shall I defend you?"

"No," I replied, dispelling my invisibility and my silence spells. It seemed rude to leave so abruptly now, and I was abashed at being caught so easily. "It isn't mine. I didn't even know about it. I'm really just passing through." I edged away from it, and it kept its flat, unblinking eyes on me.

Rija's parents had joined us, and they seemed amused by my discomfort. Rija's mother brushed off the golem's shoulder and smiled maternally at the blank glance it returned. "Of course, she's yours. She's only been collecting dust here, waiting for her mistress. Her place is with you, Protector." Rija's mother reached her tawny hand out to me and said, "We can discuss the details during the feast. Mareos, why don't you and Rija finish the preparations, and I will show our honored guest around."

Rija's father nodded agreeably. "As you say, Rijena. There's no time to waste. Our guest looks as though she hasn't had a fair meal in months." Mareos and his daughter bowed their heads to me and left me with Rijena.

"Oh, no, this isn't necessary," I insisted, but my words were as wasted on Rijena, as they had been on the golem. I sighed and asked, "Is there anything I can do?" Whether or not I trusted them, I could at least be polite. Besides, with my time in isolation, I actually missed the mundane satisfaction of chores, especially cooking.

"No, dear," Rijena shook her head. "My husband is quite proud of his independence in the kitchen, and he doesn't delegate well. Come with me, Protector. Mareos will send for us when everything is ready."

Thus, I became an honorary Dweller of the Fringe for the day. Most of the people we encountered called me "Protector", but the mages called me

"*Keeronae*", no matter how often I rebutted. The Fringe Dwellers had noticed an increase in wolf activity in the Sighing Field, as the homestead ruins were called, so they knew to expect some kind of visit soon. In addition, my arrival had been foretold by a communally-shared vision, so it was no accident that Rijena and Rija had found me on the mountainside that morning. Everyone had been waiting for me.

Rijena was an attentive hostess, and an esteemed leader of the village. She and Mareos were well-regarded for more than their power as mages; they were, in fact, only two of several mages who lived in that village, and a fraction of the number that lived scattered throughout the Fringe. I recalled Grey-Eye's account, that these people had successfully defended themselves against the marauders from the west. With mages among their ranks, it was no wonder.

Just as it cherished its mages, the Fringe community also revered its women, despite or because of their smaller number. It was common for a woman to have two or three husbands, and for her husbands to take her name. Mareos had indeed taken Rijena's surname for his own, but he remained her sole companion.

"You are young, you don't yet understand all the ways of the mages," Rijena said kindly, drawing a warm bath for me in the common bathhouse. As expected, my golem stood watch.

"I think I know enough," I replied, testing the bath water for myself. "As mages, you and Mareos share a bond that would be tainted if you were to bond with anyone else." I smiled at her speculative stare. "No, I haven't chosen a partner, but unfortunately, I have bonded with someone. I was unconscious at the time, so I didn't have a say in the matter."

She looked at me worriedly, as I stripped off my clothes. In the Haven, I had survived mostly on conjured food and drink, but my body had desperately needed real and regular sustenance. My malnutrition showed in the gauntness of my figure, in the way my ribs protruded against my skin, the way my hips were angular instead of curved. Someday soon, I expected my stamina to be depleted, but as long as I could cast a spell, I could go a little longer.

"How awful for you," she said. "To be physically violated—"

I flushed, realizing the kind of bonding she had meant. "No, it wasn't like that! I'm still … I haven't … no, not yet." I slipped into the water quickly and dunked my head under in my discomfiture.

I resurfaced and quickly explained, "I don't blame anyone for what happened, but perhaps I still harbor some resentment for the circumstances."

Rijena nodded. "That's understandable. Any kind of bonding is intimate, some more so than others, and not an experience to be casually undertaken."

"It wasn't intimate," I said. "He tasted my blood."

Her eyes narrowed. "The old *keerons* used to do that to their apprentices during their adjustments, as a means of knowing their whereabouts and intentions. Mareos was fortunate that his master didn't subject him to the same."

"And your *keeron*?" I pried.

"Mareos was my *keeron*," she said. "We came to the Fringe forty years ago from the Realm, after he left the service of his master. He had stolen a magestone from his master's store as a gift for me, and he was exiled for what he did. His master was merciful, though; he let us keep our stones. Why did your *keeron* bond with you?"

"My mistress wasn't the one who bonded with me, she only orchestrated the encounter during my adjustment," I clarified, sloughing the layers of dead skin from my body with disgust. Hygiene spells are rarely as effective as plain soap and water. "The mage who bonded with me was to be my guardian," I recounted. "I don't think he took very much; our bond has probably dissolved over the years."

"Perhaps," Rijena said solemnly. "A transfer of blood is a very significant act between mages. Such a bonding can last a lifetime."

Poor Sarc. "I hope not, for his sake. Besides, the magestone I had hosted at the time has since been supplanted and absorbed by another. Isn't the bond severed once that happens?"

Rijena's eyes widened. "I'm not sure, Protector. Your situation is singular; I've never known another mage who's been a host to two stones. With magestones being so rare, most mages keep one for their entire lives, and the mages that we know here in the Fringe are the first hosts of theirs."

If only Rijena knew the history of mine! Looking to change the topic, I glanced at my golem by the door. "Speaking of rare, how many of those are still about, I wonder. I've never seen anything like it."

Rijena gazed at the golem for a good while. "Before we found her, I had never seen a golem. We only knew what she was by the runes on her. We certainly didn't know that she could speak. When I was a little girl in the Realm, I had only heard stories about such creations."

"I don't suppose you recall the name of the maker," I asked.

Rijena shook her head. "Lost to the ages, I'm afraid."

I glanced at the golem, who was very aware that we were talking about it and seemed to be listening. "How long have you been its caretakers?"

"Some of the others found her in the Sighing Field almost thirty years ago, buried under the rubble. They happened upon the ruins during their foraging, they had no idea that anyone had ever lived there. In the Realm, we had heard rumors about the disappearance of Princess Aelora but never knew her fate, until we found the princess's belongings. Disturbing the ruins stirred something, and we began to have visions. We realized then that Aelora had managed to escape Malya's attack, so we've kept her things safe, for the day she takes the throne that is hers by right."

"Do you know where Aelora is now?" I asked.

"I'm not sure if anyone knows," Rijena shrugged. "She must be somewhere in the Dark Lands, otherwise the wolves wouldn't have continued their watch so long. I'm sure she'll emerge when the time is right, to take her mother's place on the throne."

Mother. Before Malya seized power, Augus had been Emperor, and he had inherited the throne from his mother… "Empress Adeliaraine was Aelora's mother?"

"Adeliaraine," Rijena smiled. "I haven't heard that name in ages. The Empress was always 'Adella' to her subjects. She had sent Aelora here to the Fringe for her own safety, on the counsel of the Imperial advisors, but the princess vanished one day without a trace. In the Realm, we had feared the worst. It was only when we found the Sighing Field that we knew of Malya's involvement."

"Do people in the Realm know about the ruins?" I asked.

"Some do. Malya claims it's slander, and thus sends her soldiers to try to find evidence to expose the 'lies'," she said with a simper. "In reality, they're here to assassinate Aelora, and you, if they can."

Looking at the golem, I felt a profound guilt. "It should be guarding its true mistress, not me. If my father had known when he found the locket, I know he would've tried to return it to her."

"Perhaps, but in the meantime, I'm sure the princess wouldn't mind that you borrow her golem for a while."

Mareos assembled an elaborate, splendid banquet for the village that I will remember to the end of my days: twenty-five generous platters of meats, vegetables and grains, accompanied by some of the finest bread and fruit that I have ever tasted. It ranged in flavors from tiny birds braised in a savory pomegranate sauce, a thinly-sliced, lacy sausage formed of assorted cuts of meat, to an air-light cake studded with candied flowers and berries.

Mareos insisted that the preparation wasn't as involved as it looked, but he was an unabashedly bald-faced liar. Just the sourcing of the animals for the feast was a gentle and solemn ritual, with Mareos and Rija overseeing the selection and slaughter, to ensure that the livestock was quickly and painlessly dispatched, and that the carcasses were utilized entirely, to respect the animals' sacrifice. Even their bones were saved for stock or split and roasted for marrow. Rija enjoyed working closely with her father, and while she seemed as tireless and unhurried as he was, it was no secret to anyone that the exertion was more taxing for her.

Unlike her parents, Rija was not a mage. She was, however, a natural telepath, with an innate ability to sense magic. She also had a talent for handling the raptors that served as the village messengers, without fear of their razor-sharp talons and beaks. She kept her left arm bound in a bracer of tough hide to provide a perch for them, and they were well-trained enough to fly directly to her upon their return to receive their treats and next assignments.

During supper, Rija's hawks and falcons made regular appearances. Once the sun had set, we were visited by the occasional owl while we dined. Rija cast surreptitious glances at her father and waited till his back was turned before tossing small morsels of meat to her avian couriers.

Unlike her ageless parents, Rija looked all sixteen of her years, and as I appeared to be close in age, she was drawn to me.

"You'll stay with us tonight, won't you?" she asked hopefully after dinner, as we cleared the tables.

"We insist," Rijena said. "The thought of you spending another night in the wilderness is unconscionable."

Before I could think of a reason to refuse, Rija grabbed my arm. "Come, I'll show you to the guest hut. There's plenty of room for her, too," she said, motioning to the golem standing watch behind my seat.

Rija half-led, half-dragged me to the hut, which was close enough to the main house that I could have found it easily enough on my own. The inside was spare, but certainly spacious. There was a cot against the far wall, stacked with pillows and linens, and a chair and table by the door. My satchel was already waiting on the chair. "It's so plain, I know. We don't get many guests," Rija apologized, shaking out one of the blankets. "Of the invited sort, anyway; we have marauders all the time."

"My village, too," I said, draping my cloak over the back of the chair and nudging the golem out of the doorway. It was a mostly-solid metal construct, but thankfully, I didn't have to exert any effort to actually move it. It understood my visual cues well enough that it knew to take a couple of steps to the right. "Your family has been very generous to me. I'm grateful for any kind of bed, after where I slept last night."

Rija smiled, fidgeting with the tip of her thick black braid. "Why did you sleep in the open? Since you're a mage, you must know how to make shelter for yourself."

"I do," I said, "but there are better ways to spend my energy than on small conveniences. Sleeping outdoors on the ground is nothing new to me." I pulled my long white locks into a loose braid and fastened it with Sarc's black muslin ribbon, as Rija watched me. She had most likely never seen hair like mine, just as her gloriously full black spirals were a novelty to me. "Rija ... I've always loved that name."

She smiled. "It's a common one here in the Fringe. There are two other girls in the Fringe that I know of named 'Rija'."

"It was my mother's name." Rija's brow rose skeptically. "Really. Who knows? Maybe she came from the Fringe; she certainly wasn't born in the Dark Lands."

"Was she a mage, too?" Rija ventured. "Or was she born after the Years of the Cleansing?" At my blank look, she explained: "Originally, people fled the Realm to the Fringe to escape the magic plagues. Then, during the Cleansing in the mid-940's, the Imperial Guard confiscated the magestones from all the mages in the Realm who wouldn't serve, and some more mages resettled here in the Fringe."

"Confiscated" was an interesting euphemism for it. "You mean they extracted the gems surgically, even if it meant killing the bearers," I scowled. "None of the history books I read ever mentioned the Cleansing."

Rija shook her head. "Very few would. It was a dark time in the Realm's history, and most people would rather forget it. My parents were young when it happened, and they remember it, but they don't talk about it."

"I see," I said, ending the inquiry, as it seemed to be making Rija uncomfortable. "My mother would have been forty-five this year, so she was born after all that happened." A yawn escaped me, and I covered my mouth too late. "I'm sorry! I must be more tired than I realized."

"The fault is entirely ours. We did wake you rather early this morning, and very rudely. I'll leave you to your rest, then. Good night."

After Rija left, I emptied my satchel onto my bed and worked briefly before retiring for the night. I mixed the herbs and flowers that I had collected in the jars with some ingredients from Mareos's pantry, in as exact proportions as I recalled seeing Clyara do. Just as I had watched Clyara in wonder so many years ago, my golem watched me intently, not understanding what I was doing, but seemingly fascinated by the procedure nonetheless.

I packed everything back in my satchel and lay down to sleep. I watched my golem watching me, with its etched, polished form glistening in the moonlight. Its metal reminded me of Imperial swordsteel, and in fact, during the feast, I had just been able to make out a worn "Imperial Guard 940" etching on the curve of its sculpted left shoulder. It was either a composition of recycled weapons, or it was intended as one itself. 940. Sixty years ago, before the Cleansing, before Clyara's return. Fifteen years before my mother was born, twelve before my father. As for the golem itself, it was impossible to tell its age. "Who made you?"

"I do not know, Mistress," it said evenly. "I am to serve you."

"Of course, you are," I sighed, sitting back up in bed. It was created to serve a mistress, any mistress who carried the locket. "If you're to serve me, then you're to follow some rules. Can you do that?"

"I can, Mistress," it replied.

"Good. Firstly, don't hurt anyone. If I want someone harmed, I'll do it myself. Secondly, you will only follow my orders, even if someone tells you to act for my benefit," I said. The last thing I needed was for someone to use my own golem against me. "Lastly, don't get in my way. I am capable of taking care of myself."

"I am to protect and follow you, Mistress," it reminded.

"You still can, unless it endangers your, ah … life," I said. Although it was just a golem, I was compelled to preserve it for its real mistress, Princess Aelora … Empress Aelora. Before the golem could answer me, I cut in: "And enough of this 'mistress' label. My name is Snowfleece. Call me that instead."

"I will, Snowfleece," it replied easily.

I lay back in bed and took a deep breath. Like it or not, I had a follower. I asked in elfyn: "You would accompany me to the end of the world, wouldn't you?"

As I had expected, the golem did not respond to the unfamiliar words. Its creator was humyn, as well. I knew at least that much.

Chapter 14: Traveling Against the Current

On the fourth morning since leaving the haven, I awoke with a start, before I realized that the figure standing over me in the darkness was my new golem. The bluish dawn light was barely visible under the closed door, but the crow of the roosters outside the hut was piercing. "Good morning, Tenn," I greeted. The elfyn word for "follower" seemed as proper a name for it as any.

"Good morning, Snowfleece," it greeted me in turn.

I climbed out of bed and struggled briefly with the covers, before I gave up and cleaned and straightened them with a quick spell. I left the room exactly as I had found it, and Tenn followed at my heels like an imposing, massive, bi-pedal steel dog.

Rijena and Rija were waiting outside for us, and they looked as though they had already been awake for a good while. They invited me to stay for the breakfast feast that Mareos had already prepared, but they did not press the point when I declined. Mareos was disappointed, but he was contented with packing provisions for me. That included a picnic that weighed more than my combined belongings, a piece of parchment bearing names and addresses of "safe houses" that would welcome me, as well as a pair of thick-soled hide boots. "You have a long voyage ahead of you, and those slippers of yours are nearly falling apart," he said sensibly.

"Thank you, Mareos." I eyed the basket overflowing with food. "You know, my appetite isn't always what it was last evening," I said.

Mareos harrumphed, "It should be," and passed the straw basket to Rija to carry. "If not for your heavy clothes, the first gust would whisk you away. Rija will take you to the ferry. You won't be able to find it otherwise."

I was still hesitant about taking the golem with me, not to mention Rija, but I couldn't desert either of them while I was still in the Fringe. The Dwellers would have been politely outraged, despite any argument from me of concern for their welfare. I resigned myself to the fact that they were my traveling companions for a while. They were going to slow me down, but they were interesting and pleasant company. At least, by the time we reached the outskirts of the village, we had not yet tired of one another's presence.

"We can follow the sun into the far mountains," Rija said, pointing to the cloud-laden peaks in the distance. "The Channel is over three hundred kilometers past the mountains. At this time of year, it will be at least a week's worth of hiking from here, twice as long for non-mages like me, even longer if you don't know the shortcuts through the mountains."

"Are you often gone from home so long?" I asked. "Don't your parents worry?"

"They trust that I can take care of myself," she said. "The birds help, too. They carry my messages home to my parents, to let them know I'm safe."

"Still, I'd rather not keep you longer than necessary," I said, taking a last deep breath. I closed my eyes and concentrated on the spell, but I didn't need the spoken words for the levitation. Rija was easy; she was lighter than she looked, even with the basket weighing her down. Tenn was mostly metal and not as easy to move, but I managed. I cracked my eyes open and saw the three of us hovering, a couple of meters from the ground. Rija was already ahead and leading, but Tenn was looking down at her dangling feet. "It's all right, Tenn. I'll carry you."

Skimming over the uneven contours of the prairie, we were crossing the plains even faster than I had anticipated, as we had the good fortune of having the winds with us. I tired quickly with the extra effort of levitating the others, but I didn't want to rest, not when we were so close to the Realm.

Rija, dressed in her thin clothes, was beaten by the strong winds, but she wanted to appear strong in my presence, so she, also, did not mention rest. It was Tenn, finally, who requested a break, and Rija and I did not object. Tenn, however, was the only one of us who did not rest and eat; she stayed within sight of me, keeping constant watch of the surrounding plains.

"Why did you ask to stop, if you don't need rest?" Rija asked Tenn.

"Neither of you were going to suggest stopping, although you are both tired and depleted," Tenn answered. "Snowfleece has overextended herself and needs time to recover her strength."

"She's a sobering presence, isn't she?" I commented to Rija, amused by her astonishment. I had expected Tenn to be nothing less than unwaveringly forthright. "If we continue on, can we cross the mountains by tonight?"

"Not all the way through, not even if we travel through the night," Rija said, peering at the hills on the horizon. "If we travel past dusk, however, we should be able to find shelter in one of the old caves. Some of the Dwellers used to live in the mountains, ages ago. Nowadays, the mages go there for isolation and meditation."

I nodded, admiring Rija's self-awareness and maturity and wondering if she realized that I was older than I appeared. I finished my last bite of fruit and took the much-lightened basket in hand. "Lead on."

After some rigorous hiking and some levitation up the sheerer slopes of the granite hills, we reached the caves that Rija had mentioned. Just in time, too, as the sun had long since set, and the sky was rapidly darkening. As it happened, I had to conjure a torch for Rija to light our way into our modest shelter.

Past its tiny opening, the cavern interior was generous. Its years of occupation seemed long past, judging by the dust-coated pottery shards and other debris littering the ground. The walls were elaborately adorned with painted murals and text, and Rija explained that most of the caves in the area were similarly decorated by their past inhabitants, mostly during the Years of Cleansing. We cleared a space for our blankets and set up a small fire, too tired to do much else. While Tenn stood watch by the entrance, and Rija lay down to sleep next to our campfire, I studied the walls.

The mage Junus Escan—Malya's unfortunate father who foresaw his daughter's violent rise to power—was also an advisor to Emperor Jaeris Thorne, who was Adeliaraine's father and predecessor. Under Escan's direction, the Imperial Guard hunted the mages who would not pledge their allegiance, forcing many to flee the Realm. The Guard was thorough, searching every corner of the Realm for dissident mages. In the end, the mages who escaped the Guard's notice left of their own accord, or hid their powers, finding that the Realm had become inhospitable and exclusive to their kind. After enduring the sterile, oppressive rigidity of the Realm, they rediscovered the freedom of the vast, lush and untamed Fringe, just as the very first mage Iavan had, centuries before.

The next morning started the fifth day of my journey. I awoke before Rija, and watched Tenn studying the wall records, her unblinking eyes seeming to record every detail. Once I sat up, she immediately came to my side, like a faithful pet. She even bowed to me. "Good morning, Snowfleece," she whispered, just loud enough for me to hear.

"Good morning, Tenn," I smiled with an effort, getting to my feet. My head was still subtly throbbing from the prolonged use of magic from the day before. "How is the weather today?"

She leaned over and looked through the cave entrance. "It is overcast." She watched me picking through the basket of provisions. "Would you like some fresh meat to supplement your meal?" she offered. "I am able to capture and butcher—"

"No, thank you, Tenn." During my isolation, I had become accustomed to a simple diet, and I was satisfied with the bounty of bread, cheese and fruit that Mareos had provided. "You're not to kill for me, and that means animals, as well. If I crave meat, I'll conjure some."

Tenn nodded obediently. "Yes, Snowfleece."

"You were looking at the walls, Tenn. Can you read?"

"No, I can recall images but not their meaning."

"But you can recall commands spoken to you, yes?" I asked, an idea coming to me, and pulled out the list of contacts that Mareos and Rijena had given me. "If I read this to you, can you recall it for me?"

"I can, Snowfleece."

"Good. Listen to me very carefully." I proceeded to read the names and addresses as they had been written down. The last was Slither, whose name was underlined as one of importance. The name had been mentioned by Grey-Eye, as well, and I remarked to Tenn: "Mareos recommended that Slither should be our first stop once we reach Altaier."

Our conversation and activity woke Rija, who was abashed at having slept so late. She quickly got to her feet and offered to help pick up our things.

"Rija, relax. We're making good time, there's no need to rush. Please, eat something." I left her the basket and walked outside, and Tenn naturally followed. "Why is she so nervous around me?" I whispered.

"I do not know," Tenn answered in kind.

I couldn't help but smile at the golem's efforts to be helpful. I stroked her cold metal arm and tried to imagine her creator's intentions for her. I had seen depictions and visions of golems, and Tenn was unlike any other. She was a creation of fine detail, from the soft curve of her jawline to the definition of her carefully sculpted, articulated fingers. "I wonder if your creator is still alive," I said, then quickly added, "You don't have to answer that. We'll find out soon enough."

I gazed out across the kilometers that we had crossed together, as far as I could see. We had a long way to go still, but the Realm was finally close enough to feel within reach. It was where the answers to all my questions lay. It was where Malya waited.

Once we were within the cradle of the Fringe mountains, it became obvious to me that we were going to stay a second night there, and perhaps even a third. To pass the hours, I practiced my faltering common on Rija and Tenn, and they coached me gently when it was warranted.

Despite Rija's warning that she often spent weeks crossing the mountains, I found myself becoming frustrated with our slow progress. The absence of a clear path through the valley made our tedious hike even slower, and the thin air of the higher altitude made me light-headed. While Rija advised me to forego my spells to conserve my energy, the lack of tall vegetation meant that shelter was sparse and infrequent, so we contended with the wind and occasional rain shower. I welcomed the cool sprays after our exhausting trek through the summer heat, but Rija seemed self-conscious about her thin clothes getting drenched, so I gave her Sarc's cloak for cover.

The sky began to darken with clouds and nightfall before we could even see an end to the range. Rija wrapped the cloak more tightly around herself to stave off the chill, as I examined Tenn thoroughly for signs of rust.

"This is an Imperial Guardsman's cloak," Rija noted, feeling the fine grey wool between her fingers. "An old one, judging from the darker color."

"Could be," I said. "I didn't ask whose it was."

"Who gave it to you?" she asked, sniffing the garment. She raised her brow with interest at its faded scent. "A boy?"

"A man," I corrected unconsciously.

"Is there a difference?" she asked with a doubtful glance.

I smiled, remembering all of Sarc's guises. "I certainly hope so." With a sigh, I watched the clouds blanket the whole sky, blotting out the last glow of the sun, as well as the moon and stars. "Unless either of you have other ideas, I think we'll be sleeping out here tonight."

They both looked at me blankly: Rija because of her clear exhaustion, and Tenn because that was her usual look.

I nodded. "Out here it is, then."

While I had slept on the open land before, that night was different. It could've been that I missed the comfort of Sarc's cloak, that Rija had borrowed. More likely, being so far from home and so close to the Realm made me feel especially vulnerable, and I slept uneasily, even under Tenn's diligent watch. When the darkest hours had passed, I watched the gradual dawn with Tenn. The sixth day of my journey looked to be as overcast as the previous.

I recounted the last five nights in my head: the first night on my parents' gravesite; the second in the company of Grey-Eye's pack; the third in Mareos and Rijena's guesthouse; the fourth in a cave; and finally, that night under the clouded sky in the cradle of the Fringe. Now that I had reflected on all that I had done, I was more conflicted and uncertain than I had been in a while. Had I really emerged too early? Was I too late getting to the Realm? Which was it: early or late! Who, or what, was waiting for me, at the end of my journey?

Both Rija and Tenn noticed my pensiveness, and thankfully, neither of them questioned me on it. Rija was focused on finding the quickest route to the ferry on the Channel. Tenn was busy experiencing the new sights of the southern valley, still lush despite the early arrival of autumn.

Having adjusted to the thin mountain air, I cast my spells with more regularity and ease. With a teleport here, some levitation there, and plenty of conjured water to slake our thirst, we traversed the last hundred kilometers out of the mountains and into the woods with relative ease. It took the morning and the better part of the afternoon, but the slower pace gave us the opportunity to catch our breath and recover some of our energy.

The woods were thick with ancient, gnarled oaks, as far as the eye could see. The foliage was lush and brilliant green and provided plenty of shade for us until the clouds arrived. During our brief rest periods, I watched the thickening clouds through the branches, for the discomfiting possibility of a sudden thunderstorm. Traveling with the metallic Tenn was tantamount to carrying a lightning rod, and I didn't want to be caught under the towering oaks with storms threatening.

Nonetheless, we needed to set up camp in the middle of the woods when the rain began in earnest and the sky darkened. Rija assured me that the trees were sturdy and would not fall, even if the wind increased. I conjured a tent for shelter and tiles underfoot to keep us dry, but I chose not to tell Rija that it cost me the last of my reserves to do so. If I had been traveling alone, I wouldn't have been as reckless, but I was beginning to place my trust in Tenn.

As was Tenn's habit, she stood watch over both Rija and me, but drew closer to me once Rija had fallen asleep. She preferred to remain close, both to observe me and to be ready to move on my command. Alive or not, Tenn played her protector's role with great conviction.

The hike through the oak forest was much more extensive and arduous than Rija had originally led us to believe, and after we stayed a second night in the forest, there was a third. To their credit, my companions did not complain about the crude accommodations I was able to provide. I could not imagine someone of Rija's slight stature managing the journey on a regular basis, but she seemed unaffected by the rough and unpredictable terrain. However, Rija did become more introspective as the days wore on, sometimes speaking more to her raptors who carried her messages, than to me or Tenn. During our last stretch of hiking out of the oak forest, which Rija finally revealed was called "The Great Oak Sea" by the Fringe Dwellers, she said only a few words.

The stars and planets were beginning to appear overhead when we neared the edge of the forest, when we first smelled the tang of saltwater and livestock. We saw the small farm and the buildings long before I heard the signs of life. Although they were short and plain, the structures stood as tall as hills on the otherwise flat coast. Rija charged ahead with renewed energy, returning to what was familiar and comfortable.

I trusted Rija, but I was wary of others. We were too close to the Realm not to be watchful of Malya's marauders or spies. It was suspicious that such an exposed, solitary settlement could have remained independent of Imperial control. With a quick spell, I changed my ghostly hues, darkening my hair to black, and lightening my eyes to a paler blue. I clothed Tenn in my spare dress and changed her appearance similarly to make her look … well, alive.

We walked to the water's edge, and I stared out as far as I could, but there was little to be seen through the clouds. Apprehensive about the unfamiliar territory ahead of us, I was only slightly disappointed that perhaps the weather would keep us from leaving that night.

A foraging chicken meandered past us on its way to the coop. The proprietor's domesticated animals seemed to have the run of the place, judging from the number of wandering swine and sheep. Behind us, a young voice said in common: "You must be Rija's friends."

It was a small boy, with wide, dark brown eyes. His hair was as dark as his eyes, and his skin only a few shades lighter. He was one of the most striking and beautiful children I had ever seen.

"Yes, we are. Are you the ferry master?" I joked.

He laughed. "No, that's my Mom. Follow me, please, Misses."

He led us to the main house and charged into the open arms of a tall, muscular man that I could only presume to be his father, judging by their likeness. His long, plaited hair and beard were as black and glossy as jet, and his skin was like caramel. Scooping up the boy with a single, powerful arm, he smiled, "Welcome, friends. Rija tells us that you want to go into the Realm?"

"Yes, Sir, we do," I smiled casually.

Rija emerged from the house accompanied by a woman who, upon first glance, seemed a taller, more mature version of her. She had the same, tanned skin and dark hair as Rija but was closer to Frost in age. She also wore trousers that allowed for her long, graceful stride, and a pale tunic that flattered her dusky complexion.

"You've met the rest of my family, I see," Rija said. "This is my sister, Delenn, her husband, Corlis, and their son, Timor."

I noted that Rija did not give our names.

"Welcome, friends," Delenn greeted with a bow of her head. "Come inside! It's good that you arrived ahead of the rain," she said with a glance at the clouding sky. "You must be tired, and we've plenty of food, and spare rooms." She turned her eyes at Tenn interestedly.

Tenn stared back blankly. "I have no need of food or rest."

Delenn's smile widened, showing her small white teeth. She seemed to recognize Tenn for what she was, but she made no comment. "All friends of my family are welcome in our home."

Delenn was an excellent and prodigious cook, similar to her father Mareos in her deftness with seasoning and technique. Even as the rich, spicy aroma of the roasted shoat tempted me, I was reminded of the wolves' feast on the doomed marauders every time I looked at the chunks of dark flesh clinging to disjointed bones, and I limited myself to the grains, vegetables and bread. Delenn was too gracious a hostess to comment on my selectiveness.

After dinner, our hosts offered us use of the bathhouse, which was in its own enclosure behind the main house, not too far from the pier. I left Tenn with Rija in the main house and ventured outside alone. Under the overcast sky, I spotted the vessel: a sleek, slender double-masted ship tethered at the small wooden pier, which was itself well-concealed in the crescent cove, safely tucked away from sight of passing ships. That was how the ferry had remained hidden for so long; it could only be seen from the Dark Lands side, and Grey-Eye and his lupine army had always seen to it that any marauders and Imperial troops crossing into the Dark Lands never left to reveal their secrets.

I stopped inside the doorway of the bathhouse and gawked at the system of levers and pipes overhead. It was all very simple, but unexpected. A lever was built into the roof of the bathhouse that released a generous shower of fresh water when I pulled it. Especially after the heat and humidity of the day, the shower was as thoroughly refreshing as a waterfall on a summer's day. After it was done, I considered waiting for the basin to refill to reuse it, but out of deference to my hosts, I decided to not waste any more of their potable water.

When I dressed, I was glad to discover that in just the few days since my reemergence, my body had already started to return to healthier dimensions, and my old linen chemise was beginning to cling to my curves again. I needed to recover my muscle, to recover my strength, and my overzealous magic use didn't help. As I pulled my damp hair back into a plait, I pledged to take better care of myself.

Tenn was waiting for me in one of the guestrooms upstairs in the main house, and Rija only said a perfunctory good-night from the door before she continued onto the next room.

"Did Rija say anything to you while I was gone?" I whispered.

"No, Snowfleece," she replied. "She did not say anything at all."

"That's not like her," I said. "Stay here. I'll only be a moment."

Rija answered haltingly when I knocked on her door. She opened the door, then returned to the bed. "How was the shower? I hear it's very popular in the Realm. I prefer baths, myself."

"It was very refreshing, thank you." I closed the door and went to the foot of her bed. "Is everything all right? You seem troubled."

"I'm not," she said, keeping her eyes averted from me.

"Yes, you are," I said, taking a seat beside her. "You've barely spoken to either Tenn or me since we arrived. What's troubling you?"

"Nothing," she insisted. She then amended herself, "Nothing important. It's just ... well, you're the Protector. You have more important things to think about than what's on my mind."

"I'm not so sure," I said. "I'm no different from anyone else, I know how it feels to be slighted and ignored, to be excluded and have my feelings disregarded," I bemoaned melodramatically. "Listen, I'm not going to see you or any of your family or friends for a while. If you can't tell me your deepest secrets, who else is there?"

Rija took a breath. "I feel so childish about this since we hardly know each other, but ... I'm going to miss the two of you."

I took her hand with a lightened heart. I had been expecting something much darker. "We'll miss you, too. It unavoidably happens with friends."

"I also had a dream the first night, in the cave, and then each night in the woods," she said haltingly, squeezing my hand. "It was horrible. I saw Tenn, broken into pieces, and you were hurt, bleeding..." She took another deep breath and shuddered. "I don't remember anything else, but I knew that you were in danger."

That was more along the lines of what I had expected, given Rija's skittish mood of the past few days. "You're afraid that we're going to die?" She nodded. "Do your dreams come true often?" She nodded again. "Always?"

"No, not always," she admitted.

"Then there's hope for me, yet," I said lightly, getting to my feet. "I don't have much experience with visions and prophecy, but I do consider warnings." I kissed her on the forehead and returned to the door.

Her eyes followed me. "Thank you for asking, and for listening."

I smiled, "You're welcome, Rija. Good night."

"Good night, Protector."

The fog lifted early the next morning. Rija joined us for a spare breakfast before she accompanied us to the pier to see us off. She planned to stay until Delenn returned, she said, before starting her journey back to the Fringe. As Delenn and Corlis carried aboard jugs upon jugs of fresh water, they waved Tenn and me away from assisting them, so we stayed with Rija and her nephew Timor. We kept our bittersweet farewells brief, and I tried my best to convince Rija that we would be fine, but she seemed steadfastly unconvinced.

We settled on a fare of twenty imperi, for both Tenn and myself, and that was after I insisted that we pay for our passage. The ferry was the family's livelihood, and supplies and maintenance cost money. Besides, I still had a bag of coins from Grey-Eye's pack that had weighed me down for eight days and over five hundred kilometers, and I was eager to shed some of it.

Once we set sail, I was nauseously reminded of my inexperience with sailing. I had ridden the small barges up and down the Yirae River, but I had never been on such a vast and turbulent body of water as the Channel. I tried my best to conceal my queasiness, but Delenn realized it soon enough when she saw me lurch over the starboard railing and disgorge my meager breakfast.

"We keep extra water aboard for such occasions," she said. "Don't feel bad. I've seen seasoned sailors lose their stomachs on these waves. Last night's storm is still passing, plus we're traveling against the current. Keep your eyes on the horizon, and have a piece of fruit, when you feel up to it."

Once I adjusted to the rhythm of the waves and trained my eyes on the land mass of the Realm in the distance, I was able to enjoy the journey, especially the cool and bracing seaspray and the breeze off the water. Despite the modest size of the vessel, it made good time in the choppy waters, and I found my seasickness alleviated by focusing on the horizon.

"My friends have joined us," Delenn called. I looked across the water for other ships, but she shook her head and pointed down at the waves.

Large, sleek grey forms were riding our waves, at least half a dozen. I had never seen such large fish; each one was at least my size, not counting its fleshy fins. On occasion, one would peer up at us, or spray us with water from a hole atop its head.

"Good morning, dolphins," she called. A few squeaked in response. "They look like fish, but their blood is warm like ours, and they bear children like we do. Some say they're as clever as people, but I disagree."

"Why is that?" I asked.

"The dolphins do not fight amongst themselves, so that makes them wiser than us."

As we approached the shoreline, the dolphins dispersed, disappearing under the waves. "Clever," Delenn commented again. "The pods stay away from the Realm. Recently, the Imperial troops have been killing them for sport and meat. The Imperials are getting restless for battle, I think."

"Do you encounter other ships often?"

Delenn shook her head. "Not in this stretch of the Channel," she said. "It's one of the reasons I choose to sail it. There are rocky shoals to the north and south that Imperial ships prefer to avoid, so they act as a natural barrier, and the dolphins and I have the deep water to ourselves."

The boat slowed to a crawl before we reached the cove where Tenn and I would disembark. The cove was simply a small sand beach, barely a kilometer in length and surrounded on all sides by rocky hills. As we approached the shore, the boat started to turn, and I realized that it would not be anchoring.

In pairs and groups, at least forty men, women and children emerged cautiously from the shelter of the rocks. From the way that they were dressed and bundled, I knew that they must have waited on the beach since the night before, at least. Many of them looked as though they had been exposed to the elements for days, if not weeks. I couldn't begin to imagine what they were fleeing, with little more than the clothes they wore.

"Head straight west for Altaier, and find Slither," Delenn called. "Send the old snake my regards. Good journey, friends ... what is this?" I heard Delenn's laugh behind me, and the jingle of coins; she had found the extra hundred imperi that I had hidden by the wheel for her troubles.

"A small token of our gratitude, Delenn. You can find better use for it than I would. Have a safe journey back." I turned to my companion. "Ready?"

"Yes, Snowfleece."

With my bag slung across my shoulders, and my new boots in hand, I leapt over the side and splashed down into the waist-high water, leaving the ropes and ladder for the people waiting to climb aboard. Many were on deck before Tenn and I even reached the dry sand.

It was pointless to try to distinguish them as either elfyn or humyn, for they all wore a look of haggard desperation about them, even the children. I counted over fifty of them, in total. I realized then that Rija was waiting for their arrival; once Delenn took them back across the Channel, Rija would guide them to the Fringe. If there were any spies mixed in with the refugees, Rija and her family would no doubt discover them soon enough and deal with them accordingly, or perhaps leave them to the wolves to dispatch.

There was no one remaining on shore for us to ask about a way out of the cove. Tenn and I trudged around for a little while before I found a steep, narrow ledge that led up to the higher ground. At one point, the pass had been a treacherous foothold for the infrequent wanderer, but now it had worn from use into something of a path.

From the higher vantage, we could see a lush, green land before us, and beautiful, sapphire blue mountains in the far distance. Patches of the land looked cultivated and inhabited, but there didn't look to be any organized layout to the land. Wherever the heart of the Realm was, it was not here. To be on the safe side, we stayed away from the settlements, and I fed off the wild fruits of the plains and drank from a canteen of fresh water that Delenn had given to me. We had been lucky with the Fringe Dwellers, but we had no way of knowing anyone else's allegiance, and I wasn't ready to start a fight. Yet.

To pass the time, Tenn and I recited the names and locations that Mareos and Rijena had shared with us, and while we knew the data intimately now, it was still as foreign to us, as it was when we first left the

Fringe.

We were able to reach the mountains by nightfall. Tenn and I settled for the night in a shallow indentation in one of the taller mountains with an eastern exposure, so that the light of the morning sun would wake me. As I fell asleep, I still smelled the salt of the Channel on my clothes and skin, and the faintest tinge of sandalwood still lingering on the cloak. I thought of the distance that we had traveled and wondered how many more lay ahead.

On this, the ninth night of my journey, nearly six hundred kilometers from home, I dreamed of dolphins.

Chapter 15: Welcome to Altaier

On the tenth morning of my journey, I awoke to the peal of a brass bell. I opened my eyes to half-darkness; I saw a band of pale pink light on the horizon where the sun would soon appear. Perhaps I had dreamt the sound. I heard the faint toll again and staggered to my feet to search for the source. I half-climbed, half-ran up the slope of the mountain where we had camped, blindly without the aid of the sun. I managed to reach the ridge and peered over to the other side.

"We've made it!" I shouted to Tenn.

The golem stood near me silently, my bag gripped firmly in her hand.

I was enthralled to see a city looming on the distant horizon before me, in all its illuminated majesty. The lights of the city formed a sparkling net, like a gossamer web after rainfall. A river ran through the city, a shimmering ribbon weaving through the center of the city. I knew it in my heart that this had to be Altaier, the capital of the Realm.

Oh, yes, and there was a small temple a little outside the city walls, with its bell solemnly ringing in the new day.

I was giddy at the sight of Altaier. This was the gateway to the Realm, and my last chance to reconsider my actions and go back to the Dark Lands. *Run back to your little Haven hole.* I imagined Malya waiting amidst the lights of the city, taunting me from afar, daring me to face her. Would it really matter so much if I didn't face her? She could stay on her side of the strait, and I could stay on mine, but how long would that peace last? It certainly hadn't worked out between Malya and Clyara, despite all the years they had to negotiate a truce.

Then there were the other lives to consider. Frost and her children did not deserve to live in the shadow of fear. The people who had scrambled onto the ferry back to the Dark Lands were desperate for escape. The wolves were willing to sacrifice their lives for me to protect the future. Wherever the humyn queen was, she deserved her throne.

My pulse quickened, and I felt my gem stirring with anticipation. I would finish my work here. If I was fated to die, then I would take Malya with me and end the war with us. "Come, dear Tenn. Altaier awaits."

We made our trek on foot, down from the mountains and across the plains. The hike took hours, but I barely noticed the passage of dawn. My mind was buzzing with questions: how had Malya's ascent affected the

Realm? Why was Malya so intent on drawing me out of the Dark Lands now? How would I even find her now? Had I really emerged too soon? Tenn and I hiked in silence, with my metal companion leaving me to ponder in peace, and for that I was glad. I doubt that a living, sentient companion would have suffered my muteness for all the kilometers that Tenn and I traveled.

After so many centuries, the gleaming white, sheer stone walls that Mother Kaylis of the Realm had commissioned for Altaier's defense still stood. The hundred-meter high battlements embraced the inner city like the arms of a protective lover, but even they could not contain Altaier's prosperity. The stone and brick buildings of the bustling city spilled outside and spread prodigiously, and some of them looked fairly new. Apparently, Malya's rule hadn't affected Altaier's economy too aversely.

Tenn and I still wore our darkened hair and blue eyes, and as I wanted to be as inconspicuous as possible, I didn't bother to change our apparent gender. The less magic I used, the less conscientious I had to be about maintaining our illusion, so hopefully we would arouse less suspicion.

To test our disguises before we reached the city walls, I led Tenn to the temple whose bell had awoken me. It was a small, unassuming place, maintained by the acolytes who worshipped and lived there. At the entrance, we were greeted immediately by robe-clad monks, who offered us tea. I declined the offer politely but donated to their collection box at the entrance.

The temple contained one central, colossal statue of a woman, surrounded by brass censers of burning incense and fresh flowers. Tenn studied the detailed bronze statue with much interest, and indeed, her molded shape did bear a strong resemblance to the giant figure, from the wide-set, long-lidded eyes to the gracefully tapered fingers.

"Welcome, friends and travelers," one of the monks greeted with a bow. "Welcome to our temple."

I bowed and said, "Thank you," then cringed internally. It was fortunate that I hadn't attempted to disguise myself as a man, as I forgot to even change my voice. I cast a spell to raise the pitch of my voice. "Do you worship a particular spirit here?" I glanced at the statue in the center of the temple.

The monk smiled patiently. "There are no spirits, only the Goddess."

Semantics. "Which goddess, then?"

"There is only one Goddess," he explained patiently. "We, the Brothers of Divine Mercy, believe that she alone is the source and mother of all that exists." Seeing that he had my attention for the moment, he continued eagerly. "She is the All-seeing and All-knowing, the Creator and Mistress of this and all other worlds. All She asks is that we honor Her name and respect all that is Hers, and we shall be allowed to spend the afterlife in Her grace."

It was an intriguing belief, that one deity would be responsible for all the workings of the universe. On matters of faith, I remained neutral and respected the fact that these Brothers of Divine Mercy found solace and joy in worshipping their Goddess. If it didn't harm anyone else, it was hardly my place to challenge their creed, especially in their own shrine.

I nodded my acknowledgment rather than agreement and pulled Tenn's arm to signal our immediate departure. Once we were far beyond the temple walls, I spoke freely. "Believing in one god. By Ajle, that must be some tea."

From the maps I had seen of Altaier, I knew there to be four entrances into the city, one at each main point of the compass. Presuming that all were equally fortified, I decided to go through the guard post in the east quadrant. Empress Malya had to realize that my intention was not to mount an invasion but to infiltrate, as the dozens of armed soldiers who were posted by the gate looked capable of little more than observation. Many of them looked weary and unfocused, even bored, but appeared too docile and well-trained to be openly insubordinate.

One of the senior officers, designated as such by a pretty sash across one shoulder, glanced at a parchment tacked to the inner wall and swaggered over to us. He looked awfully young for his high ranking. "State your business in Altaier," he addressed us stiffly.

"We are visiting family," I replied innocently, looking at the grim faces all around. A very crude, unflattering line drawing portrait of me with an unruly shock of white hair stared from the wall. "There certainly are many soldiers about."

"Her Imperial Majesty has ordered reinforcements to protect her subjects from the enemies of the Realm. Your papers, please," he requested with his hand outstretched.

I looked around at a few travelers stopped at the gate on their way out to see what their papers looked like, then cast a subtle illusion around us. It would have appeared to any spectators that I had presented papers of identification to him for Tenn and me, and that he had glanced at them and passed them back to me. *Our papers are in order,* I suggested to the young soldier. *We're just typical, unremarkable travelers.* Aloud, I asked, "Who could possibly be so dangerous?"

"No one dares question Her Imperial Majesty's command," he said dully, stepping aside. "Everything appears in order. Enjoy your stay in Altaier."

Inside the walls, the city was crackling with energy and activity. I felt a deep and visceral thrill to be in such close quarters with so many people.

The buildings were packed tightly together, too, like cells of a hive, and the humyn drones swarmed throughout. We were jostled regularly by passersby, who looked as though their lives depended on their frenetic paces. Once, a young woman pushed against me so quickly and roughly that I might have thought that she was trying to dislodge my satchel purposefully. When I succeeded in keeping hold on my bag, she gave me a furtive glance and darted away without the briefest word of apology.

With so many people about, it was difficult to determine where to start looking for the legendary Slither. It seemed imprudent to start questioning random passersby, as it was likely to draw unnecessary attention, especially so close to the city gate. I led Tenn deeper into the city, but I was just as lost as she was. Perhaps, I hoped, we could find a map of Altaier somewhere and try to get our bearings. If that proved fruitless, I was not beyond peeking into people's thoughts for possible clues.

The barrenness of the city was disheartening. The few trees that we did see were bound by pots, or by tiles of pavement. Few birds filled the air with their songs, and everywhere, the ground was hard and dead. Every new street looked the same as the last, and the lifelessness reminded me of how much I missed home. My one-time acquaintance Jaryme had told me once about how bleak things were in the Realm, compared to the verdure of the Dark Lands. I was sorry to see that he had not exaggerated in the least.

We did find a park, eventually, where the stunted, sickly bushes and trees were trimmed into artificial neatness. At the gate was a metal plaque, stating that the Imperial residence at one time stood on the site, but that it was destroyed in a fire in 996. The same tragedy also claimed the lives of the beloved Emperor Augus Thorne and Princess Glory. *Not Glory Thorne, just Glory.* Four years ago. This park was constructed "in loving memory" by the newly coronated Empress Malya. In the center of the park, a commemorative clock tower stood in a paved square, and the time read as eight on the clock—or "o'clock," I was hearing people say. Near the clock, a posted map of the area drew my eye.

Tenn noticed the stranger just as I heard the footsteps. I had sensed more than once that we were being watched, so my surprise was less about being approached than the individual who came forth.

She strolled towards us indirectly, as casually as any pedestrian passing another on the street. She was tall but moved gracefully, and she was adorned with wildly, splendidly marigold-red hair and a sweeping green cape that fell to her slender ankles. Balancing on her toes in delicate shoes, she stopped next to me, peering up at the clock tower. "It's tragic, isn't it?" she asked, with a rich, smoky voice, casting a brief glance around us.

"Pardon me?" I asked.

She stepped closer to me, looking at Tenn with a superior, dismissive smile. "The Great Fire," she said, peering at the map with me. "Since then, since the Empress moved to the north, Altaier has never been the same. It's not safe to be in this part of town, even at this early hour, especially young women like ourselves."

"It's not always safe to talk to strangers, either," I said.

"I don't think you count as a stranger," she said. Her stare and predatory smile were sexually charged, and I felt my face heating under her thorough, assessing gaze. "But I can see that you're not alone," she said, nodding indifferently towards Tenn. "Why don't we go someplace more private?" She leaned in closer and whispered, "Where your guardians can speak with you about your plans."

"You've mistaken me for someone else," I said, turning to Tenn.

"I know who you are, Protector," she said without concern, setting her gloved hand on my wrist. "We've been awaiting your arrival for some time."

"You have me at a disadvantage," I said amiably. "Who are you, and where is it that you're thinking of taking us, exactly?"

"My name is Renay," she said, the fabric of her glove warming my arm. "And I'm taking you to some people who are very eager to meet you."

Her last words sounded distant and tinny, and I realized too late that Renay had done something to me. Something in her glove was affecting my head. I turned to Tenn while I still had the will, but I could not form words to command her.

It was too late, anyway. Everything went dark.

"Aren't you a clever golem," said a peculiarly accented voice, speaking elfyn. "Now let's-s take a look at your mistress-s."

I felt a smooth, warm hand on my forehead. It felt slightly textured, like scales? Instinctively, I reached for it.

I opened my eyes and was caught in the hypnotic yellow gaze of a sinewy, milky-pale man with a kind smile. His warm grin did not waver despite my surly manner, and the vise-like grip of my fingers on his, inches from my head. He looked impossibly slender, but there was enough strength in his thin hand that cautioned me not to underestimate him.

I glanced around the darkened room and saw that we were in a tavern. The establishment wasn't yet open for business, judging by the upturned chairs on the tables, and stools inverted onto the counter. I was seated in a cushioned wing chair by a smoldering fireplace, with a dark grey cloak over me like a blanket. The aforementioned golem was standing next to me, patiently vigilant.

"Forgive me, Miss," the man said blandly, his forked tongue flashing briefly. His silvery yellow hair was slicked back from his forehead, giving his long, slender face even more of a reptilian demeanor. "I am not in the habit of touching people without first asking, but your companion here seemed concerned about your well-being, although she did not say so," he said, with a glance at the statue-like metal figure looming over us. He spoke elfyn fluently, with an interesting hiss of a lisp. His eyes gazed into mine, captivating me with all the incandescent shades of gold and sunlight in his irises.

I released his hand, cautiously. "We don't know each other," I said at last, in elfyn. I looked up at the golem, and my head was still clouded. "But I know you." *Didn't I?*

"I am Tenn."

"By Ajle, it speaks," I said, my mouth falling open. "Wait, I knew that," I said, pressing on my skull where the headache was lingering. "I should know who you are, too," I said to the man.

"Yes, you should," the man said. "Your golem handed this to me when you arrived." He set down on the arm of the chair a piece of parchment with names and addresses. "That would be my name underlined at the bottom." He turned his attention back to Tenn. "Golems are rare, and speaking ones even more so. I'm going to hazard that you're not her creator," he said to me.

"'Slither,'" I read, then looked back at Tenn. "How did we get here? Did you carry me?"

"I did not need to," she said. "After your attacker was subdued..."

"My attacker," I mumbled, remembering. "Renay? What do you mean, 'subdued'?"

"I placed her hand on her face," Tenn said. "Just as she had put her hand on your arm to sedate you. I did not need to harm her, as she was not expecting me to act quickly, so she did not struggle much. Did I do something wrong, Snowfleece?"

I wanted to give her a hug, so guileless and magnificent she was. "No, Tenn, you did nothing wrong. If you didn't bring me, how did we arrive here?"

"Your guardian brought you both," Slither rejoined. "You can ask him for the rest of the details when he returns. Perhaps you'd like a drink while you wait?" he asked casually, as though we were regular patrons.

My throat felt like sandpaper. "I could use some water, please."

"*Bien sur*," he nodded and slipped away, back behind the bar counter.

"What did he say?" Tenn whispered.

"I haven't the slightest idea," I replied. "So, Slither, where did my guardian go?" *What in the world — what guardian?*

He shrugged his sinewy shoulders and returned with a glass of cool water for me. "Who can say, *cherie*? But he will not be gone long." He

161

waited until I took a drink before continuing, "I won't insult your intelligence by pretending not to know you, but how did you— Snowfleece, daughter of Moonteyre, Protector of the Line, and so forth— come to seek me?"

"Mareos and Rijena of the Fringe," I said, "and their daughters. They provided the list of names and addresses."

"Oh, them," Slither grinned. "Interesting folk, aren't they? The ride over wasn't too rough, I hope. Delenn knows the Channel like Mareos knows his kitchen; you may get what you ask for, but not necessarily what you expect."

"I don't remember what I expected of you, either," I confessed. "Except that I was advised that you could be trusted. Even Grey-Eye recommended that I find you."

Slither's grin broadened further to fill most of his face. "Ah, Lord Fluffy-Bottom does like me, then."

"You don't call him that to his face, I gather," I said.

"I don't have to. That's the fun of dealing with telepathic creatures." He returned to the bar and began to take inventory of his shelves. "Don't mind me, I'm just checking stock. I need to keep my patron Guardsmen happy." He smiled at me reassuringly. "Don't worry, you're safe here. Locally, I am considered a harmless freak who pours a more generous drink than most, so I remain unmolested and in business. Some of the senior officers like to bring their recruits from time to time, to show me off as a warning."

"How is that?" I asked.

"I was not always like this," he said, flicking his forked tongue once more. "I was once a man, a Guardsman, in fact. One day, I crossed paths with another former Guardsman, who also happened to be a mage and was very mad, and… It's a long story for another day. In the years since, I've grown into my skin, so to speak. As a deterrent for disobedience, I'm much more effective than anything the Imperial Guard can devise nowadays, *cherie*."

I frowned. "All these years, no one has been able to change you back?"

"Not entirely, but this is better than I was. I used to be fully scaled and hairless." His thin lips curled in a self-deprecating smile. "I am not a mage, Protector, so my body wouldn't survive the strain of further metamorphosis. Perhaps I am a coward, but I would rather live as a demi-reptile than die a whole man."

As I pulled the cloak around myself and joined Slither at the bar, he ambled into a back room and reappeared a moment later with a tray of bread, cheese, grapes and shelled hard-cooked eggs. "If you're hungry, you're welcome to share my humble breakfast, while you're waiting. It may help clear your head." He took one of the seasoned eggs and ate it whole.

I had been too excited all morning about being in Altaier to think about food, and after the encounter with Renay, my head was too muddled. Now that I had been reminded, however, I was ravenous. I tore a piece of the warm, soft bread and practically inhaled it. As for the grapes, I ate a handful with the pits intact. I stopped at the spiced, marbled eggs.

"It's a family recipe. I did try first to follow in the family business of chicken farming, but after my change, the chickens just didn't seem to trust me anymore," he said.

I took an egg out of courtesy, but once I took a bite, I was pleasantly surprised at the complexity of flavors, which included molasses, savory anise and tea. "This is delicious, Slither."

He lowered his eyes modestly. "Your compliment honors me, *Keeronae.*"

I wasn't surprised by his address, but I still cringed. "I wish people would stop calling me that."

"It is your title, wear it proudly." Slither turned to his well-stocked shelves before I could comment and picked out a cut-glass decanter of a dark red liquid. "Your arrival, however premature, warrants a celebration with a proper toast. You've had wine before, yes?"

"Sure, on occasion." I thought my tolerance was average, from what I recalled. Especially with my stomach full, what could one drink possibly do to me? "What do you mean by 'premature'?"

"I'm told that you were not expected to arrive before five years had elapsed. You are two years short."

Slither poured a bit of the decanter's syrupy ruby-hued contents into two glasses. He picked up one and handed me the other, with an apologetic nod to Tenn, who had come within an arm's length of me to continue her vigil. "Sorry, golem. None for you." He turned back to me. "The best that the Realm has to offer. To the future."

"To peace." I clinked my glass against Slither's and pondered Slither's comment before draining the glass.

The generous pour burned its way down my throat. My heart beat in a panic, as my body tried to process the alcohol as quickly as possible. My head was buzzing immediately, with all the blood that rushed through it. My tolerance was apparently no longer what it once was, especially with my prolonged abstinence in the Haven.

But along with the side effects, there was a warm exhilaration. Nothing was impossible, and my objectives seemed as clear and simple as a child's game! Why was I ever worried? So what, if I was a little early? Feeling warm, I took off the cloak and set it on the stool next to me, giggling when it slid to the floor.

"Are you all right, Snowfleece?" Tenn asked, her eyes unblinking.

I patted her on the head and calmed the beating in my heart, and listened for the door. Someone had arrived.

The door swung open, and a crowd of Imperial Guardsmen poured into Slither's, with weapons drawn. We were surrounded in seconds, before I could even fathom what was happening. Still placid and relaxed from the wine, I looked at the stern faces with casual curiosity. *They look like they could use a drink, too.*

Slither greeted the new arrivals with wide and welcoming arms, ignoring their brandished weapons. "Noble servants of her Imperial Majesty, what can I get for you this fine morning? Mind you, no spirits before noon, by her Majesty's order—"

The captain of the squad stepped forth, a man of no more than thirty. "Quiet, Slither, our business is with your customer." In his proud bearing and stance, he reminded me of Tracker's acquaintance Ohynn, who had once endeavored to win my affection by overbearing me with his overinflated ego. I chuckled at the memory of Ohynn's conceit, and all that followed on the night of the Harvest Feast years ago.

"What's so funny?" the captain scowled.

I shook my head, fighting a giggle. "Nothing, you just reminded me of someone I knew once."

"You'll have to come with us," the captain said, then seemed to notice Tenn for the first time. "Both of you."

Behind me sounded a mechanical, metallic click, and I knew that Slither had drawn a weapon. "You can at least let the young lady finish her drink," my new friend said. The other Guardsmen looked at each other uncertainly and kept their weapons trained on me, as Slither had his firearm aimed at the captain's heart.

"You're not a Guardsman anymore, Slither," the captain said with a patronizing smirk. "This doesn't concern you. If you put down your weapon, I won't have you arrested for interfering with official matters."

I ignored the men around us and leaned over the bar to whisper to Slither in elfyn: "I can come back later, if that's easier. I don't want you to have to shoot anyone on my account."

He replied in elfyn: "It wouldn't be a bother, really."

As I stared into Slither's yellow eyes to try to convince him to lower his weapon, I heard the strange, unexpected noise of several bodies and weapons hitting the floor simultaneously. Out of the corner of my eye, I saw Tenn looking intently towards the door. Slither lowered his pistol, at last.

I turned around slowly, wary of what I would see. A single tall silhouette stood just inside the open door, looking down at the still figures of unconscious Guardsmen littering the establishment.

"Looks like I returned just in time," he remarked.

"You've done worse," Slither commented, sliding his pistol back under the counter. "Shut the door. You're letting in fresh air."

That voice, I know that voice. As he approached the bar, I started to remember, and I smiled with nostalgic recognition, "Sarc." My mind was still clouded and slowed, but he was a spot of bright clarity. *My guardian.*

Coming into the light, Sarc looked much as I remembered him from three years ago, except a little scruffier, and perhaps a couple of kilograms heavier. He stepped over the prone figure of the Imperial captain and picked up his old cloak from the floor where I had dropped it, draping the thin wool garment on the counter between us. "Good to see you up and about, Apprentice." He nodded to Tenn. "You, too."

It was nice to see a familiar face, and especially nice to hear his voice, after years of absence. "You're the one who brought us here, I presume," I said. "Thank you."

"'I'll only be a few minutes,'" Slither mocked. "Cutting it a little close there, *mon ami*."

"Some things take time," Sarc said. "I knew you would be able to handle things until I returned."

"Well, I don't have my name for nothing," Slither said. He slipped the cut-glass decanter under the counter and offered a glass of water to Sarc. "Have a drink, Sarc. No need to rush off."

"I just came to check on our guests. I'll return later." Sarc glanced at my empty, red-tinged glass, then glowered at Slither. "You didn't."

"Relax, I just had a little bit. I hardly felt anything," I pouted. "Are you always so serious?"

Slither threw up his slender hands in surrender. "What? She said she'd had wine before."

"Elfyn sweet wine, old friend," Sarc said with restraint, taking the glass of water in hand. "The stuff you once mistook for fruit juice. Not fortified ramsblood."

Slither rolled his eyes with a begrudging nod. "Fair point." He looked at me. "How are your hangovers, *cherie*?"

"What's a hangover?" I asked.

Sarc grimaced and swirled his water glass, frosting it until ice began to form. Slither refilled my water glass to the top, and said, "Maybe you're one of the lucky ones who don't feel them."

My mind was settled, but my stomach was not. I took a big drink of water and watched Slither refill it. As I took another sip, I felt a headache starting to take hold. To distract myself, I watched the unmoving Guardsmen all around us. "Are they...?"

Sarc followed my eyes while he sipped from his glass. "They'll be up in a little while. With any luck, they won't remember a thing."

He seemed different somehow from the last time I had seen him, and not just physically. He seemed older, more dour. What had happened to him since our last meeting? "Are you angry with me, Sarc?"

"No, *janya*, I am not," he said. "You're old enough to decide what you want to eat and drink. I'm sure you don't need my guidance for that."

I bristled that he called me an "innocent," but I held my tongue. *He had a point about the ramsblood, didn't he?* My lingering headache and vague nausea attested to his better judgment.

He looked around me, at Tenn, and remarked: "She's handy, isn't she? She saved your life."

"I am Tenn," she answered for herself.

"So you told me. Your maker will be pleased that you're staying busy, and you've been well-maintained all these years." He turned back towards the counter and remarked, "You were smart not to come to the Realm alone, *Keeronae*."

He had called me "apprentice," then an innocent, and now "master of masters," again. It was as though he was trying out different names for me, to find one that he preferred.

As he took another drink, I studied Sarc's profile, getting my first real close look at him. I was struck by his serious eyes, with their long, spiky dark lashes, and his dark gold and bronze coloring. His hair was still near his shoulders, and his face was shaped by smoothed edges where a classically handsome face would have borne harder angles. He bore a faded crescent-shaped scar along the outside of his left eye—it was the first scar I had seen on any mage, and it was odd to see it on Sarc.

Focusing on him helped me to ignore my hangover, and eventually my head and stomach were almost back to normal. I took a last drink of water to be sure, and noticed that Slither and Sarc were both looking at me. "Did I do something?"

"You were staring like you've never seen me before," Sarc said, looking at me askance over the edge of his glass. His eyes were the same as I remembered: the color of dark amber, with generous flecks of copper and gold.

"It has been almost three years," I blurted, then remembered that we had an audience. I looked over at Slither, whose eyes flicked back and forth between Sarc and me with great interest. "I got tired of waiting in the Haven."

Sarc tilted his head in acquiescence. "Yes, and you managed to break out, congratulations. I should've made the password harder to guess. Still, traveling all the way from the Dark Lands was perhaps not the wisest move you could have made. We would've come for you."

"In another year and a half, perhaps," I said, "but the longer I lingered in the Dark Lands, the stronger Malya was going to become. No one here even seems aware that they are under the rule of a gemwraith." I struggled to read Sarc's expression. He had been a friend to me, once, and perhaps still the closest I had to an ally in this alien place. "She won't stop sending marauders to the Dark Lands, and I need to keep my family safe."

"Grey-Eye couldn't convince you to return to the Haven?" Sarc said.

"He told you I was coming, didn't he, somehow?" Thinking back, I recalled seeing a barn owl carrying off something in its talons during my brief stay with Grey-Eye's pack. "He didn't write you a note, so how…"

"He sent me a sprig of creeping sage," Sarc said.

Slither cleared his throat delicately. "I hate to break up this lovely reunion," he said, "but the men littering my floor are beginning to stir."

"Yes, they are," Sarc said, looking at the sleeping Guardsmen with vigilance but not concern. "They certainly arrived sooner than I would've expected. They're usually not so quick to pick up on a trail." He looked at me and Tenn. "Did Renay say anything to you?"

"Just that my guardians had been expecting me, and that she was taking me to them," I recalled, suddenly feeling quite small under Sarc's scrutiny. "She may have said something else after she poisoned me."

Sarc's eyes narrowed with something that resembled disapproval, and he looked at Tenn. "What about you? What else did you hear?"

In a perfect mimic of Renay's smoky lilt, Tenn said: "'He should have been mine, you filthy elfyn whore. Oh! What did you do, you stupid hunk of metal!'" Without a pause, she added, in her own serene voice: "Then she fell asleep."

Slither covered his mouth with his dishtowel in a vain attempt to hide his amusement. "That certainly does sound like Renay."

Sarc ignored the quip. "What else happened before I arrived?"

"A crowd began to gather, so I stood guard over Snowfleece," Tenn reported. "I was waiting for Snowfleece to awaken when you arrived and brought us here. I did not see Renay regain consciousness."

"But she was gone when I went back for her now," Sarc said.

"Good riddance, the woman is toxic," Slither grimaced. "She is undeserving and incapable of redemption. It might've been better if Jeysen found her, he would've done us all a favor and ended her."

"Who's Jeysen?" I asked.

Sarc seemed lost in his thoughts and ignored us both. "Stay here with Slither," he said. Just as the first of the Guardsmen began to pick their heads up, Sarc waved his hand, and they collapsed back onto the floor, unconscious. "I'll be back before these fellows wake again. And you," he said to Slither, "are not to serve her ramsblood again, or I'll put you lower on the food chain than Leis had."

"What happened to letting me decide what to eat and drink?" I replied smartly. I caught a fleeting comment in Sarc's mind and snapped,

"Stop calling me an 'innocent'!"

Sarc vanished too quickly for me to know if he had heard me. Slither was quietly clearing the glasses from the counter and was looking to disappear into the back.

"What can you tell me about Renay?" He hesitated, and I implored, "Please."

Slither swallowed with discomfiture. "Renay was an acquaintance of Sarc's. When he returned from the Dark Lands, from escorting you to your Haven, he found a woman in his flat, murdered brutally. She was dressed like Renay, had the same build and red hair, so one could presume."

"But it wasn't her?"

"No, however, it was her handiwork. Sarc had wanted nothing to do with her, despite years of her repeated overtures, so she decided to mark him in other ways. She made it appear as though Sarc was the murderer, and he had no alibi since he had been off in the Dark Lands, so he had to endure the indignities of an inquiry. The charges were dropped, once witnesses came forth attesting that they had seen Renay alive."

I must have looked bewildered, as Slither clarified: "As cold and cruel as the killing was, she thought little of it, and she made no effort to hide herself during the investigation. She considered it little more than a prank. But, there was no evidence to link Renay to the dead girl, so she remained free."

"What happened to the victim?" I asked. "Did Renay actually kill her?"

"Funny thing. After Sarc was vindicated, the body vanished before it could be reexamined. You know how things can disappear where mages are concerned. Without the victim, there was no further inquiry." Slither shrugged. "As I said, Renay is beyond hope of deliverance. You're fortunate to have come away unscathed."

"Do you think Sarc is looking for her? Where would he even start?"

"She may be with the black-haired man," Tenn volunteered.

Slither and I both looked at her. "What man?" he asked.

"When your guardian was checking that you were not seriously hurt, a man with black hair appeared in the crowd near where Renay had fallen. He watched us but did not speak to us."

"Why didn't you say anything earlier?" Slither asked, agitated.

"He appeared after Snowfleece's guardian arrived," she said innocently. "Your guardian did not ask me to provide those details."

"You know who it is," I said, watching Slither. "Where can I find him?"

"I would not tell you, even if I knew," he said. "Sarc wants you to wait for him here." He looked anxious, however, seeing the men on the floor stirring again. Sarc was taking longer than expected.

"It's probably better for you, if we're not still here when they wake." I stood, checked my bark-brown hair in the mirror behind the bar and motioned to Tenn that we were leaving. "We'll return when everything's settled down, maybe tomorrow." I left Sarc's cloak on the counter and left a fifty-imperi coin next to it for Slither's hospitality, before weaving through the minefield of bodies to the door.

"Wait," Slither called after me, sliding out from behind the bar. "What will I tell Sarc when he returns?"

I held the door for Tenn to exit first. "You can tell him the truth. He knows I'm not the sort to wait patiently," I called back, and closed the door behind me. As Tenn and I walked away, I listened for Slither, but the door remained closed.

What a mess. I felt like a guest of honor showing up at my own surprise party earlier than expected—in this case, two years earlier. I had wanted to prove my worth by demonstrating my initiative and readiness, but I had done so without thought as to the disruption to any of my guardians' careful plans, and now my sudden arrival in Altaier was one complication after another. It seemed better, for the time being, to avoid everyone. *I can stay out of trouble for a few days, while I sort this out, can't I?* I reassured myself that I could, as I shivered against the breeze piercing my clothes. Perhaps I should have taken Sarc's cloak, but I wanted to owe him nothing. Besides, I felt sheepish about reentering Slither's bar after making such a dramatic exit.

Tenn and I traveled on foot, as I wanted to leave no trail for Sarc or anyone else to follow. We did not converse until we turned onto a more populous street. It was lined with tiny shops and pushcart vendors, leaving little room for walking, but somehow pedestrians managed to continue moving. Thanks to our less eye-catching appearance, people passed in front of us without even a sideways glance. *Have I come all this way just to hide behind illusions? Why come at all, then?*

"You're crying," Tenn observed. "Are you in pain?"

I laughed despite myself and wiped my tears dry. "Nothing gets past you, does it? No, Tenn, it's just a speck of dust." I was glad that Tenn knew nothing about lies. *Speaking of lies.* A head of dark hair decorated my reflection in a shop window, taunting me about my artifice. What would happen if I canceled my spells right here? Would people have screamed at the sight of the white witch and her metal companion? Or, would they have even noticed?

A small group of Guardsmen marched stiffly past us, and I thought better of revealing myself, even as the desire continued to gnaw at me. Malya had to know already that I was in her domain, but I didn't need to advertise my presence. I had to keep her guessing at least a little bit, until I had figured out my next move.

169

The population of Altaier as a whole seemed rather unaffected by the affairs of their political leaders, even as they loved to gossip about those in positions of power. Mainly because Altaier was the commercial center of the Realm, most of its citizens believed that their city would survive even if the rest of the Realm crumbled to dust.

Even the most jaded, however, noticed the sudden mass exodus out of the Realm. Perhaps not in Altaier, but elsewhere in the Realm, there was a sense that something catastrophic was imminent, and people were fleeing before it was too late. Many retired or discharged members of the Imperial Guard, also, had apparently left the Realm in favor of other, less volatile lands, to avoid the possibility of being recalled to service. Even the weather was atypical, with the cooler temperature across the Realm being closer to that of winter than autumn.

While no one dared to speak their minds in the presence of the omnipresent Imperial Guardsmen, most people invariably compared Empress Malya with Empress Adella, the late Augus's mother and predecessor. Adeliaraine Thorne Mareni was a beloved, iconic figure to her subjects, and she had died after her fifty-year reign only five short years ago. As the first-born of Emperor Jaeris, Adella was considered one of the greatest rulers of the House of Thorne. She had two younger brothers: Jaryme and Jeysen.

For the first decades of their sister's rule, Prince Jeysen was commander of the Imperial Guard, while Prince Jaryme had served as Adella's advisor and chief envoy. The brothers were believed to have died years before the end of their sister's reign, but as their bodies were never presented or publicly interred, there were conflicting accounts and even some doubts about the truth of their passing.

The math was simple enough: if Adella had only died five years prior, then her son Augus had only ruled for a year or so before he perished in 996. Without other members of the Imperial line to take the throne, the widowed Imperial Consort Malya's ascension was swift, bloodless and uncontested. It seemed to be further evidence of Jaryme and Jeysen's demise, that neither came forth to challenge her right to rule.

It would have been an odd coincidence for Jaryme to be the same that I had encountered in the forest, and for Jeysen to be the same that Slither had mentioned in the bar, but not impossible. I couldn't jump to too many conclusions; the names were popular ones, after all. But what if they were mages? The brothers would have been in their seventies, but with their magestones to rejuvenate them, they could appear as young men. Certainly, the Jaryme that I knew could fit the profile well enough.

The mage I sought was the one that Sarc had mentioned — the one who had created Tenn. Such a venerable and powerful mage would be an excellent ally, or at the least, a source for knowledge about the true Empress Aelora. I regretted not pressuring Slither for information when I had the chance, but I was confident that I could get what I needed through other means.

At five o'clock, many of the shops started closing for the day, even though the sun was still bright. Tenn and I watched as the faces in the crowds changed from solemn to carefree. The hours of leisure seemed to begin with the gradual fading of the sun.

Before long, the sun dipped behind the cover of buildings, and the evening establishments lit torches and lamps in front to promote their offerings. Municipal lamplighters went from one streetlamp to another, adding each lantern's soft glow to the collective. When their work was done, Altaier's night looked almost as bright as its day. The two halves of the city were knitted together by bridges that spanned the river Prosper, and strings of lamps adorned Prosper on both banks like pearls. Even at night, the river was teeming with cargo ships and ferries, yachts and commercial clippers, with the lapping of waves muffled by the raucous crews and passengers.

Snowfleece, my dear! Jaryme's voice called in my mind. I looked at all the strangers around me and finally saw his handsome smile. He moved through the crowd easily, his eyes never off me for a second. He looked the same as I recalled, with his full black hair and piercing blue eyes. "I would recognize you no matter what your colors were. Here in Altaier, of all places, after all these years! And as lovely as ever."

His smile cheered me. "Jaryme! What are you doing here?"

"Me? I live here." Jaryme shed his cloak and wrapped it around my cold shoulders. "You must be chilled, standing out here without a cloak. Why aren't you with Slither?"

"It wasn't safe to stay," I said. "How did you know that I was there?"

"Slither's place is as a known safe haven for mages, and the most natural place for you to go."

"Then, how were you able to find me here?"

"It wasn't easy, but I managed. Didn't I tell you Altaier was an interesting place?" Jaryme said. *Snowfleece, you should be careful, the Empress has spies everywhere looking for you.*

I am careful. "It's very much as you had described it," I said. I felt comfortable with Jaryme, eased by his kind smile and gentle disposition. "I'm glad that you're all right, after the … incident at your camp."

Jaryme shrugged. "It wasn't the first time, nor the last. I was worried when you left so suddenly," he said quietly.

"I can take care of myself."

"Yes, you certainly can." *I feel that I should warn you, however,* he said with a sudden gravity. *I have a brother who is in league with the Empress, and he, too, knows that you are here.*

Your brother wouldn't happen to be Jeysen Thorne, would it?

Jaryme wasn't surprised by my guess. *Catching up on humyn history, I see. Yes, I am Jaryme Thorne, and my brother Jeysen and I were once part of the royal line. Now, we are relics, little more than historical footnotes.*

It must have been hard to leave your Imperial life behind.

He took my provocative remark in stride. *I never wanted our father's throne, although Jeysen may tell you differently. If you do ever encounter him, take care. Don't underestimate Jeysen's abilities, or his ambition.*

I'll consider your advice, I said. I shed Jaryme's cloak and draped it over his arm with a grateful smile. "I didn't come all this way to hide."

"Of course not," he smiled easily. "I'm sure you'll be fine. But if you change your mind, I'll be here for you," he said, pressing a card into my palm. "Please don't wait too long." With that, he blended back into the crowd. I watched him disappear into the shadows before I looked at what he had given me, before I could ask another question of him.

I read the card as Tenn rejoined me from where I had positioned her several meters away. "It's an address. Apparently, I am to follow him if I want any more information from him. Did you feel anything?" I had come to realize over the past days that her creator had imbued Tenn with the wonderful, invaluable ability of sensing all types of spells.

"He charmed you, very effectively," Tenn reported.

"I thought he might. Did you recognize him?"

Tenn commented quietly: "Yes, he was the man who came for Renay."

"I suspected as much." I glanced at the note one final time and let it slip through my fingers, into the dark waters below. I had wanted to find him, but on my own terms. I wasn't going to underestimate either Jaryme or Jeysen Thorne, and I certainly wasn't going to either of them anytime soon.

Not too far from the water, we found a small inn that was as spotless and spare as its proprietor was unkempt and ungainly. He looked at our plain dresses with some disdain, but a subtle persuasion spell and three hundred imperi up front were enough to acquire for us the best available room, the only one remaining with a private washroom.

It was an effort for the lumbering innkeeper to ascend to the upper floor, and Tenn and I stayed a few steps back, just in case we needed to catch him or jump out of the way. He managed to reach the top landing, finally, and handed me the key.

I asked, "How far is the Arch of Kaylis from here?"

"The Arch? It's almost six kilometers from here, on the other side of the river. Why?"

"I have a friend who lives nearby," I said, recalling the address that Jaryme had given me.

The innkeeper looked impressed. "The area's very exclusive. Your friend must have some wealth," he said speculatively.

"It looks that way." As soon as the innkeeper left us, I dispelled my illusions. It felt good to wear my own colors again, and I preferred my hair silver-white instead of the dark brown I had tinted it. It reminded me of my sister and father, of what I had left behind.

To clean the last traces of the perfume from Jaryme's note from my skin, I had to scrub my hands until they were almost raw. I extinguished the fire and sat by the windowsill in the darkness, watching the Prosper River shimmering under the radiant swarms of lamps.

Sarc was out there, perhaps, looking for me, although I suspected that his life was busy enough without the challenges brought on by my arrival, if the morning was any indication. He must have been cursing the day that he agreed to be my guardian, as a favor to Clyara or not. Surely, she didn't intend for him to keep watch over me for the rest of my life, when he had his own to manage. I was going to miss him, but it was better this way.

Tenn stayed faithfully by my side, silent and austere, until I was too tired to keep my eyes open. When I tucked myself under the covers, Tenn dutifully took her place at the foot of my bed. Her feminine metal form glimmered with the dim light shining in through the window.

"Tomorrow, we plan for the Empress," I said with a yawn, too tired to even disrobe before slipping under the covers. "We'll finish this, and go home to the Dark Lands. Unless there's someplace else you'd rather go."

"No, Snowfleece," she replied quietly. "I shall follow you."

"Thank you, Tenn," I smiled, closing my tired eyes. "I'll welcome your company. When everything is finished, I'll get you cleaned up and take you home to your mistress, as good as new."

Chapter 16: One Step Closer

The acrid, choking smell of scorched metal thickened the air, along with the sounds of shattering glass and breaking furniture. Disoriented and groggy, I forced my eyes open against the blinding magical flares, the light stinging and blurring my vision. My mind struggled to make sense of the confusing images before me. "Tenn?"

She did not reply. By the time I focused on the figures of Sarc and another in the room, the screeches and groans of wreckage had dwindled. Images from my dreams, too, had faded as quickly. Sarc helped me upright, and his companion crouched over a pile of mangled, blackened ... *Tenn?*

I stifled my cry and stumbled out of bed and over to where the golem lay, broken apart and unmoving. Her decapitated head faced away from me. Her hollow hand was still warm, blackened but still heavy in my grasp. *Rija's vision is coming true.* I was too stunned to even shed a tear, but I felt a tightness knotting in my stomach like a clenching fist.

The stranger's ice-blue eyes bore into me, and I faltered. I dropped Tenn's hand back into the pile with the rest of her remains. "You."

His black hair was longer and tousled, and his cheeks and brow were marked with healed cuts, but his handsome face I could never forget. He was the man who had freed me from the hunters' cage the night before Sarc delivered me to the Haven. *Damn, he does look like Jaryme.* "You must be Jeysen Thorne."

"Ever at your service, *Keeronae*," he replied evenly in elfyn. His voice was soft, clear and beautiful: a cross between Jaryme's light pitch and Sarc's deeper, warm timbre. "Are you done with my golem now?"

My jaw dropped. "Your golem? You created Tenn?"

"You named it." Jeysen glanced at the remains of the golem, then back at me. "Are you all right? You're as white as death."

"This is how I always look," I said, rising to my feet.

Jeysen seemed so earnest that it was hard to believe that he could have wanted to hurt me. Or that he was allied with Malya, as Jaryme purported. "I'll leave you to discuss the arrangements." Jeysen vanished from the room, taking Tenn's remains with him. The room dimmed a little with his departure. I had wanted to find the mage who had created my talking golem, but now that I knew that Jeysen Thorne was her creator ... I was so struck by Jeysen's presence that I started when a blanket dropped over my shoulders. I had forgotten that I was not alone.

"Sarc, what—"

He glanced at me with his finger against his lips, before heavy footsteps crossed the hallway outside, and a pounding shook the door. "What's going on? What's that noise?" barked the innkeeper. Through the door, I heard him fumbling with his keys.

Sarc cleared his throat quietly and replied aloud in my voice, "Nothing. Go back to bed." The suggestion took immediate effect, and the innkeeper promptly shambled off, grumbling but otherwise satisfied.

I sank back onto the mattress, stunned by the loss of my *tenn*. *What in Ajle happened?* I had been oblivious, helpless against whomever or whatever had invaded my room and demolished my golem. Aelora's golem. *Jeysen's golem.*

Sarc looked down at me. "How do you feel?"

"I feel violated and angry. How should I feel?"

"I mean physically." He frowned at the dried blood that spotted the front of my dress, just as another of the magical flares extinguished. The room darkened significantly. "I'm sorry we were too late to save her."

I shook my head tiredly. "Maybe I should have stayed at Slither's after all … never mind. How did you find me? What happened here?"

"Jeysen honed in on the golem's distress beacon, and I followed him."

"Distress beacon?" I asked uncertainly.

"That's what he calls it. It's the residual energy burst that his golems send out when they're damaged or destroyed. He can track it within a fifty-kilometer radius. He was already fighting with Jaryme when I arrived."

"Jaryme was here, too?"

"You don't think Jeysen destroyed his own golem, do you?"

I had a terrible headache trying to recall what had happened. My thoughts were muddled, at best. "What was I doing? I don't remember a thing."

"What's important is that you're safe," he said. "Collect your things, let's get you out of here."

I didn't need any more prompting than that, going directly to the dresser to start packing. I wasn't going to spend one more hour in the room, not with the metallic smell of Tenn's destruction lingering in my every breath. Whom was I kidding? I was nowhere near ready for Malya, and I was sorry that it had taken Tenn's demolition to make me realize my unpreparedness. I shuddered under the blanket, desperate to think about something else. Anything else. I blurted: "Did you find Renay?"

"I didn't bother looking," he replied. "But I'm sure she's fine."

Unlike Tenn. I cinched the satchel closed, and I turned and nearly crashed in Sarc, who stood unmoving at the foot of the bed.

175

"Right now, I have other, more important matters weighing on my mind." He brushed a lock of hair back from my face and lifted my chin, and my insides fluttered. "Listen to me. Like it or not, I am your guardian, and as awful and as patronizing as it may sound to you, I am responsible for your welfare, above all else. Do you understand what that means?"

"No companionship for you until I'm gone?" I said.

"That, too, I suppose," he smiled unwillingly. "But mainly it means you can't run off again. I'm sorry that I was a little curt this morning, but you have to trust me. Can you do that?"

I had trusted him, once. That was before I knew that Sarc was Jeysen's friend. That was before I knew he had taken my blood in a secret ritual. A part of me insisted that I was better off in Jaryme's care, but it was Sarc who had taken care of me during my adjustment. It was he who had delivered me safely to my Haven. It was he whom Clyara had trusted to bond with me. I answered finally: "I'll try."

"Thank you, that's as much as I ask," he replied, withdrawing his hand. I hadn't even noticed that he had brushed my cheek. "All your silver grew in finally," he smiled, studying my white locks. "I didn't have the chance to see your hair before. It suits you."

He looked at the bag in my hands. "Good, you travel light. I'll clean up here and join you after I've gotten the rest of my affairs in order. Wait for me this time. Please."

The air swirled and shifted around me, and the scorched metal odor gave way to the familiar aroma of seasoned wood and stale wine. The dim flare light of the rented room brightened into the lamplight of Slither's tavern. The tavern was closed for business, but Slither was up. He was wiping down the counter, looking at me with a measure of sympathy. "Lost your golem?" He placed a glass of water in front of me. "I'm still under orders not to serve you ramsblood."

"I understand," I said, keeping my blanket around my shoulders. My satchel was on the counter next to my glass. "I think I prefer being clear-headed." I iced the glass as I had seen Sarc do and sipped the pleasantly chilled water. "I actually don't feel as bad about what happened as I think I should. Maybe Sarc did something to better my mood," I said. "A charm, or something."

Slither grinned. "Ah, well, that's what he does for a living."

"Charm people?"

"If he needs to." At my continued blank stare, he continued, "Mostly, he cures people, emotionally, mentally. Sometimes physically."

I tried to fathom it. "He heals minds?" Slither confirmed with a nod. "That's how he earns his living?"

"Or, it's a hobby, it's hard to tell with Sarc," he shrugged.

That explained Sarc's effortless magic, as well as his refined

176

appearance. He must have been generously compensated for his services. Part of me found it upsetting that healing in the Realm was only available to those who paid. It wasn't like in the Dark Lands, when Clyara was Healer, where it was available to all. Then again, the elfyn had become too complacent over the years, too dependent upon Clyara's magic, and it was only by my leaving that they had regained their self-reliance.

I stirred from my reverie, when Slither began moving the furniture about. I made myself useful by helping Slither set up the tables and chairs, despite his half-hearted protest. Afterwards, I cleaned my blood-marred dress and took a nap in one of Slither's two guestrooms in the back. Whatever wounds I had suffered during the night had long healed and faded. Still, I kept a sentinel spell active, to keep out uninvited guests, to avoid a repetition of the previous night's disaster, whatever had transpired.

I got up just as Slither unlocked the front door for business, at noon, the earliest legal hour for taverns, as indicated by a decree posted on Slither's wall. Before the first customer entered, Slither reminded me to restore my darker illusionary colors, which I did grudgingly. "Personally, I think you would be fine as you are, but your guardian insists."

By two o'clock, Slither's tavern was populated with an assortment of characters, and the air was tinged with the smell of alcohol. I stayed on my seat at the counter, not daring to move in case of Sarc's unexpected return. Despite how unsavory most of them looked, the patrons were decidedly respectful to Slither and, by our extension, to me. Slither served everyone at the counter, and his customers took their own drinks to their tables.

By four o'clock, the bar was reeking of ale, wine and harder stuff, but most of the clientele looked sober enough. Slither's rule was: if you became too drunk to carry your own drink to your seat, you were done for the day. Some of the patrons had hushed exchanges with Slither at one secluded end of the counter or the other, and my gracious host listened intently to his clients' concerns. He always kept a stack of paper and quill handy, for drawing maps and writing notes. There were the occasional uniformed Guardsmen who drank their fill from Slither's taps and bottles, in return for their deafness and inactivity during his private consultations.

I was far more restless, and to pass the time, I did peek into some of the customers' minds. One man was thinking about his wife and children waiting for him in the Fringe. Another, older man was reminiscing about how much simpler and more prosperous his life had been before Malya's reign. A young woman was planning on leaving that evening for a place called Ruvyna.

By six o'clock, I had had enough of eavesdropping on thoughts. I was tired and feeling antisocial from the glut of telepathic empathizing. Slither noticed my unsociability and asked, "Can I get you something?"

"No, thank you. May I ask you a question, Slither?"

"Of course, *cherie*."

"Where is Malya now?"

He hesitated, then responded. "Far from here. Really, really far. Thousands of kilometers far."

I smiled at his dissuading tone. "I give you my word that I won't run off again." *Tonight, anyway.*

Sighing, "If you do, Sarc is going to going to finish what Leis started," he pulled a scrap of paper and began to scrawl a jagged outline. "This is Altaier here." He slashed an "X" near the bottom of the page. "You came from the east, across the Channel, here," he indicated with a bold stroke to the right of the first mark. He then drew a meandering line that went far up and across the middle of the paper. "All around the edge of the continent is the Inearan Sea. The Inearan Peninsula is out here, and there is where she has made her fortress." He pointed to a spot near the top left corner of the paper. "All told, roughly two thousand kilometers, or well over a thousand miles, a good part of it water."

It was more than three times the distance I had traveled from the Dark Lands to reach Altaier, and this time, there was no Tenn to keep me company on my journey.

Slither must have read something in my expression that revealed my despondence, and he said, "Perhaps you'd like to rest a while before Sarc returns. The other room has a private bath, if you're interested."

I kissed him lightly on the cheek. "You certainly do know the way to a girl's heart. Lead on."

With a resigned, half-hearted shout to his patrons to stay on their side of the counter, much like a tired mother warning her children to stop sneaking sweets, Slither led me to the rear chambers. On the way, he explained more about the water towers on the roof and the rest of the municipal plumbing system than I needed to know, as well as his modifications for heating the bath water in his rooms. He was justifiably proud of his handiness, and I followed his explanation as well as I could. "People still use the public bathhouses, but I've never felt comfortable there, given my … differences. So, I stay here, and I can warm the water from the tanks to my own liking by running the pipes behind the fireplace."

He showed me to a small room with a large porcelain tub and matching sink against one wall, and a spacious bed opposite. I was more fascinated by the labyrinthine network of thick metal pipes that ran along the ceiling than the luxurious fixtures. "Do you offer this to all your customers?" I asked with a sideways glance.

Ambling back down the hallway to his business, he chuckled: "Only the ones who manage to rile Sarc."

I locked the door behind him and took a moment to marvel at the renovations that Slither had made. For a chicken farmer's son, he certainly had a knack for plumbing. I snapped my fingers to start a fire in the fireplace and warmed myself in front of it for a while before I drew my bath. Sure enough, the water was pleasantly balmy when it emptied into the tub.

The boisterous sounds from Slither's evening crowd out front were a comfort to me, assuring me that I was not alone, even in the solitude of the room. I drew the blinds and disrobed in front of the full-length mirror that stood behind the door to look at my body critically.

I was glad that my body looked normal again. My limbs weren't angular and bony anymore, and my breasts had regained their fullness. More importantly, I felt stronger. Once I lowered myself into the steaming tub, I stripped my hair and skin of their artificial colors to relax every part of my mind. My long white locks floated stubbornly on top of the water until I dunked my head under.

From the tub, I saw myself in the dressing mirror. Even with my wet hair matted against my head, I looked better in my natural hues. Despite how non-elfyn we looked, Frost and I were always content with our colors, with our night-blue eyes, dark lashes and our ivory complexion. Our father used to call us "the two halves of the moon," with Frost's hair silver and mine jet. Frost would have been beautiful regardless, with her natural grace and delicate features. I, on the other hand, was never her peer, with my visage too serious, eyes that were too keen and over-plump lips that often said too much.

I extinguished the lamp with a glance. The glowing fireplace provided plenty of light, especially at such a late hour. I stepped out of the bath, and a breeze through the open window sent a delicious chill up my spine. I pulled the drain stopper reluctantly and watched the water drain counterclockwise away, back to the Prosper.

As I wrapped myself in one of Slither's towels, I heard voices through my wall, coming from down the hall. I easily recognized one of the voices as Sarc's. He was speaking with a woman, but the voices were too muffled and garbled with the other voices outside for me to discern the conversation. I should have been ashamed of myself for even trying to listen.

It seemed that I had made a habit of inconveniencing Sarc. *If he wants to spend time with his latest companion, it's certainly none of my affair,* I thought petulantly. *Jealously?* I scolded myself for even thinking the word.

I heard their shared laughter through the wall. I just hoped that I wouldn't have to hear more amorous noises all night. I grabbed my comb and ran it through my hair vigorously, mercilessly. Maybe the effort of untangling my unruly hair would distract me. I jumped at the sudden sound of a quiet knock at the door.

Are you still up? Sarc called.

"Who can sleep with all that noise?" I replied in common.

His laugh filtered through the door. "May I come in, briefly?"

"Yes, I just need a moment." I threw on a dress, with my hair still tangled and soaking wet, but under the circumstances, I didn't think it mattered. I didn't much care what Sarc's friend would have thought about his visiting a strange woman in the back room of a bar.

I went to the door to unlock it, and Sarc filled the doorway, holding a covered reed basket in one hand and a satchel over his other shoulder. "How are you feeling? Slither said you didn't eat today."

"I wasn't hungry, just tired."

"I understand. You should eat something, anyway, if you want to keep up your strength. I brought a little something," he said, holding up the basket. Taking the hint, I stepped aside and let him enter. He set the basket on a chair near the fireplace, and the savory smells wafting up made me reconsider my words. Sarc dropped his satchel and crouched next to the basket, lifting the cover for a tantalizing peek.

I perched on the edge of the chair and peered into the basket, its reed fibers infused with the faint smells of lavender and lemon. I was taken aback by the amount of food inside. A great assortment of whole fruit and sandwiches filled the basket almost to the top. "A little something, you say?"

"It's not all for you." Sarc reached into the basket and grabbed a peach. "And it doesn't have to be finished tonight."

"Oh." Considering that, I took one of the dainty sandwiches and took a tentative bite. The seasoned vegetable filling was perfect: tender and bursting with fresh, herbal flavors. "Who made all this?"

"A kind and gentle woman who was good enough to repay me in food for my recent services. She insisted on delivering it in person."

"One of your patients?" I asked casually.

"My patient's grandmother," he smiled, unfazed by my knowledge. He had probably assumed that Slither would let the information slip at some point. Sarc tasted a morsel of bread from one of the sandwiches and grinned his approval. "If only she were unmarried, or her granddaughter ten years older," he sighed.

"It's not ethical to get involved with patients," I teased.

"Pity."

"Is that a habit of yours? To receive payment in food, I mean?"

"Food, clothing, whatever my patients can offer, and whatever they feel my services are worth. Healing shouldn't only be for the wealthy, don't you agree?"

"Absolutely," I said, impressed by his philosophy. "Pardon my curiosity, it's just that I've never heard of mind healing before," I confessed. "There are no books for it. How does it work? Do you absorb your patients' pains, or do you … how can I put it?"

"Give them to someone else?" he completed for me. "In Aron's tradition of 'passing the pain'? That would be horrific. I couldn't do that to so many people. My *keeron* would've revoked my stone, besides."

"You absorb your patients' thoughts and emotions yourself, then. How can you do that without literally going mad?"

"It's a trade secret."

It was a less-than-subtle hint to not bother asking for any more details. Even by the firelight, I could tell by his eyes that he hadn't rested since the morning. "Maybe you should go home and get some rest."

"And leave you here again, unsupervised? Not likely," he said. He got to his feet, satchel in hand, and smoothed down my cowlick. Just his fleeting touch made me smile, and I found the idea of him staying with me strangely compelling. "I'll be in the next room, if you need me. We'll start on our way in the morning."

"Oh," I said, a little disappointed that he was leaving after all, but then his other words settled in my head. "Wait, you're leaving with me?"

"I am your guardian," he reminded gently. "Besides, for your first visit through the Realm, you'll need a guide, and your other traveling companion is currently in her master's shop for repairs."

"You're going to escort me all the way to Malya's fortress?"

"If that is where our path leads."

"Haven't you tired of my company yet?"

He paused with his hand on the doorknob. "Tired of it? I've hardly seen you since you arrived," he said. "Good night. We'll talk more tomorrow."

I closed the basket and extinguished the flames in the hearth. In the pitch darkness, I felt the exhaustion weighing down my limbs, urging me to finally rest. I just managed to finish combing my hair before my eyes started closing on their own. Overwarmed by the fire in the hearth, I shed my dress and slipped under the covers, trying to keep my mind clear. I hoped that Tenn would not haunt me in my dreams, and I hoped even more that her killer wouldn't be there when I awoke.

The maze of towering, spiraling black pines stretched endlessly in all directions. Tenn's metal limbs and chunks of her horribly disfigured torso were tangled in the high branches around me, writhing pitifully, out of my reach. My voice was gone, and I could say nothing to console my dear friend.

Be strong, my girl, her molded lips echoed Clyara silently.

You cannot defeat me, Apprentice, boomed a voice from above. Empress

181

Malya's presence seeped into the forest in the form of a black mist, enveloping Tenn's broken body and rending it further. My golem's wide eyes remained open to stare helplessly at me.

I did not want to watch, but someone held my head in place, their fingers forcing my eyes open. A cold, cruel whisper rasped against my ear, *You did this, little witch. You bring destruction. You bring only death.*

There was another voice, soothing and gentle, and I struggled to find its source, as though I were drowning and desperate to surface. Just as I felt blackness closing in on me from all sides, Sarc's voice sounded in my head, filling it, and all was bright and clear again: *Aylonse, let it go.*

"Are you awake?"

At the sound of his voice, I did start to wake, and I pulled myself upright. With my eyes still closed, I grasped for him and felt his arm next to me, and without a word, I lay my head against his shoulder and took deep, life-restoring breaths. My hands remained balled into fists, and my eyes flickered open and shut. The images of the dream remained vivid in my mind, returning as soon as I closed my eyes. "Tenn, everywhere…"

Sarc let me rest against him, and he pulled the sheet around my cold shoulders. "Hush. You're safe," he whispered, brushing my hair back from my face. "It was just a dream. Open your eyes, let it fade." He waited for me to acknowledge his words with a nod, and I let go of his shirt that I had so steadfastly gripped. He still wore his clothes from the evening.

"I'll be fine," I said groggily. "I think I should have meditated before going to bed." I pulled the covers closer around myself, realizing that the thin sheet was all that stood between me and Sarc. *Wrong night to sleep unclothed.* I closed my eyes, and the visions resurged. "Damn it."

Sensing my consternation, he frowned. "Would you like me to stay with you, until you fall asleep?"

I lay down, with the cover pulled up to my neck and my body rigid. "That depends. Are you going to drink from me again while I'm unconscious, or lock me away for my own protection?" I replied, regretting the words almost as soon as they left my mouth. I felt the intensity of his gaze as he stayed at the edge of my bed, unmoving and unmovable.

I turned onto my side, facing away from him. "Forget I said anything."

"I am sorry for what was done to you," he said, getting to his feet. "What I did to you."

"It's done. It was a mistake for me to mention it."

"If it means anything, our bond was broken as soon as your adjustment to Clyara's magestone was complete, so there's nothing left between us. I won't force another one with you," he said. "As for locking you away … apparently, you won't stay in any one place no matter what I try, so I don't see the point of attempting it again."

The room was dark, lit only by swaths of moonlight through the drapes, and Sarc's large figure loomed over me. He could see clearly that I was nowhere near the point of relaxing. He stroked my brow and rested his hand over my closing eyes. "Let yourself rest. Think of happier things."

At the sound of his calming voice, my mind and body stilled. My eyes flitted closed, and the assurance of Sarc's watch allowed me to relax. Just as it was years ago, his hand on mine now was so warm, so comforting. Even without a bond between us, he managed to soothe me. So long as Sarc was there, I thought as I drifted to sleep, nothing in the world could hurt me.

When I awoke, it was still mostly dark, and I slipped quietly out of bed. As I dressed and packed the rest of my things away, I recounted the days since I had left Moonteyre. It was my twelfth morning away from home.

Moonteyre would have been beginning the second harvest soon. If the tradition of the Harvest Feast had continued, Frost would be sure to join the planning party, even with the responsibilities of raising her children. Then there would be her pilgrimage to the graves, before the end of autumn.

We always shared news with our parents during those times. "'Fleece has run off to the Realm," Frost could have said. "I don't know when she's coming back, but I hope she does soon. Things have been peaceful around here without her, though… Come to think of it, maybe it's better that she stays away. She's gone to find your murderer, Da, and exact vengeance for all that's happened for over the past hundred-fifty years."

Frost would've said something different, but maybe not.

A rhythmic knock stirred me from my reverie and reminded me of Sarc's plan to accompany me on my quest. For a moment, I considered not answering the knock and sneaking away to make my journey alone, but then I realized that Sarc would most likely track me down somehow and scold me again.

A second knock sounded, more urgently staccato.

"Come in." I smoothed down my dress and hair and unlocked the door with a mental command. I tried not to think about the fact that Sarc had seen me undressed just hours ago. I returned to the bed and stripped the linens.

Sarc entered and closed the door behind him quietly. "Sleep well?"

"Eventually." I was glad that his eyes weren't bloodshot either. "Let me just put on my face." I glanced in the mirror and changed my hues to shades of brown, becoming the dull wren to Sarc's golden eagle. Even his clothes, simply tailored but well-constructed, were natural-hued leather and linen. I checked that my locket was still against my skin, under my clothes; it was my one irreplaceable possession. With Tenn gone, it meant even more to me.

Without a word, Sarc picked up my satchel in one hand and our picnic basket in the other. He kept his own bag, as compact as mine, slung over one shoulder.

"Please be careful with that," I indicated my bag, opening the door for Sarc. "Nothing in there is worth much, but it's practically everything I own."

Sarc weighed the bag in his hand, and I cringed at the sound of a couple of the jars clinking together, along with the muffled jingle of coins.

"All right, there's a pouch of coins that's worth something. Maybe a year's wages for someone, from what I've seen in Altaier," I said, eliciting a laugh from Sarc. "Grey-Eye gave it to me, I didn't know how to refuse it, and I've had few occasions to spend it."

"Let me take care of our expenses; there's no point in both of us being weighed down. Slither can hold your stash for you, in the meantime." He stopped in the doorway and looked at me with a raised brow. "Is the thought of traveling with me really so distasteful to you?"

I realized at that moment that I had been scowling since the moment I awoke, with my jaw tightly clenched. "I'm sorry," I said in earnest, forcing my face to relax. "It has nothing to do with you. Well, maybe a little bit."

Sarc did not budge.

"I was just thinking that it may be better, if I went alone."

"Better in what way?"

"Safer?" I couldn't say anything more without sounding insulting or condescending, but I had to try. "Not that I don't trust you, but I've already lost one companion, and I would hate to lose another."

Sarc seemed to accept my answer and continued out. He called over his shoulder, "Have some faith. I'm a little tougher than I look."

While Slither refreshed our basket and made certain that I ate a hearty breakfast, Sarc saw to our transportation and returned with a carriage and driver. The driver, a wiry man by the name of Flyn, helped me into the carriage, while his chestnut-coated draft horse idly gnawed on the carrot Sarc offered, seeming engaged in a wordless conversation with him.

Once on our way, Sarc took out a more detailed map than what Slither had scribbled for me and traced the northwesterly route for me. We were setting out for the coast first. It was the better part of an overnight trip, usually, to reach the coastline on the Inearan Sea from Altaier, since we had to cut through a mountainous ridge running alongside the shore, in order to reach any of the coastal towns. Afterwards, we would start the next leg of our voyage, across the sea to the Peninsula of Inear, where Malya had built her fortress.

The memories of the ferry were too fresh. "Can we teleport any of this?"

"Perhaps, but it's not worth the effort for the distance we have to travel, and we shouldn't be so conspicuous as to appear out of thin air," he advised. "The Realm is too populated to take the chance of people seeing us; we would be dodging both the Guard and mage hunters the whole time. Besides," Sarc said, putting the map away, "there's someone I have to see on the way."

The carriage was stopped at the western guard post, and Sarc handed our forged papers to one of the sentries on duty while several of the others did a cursory inspection of the coach. The horse seemed the most impatient of all of us to get going. The attending soldier glanced at us, then at the papers, and waved us on our way. "Enjoy your trip," he said, blandly. Sarc and I smiled our gratitude weakly as Mister Flyn took us out of Altaier.

Sarc took a final inventory of what we had with us, and he shook his head at Slither's furtive departing gift: a full bottle of ramsblood.

Sarc and I spoke little; I enjoyed the silence and the chance to see the reawakening Realm, and he seemed lost in his own thoughts.

In all the kilometers we traveled, the road was even and paved, straight and wide, but in need of some maintenance. As the passing traffic changed during our journey, so did the landscape change from intricate buildings to rolling hills, to tall, golden fields with farmhouses and livestock. The warm, dark amber hue of the ripe grain reminded me of Sarc's hair, weirdly enough. I looked to Sarc to see if he had caught my unspoken comment, but he had fallen asleep, with his head leaned against the coach door window.

Chapter 17: Obligations

Shortly before noon, we arrived at the walls of a small city. It was perhaps the size of Moonteyre geographically, but once we entered the gates, I realized that the dense population numbered easily over five thousand.

"Welcome to Bliis," greeted a heavily-painted and bejeweled young woman who passed by while we alighted. She raked her eyes over Sarc's figure without the least bit of subtlety. Practically everyone greeted us with suspicious, leering smiles and similar stares. It was intensely disturbing to me, and Sarc could tell from my visage.

"We're not staying long, Snowcap," he said. "We just need a few supplies, and I need to pay a quick visit, then we'll be on our way. Believe me, I don't want to be here longer than necessary, either. Bliis may be mostly free of Imperial influences, but it's still a den of cutthroats and thieves."

"And mage hunters?"

"Always those," he said.

I accompanied Sarc to a sprawling outdoor marketplace, where vendor stalls stood tightly adjacent to one another, almost overlapping. I learned quickly to avoid staring at any one object too long, as the keen-eyed merchants misread my passing curiosity as genuine interest and would shout gradually decreasing prices at us. At a linen seller's stand, Sarc glanced casually at a stack of fabrics, neatly-folded and unpriced.

"Fifty imperi," came a voice, deep and strong. I followed the voice to a large man with a shock of red hair and an equally impressive red beard, tinged with white. He sat atop a pile of thick rugs, a cut crystal glass in hand, sipping from it as though he was at a garden party instead of a boisterous marketplace.

"For this pile of rags?" Sarc quipped. "I would be generous to give you ten for the pile."

The big red man took another sip. "I've broken men's arms for lesser slights, but I see you're a little slow, and I would spare the lady the sight of blood, so I will let you go for a bargain price of forty apiece."

Sarc flashed me a quick, playful wink. "Only an imbecile would agree to such a price, but I can see you're desperate for business, so I'll offer you fifteen for the dirt-brown one."

And so the banter continued, with insults lobbed until the price was settled at twenty-five imperi for what appeared to be plain, thin wool, but was actually densely-woven silk, light in weight and incredibly warm. Completing their transaction, they shared an easy humor and conversation that seemed more a brief reunion between friends than a simple exchange between customer and seller. As we continued on our way, the man stroked his luxuriant red beard and raised his glass to me wordlessly.

"What was all that about?" I asked, once we were out of earshot.

"He was a friend of my father's," Sarc replied. "The two of them could converse like that for hours."

We had stopped in front of a vintner's stall, where a heavy drape hid the back room from passing view. A young, plain-dressed woman bowed to us and started to pull the drape aside for us, and I looked to Sarc. "I will only be a few minutes," he said to her. "Can I trust you to wait here, Snowflake?"

"Where would I go?" I asked, intrigued about what was hidden from view.

"Just checking. Don't wander off too far," he cautioned paternally.

I didn't, just to the neighboring stands to admire some of the goods. After being in Sarc's company all morning, I needed time alone with my thoughts, albeit amidst the throngs of the market. While I appreciated his companionship, the separation gave me time to reflect on the direction that my life had taken, and about what was to come. I stopped in front of a clothing display and imagined how my life would have been, had Clyara not chosen me to become her apprentice. Among the wares was a bridal nightgown, which was little more than a translucent, lace-trimmed muslin handkerchief.

"Anything catch your eye?" came Sarc's whisper behind me.

I turned with a yelp and slapped his arm, as irritated and embarrassed by his timing as by his suddenness. "Hardly," I sniffed, marching from the stall as quickly as I could without drawing too much attention.

"Just thought I would ask," he said, his long strides allowing him to catch up to me in a mere couple of steps. "Did I startle you?"

"No, just..." His eyes were reddened, and I fought the urge to touch him. "Are you all right?"

"Fine," he said, although his smile was slow to return. He nodded back towards the vintner's stall. "It was a quick visit, as I promised. Ready to go?" He smiled at my vigorous nod and led me out of the market square towards a quiet sidestreet, back towards our carriage.

As we entered the mostly-empty alleyway, I suddenly felt uncomfortable, as though I sensed something dangerous, yet intangible. Someone called me, and when I spun around, my heart kept going. Jaryme stood at the edge of the marketplace where we had been, watching us. I met his eyes, through the crowds, and I was riveted.

Sarc passed his hand in front of my face. "What is it?" he asked. He wasn't seeing Jaryme as I did, and he didn't see Jaryme holding his hand out to me, calling me to him.

Sarc jerked me aside, breaking the spell, just as something small and dark shot past us and circled back. I tried to keep the insect in sight, but it was too fast and blended into the shadows too well. I looked back over at Jaryme, but he had also disappeared.

Sarc brought his arm up around me, and he growled with annoyance as the tiny creature stung him. "This way," he said with an effort. He plucked off the bug that had latched onto his arm and crushed it underfoot. Only a handful of men were in the alleyway with us, and by the way that they eyed us, I expected trouble.

All at once, the men intercepted and surrounded us. Before I could cast a spell, something struck the back of my head, unbalancing me. Two of the men quickly bound my arms behind me with rough twine. Another three held Sarc immobile, though he looked a little too dazed to offer much resistance, and I realized that he had been poisoned. The sixth addressed Sarc: "Don't struggle, friend. We're just going to have some fun with the lady here."

Sarc shook his head to try to clear it. "You have no idea what you're doing," he warned them. "You're all going to die."

Our captors laughed, and the leader drew a small, serrated dagger from under the folds of his dark tunic, as he approached me. The sight of the gleaming blade stirred a distant memory in my mind, and I began to slip into a trance, with everything around me seeming surreal and immaterial.

I heard Sarc thinking to himself, *Idiots. They can't say they weren't warned.* His suddenness took his captives by surprise and he threw them off his back easily. He struck the leader's hand, knocking the dagger skittering across the cobblestones. Sarc moved gracefully, swiftly, despite the effects of the toxin. He managed to thoroughly disable three of the men before he staggered, and fell.

Without Sarc's calm to influence me, and seeing him unmoving on the ground, my indignation swelled into wrath, and I acted on instinct. I unraveled my binds from my wrists with a thought and whirled on my captors, brushing them off like leaves. I fought the overwhelming urge to kill them outright and instead commanded the ground to open and trap their legs. I cast a cloud of fog and silence in the alleyway, so that I could continue my work undisturbed.

I'll make them suffer. My heart rate quickened, perfectly matched by the throbbing of my magestone. I unleashed its destructive power so infrequently that it seemed to enjoy my release.

The leader tried to escape, casting a spell of invisibility around himself. The smell of his sweat gave him away, and I paralyzed his limbs to keep him at hand. *Stay, I'm not finished with you*, I said. I looked down at one of the men by my feet, who looked barely older than me, and who was clearly regretting his recent life decisions. I chose to show some mercy, and I lifted him from his trap.

I looked at him and said, *Never cross my path again, and find some new friends. You have seen these for the last time.* I watched his flight just long enough to be sure that he had gone, then continued my work.

A white-hot ball of flamed enveloped my fist, and I was close to torching alive the men who sought to hurt me, but I hesitated. For a moment, it seemed enough that the men were petrified with fear, and I could reason that they would see the error of their ways, but then I reconsidered. If they hadn't accosted us, they would have found other, more vulnerable prey, and they didn't deserve another opportunity to harm anyone else. With a wave of my arm, the ground liquefied around their legs and swallowed them whole before hardening again, encasing them in stone and killing them more quickly and mercifully than they deserved.

As for the leader, I picked up his dagger from the ground and pinned him against the wall with a force. He was whimpering with fright, his eyes wide at seeing how his cohorts had perished. *How does it feel to be on the receiving end of magic?* I asked, scratching the blade against the brick wall next to his head. *Who gave you your magestone?* He opened his mouth, but his eyes avoided me, and he said nothing.

You shouldn't test my patience, I said, digging the tip of the blade into the hardened mortar, inches from his throat. *Who was it?*

Jeysen Thorne, he squeaked soundlessly.

You're lying. I sensed it in his hesitation. *Why would you lie about such a simple thing as that?* Before I could interrogate him further, his face turned purplish from some unseen constriction, and he died there, pinned there against the wall. *Damn.* I plunged the dagger into his flesh and gouged out the tiny magestone; it would've been easier if his eyes weren't bulging at me.

With his stone in my hand, I let the dead man drop and set the body on fire to prevent its reanimation. What good was a magestone, when I wanted answers? I dispelled the fog and silence, stuffed the stone in my pocket and flung the dagger away in my frustration. In the distance, I saw Sarc's unconscious figure. Past him, Jaryme came slowly into focus. He crouched over Sarc, ignoring or unaware of my presence. "Where did you go?" I called.

"Making sure your path is clear," he said, raising his eyes to me. "Get out of here, 'Fleece. The Guardsmen will be here any minute now." He noticed my stare at Sarc. "He'll be fine, but he may not be so lucky next time," he warned. "Come with me, or leave us both, but staying with him isn't safe for either of you."

I heard voices coming from the main street, so I knew that we would not be alone for long. "I can't, not now," I said. "Thank you, Jaryme, but I have to stay with him. Another time, perhaps." As I knelt next to Sarc, Jaryme disappeared from my periphery. Already, the memory of his appearance was slipping away like a fragment of a dream.

I kept a hand on Sarc and the other on our packages and looked to the end of the alleyway, where Mister Flyn had just pulled up the coach. Upon seeing us, he reached back and opened the coach door, and I phased us inside and slammed the door shut. Flyn snapped the reins, and the carriage shot forward.

I glanced through the rear coach window and saw a team of a dozen Guardsmen approach on horseback. Some of them had their pistols aimed at us. "Keep your head down!" I shouted.

"Don't worry about me, Miss," Flyn replied with strained ebullience, as pistol shots crackled behind us. "How's Mister E'lan doing back there?"

"I think he's coming around," I said with great relief, as Sarc's eyes flitted open briefly. Sarc was cool to the touch, and breathing shallowly, but he looked otherwise unhurt. Propping his head on my knee, I pricked my finger on something on the back of his neck and plucked off the offending barb, a second stinger that had struck him. While the insect itself was long dead, its stinger still held enough toxin to affect me.

Luckily, Sarc was fully awake by then. He caught me before I slumped, but my eyes continued to close of their own volition. Even as he shook me to try to keep me awake, my head was swimming. The streets of Bliis were a blur through the windows. My vision dimmed, and my body felt heavy and numb. Faintly, I felt admiration for Sarc that he had been able to fight as long as he did when he was stung, as I could barely stay conscious. Sarc glanced out the back window and called, his voice thin and distant to me: "How are we doing, Mister Flyn?"

"Oh, welcome back, Mister E'lan," Flyn replied brightly. "I may need assistance once we clear the city walls."

"I'll be right there," Sarc assured, keeping me upright. "Oh, no, you don't," he said, catching me as I teetered. "You haven't come this far to let a thug's assassin fly defeat you."

"Just for a few seconds," I mumbled. "Please, Sarc, let me sleep."

I let out an ear-piercing shriek as an ice-cold torrent poured down my body. In an instant, I was drenched from head to foot, and chilled to the bone, and wide awake again. Through my soaking tresses, I saw Sarc's apologetic expression. "All right, I'm awake now!" I barked.

"Good. Don't let anyone in." Sarc climbed nimbly through the open coach window, as the carriage jostled over the paved roads. Over the sound of gravel and stone under our wheels, the screams of the scattered pedestrians, and Sarc's quick footsteps on the carriage roof, the sound of the pursuing horses grew closer.

I spun to my right and saw a grey-uniformed Guardsman on horseback, aiming his pistol at me through the window.

I cast a shield instinctively against the carriage door. When the pistol fired, the shield shook and sent the discharge back, wounding the Guardsman and knocking him off his mount. Another pistol fired overhead, outside the carriage. A gloved hand diverted me, as it latched onto the frame of the carriage window to my left. A young Guardsman's face soon appeared in the open window. I shoved the heel of my hand against his chin. When that alone did not dislodge him, I heated the metal window frame until it was red-hot. He released it soon enough and fell back into the dust.

Out of the corner of my eye, I saw Sarc's boot connecting squarely with a Guardsman's jaw, knocking the man loose. There was a last pistol shot, then stillness, while the carriage itself maintained its steady speed.

"Sarc!" I cried. The hem of his jacket dropped into view, before Sarc grasped the window and slipped back inside the coach. The red stain by his shirt collar was glaring and fresh. "You've been shot!"

"I know," he said shortly, stripping off his jacket. "Give me a hand, before the wound seals." He unbuttoned the top of his shirt and pulled it back from his injury, and I saw the round pellet that was lodged in his collarbone. The hole was closing before my eyes. "How do we look, Mister Flyn?" he called with a grimace.

"All clear, Mister E'lan," came the cheerful reply.

With a spell, I pulled the shot free just as the hole disappeared. I exhaled my relief and conjured a wet cloth for Sarc. As he cleaned himself, I raked my cold, dripping hair out of my face. My fingers stopped at a stiff patch on the back of my head. When I pulled my hand away, it was stained rust and smelled of my own blood.

Sarc saw my surprise and turned me around to get a better look at the healed wound. "You don't remember getting hit?"

I shook my head. I didn't recall much of our earlier encounter with the thugs in the alley, but the leader's blood was still encrusted under my nails from when I had gouged out his magestone. My memory of the encounter otherwise seemed as dim as a faded dream. "They're all dead, aren't they. I killed them all, save one."

"I'm sorry," Sarc said. "I should've been the one to do it. I won't fail you again."

"You didn't fail me. I should be able to take care of myself." I combed my fingers through my damp hair to dry it and clean the blood from it. Without thinking, I reached out and stroked my hand across Sarc's punctured shirt, cleaning it and feeling its warmth and soft drape under my fingertips. "Besides, you're a healer. It's against your nature to harm anyone."

"What about you? Aren't you also a healer?"

"I don't often feel like one," I said, dropping my hand.

"I understand," he said. "That happens to all of us, at one time or another." He took the silk blanket that we had purchased in Bliis and wrapped it around my chilled shoulders, then reached into his satchel and pulled out a pair of black gloves. "Here, maybe these will help keep you warm."

The thin black leather molded perfectly to my fingers. "Thank you, these are beautiful," I said staidly, still thinking of what I had done.

"Too plain?" he asked, judging by my unenthusiastic response.

"No, of course not," I said, forcing a smile for his sake. "It was very thoughtful of you, really. They're perfect. Simple is always best." At Sarc's uncertain glance, I joked, "Well, you can clearly see from the clothes I wear that I'm not much for frills and froth."

"That's true," he mused. "How very non-elfyn of you."

"I'll take that as a compliment," I smiled, brushing back an errant curl. "I've never looked elfyn, so why should I think that way?" Not that it really mattered anymore, but I would've loved to see the Elders' faces when they learned that the idea of elfyn purity was a myth. "What?"

Sarc had an unguarded smile. "What a child you must have been," he said. "The boys must've flocked to you. Or avoided you like a pox."

My lips curled. "There was one boy who approached me, when I was thirteen. I had my hair under a scarf and was wearing Frost's cast-offs, so he mistook me from the back for her, then muttered an apology when he saw that it was me and ran off. That sums up my life nicely." My sister was the sweet-natured beauty, and I was the feral tomboy. Perhaps to spare me from distractions, or maybe humiliation, Clyara had removed me from the list of eligible maids before I was even considered on the market.

Sarc shook his head. "I recall dancing with an exquisite raven-haired maiden at a certain harvest celebration, and being the envy of every man in attendance."

I smiled at the memory, too. It didn't seem it in the moment, but it truly was a more innocent time. "If anyone envied you, it was for the fact that you were an old man dancing with women young enough to be your granddaughters."

"You remember it your way, I'll remember it mine. The fact is, if your life had been different, you could've claimed every heart in Moonteyre, and the bards of the valley would be composing ballads in your honor."

"I doubt it," I said. "I'd either be married or dead. Not much of a choice, and some would say they're the same thing."

His grin broadened at my cynicism. "Your life is what you make of it, and it's certainly not over after a mere twenty years. You should be looking forward to the years ahead." He read the unspoken question from my face. "I'm not as young as I seem, *Keeronae*. I don't plan for much anymore."

His voice was tired, and his smile waned. I picked up his hand and studied its smooth back against the deep black of my glove. The blue cabochon in his gold and black ring shone brilliantly. "You told me once that you were fifty years older than me, so you've lived a full life, yet you must be looking for something more. Just the fact that you're here with me, means that you still have some hopes for the future."

"Perhaps," he said. "When I was young, I planned to roam the world someday with a lovely princess by my side, and I would show her all that nature and man have to offer."

"So, what happened?" I teased, charmed by his romantic notion.

He slipped his hand from mine, and his smile returned, more cynical this time. "It didn't work out that way," he said, looking out the window. "She had a country to rule and married someone else."

"We've arrived," Flyn announced as we approached another settlement, one without walls. A sign greeted us at the limits: "Bin'vni a Ruvyna." It was a small town. Rather, it was more a sparse collection of quaint, two and three-story wooden houses and stores painted in pastel hues, nestled amongst towering trees. Its streets weren't even paved like those in Altaier and Bliis; that alone gave me a good feeling about Ruvyna. Ubiquitous flower boxes perched on windowsills and staircases, spilling over with ivy and lush blooms that filled the air with chromatic splashes and fragrance.

The hansom stopped in front of a two-story light blue house with white trim and a white porch. I followed Sarc out of the coach, captivated by the simple beauty around us. Ruvyna looked perfect in every way, except for the lack of people in the pristine streets.

"First time in Ruvyna, Miss?" Flyn asked as he carried our bags out and set them on the dusty ground.

"Yes, it is," I answered, peering into the windows of neighboring shops. They were dimmed, but furnished and seemingly in business.

"Ah. The locals are resting presently. They take a break in the afternoon, when it's the hottest. They'll be up shortly to reopen shop." He caught Sarc's attention with a wave and approached him. "Will that be all, Mister E'lan?"

"Yes, thank you, Mister Flyn. We'll find our own way from here. Please return the basket to Slither and tell him 'thanks' for the picnic, and give your father my regards." Sarc reached into his cloak and pulled out a fifty-imperi coin. Flyn received it gratefully and tipped his cap to us, before he climbed back on top of the hansom and left our service.

"Drives like a lunatic," Sarc muttered, watching him go, "but he makes better time than anyone I know. He's already saved us a half-day's travel."

Sarc slung our bags easily onto his shoulder and walked to the light blue house, and I followed close behind. Boxes of herbs lined the porch railing, and waist-high rosebushes stood guard on either side of the door. As was customary with elfyn homes, a small white ceramic tile was set into the frame above the door, with sharp blue enamel lettering that read: *Bin'vni.*

"Wait here," Sarc whispered, opening the door and disappearing inside, with the bottle of unopened ale from Bliis. I waited, studying the aromatic plants all around, and Sarc reemerged a moment later, empty-handed. "You can come in now."

Walking in the door, I was struck by old memories. The home was filled with books, bottles and jars... It was like Clyara's cottage, but brighter and far less cluttered, with everything set neatly into spaces against the walls and nothing on the floor. Sarc closed the door behind me, sealing us into a cocoon-like silence.

An aged, white-haired man stood in the alcove, facing me with blank, staring eyes on a thin, pale face. "Come closer, child," he said in elfyn. "Don't be afraid."

I wasn't afraid, just wary. He approached me with his hand outstretched, stopping when his fingertips brushed my hair. I glanced at Sarc, who stood next to me with his head bowed reverently. *Who is this, Sarc?*

"For shame, Alessarc!" the man rumbled, in a voice much bigger than I had expected from such a small frame. "Have you told her nothing of me?"

Sarc took the comment in stride and even allowed a small smile. "I wasn't sure of what you wanted her to know, *Keeron.*"

"Never stopped you before, boy," he muttered in reply. "Relax, child," he said to me in elfyn, "no harm will come to you under my roof." His touch had been so gentle that I had not realized that his fingers still rested on my head. He stroked my hair softly and steadily, and his fingers traced downward, along the edge of my jaw. "You are so young, my dear, and I must look hideously old to you."

He didn't look that old, now that I saw him closely. I would have estimated that he was in his eightieth year, unless he was a mage. In that case, who could guess? "No, you don't."

"I should," he insisted, dropping his hand. "I *am* hideously old." His pupils were so pale that they seemed almost invisible against the blue irises. His eyes opened and closed normally, but his eyes did not move. He was blind. "My dear girl, it's an honor to meet you at last. I've waited for you for so many years, I thought I'd never live to see the day, so to speak."

I smiled weakly. "I'm sorry, I still don't know who you are." Sarc's silence didn't give me any hints.

"I'm sure it'll come to you," he said patiently. "A couple of hints, perhaps? Like you, I'm a mage, trained in the arts in the elfyn tradition. It's my prophecy that you're helping to fulfill. My name," he said with a courteous bow, "is Junus Escan."

I flinched, and I might have gasped. *Junus Escan.* He was Sarc's *keeron*? The Imperial Advisor who exiled the Realm's mages to the Fringe. Junus was the sightless mage with the vision … whose daughter was Malya. *Hilafra.*

Junus chuckled. "So, you do know of me. Is that just my apprentice's doing, or from Aron's colorful account, too?"

"Aron's journal mentioned…" A young man, a humyn apprentice who stole the secrets of the elfyn sorcerers to take to the Realm. "You're Jyrun Uscari!" Junus grinned broadly at the name. Alive after all these years! The man who stood before me didn't seem old enough to be either Escan or Uscari, but I sensed no deceit from him.

"Not what you expected?" Junus guessed. "I was born in the year of the Emperors 800. I finished my two hundredth year this past spring. You were expecting me to be dead, perhaps?"

"Y-yes," I stammered artlessly, abashed at being so easily read by a blind man. "Aron wrote about exiling you. But that was so long ago…"

"It was," Junus said. "I assure you that I am who I claim to be."

We'll have time for questions later, Snowflake, Sarc said softly. "We're sorry to have interrupted your meditation, *Keeron,* but Flyn beat his record today. We can come back later if you wish."

Junus thinned his lips with disapproval. "Still the impudent brat, young E'lan. You've already interrupted me once, so are you thinking to do it a second time today? Who'd think an apprentice could be so rude to his old blind *keeron*? I can sit quietly by myself anytime I want, but I rarely ever get visitors. You wouldn't deprive an old man of company, would you?"

Junus snapped his fingers and a tray of biscuits appeared on the table, on a silver platter with a teapot and three cups. "I sense residual magic around you, child. You needn't keep colors up around me."

"My apologies, *Keeron* Escan." Feeling suddenly self-conscious, I dispelled my artificial colors and poured tea for the three of us. Not since my years with Clyara had I felt so scrutinized, and the back of my neck heated with my chagrin. *Watched by a blind man, that's a first.* Junus held out his open hand, and I placed the teacup in his hand with trembling fingers.

"How long have you …?"

"Been blind? Not long, just a few decades," he said, without sarcasm or regret. "My daughter did this some years ago to punish me for being a bad father. Malya always did have a quick temper, didn't she, Alessarc?"

Sarc half-smiled. "You would know better than me."

"She knows I'm here, but the sentinel spells keep her and her Imperial brutes out," Junus said to me. "The common offal stay away, out of fear and superstition, and the mage-hunting mercenaries stay clear, out of fear of *me*," he smiled darkly. "Ruvyna would be overrun by the trash of the Realm otherwise."

"How fortunate that your reputation precedes you," I said evenly. "You can hide here in safety while your daughter sends the rest of the Realm into ruin." I could not envision the frail-looking man before me overseeing the execution of hundreds of mages during the Years of Cleansing, but he certainly sounded like he could be Junus Escan. He was also Jyrun Uscari, who betrayed Aron's trust to bring magic back to the Realm, with whom Aron started the sequence of events that cost the lives of hundreds, if not thousands, of innocents.

"Hah, you are most definitely Clyara's apprentice!" he laughed, patting my cheek, before I even realized that his hand was by my face. "I wish you were my daughter, instead of that rotting corpse of a witch. She wasn't much better when she was alive."

I shook my head in dismay. "You're a seer, you must have known what was going to happen. Why didn't you stop her when you had the chance?"

"We did what we could," he said, more seriously. "I warned Adeliaraine, and she protected her Realm as well and as long as she could. I warned Augus, and fool that he was, he thought he could prevent it through compromise. My apprentices and I," he said wearily, gesturing in Sarc's direction, "tried everything to thwart her ascension, but in the end, fate will not be averted. And, it can be argued, some catastrophes are best left to run their course, so that people can learn from their mistakes."

I had not intended to enter a philosophical debate with him, much less try to sway him from his mindset, but I found I couldn't help myself. "Your presumption, *Keeron*, is that there will be people left after such a catastrophe to learn from its lessons."

He chuckled again, with more warmth. "People are the vermin of this world, *Keeronae*. As a whole, we will not be easily exterminated. You, as an elfyn, are living proof of that."

I looked over at Sarc, who looked amused by our exchange. *Did he just compare me to vermin?*

"Only in the best possible way, dear little girl. You seem resilient and resourceful, although your environment and choice of company are sometimes questionable. You came through Bliis today, Alessarc, if that pungent tang on that bottle of ale is any indication. Let me guess: you had to see a patient. And, why did you bring the *Keeronae* by coach, anyway?" he demanded of Sarc. "Where's your amulet?"

"You've never given me one, *Keeron*," Sarc replied.

"Pardon me for overestimating your resourcefulness," Junus replied acridly. "I would've thought you could find a way to craft one of your own, or steal one from me. I am blind, you know."

I sat stock-still, uncertain of how I was to respond, if at all. Sarc's bemused smile contrasted starkly with his *keeron*'s indignant glower. "I don't find that your blindness has ever affected your powers of perception, *Keeron*."

Junus harrumphed at Sarc's easy acquiescence. "You say that with your tongue firmly in cheek, no doubt, but at least you don't take me for a fool like others I could name. I only regret that I can't see the *Keeronae* for myself, after all these years of waiting. I do smell mountain jasmine on her sweet skin. And orange blossom … no, honey. Her voice is richer than I would've expected, older than her years. Is she as lovely as she sounds, Alessarc?"

Sarc gave me a careful, assessing glance before he replied, "I wouldn't describe her as 'lovely', exactly."

I flushed but bit down on my lip to keep silent, and out of the corner of my eye, I saw Junus's eyes narrow.

"'Lovely' is a word to describe clear spring days, and tidy homes like yours, *Keeron*. The *Keeronae* is more like the first ray of sunlight piercing the black sky after a hurricane, or the view of the valley from the summit of Ajlekuun on a bright autumn morning—the proper word escapes me at the moment, but I would never call her 'lovely.'"

I saw the trace of a genuine smile on Junus's face before it vanished. "A simple 'yes' would've sufficed," he murmured, sipping from his cup. "He gets that tendency for drama and hyperbole from his elfyn blood. Has your hair turned silver, finally?"

I was surprised by the question. "Yes, it has. How did you—"

"Good, finally." In the next breath, he said, "It's his sentimental elfyn side that ignores me when I tell him to stay out of Bliis, regardless of the quality of its ale."

"And you would have berated me as a coward had I brought you anything less," Sarc responded, taking his *keeron*'s topic switches in stride. "And you're right, I did need to see a patient."

"Knew it," Junus barked. "You care too much. Make your patients come to you, maybe you'll stay alive a little longer. And if they're from Bliis, have them bring you ale, or better yet, have it delivered directly to me."

Sarc shrugged helplessly at me, as if to say, *No point in arguing, ever.* "As fascinating as this conversation is, would you please excuse us?" Sarc said gently to me. "I need to discuss something with my *keeron*."

Junus sighed, "Impatient to the last. I don't think he ever makes social visits, at least not to me," he whispered aside to me, squeezing my hand gently. His was a warm hand, withered, spotted and soft with age.

"For the elfyn, all visits are social, by definition," I whispered back, slipping my fingers from his grasp.

He patted my head a last time, making a sound somewhere between a laugh and a cough.

I recast my wren-brown colors and left to give Sarc and his *keeron* some privacy. The town was reawakening, little by little. The hottest hours of the day had passed, and the shopkeepers reopened their doors for business. People reemerged from their houses to bask in the afternoon sun.

I passed the shops with keen interest, taken in by the brilliant colors and bold displays of artistry. The shopkeepers seemed welcoming enough, with wide toothy smiles, but they were far more reserved than their counterparts in Bliis. They moved at an unhurried, placid pace, greeting me and each other with seemingly genuine civility. Ruvyna seemed to belong more in the Dark Lands than in the Realm.

A grey-headed woman who looked older than even Junus, rocked in a chair on the porch of a linen shop. She spoke the common tongue with a lilting elfyn accent. "Come inside, child. You're sure to find something you like."

I shook my head with a genial smile. I had had enough of going into strange places without knowing what to expect. "I don't have a lot of money."

"Money! You don't need money to appreciate beautiful things." She began to rise from her seat precariously, and I rushed forward to catch her in case she tottered. Once I stepped foot onto her porch, she steadied and grinned, "Since you're here, why don't you go on in and look around?"

I was won over by her gregariousness, and I was glad for it when I entered the teeming shop. It was filled to the rafters with clothes, linens, earthenware and other household items, plus some more whimsical items like wooden dolls and toys. The designs and engravings on most of the items were distinctively elfyn, such as those decorating an etched reed flute dangling from one of the many wall hooks. It reminded me of the one we buried with my father, that he had used to teach me to play. At the other end of the shop, an old marriage sash was preserved under glass, its intricate, swirling threadwork still vibrant against the yellowed muslin.

The old woman shuffled in, her long grey hair falling in waves to her waist. She was slender, and slightly hunched. "That was my sash, woven by the women of my family for me when I married into the North Woods folk."

"It's beautiful." My eyes fell on the flute again.

She noticed the direction of my stare. "Do you like it? I found it on my doorstep here one day. Never found out who made it," she laughed, and for a moment she was young again. "Ruvyna is full of artisans and mystics."

"It's remarkable," I admired. "I haven't seen its like in years." The night Frost was married, to be exact, being played by a master.

"Do you play?" she asked, picking it gingerly from the hook.

"I used to play, but very little," I said, remembering when Winter taught me. I was barely ten at the time.

"Let's see what you remember," she smiled, pressing it into my hands. When I balked, she closed her hands around mine, keeping the instrument in my grip. "Grant an old woman a modest request."

"You wouldn't ask if you knew how badly I play." I held it with stiff fingers and sighed. When did I play last? The night before we buried Da. My fingers relaxed, I closed my eyes and took one deep breath.

I began to play the first song that came to me, which was about a Moonteyre woman on her way to reunite with her lover on the bank of the Yirae. The tones resonated through me and through the flute, as though we were one being. With every breath I expelled into the reed, the melody filled my head and coaxed my thoughts towards home, and when I stopped, I discovered that my eyes were damp.

The old woman was moved, too. "That brings back memories, child. I come from Moonteyre, also. The most beautiful place in the world," she sighed.

"Why did you leave the Dark Lands, then?" I asked.

"For a chance to live without fear," she said. "Hundreds of elfyn were killed and maimed, my husband and son included. Before then, I would've never dreamed of leaving home, but it seemed better to face the unknown perils outside the Lands, than to wait for certain death within. Some of us only came as far as the Fringe, some settled here in Ruvyna. Once we came, we realized that the plague was here, also. When Junus came to Ruvyna, he told us the truth about the healing magic, of the conflict between Malya and Clyara. He swore to keep Ruvyna safe, as a haven for all the elfyn who wish to stay in the Realm."

"As a penance for the Cleansing?" I asked.

"That, I wouldn't know," she said. "I have only known Junus for as long as he has been in Ruvyna, and for what he cares to share of himself. To all of us here, Junus has always been kind and wise, a gentleman of his word. He wanted to keep as many of us safe as possible, after his pleas to Malya and Clyara went unheeded."

I said out of deference to my dead mistress, "Clyara thought she had no choice in the matter. She thought the elfyn would be destroyed without her involvement and efforts to keep the elfyn in the Dark Lands hidden." I needed to say it, if only to try to convince myself.

The old woman looked at me squarely. "You know about Clyara, then?"

"I discovered her secrets, yes," I replied, careful not to reveal myself. "The others will also learn the truth, in time. Already, back home, the humyn have blended with the elfyn, into one community with common goals." *And common enemies.*

"Humyn and elfyn together, who would have thought it?" she sighed. "When I was your age, few of us ever admitted to believing that the humyn existed, and people were still afraid of outsiders. When Clyara appeared in the 940's, without kin and without possessions, we in Moonteyre were the only ones to accept her."

"A few people are still slow to change," I admitted, remembering Tracker, "but the rest are no longer afraid. They know that they're not alone."

"I'm glad, my dear. One should never hide from the truth, however terrible," she said. "Well, don't let me keep you from your business. Come back whenever you feel the need to reminisce." I held the flute out to her, but she shook her head. "I told you, you don't need money to appreciate beauty. Accept it as a gift, child. It belongs with you more than in a dusty old shop."

Sarc and Junus were waiting outside the old *keeron*'s house when I returned. Sarc was stroking the mane of a massive, coal-black mare that seemed to listen intently to his whispers. Sarc looked at my new flute with interest.

"It's a gift," I replied, tucking it into my satchel behind the saddle. "I was just in the shop across the way, chatting with someone about the way things used to be."

"Mistress Belladonna is still at it, I see," Sarc sighed, slipping a small black pouch into the deepest of his pockets, close to his heart. He turned towards the venerated lady, who was rocking in her porch seat once more, and he executed a very formal bow, which caused her to let loose a girlish guffaw. She blew Sarc a kiss and waved her hand dismissively for his cheek.

"You best leave before she empties half her shop for you," Junus advised dryly. "As it is, she will most likely take it upon herself to visit me this evening and recount the day's excitement in excruciating detail."

"It's good for you to have company, *Keeron*," Sarc said. "This way, you won't have to drink the ale by yourself."

Before Junus could respond, I set my hand gently on his arm and said, "It was an honor to meet you, *Keeron* Escan."

When he turned his unblinking eyes to me, his expression softened. "The honor was mine," he said, laying his hand on top of mine. "I hope the next time we meet, we can speak at length. May the stars guide you both, *Keeronae*."

Chapter 18: Home by the Sea

Once we left Ruvyna, our horse picked up her pace without much coaxing from Sarc. I opted to sit behind Sarc in the saddle, and I started to regret my decision when our horse broke into her first trot, but I remembered quickly how to stay upright. At the first lurch, I let out an unseemly squeak, and Sarc slowed us to a stop.

One look at my face, and he realized. "You've never ridden with someone else."

"Is it that obvious?"

"You look terrified," he said. "You should've said something, if you preferred having your own mount..."

"It's fine," I said. "It's just something else I'll have to get used to. I'd rather not waste any more time."

Sarc looked unconvinced, but he clicked his tongue to signal the horse to continue. "We'll try to make the best of it, then. If you feel yourself moving too much, just hold onto me."

Once we resumed, our mount cantered tirelessly across the plains, almost joyfully, barely breaking into a pant, and Sarc seemed accustomed to her jostling gait. I held onto him for balance, perhaps too tightly at times, and I learned quickly to lean forward against him to lessen the discomfort. Our mount slowed her pace once we reached the rougher terrain closer to the mountains and ascended the rocky slopes with nimble, confident steps.

With jagged rock spires standing menacingly erect all around us, bare of vegetation or even soil, it was obvious why the ridge was named the Devil's Spine, but our mount picked her way along the path with little consternation, as though she had traveled this way often. While the ride through the barren ridge was slow, it would've been impossible with a coach. The path was far too narrow and steep for anything but a single animal. To avoid the view of the plutonic spikes jutting up at us from the bottom of the ravines, I watched the setting sun instead, as we proceeded westward. The fading sunlight caught in the flecks of the volcanic stone, lending to them a vivid, eerie orange glow that was reminiscent of lava.

"She'll be ten next month." Sarc's voice startled me, although I had been fully aware of his nearness throughout our ride. Now that our mare was traveling along a sheltered section of the Devil's Spine that was not buffeted by constant winds, it was quiet enough to have a verbal conversation. I relaxed my arms around his waist. "Her name is Brahn, by the way."

"That's an unusual name," I remarked.

"Her namesake was an unusual woman. How are you feeling now?"

"About the ride? Much better now, thank you," I said. I hadn't been on the back of a horse since I was a child, and I was rediscovering the sense of calm from being close to an equine. "Brahn's very gentle."

"When she wants to be," Sarc said indulgently, patting her neck. Brahn snorted her reply. "She has her grandmother's spirit." He pointed to the hill ahead of us. "Just over that, then we'll settle for the night in Mione," Sarc said, watching the sunset with me. "Tomorrow morning, we'll set out to sea, for three more days, if the winds are with us. Our destination isn't far from there."

"Do you travel this way often?"

"Now and again. My vocation takes me all sorts of places."

"Like Bliis?"

"If there's a need, yes."

"I didn't realize mind healing was so much in demand," I remarked. "It's a wonder more people don't practice it." Sarc shook his head. "Yes, I'm sure *Keeron* Junus was very selective about teaching it. Still, others must know it." As obscure as regular mages were, Sarc was even more of a novelty. "Did Junus have other apprentices?"

"Certainly, Junus had many, but few who were ever taught mind healing."

"Like Jaryme Thorne."

"How did you guess?"

"He's very proficient with charm spells, and I sense that there's something between the two of you. Maybe some rivalry left over from your apprentice days?" I ventured, as a cold mountain gust blew against us.

"Something like that." Sarc reached into his satchel and pulled out the silk blanket. He shook it out with one hand, careful not to startle the horse, and passed it back over his shoulder to me.

"Something to do with Jeysen?" I asked, pulling the blanket around myself.

"Not in the way you may be thinking. Jeysen and I have been friends since we were boys, and Jaryme's never shown anything but contempt for me, but Jeysen's endured his brother's arrogance and ire as long as he can remember. But if not for Jeysen, I would've gotten myself killed long ago fighting with Jaryme. I guess you could say that Jeysen tempers me."

Jaryme's warnings about Jeysen echoed in my head, cautioning me to the possibility that Jeysen was using Sarc. "Do you think that Jeysen wants to be Emperor?"

"Jeysen, an Emperor?" Sarc laughed. "Not unless the fate of the Realm depended on it, and even then, he'd have to think hard about it. He enjoys his seclusion far too much."

"But he does venture out from time to time to rescue damsels from certain peril, it would seem. He's already saved me twice."

"Well, Jeysen's not so much a hermit as he is a curmudgeon. He's been much happier since he faked his own death. He still goes out and does what he must, but he travels in anonymity. Like Junus, he loves the idea of humanity, he just doesn't enjoy being around people most of the time."

"What a shame," I murmured, too quickly, once again.

"Oh?" Sarc chuckled at my lamenting tone. "You have noticed the handsome young prince, then."

"I'm just thinking of the future for the Realm once Malya is gone." I tightened my grip around Sarc and whispered dreamily, "Young men don't interest me, or don't you recall?" I enjoyed feeling Sarc's laughter through my embrace, and hearing his voice so light and unconcerned.

"Jeysen's older than I am, just slightly. And there's always Junus…"

"Why did he ask about my hair turning white?" I asked, recalling our strange, brief conversation.

"When he first saw you in his visions," he said, "he was quite struck by your silver hair. He thought Clyara was mad when she told him that your hair was black, and she had to assure him that the silver would come later."

"Much later. My sister and my father's hair had both turned entirely white when they were children. I was thinking that it would never change."

"It probably helped to keep you hidden," Sarc said. "Anyone that Malya sent would have looked for someone of your age, the way Junus envisioned you. Your hair started changing quickly after Clyara was gone, so I wouldn't be surprised if she had suppressed the color somehow, to keep you safe. There's nothing she wouldn't have done to protect you."

By the time we reached the town outskirts, the sky had turned to indigo. The tiny, close-set buildings twinkled with the occasional lamp. Even from a distance, we could see hundreds of lights from the ships that dotted the shore and from the piers of Mione, still bustling with activity.

Inland, the town itself was homely. The buildings and streets were utilitarian, devoid of ornamentation and color. The bracing air, however, was rich and aromatic with the invigorating combination of brine and lumber.

"It's small even compared to Ruvyna," Sarc said. "There isn't much to see, except for the ocean. The pink beach is especially pretty at dawn. Most of the people here work in shipbuilding, some are sailors who transport along the coast, mainly ramsblood wine shipped from further inland."

"You sound like a guide book. Is there any town along this way that you don't know?"

"Maybe, but I certainly wouldn't take you there. Until recently, I wouldn't have brought you here to Mione either, except that the Empress hasn't commissioned any new ships as of late."

"So, we shouldn't encounter many Guardsmen here."

"That's the hope."

We stopped in front of a public house, where other horses were tethered. It was two stories tall, brightly lit throughout, with an old wooden sign out front that was splintered and rendered illegible by the elements. Sarc dismounted and helped me down from Brahn before he tied her to the post with the others. "Thank you, Brahn," he said to the mare, "I'll visit as soon as I can."

She brayed doubtfully and turned her attention to an adolescent boy who emerged from the tavern and tipped his cap to Sarc and me. "Good evening, Miss E'lan … Mister E'lan. It's good to see that you've arrived safely. Are you done with Brahn for tonight?"

Sarc smiled at the boy's practiced formality and nodded. "Yes, thank you, Rhys. Is your father inside?"

"Yes, sir," the boy said, as he took Brahn's reins in hand. He produced an apple from his pocket for her, which she gnawed with interest. "He's expecting you."

"'Miss E'lan?'" I asked under my breath.

Sarc stopped and looked me over for a second, to check that my brown shades were intact. "That's what the boy said. Come on, Sister."

Sister? I followed him closely into the tavern, my legs unsteady from our long ride, and my eyes needing to adjust to the sudden light. The tables were crowded with rowdy, half-drunk patrons, but none of the furniture or customers seemed in any immediate peril. Sarc sat me down at the counter and went to speak with the barkeep, who greeted him warmly with a drink ready.

I glanced at a wall map of the Realm. We had traveled almost two hundred kilometers since our morning start in Altaier, further west than north, through terrain that looked nearly impassable on paper.

The hair on my neck rose, as someone's eyes settled on me.

"Let me buy you a drink, Miss." A tall, burly man took the stool next to me and looked me over with a lustful grin, his gaze finally settling on my bodice. Each of his forearms looked about the size of my head. "A delicate little thing like yourself shouldn't be left alone in a dump like this."

"Thank you for the offer, but no." I made a move to get up, only to have the man latch his huge hand on top of mine. His paw was warm and clammy, but the leather of my glove repelled his dampness admirably. It did nothing for the sour stink of alcohol on his breath, however. "Let go, please."

"You're elfyn, aren't you?" he asked sinuously. "I haven't seen much of your kind around here lately. I suppose you think you're too good for a filthy humyn like me. Well, I'd bet a few minutes with me would change your mind about that—"

"Excuse me," Sarc interrupted. He locked his hand on the man's shoulder, which lingered just a few inches above his chin. "She's asked you to remove your hand." The brute tried futilely to shake Sarc's grip, and Sarc seemed amused by the effort. "You should really consider it, Ox."

A moment of lucidity finally pierced the man's drunken haze, as he appeared to recognize Sarc finally. Ox lifted his meaty mitt and dropped his eyes, backing away from the counter and bowing to me with a muttered apology, before slinking off towards a corner. Several patrons stared after him, and us, but only briefly. I dried my glove and shuddered.

What is it with you and drunken men? Sarc did not take the vacant seat.

Very funny, 'Brother.' "Where do we go, now?" I wasn't at ease in these public spaces. There were too many eyes on us.

Sarc picked up on my mood when he pulled me to my feet. He stayed close to me, shooting glances here and there to check that we were unobserved, then showed me a small key. *Settle in for the night.*

Our lodging for the night was down the road from the pub, less than a kilometer from the beach. Sarc brought along a small lantern to illuminate the sandy path, but it was flat and even enough to traverse without the extra light. We reached the road turning up to the house just as the rain started. Walking up to the house, we were serenaded by the gentle drizzle and the rolling waves, and I was disappointed that the night wasn't clear enough for me to get my first peek at the ocean.

The house was boxy, with small windows and a rough stone exterior, just like the others around it. Ours, however, was the only one with wild roses and sea holly growing around it. The flowers imparted a fruity, spicy sweet scent that dominated the saline and lumber smells that were so pervasive in Mione. An assortment of smooth stones, decorated with carved runes and glyphs, lay scattered across the ground.

"Protection spells?" I asked.

"Just sentries," he said. "I like to know when visitors come."

Sarc unlocked the door and let me enter first. The cool air was graced with the faded aroma of juniper, cypress and sandalwood. Sarc passed the lantern to me and passed easily through the dark interior, casting magical flares to light the corners. He lit another, larger hurricane lamp that stood on a counter at the far end of the room and added its soft glow and warmth to the open, airy space. As I set the smaller lamp on the counter next to the larger one, I pulled out the old, embroidered handkerchief that I kept in my pocket, to dab the rain from my face.

The house was modest and comfortably worn. A chair upholstered with black brocade rested against the left wall, and a wrought iron daybed strewn with books stood opposite, under one of the windows. A table fashioned from a wooden crate sat in the middle of the room. In the partially-obscured far corner lit by the hurricane lamp, was the kitchen. The shadows and a staircase to my right obstructed my view down the hall, but I caught the smell of old paper and vellum from that direction.

Sarc placed our bags on the daybed between piles of books and magically closed the door behind me. "It's not much to look at, but it's home."

"You live here?" I noted the personal effects scattered throughout. A small red sculpture sat on the kitchen counter, and a woman's portrait hung over a mantle. A muffler and a tunic lay strewn on the floor before Sarc scooped them up and dropped them on the daybed, along with his jacket, on his way to the kitchen.

"Every once in a while. It was my father's summer home, when he wasn't teaching or dispensing advice."

"He was a counselor, then?"

"One could say that," he said, picking pans and dishes from his cupboards. "After Jeysen and I joined the Guard, my father and the Emperor became acquainted. He never served in any official capacity, but my father was always one to offer his opinion, whether or not it was solicited." He smiled, noticing my interest in the portrait over the fireplace. "Isn't she beautiful there?"

"She's stunning." She peered out from the wall with a coy expression, her brown eyes wide and trusting, her dark curls piled on her head elegantly. A crimson stole draped around her, leaving her golden shoulders bare.

Sarc simply nodded and disappeared behind the counter, leaving me alone with the portrait. "You can drop your glamour, if you'd like," he called, "and make yourself at home."

Another of his female friends, perhaps? I thought with a slight pang of envy. I shook my head to clear that thought from my mind. *What reason do I have to be jealous?* My relationship with Sarc, if it could even be called that, was strictly one of necessity. When he had chased off the brute in the tavern, he had done it to accommodate "the Protector," nothing more. *What reason do I have, to think otherwise?*

At the sound of clanging metal, I followed Sarc into the kitchen, where he was surrounded by an assortment of spice bottles and fresh produce. At the opposite end of the counter was a small towel, draped over the edge of a basin of steaming water. "For you, in case you wanted to wash up," he said, his attention focused on a teapot that he was filling from a kettle.

I reverted my colors back to my own and washed my hands and face, then helped set the table with dishes and cutlery that Sarc had laid out. He brought the pot of tea and a beautiful arrangement of fruit and vegetables, as well as a basket of freshly-baked bread. He set down a glowing glass lamp on the table and pulled out a chair for me. "*Keeronae* Snowfleece of Moonteyre, as you are my guest, everything in my home is yours."

I settled into the seat and waited for Sarc to sit before I picked a blackberry from the tray and savored its tart succulence. "'Snowfleece', now, is it? I was starting to think that you didn't know my name at all."

Sarc raised his eyebrow, as he poured tea for both of us. "How can I miss a name like that? Someone in your family obviously had a sense of humor."

"That would be my father. While we're on the topic of names, *Alessarc E'lan*, what does the 'N' represent?" I asked, holding up the folded handkerchief, with the initials "A.N.E." still crisply darned into one corner.

"I can't believe you still have that," he said sheepishly. "My middle name is Nahe. Doesn't it mean 'sunburned' or something equally precious?"

I chuckled. "It means: 'touched by the sun.' It's very elfyn."

"It was my grandfather's name." He nodded to the woman's portrait on the wall. "Mother insisted."

"Mother?" I swallowed. I felt awful about my pettiness a moment ago.

"Her name was Sariah. My grandfather came from the North Woods, but he raised his family near the Red Lake. My father was born and raised here in the Realm and managed to find his way to the Dark Lands, where he met my mother."

"You're a mongrel?" I said in jest.

"Rumor is that we all are, to varying degrees," he grinned.

"Cheers to that." I served myself a portion of the vegetables, savoring the aroma of the fresh herbs. "Did you conjure this?"

"No, actually. I sent word ahead that I would be coming home, and my friend stocked fresh ingredients for me. It would've been fresher, had we arrived last night, as originally planned," he said pithily.

"But you cooked this?" I asked, hesitating before the first bite.

"Are you surprised that I could?"

"A little," I admitted, then took a nibble. It was savory with a sweet hint of juice, its firm texture yielding to the gentlest bite. It was a modest, humble offering, but after the day's travel, it was just perfect. Across the table from me was a paper-lined box filled with what looked like small balls of mud. *Forget the food.* "Are those truffles?"

Sarc nudged the box closer to me with a mischievous grin. "Isn't there a rule about not having dessert before finishing dinner?"

"It's a stupid rule." My dish abandoned, I took a morsel from the box and savored it, letting it warm and melt on my tongue. "You made these, too?"

"Not this batch, but I could, with the right tools and ingredients."

"You could give up healing and become a confectioner," I teased.

"Perhaps, if I took more after Nahe," he said. "The techniques he learned from his adopted mother, but his perfectionism and gift for alchemy he inherited from both of his birth parents." He watched my expression carefully, as though waiting for a reaction of some sort. "Clyara really didn't tell you much about her life, did she?"

"What does your grandfather have to do with..." I stopped breathing for a moment. "Clyara was your great-grandmother?" He waited for me to finish the puzzle on my own. "But she never married. When was your grandfather born?"

"He was born in the year 881, when Clyara was forty-one."

"She said she killed Aron because he wanted her to give up something," I recalled. "He didn't want her to keep the baby?"

"Aron didn't want a child at all," Sarc clarified. "He even accused her of betraying him with another man, to deny his role. In the end, he raised his hand to her once too often, and Clyara did what she needed to, to save herself and her son."

"It's strange what Clyara considered note-worthy for her journal," I said, taking a drink of tea. "She made no mention of any of it."

"It was one year's time out of a very long life," Sarc said. "Clyara did agree with Aron that she couldn't give a child a normal life, so she gave him up almost as soon as he was born, so that he didn't have to live in a cave."

"Nothing's worse than living in a cave," I joked. "I should know."

My quip sounded harsher than intended, and Sarc looked pained.

He and I didn't speak for a moment and just listened to the rainfall against the windows and roof. I recalled many nights I spent as a young girl, wrapped in a blanket on my father's lap, falling asleep to the sound. Rainfall was among the things I missed most while I was in my Haven.

"It gets very quiet in the Haven sometimes," I said at last. "It almost feels like a tomb."

"I'm sorry."

"Sorry that I was trapped there, or sorry that you were the one who delivered me?" I said, with more bitterness than I realized I felt. I closed my eyes and took a breath. "It was almost three years without daylight,

Sarc. And it would've been even longer, had I remained. Without seasons, without rain, without another living soul for company..."

"I know," he said, his head bowed. "But it was necessary."

"It was necessary to isolate me?" I demanded.

He seemed ready with an immediate answer, but he reconsidered and took a second to collect his words. "It was necessary because Clyara and Junus wanted you to have more time to prepare," he said finally. "They chose a location that would be free of any distraction, even companionship. I disagreed but was overruled," he said with a frown.

"There were days when I thought I would be trapped there forever, and no one would ever know if I had perished."

"You wouldn't have perished. I wouldn't have allowed it."

"How could you know? You said yourself that we no longer have a bond."

"You may have lived there by yourself, but your guardians never left you alone," he said. "We left spells and sensors, devices and machines, everywhere throughout the Haven. Had you been in distress, I would have retrieved you, no matter what Clyara had wanted, but you thrived on your own. If you hadn't found your way out, I would have come for you."

I believed him. While I was still learning about Sarc, one thing I noticed was that he rarely lied. He was evasive at times, but he was always sincere, if not entirely truthful. "Devices and machines," I grimaced, "including that infernal thing with the wires and headpiece. That was your contribution, too, I assume? It certainly doesn't strike me as being Clyara's kind of trinket." I shuddered, recalling the hours of headaches that often followed the lessons administered by the device.

"Something I picked up during my travels, just like chocolate. I could have either left you the trainer, or more textbooks to study," he said, absently levitating the red clay sculpture from the counter to his open hand. "That would have left less time for you to devote to your other instruction. It's a form of cheating, but I exploited every advantage I could."

"It was effective, just uncomfortably rigorous," I admitted, watching him stroke the smooth lines of the sculpture. "Did you make that?" I asked. "Please don't take this the wrong way, but what is it supposed to be? It looks like it has wings, but it's not a bird, nor a bat."

Sarc passed it to me for my study. "You're right, it's neither. It's a ship for traveling amongst the stars."

"Fine, don't tell me. Serves me right for prying," I laughed, admiring the sleek, fluid lines of the vaguely avian shape before passing it back to him. "Next, you'll tell me that you've ridden in one of those?"

"In a larger version, of course," he teased, flying the strange "starship" sculpture back and forth between us like a moth. With a flick of his

210

finger, he sent the sculpture back to the counter, where it hovered briefly before settling softly on the countertop. "I've traveled here and there. Let's just leave it at that."

"Good enough for now. Any other secrets I should know?" I asked.

"Perhaps," he said slyly. "All in good time."

He gestured to his satchel on the daybed and levitated it to his lap, pulling from it a large paper-wrapped bundle, which he offered to me.

"What is this?" I asked, feeling the heft of the package.

"A gift."

"Another one?" As I folded back the layers of paper, I felt the warmth of the bundle. Finally, I saw the rich, night-black fabric of the cloak, the edge of its silk-lined hood trimmed lavishly with gold and silver embroidery. The color of the cloth was so deep, so pure, that no light reflected from its surface. "Oh, Sarc. It's ... *naehin*." I could think of no word in the common tongue to aptly describe its beauty.

I jumped to my feet and wrapped myself in the seductive softness of the cloak. I turned around for him to see its cut and color on me. "You shouldn't have," I said, luxuriating in its sensuous folds.

He sat back. "I had to. Your barbaric treatment of my old cloak was more than I could bear," he said lightly. "More importantly, *Keeronae*, you are a lady in manner and by reputation, if not by birthright. It's time that you had some clothes that befit you."

He got to his feet and cast a cleaning spell to clear the dishes. "We're going to have another long day tomorrow, and it's getting late. Let me show you to your room."

I shed my cloak and folded it carefully before setting it on the daybed. "I thought I was sleeping down here?"

"Now, I wouldn't be a very good host, if I allowed that," he said. He directed me up the stairs, into a small, well-kept chamber with mahogany furnishings. The sweet aroma of sandalwood was subtle but distinct.

I touched the dark wood adorning the familiar four-poster bed and the ivory-colored linens. "You summoned this for me the night before my adjustment."

"Yes," he said, pleased that I remembered. "It was the end of a long night, and it was just easier for me to summon something than to conjure it from stones and dirt. It was just sitting here unused, anyway." He set my bag by the door and materialized a towel and a standing water basin for me.

On the dresser was an array of personal items: a brush and comb, a straight-edge razor, a couple of lengths of black silk and muslin and a few jars and bottles of various salves and oils. As well as other objects that I couldn't begin to describe, much less name: more souvenirs from his extensive travels, perhaps. "Is this your room? You don't have to give up your chamber for me. The daybed downstairs is fine."

"Stay. I'll be next door, if you need anything," he said, knocking on the common wall. "Good night, 'Fleece. I'll see you in the morning." He bowed his head to me and closed the door behind him.

Shadowy ghouls were circling closer around me, hordes of them, some misshapen beyond humyn semblance, enmeshed into an impenetrable mass of flesh and bone. I recognized some faces to be those of the men that I had killed in Bliis, returning to seek their vengeance. They pressed against me, pulling my arms and hair in all directions. They tried to lure me into their midst with hideous, bloody offerings, including limbs that they had cut from their own bodies. All they wanted, they said, were the gems. The ghouls changed into Guardsmen, who descended upon me savagely, gouging me with their claw-like fingers and knives. They retreated, turning on each other for possession of my gem that they ripped from my chest. I looked down at the gaping chasm between my breasts where my gem had been uprooted, and I wept knowing that I would die in pain, and alone.

I awoke to the sounds of my own whimpering cry. I sat up and reassured myself. It was just a dream. Still, I placed my hand against my chest to feel that my gem was still there. My heart beat rapidly, in time with the lashing rain. I tried to calm myself, burying my head against my drawn-up knees and fighting the temptation to call Sarc.

The last time I had slept in that bed was three years ago, unaware of what was to become of me. I was unaware that a woman named Renay in Altaier was plotting a gruesome surprise for Sarc's return. I was oblivious to how inextricable my life would be from his, at least for a while. I was ignorant of the intimate familial ties he had to Clyara and her master. I had yet to discover the conflicting emotions that arose from taking another person's life.

I summoned into my hand the magestone that I had taken from the fledgling mage in Bliis that morning. It was crusted with dry blood and fibers from the inside of my dress pocket. Was what I did so different from what Junus Escan effected during the Cleansing? I, too, had confiscated a magestone from someone that I had deemed unworthy. I tossed the magestone onto the nightstand and lay back down. It had been a matter of survival, and I was certain that the mage whose gem I had reclaimed would've killed Sarc and me without losing sleep, as I was doing.

In the stillness, some voice gnawed at my subconscious. There was no physical movement that I could sense in the room, nor was there any telepathy, but I sensed distress, coming from the other side of the wall.

I threw aside the covers and listened at the wall, but I could hear nothing. I opened my mind and felt an intense but unfocused pain, a deep-

212

rooted kind of suffering that was not tied to any single source, but tangible enough that Sarc's mind was filled with it. I rushed through the wall and saw him clearly by the glow of the lamp still lit on the nightstand. He lay still, but his brow was deeply furrowed, and he was speaking in murmurs too low to understand. He was tangled in his sheet from the waist down, as though he had been sleeping fitfully.

I sat on the edge of the wide bed, wiped the perspiration from his face with my sleeve and took his hand in mine. *Wake up, aylonse.* "Sarc?" My voice was deafening to me in the midst of the silence, but he did not wake. Seeing that he was still deep in his nightmare, I placed my palm on his brow and tried to see what he was dreaming.

I fell back with a scream. My mind was engulfed in thoughts, memories, fears, ecstasies—none of which were mine. Or Sarc's, for that matter: one moment, I was a young man embracing the woman that I wanted to marry; the next, I was a toddler boy watching his parents drown, then I was a little girl hugging my beautiful, weeping mother for the very last time. I was a man looking down from the edge of a cliff, petrified that I might fall, and I was an old woman near the end of my years, missing my husband who had died decades before, yet not quite recalling his face. The memories were incredibly, painfully vivid, some terrifying, all belonging to other people.

I opened my eyes but only saw more to confuse my mind. I had clarity for just a second, when Sarc grabbed hold of me to keep me still, as I fought screaming to get away from him. I was sixteen, and a man came into my room while I was sleeping. He was lying on top of me, whispering words of love and stroking my golden hair. It was Jeysen, and his face was beginning to blur ...

The vision was gone, along with all the others. Illuminated by the lamplight were only Sarc and me, sitting on the woolen rug next to the bed. He brushed my hair back from my face. "Inquisitive little Snowball," he said gently. "Are you all right?"

My heart was still beating so fast, I had to catch my breath, but I nodded. "You were in pain, I just wanted to help." My head was clear of visions, but pounding wickedly. "I've never felt anything like it before. What was that?"

He got to his feet and pulled me up, with one hand on the sheet wrapped around his waist. "Nothing of concern, just some stray thoughts and memories from the healing. Junus taught me how to purge most of them and bury the rest, but sometimes the latent ones emerge when I sleep."

"You take the memories into yourself, like wounds?" I marveled.

"Not exactly," he said, going to the washbasin to splash his face with the sheet tucked around his waist. "With all of us, our memories help to shape who we are, for better or worse. But some experiences are too painful to revisit alone, so I help my patients endure and recover by sharing their memories and emotions. I would never strip someone's recollection from them unless I'm given a very good reason."

"I'm heartened that you didn't say: 'unless I am paid handsomely.'"

He chuckled and rinsed his face and throat. "Well, my fee is commensurate with the uniqueness of the service I provide, and I select my patients carefully. I've been busy the last few days, so for your own sake, I would recommend that you stay out of my head."

"So, that's where you've been spending your time, visiting your patients." As my breath and pulse steadied, I glanced around the plain chamber. The furnishings were similar to those in Sarc's room, but older and more austere, except for a crowded desk and packed bookshelves that lined the wall through which I had stepped. "If I'm staying in your room, then this must be your father's room?"

"Yes. Don't touch anything, or you'll get a memory surge," he cautioned. "My father spent much of his free time in here, and most of his things are imprinted with his presence." With one hand, he doused his face liberally a last time and picked up a towel to dry himself. "I replaced the floorboards and rug a few years ago, so those are safe to touch."

"Oh." My eyes eventually settled on Sarc's muscled shoulders and lean torso, down to where the sheet was tucked. With his workload of the past couple of days taking its toll, his figure had become lean, and even his face had become more sculpted. On his muscled back, between his shoulder blades, was a round, dark blue tattoo. I was studying it when Sarc turned suddenly, and his hooded eyes met my gaze.

"You'll have to excuse me, if I'm not exactly dressed for company."

"Hmm? Oh!" I realized then why his hand was still clutching the sheet to his hip and dropped my eyes quickly. I avoided looking at Sarc, but all I could do was wonder about what was concealed. "Sorry, I didn't mean to stare."

"It's fine," he said, and tossed the sheet back on the bed behind me to cue that it was safe for me to look at him again. He had somehow found a pair of loose trousers to wear, from somewhere in the pile of upturned bedclothes. "I take it that you haven't seen a half-dressed man in a while."

"An uninjured one, yes. During my time with Clyara, I saw plenty of people in various stages of undress."

"So, you eventually overcame your modesty and learned to look at bodies objectively," he said with a sober nod and a skeptical smile.

"I had to," I said. Most of the men I had seen could have only dreamed of looking like Sarc, with his golden colors and lithe build. By Ajle, even the sprinkling of hair on his bared chest glimmered like gold thread in the lamplight... I forced my eyes back to his face with an effort.

214

"You never bothered with looking at anyone, outside of your duties?"

"No," I said too quickly. "Never saw the point. Does that matter?"

"You tell me." He stepped forward, and I automatically stepped back. He smiled, knowing that he had called my bluff. "How do you fix something that's broken, when you don't know how it looks and feels when it's working?"

He was deliberately provoking, but I couldn't help responding. "I've managed so far without a problem. Why, are you offering yourself as a 'working' specimen?"

He laughed, "If you think I'm an acceptable subject, then you're welcome to use me anytime." There was a double meaning to his words that I was too flustered to catch, and he shook his head, as he headed back to his bed. "It's late, though. Maybe another time."

As he turned his back to me, I saw again the blue tattoo between his shoulder blades. "What is that mark on your back?"

He reached back and touched the mark. "This? A souvenir from my apprenticeship days."

He stood still to let me examine the indigo mark more closely. It was a beautiful, intricate design, no larger than an imperi coin, with organic-looking curves interwoven into a knot pattern. His skin there was supple and uniformly even. "I would've expected an Imperial seal, or something like that, but it doesn't look familiar at all."

"I didn't get it to commemorate my apprenticeship, it was just something I got during that time," he clarified. "It's a metallic dye, injected under the skin. I wouldn't recommend staying conscious for the process."

"Why did you get it?"

"I'm told that it was put there for my own protection," he said. "My consent and knowledge were not required."

"Sounds a lot like bonding," I remarked. "Protection from what?"

"It doesn't matter anymore," he said. "But the mark is indelible, so I'm stuck with it for the rest of my days. It's more permanent than bonding."

I dropped my hand once I realized that it still rested on his back, my fingers warmed by his unblemished skin. "If you're sure you're fine, I think I'll go back to bed now," I said quietly.

He turned slightly, but did not bother to face me. "Good idea."

"Good night, Sarc." I hastily phased back through the wall, back into the safety of my room, which was technically his room. Back in the solitude of my room, I felt relief from the cool darkness on my flushed skin. I smelled him in the air around me and on my fingertips, and the image of his handsome form was burned into my mind. *Wait just a while longer*, I rationalized. *Soon it will all be over, you'll be home in the Dark Lands, where you belong, and he'll be gone from your life.*

From the window of Sarc's room, I watched the lightening of the sky over the sea. The sun had not yet cleared the eastern horizon, and the beach was still dark with shadows. Staring across the water, I couldn't tell where the sky ended and the water began. Gradually, the impenetrable darkness rolled back, exposing a clear sky and calm waters. I dressed quickly, slipped a note under Sarc's door and left for the beach, inspecting the brown hues of my skin and hair before I stepped outside. I did not intend to be gone for long, and I was impatient for my first taste of the open sea. The rocky, secluded beach was deserted and perfect for my solitary exploration.

I fell in love with the magnificent blue expanse before me. It was beyond anything I could imagine. It was an impossible shade of brilliant lapis, extending to the horizon. I was seduced by the feeling of the cold, soft pink sand between my toes, and the bracing scent of sea salt in my every breath. Growing up in a land surrounded by mountains, I was in awe of the vastness of the Inearan Sea. The gentle crashes of the waves around me lulled me into tranquility, their voices drawing me into the water like a lover's whispers amidst the soft rustle of the sea grass behind me.

"The ocean is beautiful, isn't it?" called a voice behind me.

It was Jaryme, joining me on the shore. He bowed his head to me.

I was at peace inside, and even the suddenness of Jaryme's presence didn't jar my serenity in the least. Even waist-deep in the sparkling water, I could see through it to my feet buried in the pink powder. I was getting drenched, but I was having too delightful a time to care. "It's incredible. What brings you here? You haven't been following us, have you?" I said in jest.

Jaryme smiled broadly, gazing far across the water. "I trust Sarc to take good care of you, as well as he can, for the time being."

"That doesn't sound like a vote of confidence," I said.

"I wonder about his motives, that is all, as you should, too. Don't you find it strange that he should want to take you to Malya's fortress when he thinks you're not ready? Is there something he's not telling you?"

Suspicious, aren't you, Jaryme? "What are you insinuating?"

"What should be very plain to you," he said dispassionately. "Your guardian is acting on the advice of my brother, who wants power for himself. If you're not ready to meet Malya, she will try to turn you. If you resist, she would think nothing of destroying you, and Jeysen can secure a position for himself at her side. If you manage to defeat her, well, it will be all the easier for Jeysen to take control while the Realm flounders without a ruler."

"I don't believe that Sarc is so impressionable, or that Jeysen is so eager to rule," I replied, more than a little insulted by Jaryme's suggestion. The moment of my euphoria had passed, and I waded out of the water to stand with Jaryme on the shore. "But let's assume that you're right; what do you recommend?"

"Leave with me," he said. "You remember what happened in Bliis; you can't possibly want to put your guardian's life at risk again. I can take you someplace where you won't be found. You can complete your training, and we can confront the Empress together."

"You're offering to be my *keeron*." A part of me was thrilled with the idea of learning from Jaryme. Perhaps, I could even learn the mind healing discipline that Sarc had been so reticent to share.

"I wouldn't venture to call myself your *keeron*, but I think I could be your mentor, for a little while, at least. We can learn from each other," he said in earnest, brushing his hand against mine. "Together, we would be an irresistible force."

It was a tempting offer. Certainly, I could learn much under Jaryme's tutelage. Also, I did not want to see Sarc hurt again on my account, especially since it was clear that he would endanger himself for me without hesitation. "I owe Sarc the benefit of the doubt."

"At the risk of your lives?" Jaryme frowned.

"It won't come to that," I assured.

"I hope you're right," Jaryme said. "For all our sakes." He held his cloak close to his body and disappeared from the shore.

Chapter 19: Secrets Close to the Heart

I watched his space after he vanished. There was something that I had wanted to ask Jaryme about what happened in Bliis, and even before that in Altaier, but I couldn't remember what. I returned to the water and dove into the crests, enveloping myself in the brisk rolling surf and enjoying the feeling of weightlessness.

Resurfacing, I spun around at what sounded like pebbles splashing, closer and closer. I braced myself, only to discover that I was being scrutinized by a school of golden fish. The glistening creatures, each the size of my open hand, swam past me, arcing into the air and plunging down in tight formation. As they dove down and circled around me, their fins tickled my legs. Their swift and graceful race around me kept me too captivated to notice when Sarc had come down to the water's edge.

"They're hungry," Sarc called from the water's edge, lobbing a chunk of stale bread to me.

I broke off a piece and crumbled it on top of the water. Immediately, the school converged on the crumbs and left no trace of them. Their scales twinkled like burnished coins, glowing with reflected sunlight. I couldn't feed them fast enough to sate them, and on occasion one would gingerly nip at me in its frenzy. Eventually, when the bread was finished, the sungolden fish moved off to find their next meal.

As I fought the undertow and sand to join Sarc, I saw for the first time how tightly the thin, wet clothes clung to me. Sarc wrapped a blanket around me without comment and retrieved my boots from the sand.

"When I was young, my father and I used to come down here every morning during the summer to feed the sunfish," he recalled. "I could swear that the fish knew his approach by the rhythm of his pace across the sand, as they were always waiting for us in the shallows." Once he was next to me, he said, more quietly: "Thank you for the note. I'll spare you the lecture about the dangers of you coming out here alone."

"I was perfectly safe," I replied, the memory of Jaryme's brief visit already dissipated. I darted ahead of Sarc to feel the warm, petal-hued sand underfoot. "I had the sunfish to keep me company."

After a modest breakfast of leftovers and fresh bread, Sarc and I packed quickly. In my haste, I forgot about the magestone on Sarc's nightstand until we were almost at the pier. I didn't mention it, confident that nothing would happen to it while we were gone … while Sarc was gone.

Aside from the attraction of the sea, Mione didn't possess much charm. The town itself was too industrial to be anything but bleak and severe, architecturally, and the treacherous, jagged shoreline had few pedestrian beaches. Once we reached the docks, however, the vivid colors and designs of the ships at the marina made for an astounding spectacle.

"Wait, what about Brahn?" I asked. "Don't we need to get her?"

"I don't think she'd appreciate it," Sarc said. "She hates traveling by water. Don't worry, young Rhys will no doubt dote on her and fatten her on apples and peaches, and she won't miss me at all."

Sarc directed me to stay on the boardwalk so that he could approach the shipmasters alone. The boisterous captains bantered and boasted amongst themselves, each seeking to eclipse the last with a spirited telling of his latest adventure on the Inearan Sea, while their crews went about their daily chores and preparing for the next transport. Most of the captains seemed to know Sarc, as they greeted him warmly. With his shadow of a beard and his long dark golden hair, he seemed at home in their company.

After listening briefly to their lively bluster and debate, Sarc left the circle of sailors alongside a stout captain and a slender young man. The young man came to me while Sarc and the skipper discussed the details of the trip. "Good morning, Miss E'lan," he greeted in a sweet, shy voice. "I've the pleasure of serving you and your brother aboard the *Serenae*."

I cast a glance at my "brother" and smiled prettily at the young man. He was handsome with the flush of youth, not much taller than I was. He had curly dark hair that covered his ears and dark green eyes. "And what is your name?"

"Aric, Miss E'lan," he said proudly. "Aric Zephyr. My father's the captain. May I escort you aboard?"

Sarc and Aric's grinning father stood by, as Aric accompanied me aboard the *Serenae*, named for the swan-shaped summer constellation, I could only guess. It was an elegant, four-mast vessel painted in shades of blue to match the moods of the sea. The rigging was cloud-white and in top condition. The senior Zephyr had a familiar look about him, but I couldn't recall the time or place. He looked at me with a lively spark in his pine green eyes as he pulled his fisherman's cap further down over his forehead in greeting.

Once Sarc had joined us aboard, Aric showed us around the ship. "Sorry we've only the one room for two of you, but if you'd like, Sarc, you can have my room," he offered, hoping to impress.

Sarc looked at me for an answer, and I indiscernibly shrugged. "This will be fine," Sarc assured. "I promised your father that we'd keep the

219

inconveniences to a minimum."

Our room near the captain's quarters was spacious, given its location aboard a ship. The few furnishings included a bed and a well-worn upholstered chair near the starboard wall. While the chamber was insulated against the noises of the sea, the briny air was sweetened by the spice cargo's aromas wafting from the hold.

"Don't let us keep you from your duties, Aric. Tell your father that Janin and I will see him shortly." Sarc dismissed with a good-natured smile. He towered over Aric, in presence and height. The youth left reluctantly, flashing a last smile at me before the door shut in his face. Sarc leaned against the door with a sly grin. "Pretty young man, isn't he?"

I blinked. Who's Janin?

Janin was my sister, he said, moving away from the door. "I've known the Zephyrs a few years, but the captain's not too fond of mages, so I've never told him much about me," he said under his breath. "Beyond that, he's the most trustworthy sailor I know. Most of them would sell their own mothers for an imperi, especially these days."

"I had hoped that we wouldn't have to travel by water at all," I said, remembering my last sailing voyage queasily. "Is this the only way?"

He tossed our bags onto the chair and draped my cloak carefully across the back. "It's the fastest course, and the least conspicuous. Ships travel everywhere up and down this route, transporting all types of goods and passengers. The same trip by land would take weeks, plus we would have to deal with the Guard, as well as bandits and mage hunters. Don't worry, I'll deliver you safely."

"I've complete confidence in you," I said.

"Well, thank you," he said wryly. "You realize, however, that by saying that you've just jinxed us both."

We reached the open sea by mid-morning, and my stomach was much hardier on this journey than on Delenn's cross-channel ferry. The Serenae was a much larger vessel, after all, despite the comparatively small crew; it measured almost seventy meters from stem to stern, not counting the bowsprit. From what I gathered, she was purchased with a loan from Sarc and Slither when the family first settled in Mione.

Aric was hoisting the sails with a few members of the fifteen-man crew under his father's supervision. Some of them stared after Sarc and me, spurring the senior Zephyr to bark: "*Bak travi!*" to impel them back to work.

I clutched Sarc's arm. *They're elfyn!*

Sarc pulled me along gingerly to continue our walk. *With a ship named Serenae, what did you think, 'Fleece? They're like all the other elfyn in the Realm, just lying low.* "The captain says that we should reach Adelleen by the evening after next. Maybe sooner, if the winds are in our favor. From there, we can either continue along the coast, or travel two or three days by land." *I think Captain Zephyr is looking for a bride for his son; you look younger than Aric, even if you aren't, and you have elfyn blood in you.*

"I can't wait." *The timing could be better, and besides, I think my magestone disqualifies me, if magic is taboo. What do you know about them?*

I know that Zephyr lost his other son some years ago. "The captain's in a hurry, too. The humidity out here spoils the spices quickly, and he has a full cargo."

"It would be a shame to lose them, then." *He told you about it?*

Briefly, in passing. "Plus, Adelleen is a major market for spices. Too bad it's been in decline these past few years. You would have liked it more during Adella's time."

"What was it like?" *Tell me about Janin. What was she like?*

Sarc smiled. "It was a gorgeous, rambling city, full of ancient spires, vaulted archways and winding roads." *She was very headstrong, very beautiful, a little too smart for her own good, maybe.* "…built with narrow, crooked streets, to discourage mounted invasions…" *She did everything I wanted to do, and I idolized her for it.* "…temples and shrines of every faith…" *She drove Dad crazy with her recklessness sometimes.*

"Sounds wonderful." By then, I had stopped paying attention to his spoken words, but I knew that he was still coherent. He was remarkably adept at carrying on two conversations in tandem. *What happened to her?*

"It was breathtaking." Sarc faced the water and closed his eyes. *She died when she was fourteen and I was eight. It happened in an instant, in a carriage accident. My mother died the following winter, but with her at least I had the chance to say good-bye.*

I touched his arm. *It must have been awful for you.*

It was harder for my father, to lose so much, so fast. He tried to nurse my mother, but pneumonia set in too quickly. He wouldn't let me near her too often, fearing that I would catch her illness, too, so he cared for her by himself. He looked down at my hand on his arm, as if seeing it for the first time, and lay his fingers on top of it. *It's fine, 'Fleece. The worst of the grief is over. It happened years ago, when I was just a boy.*

Some of it still lingers, doesn't it, and always will?

He heard something in my query that made him wrap his arm around my shoulder. He knew that the question was for myself, as well as him. *Yes, some of it always does, as long as we still care for what we've lost.*

Sarc and I joined the crew below deck for lunch, which consisted mainly of bread, pickles and cheese from Mione and a few fish that the crew had caught. I was able to gather from the conversation that, while they had been acquainted for years, theirs was more of a business relationship, and Sarc and the Zephyrs did not speak often of personal matters. Once the rest of the crew had left, Sarc explained to Aric and his father that we were on our way north to visit friends. I listened to Sarc attentively while he spoke elfyn; his voice was low and soft, fluid and lyrical.

"You speak like a native," the captain marveled.

Sarc responded without a hitch, "Mother taught us well."

The captain sighed. "After so many years in the Realm, you probably don't even remember your land."

"Of course, we remember," Sarc said. "We used to make figurines with clay from the Red Lake, and go fishing on the Yirae."

Captain Zephyr nodded. "I remember trips to the Red Lake. We're from further south, originally from Moonteyre." At the mention of my town, I listened more closely. As he spoke, I focused on his name again: Zephyr. It was not an uncommon name, but a Zephyr family from Moonteyre… "In the morning, from the peak of Ajlekuun, you could watch the dew clouds lift from the green valley, and rise into Ajle. The Yirae River carried the sweetest and clearest water in the world. I will never forget Moonteyre, for as long as I live."

"Why did you leave?" I asked, even as the answer came to me. *Hilafra, I remember his family now.* I reached for Sarc's hand and felt it close over mine.

The captain became still, staring at his gnarled fingers, while Aric averted his eyes, a flush rising to his cheeks. The entire table fell uncomfortably silent.

"My town had a so-called healer," the captain said stiffly. "A duplicitous witch is what she was! My first-born son discovered the truth and chose to end his service as her apprentice, and she cursed him for it. She killed him!"

He means Clyara! I said to Sarc, squeezing his fingers. *His elder son was her apprentice before me. I didn't know he had died.* I couldn't imagine the pain he felt, but I heard the anguish in his voice.

He needs to voice his grief, Sarc replied. *Will you let him finish?*

I nodded for Sarc, but my eyes were trained on Zephyr, who read my gesture as a cue to continue.

"My son told us that we had to leave Moonteyre, and quickly, so of course we did. We had no family remaining in the Dark Lands, so we told no one where we were going. Everyone would have thought we were mad, but my son swore that the Realm existed, and this was where he wanted to be."

'Where he wanted to be?' The captain had decided to uproot his family at the sole request of his elder son? What about the rest of the family? I glanced at Aric, who sat silently, twisting his napkin tightly around his

knuckles.

"During the journey, my beautiful boy fell ill, and it was that witch's curse that—"

"No, it wasn't, Father!" Aric broke in finally, throwing down his napkin. "It wasn't the Healer, it was his own reckless ambition that killed him."

"How could you say that?" the captain growled.

"Because he told me what he was going to do," Aric said, as much to us as to his father. "And he made me swear to never tell anyone else. He had discovered the secret of the Healer's power and was going to use it himself, and she would be furious when she found out. That's why we had to leave right away, Father." He met my sympathetic eyes.

"He stole something from her, didn't he?" I asked Aric.

"My boy was not a thief!" the captain roared.

"Well, he was, that time," Aric spat, showing his father a pendant that he wore around his neck, hidden under his shirt. From the thin leather strip hung a glossy black pebble inside a metal wire cage. A magestone. "This is what he stole.

"When we found him that morning vomiting blood, he coughed up *this*," Aric said. "Before he died, he confessed to me that he took it from Healer Clyara without her knowing."

I understood then what had happened. The elder son had taken the magestone, but it had rejected him when he tried to host it. From the look of shock on the captain's face, it was clear that all of this was new for him.

"Why didn't you ever say anything?" he said, his voice a whisper.

"You wouldn't have listened, Father," Aric said wearily, getting to his feet. "You never do. He was the only son who mattered to you." Without another word, he grabbed several of the dirty dishes and retreated to the galley.

I wanted to express my condolences, but there was nothing on the captain's stunned, red-faced mask that suggested that he would hear me, much less acknowledge my words. It was plain that he was in need of mental and emotional succor, so I rose to my feet. "Will you please excuse me? I'll help Aric with the dishes," I said, glancing down at Sarc. *You'll help Zephyr, won't you?*

Sarc nodded, in response to both my spoken and silent words.

I took the last of the dishes with me into the galley and found Aric leaning his head against the wall, exhausted. As soon as he noticed me, he stood at attention again.

"I'm sorry you had to witness that," he began. "I said what needed to be said, though whenever I had rehearsed the words in my mind, I hadn't planned on having an audience present."

"Anything I can do to help?" I offered.

Aric nodded his head towards the stack of dishes. "Do you want to wash or dry?"

We began the chores in silence, and I noticed after a while that it was silent in the dining hall. Aric peeked through the door and reported back that Sarc and the captain had both gone.

"We'll revisit the topic another day, I'm sure," he said. "It will take a while for my father to get past what happened, but he's strong. He's a proud man with a generous heart, but he tends to hold a lot inside."

"You're very observant for your age," I remarked. "Do you remember much about Moonteyre?"

"A good deal, actually," he grinned. "I remember you, 'Fleece."

I looked up sharply at him. "What did you call me?"

"You are Snowfleece, Winter's daughter, aren't you?" he asked innocently. "Your voice and face are unmistakable. You haven't changed much in four years, except maybe you're a little taller than I recall. Your hair looks lighter than I remember."

If only he knew, I thought, brushing back a lock of my oak-brown hair. "I didn't think anyone would remember me," I said. "Plus, I don't quite look myself in this … wig."

Aric smiled, drying the last of the dishes. "Don't worry, I'm not as cynical about mages as my father is, and he doesn't even remember you, clearly. Your secret is safe with me."

"Thank you," I said. "That's very considerate of you."

He shrugged with a bashful smile. "I'm good at keeping secrets."

Aric and I reemerged from the galley to find everyone preparing for the next shift. We passed his father on his way down to his quarters, but no words were exchanged, which Aric seemed to take as a good sign, judging from his relieved smile. Once we were topside, Aric excused himself to supervise the crew, and I went to watch the sunset alone.

The glowing reflection of the sky off the water was mesmerizing. I always did prefer sunsets to sunrises, and this one was magnificent. From one end of the horizon to the other, there were only dazzling hues of citrines, rubies and amethysts playing on the waves, blending and changing before my eyes. I opted to skip dinner, as I was still full from our prolonged lunch. Only when the sky was dark enough to see the faintest stars did I retire to our room.

While my eyes adjusted to the pitch darkness, I fumbled for the bed, which I found by almost tripping over it.

"This may help," Sarc said from the shadows, and cast a gentle golden flare to illuminate the room. He was stretched out in the chair, still dressed but otherwise looking quite relaxed.

"You missed a beautiful sunset, Sarc."

"And we missed you at dinner. Are you hungry?"

"No, thank you. How is the captain faring?"

"A little embarrassed that he and his son caused such a scene, and disappointed that he couldn't apologize to you personally at dinner. Apart from that, he understands that he is fortunate to still have a son who cares so deeply for him."

"You've known all along who they were, haven't you," I said, taking a seat on the edge of the bed near him and passing him one of the blankets. "You knew that Aric's brother had been Clyara's apprentice before me."

"Yes, I did," he said. "It was perhaps not the wisest move on my part to bring you aboard this ship, but Zephyr really is the most reliable..."

"No apologies, Sarc," I said. "You shouldn't second-guess yourself about your choice, any more than you should blame yourself for not saving Clyara's apprentice from himself. If Clyara couldn't stop him, it's unfair to expect anyone else to do it." At his silence, I said, "That's not why you're sitting here in the dark, is it?"

"No, it's not. I just needed some time alone to clear my mind and think, and plan." He peered at me. "Are you nervous?"

"A little." I slipped off my boots and tucked myself into bed just as the flare extinguished, and the room returned to darkness. I took a heavy breath and drew my legs up to my chest. "Maybe more than a little. I promise you, though, I'll defeat Malya even if it's with my last breath."

"I didn't bring you all this way to die."

"I don't like the idea, either," I said tiredly. "But it's a possibility, isn't it?" It was too late to go back to the Dark Lands now; the gemwraith empress was waiting. I lay down and closed my eyes, telling myself over and over what Sarc and I both wanted to hear: *I'll be ready. I must be.*

Sarc was gone from the room by the time I woke the next morning, and he spent the morning perched in the crow's nest. We had sailed through the night, now cruising hundreds of kilometers from shore, with nothing to see but water, but remained aloft. He seemed untroubled by the occasional pitch of the ship, despite his precarious position at the top of the mainmast. Aric's chores kept him on deck, so he kept me company, as I watched Sarc to make sure he didn't fall overboard.

While the sun was intense overhead, the sky ahead of us was growing darker by the hour, with a storm quickly approaching. "It's too large to avoid," Aric said, "but the *Serenae* will be fine. She's sailed through worse."

"That's reassuring," I said, "but I hope Sarc's not still up there when the storm arrives."

Aric chuckled. "Probably not. He's been up there since dawn. If you want to get some rest and shade, I'll keep an eye on him. If he doesn't come down soon, I'll start throwing things at him, for you."

Once I went below deck, I realized that my fair skin had burned with my exposure to the elements, and that my gem was trying to heal me as quickly as possible. An illusion of a golden complexion isn't quite the same as the real thing, after all, and does not fool the sun.

I returned to the room and lay down with the blanket up to my neck, shivering under the covers, thinking of the days ahead with as much dread as excitement. *The Protector, ha! Huddled under a blanket with a raging sunburn.* We were getting closer to our ultimate destination, and I could almost feel Malya's presence emanating from the northwest, from across the Inearan Sea, taunting me and daring me to challenge her might. *Sure, she doesn't have to worry about sunburns anymore.*

The rain was falling in thick, heavy sheets when I awoke before dusk. I was wakened by the stomach-churning lurching of the *Serenae*, as much as the thumping rhythm of the rain against the deck and hull. In an effort to stave off the growing nausea, I climbed up on deck and was careful to stay out of the crew's way as the men worked to keep the ship steady and upright.

"It's better if you stay below deck for now," Sarc shouted over the deafening wind when he spotted me. He was helping the crew manage the rigging and was already soaked through, with a rope secured around his hips. "We should be through the worst of the storm soon."

"There must be something I can do," I called lamely, although I was struggling to stay on my feet.

Sarc noticed my effort and smiled. "If you insist, you can work the galley. The crew will be famished after this." *And I'd feel better knowing you're safe below deck.*

Looking around, I realized that all hands were on deck, including Kelu, the dark-haired boatswain who was also the Serenae's cook. I nodded to Sarc and went back below to make myself useful.

My job was made easier for the fact that the menu was already planned, and Kelu had started some of the supper preparation before the storm had hit. On a small ship with limited supplies, the provisions were closely and carefully managed, so nothing was to be wasted, but I found some herbs and spices hidden unused in a drawer. The greatest challenge was having the food and utensils moving constantly around me, but having to concentrate on something as simple as cooking at least helped to keep seasickness at bay.

The storm had lessened by the time I had taken the rolls from the stove. I heard the men's appreciative comments and rushed footsteps before I turned to greet them with a smile. They were a ragged bunch, drenched and clearly exhausted, but too ravenous to delay their meal any longer. My smile slipped a bit when I saw that Sarc was not with the few who arrived.

The captain seemed unaware of anything amiss, but Aric met my searching glance and took the serving tray of roasted fish from my hands. "Sarc is perfectly fine," he began.

My fixed smile faded. "Why wouldn't he be? Did something happen?"

"Don't scare the girl, Aric," the captain huffed, drying himself with one of the cloth napkins. "Janin, your brother went into the water after Kelu, when the fool tripped over the rigging and fell over the port side. They went to change into some dry clothes, is all."

"Is Kelu all right?" I asked, setting the potatoes down.

"Better than he deserves to be, the idiot," muttered one of the crew between hearty bites. "Though if he's bed-ridden for another day, I wouldn't miss him the least. With all respect, Miss Janin, this is the best food we've had on board in a long, long time."

"Then you should get a better cook," I quipped. I hadn't cooked for a crowd in years, and it felt good to know that I still knew my way around a stove. I was still basking in my modest triumph, when another of the crewmen wrapped his arm around my waist and pulled my hip hard against his shoulder.

"Would it be too forward for me to ask your brother for your hand?" he said laughingly, although I wasn't entirely sure that he was joking.

"Yes, it would," bellowed the captain from the head of the table. "If anyone's asking for Janin, it should be Aric!"

The table erupted into heckling cheers, and I found myself pushed onto Aric's lap. He was just as uncomfortable as I was, an awkward grimace frozen in place as he avoided touching me, as though I was coated in mud. I rolled my eyes at the crew's half-hearted matchmaking and got back to my feet.

"I see what you're trying to do," I reprimanded mildly, taking an empty dish in hand. "You're trying to distract me, so you'll finish everything before my brother and I even have a chance to start. As it is, it looks like I'll need to make a second batch of everything just to make sure your crewmates eat." I took a portion of everything while the platters were still half-full and snatched a roll from Aric's nimble fingers, when Sarc appeared in the doorway.

His white shirt glowed against his sun-darkened skin, and he was still fixing his cuffs when he came to the table. Taking his seat next to the captain, across from Aric, he remarked, "I see my sister has outdone herself. I was hoping that those wonderful aromas were coming from here and not just from the hold." He gave me a smile, as I set his dish before him. "Thank you."

I gave him a sisterly peck on the top of his damp head and caught his clean, freshly-washed scent, as I straightened his collar. "It's the least I could do for the brave hero."

"Mind her, Sarc," the captain warned. "If she continues to charm my men with her cooking and that pretty, sassy little mouth, you'll have to fight them off to defend her honor."

At the captain's mention, Sarc's gaze traveled to my lips and lingered there for a moment before he turned his eyes back to him. "They should be forewarned that she's quite capable of defending her own honor."

Sarc and I stayed until the first shift left to relieve their crewmates, which gave me some time to make some extra potatoes and bread, and Aric insisted on overseeing the cleanup afterwards. We bid everyone a good night and managed to get back to our room with minimal bruising, despite the continued heaving and pitching of the ship, as we rode through the rest of the storm.

I was thrown against Sarc just as he closed the door behind us, and he caught me around the waist with a laugh. *Poor Snowfleece, still haven't gotten your sea legs, I see.* Instead of setting me back on my feet right away, he walked with me to the bed. Before he let go of my hand, he brushed his lips against it. "You smell like thyme and rosemary."

I wiped my hands on my skirt. "I might have been a little heavy-handed with the seasoning."

"Everything was perfect," he said. "Better than I could have done. Maybe you were trying to charm the crew, after all."

"Hardly," I said, perching on the bed to take off my boots. "But maybe some of them haven't been around women in a while and are feeling desperate."

"On the contrary, I think most of them have been around long enough to recognize an attractive young woman of quality," he said, easing back into the armchair. "Why do you cringe at compliments?"

"Do I?" I asked lightly, tossing him a pillow and blanket.

"You know you do. Why?"

I slipped under the covers. "I'm not sure you can understand this, but I'm not accustomed to flattery, except when it's expected. My father and sister called me pretty, but they were my family, and they loved me, so what else would they have said? I don't mind that people praise me for what I do well, but how I look is another matter."

"You don't think you're pretty?" he frowned.

I shot him a wilting glance. "I've been told I have eyes like a falcon, a mouth like a hornet sting, that my neck is too short and my legs are too long. So, no, I wouldn't consider myself anywhere close to the elfyn definition of 'pretty.'"

"It's unfortunate that you would listen to such fools," he shot back, "rather than to the people who care about you and who know you best."

"Which one are you?" I asked.

"I'm your guardian," he smiled, lying back and closing his eyes, "which means I have to be a little of everything, I suppose."

He laughed when he noticed that I was still analyzing his response. "Sometimes, a compliment has no ulterior motive, and you should just accept it in good faith. Good night, 'Fleece."

Get up, 'Fleece! A sudden cacophony of noises stirred me from my slumber, the dissonant clash of ... swords? I forced my eyes open to the dim lamplight and focused with an effort on the figure of Sarc fending off two attackers who were dressed like members of Zephyr's crew. I jumped off the bed in time to avoid the edge of a third attacker's sword. I grabbed the iron lamp next to the bed and swung it, but in my grogginess, I missed the arm I had aimed for. *Good, you're up,* Sarc telepathed. *Scream.*

"What?" I yelled, hopping back to avoid another sword swing.

Shout. Ventilate. Whatever. It'll bring the others.

I was reading Sarc's lips as I heard him in my head; someone had cast a spell of silence around him. I took a breath and did my best impression of a child shrieking for her parents, and it really did make me feel better, so much so that I screamed again. I pivoted and kicked my attacker in the jaw, knocking him to the ground. I screeched at him, too. A few feet from me, Sarc disarmed one attacker and ran him through with the man's own sword.

My attacker was getting to his feet, and I prepared a spell to—

No magic, if you can help it, Sarc interrupted.

A third man was focused on me, and he had no such concerns; he whispered a spell that anchored me in place, weighing me down until I fell to the floor. He drew his pistol and aimed it at my head. Sarc took off his head with a graceful stroke, so quickly that blood didn't flow until the body hit the floor. Sarc's other opponent was staggering back to his knees and uncorking a vial of ink-black liquid with his shaking hands.

Oh, no, you don't, Sarc said, waving his hand in front of the man's face to put him to sleep, and kicked his sword out of his reach. The vial emptied on the floor, staining the boards. Three of the crew rushed the door then, led by Aric, who was still disheveled from sleep. I glanced through our porthole and noticed that the sun's pink glow barely skimmed the horizon.

"Are you all right, Janin?" Aric exclaimed, his eyes bulging at the disorder of the room. He picked up the sword that had skittered across the floor to stop at his feet. "By Ajle," Aric gaped at the sword. "How did that— Sarc, behind you!"

Sarc whirled with the sword in hand and cut a gash down the

headless gemwraith's chest, knocking it down with the force of the blow. He anchored the sword between its ribs to control its thrashing and plunged his hand into the corpse for its gem. Amid the process, the silence spell lifted from Sarc, and his annoyed mutter became audible. I only understood half of what he said, as his words were an angry jumble of different tongues.

Aric and his crewmates watched in horror, and I covered my mouth to stifle my laughter at the spectacular grotesqueness of the scene. They stared with their mouths agape, as Sarc found the medium-sized gem and bound the convulsing decapitated gemwraith with its own tunic sash. Aric recognized neither of the dead men. "Who are these men? They're wearing…" He grabbed the unconscious man off the floor and shook him with atypical vehemence. "Hars, wake up! Where are Kelu and Hedj?" he demanded.

The man stood unsteadily, held up by his fellow crewmen. He replied deliberately in common: "Dead, as we'll all be, unless you surrender the mages to the Empress. They've killed her agents now, and you're all accomplices."

Sarc pulled the sword out of the gemwraith's body and passed it to me. "Let's take this matter topside," Sarc said to Aric. "We'll let your father decide what's to be done."

"I agree," Aric said. "Janin should stay here." He was stronger than he looked, as he easily dragged the body of the third man out of the guestroom by himself before the other crewmen assisted.

I watched the gruesome procession with mixed feelings of disbelieving shock and morbid amusement, and I looked to Sarc for some assurance that everything would be fine. He was last to go, pulling the bloodied ex-gemwraith behind him with one hand and carrying its head by cradling the scalp in his palm, to minimize bleeding.

"I'll help you clean up when I return," he offered.

Once I was alone, I looked down at the bloody sword that he had handed to me and saw the Imperial markings on the blade and pommel. I tossed it aside and got a bucket of water and rags from the galley. My head was throbbing from the sweet, metallic stench of blood, but Sarc's reminder to refrain from magic stayed with me, so I cleaned as quickly and thoroughly as I could by hand.

I picked up the empty vial where Hars had dropped it, just as Sarc returned from speaking with the captain. He looked stolid, but not grim. "We're on our own after Adelleen."

"The captain knows the truth about us?" I frowned, remembering my conversation with his son on the first night. "Did Aric say something to him?"

"By Ajle, no; give the boy some credit! I confessed to the captain that I

230

was a mage. Honestly, I don't think he was very surprised to hear it; he's probably suspected for a while now." He wiped my cheek, and I saw the dry blood that had flaked from my skin. "How are you?"

"Good, fine," I replied, still fiddling with the empty vial in my hands. I was shaken by this latest attempt on my life, but I was recovering. Perhaps I was starting to get used to it. "What's going to happen with Hars?"

"He readily confessed to helping Malya's mage hunters stow on board in Mione, and aiding in killing Kelu and Hedj earlier, before the rest of the crew had arisen. They had planned originally for late last night, except the mage hunters apparently hadn't recovered yet from their seasickness."

"How did they know we were aboard?"

"Hars said that he was approached by someone shortly before we set sail, but didn't see his face. Couldn't see past the sack of imperi he was handed, perhaps. He'll be delivered to Kelu's family in Adelleen, and they can decide his fate. We burned the hunters' bodies and scattered the ashes overboard," he said, taking the vial from me. "Nightshade syrup?"

I nodded. "A sip would've killed him in seconds."

"For the hunters, failure can mean a painful death. They all carry a vial with them, for a chance to escape a more agonizing end." The vial vanished from his hand.

I shook my head in bewilderment. "The rewards must be considerable, if the hunters serve her at such risk."

"There's the allure of magic, for some," he replied. "Mostly, it's just more lucrative than the standard Guardsman's stipend."

"They can't all be that mercenary," I said. "Maybe some of them are driven by fear, or desperation."

"Some, but I think you can tell the difference," he said. "You're fairly intuitive, usually, and I'll be here when your intuition fails you. I can't think for you, but I can help keep you alive."

"Because that's what guardians do," I said stiffly, irked by his haughty tone and still plagued by my headache from mopping up the blood and cleaning the remaining traces. "It's your job to protect me from myself, isn't it?

He straightened. "That's what friends do, too," he said stonily. "I see you've cleaned up here already, so if you'll excuse me, since we're short a couple of crewmen with the wind against us, I'm going to help with rowing."

I offered to assist on deck, but was relegated to the galley once more. I was, in the crew's eyes, a simple innocent who was still in shock from the terrible events of the morning and needed to recover. I wondered if the good captain even understood that I was complicit in Sarc's deception, and was not just an unwitting sibling. I went back and forth between our room and the galley, keeping busy with packing and preparing meals for the crew. Sarc remained on deck for the day to help where he could, not even coming below to rest or eat.

I went topside shortly before dusk. From the starboard side, I barely made out the shadowy mass on the horizon, just under thirty kilometers away. It was the city of Adelleen, named for the late Empress Adella. A few minutes after I spotted land, Aric announced the same from the topmast.

The *Serenae* docked at one of the busy piers just as the sun hovered above the horizon. The sky was filled with shades of crimson and violet in the last moments of daylight, and from the bulwarks, I watched the first stars of the night emerge.

"Miss E'lan," Aric called behind me.

"Good evening, Master Zephyr," I smiled. His reticence was endearing, especially after his display of calm authority that morning. "Thank you, again, for your discretion," I said, once he joined me on the foredeck.

"I wish we could have taken you further," he said. "I don't agree with my father's decision, but I must support him," he said in elfyn. "He doesn't blame Sarc and you for what's happened, of course, but…"

"I understand," I said in kind. "Don't worry about us, we'll manage."

"I don't doubt it. You handled yourself very well before, in your room. You're really extraordinary."

I almost blushed. "You're too kind."

"I mean it." He drew some courage to step closer, as I gazed at the setting sun. When I did not back away, he came closer still and leaned over to whisper, "Alessarc is lucky to have you, 'Fleece."

I smiled despite myself. It was nice to hear my name spoken again. "I'm the lucky one, I think. I could not ask for a better friend."

"A friend, of course," he nodded slowly, mockingly.

I flicked his shoulder for his insolence, and he only laughed. "Yes, a friend! He may not be my brother, but I doubt I could find a more fraternal, stalwart companion."

Aric smiled sagely. "Oh, I'm certain of that. It's just that I've seen the way he looks at you, and it's not a brotherly kind of gaze." He paused for my response, but I refrained. "Can I confide in you, 'Fleece? You must promise not to tell Sarc. I've never told anyone."

"Sure, I owe you one secret," I said, intrigued by his hushed tone.

Aric took a deep breath and said: "I've loved Sarc, since the day I first met him." He beamed, as though a great weight had lifted from his shoulders. "I've never said anything because I know that he'd never reciprocate my feelings. His heart and mind always seemed to be elsewhere." He looked at me squarely and said, "Now I see where they've been all this time."

"Aric, I assure you that there is nothing between us. By Ajle, I hardly know him!"

Aric bumped against my shoulder playfully. "Then maybe he's not as lucky as I had thought. Here, I want you to have this."

He pressed a tiny object into my hand, and I recognized the thing immediately outside of its metal wire cage. "Your brother's magestone."

Aric shook his head. "Not his. He was never meant to have it, and I would rather not keep it. There are better ways to remember him."

I slipped the stone into my pocket and touched his hand. "Take care of yourself, Aric. And take care of your father."

The captain announced his nearness with a cough and emerged on deck a moment later. He nodded his cap to me. "It's been a pleasure, little Janin." The captain gave Aric and me a regretful smile, oblivious to his son's deeper feelings. "I wish the situation were different, and I hope you understand—"

"I do, really," I said, sparing him the trouble of explaining why we were parting ways. I did understand, too, that his decision had not been easy. As fond as he was of Sarc and me, he was dedicated to his loyal crew, and our presence put them all at risk. "Thank you for your hospitality, and may Ajle watch over you and keep you safe. I hope our next meeting will be during more pleasant times."

When Sarc emerged with our bags in hand to bid farewell to Aric and his father, I realized for the first time that it had been Sarc that Aric had always watched so intently, and not me. "Ready to go, Janin?"

I nodded and took my bag from Sarc's hand, as we disembarked from the *Serenae*.

Chapter 20: City of Adeliaraine

Just off the busy pier stood a painted wooden sign that read: "Welcome to Inearia" in faded golden script. *I remember when they erected this.* Sarc tapped the sign, as we passed it. *It was the week after Emperor Jaeris incorporated it into the Realm and renamed it 'Adelleen.'*

I recalled the date from the history books. *You would've been about fifteen at the time.*

Yes, and still giving Junus a hard time during my apprenticeship.

While most of the cities on the Peninsula of Inear benefited from increased trade and a population influx during Empress Adella's rule, Adelleen and her sister cities went into sharp decline when Malya took the throne. It showed in the dingy and neglected streetlamps and broken roads, and the evening pedestrian traffic was sparse. The winding streets that Sarc once admired were demolished, straightened and repaved to accommodate Malya's occasional troops. Whatever buildings stood in the way of her plans were razed, either wholly or in part, leaving behind ruin that looked almost like raw, open lesions on the desecrated structures.

Sarc regarded the decimated city with a profound sadness. The expression hardened when we saw a troop of Imperial Guardsmen march across our path in perfect lockstep. The small crowds that did manage to gather dispersed quickly, taking care to stay out of the Guardsmen's way. *Malya needs to keep the Inearan ports open to keep her troops fed, but she does not allow non-sanctioned assemblies.*

I slipped my gloved hand against Sarc's cool palm and averted my eyes. *Has she instated martial law here?*

Not officially, yet, Sarc said, as we left the pier. *However, anyone heard speaking elfyn is automatically branded a conspirator; assets are seized for the Empire, and exile is immediate. Slither and his connections usually try to help the banished keep something of their property here for the day when they're free to return.*

We walked in silence for a few moments, onto one of the more intact streets, lined with small shops and busy taverns. "The better inns are up this way," he said. "You deserve some pampering after the *Serenae*."

"It was fine, really. Until this morning, anyway," I said. "Aric was especially kind."

"Naturally," he said. "I saw the two of you chatting, as we were getting ready to go. What were you and Aric whispering in elfyn about?"

We turned the corner, onto a quieter passage, and he read into my prolonged silence. "Thinking of joining the crew?"

I laughed at the suggestion. "If you must know, we talked about you."

"I can't imagine why."

I remembered my promise to Aric, and I watched what I said and thought. "Aric admires you greatly."

"Of course, he's a young man of good character and impeccable taste," Sarc said half-jokingly. "He's a beautiful and thoughtful boy, who deserves to find someone to make him truly happy." At my silence, he said quietly, "And he knows that it won't be me."

I slowed. "You've known how he feels about you?"

"I may be preoccupied sometimes, but I'm not blind. Nor is he, which is why he will never say a word to me about the matter." He looked up at the building façade in front of us. "How is this one?"

It wasn't the first respectable-looking inn we'd encountered, but it seemed non-descript and unpretentious. I followed Sarc to the foyer and waited, as he asked for two rooms with fireplaces and baths. Unfortunately, there was only one available, and it was the best that the vivacious innkeeper with the long, honey-colored hair could manage. From how her wide blue eyes devoured Sarc, it was fair to assume that she would try her very best to make his stay a very comfortable one.

"It will do," I said, too tired to succumb to petty jealousy and try elsewhere. I passed my bag to Sarc and signed a false name into the guestbook.

"'Lord and Lady Thorne,'" she smirked at my pseudonymic signature, pressing the key into Sarc's open hand, more slowly and carefully than necessary. "First room on the left at the top of the stairs, your Highnesses." Watching us go, she called after us, "Will you need anything else?"

"Maybe later," Sarc said, herding me up the stairs.

The suite was larger than our room aboard the *Serenae*, and as promised, it had a fireplace against one wall. Near it, next to an oversized plush wingback chair by the closed window, was a doorway that led to a small washroom. A vanity with a bench with a matching dresser and mirror stood at the wall opposite the bed, which was generously sized but stood alone.

"I can take the chair," I volunteered.

"No need," he said, dropping our bags by the dresser. "The chair will let me keep watch more easily on the door and the window. We can go back out, if you prefer—" He watched me stretch out on the bed and close my eyes to the world. "Or not."

"You go on without me, and let me enjoy this," I murmured. After sleeping aboard the Serenae the previous couple of nights, the well-appointed, stationary bed was heavenly, with its silky sheets and overfilled pillows. I dangled my head off the edge of the feather mattress and looked at Sarc upside-down. He was a handsome figure, viewed from any angle, and I missed seeing his smile. "About our conversation this morning…"

"What about it," he said from the foot of the bed.

I replayed our exchange in my mind, as I sat back upright and took Sarc's hand. "I didn't mean to insult you. You've been very good to me, and perhaps, I've taken your friendship for granted."

"You've every right," he said. "You should never have cause to question my loyalty, and I took no offense."

"Of course, you wouldn't," I rejoined. "You could've fulfilled your duty without being kind, yet you've shown me compassion and patience. I didn't need to speak so harshly to you."

He chuckled. "That wasn't harsh. That wasn't even close to it. You said what you thought, and I replied in turn. You should feel free to speak your mind to me all the time, if this arrangement is to work."

"Why do I feel like you're not allowing yourself the same liberty?" There was a part of him that seemed cloistered from me. "You don't always have to be accommodating and complimentary to me."

He looked down at our joined hands and smiled. "Is this because I called you beautiful?"

I laughed. "There is that, too. You said that to me the first time during my adjustment to Clyara's stone, while I was paralyzed and propped between two tree roots, as I recall." I remembered the final hours clearly, and how I clung to Sarc's presence with everything I had, until I had nothing. Returning to the present, I tried to pull my hand away, but he held fast, and I met his gaze.

"I wasn't just being kind, then, not entirely," he said. "I needed to distract you from your condition, and I said what came to mind. You were sweet and vulnerable, and in need of a friend, and all I kept thinking was how easy it would have been for a less principled man to take advantage of you." He slipped his hand from mine and stood away from the bed. "I just want you to know, while my thoughts may not always be pure or open to you, you should never have cause to doubt me."

"I know that," I said, curious that I had even managed to evoke that kind of feeling from him. "So, are you planning to indulge your baser instincts here in Adelleen, then, while you have the chance?"

"Are you kicking me out? Tired of my presence, already?"

"Hardly, but that doesn't mean you need to stand guard. I won't run away, I promise."

He seemed to consider his response before he said, "I'll just be gone for a little while, maybe pick up some food. Sure you don't want to come along?"

I nodded my head and lowered myself back onto the mattress.

"Don't go to sleep yet." He leaned over and gave my forehead a quick peck. "Lock the door, and don't let anyone in. If you behave, I'll bring you back a present." He closed the door behind him, and I heard his quick, light footsteps down the stairs.

I crept to the window once I heard the door close downstairs. Between the drawn curtains, I watched Sarc, his tailored silhouette moving with efficiency and grace. His long hair was loose in the wind, and the stubble on his face was thick. *Perhaps he'll visit a barber in town.* His beard had tickled my skin, and I still tingled where he had kissed me. Aric's words had stayed with me, and while I didn't dare recount our conversation to Sarc, I couldn't help hearing it again in my mind.

And now Sarc was enjoying his temporary freedom from my company, with my blessings. I had noticed the flirtatious glance he had bestowed on the innkeeper downstairs, and I was aware that he must have had needs to satisfy, like any other man. In fact, the only man that I had ever known to not have an active libido, to my knowledge anyway, was my father, and I had no interest thinking of Sarc in any paternal way...

What was I doing, even thinking of Sarc, anyway?

Forcing him from my thoughts, I locked the door, started a fire in the hearth and went into the washroom to indulge in a bath. After our time on the *Serenae*, I found the bounty of fresh water rejuvenating, especially as the water was warm from flowing though the pipes near the fireplace. I dispelled my illusions and let the water soothe my body and spirit.

Afterwards, I pampered myself with some infused oil from one of my bottles, indulging in its sweet scent. I needed something to help lighten my mood after the encounter that morning on the *Serenae*. I also wanted to remind myself that I was a young woman, and not a sexless, mindless vessel for a magestone. How many such opportunities would I have remaining before facing Malya? Who was to say that I would have any more such opportunities?

I had just slipped into my nightdress when the doorknob rattled. The door creaked open, and Sarc entered with paper-wrapped packages in one hand and the key in the other. His hair still fell almost to his shoulders in a dark golden wave, but his stubble was trimmed neatly into a short beard. He had also exchanged his jacket for a longer coat. "Good evening, *Keeronae*," he whispered, shutting the door behind him.

"Good evening, *Keeron*," I returned with a smile.

Sarc slipped off his coat and tossed it carelessly on the bed to focus his attention on the packages. As I went closer to see what he had brought, Sarc sniffed the air around me. "Jasmine becomes you," he said, wrapping one of my curls around his finger.

"Thank you." I liked his flirtatious whisper and leaned into him to peek around him. He didn't back away from my deliberate contact, obviously enjoying our playful exchange. "What do you have there? Berries!"

He laughed and unwrapped the smaller package, to reveal a paper cone teeming with delicate, jewel-toned fruits. "I found them at a fruit peddler's stand." He picked a sweet-scented purple nugget from the cone and held it out for me. "Would you like one?"

I snatched it from his fingers with my lips. "That one, and the rest, too, please," I sighed, relishing the honey-like nectar of the fruit.

"I thought so," he said, setting the berries aside. "You can help yourself in a moment. Close your eyes," he said and pulled my hands in front of me. I tried to listen for what he was doing, but I heard only the rustle of paper.

At the touch of something flat and rigid, yet warm and pliable, on my palms, I opened my eyes. Sarc had given me a book, bound in supple black leather. I opened it at once and saw that it was blank. "My own journal?"

"It's only proper that we mages become the recordkeepers of our times," he said. "One day, people may want to know the story of the Guardian of the True Empress, Protector of the Line, and it would be nice if you were the one to tell it."

I turned the plain, unadorned volume around in my hand, and I enjoyed the buttery softness of the leather under my fingers. "It's beautiful," I said, taking Sarc's hand in mine. "Thank you, *aylonse*." At the touch of his hand, I recalled the comfort of his presence in the middle of the Red Lake wilderness, and after waking up from a nightmare during a restless night in Altaier. So priceless that sense of security was.

"Wait, there's something else," he said. He returned to his coat briefly and pulled from one of its pockets a thin, tapered metal rod that he passed to me. "Retractable ball-point pen; I hope you don't mind black ink. Only one in all the world, at present, so please don't lose it."

"I'll try not to. Thank you," I said. I played with the pen in my hand, clicking and unclicking the mechanism and watching the inked tip extend and contract. "I would ask you where you found this, but I'm not sure I would appreciate the answer."

"Probably not," he laughed. "Perhaps you should play with it later and finish combing your hair first."

"My hair ... oh, my hair!" I set the pen carefully atop the journal and placed both on the bed, snatched up the berries and returned to the vanity. I took the seat and picked up my ebony comb, peering at Sarc's reflection. "First, my gloves and cloak, now these. You know, if you keep showering me with such exotic gifts, people will think that I'm your mistress."

"I wouldn't disabuse them of the idea. I'd consider myself a lucky man, if that were true." He watched me with amusement, as I struggled with my damp, curling hair. He waited for me to offer my comb in defeat before he plucked it from my fingers. "Eat, and let me take care of this."

It had been many years since anyone except Frost had combed my hair for me, and now it felt as though it were happening for the first time in my life. The feel of Sarc's fingertips against my skin and hair was almost too much to bear, as brief as the glancing touches were. It was too easy to imagine his hands moving across the rest of my skin, and I closed my eyes to avoid watching him touch me. When he was finished, I was almost breathless.

Sarc didn't seem to notice, much to my relief. He admired the comb's Fringe-crafted design briefly before setting it back on the vanity and brushed his fingertips down the length of my tamed silver tresses. "I'm a little out of practice, but I managed to keep most of your scalp intact."

Before I could comment, he was already at the drapes, peering outside with serious eyes. "Sarc? What's wrong?"

"Probably nothing," he said, reaching for his coat.

"You're going back out?" I asked, rising from my seat.

"I'll be back as soon as I can, 'Fleece," he said, slipping his arms through the sleeves. "Have to see to some details for tomorrow, anyway. I have the key. Don't wait up."

Once he shut the door, I released the breath that I hadn't realized I was holding. I went to the window again and watched him between the closed drapes. Sarc stopped in his stroll to look up at the window where I stood, and I froze thinking that he saw me, but he continued on his way. His stride was long and quick, and he was gone from my view within seconds. I missed him immediately.

I was a fool, I realized. I barely knew him, and already I couldn't be without him. Was I really that naïve and starved for attention, that I was already so charmed by his smile, his words and his gifts? *You forget who you are.* If I didn't watch myself, there was a chance that I really would do something foolish, or say something that I would come to regret by morning.

I stood before the mirror and looked at my reflection critically. What would he want with someone like me, when he didn't even want someone as stunning as Renay? He was sparing my feelings as much as he was sparing Aric's. It was time to forget him! The fate of the Dark Lands came first. I was Snowfleece of Moonteyre, the daughter of Rija and Winter. I was Aelora's Protector, and she needed me to clear the path for her return.

After I finished the berries—I was hungrier than I had thought—I climbed into bed and drew the covers up over my head, trying in vain to hide from my conscience. I tried for a while to concentrate on a strategy for dealing with Malya, but I couldn't. My mind kept returning to Sarc, and to the suggestion that Aric was right, that somehow my guardian's feelings for me were not entirely platonic.

I tried to relax, to try instead to sleep, but I failed there, also. I watched the fire dwindle, until there were only the glowing embers and the single candle to light the room, but even the darkness didn't help me to drowse.

The luxurious feel of the silky sheets against my skin only made things worse. The more I squirmed, the more roused I became, but lying still was just as useless. I could not avoid envisioning Sarc's hands on me, as gentle and teasing and inescapable as the covers, now marked with his scent from his coat. I parted my lips to take a deep breath and made the fatal mistake of imagining his kiss. My fantasy got away from me and took on a life of its own, until all I could think about was how he looked and sounded, how he smelled, how he would taste ...

What was I doing! I clenched my hands into fists at my sides and struck the bed. I wanted to scream my frustration, but I fought the impulse and instead, pulled my blanket over my head, and in one breath, I released a stream of elfyn obscenities that would have made Aric's father blush purple. Overcome by how uncomfortably warm my tossing and ranting had made me, I flung the covers off the bed. I shut my eyes in mortification.

"Such language for a lady," Sarc said in mock outrage, leaning against the closed door with his arms crossed. Lit only by the candle, his features were difficult to discern, but I imagined that he was grinning.

"I didn't hear you come in," I said, sitting upright in bed and smoothing down my hair and nightdress. I snatched the fallen covers from the floor and hauled them back onto the mattress. "How long have you been standing there?"

"Not long." Sarc threw his coat over the back of the upholstered chair by the window and fixed the drapes where I had left them slightly parted during my earlier covert surveillance. "You look flushed. Rough night?"

"You startled me. You should've knocked." I gathered up a blanket and threw it at his head, but he caught it easily. I took a deep, calming breath and caught the acrid odor of smoke. Alarmed, I jumped out of bed and went to him. "What is that smell on you?"

"That's a pretty rude question," he replied lightly, tossing the blanket on the seat of the wingback armchair. "And vague, too."

"You know what I mean," I snapped, imagining him in the middle of an inferno, battling flames and choking fumes. I intercepted him on his way to the washroom and ran my hands up his arms to make sure he wasn't singed, even touched his hair before I stopped myself. "You're not hurt, are you?"

"I'm fine," he said quietly with an amused half-smile, assessing me with his golden eyes. When I didn't drop my hands from his shoulders, he grasped my arms gently and nudged me out of his way. He entered the washroom and shut the door without further comment.

He would divulge nothing about where he had gone, and it was pointless to ask. He expected me to trust him. I returned to the bed and closed my eyes.

Shortly, I heard the washroom door opening, followed by the quiet rustle of fabric and the muffled springs of the chair as Sarc settled into it. He extinguished the candle, leaving us with only the dying embers in the fireplace.

Is there something troubling you, 'Fleece?

"Nothing to concern you," I whispered. "Stay out of my head." If he was keeping secrets from me, I was entitled to my own.

"You know you can tell me anything," he coaxed in the darkness.

"Almost anything," I said, turning to face him. By the dim glow, I saw his silhouette facing me. He was making no attempt to read my mind, not that I could sense, and I could only trust him to respect my privacy for the rest of the night.

Perhaps it would have been better if he had read my mind after all, as it would've saved me the trouble of sorting my thoughts out by myself, but that was not his burden. After a night's rest, I assured myself, my mind would be clear, and all my madness would be behind me.

I dreamed of being Sarc's lover. I dreamed of stirring kisses and provocative touches. I had never felt anything so exquisite before. He was hard, smooth and sweet against my lips, and the slow rhythm of his breath against me was as hypnotic as the dark ocean waves swelling around us. I trembled in my rapture, feeling his hands and mouth moving across my bare skin. Every part of me came alive at his penetrating caress.

Please, Sarc. I received his deep kiss hungrily and ran my fingers through his hair and along the contours of his body. *Please, now.*

Soon. His mouth traveled down my neck and along the curve of my shoulder. He traced his fingers along my jaw and gazed into my eyes, into my soul. *But not yet.*

He vanished from my arms.

I opened my eyes to the harsh morning light of the conscious world. *This is so unfair.* I punched my pillow furiously and cursed silently into it until my breath ran out. Instead of being refreshed from the night's rest, I was now more distracted and off-balance than before.

I stared across at Sarc, asleep in the chair. As he had done aboard the *Serenae*, he slept fully clothed, but with his shirt loosened, to reveal a sliver of the lean midriff that I had touched in my dream. His dream must have been interesting, too, judging by the grin on his face. Now with his trimmed beard, Sarc looked even more roguishly handsome than before. Just looking at him, a part of me despised him for the power he had over me, while the rest of me wanted him at any cost.

I finally comprehended that it had been that way from the start. Even during our brief initial encounters in Moonteyre, I had felt his irresistible pull. Perhaps my attraction to him had been strengthened briefly by my temporary bond to him, but I recalled always feeling drawn to him, even during my time as Clyara's apprentice, despite our obvious difference in age and the infrequency of our meetings.

I stepped to his side silently. What would one stolen kiss hurt? If I got it over with, chances were that I would be unaffected by it... *Whom am I kidding?*

He turned in my direction, before he opened his eyes. He blinked, but he didn't look surprised to see me standing over him. "You're up early."

"I couldn't get back to sleep."

"And you thought watching me sleep would help?"

"It was worth a try." I lowered my eyes and saw that the slip had shifted during my restless slumber, leaving more of my skin exposed than I would have liked. I turned to adjust myself and to hide my reddening face from Sarc. Though he said nothing, I felt his eyes. I tried to be unconcerned and asked, "Did you sleep well?"

"Yes, when you weren't talking in your sleep."

"You're a lying *frejyk*!" I laughed casually, shoving the more carnal images from my dream to the back of my mind. "I've never talked in my sleep, in my entire life." I walked to my bag to put some distance between us, and to get my things ready for the morning.

"Maybe you've never dreamed like you did last night," he suggested.

"You flatter yourself," I said, carefully packing my bag. Once again, my mouth had moved faster than my brain.

"So, I was in your dream? I'm honored."

"Forget it," I said, feeling the blood rushing to my head again. "It was just a dream." *Oh, but what a dream it was!* I stood unsteadily just thinking about it.

"Of course. Still, what was I doing there?" I heard the soft whisper of linen, as he took off his shirt.

"Nothing," I said instantly, even as I recalled his imagined kiss.

"That's a shame," he joked. His voice was closer now, he was standing just behind me. "'Fleece?" His hand rested on my shoulder. "Is something wrong?"

I stood very still, lest I ruin the moment and cause him to retreat. He eased me around to face him. I had dropped my eyes as I turned, but that just forced me to look at his enticing torso, so I lifted my eyes unwillingly. I tried not to think about how I wanted to touch him, everywhere.

"If something is bothering you, I need to know."

He was using his patrician Guardian's Voice, which sobered me instantly. I batted his hands away and snapped, "There's nothing to tell. What's the plan for today?"

He raised his brow at the abrupt change of subject, but he allowed it. "Since we know Malya's hunters are searching the ships, we'll travel overland. We won't encounter much Guard presence once we're outside the city, but it will take a little longer to reach our destination, by a few days perhaps—"

We were interrupted by a knock on the door. "Good morning," he said brightly, upon opening the door.

"Good morning," came the innkeeper's warm response. "Your wake-up call, as requested." Through the vertical slit between the door hinges, I saw her obvious perusal of Sarc's half-dressed physique. I also saw the image of another man in her mind, an older man, and glanced down at the wedding band on her finger. "Hope I wasn't interrupting anything," she said coyly.

I emerged with my darker colors intact, and I set my hand on Sarc's arm. "Nothing that we can't finish later," I said, resting my head against his bare, sculpted shoulder. "Thank you for the reminder."

Her smile froze on her face. I felt her envy acutely and enjoyed it immensely. She flashed a last glance at Sarc and continued down the corridor.

Sarc watched her briefly, then shut the door. By the time the door clicked shut, I was already back at the vanity, changed into my dress and weaving my darkened hair into a braid. Sarc leaned against the door with his arms folded. "That was unexpected, on your part."

I packed my nightdress and touched my locket out of habit, making sure that it still hung around my neck. "You should be ashamed of yourself, flirting with a married woman." I reached over to his bag and flung a clean shirt at him, more aggressively than I needed to.

"She happens to be a recent widow." He pulled on the shirt and returned the other one to his satchel.

"Can't be too recent, then. Widows in mourning don't wear that shade of red on their bodies or their lips. Besides, I don't care who you choose for your conquests, I just don't want to be a witness. It's distasteful…" I saw the corner of his lips twitch with amusement. "I'm not jealous!"

"No reason you should be. You're the one sleeping in my bed." He took my bag in hand and reached for the door, but as I approached, he blocked it and faced me. "What's wrong? Really?"

Nothing. Everything. Overnight, it had become painful to look at him, as he was a reminder of everything I risked losing in confronting Malya. Then again, I rationalized, what was I without my mission? What reason did Sarc have to stay with me, if not to ensure that I lived long enough to fulfill my purpose? "Nothing's wrong," I said finally, hoping that I sounded convincing.

Sarc shook his head. "Never lie to me, 'Fleece. You're awful at it."

"I don't know if I can do this," I said unsteadily. "I'm sorry I didn't say anything sooner, but it's happening so fast! And so many people are counting on me..."

"Shhh." Sarc dropped the bags and gathered me to him. He said nothing for a minute, letting me settle first. "You may not think so now," he said finally, "but when the time comes, everything will be clear, and you'll know what to do."

"How can you be so sure?" I asked, leaning my head against his shoulder.

"Because I have faith in you, *Keeronae*." He set me back on my feet, much too soon. "And I ask that you have some faith in me, too. I also know exactly what I need to do."

Little about Adelleen seemed to change from the night before, except that the sky had become overcast. The dock was still overrun with ships loading and unloading cargo of produce and seafood. The *Serenae* was long gone. The market and streets were busy with dealers and consumers of every imaginable product, alive and dead. The gaudy colors and smells of all the exotic foods and spices made for a showy, heady treat for the senses. They stood in stark contrast to the bleakness of what remained of the city itself.

Sarc bought some fresh bread and curious-looking fruits from a few of the street vendors. "For tonight, I would recommend that we stop near Dejàl, which is about three hundred kilometers from here if we go through the mountain passage," he said, breaking off some of the crusty, fragrant bread for me. "It's not well-traveled, and the people are friendly enough, if we need to find shelter. Otherwise, we can travel along the shoreline, then cut inland, which would be an easier route, but a longer one, and we run a greater risk of encountering the Guard. Do you have a preference?"

"Whatever you feel is best," I answered. I was not in a rush to say good-bye to Sarc, but I couldn't be sure that he felt the same.

"Through the mountains it is, then." He took one of the homely, gnarled fruits and snapped its hard stem off the top, then passed the gourd-like remainder to me. "The stable's this way. Come on."

I looked at the hard, bumpy, mottled thing in my hand, seeing through the opening to its liquid center. "What is this?"

Sarc chuckled. "It's an Inearan gourd, *janya*. You drink from it." He prepared another gourd for himself and took a confident sip. "Go on, try it. Just drink through your teeth to catch the seeds. If you like it, we'll have plenty to pick on the way north; they grow wild on the peninsula."

As I kept up with Sarc's long gait, I took a sip from the gourd. The thin nectar was mildly sweet and creamy, almost like fresh milk mixed with honey and water, and surprisingly plentiful for such a small fruit.

The briny smell of the docks gradually gave way to the organic odors of hay and horses, mixed with the familiar smoky stench from the night before. The ground was splotched and muddy with wet ash and soot, but Sarc seemed not to take notice. He waved to the stable mistress, a slim young woman with her auburn hair pulled back, who was watering a powerful black draft horse in front of the stable. In the distance, I could make out some blackened structures and frames, but the slender, red-haired stable mistress seemed unperturbed, greeting us with a smile.

"Is this where you were last night?" I whispered to him.

"Yes," he said briefly, nodding his greeting back.

"Why didn't you tell me? I would've gone with you."

"That's precisely why," he said, then beamed at the pretty young woman who walked with the horse towards us.

"Good morning," she said. "I don't think it looks so bad in the daylight."

"You were lucky this time," Sarc said, holding his hand out to the stallion, who flared its nostrils and gave Sarc's fingers a deep, satisfied snuffle. He looked very much like Brahn, our previous mount, right down to a small notch on his left ear.

"Well, your impeccable timing last night helped, too," she said, her green eyes twinkling with good humor. "Father's out getting some lumber and supplies, but he thinks all the animals will be fine."

"I'm glad, Laurel," Sarc said, stroking the stallion's withers. "Paol would never forgive me otherwise. Would you, boy?" The horse answered with a thoughtful glance, as Sarc took his reins in hand. "Has he behaved himself these past months?"

"He's been the perfect guest, as long as I can keep him from the breeding mares. He's only one more mouth to feed, even if he is a mouth connected to a bottomless pit of a stomach." Laurel watched the interaction between the stallion and his master with some amusement. "I would almost say that Paol's been pining for you."

Sarc looked into the creature's large black eye. "Have you really now, old friend?" He turned back to me and introduced, "Paol is Brahn's sire, and my old traveling companion. This is Laurel; her father and I served in the Imperial Guard together."

So, the cloak he had lent me was his, after all. He was a Guardsman, or had been at one time. "It's a pleasure to meet you, Laurel." I bowed my head to her, and she curtsied deeply to me.

Her formality took me by surprise, as did her fluent elfyn: "The pleasure is mine, *Keeronae*. All we have is yours. What kind of mount would you prefer?"

I turned to Sarc with a dubious scowl. "Something slow, and low to the ground?"

Sarc stifled a laugh. "I think for the safety of all concerned, we'll just take Paol this time. He can carry us both." He gestured to the burnt-out structures. "You know, I'm more than happy to cover the costs for this mess..."

Laurel waved his offer aside. "Forget it, this has nothing to do with you. Insolent Imperial thugs," she spat. "They have no sense of honor left. This is what they do when they don't get their way, like spoiled, spiteful little children. It's bad enough that they take our best mounts whenever they please, but to even think of taking Paol ... I told them, over my dead body."

"It is not worth risking your life or livelihood," Sarc replied. "Paol can manage in the Imperial stables, until I retrieve him, if necessary."

Laurel scoffed. "We can always rebuild our stables, and Father won't take a single imperi from you, you know that. He'll probably just ask you for rights to Paol for the next breeding season."

Sarc shrugged, "Your father's welcome to try, but he's not really Paol's type ... or species." He laughed when Laurel punched his shoulder viciously. "If your father mentions it, tell him that Paol will be happy to oblige. In the meantime, I have something that will hopefully ease your pain." Sarc reached into his satchel and pulled out Slither's unopened bottle.

At the sight of it, Laurel burst into merry giggles. "Ramsblood! Sarc, you remembered! And look at the vintage: it's older than I am. You shouldn't have, Sarc—it must have cost a fortune."

"Actually," Sarc admitted, "it's from Slither, in a way. You and your father would get more use from it than the *Keeronae* or I would."

Laurel admired the bottle, then clutched it to her heart with a smile for both of us. "Thank you. It's very generous of Slither, too, and Father will be delighted. He'll be sorry that he didn't have a chance to say good-bye in person, though he'll insist that he didn't miss much. Something about how you never change, never look any older, for all the years he's known you."

Chapter 21: Ghosts in the Sanctuary

We reached the Inearan plains north of Adelleen before mid-morning, thanks to Paol's energetic, jarring pace. The Greater Blue Range of Inear loomed on the horizon. Sarc kept me in front of him the whole way, for my own comfort and warmth. While the chill in the morning air confirmed that autumn was approaching, the wild landscape was still lush and green, except where the rambling, browning vines marked the prodigious growth of the wild milk gourds.

The tumbled remains of ancient stone cottages dotting the land testified to the age of abandoned settlements. An awful shudder went up my spine, as I saw my beautiful Moonteyre broken and burned, reflected in the neglected structures. I counted off the days in my mind from when I last saw Frost and the children. This was my sixth morning in Sarc's care, and I had traveled another ten days before that to reach him. The time had gone so quickly, and now Malya seemed alarmingly near.

Sarc would be gone, too, once our goal was accomplished. He would return to his mind healer's life, and I could return to Moonteyre, hopefully, to enjoy the rest of my years. I could eventually marry, if anyone would have a hellion like me, and bear cherubic offspring like a good little wife. But that didn't feel right for me. I wanted to see the world, unfettered by traditional ties and expectations. I peered at the grey sky above us and saw a pair of hawks soaring together, circling each other in a mating dance. I wanted that kind of freedom…

I must have fallen asleep at some point during the ride, nestled sideways against Sarc under the warm cover of my cloak. I was jostled awake by Paol's rough landing on a patch of rocky ground, and I instinctively gripped Sarc's shirt to avoid being thrown, inadvertently tearing the front of it. I quickly realized that we were racing across the open plain, as I felt the stallion's powerful body roiling beneath us.

"What's happening?" I asked. Sarc's eyes were focused on the landscape ahead, and I could tell by the set of his jaw that his teeth were gritted. "Sarc?"

"Hopefully nothing," he said, his eyes still staring forward.

I looked around and realized our bearing was wrong. The jagged blue peaks of the Greater Range were nowhere in sight, and the sun was just past the zenith. "We're not heading to Dejàl anymore?"

"Change of plans," he said casually. "We're heading towards the southwest coast of the peninsula."

"But that's in the opposite direction of the fortress. Sarc, where are we going?" I asked, wrapping my hands over his to stay the reins. "I don't understand. Can we please stop, just for a moment?"

Paol slowed to a stop, his breath labored. I slipped off the saddle before Sarc could stop me, and I stroked Paol's cheek, conjuring an apple for his efforts. "You poor thing," I cooed. "How long have you been running like that?"

"He's run harder than that," Sarc said curtly, dismounting and stalking off towards an outcropping.

I conjured a trough of fresh water and patted the stallion's lathered, velvety black coat. He was a handsome creature, thoughtful and strong like his master. "So, did he get surly like that when he was in the Guard, too?" I muttered to Paol, who shook his mane with seeming exasperation.

I found Sarc leaning against the outcrop with his head bowed. He was exhausted, I saw from his eyes, but he seemed determined not to falter. He straightened when he saw me but still offered no words of explanation, so I spoke instead.

"This was never about taking me to Malya, was it? You don't believe that I can defeat her."

"You can, just not yet," he said carefully.

Well, at least he hadn't dismissed my abilities outright. "So, where are you taking me, if not to her fortress? Are you returning me to the Dark Lands, or —"

"I can't tell you, as much as I would like to," he said, his expression a regretful one. "I just need you to trust me a little longer."

"I think I've trusted you enough, given how little I know about you." I went to his side and looked deeply into his golden eyes. They were usually warm, clear and soothing, like honey, but today they shone hard and cool like amber. The inscrutability of the gaze was startlingly like Clyara's. "I don't need to hear the story of your life. Just give me one good reason that I should follow you blindly to whatever Ajle-forsaken place you've chosen for me this time. You owe me that much."

He seemed surprised by the request. "You just want one reason..."

"A good one," I emphasized. I stepped closer, and he stood his ground. "Why should I go with you? Out of everyone Clyara could have chosen, why are *you* the one stuck accompanying me everywhere? Just awful luck?"

"It's because I insisted," he said. "I trusted no one else to guide you safely, so I told Junus and Clyara that I would do it, even if it meant that you might hate me by the end of the journey."

"I don't hate you," I said, "but I'm starting to feel annoyed."

He laughed without humor. "That's natural. Even my friends often

248

feel that way about me."

I doubted that most of his friends felt the same way about him that I did. "You still haven't told me why I should follow you."

"I don't have a reason to give you," he said. "Not one that will make much sense to you, in any case."

"Oh, for Ajle's sake," I snapped. "Tell me, anyway."

"Fine," he said. "You should trust me because I know you better than anyone, and I will never betray you. Long before you were born, I swore to protect you, with my dying breath, if necessary. It's curious, for that same reason, I'm not as eager to give up my life so readily anymore."

Before I was born? "You're right, I don't understand," I said.

"I'm not sure I do, either," he mused, taking my hand in his. "I trained for years under our *keerons*, but when I finally met you, I realized that I wasn't prepared for you at all." He gazed down at me, and it was only then that I realized how close I was to him, that I had to look up to meet his eyes. "Well, if you're going to be annoyed with me, anyway…"

He lowered his head slowly and released my hand, allowing me a chance to rebuff him or flee, and when I only braced my hands on his shoulders, he smiled and pressed his lips to mine. It was only a gentle, teasing glance, but it drained my mind of every coherent thought. I never drew boys like Frost did, so I had never been kissed, but even if I had, this one would have eclipsed any other experience.

When he drew away, I pulled him back down, and he responded by wrapping me in his arms. I felt a terrible thirst that had never existed before. His second kiss was deeper, more possessive, and I reveled in the feel of his bristly jaw under my hand, and his soft hair between my fingers. A sigh of euphoria escaped my lips, but when I looked to see whether he was feeling the same, there was pain in his expression. Perhaps it was regret.

He dropped his arms slowly, and I stepped back from him but refused to avert my eyes. "I won't apologize for that," I said.

"I should," he said. "I knew better than to kiss you, but I did it anyway. Now, 'Fleece," he said stiffly, "we should travel while we still have light. If we ride through dusk, we should be able to make up for time we've lost."

With a dismissive nod, he strolled back to get Paol ready for the rest of the journey without another look back at me.

I followed at a distance, my lips still tingling at his touch. What an interesting trip this was turning out to be. And I still didn't even know where we were going.

Paol tore across the plains at incredible speeds for a draft horse, but when we traversed the Minor Southern Range to reach the southwest shore, he slowed considerably. The roads, such as they were, were steeper, narrower and more treacherous, and as the fog rolled in from the coast, Paol became skittish. I didn't begrudge him the least, as I could hardly see five meters ahead myself. Even when I cast a spell to clear our way, Paol was hesitant about going forth.

"Behave yourself, Paol," Sarc scolded. "You remember what happened the last time we were stuck here past nightfall, don't you?" Paol glanced back at Sarc with a snort and flattened his ears. "Of course, you do."

"What did happen?" I asked.

"It was years ago, when he was still a colt. Something spooked him, he lost his footing and fell, snapping his right front leg. The bone actually broke through the skin. He's lucky he serves a healer; most people would more likely put him down than treat him," he said pointedly, and Paol bobbed his head sheepishly. *Actually, even most of the mages I know would have just left him out here for the vultures*, he added. "It felt even worse than it looked."

"You took a broken leg for him?"

"An arm, technically, but certainly, yes. I'd do the same for anyone willing to carry me on his back for hundreds of kilometers without complaint." He patted Paol's neck and whispered, "All the same, old friend, I'd prefer not to do it again."

We reached the foothills just after nightfall, before the rain began in earnest, and stopped at an abandoned monastery that looked sturdy enough to shelter us for the night. It reminded me of the houses in the Fringe, with their stone frames and thatched roofs, and most sections appeared intact, if a little neglected from disuse. The peaceful, secluded solemnity also reminded me of the temple to the Goddess outside Altaier that had first welcomed me and Tenn to the Realm, seemingly ages ago.

Sarc chose two adjacent rooms on the ground floor of the main house that looked in better condition than the rest, and I conjured lamps and candles to light our way. The monastery structures were simple, befitting their humble and ascetic former occupants, but they were soundly constructed. Even the furniture appeared to be in good shape, underneath the dust and cobwebs. Paol had remained outside, feeling more comfortable in the dry, open and empty stable that stood near the main building. Sarc saw to his horse's immediate comfort with an abundance of hay and alfalfa and a troughful of water, before coming back inside.

Sarc was setting out a dry shirt from his satchel when I entered his room. He didn't notice that I had brought a stacked armful of clean linens, pillows and blankets, held steady by my chin. "I was going to check Paol's shoes and give him a thorough grooming after all his hard work today," he

250

called over his shoulder. "It shouldn't take long."

"He'll appreciate that," I said, snapping a pillowcase before easing it over the feather bolster.

At the rustling of the cloth, he turned. "Where did you find those?"

"In a storage chest in my room," I said, shaking out the sheets to cover the mattress. I glanced back at him when I heard him laugh. "What's so funny?"

"The sight of you making my bed," he said. "I wasn't expecting maid service tonight. Thank you."

"I'm very capable. I kept Clyara's house, and my father's before that," I said smartly, billowing one of the blankets.

"I remember," he appeased. "But it's the thought of you making *my* bed that I find especially appealing."

I turned to look at him, but he was gone. It was an admittedly domestic and intimate chore for me to do, and it was a harmless sampling of the kind of tranquil, domestic life that I had been considering for my future.

I closed my eyes and put aside all thoughts of prophecy, pretending that I was home, in Moonteyre, getting ready for the Harvest Festival. I imagined the distant melodic strains of the minstrels tuning their instruments and children playing in the fairground. Passing outside my window, the matrons gossiped, as they carried their baskets of delicate, savory treats to the Festival. Mistress Mallow's mince pies and cherry biscuits were my favorites, and their warm, zesty aromas beckoned me to hurry before they were all claimed. Frost's voice and the sweet rose scent of her perfume wafted to me from down the hall, along with the giggles from her children and the sounds of their tiny padded footsteps fast approaching my door.

The blissful illusion faded as soon as I opened my eyes. I was far away from Moonteyre, at a site of utter solitude and desolation. Instead of a pampered young maiden, I was a frazzled, disheveled witch with delusions of gentility. Even the home that I had romanticized no longer existed, but had been demolished and picked apart for salvage. It was about time I accepted the fact that my life was destined to be quite different from that of my ancestors.

The air was no colder than a brisk mountain breeze, but the damp made it bone-chilling. A small fire and a bath were just what I needed to clear my mind and warm myself up, so I quickly finished making Sarc's bed and my own in eager anticipation.

I started fires in the small stoves in each of our chambers and went in search of a tub. The only piece I found intact was a heavy oak basin on a matching stand, in what must have the laundering room, not far from the chambers we occupied. I sighed; it wouldn't be a soaking bath, but at least

I would be clean and warm.

I brought it back to my room, set it on the stand and filled it with steaming water, while I stripped away my false colors and damp clothes, except for the slip that I needed to keep warm. I added a few drops of jasmine oil to the water before I washed myself. Last night, I had used the perfume to please myself, and tonight, I used it for Sarc. I was unaccustomed to the idea of doing anything frivolous for attention, and I felt ridiculous for doing it now, but I was also honest enough to admit that I would try anything to draw Sarc's notice. Still, it was nice to feel the warm water coursing over my chilled skin, for whatever the reason.

It was no more than a small shift of air, but I felt the presence of another in my room, and I stopped mid-splash. I looked over my shoulder and saw Jaryme, leaning against the doorjamb with his form framed by the doorway. He looked at ease, as though he had already had a moment to study the surroundings.

Presently, he smiled. "Good evening, Snowfleece."

"Jaryme." I conjured a towel to wrap around myself. "You surprised me."

He was dressed simply, appropriately for the cool weather, and his well-formed mouth curved handsomely. "My apologies," he said, taking a desultory look around. No detail escaped his notice. "Your guardian is clever, I will allow him that. I wouldn't have expected him to bring you here."

"So, how did you find us, then?"

"I've been following you to ensure your safety," he admitted. "And I must warn you: the Empress is intent on finding you, and Dejàl and these outlying regions of Inear are thick with mage hunters."

"We'll be careful," I said. I reached for my bag that Sarc had set at the foot of my bed, but Jaryme blocked me.

He was shaking his head. "Please, 'Fleece, listen to reason. I've tried to be patient, but it's really not safe for either of you here," he said. "Come with me, let me help you, and we can end this together. We can destroy Malya, unite the Realm and the Dark Lands, and no one else needs to die."

"Like someone did for Renay?" I said, refusing to yield any ground, despite his closeness. Jaryme didn't flinch at the mention of her name, he even smiled. "She's one of your followers, isn't she? She intercepted me in Altaier, on your order?"

Jaryme sighed. "All Renay ever wanted was a chance to prove herself, and Sarc refused to give it."

"Did that include the chance to murder an innocent girl?" I frowned.

"I don't know what you've heard," Jaryme said, "but all I want is to help you complete your quest, and everything I have is at your disposal, but Sarc won't allow it. Has he even told you where he's leading you, and how much he's risking by taking you there? He's being entirely unreasonable, to the point of obsession."

"That hardly sounds like the Sarc I know," I said.

"But that's the point, isn't it?" Jaryme returned. "You don't know him, really, do you? Aside from what he's presented to you these past few days, what do you know about him and what he's planned for you?"

I don't know much about you, either. Before I could voice the thought, it slipped from my mind. "You've thought a lot about this," I said. I lifted my chin and met Jaryme's piercing blue gaze.

"Of course, I have," he said, softly. "You're very special to me, 'Fleece, and I care deeply about what happens to you. I can protect you, if you come with me."

I was drawn to him, as anyone would be drawn to a charismatic, powerful presence, but I recognized that it was different from the primal, intuitive attraction I felt with Sarc. I felt Jaryme's fingertips against my cheek, and I closed my eyes, helpless to move away from him.

"Am I interrupting something?" came Sarc's voice from the doorway.

I jerked back from Jaryme, the spell broken, and he barely turned his eyes from me to address Sarc. "I was trying to appeal to the young *Keeronae*'s sense of reason. We both know that Malya would destroy her."

"You're wasting your breath, Jaryme," Sarc said evenly. "There's already a plan in place."

"I know all about your plans with Jeysen!" Jaryme exclaimed, finally turning to face Sarc. Taken aback by the break in his calm, I took another two steps away, but Jaryme didn't seem to notice. "Don't you think 'Fleece is in enough danger as it is?"

"Danger," Sarc said thoughtfully, stepping between Jaryme and me. "If you really want 'Fleece to be safe, keep your distance, and stop sniffing around her! With all the residue from your spells, you might as well set off a barrage of fireworks every time you visit, so why don't you save us all some time and just bring Malya with you on your next visit, you sneaky *kuranyo-eha!*"

I won't bother translating, except to explain that it is an extremely impolite elfyn term for an anatomically-improbable act. I was stunned at Sarc's outburst, but Jaryme seemed unperturbed. "Does he speak for you, 'Fleece?" Jaryme asked, peering around Sarc at me. "Is that how you feel?"

How could I choose between them? I could sense no deceit from Jaryme, but nor could I leave Sarc, feeling as I did. I hesitated too long in my answer, and Jaryme's face showed his disappointment. "As you wish, *Keeronae*," he said flatly, and vanished from sight, leaving a cold void in his wake. Even after he left, Jaryme's presence seemed to linger in the room.

Sarc seemed to notice for the first time that I was only in my slip and a towel, and he averted his eyes. "I'll let you get dressed." He left the chamber without another word.

"Sarc, wait." I followed, but I had no idea what I planned to say.

I had just stepped into his lamp-lit room when he whirled on me. His golden eyes darkened whenever he was angry or upset like he was now. "You should have called me!" he said. "Just a minute later, and you would've been gone."

I shook my head. "He asked me to go, but I was going to refuse."

"Really. It looked more like you were going to kiss him," he said, conjuring a basin of soapy water and towel to wash off the lingering smell of horse and hay. He was damp from the rain, and I watched the firelight play off his darkened hair as he stripped off the tunic. His skin was glistening with rivulets, and bronzed from his long hours working on the *Serenae*.

"Maybe I was," I admitted finally, earning another black stare from Sarc. He looked ready to pounce, and I couldn't think of anything to say that wouldn't worsen his dark mood. *Would it be better, if I were pretending that it was you instead?* I thought to retreat to my room until Sarc had calmed down, but when I turned to leave, I collided with him.

He blocked my path, and he held my arms to keep me from blinking away. "Please listen carefully," he said. "Don't toy with him. Unlike me, Jaryme's used to getting what he wants, and he won't take your rejection lightly."

"Unlike you? I can't imagine you ever not getting your way," I said, reaching my hands up to push at him, to free myself from his hold, but I lost my resolve at the feel of him under my fingertips.

"If I had my way now," he said, looking down at my hands splayed across his chest, "you would be over there in my bed, with me." His words evoked the image with perfect clarity in my mind, and I warmed with the sensations flooding through me. "I would rip off that little scrap of linen you're wearing and explore every curve of your jasmine-scented body until morning."

From the intensity of his gaze, there was no doubt that he meant what he said, yet he pulled my hands off of him. "But it won't happen," he said. "It can't. You deserve much better than that." He kissed my palms tenderly and lowered them to my sides, and stepped aside to let me pass. "You should go back to your room. I'm sorry, if I shocked or offended you with my audacity."

I nodded dumbly, and went to the door before I could do anything to embarrass myself, or him. Out in the hall, I tossed over my shoulder, "For the record, I think I would have enjoyed your way very much."

I wish there was an easier way to do this, but it's better than the alternatives. The man was petrified, and I couldn't blame him. Keeron Escan made no exceptions, and I was beholden to my pledge, and to my Empress. A glance at the blue stone on my finger reminded me of my duties to her. "I will make it as painless for you as I can, but I can't let you leave here intact." I hoped that my voice was strong, that the man didn't hear my reluctance.

"I have to take care of my family, please!" He watched in impotent terror as his wife and twin daughters were ushered from the room by the trio of indigo-robed Sons of Mercy. The girls were in their teens, nearly my age. I had told him that none of them would be harmed, but his fear and panic blotted out his ability to accept my assurance.

"The extraction is brief and will not cause a mortal wound, I give my word. The monks here will see that you are well enough to travel before you rejoin your family in Adelleen."

"Keeron E'lan," he sobbed, falling on his knees. "I'll surrender the stone, I'll give you anything you ask, if you let us all stay. My wife won't be able to survive the journey alone."

"This is not a negotiation!" I snapped, furious at him for trying to appeal for mercy. "You took something that doesn't belong to you, and you're lucky to still be alive." I bit the words off, as I could tell that I was wasting my breath. He had most likely scraped together money to buy the stone from a fence in some desperate attempt to try to heal his wife. Treason or not, if he could save her, it was worth any cost. "Do as you are ordered, and you may be granted mercy."

The monks were back, for which I was glad. One of them offered the man a cup of a special tea, and he drank it without questioning. The sedative took effect quickly, and the monks caught him with practiced care. Quietly, efficiently, the monks moved his body to the raised bed and brought to my side a tray brimming with surgical tools and various dressings.

I hated this part the most. I took the scalpel in hand and made a small incision in the center of his chest, careful not to pierce the sternum or his internal organs. He jerked with pain, of course, as he wasn't completely unconscious, but the worst was almost over for him. I set down the scalpel and held my hand over the open cut until I felt the stone burrowing its way out to me. Once the gem was free, I stitched the wound closed, dressed it and gestured to the monks to return him to his room to recover.

"How long will he be with us?" Brother Flyn asked. "And his family?"

I set my hand on the man's chest, just as I saw my partner arrive out of the corner of my eye. "However long you are inclined to keep them, Brother. If you can spare the room, you can send them on their way together the morning after tomorrow."

"We will keep them together, Keeron," Brother Flyn nodded. "What about his wife?"

I shook my head. "The cancer's spread throughout her body. All we can do is ease her pain until she succumbs. It will be soon, weeks at the most."

"In that case, Keeron, we can shelter them until she passes," he said, and the other monks in the room nodded their agreement. "The family should be allowed to spend their last days together peacefully."

I smiled at their kindness. "Thank you, Brothers."

The monks nodded and left, supporting the weight of their patient between them, and I sagged against the bed as soon as the door closed. Now came the hardest part for me. Jeysen was there to catch me, as always, and he eased me onto the bed. He shook his head as the blood began to soak through the front of my uniform shirt, and he quickly pressed a wad of gauze to my chest where I had taken my patient's surgical wound.

"Junus would kill you himself, if he knew you were doing this," Jeysen hissed. "We're collectors for the Cleansing, for the Goddess's sake. Mercy is for the monks to grant."

I took slow breaths to keep my body still while the self-healing neared completion. The sharpest pain was over, more quickly than last time. "Look at it this way: if word gets out that extraction doesn't mean a death sentence, we may have more people surrendering. The Cleansing will be done that much sooner."

Jeysen scoffed. "Ever the optimist, aylonse. Power is addictive, with these gems even more so. I would bet my sister's shiny new throne that the vast majority of hosts will fight us till their last breath."

I sat up and touched my chest. The healing was complete. I cleaned my shirt and stood from the bed. "You're probably right, Jey, but shouldn't we give a second chance to those who have committed no other crime than this?"

"Treason is serious enough by itself," he muttered, running his fingers through his hair as he always did when he was contemplative. "But if you insist on this method, I can't let you do this alone, or you'll never reach your sixteenth birthday."

I was wary of his look of determination. "What are you suggesting?"

"We do this together, in turns. I'll take the next one."

"'Fleece?"

It was my voice calling to me, sort of. It was a gentle awakening, and I realized gradually that I was stretched out on the bed in my room. I was still in my slip, having fallen asleep before I even had the chance to dress. Sarc was seated on the edge, and looking at him felt like looking into a mirror. Gone were his dark grey Guardsman uniform and white shirtsleeves, replaced by a simple white tunic and dark trousers. I had become him during my dreams, somehow connecting to the remnants embedded in the structure around us.

I sat up and saw the platter of food and drink that Sarc had left on the side table. "I must have dozed off," I mumbled.

"I didn't want to wake you, but I hadn't given you a chance to eat since the morning," he said, levitating the platter to rest on the mattress next to us. I must have made a face, as he then added, "Not hungry?"

"I guess not," I said. "I saw you in this place, sometime during the Cleansing, when it was still a monastery for the Brothers of Mercy. You

256

had done an extraction and taken the wound yourself."

"The good old days," he said wryly, popping a grape into my mouth.

"You're being facetious, aren't you?"

"Of course, *janya*," he said. "It was awful, but necessary. And I was young and impulsive. Junus had brought more than a hundred gems back with him from the Dark Lands, and a third of them were stolen by Malya and her agents by the time I became an apprentice. If you can imagine even a handful of them mastering the kind of magic that you and I possess..."

"It would be chaos," I said, although I recalled the mages of the Fringe as part of a civilized society despite their power. "So, did the Imperial Guard manage to retrieve them all?"

"Not all, but most of them. There were only ten of us who were chosen to be collectors," he said. "We were paired into five teams, with nearly all of us being mages selected and trained by Junus."

"I saw that you were partnered with Jeysen. Did you choose to work together?"

"It made the most sense, since we were already friends," Sarc said, handing me a cup of water. "Are you going to keep me up all night talking, or are you going to eat and get some rest?"

I flashed him a wicked smile between sips, and he shook his head, though his half-smile betrayed his pleasure. "How about this," I countered, biting into a biscuit. "You keep talking, and I'll eat and listen. I think I can manage both."

He laughed, "How could I say 'no' to you?"

"Would you say 'no,' if I asked you to kiss me again?"

He sobered. "I don't think kissing you was a smart move on my part."

He hadn't tried it again, so maybe he felt that it had been a mistake. He was so deliberate about keeping his distance from me despite our flirtation that I had to ask: "Is there someone special in your life? I don't want to interfere, if there is. I would understand."

"No, 'Fleece," he said somberly. "There is only you."

"I know I'm keeping you from your life." I bowed my head in resignation. "I'm sorry to be a nuisance, Sarc. I really am. You must think I'm a fool for even saying anything..." I stopped speaking when he stroked my cheek and lifted my chin, but I would not look at him. It was too painful to consider what kind of pity I would see in his eyes. Perhaps he liked me enough to banter with me, but I could hardly expect anything more. I felt his thumb play across my lips, easing them apart.

"You misunderstand. It has always been you," he said. "For as long as I've known about you, I've never wanted anyone else." Before I could think of a suitable response, he pulled me against him and kissed me for the third time that day.

257

The kiss was sweet to the point of intoxication, and my mind did in fact start to cloud. I was vaguely aware of him levitating the tray off the bed, as I was more focused on the way his hands coursed down my shoulders and back, and how he pried my mouth open with his tongue to taste me. I trembled under his stirring touch and moaned in protest when his mouth left mine.

I tried to pull him back as I had the first time, but he only grasped my hands and pinned them to the mattress at my sides. Immobilized, I felt my pulse quicken further at the dark, dangerous glimmer in his eyes as he studied my curves, barely covered by the thin fabric. "You're testing my resolve, 'Fleece. What am I to do with you?"

"Anything you wish," I smiled with a deliberate shrug, which nudged one of the straps off my shoulder.

"If only I could," he murmured, kissing my cheek. His mouth moved to the slope of my shoulders and throat, in slow sips, as though committing me to memory, before he returned to my lips and felt the tip of my tongue against his.

Through his deep and penetrating kiss came his memories, and I felt his years of emotional isolation as acutely as though they were my own, as well as his elation that he was no longer alone. He uttered a primitive groan of pleasure and touched his forehead to mine. "*Ajle'xon.*"

"Heaven and earth" is what he called me, and at that moment, I would've answered to anything. I wanted to be anything he wished. Outside of him, nothing in the world mattered. I existed only for Sarc: to tease, to touch, to worship ... to use however he pleased. I opened my mind to him, to let him read for himself how I adored and wanted him, to let him know that I was his, unconditionally.

He straightened, releasing my hands, and the familiar pain returned to his eyes. To salve it, I wrapped my arms around him and rested my head against his chest, and felt for the first time his racing heartbeat, as well as his feverish skin. I lifted my head to look at him, but he had closed his eyes.

"What's wrong? What's happened to you?"

"Not to worry, 'Fleece," he soothed, stroking my hair. "It will pass soon enough. It's better that you and I get some rest tonight, and continue this another time."

He rose to his feet, but I grasped his hand before he could leave. "Can't you stay here with me tonight? Even if nothing else happens, I like having you close." I lay my head on the line of his hip and caught his subtle scent, and I knew it would haunt me. "Please."

"Just for a little while." He sat back down and touched my brow. "I remember the first time I did this, to soothe you to sleep."

"The night at Slither's before we left Altaier?" I recalled groggily, lying back onto the bed, tingling at the touch of his gentle fingers across my forehead and cheek.

"Long before that," he said. "The very first time was during your apprenticeship, when you were going through your first adjustment. You were still so young, then. You dreamed about the death of your father, and it was as though you were reliving your loss again." His voice seemed distant with my sudden exhaustion, and all I could do was listen while Sarc lulled me to sleep.

"Your pain was still raw and deep, so I helped you find solace, and now your grief is part of me." I felt his lips brush against my cheek one last time. "It has been my privilege to serve you, sweet *Keeronae*, Snowfleece of Moonteyre. You will always be my *Ajle'xon*."

Sarc's voice sounded in my dreams. *You should take her before she wakes up.*

In my dream, Tenn stood on the plains of the Fringe, looking so lost with her pearly, metallic eyes.

I'll hold them off as long as I can, Sarc said. Piece by piece, Tenn's body fell apart. Within moments, the golem was merely a pile of weapons. It was, after all, all she ever was. *Yes, it's a mess, and it's my fault.*

I looked around for Sarc, hearing his voice, but he was nowhere to be seen.

Thank you, Jeysen. Let's get this over with quickly.

My eyes snapped open in full alertness.

She's inside.

I was out of bed and dressed, though my satchel was nowhere to be seen. When the door to my room creaked opened, I was already outside in the main yard with Sarc and Paol, who was saddled and packed.

Jeysen emerged from the main house behind me with a look of annoyance, holding my bag in his hand. His physical resemblance to Jaryme was unmistakable, with the same dark hair and striking blue eyes, but his gaze was cool and unforgiving. "This is not the time to discuss this," he said, casting a portal with a wave of his graceful hand. "We have to leave, now."

The yard exploded with smoke and flames, and Paol brayed his surprise. The rain-soaked weeds around us smoldered with dark billows, so acrid and thick that I had to shield my eyes. I dispelled the flames and saw dozens of hunters emerging from the heavy smoke, through the main gate, coming towards us like a wave. Some stood back from the charge, aiming their guns.

Go with him, 'Fleece, Sarc said, turning away from me.

"Now, *Keeronae.*" Jeysen pulled me towards the waiting portal.

"No! I won't leave him!" I struggled against Jeysen and succeeded in firing a wave of lightning that washed over the land and cut down many of the hunters. Panicked by the fire and lightning, Paol reared and kicked, his heavy hooves connecting with anyone who came near. Shots cracked all around, and bullets riddled the shield that surrounded us. Paol brayed and stumbled, and Sarc dropped to the ground, unmoving.

"Sarc!"

"He'll be fine," Jeysen insisted. "We need to go."

There was no time to argue with Jeysen. I scorched him to spur him to release me. When he still held fast, I drove my elbow into his stomach, forced my bag from his grip and shoved him into the closing portal. *You're not ready. Stay close to him,* Jeysen warned, and the portal vanished.

The hunters seemed oblivious to my presence; they were busy dealing with Paol, who although wounded, stayed with his unconscious master. It was only when I looked down at my hands that I realized that my satchel and I had become invisible — a parting blessing from Jeysen. I moved through the ranks of the hunters undetected and cast a general spell over them to make them all sleep. Unfortunately, Paol fell under its effect as well, and the stallion fell heavily on top of two of the hunters. "*Hilafra.*"

Alone with Sarc, I knelt at his side and parted the blood-soaked layers of his shirt. He had taken two wounds: a graze on his right side and one to the left of his heart. They were open and glaring, showing no sign of closing on their own, but nor were they bleeding heavily. I scowled, recalling how quickly he had recovered from his injuries in Bliis. As I extracted the bullets from his wounds and got ready to heal them, it came to me.

"*Hilafra,*" I muttered again, and sat back on my heels. "You're going through a damn adjustment, aren't you?" I growled, rhetorically, fighting the urge to shake him. The symptoms were all there: his fever the night before, his silence just before the ambush and his helplessness during. There was no response from him now. "Why didn't you just tell me, you stubborn *frejyk* bastard!" I yelled and bolted to my feet, tripping backwards over Paol.

"Sorry," I said to the unconscious steed. "Well, boy, let me see what they did to you. I need to think for a moment." I found a six-inch gash along his right flank where a shell had pierced him, and a smaller bullet in his right shoulder. "That doesn't look so bad," I said, pressing my hand against his side and extracting the bullet with a spell. As the energy flowed between us, his wounds vanished and reformed on me, and I winced. "Oh, that was actually pretty horrible. Good boy, Paol, you get extra treats for that one."

As the wounds bled through my dark dress, I lay against Paol and waited for my injuries to heal. There was little that I could do for Sarc without disrupting or corrupting the adjustment process. "I'll have to treat him the traditional way, while his gem takes care of the rest," I said to the sleeping horse.

As my magestone methodically repaired me, I found my invisible satchel on the ground and rummaged through it for some comfrey and achillea. I was aware of the hunters still unconscious on the ground all around us, but I couldn't move Sarc without dressing his wounds at least superficially. I conjured a basin of scalding water and some towels and got to work.

I tried to be gentle, knowing that if I hurt him he would have been unable to flinch. I rejuvenated the dried herbs with my own energy to make them fresh again and smudged some of my *rijkil*-infused ointment onto the gashes to naturally boost his body's own healing abilities. I crushed the cuttings to release their oils and applied them, then covered my handiwork with a thick layer of bandages. The old knowledge returned easily; I could almost feel Clyara within me, guiding my hands and keeping my mind focused on the task. At the last, I whispered a brief prayer to the spirits of Ajle to watch over Sarc and looked over at Paol, who had just picked up his head. "All we can do is wait."

Paol's ears perked, and he snorted at something in the air. Some of the hunters were stirring from their slumber, as well. I dispelled the basin and towels and packed my things quickly. *But we can't wait here.*

I got Paol to his feet and tossed my satchel over his back; Sarc's bag was already fastened to the saddle. I levitated Sarc into the saddle and spotted the jagged, craggy mountains of the Minor Southern Range behind us, not too far away. "That will do nicely."

Paol started at our sudden displacement into the cavern, but Sarc's presence in his saddle kept him from rearing. I cast a spell of silence around us to keep Paol's anxious braying from giving away our location. Immediately, I conjured a bed and moved Sarc onto it, and pulled in shrubbery from outside the entrance to change into some forage for Paol. I grabbed a fistful of grass blades and made a biscuit for myself, to help replenish my energy after my rigorous use of magic. As I ate, I watched the activity stirring several kilometers away; the mage hunters were regrouping, some of them spreading out from the monastery to look for clues of our direction. As careful as I was to cover our trail, it was only a matter of time before they would discover where we had gone.

From the suddenness and boldness of their attack, I had to guess that there had to be at least a mage or two among their numbers. From their lack of strategy in their attack and their plain dress, I deduced them to be mercenaries and not Imperial Guardsmen. While I was certain that I could defeat them again, I preferred to avoid a second confrontation altogether, especially with Sarc and Paol in my company.

I stayed close to Sarc and tried to reach him mentally, but still no response came. Six days ago, I was leaving Altaier under Sarc's supervision. I would've never imagined that on that seventh morning, I would be overseeing his care. I kissed his brow lightly and told myself that I was right to stay with him. I would've done more, if I could. I would've given anything to switch places with him, to suffer his adjustment for him. How could such a thing have happened?

He was too strong of a mage to need a more powerful gem, if such a thing even existed, so he wouldn't have done this to himself. So, was this forced on him? And if so, by whom? And when?

I started counting back from last night: Dejàl, Adelleen, Mione ... Sarc could have gotten the new magestone when we were attacked in Bliis, maybe on our last night in Altaier or even before. Whenever it had happened, Sarc had told Jeysen, but not me. Despite how he seemed to feel about me, he did not entirely trust me.

The only way I was going to get answers from him in his present state was to take them from his mind. Sarc was having a troubled dream, apparent from the twitches of his closed eyes and the unevenness of his breath. Perhaps later I could tap into his thoughts, but for now my attention had to remain on keeping us hidden.

I returned to the cave entrance and saw that the hunters had gone. Or rather, gone from my field of vision. That's not a good sign. I retreated from the opening and listened for approaching footsteps, but there was nothing, not even a breeze. Then I saw it: a flash of metal on the ridge below us. The hunters were approaching slowly, silently from the foothills. They would arrive in moments.

Stay and fight, or retreat further? I glanced over my shoulder at Sarc, and Paol looked back at me with interest. I wanted to move Sarc minimally, and Paol didn't seem to care for the teleportation experience. I could more easily deal with the hunters if I faced them alone, without Sarc and Paol's well-being to concern me. I silently erected a stone wall behind me, sealing Paol and Sarc inside for the moment. I leaned back against the granite face, made myself invisible, and waited.

I didn't have to wait long.

"They must have come this way," called one. He passed underneath me without sensing me, examining the walls instead of the ledge where I perched above him. "I can smell the witch, and the horse."

"We're not looking for the girl; the Empress wants the healer."

"If we find her, we'll find him," the first reasoned. "Where's our conjurer? She should be testing this wall." *Useless bitch, she should have been watching our backs down there.* "Well, there you are. It's about time."

Renay? Her lush, fire-red locks and vivid eyes were too distinctive. Why was Jaryme's follower allied with the Empress's hunters? It was definitely Renay, though. She carried herself proudly, disdaining to let the men around her get too close, lest they soil her pristine green and white robes. She approached the wall and lay her open palm against it for a couple of seconds. "The stone is real," she said. "I can feel nothing beyond it."

"Another dead end," one of the men grumbled, as the group turned to go.

You're all worthless at tracking. This chore is beneath me.

"What did you say?" the first man snarled at Renay.

"I didn't say anything," she replied hotly, shoving her way past him.

She really didn't say anything; I planted the thoughts in the hunters' minds. *Incompetent dogs, the lot of you. No better than the Imperial Guard, and a lot smellier.* I grinned at the seething visages that surrounded Renay.

"You conceited bitch!" one of the other men yelled.

"What is wrong with all of you?" she said. "I'm here to help you."

"We can hear what you're thinking," he said. "Incompetent, are we? We'll show you how incompetent we are." A couple of them drew their swords and guns.

"I wasn't thinking any such thing," she shot back.

"Don't insult our intelligence, Renay."

Intelligence? That's rich!

"Of all your sanctimonious—"

Impressive! How long did you have to practice your pronunciation?

Renay glared at the faces around her, sensing that another force was at work. "That wasn't me! I would never think such a thing about any of you. It must be the elfyn witch. She must be close." She charged out of the cavern before the situation could get any worse, and the others followed closely. They weren't going to let her out of their sight any time soon.

I watched them from my hidden perch, making sure that they were actually leaving the area, and not just scouting nearby. It would just be a matter of time before they returned, possibly with reinforcements. In the meantime, I had a few moments to return inside to check on Paol and Sarc, then I would decide how to deal with Renay and her friends.

I picked up my head from the mattress and glanced around the cavern. I hadn't even remembered feeling tired enough to sleep. I got up from the ground slowly, not wishing to disturb Paol, who was nodding off even as he stood against the wall. Sarc still lay unmoving, but his wounds were healing quickly. His bandages were heavily stained, but they were dry.

My mind was brimming with disjointed images from feverish dreams; there was Renay lying dead in a pool of blood, which was actually a bed in Altaier, except that it wasn't Renay, and I wasn't myself when I looked in the mirror. I turned into Sarc again, and the dead woman became me. That is, she looked like me, pale with silver hair. Then Jeysen arrived and reminded me of the prophecy… It was all very strange.

It makes perfect sense to me, Sarc replied.

I looked down at him. *You're awake!*

Yes, and you were sifting through my dreams again. I sat on the edge of the bed and picked up his hand, and it dropped limply to his side again. Aside from his thoughts, there was no sign that he was conscious at all. *Yes, I'm still in the throes of the adjustment. How long have I been out?*

A few hours. It's still bright out, or at least it was when I last checked.

Where are we, anyway? I can't tell if we're moving, or if it's even hot or cold where we are. His frustration touched me, and I tried to transfer everything that I was sensing to him. *So, you're not really sure where we are, either.*

Not yet. It's only my second time this way. When you're well enough to travel, we'll get you someplace more secure, I said.

No, he said sternly, *when I'm well enough to travel, I'm entrusting you to Jeysen, as planned.*

But once you've recovered, why can't you stay with me?

Sarc sighed, mentally. *Ajle'xon, listen to me. It's not just because of my condition that you have to go with Jeysen; there are things that you can learn from him that I could never teach you. If you care for me, and if you believe in my best intentions for you, then you'll go with him.*

You're not playing fair with me.

It's not about being fair, 'Fleece. It's about preserving the Realm and keeping your family safe. I've taken too many chances already, and you need someone with a cooler head to see you the rest of the way.

Like Jeysen. You told him about your predicament but not me, I said petulantly.

As I continued to watch him, I caught my breath. He moved! It was a jerk of irritation, but it was still willful movement. *I didn't have to tell him anything. He's bonded to me, and he knew about my adjustment as soon as I realized it.*

And you meant for both of us to leave you like this? What would you have done had I not remained behind?

I would've been fine. No harm would have come to me, he said with what I felt was a superlatively self-delusionary level of confidence.

We were surrounded by mage hunters, and you were defenseless! I snapped, then took a deep breath. *Unless their goal was not to kill us, but to capture us. They must have known that I wouldn't let you fend for yourself, so they had to know that you were prone. Somehow, they knew that you had been implanted with a second stone.*

Yes, 'somehow,' he said, ironically.

But they had to realize that your gem would've dominated any new introduction, and the adjustment wouldn't last more than a few hours before your gem reasserted itself.

A few hours are all they would have needed. We were lucky to get away.

It had to be done by someone strong enough to catch you off-guard, and knowledgeable about gems. You know who did this to you, don't you?

I have an idea. Is anyone tracking us?

Yes, they're searching the hills, but we're walled inside.

Hunters or Guardsmen?

What difference does it make?

Guardsmen act out of duty and will only venture far enough to ensure that the population is safe, but the hunters will do whatever is necessary to earn their commission. The more dangerous of the two.

I think they're hunters. They're not very disciplined. I didn't see the point of mentioning that Renay was with them. *Whoever did this to you will pay, regardless*, I said.

I brushed my fingers across his face to sweep back an amber-colored lock and uncovered the small crescent scar that followed the outer contour of his eye socket. *How did you get this?*

An ill-tempered rosebush. I got it in the spring of 944, falling off a second-story balcony when I was thirteen. About two weeks before I took my magestone.

Thirteen years old. You started training so much earlier than I did. How old were you when you first learned about me, then?

Even younger. I saw you in a dream, one of those special dreams teenage boys sometimes have.

I smiled at the thought of Alessarc Nahe E'lan as an adolescent boy. *You had the power of foresight, even without a gem.*

It was one of the stronger traits passed down from Clyara and Aron, I suppose. Junus sensed my talents early on and couldn't draft me into the Emperor's service fast enough.

It wasn't as gentle a recruitment as mine, was it.

No, it wasn't, he said. *I was pulled off the street, dropped into a uniform and gifted my first magestone, in under a week, but I came to appreciate the expedience and discipline of my apprenticeship. After thirty-five years, I decided that I had had enough, and I retired from Adella's Guard with a generous pension.*

I did the simple math in my head. The Cleansing had started the year prior to his apprenticeship. *You must have been very young during your service as a Collector.*

Sarc eased himself up onto his elbows. *I didn't need to be physically strong or particularly wise, just fast on my feet. I only served for a couple of years. I volunteered when I learned that Jeysen had been selected; I couldn't let him risk his life, alone or partnered with anyone else. Clyara and Junus mentored us both, so we served together, but my duty was always to my Empress. When she no longer needed me, I was free to fulfill my remaining obligations to my keerons.*

The more he revealed, the less I apparently understood. It was a mind-numbingly large puzzle, of which I was one small fraction. Sarc, on the other hand, knew where the all the pieces fit together. He had seen and

265

experienced things that I could only know anecdotally. I recalled our first conversations, and how worldly and imposing he had seemed back then.

What could I possibly have to offer such a man? *It's no wonder you call me 'janya' all the time. I must seem practically infantile to you.*

Hardly, Sarc refuted thoughtfully. His fingers found me easily, and he stroked my jaw with his thumb, thrilling me with his soft touch. *No one with a life like yours stays a child for very long. Still, the woman you've become is very different from the girl who was Clyara's apprentice, or the fantasy of an adolescent boy.* His simple contact galvanized me, but as quickly as he had reached for me, he dropped his hand. *However, you are still painfully young, and you deserve better than me.*

Younger, you mean? I frowned. *Fifty years between us or five thousand, it'd still be irrelevant. I can't think of any man I'd rather have than you.*

Even after everything you've endured with me? You're clearly not thinking hard enough, he said. *To be fair, you also haven't been given a broad selection.* He sat up in his bed with an effort. Following his nose, he leaned over the side and fumbled with the bottles of ointment that stood on the floor. *Home brewed?*

Clyara's recipes, my interpretation. I fought the urge to reach across and wait on him; Sarc needed his moment of independence. I held my breath as he opened the wrong jar; he sniffed it tentatively, then exchanged it for the almost-empty jar of *rijkil* oil. He stopped as the jars clinked together.

I heard that! He turned in my direction and opened his eyes. *I can't see, yet, but I'll take it. Say something.*

"Welcome back, *keeron,*" I smiled, and kissed his cheek. I swept my fingers across the soft fabric over his chest, elated at the vibration of a strong, steady heartbeat beneath my fingertips.

Thank you, Ajle'xon. He grinned at my warm greeting. *You didn't ravish me while I was out, I hope.*

"Why bother? It wouldn't be as fun without your participation." I helped him unwrap the soiled dressing off the shrinking, bruised scabs on his chest and under his ribcage, but withdrew to let him redress his wound by himself with fresh salve and bandages. Despite his temporary handicap, his manual skills as a healer were impeccable. He even repacked my supplies when he finished.

Paol was stepping in place with nervous energy. "I'll take Paol outside for some fresh air, and let you rest." I gave Sarc a parting peck on his forehead. "Don't go anywhere."

I led Paol by the reins to the entrance and felt the wall to sense whether the hunters were waiting in ambush. The other side was still clear of noise and movement, as it had been for the past few hours. I dispelled the granite barrier from the entrance and squinted against the warm afternoon sunlight.

Next to me, Paol whinnied at the sudden brightness, and inside my head, a voice greeted me: *Hello, 'Fleece.*

Chapter 22: Home, Again

Jaryme! My eyes only took a moment to adjust to the light. By then, he had formed next to me, with a finger to his lips to gesture for silence. It was more than a gesture, as I was frozen in place, unable to speak or even turn around. It was as though I was encased in stone up to my nose, free only to breathe and move my eyes. Paol twisted in his bridle uncertainly, but he remained calm at my motionlessness. *What are you doing?*

"Just making a point," he said. "If I had been Malya, you would be dead now." He left my side to venture deeper into the cavern, to where Sarc was waiting, and I crumbled inside; *how could I have been so careless?*

As I waited for control of my body to return, I watched another figure enter the cavern: Renay. I was surprised to see that she was alone. She passed from one side of me to the other, staring at me critically, with her stunning blue eyes. "What a tricky little witch you are. It took longer than expected to find you, but Jaryme always finds a way. You didn't think you could evade us, did you?"

She wasn't expecting an answer, and I had none to give. My thoughts were focused on Sarc, and what Jaryme would do with him.

Concentrate, and break the spell. Sarc's voice in my mind stirred me, and I ignored Renay's baiting chatter as much as I could.

"It's because of you that he wouldn't touch me," she said in disdain. "And you were just a child years ago, but I guess you were grown enough in all the ways that count. After that kind of humiliation, it seemed only fair that I leave him in a memorable way. What does he see in you, I wonder? Would he still want you if you couldn't..." She drew a long, painted fingernail down between my breasts to the center of my chest, where my gem churned frantically to free me.

Finally, the irresistible weight fell from my limbs, and I willed myself to move. My first act was to shove Renay against the wall and mold the stone wall around her head to shut her up, as I planned my second step. She shrieked pitifully at the prospect of being buried alive inside the stone, but I couldn't stand her voice any longer. If she stopped screaming, the air pocket I left could sustain her until I figured out what to do with her. For her selfish brutality, and the pain that she had caused Sarc, not to mention her murderous inclinations, she deserved a very bad death. *But first...*

I dropped Paol's reins and blinked inside, back to Sarc and Jaryme. Sarc lay on the bed, with Jaryme standing over him, and a lost memory returned to me in a flash. "You gave Sarc the magestone, in Bliis. You let me kill those thugs, and you killed the mage when he was about to reveal that you were his source."

Jaryme looked pleased. "Well done, 'Fleece. I was wondering when those memories would emerge."

Because of Jaryme, Sarc had nearly died. To what lengths was Jaryme willing to go to have my cooperation? "Let him go, Jaryme, and I'll leave with you," I offered. I didn't dare step towards them, lest Jaryme sense a threat in my move.

No, you won't, came Sarc's angry retort.

Jaryme clamped his hand on Sarc's throat in a reprimand, and I suddenly recalled the image of my father's shattered neck under his cerements. "Please, Jaryme, don't!"

Jaryme dropped Sarc back on the mattress, vanished and reappeared before me, his blue eyes cutting me like steel, his lips set in a hard line. "You would surrender yourself to spare him?" he growled. I nodded silently. "You love him?"

Jaryme wanted to make the words sound ugly and alien, but I could not deny them. I had nothing of which to be ashamed. I looked him in the eye, ready with my answer, but my defiance was already more than he would tolerate.

The suddenness of the blow stunned me more than the force or the pain did. I supported myself against the wall, feeling the swelling of my cheek where Jaryme struck me. I turned around to face him, only to feel the back of his hand against my head a second time. I lowered to the ground, out of his reach, readying my spells to retaliate.

"You could have the world, but you'd rather give yourself to *him*," he snarled, unwilling to even utter Sarc's name. Jaryme's voice filled my head, dampening my concentration. He reached for me, only to jerk his hand back in pain when he touched my shoulder. I looked to Sarc in my surprise.

"You will not touch her again," Sarc warned, standing steadily, his eyes clear and focused. Sarc's countenance was inscrutable, but his mind was buzzing with violent thoughts. If I sensed it, I was sure Jaryme did, too.

"So, you have recovered," Jaryme said lightly. "Good, then it's just a matter of time before my brother comes to take her off your hands." He looked at me with a cruel smile. "And Jeysen is *really* looking forward to spending time alone with you, 'Fleece, while Sarc goes off to war. It's still not too late to change your mind."

"Get out!" Sarc raged. A burst of energy exploded from his fingertips that swept Jaryme up like a leaf, out to the cavern entrance and beyond.

Jaryme did not return, but I kept my eyes on the entrance to be sure.

His words continued to haunt me, filling my head, and I shuddered, even as Sarc pulled me up into his embrace. I tried not to think about Jaryme's words, but they would not leave me. "War, he said." I clung to Sarc. "You're leaving me; you're not coming back. You're never coming back." If Sarc hadn't intervened, I would have certainly perished at Jaryme's hand; what was I going to do without him? "What will I do without you? What can I do?" *Scream, cry, yell…*

Sarc did not answer me as we settled back on the bed. He merely held me, cradling my head to his shoulder. Still, the cavern was far from silent. There were footsteps quickly approaching, and I knew that our time was almost over. Voices and memories flooded my head, and only through Sarc's anchoring touch was I able to distinguish reality from vision.

"What has he done to me!" I cried, clenching my fists against Sarc's shirt. I remembered the shirt; it was the same that he had worn the morning we left Altaier, except that it had been pierced by bullets. What a day that was! And the day after that … was that when I first realized that I had fallen in love with Sarc? Every thought that leapt to my mind was accompanied by others, too many others. "Why can't I think straight?" I screamed, pushing aside all other thoughts.

"Jaryme's cast a spell on you," Sarc tried to explain, but his words sounded confusing and strange to me. "You'll be fine in a couple of minutes."

"Minutes," I echoed. "Hours. Seconds. Where's Renay? I left her a few seconds ago." I teleported from Sarc's embrace, out to where I thought I had left Paol, and Renay pinned to the wall. Paol was there, alert and anxious, and Renay was unmoving on the ground, surrounded by a band of mercenaries. "By Ajle, I've killed her! I was angry, and she was mean to me, and I killed her!"

I was saved from a hunter's bullet by a timely shield that was cast in front of me. I stared wide-eyed at the pellet that still pointed at my head, until Sarc pulled me aside and positioned behind Paol's massive flank. "She's dead, Sarc; I killed her," I said in a daze, feeling some of the pain that I saw in his eyes. It didn't even register at the moment that Renay had a bleeding gash across her throat that I hadn't inflicted, and that her limbs were beginning to twitch. In my head, it was all my fault, she had died because of me, and I made Sarc sad. I started to cry, barely comprehending anything else that was happening around me. I certainly couldn't fathom that the hunters around us wanted me dead, or at least unconscious.

In the periphery of my sight, there was a vision in black and the flash of gleaming steel, cutting down the hunters more quickly than they poured through the entrance, until the cavern was clear to the entry. The black hair and ivory skin … *Jaryme?* My protector turned his head slightly, and I finally recognized Jeysen. *Sarc, get the gem.*

Sarc was a golden blur around me, as he crouched next to Renay's reanimating body and immolated it. Silhouetted against the white glow of the flames, Sarc resembled the elfyn warriors of lore, the *nahe,* granite forms sculpted from the Ajlekyrn and brought to life by the divine light of a thousand golden stars. Extinguishing the flames, Sarc rose from the ashes with Renay's magestone in hand and returned to me.

"You have to go now, 'Fleece," he said urgently.

"Come with me!"

"I can't, *Ajle'xon,*" he said, cupping my face in his hands. "This is something you have to work through on your own. Do you understand?"

I dried my tears and shook my head, but I understood well enough. I just couldn't form the words that I was desperate to say, that I loved him and would've given anything to stay with him. Instead, I locked my arms around him and kissed him. Our minds touched, and in that moment, everything in my world was perfect. There was no fear, no pain, no loss, no sadness. There was only Sarc, and my peace in knowing that I had found in him everything I had ever wanted. I clung to him tightly, feeling his arms around me and his breath in my hair. It all happened in mere seconds, which felt like an eternity.

His arms wrapped tighter around me. "I believe in you, Snowfleece of Moonteyre, so you must do this for me. For us."

A portal swirled into being just steps from me, and Paol brayed his annoyance at the new disturbance. Sarc stood away from me with a reassuring smile, as Jeysen joined us and proclaimed gruffly: "It's time, *Keeronae.*" Just in time, as Jaryme's figure reappeared in the cavern entrance, crooking his finger at me in a mockery of playful coaxing. I took an automatic step back and bumped into Jeysen.

"Go on ahead," Jeysen said, with his sword raised, placing himself between the portal and his brother. "I'll follow when we're done here."

"Sarc?" I called uncertainly.

Sarc's eyes were focused intently on Jaryme, while his hands sparked and crackled with a growing tangle of lightning. "Go," he said solemnly, taking position next to Jeysen.

After a last look at my two guardians making their stand, I darted through the portal to step out into a warm, quiet chamber. Feeling guilty for leaving the battle, and wanting to see Sarc once more, I considered returning through the portal, but it suddenly vanished before my eyes. "No!" I cried, waving my arms through the empty air where the portal had just stood.

I stopped and calmed myself. *Nothing to do now, but wait.* I looked all around me at the sumptuous room where Jeysen's portal had brought me. It was a study, of sorts, with bookcases and maps lining the walls, and several upholstered and leather chairs and couches scattered about.

Through the sheer drapes adorning the ceiling-high windows, I saw that it was early evening; in fact, I could see the sun disappearing behind a distant ridge. Wherever I was, it was east of where we had been, but still somewhere on Inear, judging by how quick the passage through the portal had been. There was a garden just outside the window, verdant and speckled white with the eerie snowball blossoms of nocturnal moonglow shrubs, and the vines and wildflowers indigenous to the Inearan Peninsula.

Feeling a stiff, chilling breeze behind me, I returned to the center of the room where another portal was forming, and I braced myself for the possibility of Jaryme's arrival. Still, I was startled when I saw Jeysen emerge; it would take me a while to get used to how similar they looked. To my alarm, he staggered and dropped his weapons on the floor, and I caught him just in time and eased him onto the nearest couch. I looked up at the portal in time to watch it close, then down at the sticky, familiar wetness on my hands where I had touched him.

"*Hilafra!*" I exclaimed, turning him onto his stomach and folding back the heavy cloth of his coat to better see the wound on his back. I peeled the charred fabric of his clothing from his raw flesh and conjured a wet cloth to help clean the wound, which spanned a section in the center of his back about the size of my open hand. With a couple of spells, I picked loose a few flakes of blackened ... *something* from between his shoulders. "If only I had my satchel," I muttered.

Without a sound, Jeysen lifted his arm and presented my bag. He had been so still that I hadn't even realized that he was conscious. As I picked out the salves that I needed, Jeysen began to get up, and I firmly forced my hand down on the back of his neck to keep him still. "Don't. You've only just stopped bleeding. By Ajle, what hit you?"

He flinched a little at the touch of the cool ointment on his burnt flesh and mumbled into the cushion: "Don't know. Jaryme didn't give it a name. Looked familiar. Felt like a carcass. Incendiary projectile type, that is..."

I let Jeysen ramble and marveled at the speed at which his body healed itself, much like Sarc's. I watched as, layer by layer, the tissue knitted itself together, until he was whole again. Cleaning the blood and char from his tender new skin, I noticed that his wound had partially obliterated an indigo blue tattoo between his shoulders, of the same pattern that adorned Sarc's back, and I caught my breath at the memory of my love.

Sensing my mood, Jeysen pushed himself up from the couch and got to his feet promptly. With his back to me, he shed his ruined coat and pulled off what remained of his shirt. Jeysen evidently saw no need for modesty. If I was offended by his half-dressed state, it was my prerogative to avert my eyes. "Thank you for tending to me, *Keeronae*."

"You're welcome." I focused on packing away my jars to avoid staring. "Where is he?"

"He's somewhere safe," he answered, slipping over his head a new shirt that was draped over the back of a wingchair. "That's all you need to know."

I scowled. "You're not telling me everything."

He faced me. "No, I'm not."

We were interrupted by a quiet knock on the door. It opened slowly, and a small, slim woman entered, carrying a tray laden with a teapot, two cups, and an assortment of fruits and biscuits. She placed the tray on a small table and proceeded to serve us a fragrant, green-tinted tea. Out of the corner of my eye, I saw a flicker around the servant where the illusion of flesh and fabric frayed, and the sculpted golem-steel showed. It picked up Jeysen's sheathed sword and pistol belt from the floor, took his ragged clothes from his outstretched hand and curtsied to us.

She moved even more fluidly and naturally than Tenn, and I was captivated watching the golem until it left the room and closed the door behind her. I tried again, "You were about to…"

"That was all." He took a biscuit and one of the cups of tea. "I wasn't about to tell you anything else," he said.

I warmed my hands on my teacup and stared at the whole leaves suspended in the infusion. I felt awkward around Jeysen, finding my words slow to come, and I wondered what was going through his mind. I tried to peek into his head, only to feel a mental block snap back violently, like a bite.

"Don't," he said, setting his cup back on the tray with a gentle hand. "It's rude, and you're not very good at subtlety. You tended to me, so I owed you a kindness, but not a second time. If I need to rebuff you again, I will be much firmer." He wasn't any taller than Sarc, but he was far more intimidating.

"I'm sorry," I managed. "I'm worried and anxious, that's all."

"I know," he said, walking around me, towards the door.

"I know nothing about you," I called after him.

"Then you will learn, soon," he said without concern. The door reopened, and the golem returned with the sword belt, the holstered pistol, and another black coat, identical to the first. "Now, if you'll excuse me, I must attend to some unfinished business," he said, fastening the clasps on his coat. Unlike the commonplace cloaks that served to conceal under volumes of fabric, his coat was similar to Sarc's: cut to fit his broad shoulders and trim body with the utmost economy while allowing him full range of movement. In the unrelieved, tailored black, Jeysen was a more somber, arresting figure than usual. He took the weapons from his enchanted servant, unsheathing the sword briefly to check that it had been properly cleaned.

"I'll be back soon, and the golems can fetch for you anything you need, in the meanwhile. They understand elfyn, also, if that is what you prefer to speak. And try to get some sleep; you look awful." Without another word, he vanished.

"Thanks," I muttered belatedly to the space where he stood. The golem left, also, by way of the door, leaving me alone in the study. I went to the windowsill, where a small vase held a freshly-picked, saucer-sized moonglow, its tender stem slightly bruised from too much handling, and its voluptuous, cream-scented petals glowing softly in the light of the candelabra. I took a seat on the sill and looked out at the lamp-lit garden and the stars. Wherever I was, I was far from Adelleen and perhaps even Inear, and still further from home.

The room was too dark, and the house was too quiet for my taste. It was unsettling to think that all the noises of activity outside were made by artificial, non-living beings. It felt strange to be alone again, after so many days in the company of others; after being alone for three years, you would think I had gotten used to solitude, but I hadn't entirely. Some part of me still enjoyed the presence of others. *We'll see if Jeysen manages to change my mind about that.*

I lay down on the settee, tired but unable to sleep. What was I even doing there? Was that what Sarc had intended for me all along? Jeysen seemed as tight-lipped as Sarc was, but I was hopeful. Things were happening around me about which I had no idea, yet, but perhaps Jeysen would be more forthcoming than Sarc had been.

The door opened again, and I peeked over the arm of the settee at the returning golem. It walked around me and picked up my satchel from the floor. *"Me tene, siv'ee,"* it finally said, in a low, staid voice. *Follow me, please.* In elfyn.

I followed it outside, and saw the palatial dimensions of the house for the first time, by the warm light of innumerable lamps. The full moon and stars shone through the glass dome ceiling a hundred feet above me, and the polished white marble of the stairs and floor below reflected their light. By the brightness of the sconces and chandeliers, I saw that the study was one of several rooms on the ground floor. The doors to most of them were wide open, as though Jeysen was inviting me to explore. The golem walked towards the grand staircase to our right and led me up the pristine steps.

The golem opened a door near the top of the stairs and entered the chamber, but I lagged behind to follow the smell of old paper and ink, wafting out from the room next to where I was being led. I stood at the threshold and peered into the library; I hadn't seen such a compilation of books since Clyara's haven. A colorful globe nestled on its polished stand,

and several glass-encased skeletons and skulls completed the decor.

"This will be your room," the golem said, seemingly unaware that I had not followed it into the adjoining room. I lingered in the doorway of my appointed chamber with my eyes wide.

The beautiful, lamp-lit furnishings were too formal for my taste. The large bed dominated the chamber, with its carved headboard against the wall to my right. A tall window, as absurdly oversized as the ones downstairs, dressed and hidden by heavy blue velvet drapes, was set opposite the door. An ornate hardwood dresser and a small portrait of a woman stood opposite the bed, to my left. I marveled at the intricately inlaid wood around the posts of the bed, its fine workmanship reminiscent of the marquetry on Clyara's much simpler guest furniture.

"Will this be satisfactory?" asked the golem.

I nodded. "Yes, it's fine, thank you," I replied, and the golem set my bag down by the dresser. I returned the golem's polite, automatic bow and watched it glide back towards the steps.

Stepping into the chamber, I studied the portrait over the dresser, whose eyes seemed to follow my every move. The subject was a woman in her prime, with night-black hair, the first creases by her sea-blue eyes, and a clever smile like Jaryme's. Their mother, I would have guessed, the one-time Empress Mother of the Realm.

Under Karina Thorne's watchful stare, I took inventory of everything I owned, most of which fit in my worn satchel, with room to spare. The locket. The heavy-soled boots I wore. My clothes, including the dress I was wearing and the thin slip underneath that. The journal and pen, gloves and cloak that Sarc had bought for me. Three small, nearly spent bottles of oils, two half-full jars of assorted herbs. The ebony comb from Mareos. The reed flute from Belladonna of Ruvyna. And one small magestone, reclaimed from Aric Zephyr.

I stripped off the blood-streaked dress and exchanged my slip for a more modest, longer gown. I emptied the rest of my satchel into the top drawer of the vacant dresser and plopped into the feather-soft cushion of the bed. I yawned, despite my best efforts to stay alert, and lay down on top of the covers. *Just for a few seconds.*

I opened my eyes when I heard Jeysen's voice downstairs. I had fallen asleep after all, and it took me a few seconds to remember where I was. After a burst of noise and activity, there was only silence. Intrigued, I phased out of my room and darted down the stairs.

Jeysen was emerging from the study with two of his golems in tow, and he froze in the hallway when he saw me. The golems stopped mid-stride as well, their arms laden with Jeysen's coat and weapons.

"Aren't your feet cold, *Keeronae*?" he asked. "I'll have one of the

275

golems bring slippers to your room."

I realized suddenly that, while I was covered modestly in the thin gown, the marble steps did feel icy against my bare feet. I watched as Jeysen slowly ascended the stairs towards me, his impassive visage gradually lightening with a gentle smile. It was strange to see Jeysen with such a relaxed, almost loving expression, and I almost made a comment.

"Did I wake you?" he said in the common tongue, looking past me to the top of the stairs.

"No, I was still up," returned a familiar voice in kind.

Glory? I looked to the balcony with my mouth agape, at the young woman in an ivory gown, with her skin as pristine and unblemished as her clothes. Even as she stood mere meters from me, she seemed like a mirage. Her golden locks, as burnished and perfect as I recalled, cascaded to her tiny waist. She turned to me with a welcoming smile and a gentle twinkle in her green eyes, and held her hand out to Jeysen, who kissed it affectionately.

Glory and Jeysen's tenderness surprised me, but as I watched them, it also looked as natural as anything else in this world. "It's good to see you again, *Keeronae*," she greeted in elfyn. "Welcome."

"Thanks," I returned in common. "I'm relieved and happy to see you alive and well, too," I gushed, still flabbergasted at the sight of her. Four years had passed since I had last seen her, and while she seemed in some ways older, she also looked exactly the same. "When you disappeared so suddenly from Clyara's that morning, I had feared the worst."

"Clyara would have never put me in harm's way," Glory said, and turned to Jeysen. "She knew that Jeysen would watch over me."

"You've been with him all this time," I realized.

While I was not envious of either of them specifically, I did covet their loving manner and contentment. Together, with their hands barely touching, they were whole. "Are you all right, *Keeronae*?" Glory asked with concern, gazing at me with her head tilted inquisitively in a gesture that reminded me of Sarc. "You must be chilled, dressed like that. Let's talk in the library, where it's a little warmer. I would have welcomed you sooner, but when I looked in on you earlier, you were sound asleep, and I didn't want to disturb you."

As she led the way into the library, Jeysen conjured a robe and draped it over my shoulders. "We can leave any discussions for the morning," he offered, "if you need to rest."

"I'm fine," I said, perching on the plush arm of one of the seats, with Glory seated across from me on the footrest. "Just worried about Sarc."

"He's resourceful," Glory smiled. "He hasn't survived this long on sheer luck. Besides, my mother wants him alive and well, if he's to be of any value to her," she said matter-of-factly.

"What kind of value?" I frowned.

"Malya's falling apart." Jeysen slipped into the armchair between us. "Since her transition into a wraith, her body has continued to decay. Her gem can barely keep her limbs and organs together, and that includes the brain. A mind healer is her only hope of slowing her madness and decomposition."

Decomposition. What vivid imagery that word evoked. "Why Sarc?" I asked. "Jaryme trained under Junus, too."

"Jaryme knows nothing about healing," Glory said coolly.

I got to my feet, unnerved by the idea of leaving Sarc to deal with Malya alone. "This is insanity! I can't just stay here and do nothing! You must know where she is, Jeysen. Take me to her, we'll end this once and for all." I glanced at Glory out of the corner of my eye, wondering if she felt any discomfort about the way we spoke about her mother, but she seemed unmoved.

"You and me, marching into her fortress, together," he mused. "Sounds like something my brother would say."

"Jeysen," Glory reprimanded, snapping her foot against his boot.

"No, he's right," I said, reconsidering my words. "But there must be something else that we can do."

"We can discuss it in the morning," Jeysen said, rising from his seat as soon as Glory rose.

"There's already a plan?" I asked.

"There's always been a plan," he said. He held the door open for Glory but did not walk with her. She looked over her shoulder at him uncertainly. "I just need a moment with the *Keeronae*," he said, then closed the door.

By Ajle! I exclaimed as soon as we were alone. *I had no idea that she was here!*

Jeysen raised a finger to his lips to remind me to remain quiet. *I forgot that you even knew each other.*

Just briefly… She really has been with you all this time?

The alternative was going to Ruvyna to stay with her grandfather.

I recalled Junus Escan with mixed emotions. *You're the lesser of evils, I suppose.*

He guided me back to the armchair and gestured for me to sit. *I'd like to set some house rules.* I nodded, and he took a seat on the footrest and bowed his head thoughtfully. *First: you have the run of the house, except for my room and Glory's. Second: you are not a prisoner here, but I would suggest that you not leave the grounds, until you've learned how to find your way back. Lastly: do not speak to Glory about Sarc, unless she initiates.*

Why? I scowled.

Glory's sensitive on the subject, despite how casual she may act. If she wishes to confide in you, that's one thing, but until then…

Not a word, I promised.

"Thank you. It's not in my nature to keep secrets, but they're necessary." He turned at the sound of one of the golems shuffling past in the hallway and returned to his feet.

"Since we're alone, you can be frank with me," I started, standing to meet his eyes. "You don't like me, do you? You tolerate me, but not by choice."

Jeysen looked at me squarely, stone-faced. "I don't know you well enough to feel anything but indifference. However, I haven't noticed anything about you that is worth Sarc risking his life and sanity, repeatedly." He tilted his head, like a raptor assessing its prey with new perspective. "Yet, you've also drawn my brother's attention, so you must have some value. One day, I'll discover it."

"That was scathing," I managed to reply. "But honest, thank you."

"I'm surprised that you didn't start crying," he said.

"Don't worry. I'm sure you'll manage to make me cry soon enough."

His expression didn't change outwardly, but he seemed less rigid. "If you'll excuse me, I wish to bid Glory good-night before retiring to my room."

"Your room?" I asked. "I thought that you and Glory … ah…"

He looked at me inquiringly, and I mumbled, "Never mind."

Jeysen opened the door for me and accompanied me to the entrance of my room. "Until the morning, then, *Keeronae*. Sleep well."

Back inside my room, I shed the robe and lay back in bed but kept my eyes on the ceiling, where the moonlight was casting curious shadows. I closed my eyes and envisioned Sarc's face easily. I had only last seen him hours ago, yet it felt like days. My hands reached out but touched only air, and I shivered at the emptiness of not having him with me. For days, weeks … months? Years! Who could say? Perhaps it was all a dream, and I would wake in his arms in the morning! Worse, I would wake and find that he only existed in my imagination.

Of course, it wasn't a dream, and he was very real. By the universe's grand design, Sarc was gone indefinitely, and I would have to find a way to cope with his absence. If Jeysen was right, and I was a hazardous distraction, perhaps it was better that we were apart.

What about Glory? What was Sarc to her, that I had to keep silent about him? Had she been in love with him, too, before she found her happiness with Jeysen?

Had she felt like this? More than merely cold, I felt devoid of all sensation now that he was gone, as though he had been the source of all my senses. My world was now colorless, bland and empty without him, except for the pain: a bone-numbing, unescapable ache, which was all that remained.

Be strong, I heard Clyara's voice from the past, from deep within. It is only pain. And this pain, like all others, will pass.

Chapter 23: House Rules

When dawn arrived on the seventeenth day of my exodus from the Dark Lands, I felt better rested than I had in days. I had no memories of any of the dreams I had during the night—also for the first time in days. Memories of Moonteyre, my beloved homeland that I had left over two weeks ago, were just as faint. Thoughts of Sarc, however, remained fresh in my mind.

I awoke in time for the sunrise over the distant mountains, and to see the retiring orb-like blooms of the nocturnal moonglows. By the time I found my way to the dining hall, Jeysen and Glory were already waiting at the opposite end of the long rectangular table, watching the sunrise through the tall windows. Jeysen rose briefly until I joined them at the table, in an unaffected show of his ingrained gallantry.

I made my way to the table slowly, as a golem brought a glass of water to my place setting. I looked at the servant askance, studying its structure beneath the illusion while avoiding glances at its expressionless face.

"Is something wrong?" Glory asked.

"It's a little unsettling," I said. "I think I prefer my golems metallic, instead of looking like soulless people."

Jeysen gave an acquiescing nod, and the illusion faded, returning the servant golems to their intrinsic, gleaming metal guises. As soon as I took my seat, I stared at the roast fowl on a platter near me, yet untouched, judging by its perfect form. I hadn't eaten any kind of meat in days, and it looked strangely unappetizing and foreign. Jeysen noticed my discomfited gaze and gestured to one of the servants to take it away.

A waste of food and life, I mused.

Glory seemed to read my thoughts. "No animals are ever killed to be served at this table," she explained. "We weren't sure about what you eat."

Recalling the dry biscuits during my first weeks in the Haven, I said, "I'm not finicky, but some tea would be nice, please."

A golem stepped forth and set down a cup and saucer, which it filled with a steaming, fragrant brew from an ornate silver carafe. It was strong, garnet in hue, with wine-like tannins and an herbal finish.

"I hope you weren't waiting long for me," I said.

"Not at all," she said, breezily. "Just a couple days later than expected, but still more than a year earlier than scheduled." I cracked a smile, and she added wryly, "You mean this morning. Well, I'm up before the sun, and I don't think Jeysen sleeps at all."

Jeysen drank his water and shrugged. "Did you sleep well, *Keeronae*?"

"I think so," I said. "My mind feels clearer this morning."

"Clearer than what?" he asked.

"Clearer than usual. I have occasional nightmares, that's all."

"Nightmares about what?" Glory said. "Things you've seen?"

"Things I've done." Flashes of vaguely familiar faces sped through my mind, of marauders in the Dark Lands and the thugs in Bliis, as well as the mercenaries in the foothills of the Minor Range. "Lives I've taken, in less than honorable ways."

Glory looked concerned, but Jeysen was stoic. I continued, "We wouldn't have been spared, if our places had been reversed, but I just don't know if I needed to take *their* lives."

Clyara used to test the limits of my self-control, and at one time, I had learned not to act rashly. Somewhere along the way, I had lost that discipline. "I could've handled things differently. I had other means, but because we were attacked, I reacted, badly."

"You acted in self-defense," Glory said.

"I was unnecessarily cruel."

"But you weren't yourself!" she said.

"She believes she was," Jeysen cut in, then looked at me. "You weren't acting like a healer, but you're not a remorseless killer, either. You acted on impulse, released your rage, but you took no pleasure in it."

"I felt removed from the experience, as though I was observing and not partaking. Does that make sense?"

"More than you realize," he said. He and Glory stood from the table, and I followed their example. "Let's get started."

Jeysen held the door, and Glory led the way down the hall to a chamber with double doors, and she waited by the entrance for me to go in first. It was a spacious room, decorated in hues of burgundy and gold and trimmed with richly-hued maplewood, with the unadorned floor tiled with polished marble. It was sparsely furnished, with a fully stocked rack of weaponry on one wall. Once Jeysen joined me inside the chamber, Glory began to close the doors.

"You're not staying?" I asked in alarm.

She shook her head and shut us in. I had just enough time to understand the implications of where we were when I heard the rattle of staves being drawn from the rack. I turned around in time to catch the staff that Jeysen had tossed in my direction and weighed the wooden weapon in my hands. It had a solid, substantial heft.

Jeysen looked me over briefly and scowled at my ankle-length dress. "Do you have anything less cumbersome?" he commented. At my puzzled stare, he elaborated, "For sparring?" I shook my head. Jeysen materialized a set of dark grey clothes in his hands. "Try these on. Old Imperial issue."

I held the new clothes against me and changed into them with a quick spell. They were a little oversized, especially the trousers, but they were fine once I rolled up the cuffs and tightened the waist. I tossed my tailored dress into a pile against a wall, and turned back to him.

Dressed in the same uniform, he was actually handsome in the drab outfit, with his long hair neatly drawn back from his face. "You know how to use a staff, I take it?"

"Just what I taught myself in the Haven. I've never fought a real opponent."

"Fine. Show me what you know."

I held the staff properly and took a dueling stance, unprepared for what was to come.

Luckily, Jeysen had suspected my inexperience, so that when he knocked me onto the marble floor, it didn't hurt much. Unluckily for me, as soon as Jeysen pulled me back onto my feet, he made me fight him again. "Pay attention to my form, anticipate my next move."

When he forced me down again, he did so with such force that I think he cracked one of my ribs. I was quickly becoming frustrated at our uneven match, but I did not want to give him the satisfaction of breaking my spirit. I stood against him again, and was beaten again. "Focus, *Keeronae*," he challenged, "you have to do better than that. You do want to put me in my place, don't you? Didn't Jaryme tell you I'm using you and Sarc to capture the throne for myself?"

The rancor in his voice, although it wasn't directed towards me, roused me. I gripped the staff tightly in my hands and swung it at Jeysen with all my strength.

He sidestepped my advance, took one hand off his staff to grab a fistful of my hair and jerked my head back brutally, throwing my balance off. Then, he swept my legs out from under me, dropping me onto my back. Pulling me up from the floor by gripping the opposite end of my staff, he asked: "How badly do you want to beat me?"

"Why? I don't foresee that happening anytime soon," I replied.

"You're letting your emotions cloud your mind. You have to set your feelings aside and visualize what you need. Think back to when you learned your first spells, how you envisioned your goals."

I focused my gaze on him and tried to focus my mind likewise. I envisioned fighting with him, and winning, and I did feel a little better for it. Then, the scenario took a more sinister turn, and the image emerged of me beating him to the floor. I was thrashing Jeysen savagely, and with a sadistic fervor. He made no sound and no effort to fight back, or even defend himself. With every blow I dealt him, with every bit of release, my anger, my fear, my hatred of Jeysen began to swell.

"*Jaeta*," he said in elfyn, signaling a formal pause. "*Keeronae?*"

His voice sounded distant, as my full attention was on the violent imagery that I had conjured. As horrific as it was, I was fixated on seeing it to its awful end, until I heard Jeysen's voice in my head. I blinked and found myself back in the stillness of the training room. "That was strange. It felt like the vision was taking on a life of its own."

"What did you see?"

"I don't think I want to tell you." The vicious images were still too fresh, and I avoided looking at him, feeling strangely irritated by his presence. "I'm ready to continue, please."

"As you wish, *Keeronae*." He scowled at my secretiveness, but he didn't press the point. He merely returned to the starting position and waited.

I slapped the tip of my weapon against his, and the resonant crack recharged me. I attacked Jeysen with newfound energy, and also found new satisfaction in exerting myself to such physical extremes. The images of a brutal victory began to seep into my mind unbidden, and I laughed aloud at the spectacle playing out in my head, all the while matching Jeysen's attacks almost blow for blow.

"*Jaeta*," he ordered, lowering his staff.

"No," I returned, and swung the staff full-speed at his head, expecting him to block the move. To my surprise, he didn't, not exactly.

He caught the full brunt of it against his shoulder and dodged my backhanded swing before disarming me. "Stop, and still your mind for a moment," he said, holding the staves out of my reach.

"Why should I, your Highness?" I said mockingly, reaching playfully around him. I was giddy with energy, and I didn't want to lose my momentum with pointless chatting. Jeysen, too, was energized by our sparring; I felt it in his warmth, the dampness of his skin and the quickness of his breath.

As I met his pale blue eyes, I realized our closeness and took a step back. The ugly visions were fading from my head as quickly as they had entered it, replaced by images of a different sort of exertion—

"*Hilafra*," I gasped, slipping around Jeysen and skirting the edge of the chamber to avoid any kind of contact with him. But the damage was done, and the fabricated image of my lying in Jeysen's fevered embrace was indelible in my mind. *I don't want this. I love Sarc, and no one else.*

"Enough! If you don't tell me what's wrong, I'll have to read it from your mind," he threatened from across the room.

"Don't!" I hissed. "I'll tell you, later, I promise. Just don't go into my head right now," I said, pacing the room like a caged beast. I avoided looking at Jeysen, as even the fleeting glimpse of him stirred new visions, and I likewise held my arms out to cue him to keep his distance.

"Fine," he said, returning the staves to the rack. "Take a break."

Feeling defeated, I returned to my chamber and locked myself in. My scalp still smarted from how roughly Jeysen had pulled my hair, and my body ached from the battering I suffered at his hands. Even the cushion of the bed did little to soothe the pains. I remembered the coldness of his expression, and the exactness of his maneuvers. *He is not the enemy, but he will show me my weaknesses. Be thankful for it.*

Thank him for thrashing me? I was trying my best, truly, and failing, disastrously. What else did Jeysen want from me? He was impossible to understand, impossible to please. If my best wasn't good enough for him, perhaps it was better that I left … to go where? If I couldn't beat Jeysen, how could I hope to defeat Malya? Like it or not, I needed him, clearly more than he needed me. I had to stay. *Maybe Glory could help…*

No. I stared at the ornate ceiling to clear my tearing eyes. *This is my struggle, I won't bring Glory into this. While I'm in his home, I must follow his rules. If only I were strong enough to face Malya on my own!* I flipped my unruly curls back from my hot face and disentangled my fingers. My tresses were like shackles weighing on my head, a symbol of my vanity and weakness and a remnant of my old life among the elfyn. Maybe Glory could afford the luxury of wearing ringlets, but Jeysen was within his rights to use mine against me. *Never again.*

With a pair of conjured scissors, I severed my hair, tight fistfuls at a time. By the time I was done, what remained of my white locks barely brushed the base of my neck, and my head felt lighter and freer for my impulsive act. I liked the cool air against my nape especially. I dispelled the shears and swirled my fingers through the cloud of silver curls all around me on the bed. *Damn, I've finally done it.*

Before I could change my mind and restore my locks, I turned the clippings of my snow-white hair into a pile of dust. I hadn't had my silver long enough to truly miss it, and I reasoned that I was more than the color or cut of my hair. It had only taken a moment, a brief fit of pique, to change something that had been a part of my identity, but that was the point, wasn't it?

If I wanted to badly enough, I could change myself.

Encouraged by my new confidence, I hurried back to the training room and approached the weapons rack with renewed determination. It had everything I could possibly want to use: epees, rapiers, stilettos, sabers, machetes, flails, maces, even claymores that were three-quarters of my height. I pulled an Imperial saber from the sword rack. It was heavy and ungainly, but good for practice. Raising it overhead, I recalled the hours that I had practiced alone in the Haven, when I would've given anything for a partner, or a *keeron*. Now that I had one in Jeysen, I had to figure out how best to learn from him. I closed my eyes and ran through the positions: *first position ... third ... fifth ... second ... fourth ... second ... first—*

Clang! I jumped back and opened my eyes. Jeysen stood poised with his saber crossed with mine. His blue-grey eyes studied my new haircut, but he reserved comment. Instead, he resumed our sparring as though nothing had happened earlier. The corner of his lips turned up slightly at my improved concentration, but still he was silent.

I blocked his last thrust with enough force to almost disarm him, and snapped, "You want to say something, so just get it out."

"*Jaeta*," he said. "I'm not sure what to say. I had expected you to plait your hair or tie it back, not ... hmm."

I ran my hand through my hair and felt the soft fringe at my nape. "It looks that bad, does it?"

Jeysen sighed and tapped his sword against mine to resume our match. "That's a loaded question, with no right answer. Let's move on."

"*Jaeta*," I signaled, and lowered my sword. "Why did you come back?"

"It's my house. Where would I go?"

"No, seriously," I frowned.

"Yes, seriously. If you want to stay, then my place is here with you. If you leave, then I can't think of a safer place to be when Malya wins."

"You certainly know how to build a girl's confidence," I quipped, touching my sword to his to continue. "So, Your Highness, how long am I to stay here?"

"Until you can defeat me." He disarmed me with a simple flick on his wrist. "Until you've earned the title of *Keeronae*."

Jeysen and I continued our sparring, verbal and otherwise, for several more hours. The time passed quickly, as once I was warmed up and in the proper mindset, our match was more balanced and less excruciating for me. I never beat him, but a few times I thought I came close to it, and I was appreciative of the fact that Jeysen spared me nothing. Once he saw that I was more focused, he corrected and advised me with calm patience. Stimulated and driven by our interaction, I could have continued into the night.

As it was, I didn't even realize the time until the golem interrupted us. It entered the chamber with a dishtowel draped across its arm and waited for our full attention. It made eye contact with us, so to speak, bowed to us soundlessly and exited.

"Dinner is ready," Jeysen said, returning our sabers to the rack.

"Is that what that means," I mused, picking my dress up from the floor. "Are we three the only living beings here?"

"Aside from the plants and garden dwellers, there are also the horses in the stable and the falcons that nest in the towers. Maybe the occasional rat or fox, too," he said. "We are the only people, yes. We are isolated from the rest of the Realm, and our privacy can only be insured if no one knows we're here."

"Hence no live servants," I completed. "Isn't it hard living like that?"

Jeysen smiled wryly, opening the door for me. "I don't know. You managed to live alone for a few years, and you turned out fine. Mostly."

By the time I cleaned myself up and dressed for dinner, the sky was already dark. I could hear Glory's voice floating from the parlor, directing the golems, and Jeysen in his chamber upstairs. I entered the parlor with a sheepish smile, expectantly.

"*Keeronae!*"

Glory stood up from the table with her pretty mouth in a surprised "o". "Your beautiful hair… What happened?"

"A great weight has lifted from my shoulders," I said blithely, taking a seat across from her at the table. My joints ached terribly, but I remained impassive. The parlor was a quieter, more intimate setting than the sedate, formal dining hall, and with a better view of the gardens from our seats near the expansive windows.

"Did Jeysen upset you?" she frowned. "I know he can be difficult at times. I must admit, though, that this is the first time I know of when he's driven someone to cut her hair."

"It's nothing," I insisted, raising my glass to Jeysen as he entered the parlor. "I'm sure it'll grow back. It's done so before."

The next morning, a golem came to wake me at dawn. My body was sore, and my head was pounding, but physically I was unscathed. *All that pain, and nothing to show for it.* By the time I left my room, I could already hear Jeysen warming up in the training room, which I learned had previously functioned as the ballroom before Jeysen repurposed it. The door to Glory's room was closed. I gulped a cup of tea and a slice of fruit for my breakfast and joined him shortly for our match.

"Your promptness is appreciated," Jeysen said when I entered the room. He tossed a staff to me and took another in hand.

Feeling the heft of the weapon in my grip, I tapped the tip of the staff against Jeysen's to let him know that I was ready.

The morning's session passed as the previous evening's had: with me losing every match, either by losing my weapon or lying prone at Jeysen's feet. As he pulled me to my feet for what felt like the tenth time, he suggested, "Maybe weapons are not for you. Let's try something else."

Setting the staves aside, we switched to hand-to-hand techniques, and Jeysen was able to observe my technique better with our closer contact. I was unaccustomed to being physically close to men, and I became self-conscious, despite the fact that Jeysen projected as much interest and emotion as any of his golems.

He aimed an open-hand blow at my head, which I blocked. "So," he started casually, "you want to tell me what's making you skittish?"

"I'm not experienced," I confessed. "Sarc is actually the first man I've ever kissed." It actually surprised Jeysen enough that my retaliatory punch connected with his jaw. "I'm so sorry!"

"No, I should have kept my guard up. Go on."

"*Hilafra*, it feels like I punched a rock." The pain was reverberating through my fist. "As I was saying, I'm not used to touching men. Although I know you have absolutely no interest in me, I start getting visions..." Even the mention of what I had envisioned the day before was making me uneasy.

"From your expression, I can guess the kind you're having."

"You don't seem surprised."

"I'm not." He looked into my eyes briefly. "But you are. You still don't know what's happened to you, do you?" At my blank stare back at him, he dropped his head tiredly. "Come with me. There's something you need to see."

I followed Jeysen into the hall, where a large, strangely garish tapestry obscured a door leading to a downward flight of steps. Guided by the steady light of wall sconces, we eventually reached the cellar, which was outfitted like an alchemist's workshop. Nearing the bottom of the steps, my breaths were saturated with the aromas of ancient vellum, chemicals and metals that filled the room and lined the shelves that defined the walls.

Jeysen lit a few more lamps and went directly to the far end of the cellar, where there stood piles of broken weapons and armor and a dormant forge with several half-finished projects, including one that I recognized. I was drawn to it immediately.

Tenn's head and torso were mostly assembled and propped on a stand, with her limbs on a table to her left. Peering into her gaping arm socket, at the shards of metal and wire within, I easily envisioned the flesh and bone equivalent. Images from past dreams flashed in my mind of Tenn's broken form, and her blank eyes confronted me, to force me to deal with my unresolved feelings of guilt and loss.

It had been mere days ago, during my first night in Altaier, when she stood at the foot of my bed to keep watch when I slept. I hadn't yet mourned her destruction, although she was a friend to me. Seeing her refreshed my memories of our short time together, and the helplessness I had felt when she was gone.

I reached towards her and stopped. "May I touch her?"

"That's why I brought you down here," he said.

I laid my fingertips on Tenn's cheek for just a second.

I did it. I was the one who destroyed Tenn. I had stirred in the middle of the night to find Malya standing before me. In my half-conscious state, I had lashed out and torn her apart with a few strikes of lightning. Tenn didn't struggle against me, her mistress, naturally. Out of the corner of my eye, I saw Jaryme next to me, seated on the bed, smiling with approval. I remained in my trance, waiting for his next command.

Ever so gently, Jaryme lifted my chin as he leaned over me and ran his fingers along the curve of my shoulder. My mind was like my body, aware of his touch, but numb and unresponsive. The room was soundless, muted by Jaryme's spell of silence.

Would it break his heart, if I had you first? He traced the edge of my jaw gingerly. *Too bad he's not here to see it.*

He traced his fingernail into my lip, drawing a trickle of blood that dripped onto my bodice. Closing his mouth over mine, Jaryme drank what he could of my blood before the wound closed itself. Next to Tenn's broken body, a white glow began to form, signaling Jeysen's impending arrival.

"Keeronae?"

My eyes opened to Jeysen's thoughtful gaze, and I dropped my hand from Tenn's face. "You were the first to arrive in the room. You've known all along."

"That you're bonded to my brother? Yes," he admitted. "And that you destroyed my golem, also, yes."

"Sarc knows everything that happened that night?" I swallowed.

"He figured it out. Sarc knew that we almost lost you that night, and that Jaryme could track you from the time you left Altaier, regardless of the route you took, so he knew there was a bond. At the monastery, Sarc saw for himself how strong the hold is that Jaryme has over you. My brother had tried something similar when he found you in the woods the first time, but your recalibration with Clyara's stone broke the connection, so he had to rebuild it."

"And now Jaryme's sending me visions? How close is he that he can get into my head like this?" Upon mentioning the visions again, I had to remind myself not to revisit them.

"Very close," Jeysen said, and directed me back to the steps. "This was once a summer home for my family, so Jaryme knows exactly where we are."

I went up the steps cautiously, half-expecting to see Jaryme at the top of the flight. "He could show up here at any time, then."

"Relax, *Keeronae*, he can't," Jeysen assured, passing me on the stairs. "I've learned from Junus how to cast protection spells along the perimeter of the property to make sure that no one comes in who doesn't have an amulet. Even portal spells need to be cast within a certain range in order to work."

Now I understood. "Sarc never intended to take me to Malya, did he? He knew I wasn't ready, but then his unexpected adjustment meant he wouldn't be able to protect me from Jaryme, either."

He nodded. "It just moved up our timeline a little, but I needed Sarc to get you at least as far as Dejàl before I could open the portal to you. My family has half a dozen properties around Inear, including the Imperial palace that Malya favors, so we could still keep Jaryme guessing about where we would eventually bring you."

"As long as I didn't know the plan," I finished. Otherwise, everything I knew would be known to Jaryme. I recalled the frustration I had felt about Sarc not trusting me enough to share what he knew, but now I knew that his secrecy had been warranted. My frustration was very different now, closer to the dreadful sensation of having an incurable disease destroying me from the inside out.

"With the protection spells in place, it's no wonder you said that this was the safest place to be," I said, walking beneath the tapestry he held aloft for me.

"After Ruvyna, perhaps," Jeysen said. "Junus is ruthless."

"Then you must be on your best behavior around his granddaughter," I said. "Or does he even know?"

"Junus knows all," Jeysen intoned. "He's advised my family for generations, and he's known me since I was born. He trusts me, as Clyara did, to keep watch over Glory."

"You apprenticed under him with Sarc, I'm guessing. Did you get the matching tattoos around the same time, too?"

"I did, *Keeronae*," he said. "The apprenticeship was painful, but worth the effort. The tattoo, I could have done without."

I remembered Sarc's remarks about the mark. "Sarc said it was for protection. From what, exactly?"

"Nothing of significance, anymore," Jeysen said.

"And your bonding with Sarc, was that part of your apprenticeship?"

"No," he said sheepishly. "That happened because Sarc and I lost a fight with something bigger and meaner than us. Our open wounds touched, our blood mixed, and from that point on, each of us could sense everything the other was experiencing. We avoided each other for days afterwards, and *Keeron* Junus eventually had to teach us how to block each other so we could regain some of our privacy and individuality. Bonding can be an awful thing, *Keeronae*."

289

"I'm starting to understand that, *my Lord,*" I said, mocking the formality of our titles. "I don't suppose you could teach me how to block Jaryme to keep him out of my head?"

Jeysen stopped in front of the training room and opened the door. "He would have to be bonded to you, too," he said, "and I don't foresee that happening anytime soon. Don't worry, we'll figure a way around it."

Dinner that evening was awkwardly silent. Glory sensed that the tension between Jeysen and me had diminished slightly, but neither Jeysen nor I were much for conversation. It had to feel strange for her, after living alone with Jeysen for so long, to have my arrival disrupt their shared life, but she was more welcoming than I could have hoped. The only woman who could have accepted me as unconditionally was Frost.

Jeysen sat at the head of the table, with Glory at his right and me to his left. He paid no attention to either of us, his mind occupied with other thoughts, and he barely touched his food.

I looked out the window at the gold and brown hues of the autumn garden. Some of the trees were almost bare, and aside from the moonglows with their waxy leaves and the roses with their scarlet hips, few of the shrubs were still green. "How are winters here?"

"Colder than in the south," Glory said, "and we're expecting a harsh one this year, worse than in years past."

"The Imperial Guard has never experienced even a normal winter in the Dark Lands," Jeysen said. "There will be thousands dead by spring, if Malya's troops manage to survive crossing the Fringe."

"Jaryme mentioned a war," I said quietly. "He was telling the truth?"

"Depends on what he told you," he said.

"That it would be soon. What does Malya want?"

"In the end, she wants your annihilation," Glory said. "She wants every trace of the elfyn wiped from existence. As the first step, she's organizing a small campaign, and when it fails, she will tap into the Realm's sense of imperial pride and outrage to justify a broader, more systematic approach to purification."

"She wants to destroy us all?" I asked, thinking of Frost and the children at home. "But they're simple people — some of them don't even know that the Realm exists! Isn't there any way to change her mind?"

Jeysen laughed, cynically. "Gemwraiths don't negotiate. War will come, regardless of your actions. The most you can do is be ready. Your early emergence from the Haven just made Malya more impatient to act, but that impatience will cost her in the end."

For countless days, Jeysen and I trained regularly from dawn to dusk, with only brief breaks in between for meals. I was more often the one who

290

insisted that our matches continue, and while Jeysen sometimes tired, either of the practice or of my company, he never refused me. Thankfully, Jaryme did not send more visions to me—he had made his point that he could.

Our extended sessions left little time for Jeysen to leave the grounds, so he relaxed with his grooming regimen a little. He had grown weary of shaving, and with his slowed rate of growth, the beard grew only a fraction of a centimeter in the first couple of weeks. The beard hid his perfect features and lent to his face a more mature beauty.

Once Jeysen got me accustomed to the different weapons in his armory, he restarted my lessons in manual combat. It was as important, he said, for me to know how to fight without weaponry, as it was for me to know how to fight without magic; such tools should never be taken for granted. Even our sparring clothes were fairly thin and loose-fitting, providing little protection or cushion.

His body was much older, battle-worn and stronger than mine, of course, so I always suffered more for the hard, jarring contact of our clashing limbs. Unconsciously, I learned to avoid the brunt of his powerful strikes rather than endure the body-crushing bruises.

He quickly caught on to what I was doing. "You're not shrinking from my touch, as much, that's something. But you won't always be able to cower, when someone tougher than me tries to put you down."

I massaged my sore limbs and flashed him an injured pout. "Tougher than you? I doubt it. Besides, I'm not a ... what's the word? 'Masochist?'"

Jeysen smiled unwillingly at my broadened vocabulary and went to the weapons rack to draw a long dagger from its sheath. He examined it briefly in the light. "None of this is about enjoyment, *Keeronae*. It's a matter of necessity, and of knowing all that you need to survive." He faced the weapon rack, absently scratching his whiskers with the tip of the dagger, looking for an alternate weapon. "Like how to mend."

He whirled around faster than I could see, and he sliced me across my midriff, through layers of fabric and flesh. I controlled my instinct to return the wound to him, only because I knew that he could have hurt me much more severely. He could have disemboweled me, had he wanted to. As superficial as it was, it still hurt, a lot. The sting gave way to searing pain, easing into a throb around the torn flesh.

My hand went to the wound at once, and my shirt became quickly stained red. I continued to remind myself that he wasn't trying to kill me; he had had plenty of opportunities for that. "How am I supposed to learn from this?"

Jeysen twisted his lip with concern and passed a conjured towel to me. "Concentrate. Don't be so passive about it."

"Look," I gnashed between painful breaths, "my body isn't as used to this as yours is. Give me a moment." My gem was repairing me from the inside out, mending and weaving the tissue back together, layer by layer. I tried to focus my energy inward, to let the gem speed the process of healing. The pain eventually became a dull, insistent ache that lingered for a few moments before it slowly faded. The long thin line of the scar was purple at first, with old blood collecting under the skin, but that too faded in time, until my skin was unbroken once more. My tunic was still drenched and warm with blood, but I was whole.

I caught my breath, gradually. Jeysen was waiting, wiping my blood from the dagger on the tail of his *gee*. We both knew that my gem had to learn to heal me faster; Malya would not be as generous with her timing. I straightened and braced myself for the next laceration. I swallowed and closed my eyes.

"At your command, Sir."

"Don't tense, you'll make it worse," he said.

As soon as I let out my breath, I felt the sting of the blade, and I tried not to flinch too much. It was going to be a long session.

In an attempt to afford Glory and Jeysen some privacy, I took my meals in my room whenever possible. Occasionally, I dined in the library, surrounding myself with Jeysen's books and maps, which reminded me of my late mistress's Haven, a lifetime away. When I began to feel lonely, I bestowed nicknames on the specimens in Jeysen's collection of skulls and skeletons.

I also became acquainted with Jeysen's extensive stables, occasionally accompanying the golems on their daily chores to feed, water and train the horses. The intelligent animals were skittish with me, initially, given my equine inexperience and general aloofness, but they gradually accepted my attention and companionship. To some of them, I probably wasn't never much more than a golem made of flesh, but a handful of them were genuinely affectionate and would affably trot across the paddock length to greet me. With few sentient acquaintances to engage in conversation, I appreciated the horses' innate, playful willfulness and strong sensitivity to my moods, honed over generations of selective breeding.

Once I made it clear to Jeysen that I had no intention of running off, and that I would train with him until he was satisfied with my progress, he gave me an amulet to his home. It was a deep blue cabochon stone set in gold filigree and steel, hanging from a fine swordmetal chain. I kept it safe in my room, next to my locket, and I never thought much about it.

I was never tempted to leave, as there was still so much left to learn. Studying the land masses and oceans of our world on Jeysen's topographical globes, I was humbled to discover that all I knew of the world, for all my twenty years, was neatly contained on a sliver of the map, on a piddling little continent in the northern hemisphere. One day, I mused, when this whole matter was over, I would try to see the rest of it.

In the meantime, I began to write. I was ineloquent and unpolished, but I needed a release for the ideas, thoughts and memories cluttering my head, and I poured my words and sketches into the black leather volume that Sarc had given to me. Using the pen and paper that he had touched, I was sustaining our connection as long as possible. To improve my knowledge of the common language, I spent my free hours in Jeysen's library, immersing myself in the works that he had collected over the decades: epic poetry, comedic and tragic plays, romantic sonnets and fanciful tales about races of mechanical people exploring worlds among the stars.

Many of the books I couldn't even read, written as they were in various strange languages. Jeysen even teased that some of them came from other worlds. Certainly, some of the diagrams and pictures seemed fantastic enough.

As expansive and extensive as it was, the library was not nearly as enigmatic as its master: given the motivation and enough time, I could eventually learn everything there was to learn within the volumes, but Jeysen would always find a way to surprise me.

Glory was just as intriguing, but in a more troubling way. Days passed without more than a few words exchanged between us. It was as though she sought to avoid me whenever possible. As I was the interloper in their home, I felt it was best not to force my presence on either of them more than necessary.

One evening, while Jeysen was out on a late errand, Glory came into the library. "I'm sorry, I didn't realize you were still in here," she said, and immediately turned to go.

"Please stay," I said, setting down my book. She looked uneasy. "Is something wrong?"

She shook her head and came in, closing the door behind her. "I was going to ask you the same. We never see you at meals anymore."

"I think I missed my solitude more than I realized," I lied, taking another sip of my valerian tea. It relaxed my muscles and prepared me for sleep better than other concoctions, and in Jeysen's favorite wingchair, I felt about ready to melt into a puddle. "Besides, you and Jeysen need your time alone, don't you?"

"Maybe at one time that was true," she said. "Now, I wonder sometimes if I wouldn't be more useful back with my mother." My expression must have given away something, as she smiled wanly. "You shouldn't believe everything you hear about her. Although she certainly deserves to pay for her crimes, she's not entirely the monster that people claim."

I sat up in my seat and gazed up at her. "Enlighten me."

She sat on the edge of the chair across from me and picked at her gown. "As far back as I recall, my mother saw to it that I lacked for nothing. Once she realized that I had inherited some ability to self-heal, and once I was old enough to understand what she was doing, she would cut me and strike me in measured doses, to force my body to recover more quickly. She always had tears in her eyes when she delivered the blows. She hated being the one who had to hurt me, but there was no one else she would trust. She called me her 'perfect child', and I always felt as though she would defend me to her last breath. She educated me about her feud with your mistress, and what she had to do to protect the humyn from Clyara's attacks. She never gave me a gem, explaining that Clyara would kill me if she knew of my existence."

"Obviously, that wasn't true," I said.

"That was one lie among many, but perhaps she believed it. I remained with my mother, though, because there was nowhere else to go. She wouldn't teach me anything of the magical arts, even in theory, in order to keep me safe from Clyara. Every time I ran away, she found me and brought me back. Finally, one day, I decided to run far enough away that I wouldn't be caught again."

"What made you seek out Clyara, of all people?"

"I don't know. Maybe I wanted to prove to my mother that she was wrong, and that I wasn't as imperiled as she believed. In any case, Clyara asked me where I wanted to be, so she brought me here."

"Then, this is where you belong. Jeysen needs you to be here with him."

"Maybe at one time," she said again. "Now, he has you."

"Me!" I laughed tiredly, leaning back in my seat. "The only thing his Highness feels towards me is a sense of obligation. He'll be eager to see me go, I'm sure."

"That's not true!" she defended. "Well, that may have been true when you first arrived, but he's come to know you better," she said reassuringly, laying her hand on mine. It was a warm, intimate touch that felt oddly familiar. It was also unsettling somehow, and it occurred to me then that we had never touched before. There was an energy that suddenly filled the room, something unleashed. My head felt incredibly heavy, and I had to shut my eyes for a moment.

Glory seemed to realize also that something had changed, and she got to her feet, withdrawing her hand. "It's not your fault. You were born into your role, just as I was born into mine. You are the *Keeronae*, and everything must yield to you. Don't worry, I won't stand in your way."

At the sound of the heavy iron candlestick moving across the marble table, I began to lift my head. Glowing white candlewax was all I saw.

Chapter 24: Good Intentions Gone Awry

My father smiled at me. "How you've grown, my little treasure."

I cried at the joy of seeing him alive and well, and I let myself forget that I was inside a dream. "I've missed you," I said between tears.

"I've missed you, as well." He touched a woolen muffler bound around his throat and coughed.

"Who did that to you?" I asked, recalling the terrible mortal wound that the scarf concealed.

"It's not important," he said.

I shook my head. "It's the most important thing in the world."

My father took my hand in his chilly grasp and gave me a sorrowful gaze. "If you're still set on revenge after all these years, then you've already lost."

"Was it Malya? Or, did Jaryme do this to you?"

Winter cupped my chin in his hand and forced me into his stare. "Let it go, janya. The matter is not yours to settle."

"But I will have to face them eventually," I said.

"You mustn't do it alone, or you will lose. You must trust your guardians to do what is best for you." He curled his arms around me and held me tightly. "This is a difficult time for you, but be brave. I will always be here, if you need me."

I felt something cold and metallic between us. Looking down, I saw our locket, which we both wore. "He must not win," he said, his eyes focusing on a gash of light forming and growing in the center of the room.

Jaryme appeared in our midst, dressed in white, with his hands sheathed in white leather. He turned his attention to Winter and smiled cruelly, "You, again." He formed a fist with his gloved hand, and my father's throat collapsed on itself. My father was dead before he fell to the ground, just like the first time.

I screamed, kneeling by my father's side, weeping. "You're the one who killed him! Why? He didn't even know you."

"He was in the way, and you didn't need him anymore," Jaryme said. "Soon, the other men will leave you, too, but you'll always have me."

I awoke with my fingers at my throat, gasping for breath. Finding myself alone and awake, I cried in silence for having lost my father again, even if it was only in my mind. It was Jaryme who had killed him. The vision of seeing Jaryme murdering Winter was indelible in my mind, more so when I closed my eyes, so I forced myself to remain awake and focus on my surroundings.

A couple of meters away stood a glass display case containing a humyn skull. The head had once belonged to an irritating little Guardsman named Leis, who had died conveniently, or so Jeysen had once told me. It was hard to tell sometimes when Jeysen was joking.

Jeysen. I sat up on the settee and picked up the candlestick from the floor and remembered what had transpired between Glory and me. *What am I going to tell Jeysen?* From the silence of the house, I knew that she was gone. I had awoken too late. I had been too careless in my dealings with Glory, and now I had lost her.

Where do I even start? How do I find her, and how do I tell Jeysen that we had quarreled? Was it even a quarrel? Glory had seemed to have her mind already set, and I hardly had the opportunity to respond. Something had happened when we touched. Something *snapped.*

I looked down at my hands when I realized that they were shaking. I forced them to be still and got to my feet. Perhaps if I cleared my head, the ideas would come to me. Perhaps if I went to Glory's room, I would find some indication of where she had gone. Jeysen's directive remained in my mind, but I reasoned that I would keep my visit brief. The door to the room was ajar, for once, and I entered before I lost my nerve.

The chamber was smaller than mine, but still spacious. It was decorated mostly in hues of cream and rose and had the distinctive character of a younger girl's room, right down to the upholstered toy animals in the corner of the room. I was reminded suddenly of Aelora's tattered doll among the ruins of her former refuge, and I realized that this had been her room when the house was occupied as the imperial summer home.

Hanging from the corner of the dresser mirror was a finely woven pink scarf. I grasped it in my hand and closed my eyes.

I turned around and brushed the copper-red curls from my eyes. I stared at the door, petrified of the commotion just outside, where my nurse was screeching orders to the golems. When my guardian burst into the room, I ran to him and hugged him around his waist. "What's going on, Uncle Jey?"

"It's time to go, Aelora. Don't be afraid." He shed his cloak and wrapped me in it. I watched him go to the shelves to pull some of my belongings from their neat compartments, tossing them as carefully as he could into a small satchel. He handed me my favorite doll, that I had for years, the black-haired one in the pink dress, and I crushed it to me.

I watched Uncle Jeysen in awe. He was like my father in his quiet strength. He was my hero, Mother called him her "baby brother," and he was more like a big brother to me than an uncle. There wasn't anything that my Uncle Jey couldn't do, and I wasn't afraid of him like I was of Uncle Jaryme. "Where are we going?"

"To the Dark Lands, where you'll be safe. I'll never let her hurt you, my

precious … my Aelora." I was yearning for my mother's comforting hug, but Jeysen's would do, and as he cradled me in his strong arms, I knew that everything would be fine.

"What are you doing in here?" Jeysen demanded.

I saw Jeysen as he was years ago, then as he was in the present, and the two images merged seamlessly. He was eternally young, eternally handsome. "You have always been my guardian," I said in awe, oblivious to his displeased frown, until the last remnants of the transference faded. Then, everything was painfully lucid.

"Where's Glory?" he asked.

"She left," I swallowed. "I think she may have gone home." I braced myself for Jeysen's accusations: what did I say to her, what did I do to upset her, why didn't I try to stop her… All he did was bow his head and leave the room. I caught up to him and grabbed his sleeve. "Wait! Aren't you going to say anything? Aren't you angry with me?"

He detached my hand from his sleeve gently. "No."

I did not grab his sleeve again, but I stayed close to him as he strolled towards his chamber. "When do we leave, then?" At his scowl, I elaborated: "To get Glory back?"

Jeysen opened his door and turned to me dismissively. "I have no intention of going after her anytime soon, and she was well aware of that," he said coolly. "Now, if you'll excuse me, I'm going to have a long evening ahead of me."

"Wait a minute," I snarled, forcing the door open. "You can't tell me that you don't care what happens to her!"

"I didn't say that," he said evenly. "Are you finished?"

"Why don't you want to save her?"

Jeysen rubbed his pale blue eyes and leaned against the doorframe. "Do you really want to have this conversation, now, *Keeronae*?" At my blank stare, he continued: "*We* are not going because *you* are not ready. If you can't even defeat me in drills, then there is no way that the two of us can infiltrate the palace to mount a rescue. Believe me, my ancestors built a very secure structure."

"So, you're going to leave Glory's fate in her mother's hands."

Jeysen stared down at me. "Until you can convince me otherwise."

"But what if—" I began desperately.

"Good night, *Keeronae*," he said curtly, and shut the door to me.

I tried to open the door and found it locked, both physically and magically. Jeysen was not in the mood for discussion that night, and who could blame him? *But what if I proved to you that I'm ready?* I had wanted to say.

And that you've just been wasting our time here these past few weeks? he would have replied.

Standing away from the door, I contemplated that possible exchange. Had I been restraining myself for some reason? Was I afraid that when the day came, I would fail? I shook my head resolutely. If not, and I really was making my best effort, then Jeysen was right, and I was far from ready.

That's what he wants you to think, the voice surfaced in my mind. *But you know the truth, don't you?*

I closed my eyes. *Go away, Jaryme.*

I will, soon enough. I've other ways to pass the time. What about you?

What do you want?

The same as always: to show you the possibilities that the others would hide from you. Images formed in my crowded mind, of a massive army camping in the Fringe, preparing for battle. Hundreds of fresh wolf pelts lay stretched on racks, drying in the late autumn sun, while soldiers sharpened their swords. On the far end of the field stood thousands of men and women from the Dark Lands, arming themselves with makeshift weapons and little more than hide and leather for armor. *This is what lies ahead for our people.*

I don't believe you, I said, even as I bristled at the thought of Frost on the battlefield. *It won't come to that. We'll find a way to stop —*

You're a fool to think that you can prevent it. Very well, then. Take some time, and think it over. My evening's entertainment awaits me, and for that, I'd like to thank you.

Thank me! What do you... I stopped short and swallowed. *By Ajle, what have I done?* I touched her. Rather, I let Glory touch me, and that simple act had cost Glory her freedom and sent her to Jaryme. *What did you do to me?*

I gave you a message to deliver to Glory, in the form of a charm, and she finally received it when she touched you. She knew you were tainted, somehow, but in the end, she couldn't help herself. Too much of her father in her. As his voice faded from my head, Jaryme let me see briefly through his eyes, and all I caught was a glimpse of Glory's despairing, tear-filled eyes. Her eyes shut tightly, and a muffled cry shattered the vision, returning me to the hallway outside Jeysen's room.

I pounded on the door, growing cold at the realization of what was happening inside.

"Go away," Jeysen eventually replied through the door, his voice barely above a whisper. "Go back to your room."

Jaryme, leave them alone! Receiving no response, I returned my attention to Jeysen's door. The door was still held fast to the frame, but that was easy to bypass. With a magical boost of strength, I tore the doorknob off my side of the door and pushed the rest of the lockset into the room. Through the hole in the door, I was able to phase into the chamber, where I saw him getting to his feet, and backing away from me.

"I'm so sorry," he said with his eyes downcast, keeping me at bay with a trembling hand. "He doesn't want you in here."

It was Jeysen's body, but not his voice, or his bearing. "Glory?" He lowered his head and shrank away even more. "It is you, isn't it. Jeysen's taken your place, in your body."

"Stay back!" he croaked. "You don't want to touch me. You shouldn't be here." He shrieked with a pain-filled sob and bolted for the adjacent chamber.

"Glory, wait!"

Jeysen stopped, but not by my command. He leaned against the bedpost and slid to the floor, his shoulders hunched and tense. "There's nothing you can do for us. He wants to punish us for keeping you from him." He took a deep breath and said, "Jaryme's gone, for now." He closed his eyes and nodded his head, as if to sleep.

I crouched next to Jeysen's unconscious body and waited. After a moment, he stirred and looked at me. "Get away from me," he said wearily in his natural voice, getting to his feet, and out of my reach. "How did you get in here?" He peered into the anteroom at his ruined door and grunted his annoyance.

"I should've guessed you were bonded to Glory."

"It would've changed nothing," he said, staggering towards his bed. "She still would have gone, sooner or later, and you'd hate yourself for not being ready any sooner."

"Jeysen, wait, there's something I have to tell you." I grabbed his sleeve and realized too late that I shouldn't have done it. Through that simple, unassuming touch, I tapped into Jeysen's consciousness and caught a glimpse of the trauma he had just experienced for her. A glimpse was all I could take before I jerked my hand back.

Glory was on her back, with her arms pinned to her sides, lying prone under Jaryme's weight. While it was her body enduring Jaryme's assault, it was Jeysen's consciousness trapped inside, feeling her physical helplessness. Jeysen saw his brother's face through his lover's eyes, and he felt Glory's presence, hundreds of kilometers away, in his own body. As much as he tried to shield her, Glory still shared his anguish through their bond.

The recollection was so intense and visceral, I could practically feel Jaryme's unshakable grip. Then, as quickly as the images had emerged, they were fading. I became conscious of Jeysen's hand on my face, and I pulled back, but Jeysen held me fast.

"It's not your memory to keep," he said softly. The last glimmer of the memory seeped away in his touch, but the discomfort remained. "I will do what I can to spare her suffering, but it's all we can do for now. Go to bed, *Keeronae*. We can discuss the matter in the morning with clearer heads."

Having lost the memory, I still felt helpless and angry about something that I knew Jeysen was keeping from me, but I couldn't figure out why. His last words were a charm on me, and I found myself nodding despite my doubts, but I fought it, remembering that I had something to tell him.

"It's my fault she's gone."

"What?" he said sharply. "What do you mean that it's your fault?"

I was oblivious to the trauma that Jeysen had just endured, so I said guilelessly, "Jaryme had cast a charm on me, that transferred to Glory when she touched me. It was because of me that she was impelled to leave. I'm so sorry, I wish there were something…"

"There isn't," he said tersely. "Let's leave this discussion for the morning," he said more mildly, and pointed me to the door.

I returned to my room with reservations, but I had to trust Jeysen's judgment until my own proved better. He was keeping his pain from me, and I couldn't force him to share it. He had shown himself to be a tenacious mentor and a formidable ally, and he deserved my confidence. He was as much a guardian to me as Sarc was, and he also cared for me, in his own way.

If only that devotion didn't exact such a high price.

I awoke after only a couple of hours of rest. I slept restlessly and dreamlessly, still tired but focused on the task at hand: getting Glory back. I dressed in the dark and listened for signs of activity in the house, but all was still.

Do I have your attention, now?

I gnashed my teeth at Jaryme's presence in my head. *Where is Glory, and what have you done with her?*

His laughter was soft and cruel. *So, my brother won't let you see. He plays the role of the guardian in every way, doesn't he? Don't worry about Glory, 'Fleece. She is more resilient than you may think. She's no stranger to my habits, and she knows that her mother wouldn't let her suffer any lasting harm. In fact, I quite admire Glory's courage to confront me and not hide behind walls, magic or otherwise.*

What do you know about courage? I said. *Does it make you feel like more of a man to hold someone captive who's defenseless against you?*

Do you have a more suitable adversary in mind? he countered.

I'm the one you want.

Oh, but you're not at liberty to volunteer yourself without Jeysen's approval, are you? Don't worry, dear 'Fleece. I assure you that Glory's presence here changes nothing between the two of us. You still hold a special place in my heart.

Should I be flattered, or concerned? I asked.

That would depend on you, he said gently. *Hopefully, one day soon, you'll come around to seeing things my way. In the meantime, I think I'll play host to Glory a little while longer. Perhaps the poignancy of the matter will move her father to act more decisively.*

At the mention of Glory's father, Jaryme must have sensed my confusion, and his cruel snicker filled my mind again. Before I could answer him, he was gone. For the moment.

I looked around the sunlit room and realized that Jeysen was probably awake. I hurried out of my room and down to the parlor, where the golems were already serving breakfast to their master. As I joined Jeysen at the table, I noticed that his food was untouched, as his brow was lined in thought. A pot of strong tea was before him, and its bittersweet, heady aroma pervaded the air.

That was odd in itself, as I did not know Jeysen to drink tea at all as of late. He claimed it made him high-strung, especially the recipe that I had taught the golems to prepare for me. Yet, he poured a full cup for himself and took it in hand. He did not look up at me, nor did he watch the golems attending him, as was his custom.

I took a seat next to Jeysen and waited for him to drink, but he did not. Finally, I broke the awkward silence with: "Jaryme visited me this morning."

Jeysen finally looked at me. "Did you speak to him?"

"Just briefly," I answered.

"And what did he say?"

I fidgeted with my napkin and lowered my eyes. "To not worry about Glory."

Jeysen raised his eyebrow at my phrasing. "Well, it doesn't gain him anything to have her permanently damaged, so I'm sure he'll see to her welfare, more or less." At my appalled glance, he explained. "It's all very simple, really. He keeps Glory because it gives him an advantage, and he'll work to keep it as long as he can. The fact that her imprisonment takes an additional toll on me may add to his sadistic pleasure, I suppose, but his real hatred is directed elsewhere."

"Then who is his intended target?" I thought about Jaryme's last words to me. "Glory's father."

Jeysen finally took a drink of tea. "He's reached the Dark Lands by now, and started negotiating alliances, perhaps. I don't know for certain, just as I don't know what his plans are now that Glory's situation has changed. Perhaps it's better that I not know."

"Has Junus been told, as her grandfather?" I asked.

"I sent a message to Ruvyna last night," Jeysen said, unaffected by my abrupt mention of his old *keeron*. "He sees the priority as contacting and recalling the Guardsmen and mages that he has dispersed over the years, to ensure that the Empress doesn't press them into her service first. He was distressed by the news, to the extent that Junus can be, but he, too, is a pragmatist. Jaryme learned that much from him, at least."

The enigma of Junus's role was becoming clear. "The Cleansing was a ploy to seed the Fringe and the Dark Lands with mages. So, it was all fictional? The Guard didn't kill anyone during that time?"

Jeysen stared into the cup of garnet brew. "No, we killed quite prodigiously. We hunted down the mages who were loyal to Malya, or only to themselves, and executed all of them who would not surrender their gems. If their loyalty was questionable, Junus felt that they were too dangerous to set free, so exile was not an option."

I recalled the vision from the monastery. "How many did you and Sarc heal and set free?"

"Thirty-four," he answered easily. "My fourteen to Sarc's twenty. Quite the humanitarian, our dear Alessarc. Non-lethal extraction was his trademark, so there were some who would only surrender to him."

It only hit me then that he and Sarc were of the same age, perhaps a year apart. The devastatingly beautiful young man seated before me, with his lustrous black hair and his glacial blue eyes, was in fact a very spry septuagenarian. I was getting thrashed daily in hand-to-hand combat with a man more than three times my age. I lowered my head into my hands and stifled a chuckle at how inept and absurd I must have seemed.

"I'm glad you find something amusing," Jeysen muttered as he drank his tea, sounding even more like an ornery curmudgeon. It was enough for me to break into open laughter, but I refrained.

I eventually stopped giggling, but not until after I pictured Jeysen and Jaryme as doddering old men hitting one another with canes. Not that Jeysen wasn't justifiable in his position, but it was the worst case of sibling rivalry I had ever witnessed. "I wonder if Jaryme is reading my mind now," I said.

"You'd probably notice if he was in your head. He's not one to listen quietly for very long. Not that anything we've said would interest him. He was Junus's prime apprentice, entrusted with many of *Keeron*'s secrets—and gems—before he decided to join Malya, and presently, he's probably busy trying to find our present weaknesses."

"Aside from me?"

He set down his cup, and I automatically moved to refill it.

"Not everything is about you, *Keeronae*. Malya still believes that she needs Sarc, for one, and she will go to any lengths to reach him, whether by threatening his interests, or by going into the Dark Lands after him."

"There has to be a way to avoid it," I gulped, recalling the visions that Jaryme has shared with me. "How are you so calm about an invasion? She's going to start a war!"

Jeysen was insouciant. "Any campaigns she attempts now are

commensurate to suicide. You and I both know the Dark Lands in the winter: it's months of crippling cold, avalanches and ice storms. If they're unlucky enough to encounter the scores of Junus's favored retired mages who now reside in the Fringe and Dark Lands, there won't be anything left of Malya's army by spring. Even if she's able to stir some nationalist outrage in the Realm, it will take time and resources to recover from the loss."

"But why expend the energy to hunt for Sarc, when Junus is still in the Realm?"

"You mean, why would she go all the way to the Dark Lands instead of stopping in Ruvyna? Our old *keeron* has made it abundantly clear to Malya that if they ever cross paths again, he will destroy what's left of her mind outright, even if it means sacrificing himself, Glory, you, me and half the Realm in the process. It's in her best interest to stay far, far away from him."

"If he's capable of that, why hasn't he confronted her first?"

"For the same reason Clyara chose not to leave the Dark Lands, to ensure the safety of their adopted homes. He trusts that we have everything well in hand, so he will not leave Ruvyna and risk exposing its citizens to danger."

I stopped for a moment and retraced the conversation. "Wait, how did we get so wildly off-topic? We were talking about Glory, and her father in the Dark Lands. And Sarc. *Hilafra.*"

"*Hilafra.* Yes, I couldn't agree more," he muttered into his cup.

"That's why you didn't want me to mention Sarc around Glory."

"That was as much for me as it was for her," Jeysen confessed. "I think you would've talked my ear off otherwise. Yes, Sarc is Glory's father, in addition to being Clyara's great-grandson, so Malya will do just about anything to get her hands on him again."

Sarc and Malya. Malya and Sarc. The very idea of their union was staggering, and I sat stunned for a moment. "I had no idea."

"No reason that you should," he said, as one entrenched amid the tangle. "It's not a part of his history that he likes to revisit, and not something for me to share, except to make clear that he was very young, and powerless to resist."

"Malya seduced him?"

"That is too kind a word. She took him by force."

I stiffened, feeling cold. "She raped him?"

"Yes, and that is all I will say. The rest is for Sarc to share, if he sees fit, but I felt you should know that he was innocent."

"Thank you," I said hollowly, feeling the heaviness in my heart give way to a new anger towards Malya. I was more determined than ever to put her down. "Are we training this morning, Sir?"

"I don't see why not." Jeysen set down his cup and rose to his feet. "This morning is no different from any other."

But that morning was different. With the urgency of Glory's predicament looming over us, Jeysen and I were more somber and focused than usual. We sparred well into the afternoon and even then, we paused grudgingly when the golem came with water.

"You have been holding back on me," Jeysen commented.

"And you haven't pushed me hard enough," I returned, taking a glass of water from the golem's serving tray. "We're both idiots."

Jeysen smiled tiredly. "So we are, *Keeronae*."

"I wish you would stop calling me that, my Lord," I said.

"I will, if you'll agree to do the same for me," he replied.

"It's a deal," I said, relieved that he shared the sentiment.

"Let's do something different today," he said, gesturing to the attending golem. The golem nodded, and left us alone.

"What do you have in mind, Jeysen?" I said, eager to address him finally by his name.

"Armory 101," he said, smiling at my befuddled stare back. "A brief lesson on the tools of our trade."

"Haven't we been using them?" I asked, glancing at the weapons all around us. The golem had returned with Jeysen's sword and pistol and held them out for its master.

"They're not like these." Jeysen started with his sword, an elegant weapon that was sleek and minimalist in design. The non-tapered blade was a little shy of a meter long, and the double-handed hilt added another three decimeters. It had a subtle curve when viewed from the side, and perfectly straight and thin when viewed directly. What looked at first to be a blackened stain that ran the length of the blade, revealed itself upon closer inspection to be a more intricate design, resembling waves rolling onto a beach.

Jeysen noticed my intent stare and held it out to me. "Try it out. Keep your hand high on the *tsuka*, close to the *tsuba*."

As my hand closed over the silk-wrapped hilt, its lightness and speed surprised me. It felt as easy to wield as a stick. I kept my hand near the ornate hand guard as Jeysen had directed, which bore the design of Jeysen's family seal. It moved almost effortlessly through the air. I could understand why Jeysen favored it. "It's a work of art," I said.

"My armorer called my *katana* her finest piece, although she thought the *wakizashi* was the prettier one of the pair. She amended the alloy to my specifications, so the metal is lighter and keeps its edge longer."

I nodded in acknowledgment, although I barely understood some of the words he used. He was using neither elfyn nor common terms, of that much I was certain. I wondered how it would feel to bring the sword edge down on the back of Malya's neck. Would it slice through it, or catch itself on her spine? When I noticed his eyes on me, I sheepishly passed the *katana* back to him.

"Where do you go, that you need to arm yourself like that?" I mused.

"I'm building bridges," he said with a cryptic smile, returning the sword to its scabbard and drawing the pistol.

"Forging alliances?" I inferred.

Jeysen smiled and said: "In a way. 'To fight and conquer in all your battles is not supreme excellence; that comes from breaking the enemy's resistance without fighting.'"

"Did you just make that up?" I asked.

"No, *janya*, that is common sense passed down through the millennia from a fabled strategist, and it's something that I try to remember before every battle. Take a look at this one." Jeysen opened the chamber of the pistol and held it out for my inspection.

Unlike the harquebus-style pistols that the marauders carried, Jeysen's pistol had rifling in the barrel, a revolving chamber in the breech, and an atypical firing mechanism. "No fuse," I noted. "It's not an Imperial weapon."

"No, it's my own prototype, based on an ancient design. When you pull the trigger, the chamber turns to set up the next bullet. At the same time, a piece of flint hits the steel in here, which creates a spark. The spark explodes the charge, which expels the bullet." He grinned at my awed visage. "Like magic."

"Ancient design from what civilization?" I asked haltingly. "Nothing in the Realm or the Dark Lands, I'm sure."

Jeysen closed the chamber with a flick of his wrist. "Not for another hundred years under normal circumstances, but I'd rather not wait for evolution to run its course for this. The other technological advances can wait until people are ready for them, especially when it comes to weaponry."

"Aren't you concerned that someone else may find it and copy your design?"

He passed the weapon to me. "They'd have to know how."

I tried to open the chamber as he had done, without luck. In fact, it didn't appear to have any moving parts at all. In my hands, the pistol had become just a metal sculpture with an intriguing design. "It only responds to you."

He nodded, taking the pistol back. "It responds to whomever I choose, and also has the same sensors as the golems, to send a beacon if it is tampered with. I'm not completely mad. I am fully aware of my responsibility to safeguard what I use, and if an opportunity presents

305

itself..."

"Take every advantage where you can find it," I said, recalling Sarc's identical sentiment.

I was too beyond bewildered and awestruck at that point to try to question what he was saying. I recalled Sarc's clay figurine back in his house in Mione that he had described as "a ship for traveling among the stars," and I gave Jeysen's weapons another look. "Your arms wouldn't happen to come from another planet, would they?" I asked, my words sounding ridiculous as I formed them.

"No, they were crafted here," Jeysen assured me, and I exhaled with relief. "But the designs originated on another world."

I stared at him, but he was nonplussed. He handed his weapons to the attending golem and turned to the rack. "You must've had an interesting childhood," I muttered.

"I had a delightful, wondrous childhood," he said in earnest. "With all the benefits of royal birth. It's my adulthood that's dubious, as I'm sure you've guessed. Sometimes I wonder whether everything would've been simpler had I not decided to serve under Junus."

"You'd be a withered old man by now, watching helplessly as your brother conspires with the dead Empress," I said blandly. "It may not be the simpler path, but I'm glad it's the one you chose."

"That almost sounded like a compliment." At my silent shrug, he said, "I'll take what I can get, then. All right, lesson over, Snowfleece. What's so funny?"

I shook my head. "Hardly anyone calls me that anymore," I said. "It sounds too precious, like I was named after someone's pet."

He raised his brow and pulled a machete from the rack. "I agree it's not the kind of name to bellow on the battlefield, to strike fear into the enemy's heart. 'Fleece' isn't any more ferocious, but I suppose it's no worse than 'Jeysen.'"

We stopped after the sun had long set, when we were both too winded to speak. Without spoken commands to drive them, the golems acted autonomously, tending to their housekeeping duties in silence.

Jeysen and I stopped in the kitchen to get something to eat. I stood silent in the pantry, watching the golems tend to their various chores without supervision, like an army of ants around their monarch. Jeysen, for his part, seemed accustomed to being ignored, and he helped himself to some fruit and a piece of bread while his golems went about their business. He lobbed a plum at me, and we watched the golems file out of the kitchen and extinguish the light behind them, as dictated by their daily routine. Without our words to cue them, they had been unaware of our presence and had left us in darkness with the rest of the fixtures and furniture.

Jeysen and I stood unmoving for a moment, then burst into laughter. We were delirious from exhaustion and hunger, and Jeysen leaned heavily against the massive marble counter while I cast a flare to illuminate the kitchen.

"I'll need to build some better environmental sensors for the golems next," he noted.

I spied a carafe at the far end of the counter, and I poured some water for both of us. He raised his glass to me and drained it in a single gulp, and in his rabid thirst, some of the water trickled past his chin, along the smooth line of his throat and into the soft ivory cambric of his shirt.

Before I even thought about what I was doing, I reached over and whisked the stray drops from his bearded jawline, and he replied with a dazzling, unguarded smile. With the same ease, he brushed back a stray lock of hair from my cheek and straightened my collar. His fingers lingered lightly on my shoulder, and his smile faded, as he met my eyes.

I recalled the first time I had seen Jeysen, from the inside of a cage, and how his intense gaze had startled and unnerved me. His ice-blue eyes were focused on me now, and while I was no longer frightened of him, I was still unnerved. I felt a tremor flow through me at his piercing stare, as I wondered what he found so interesting. He sensed my tension, and he withdrew his hand and dropped his eyes.

"Jeysen." In the stillness of the kitchen, my voice boomed, even at a whisper. I wasn't sure what to say next.

He did not raise his eyes again and instead turned to the door. "Good night, 'Fleece," he said quietly. Before I could rejoin, he vanished.

The next morning, I was dressed in the Imperial uniform, ready for a full day's work, but instead of the practice room, I went to the courtyard to spend some time in Jeysen's herb garden. I needed some time to mull over what had transpired during the hours since he and I had last spoken, and what to do next as a consequence. I had heard him in his chambers upstairs when I retired, and I knew from the low muffled voices that he was again trying his best to ease Glory's torture at Jaryme's hands. *All of this is wrong. I shouldn't be here, while she's suffering.*

The savory scent of the new sage mixed pleasantly with the heady aroma of lavender, but their cool, silver hues saddened me. The sprouting of silver sage meant that winter would soon arrive, and that meant that time was running out. I had to think of a way to buy us more time, for Jeysen would not last the season. His brother would see to that.

In my periphery, I saw Jeysen by the door. In the last few weeks, I had learned to sense his presence nearby, even from the other end of the house sometimes, but few things captured my full attention like the actual sight of him. Conditioned to his ways, I awaited his orders with a straightened stance, as a soldier awaits the commander.

"Is something the matter?" he called across the garden.

"Why don't you tell me?" I countered, meeting him halfway. I looked at him squarely, and I cursed myself for not intervening the night before. His face was white, except for the darkness underneath his blood-shot eyes. "*Hilafra*, Jeysen, this is going to kill you," I said, catching up when he turned to go back inside. "Please," I said, catching his arm, "let me help."

"I won't have this conversation with you again. There's nothing to be done about it," he said vacantly, removing my hand.

"There must be something I can do." I stopped short, and he turned to face me.

Jeysen's expressive eyes were unused to harboring secrets, and I saw his internal conflict easily. "Nothing to which I'll be a party," he said evenly. "I swore to protect you, to the end."

"Which will be soon enough, if I can't stop this madness," I snapped, then tried to appeal to his practical mind. "Jeysen, you can't function like this, day after day. To be anything but your best would do us both a grave disservice."

He laughed without humor, "I'm sorry to disappoint, but you've never seen me at my best."

"But I'm sure Glory has," I said, having made my decision at last. "And she deserves to come home to you," I resolved, stepping back from him and reaching into my pocket. His eyes grew wide, and he realized at that instant what I meant to do. He lunged forward, too late, as the vial of soil shattered on the marble tile, and the portal engulfed me.

I took a moment to get my bearings in the new space, to steady my stance and take in my surroundings with a clear head. I took a breath and smelled a mixture that was decidedly masculine, something with smoke, leather and faint musk. It was not unpleasant, but it was also familiar in an eerie, hair-raising kind of way, and I remained on my guard. The opulence of the antechamber was impressive, gilded and festooned with billowing waves of jewel-tone fabrics on every wall and window. Somehow, I had expected something more sinister, more gruesome: bone furniture and drapes of animal and humyn skins, perhaps. The room was silent and still, but not empty. It was hardly that.

"Welcome, Snowfleece of Moonteyre," he said warmly. "It's good to see you again in the flesh."

I did not face Jaryme, but I felt him approach from behind. "I wish I could say the same."

"You may, in time," he said lightly, untroubled by my coolness. He brushed past me and towered over me, taking my scent deep into him. He looked at my short hair with a slight, inquisitive smile, and I recalled why I

308

had once found him handsome. "I trust that you encountered no trouble coming here."

"None," I said shortly, and his charming smile became a knowing smirk. "Everything was where you said it would be." While Jeysen had been distracted last night by Jaryme, I had stolen into Glory's chamber and found the ingredients under the bed exactly as Jaryme had described during one of his nocturnal visits. It had been Glory's stash, the components she had used to make the same trip here, the palace in Inear. I wondered briefly whether she had stood where I was now, and was as wary of Jaryme as I was, watching him circle like a shark.

"Now, I've kept my end of the bargain…"

Jaryme brushed his fingers across my cheek, where he had so angrily struck me weeks ago, and bobbed his head. "There is time for that, my dear. You've only just arrived."

"I want to see Glory first, now. I want to know that she's safe."

"Naturally." He seemed amused by my resolve, now that he had me where he wanted me. He looked towards the heavy velvet drapes that separated the bedchamber from the anteroom and reached out his hand. "Glory, look who's come to visit."

I turned my head, expecting to see a pale, cowering waif lurking in the shadows, petrified of her captor. Instead, I saw Glory as fresh and lovely as ever, and for a second, I was horrified that I had been duped by a simple, cruel prank. Meeting her pale green eyes, however, as she drew aside the drapes, I felt a chill overtake me.

Her expression was blank, her eyes nearly lifeless. Although her body seemed untouched, her spirit was all but absent. I fought the urge to touch her, as I was certain that she would cringe from me, and I could not bear inflicting more pain on her than she and Jeysen had already endured.

"Why have you come?" she said, her voice light and lyrical.

"Jaryme has agreed to let you go," I said gently.

Glory turned in Jaryme's direction, but she did not look at him. "Thank you, *Keeronae*, but I want to stay."

I bit back my anger, recalling how Jeysen had suffered, and I tried to reason with her. "There's no reason for that. Jeysen needs…"

At the mention of Jeysen's name, she visibly stiffened, and her beautiful pale eyes narrowed. "I don't care what he needs! I can't stand that house, or him," she growled, and she grabbed my sleeve before Jaryme could intervene.

As with the last time, I was flooded with Glory's thoughts, her tangled memories and imagined fantasies, until her mad visions drowned my own logic. She remembered being the victim of repeated brutality, but in her confused mind, it was Jeysen who was assaulting her, and not the monster in the room with us. Glory's thoughts were so tangible, so detailed, that I could almost believe that there was truth there, but then I remembered Jeysen—*my* Jeysen—who would sacrifice his own well-being to ease her pain. I also remembered Sarc, who loved Jeysen better than his own brother did, and trusted him in some ways more than he did himself.

I ignored Glory's crippling vise on my sleeve and glanced at Jaryme, who seemed faintly amused by her break and my attempt to tug free of her frantic grip. I saw through Glory's madness to Jaryme's cruelty, and I resolved to never submit to him, nor his gemwraith mistress.

"I'll give the two of you a moment to get reacquainted," he said breezily and swept from the room. He was confident that Glory would sound an alarm the moment I attempted to take her back with me to Jeysen's home.

I had to find a way to convince her to leave of her own free will, as I couldn't send her back to Jeysen in her present condition. Leading Glory to a daybed beneath one of the large palladian windows and gesturing to her to sit with me, I steeled myself for a long, discordant and potentially unproductive discussion about what was to come.

"You should not have come, *Keeronae*," she whispered hoarsely, her voice sounding stronger, more certain. "Now, things are worse."

"I'm sorry to have been your trap," I said. "I had no idea…"

She shook her head. "It's not your fault. Jaryme tricked us all, and I was too weak to fight his spell. I should have been more careful around you."

"How has Jaryme been treating you?" I asked plainly.

"I suffer no permanent scars, if that's what you mean," she said with an even voice. "He hasn't taken me to see my mother, although I have asked on several occasions."

The idea of leaving Glory in the company of her undead mother troubled me. "What do you hope to achieve by seeing her?"

"I can convince her to stop this quest. She has no hope of winning, but no one here will challenge her command. Jaryme says that she won't be swayed from her cause to exterminate the elfyn, but I have to try. She needs to rest, finally, and accept her passing." She sat with her hands demurely on her lap, shredding the tip of a ribbon cinching her tiny waist. "How is Jeysen?"

"He is doing as well as he can," I said, realizing that she had not been tricked by Jaryme's lies. "You had me fooled there for a while."

She smiled. "Something Jeysen helped me master, and Jaryme is so confident in his own skills that he doesn't question why I would choose to remain here."

"You have to return home," I said urgently. "Jeysen does need you."

"I know, but you still shouldn't have come for me." She seemed sad, staring down at her loosely knitted fingers. "It's wrong for you to be here."

Automatically, I reached across and set my hand on hers. Again, as before, a shimmer of energy passed between us. Glory tried unsuccessfully to pull free, but I held fast and worked quickly with my free hand. I cast a spell of silence around us to stifle Glory's cry of alarm and the shattering of the vial of soil at our feet. As the portal bloomed next to us, I wound around her wrist the metal chain that held the amulet that Jeysen had given me weeks ago, and I shoved Glory through the magical passage.

I turned the soil and broken glass at my feet into dust, destroying the portal and eliminating all traces of its components. Without the amulet key, I had no chance of returning anyway, but I had to be sure that Jaryme was cut off, as well. At the least, I would try to distract Jaryme and buy Jeysen more time to shore up his defenses.

I looked across the empty chamber, to the open doorway, where Jaryme stood glaring, with his fists tightly clenched at his sides. "Now that you've had your fun, 'Fleece, it's time to meet your new mistress."

Chapter 25: The White Witch

The palace was grand, certainly, but cold and drafty, as old castles often are. Jaryme led me through the maze of marble corridors for a long while before we stopped at a set of large oak doors, attended by two strapping Guardsmen. Jaryme signaled to them to open the doors, and neither of them seemed to notice that my arms were tightly shackled behind me, or that a streak of blood decorated my left eyebrow where Jaryme had struck me.

He was displeased that I had managed to send Glory home without his notice or permission. He cast a spell to muddle my thoughts again, so that I couldn't be a threat to him magically, and he bound my arms to keep his physical advantage. I had managed earlier to free myself from the first set of shackles, but he had another, stronger spell ready and a heavier, tighter set of restraints to bind me.

The doors opened to a silent chamber. To the courtiers in attendance, I must have been a strange sight, with my old-issue Guardsman's attire and halo of white curls, chained like a common criminal, being presented to her Imperial Majesty like a trophy animal. I took a deep breath that caught in my throat, as I smelled something cloyingly sweet that seemed to cling to me, something elusively recognizable, as though from childhood. I looked around the sumptuous throneroom at all the attendants and courtiers, trying to find the source of the odor.

It was something from years past, but not my childhood. The last time I had smelled it, was the day my *keeron* died.

The scent came from Malya, who gazed upon me from her throne. She dismissed her guards and her court, so that there were no witnesses aside from Jaryme. Perched on her royal dais, she was as imposing and beautifully regal as always to the eye, but the stench of death pervaded her perfumed illusion, however well-masked. Even her eyes, pale green and focused on me, were soulless, blank and empty. Sparkling and clear like glass, but just as hard and dead.

When the doors shut behind us, Malya rose from the throne and came down the steps to us. She raised her hand to Jaryme, who brushed her fingers against his lips with great reverence. She stepped closer still to me and reached her hand out to touch me, and I did not flinch. Even as her white, dimpled fingers touched my cheek, I did not cringe from her cold and leathery touch. I kept my revulsion in check and forced myself to keep my expression bland, yielding nothing to her.

"Little elfyn girl," she breathed, and her putrid air seized my nose and throat. "You are the one who shall destroy me, then?"

"So, I've been told," I replied.

"You believe it, too," she said, then looked down at my mannish, grey Guardsman's uniform. "What gives you the right to wear that, little white witch?" With that, she raked her nails down the front of my shirt, tearing through the fastenings and some of my skin as well.

The uniform did not yield easily, and neither did I. I had suffered worse injury at Jeysen's hands, and I was secretly grateful that I would not break easily at Malya's. I caught a glimpse of Jaryme and saw his amusement, even arousal, at the sight of my bloodied state. It was no more than an instant, as the scratches healed quickly.

Belatedly, Malya looked down at her fingernails and noticed the spots of my blood underneath them, and she licked them daintily, taking that miniscule piece of me into herself. "Mm," she said, licking her lips. "She's so very sweet."

"Yes, I recall," Jaryme smiled, watching her enjoyment of me. He was eager for his own opportunity to dominate me, I could see in his eyes, but he would wait for a more intimate setting. "She can serve you well, very soon."

Malya nodded, looking into my face with her wide, expressionless eyes. "You don't think so, do you?" she asked. "Sarc thought he could fight me, but in the end, he served me very well, too. And he will again, soon."

My mind was abuzz with ideas of how to destroy the gemwraith witch standing less than an arm's length from me, but I remained silent and just let myself savor the news that Sarc had managed to evade her, still. I was hardly in any condition to act effectively, with Jaryme's spell dampening me. I hoped that there would be another opportunity, the next time his spell wore off and my abilities returned.

In the meanwhile, Malya was already returning to her throne, as unconcerned with me as she would have been with a fly buzzing about the room: I was a nuisance, perhaps, but no serious threat. Strangely, I had no sense of her in my mind. She had tasted my blood, but there was no sign of her presence inside me that I could feel.

Jaryme lay his hand on my back, between my shoulders, and led me back out of the throne room. "Shall I show you to your new room?"

I refused to turn in his direction. "In the dungeon?"

"Not unless you forget your place," he said. "However, little *Keeronae*, if you behave as you should," he smiled, bringing his lips to my ear, "I can see to it that you are rewarded justly for your allegiance."

I did not reply, and in fact, I said nothing at all until we stood before an ornate oak door, adorned with intricate tracery. Jaryme opened the door inwards and herded me inside. "This was my sister's room before she was made Empress. She had impeccable taste," he said casually, as though he were leading me on a tour.

I have to admit that the chamber was spectacular. The high ceilings boasted additional tracery and provided a stunning complement to the towering posters that surrounded the bed. The walls and linens were done in a deep green hue that reminded me of dense pine groves at their peak of growth. It was not the kind of accommodation that I expected was often provided to an enemy of the Realm.

"Are you angry?" he asked. "Are you still holding a grudge against Malya for killing your mistress?"

He was addressing me as though I was having a childish tantrum, and I was in no mood for his superciliousness. Clyara's death was only one on a long list of reasons why I wanted Malya destroyed. "I may be angry for a good long time."

"I see," he said. "So, you sacrificed yourself to come here and are hoping that somehow Malya lets her guard down long enough for you to assassinate her? Was that your grand plan?"

"I had no grand plan," I said, straining at the shackles to get more comfortable. That was true; my only goal had been to save Glory, and I had not had the time to think through a strategy for escape.

"Perhaps you would consider my more modest one," he said, circling me. "I did suggest to you once that I would be willing to teach you. Who knows Malya's weaknesses better than I do?" He paused in front of me and looked down at my torn clothes. "I could have destroyed you at any point since you arrived, but I'd rather not. One day, I hope you'll see the wisdom in the path I've chosen. One day, perhaps, you'll travel the path with me."

"At your heels, or at your side?" I asked, unable to ignore his intimate perusal of me.

"Or with me at yours," he said softly. "You would be a magnificent Empress, and you've seen for yourself that I'm happy to serve, to exist in the shadows for the harmony of the Realm."

"You'd be as happy to serve me, as you do Malya? What use would I have for an advisor with no loyalties?"

"A pragmatic advisor who is open to new opportunities," he corrected. He ran his hands down the length of my body casually, to check for additional amulets and vials of soil, and when he was satisfied that I had smuggled nothing else aside from what I had used for Glory, he released my shackles. He tapped my head before I could dodge his hand, and again my mind swarmed with innumerable ramblings and thoughts that prevented me from being able to concentrate on any spells. They

314

weighed more heavily in my head than any manacle he could have clamped onto my limbs.

Satisfied with the look of annoyance that I wore plainly, he smiled. "Now that I can trust you not to run away, I'll give you some time to think about my offer."

Jaryme did not visit me until the evening, after the tailors and groomers had done their appointed work on me. The women he charged to outfit me did not respond to my questions or statements about him or the Empress, and only by their skittishness and cowed expressions did I know that they were really women and not just golems like Jeysen's servants. By the time the maids came to scrub and wash me, I had realized that I was endangering them all by speaking with them, that their willful silence was their only defense against any charges of treason brought on by my mutinous rhetoric. As the maids also did not deign to start conversation with me, my grooming ritual was completed in utter silence.

The door to my chamber opened wide just as a silver and blue ribbon was tied into a delicate bow around my throat. My locks were too short for my dressers to do anything but to wash and pin it. The maids rushed out, curtsying to Jaryme on the way, leaving me alone with him.

He greeted me with a smile and lingered in the doorway, his blue eyes taking in every detail about me. He was dressed neatly, in a pristine white shirt and a silver and dark blue brocade waistcoat, complemented by a coal-black coat and trousers. He looked polished and refined, and not at all dangerous or even capable of violence, but I knew better.

I recognized the beautiful silver and dusky blue cloth of his vest, as it was the same for my gown. Even the ribbon that adorned my throat bore the same colors. The tailors had gone to great pains to see that my dress fit snugly against my body, so that little of my shape was left to the imagination. The neckline of the frock was cleverly cut to tantalize with a peek of my cleavage, and the undergarments fashioned from silk and wire also served to prominently display my curves. The dress was sleeveless, and the ankle-length skirt billowed, which meant that easily-accessed weapons were out of the question.

I didn't dare try to amend my clothes, on the off chance that my outfit was Jaryme's selection. If he noticed any alteration to it, he was more likely to retaliate against the innocent dressmakers rather than me, and I didn't need that kind of indirect guilt on my conscience.

It was too late to fold my arms for modesty's sake, so I stood with my hands at my sides and my chin raised proudly, defiantly. I had not recovered my magic, but I had long since recovered from the indignities of being handled and finished like a prized sow. Instead of irritation at my composure, I saw satisfaction and appreciation in Jaryme's expression as he took my hand in his.

"As I suspected, you're better suited to this life than you realize. When I present you before Malya's court tonight, none will question your right to be there." He pressed his lips to my fingertips as I had seen him do earlier with Malya, and a shudder ran down my bare back. "You belong with us, 'Fleece. You'll learn that soon enough."

"Behold, a rare albino elfyn maiden from the Dark Lands!"

I entered the hall alone, but Jaryme stood nearby, to take my hand and walk me to the dais where Malya awaited. I chose not to tax my energy fighting Jaryme's control over my limbs and my ability to speak, as he was unlikely to take advantage of my weakness and raise his hand to me in full view of the court. As my mind was still muddled by Jaryme's spells, the thoughts of those around me were hidden, but the leering and assessing glances were telling, and some did not bother to lower their voices.

"I heard that she was found in the gutter in Altaier."

"The wretched thing is so uncivilized that she can't even speak or understand the common language."

"What fierce, savage eyes! She doesn't even know how lucky she is to be here."

Once Malya acknowledged us with a nod of her head, Jaryme directed, *You will curtsy to the Empress.*

I did fight that moment. She was not *my* Empress, and I did not recognize her sovereignty.

You will show respect, or every servant who came to your chambers today will be executed by the end of the night. Jaryme nodded with a pleasant, encouraging smile. *I would see to it personally.*

A few awkward seconds had passed, and there were some chuckles of discomfort as the court anticipated my performance. I nodded my head to Malya and executed a formal Guardsman's bow instead of the customary ladies' curtsy. When a few giggles erupted at my faux-pas, I feigned a look of confusion and stepped to the side before Jaryme could force me to correct myself.

Luckily, Malya had already turned her attention to the next guest in line, and she did not stay much longer. The nobles in attendance seemed to take her aloof behavior in stride. In fact, they seemed to find her presence unsettling and avoided looking in her direction. The mood in the ballroom lightened considerably, after she retired for the evening, and the wine flowed more freely. In fact, the evening's festivities gradually took a more debauched turn, with the guests engaging in behavior that was more suited to the bedroom, or the barnyard.

Jaryme was utterly clear-headed, as was I, at first. He left me free to move about the ballroom as I pleased, but he returned to me from time to time to reinforce the blocks that he had set up in my mind to prevent me from casting or speaking. With his constant hail of spells, layers deep, I found my mind becoming even more clouded as the evening wore on. I watched numbly as various ladies of the court threw themselves at Jaryme, but I was lucid enough to avoid the drunken groping and propositions from the lords of the court, some of whom were married to the aforementioned ladies.

I had just dodged the grasps of both a portly gentleman and his drunken wife when I felt a hand seize my arm. Expecting to see another inebriated nobleman, I was almost relieved to see that it was Jaryme.

Does this happen every night? I asked, as he pulled me behind a column.

"No, tonight's a celebration," he said. "The Empress wanted to hold a ball in honor of the brave men who are marching off to war in defense of this great Realm. The troops deploy at dawn." He looked down at my rigid expression. "The Empress will not stop, whether it takes five thousand or five hundred thousand troops to conquer the Dark Lands. Now that she's certain that you're not there to defend them, this would seem the best time to strike."

It doesn't have to happen this way, I said, thinking of the visions that Jaryme had once shared with me. *You could advise her to call off the attack. She would listen to you.* I touched his sleeve gently, in a silent plea. There had to be something that I could do or say to sway him.

He looked at my hand, then at me, more intently. "What are you willing to sacrifice for your home?"

I jerked my hand away. I wasn't a fool, not entirely. He wanted my loyalty, which I couldn't give, nor could I allow him to hold the threat of invasion over my head, to use whenever I resisted. *This is insanity, Jaryme. The Dark Lands will never succumb, but the Realm will be crippled in the attempt. This empire won't exist for much longer, if you let her proceed.*

"So, you're thinking of the Realm, as well," he said. "How very altruistic of you, *Keeronae*. What are you willing to give, in return for my support?" he demanded, taking my arm again. At his touch, I began to waver, and I knew that he had cast another spell to befuddle me.

We were interrupted by a colorful lady with bright plumage. That is, she wore vibrant feathers as part of her outfit, but I could almost mistake her for a large exotic bird, especially as she opened her painted mouth and spoke in loud, irritating squawks. "There you are, Lord Jaryme! I thought perhaps the two of us could go into one of these quiet little rooms for some … conversation, but I see you're busy. You must come visit me sometime. You would always be welcome in our home." With a dramatic fluff of her elaborate headdress and a raucous caw of a laugh, she moved on, her tail feathers swaying in her wake.

317

I giggled despite Jaryme's tight grip on me, as I was too lightheaded to react otherwise. I peered up into Jaryme's unsmiling face and sobered instantly.

"What a wonderful idea, 'Fleece," he said, pulling me towards the door. "Let's find a quiet room for some 'conversation.'"

The air shifted around me, and I felt the cool, silky cover of a bedspread against me. I pushed myself upright immediately. It was an unfamiliar room, but similar in scent to the chamber in which I had arrived that morning. *By Ajle, I haven't even been here a full day?* It was a bedchamber, obviously, judging from the oversized piece of furniture that lay underneath me. It was Jaryme's bedchamber, I deduced. The furnishings were made of the same dark woods that filled my chamber, but the linens on the bed were brilliant white. The room was silent, aside from my breathing and that of Jaryme who stood beside me, next to the bed.

"Why do you fight me, 'Fleece?"

His words didn't sound angry, but I could hear his temper in his breath. He grabbed me easily and yanked me off the bed, towards him, and I was too off-balance to struggle. He pulled my head back by my hair to lift my chin and kissed me. Desperation mixed with seduction in his deep kiss, as though he was trying to turn me still. For a brief moment, he was not domineering, only yearning. Had he not locked me in place with his magic, I might have granted the kiss freely.

But he did force himself on me, and I could not let that behavior go unanswered. I stopped struggling long enough to let him enjoy his dominance, then sank my teeth into his tender lips, hard enough to draw the blood I wanted. He growled and squeezed my mind until I let go, but he was too late, I had taken what I needed. I would have taken more had his body not healed so quickly.

Fair is fair, Jaryme. Now, we're even.

He watched me lick the last drop of his blood from my lips, his eyes narrowed with rage, and slapped me for my insolence, hard enough that I fell back onto the bed. He seized me while I was dazed and flipped me face down onto the bed. I felt cool air against my legs as he yanked up the skirt of my dress, then his weight on top of me.

"You treacherous little bitch," he whispered, as sweetly as an endearment. "If you wanted a part of me inside you, all you had to do was ask."

I braced myself, his vicious intentions obvious to me even without our new bond, but now I heard and felt his thoughts and mood deep inside my head. I had expected things to come to this eventually, and at least now I had a fighting chance. Jaryme pulled the silken ribbon that was wrapped around my throat, tightening it under my chin, before I could teleport away. He didn't want to kill me, but he knew better than to leave me conscious.

With a tiny spell, I snapped the ribbon and fell back on the bed, and I heard my name called from the anteroom. Jaryme had not loosened his grip on me, but he was distracted enough by the sudden intrusion that I wrested free of his control and phased into the other room. Disorientated but liberated, I spun wildly in the direction of the voice and crashed into someone.

He was golden, like autumn leaves, warm like afternoon sunlight. He took hold of my arms gently and looked at me. *'Fleece.* His lips moved, but I heard his voice deeper inside me, and my body tingled and hummed. Who was this man who affected me so? How did he know my name?

He had not come alone, my golden savior. The other man was both dark like jet and pale like alabaster, and he stayed by the swirling vortex of light and wind. I knew him, also, didn't I? He looked so much like Jaryme, and his name was similar, too, wasn't it?

Jaryme appeared instantly in our midst, with a fiery mortar in his hand at the ready. He fired the missile directly at the portal, but the one who looked like him tossed up a shield, and the fireball bounced off, instead igniting the seat cushion of the armchair next to it. The black-haired man by the portal raised his hand and pulled the trigger on his weapon without hesitation, and I cowered from the loud, sharp, explosive snap. Jaryme jerked with pain, catching the bullet in his chest, just centimeters from his heart. The first bullet was followed in quick succession by a second, then a third, and I turned automatically to shield my face.

With Jaryme's attention focused on defending himself, the golden one pulled me alongside him though the portal unobstructed. Once through, my thoughts began to clear, but my body was still weak from the effects of Jaryme's spells, and I sagged in my rescuer's arms. I looked into his face and smiled with relief and recognition, cursing the fact that I was too tired to give Sarc the welcome and thanks he deserved before I fell unconscious.

It was the aroma of Jeysen's parlor that stirred me, all warm spice and fresh greenery, mixed with the faint perfume of Sarc's home in Mione: sea spray, cedar and wild roses. It was a seductive, comforting and welcoming mix of scents. Immediately, images came to mind of bright summer days on pink sand shores, with cool shade under a seagrape tree, followed by evenings in front of a toasty hearth, with a pot of Clyara's special whole-leaf tea, and a comb of raw white cherry honey to sweeten it. The room was still and silent, but I heard telepathic whispers at the edges of my consciousness.

There was also a fainter, more elusive scent of leather, smoke and musk that was slowly dissipating from the air, along with the mesmerizing voice that accompanied it. Calling me back from elsewhere on Inear ... *Come back to me, 'Fleece.*

Get out of my head, Jaryme, and never return. With a concentrated thought, I shoved Jaryme out of my head. For the first time in weeks, since my departure from Altaier with Sarc, my mind felt clearer, and entirely my own.

The voices stopped, and I cracked my eyes open. "I must be dreaming," I said drowsily. "I've never seen a more handsome sight." The two men I loved most were at my side, gazing at me with care and concern, and I couldn't believe my good fortune. My eyes fluttered shut, and I smiled groggily before the fog completely dissipated from my mind, "Although, if I were truly dreaming, you wouldn't both be standing there just looking at me."

I felt Jeysen cringe. "She's fine," he muttered, and stepped to the door. "I'll be down the hall, if you need me." With that, he left Sarc alone with me in the parlor.

"I've missed you," I sighed, feeling Sarc's hand on my brow. He was clean-shaven, and his skin was even more sun-darkened since I last saw him. I touched his smooth cheek and smiled. "It's been years since I've seen you like this. You look so ... reputable."

"It was your sister's idea, *Ajle'xon*. She wanted to make sure I made a good impression on the Elders and gained their support first, before I came back bearing weapons and armor like a barbarian." He pulled a hairpin from a short curl behind my ear. My hair was no longer the shorn mess it had been weeks ago, but even the longest locks were barely grazing my shoulders. "This is a very different look for you, too, isn't it?"

"Surprise," I murmured. "How long have I been asleep?"

"Not long enough, judging by your red eyes," he said, helping me upright. "It'll be light soon."

"What?" I turned sharply to the window, where the dim bluish morning light filtered through the curtains. "There's no time to waste, the troops will be deploying soon!" I said, fighting the full skirt of my gown to get to my feet. "We have to send word to the Dark Lands, to get our defenses—" I stopped when I saw Sarc's bemused smile. "What's so funny?"

"Jaryme told you the invasion is beginning today?" he asked indulgently.

"Yes, at dawn," I replied uncertainly. "How do you know it won't?"

When Sarc rose to his feet, I noticed for the first time the weapons on the table beside him, and that he wore a full suit of dark grey—his old Guardsman's uniform. I noticed, too, that his face and what I saw of his form were lean and hard, and I understood. I sank against the sill and felt my stomach knotting. "By Ajle, I'm too late, aren't I? It's already begun. I failed and didn't even know it."

"No, *Ajle'xon*, not at all," he soothed, wrapping his arms around me.

"So, the invasion hasn't started?" I asked hopefully.

"Malya sent the first wave last month," he divulged.

"Last month!" I cried, breaking out of Sarc's arms and blinking into the training room where I knew Jeysen would be.

"Why didn't you tell me!" I cried, my voice echoing through the open chamber. "How could you let me stay here while the Dark Lands were under attack? Sarc could've been dead somewhere, my home could've been torn apart, and I would've never known about it. And Jaryme must have thought I was an imbecile! I didn't even have the common sense to ask the servants about current events. Surely, someone would've been likely to let slip that there was a *war* in progress, had I only asked!"

I paused to catch my breath, as my organs were still being crushed by that disaster of a gown that I was wearing.

"And what would you have done if I had told you?" Jeysen demanded, his voice as icy as his eyes, his hands playing on the edge of a stiletto he had been juggling. "Would you have tried harder to be ready sooner? Or, would you have become distraught and distracted, or hysterical, as you are now? You could barely hold your own against Jaryme last night, so how would you have fared a month ago?"

He was right, but I was too stubborn and upset to admit it. Sarc had joined us in the training room by that point, and I couldn't figure which of them infuriated me more, so I railed at both of them. "You've taken your guardianship too far. I've had enough of this coddling and secrecy, from both of you! Jaryme's bonded to me now, so I've shoved him out of my head for good. You may as well tell me what else I need to know, now!"

"Bonded?" Sarc snarled, his temper flaring faster than I had ever seen before. "When the hell did this happen?"

"What does it matter?" I shot back. "Or, are you just upset that he offered himself to me first, instead of you?" I knew the kind of bonding he was assuming, and I was too furious to correct him. I wanted to let him think the worst, to let him feel some of the rage I harbored at what he had suffered with Malya, and the impotence I felt at not being trusted enough to know his secret.

But it went horribly wrong, and instead of merely making him irate, I realized that my words had cut him deeply. Before I could apologize, Sarc vanished from my sight and mercifully, so did Jeysen, letting the stiletto clatter on the marble floor. After how I had hurt Sarc, I wouldn't have expected any compassion from his friend, guardian of mine or not.

The one I didn't expect to see was Glory, who stood silently in the doorway watching me. From her expression, it was obvious that she had

321

witnessed most of the exchange. Now that I knew her lineage, I found it difficult to meet her incisive, inquisitive gaze without seeing some part of Sarc in it, and even Clyara.

"I came to see about all the yelling," she said. "Are you all right?"

"*Hilafra.*" I wiped my eyes and joined Glory at the doorway, but I avoided contact. "I said awful things to your father and Jeysen, so I don't think they're very happy with me right now."

Glory dismissed my words with a wave and wrapped her arm around my shoulder. "They'll forgive you in no time, if there's anything to forgive. If they didn't hear some element of truth in your words, they would've just ignored or dismissed them outright, or laughed. That they're angry means you've struck a nerve with them."

I looked at Glory's soft white hand on my shoulder. I realized then that I hadn't spoken to her since I sent her home the day before. And here I was, wallowing in my own self-pity. "Please forgive me. How are you feeling?"

"Me?" Glory said, slipping her hand away. "I'm better than I was yesterday at this time, if that's what you mean," she said. "When Father arrived yesterday afternoon, he helped purge any residual traces of Jaryme's charms. He said something about 'detoxification.' Jeysen said he'll need to work with me, too, when Father leaves. Whatever spell Jaryme had cast on you to pass to me was swift and insidious. It feels so strange to recall the last few weeks, after your arrival, like I was seeing myself from the outside."

"I'm sorry you had to go through all this."

"Don't be," she said. "I've been through far worse and survived it all. It takes more than Jaryme's malice to destroy what Jeysen and I have together," she said proudly. "I'm so glad to have you back."

She grasped my hand, as her eyes lit joyfully. "I had the kitchen golems make Father's favorite pie last night. Should we see if there's anything left?"

"Shouldn't I go after Jeysen and Sarc and discuss this war business first?"

She wore her father's wry half-grin. "I'd let them cool off first. If it's already gone on this long without your intervention, I'm sure it can keep for a few hours longer. It's time we took care of *you.*"

While in the kitchen, Glory declared that she had an epiphany and that she intended to address some oversight immediately. She found a half of a berry tart and two forks and ordered me upstairs to the library, where we were less likely to be disturbed. Curious about her reasons, I blinked us upstairs and took a seat on the couch as directed. Glory sat beside me and handed me a fork and invited me to help myself to the dessert.

What ensued was an hour of nearly unabated conversation and laughter, as Glory shared with me anecdotes and acute observations about members of her family from both lines, as well as about Jeysen and Slither, that they probably would have preferred forgotten. Glory was well over fifty years old, though she looked half of that, and she had seen and heard too much in those years. She was a charming and engaging storyteller, as well as an uncanny mimic, and I listened to every detail in fascination. I also laughed until my sides hurt, which was something I hadn't done in years.

"Now, do you feel better about this madhouse you've entered?" she asked. "We're all flawed, absurd people in this place, in this situation, and I've noticed that few of us see the ridiculousness of what's happening around us. We've lived so long waiting and preparing that we've almost lost sight of why we're doing it. You, most of all," she said gently. "That was my epiphany, when I was trying to understand why you were so furious, and why the boys were so taken aback by it. My goodness, Jeysen gets an earful from me almost every other day. But you: when was the last time Jeysen gave you a day off from training? When was the last time you asked? Did it occur to you to ask him, or challenge him on any point?"

"Lately, it wasn't as important as finding a way to save you," I replied, trying not to be defensive. "I needed Jeysen's cooperation for that."

"I appreciate that," she said, laying her hand on mine. "But even before then, while I was here, I saw the light go out of you, slowly but surely. You became so focused that you became hard and humorless, not unlike Hephaestus over there," she said, gesturing to the male golem who had cleared away our dishes and crumbs, and was now dusting and straightening the books. "I was looking for the wide-eyed girl I met in Clyara's cottage years ago, who wanted to learn about the humyn and was dreaming beyond her borders, but she never emerged."

"She's been gone a while," I said. "A lot has happened since."

"That's true, and I think when you first arrived here, you were feeling lost without my father," she observed. "I understand he's become very attached to you, as well, so I'm happy for him. Mostly," she shrugged.

I shot her a questioning look.

"Do you know that this is the first time in months, that you've actually worn a dress?" she remarked. "You've worked so hard to prepare yourself, at the cost of your identity. My father fell in love with a beautiful young woman, and I think you forget sometimes that you still are one — the fact that you're young enough to be *my* daughter is beside the point. I've seen your heart and your potential, and I've no doubt that you are the *Keeronae*, and the true Empress's prophesied Protector, but there is also power and pleasure in simply being a girl. I'm fairly sure that aspect about you attracted my father more than the rest of it."

The dispassion of her statement made me smile, which in turn made her chuckle, which sparked an undignified chortle from me. In moments, we were giggling like frivolous, carefree schoolgirls, and I had to hold my aching side again. We checked it when we saw Sarc at the library door, but at seeing his stoic expression, we relapsed into unfettered, snorting fits.

Glory swept to the door, tossing over her shoulder, "I'll catch up with you later, 'Fleece." She gave Sarc a peck on the cheek, pushed him towards the couch and said, "Behave yourself, Papa. I like her."

Glory gestured to the golem, "Come along, Hephaestus. I think I spied Father's pistols and swords in the parlor. Let's give the antiques a good cleaning before they disintegrate." She waited for the golem to shuffle out and closed the door behind them, leaving Sarc and me alone in the library.

He perched on the arm of the sofa, his expression inscrutable.

Before he could speak, I began. "I want to apologize. I understand that you're upset," I said, standing to meet his gaze eye-to-eye. "But you were wrong to keep the truth from me about the war and everything else, about Glory, and about Malya. If you had trusted me enough to tell me … then I wouldn't be tripping over this damn skirt every five seconds!" I snarled as I tugged the hem free from the scrollwork on the low table, hopping the last step over to him.

"You don't make apologies often, do you," Sarc commented.

"No," I said, taking a deep breath. "I certainly don't, so remember this moment." He remained balanced on the arm of the settee, as I wrapped my arms around his neck, relieved that he allowed it. "I'm sorry for not thanking you properly for my rescue."

I kissed him, reveling in his scent and taste that was everything I loved. Even his uniform now smelled of the woods, earth and water of the Dark Lands, and I felt as though I was home. I touched my tongue to his, and I heard his low, primal groan, as his arms tightened around me, pulling me hard against him. The touch of his fingertips on my bare back sent a quiver through me, and for once I was happy to wear the infernal dress, if only to give him that easy access. I lifted my head finally, to catch my breath, but he kept his arms around me.

"You're welcome," he murmured against my ear. "So long as you don't make it a habit, although…" He leaned back to look down my full length. "You do make for a ravishing damsel in distress."

"Really? I was going to burn this ridiculous frock, but maybe I'll keep it, after all."

"Of course, I'd much rather see you out of it," he returned. "May I?"

"I thought you'd never ask. I can hardly breathe in this!" I turned my back to Sarc, and I trembled as he pulled the pins from my hair and tasted my neck, gently and unhurriedly, while he deftly unbuttoned and peeled the brocade from my body.

After what felt like some of the longest minutes of my life, I was left cinched from bust to hip in a rigid layer of wire-shot white silk, with my legs still clad in gossamer-like stockings and ribbon-adorned slippers. I watched with feminine pride, as his eyes darkened with hunger and desire mixed with a tinge of anger, and he grabbed me roughly when he kissed me again.

I allowed it because I understood his reason. For the moment, he had let down his guard, and his thoughts were open to me. Sarc despised the idea of Jaryme touching me and seeing me that same way. Giving in to a primitive instinct, Sarc was reasserting his claim on me as his own. He wanted to obliterate all traces of Jaryme from me if he could, but it was not in his nature to be cruel. As much as his mind was enmeshed in fury, pleasure and lust, his every touch was a tender caress.

To soothe him, I stroked his hair and face gently as our mouths and hands continued to explore. He nudged me backwards, until I was on the couch with my back against the corner. "You need to know, Sarc," I said between breaths, "that you will still be the first."

He raised his head. "What?"

"The bonding with Jaryme happened because I bit him and took his blood. You arrived before anything else happened," I confessed. I felt him beginning to withdraw, and I panicked, clinging to him. "I'm sorry I led you to think otherwise, earlier. I was upset before, and…"

Sarc quieted me with a gentle kiss. "I know. I was there."

His calm should have assured me, but it didn't. He resumed his leisurely, skillful exploration as though I hadn't spoken at all, but his mind was closed to me. His scent and his warmth enveloped me, and I could feel every line of his body through his clothes, but I couldn't read him. He was as solid and impenetrable as a wall.

"You're not angry with me?" I asked, managing somehow to undo the last buttons on his shirt, despite my unsteady fingers.

"On the contrary," he whispered, nipping my ear. "I'm furious with you for letting me believe the worst. I'm incensed."

"Oh," I said, starting as a question and ending as a sigh.

"I'll deal with that later, just as I'll deal with you for pilfering the last of the tart. You still taste of berries, little thief." He hovered over me and idly sampled my skin where the silk left it exposed, eventually returning to my mouth. "But I'd rather concentrate, *Ajle'xon*, on what I should do with you right now."

I looked down at the stack of journals that I had just set down and heard a weapons rack being moved in the adjoining room. I glanced down at the blue stone of my ring and thought of the Empress who had favored me enough to entrust it to me for safekeeping. The ring bore the design of the Imperial seal, and it was intended for the Empress's first-born, so it would remain on my finger until her heir regained her birthright.

Jeysen and I were surveying the inventory in Clyara's Haven, to ensure that nothing was missed. Everything needed to be in place, or the plan was doomed from the start. I needed to check the tapestry once more, but first, I opened the small chest at the foot of the bed to check the metal fittings of the appliance again.

"Leave it, Sarc; she'll find it," Jeysen scolded, emerging from the other room.

"If she's going to be in here for five years, I hope so," I said. I saw Jeysen's concern for me clearly on his face. "I promised Clyara that I would stay away, so I will, but what if something goes wrong?"

Jeysen shook his head. "Something is bound to go wrong, if this girl is as much trouble as I suspect, if she's anything like her mistress, or your daughter or any other woman. We'll just have to figure it out along the way."

"This is beyond cruel, Jeysen, and you know it. I wouldn't imprison Malya in solitary confinement for this long, much less the woman I ... I just wouldn't."

He gave me a knowing smile. "I've heard that the girl is tenacious and indefatigable, sharp and stubborn to a fault."

"'Fleece? There's nothing she can't do if she puts her mind to it."

"Then she'll manage. Set aside your doubt, and let her become Keeronae."

"I'm not the only one who worries. Her hair is still black. Clyara said she won't let it turn white while she still draws breath."

"All the better to protect her, Sarc. Once she actually comes to resemble Junus's vision, she'll be impossible to hide. Her sister comes close, but thank the Goddess that she's the wrong age." Jeysen stepped closer to me and thumped me soundly against the old scar next to my eye. "Let her go, Sarc. If she is meant for you, then let her find her way to you. You waited for her for all these years, you can survive five more without her."

I opened my eyes a sliver but knew from the rhythm of his breath that Sarc still lay asleep underneath me. Jeysen's library was very different from the one in the Haven, but the smell of paper, vellum and lignin was just as potent. I was still dressed, but just barely, and Sarc drew the blanket up over my chilled skin to warm me, seeing to my comfort even as he slumbered.

I took a breath, taking in his scent and imagining how different it would have felt had we decided to bond more deeply, instead of postponing our consummation. With our respective links to Jaryme and Malya still active, the situation was complicated enough without us linking to each other. Our timing was terrible, but we would have another opportunity. At least, we hoped so.

I closed my eyes and tasted him on my lips, and felt his presence in my mind, separate and distinct from me. His energy was potent, but I was not overwhelmed by him. I loved him, but I could be strong and whole, independent from him, just as he did not need me to make him complete. He had known that for a while, but I had been slow to catch on.

"I may not need you in my life to give it meaning, Sarc," I whispered as I drowsed, resting my ear close against his heart, "but my life is certainly more interesting with you in it. Even if you did intend to lock me up for five years."

Chapter 26: The Gift of Clarity

It was dark when I awoke, and Sarc was gone, but not far. It was his voice that had woken me, along with Jeysen's, as they passed in the hallway outside the library. I left the ballgown in a wrinkled heap on the floor and hastily summoned one of my old dresses and my slippers to pull on before cracking the door open.

They were headed towards the chambers and didn't notice me. "I told you she would sleep till nightfall," Sarc said.

"Given her mood this morning, I thought she would've enjoyed the opportunity to beat us to a bloody pulp." I noticed then the bloodstains and tears in their sparring uniforms and the healed scratches on their hands and faces.

"Hephaestus has enough serious cleaning to do in the ballroom tonight, as it is. It's a good thing that your head is still harder than the floor," Sarc commented. "She keeps you on your toes, then?"

"I'll admit, 'Fleece has her moments," Jeysen said. "She's more resilient than your cosseting of her would suggest. Then again, you've been hopelessly smitten with her for decades now; you probably couldn't help yourself." Jeysen stopped at his door. "You know, you've had that ridiculous grin on your face all afternoon. Considering that you haven't even bonded, I can't imagine why."

"It was enough for now, and you know I have my own reasons for waiting."

"Yes, because you're an idiot," Jeysen rejoined.

"Nice. Why don't you get washed up before Glory sees that I've thrashed you ... again?" He wiped a streak of dried blood from his brow, as Jeysen entered his chamber and shut his door.

Sarc passed my room and entered the next chamber, which had been vacant for the whole time since my first arrival. He closed the door partway, and I heard the sound of running water coming from inside. I entered the room silently and looked around. Sarc was rinsing off in the adjoining bath chamber.

To the eye, the room seemed as unexceptional as I had found it initially, when I explored it during my first days in Jeysen's care. But with Sarc's presence within it, it now felt more like a serene, austere sanctuary, with its minimal, colorless décor and only the large window and a single lamp to light the vast space. The air was now faintly infused with Sarc's scent, and his scattered clothes marked the space as his. I settled in the center of the spacious platform bed, feeling the stiff fabric of the crisp uniform he had set out.

I froze when Sarc emerged from his bath chamber, still drying himself and unaware of my presence. By Ajle, he was beautiful, and I looked my fill of his splendid naked form, from the top of his dark golden head to his long, lean-muscled legs, and back up to where he bore a thatch of curls a few shades darker than on the rest of him. My eyes moved back up to his face, and I was greeted by his wry half-smile and mischievously raised brow.

"I suppose I should get used to seeing you undressed," I said, my voice quavering.

"Just as I should get used to seeing you sprawled across my bed, with your hair all tousled and wild?"

"Just like that," I said, smoothing down my locks belatedly. "I will miss you, Sarc."

"Good," he said, reaching for his clothes draped across the bed in no particular hurry. "I don't want to hear that you've run off again, unless Jeysen's tagging along."

"Then tell your daughter to stay put," I said, trying very hard to focus on just his face until he was fully dressed. "And don't get too distracted by those exquisite elfyn maidens while you're in the Dark Lands—"

Sarc laughed and kissed me soundly on the mouth to silence me. "Now that I've had a taste of you, why would I want anything else?"

"Why not? Moonteyre women are renowned for their grace and beauty."

"And you, *Ajle'xon*, are the most flawless gem amidst the fine jewels."

"They especially love pretty words like those," I said, unmoved.

"I'm not interested in women who can be wooed easily by words, nor women who have no goals beyond marrying well and living comfortably," he said.

"Your life would be much easier, though, and probably longer for it." Seeing that he was in no rush to button his shirt, I raised myself onto my knees to fasten it for him, and he watched me closely. "What?"

"Can you forgive me, 'Fleece?"

I continued down the row of buttons. "For which offense?"

He grimaced. "I have done a lot, haven't I?"

"You've imprisoned me, you've manipulated me, you've kept secrets and deceived me, on multiple occasions and levels..." I buttoned the last fastener at his midriff and looked up at him. "I forgive you, for all of it, even for the things that I don't even know yet, of which I'm sure there are some."

"Why would you do that, so easily?" He seemed stunned.

"It wasn't easy," I admitted, "but I realized that my energy should be focused on the present, not wasted on grievances about the past."

Sarc smiled and kissed my hands. "I love you, too."

I had felt it, but it was still nice to hear his words. "Does this mean that you're no longer angry with me for misleading you before?"

"I enjoy your company far too much to stay angry at you," he said.

"Too bad," I said. "I might have been convinced to debase myself to regain your favor—"

He groaned and held me at arm's length. "If I don't make it back to Moonteyre by tonight, it will be entirely your fault, and I'll have to explain to your sister in great detail about how insatiable you are."

"She'd be happy to hear that I'm enjoying myself." We both turned at the sound of Jeysen's door opening, and I let Sarc pull me up from his bed. "You will take care of Frost, won't you?"

"I'll try, but she's more like you than you may realize," he said, heading for the door. "She takes more risks than she should, even if losing means making orphans of her own children."

The thought of losing Frost left me cold, and I froze with my hand in Sarc's, diverting his attention back to me. He saw something in my eyes that caused him to pull me into his arms. "I'm sorry, I shouldn't have said that," he said, kissing my forehead. "I'll do everything in my power to keep her safe, I promise."

"I know," I whispered back, breathing in his scent for strength. "Just don't let her catch you doing it, or we'll never hear the end of it."

Glory insisted that Sarc stay for supper, and he didn't have the heart to deny his daughter. Despite their seeming closeness in physical age, Sarc took his paternal role very seriously, and it was amusing to see his close scrutiny of Glory and Jeysen's exchanges. He had been denied a regular presence in Glory's life during her youth, but he still felt a duty to see to her happiness.

Likewise, Jeysen watched the interplay between Sarc and me, and I suspected that it was Sarc for whom he was more concerned. I was a distraction for Sarc, at the very least, and the situation in the Dark Lands was too serious for Sarc not to be entirely dedicated to his task.

We gathered in the parlor for Sarc's departure, his portal was already open and waiting for him there. He had traveled lightly this time, as he knew that he could not be gone for more than a day. He took with him only the clothes he wore and his weapons, with the rest of his possessions somewhere in Moonteyre. I gave him my locket as a token of luck, and to let Frost know what he meant to me.

After he had gone, Glory walked with me to my room and returned my amulet. "You took a terrible risk coming for me. Please don't do that again."

I rubbed the smooth blue stone of the talisman between my fingers. "I did what I felt was necessary. I didn't plan as well as I should have, but I don't regret my actions."

"It's funny, Clyara said the same exact thing to me once," Glory said. "When we were talking about you, and what she prepared for when she had to leave you. I don't think she expected my father to fall in love with you, or that he would remain that way."

"Feelings are difficult to anticipate," I remarked. "And your father is a very special man."

"You must be disappointed that you weren't able to bond," she said frankly. "I can tell that he is, although he's too discreet to say it."

I lowered my eyes, realizing that privacy was nearly impossible in a house with mages and almost-mages linked to one another. "It was for the best. The time wasn't right."

She nodded in agreement. "If there's one thing that I've learned from my parents and from my own experience," she said, "it's that intimacy of body and spirit are distinct, and controlling one doesn't necessarily mean achieving the other. You're more important to him than my mother could ever hope to be. Good night, 'Fleece."

I lay in bed for a long while, reliving the day in my head, almost afraid to fall asleep and risk losing the memory. I finally gave up trying to sleep and made some notes in my journal to clear my mind, then went downstairs to the courtyard.

The air outside was frigid and bracing, and I stared up at the clear blue-black sky. It was the color of Frost's eyes and my own. It was the color of limitless space, filled with infinite worlds. If it was indeed true that there were other planets teeming with life up there, as some of Jeysen's books suggested, I would bet my gem that those wondrous creatures were thinking of their own survival and wouldn't know or care about my situation. My problem was my own, and it was time I found my own solution, but I could benefit from some guidance on the matter.

I missed Clyara more than ever.

I closed my eyes and remembered the day of her passing: the moment I destroyed her body, the moment her gem chose to accept me as its new keeper, and when I destroyed the wraiths I had inherited and breathed in their ashes, feeling them permeate my being...

You're a mere girl, what can you possibly know to do with the power you've been given?

So, you're the one that Clyara chose for her successor. How have you managed to survive this long?

The thoughts that surfaced were elusive and distinct from my own, and I purposefully kept my mind silent, and listened to what else was emerging. There were two male voices vying to be heard in my mind, and I knew without thinking about it that they belonged to Set and Aron, the preceding hosts of my gem before Clyara. The magestone is an object like any other, after all, as receptive to imprinting as any physical thing.

Well, girl, why have you summoned us?

Summoned them? I opened my eyes and was relieved to see that I was alone, and that the voices dwelled only in my mind. Well, more relieved, in any case. *I need your counsel on how to defeat Malya.*

I felt clear disdain and resentment, manifested in their momentary silence. *The gemwraith humyn witch would destroy you in moments,* Set finally said when I refused to elaborate on my plea.

You're too young and undisciplined to win against the daughter of Uscari, Aron rejoined. *It's a futile effort.*

You'd better hope not, I quipped. *Because if I die, this gem will not be allowed to exist. So, this 'mere girl' is all that keeps you from total oblivion.* That seemed to get their attention, for the moment, at least. *And it apparently knows better than both of you of what I am capable, otherwise it wouldn't have chosen me to bear it this far. Now, keerons, if you'd please?*

They did not bother with words, since the knowledge was already imprinted on my magestone, waiting to be tapped. Whatever they knew was known to me, and I learned from their combined experiences very quickly how to deal with gemwraiths: what kind of physical force to use, which spells would actually feed into their strength, how to destroy their stones to prevent their reconstitution ...

Something was still missing. I needed more. *Where's Clyara's memory? Her body is gone, but her imprint must still be here, somewhere. I need to know what she knew about Malya.* I was asking the gem more than I was asking the ghosts inside my head, and that was all they were. They were echoes of their former selves, without substance or real consciousness once their bodies were disconnected from the source of their power. Even what had seemed like Set and Aron's observations about Junus and Clyara were limited to what they had learned during the lifetimes, and what I had added to our collective knowledge.

Clyara, where are you in here?

My girl, came Clyara's voice into my head at last. *How you've grown.*

She was the same as the others, a shadow of what she had been in life, but her shadow eclipsed the others. It was as though she was standing right behind me, unseen but present, whispering directly in my ear.

How do I defeat her, Clyara? What am I missing?

You're not missing anything. You have everything you need to end it.

How can that be? I haven't been able to defeat Jeysen...

Ah. But Jeysen is not your enemy.

No, he isn't, is he? So ... WHAT DO I DO?

While I yelled the words in my head, the actual words sounded considerably more garbled to Glory, who looked at me with alarm. She was seated in the armchair facing my bed, her slender legs tucked neatly under her, with her fingers still poised to turn the page of the book she was reading.

"Jeysen, she's awake!" she cried, tossing her book aside and darting to my bedside. "By the Goddess, what happened to you?"

"Why?" I sat up in time to see Jeysen in the doorway. I was dressed in a robe and gown, which was more than I recalled wearing in the courtyard. I saw through the window that it was dark outside, but getting close to dawn, judging from the sky. "How long have I been asleep?"

"A week since we found you nearly frozen in the garden," Jeysen replied, his eyes narrowed and fierce as he strode to my bedside. "What in the world were you doing out there in the cold, in just your slip?" Before I could answer, he grasped my head in his hands and kissed me on my forehead. "Don't ever scare us like that again, 'Fleece."

"A week? It barely felt like hours," I said.

"What happened?" Glory asked, touching her cool hand to my head to test for fever. "You were so unresponsive that we first thought you might have been going through an adjustment. When the second day passed and you still hadn't awoken, we knew it was something different."

"It was different," I admitted. "Still ... you let me sleep for a week?" I looked squarely at Jeysen and understood at once what "Clyara" had been trying to tell me. It was as clear and wondrous as the vivid blue of his eyes, except that Jaryme's presence in my mind had obscured my sight before then.

"If you didn't wake by tonight, we were going to try to revive you, but it seemed better to just let you rest," Glory said casually, as though I had been taking a quick nap. "You weren't wasting away, you just seemed ... inert. So, what *did* happen?"

"I was communing with my predecessors," I said shortly, trying to find more precise words. "I tapped into the remnants of their consciousness within the gem and found their knowledge. Their experiences, if you will."

"You can do that?" Glory marveled, then looked at Jeysen. "Can *you* do that?"

Jeysen shook his head slowly. "Most of us are the first hosts that our stones have ever had. None of our stones are as, ah, seasoned as hers."

"Yes, my magestone seems quite the tomcat by comparison," I joked at Jeysen's diplomacy. "I know what I have to do," I said. "And here's what I need."

After I gave my instructions to Jeysen, I got up from bed and consulted with Glory on what I wanted from her. Glory was sweet, trusting and somehow unjaded by her past, and I disliked bringing her into my plan, but I needed her. She listened first with amusement, then with concern when she realized that I was truly sincere. Finally, she excused herself from my room, and I wondered briefly if she had thought I had lost my mind and had gone for help, but she returned shortly.

"I sent one of the golems on an errand to gather what we need," she said. "Are you certain this is how you want to do this?"

I took a deep breath. "If it is to be done on my terms, then this is how I would choose."

"Do you have a secondary plan, if this doesn't work?"

"Of course," I smiled, "but I'd rather not implement it, which is why it's secondary."

Glory saw something in my smile that made her stiffen. "Do I want to hear what it is?"

I laughed, and I was surprised at how harsh it sounded. The secondary plan mostly consisted of my waging a direct, personal assault on the palace that would probably result in casualties on a catastrophic scale. As I considered it in detail, I looked at Glory's open, trusting expression and knew that I did not want her to know any of it. "The backup? No, you most certainly do not."

Glory left me to join Jeysen in the parlor for breakfast, while I took the opportunity to wash and change into clean clothes. Looking into my dresser, I chuckled at the assortment of new dresses that had somehow accumulated during the week that I was asleep. I pulled from the drawer a long-sleeved, burgundy-hued gown that fell to my ankles but was otherwise remarkably comfortable. In the next drawer underneath, there were slippers to match, so I wore them out of necessity, since my threadbare slippers and dusty boots were nowhere to be found.

Descending the stairs to make my way to the parlor, I felt strangely clear-headed and serene, and I marveled at how different it felt to not have Jaryme lurking somewhere in my mind. I entered the parlor with a new admiration for the bright easterly view of the garden at morning. I was looking forward to the hours ahead, now that I knew what awaited.

I curtsied to Glory as well as Jeysen, who rose to his feet per his usual habit. He glanced at my new clothes, then at Glory with a curious smile, but his smile was replaced by a concerned frown when his eyes returned to me.

Mercifully, Jeysen waited quietly until the golems served me and poured my tea. It was my first meal in a week, and I was famished. I even helped myself to the cured meats that were set out anew each morning but hardly ever tasted by any of us. It was surprisingly rich and satisfying, and

I briefly forgot that meat was a conjured food at Jeysen's table. Once I remembered, I served myself a second helping.

"Your predecessors told you that you were ready?" Jeysen asked finally.

"Well, technically, I guess it's my magestone that actually communicated the sentiment, if not exactly in those words," I said between bites. "What do you think?"

"You know my criteria," he said.

"Fair enough," I nodded. "If your schedule allows it, perhaps we can meet in the ballroom. I'm sure I can use a refresher." I took a long drink of tea. "Does this mean you've held off on the preparations we discussed this morning?"

Jeysen shook his head begrudgingly. "No, 'Fleece, everything will be ready as you've requested. The messages have been sent."

After the meal, I accompanied Jeysen to the converted ballroom and smiled at his brief confusion that I wasn't changing into my usual sparring outfit. I noticed that he, too, was still in his typical, finely tailored and expensive clothing.

"I should get used to fighting in regular clothes," I said.

"The fabric alone for that dress cost me over 200 imperi."

I touched the fine burgundy silk of my sleeve. "I can tell, and the tailoring is exceptional." I gave him a mischievous wink. "Don't worry, Jeysen. Bloodstains won't show much against this color."

Jeysen wordlessly passed a saber to me as he took another in hand. As my fingers enclosed the grip, I felt a tingle travel through my arm and a fluttering beat in my chest around my magestone that I was not expecting. My focus returned at the touch of Jeysen's swordtip against mine, and did not stray again.

However, I couldn't say what attacks and defenses I used that morning if my life depended on it. I was moving almost out of reflex, with little conscious effort, yet I somehow responded to Jeysen's every attack with the right counterattack, and I managed to disarm him finally. Demonstrating that he was not being lenient with me, he continued to defend against me, striking me with his open hands a couple of times so hard that I felt the jarring in my bones. He stunned me enough with the force of one such blow that he managed to knock the saber out of my hand, so we switched to fighting without weapons.

I owed the first strike I landed against his head to luck. The second punch was an uppercut, followed by a kick to his ribs that incapacitated him enough that he looked at me in surprise. Seizing the advantage, I swept his leg out from under him, and his head landed on the marble tiles with a wince-inducing "crack".

I knelt next to Jeysen to make sure that he was not seriously hurt, with the understanding that what I had just inflicted would have knocked unconscious a lesser opponent, or worse. He wasn't sitting up, but he was moving.

"You'd better say something, or I'll have to answer to Glory," I said, keeping my hand fisted, ready to hit him again in the case that he was feigning his incapacitation.

"She'd say I deserved it," he whispered hoarsely, opening his eyes. They were slightly dilated, but the clear blue returned quickly. He sat up and saw my fist poised to strike. "Best two out of three?"

"Fine with me." I relaxed my hand and offered it to him to help him to his feet. "I can finally pay you back for all the times you beat me, these past few months."

"Two out of three" stretched into "best of seven" before Jeysen was willing to concede the match. I was scratched and bruised, but my dress remained relatively unspoiled, except for spots of our blood. As the morning progressed, it had become less a duel of brute force and more about outwitting and outmaneuvering each other, but neither of us left the chamber unbloodied.

We returned to our chambers to change and regrouped in the parlor, where Glory gave Jeysen a satisfied little smile and congratulated me on my success before we sat down to lunch.

Jeysen, for his part, looked justifiably humbled, yet relieved and relaxed as well, that all his work to prepare me was almost done.

After lunch, it was time to work with Glory. Whereas Jeysen was my mentor for the skills of combat, she was my muse for the art of influence. The golems fulfilled Glory's request to the letter and delivered everything to my chamber. She and I remained behind closed doors for part of the afternoon, and Jeysen seemed thankful to be excluded from our female conspiracy. He also had a last task that promised to take the rest of the day to complete.

I turned my back to the mirror. "I shouldn't look at myself until we're finished," I declared.

"Don't be preposterous," Glory chastised, looking over the garments that had been brought up. "You have to oversee the progress in the case that anything needs to change."

"I don't need a mirror for that," I said. "I know what I need to do."

Glory raised her brow at me, with one of the pieces in hand. She was seeing through my bravado to my nervousness, as clearly as if she were her father, but she chose not to respond. She merely nodded her acquiescence and proceeded to direct the golems on their tasks.

The chamber was busy with activity, but it felt very unlike the afternoon in Malya's fortress, when I had been primped and groomed under a stifling cloud of fear and oppression. Here in my chambers, attended by golems who were efficient and emotionless, I felt like a machine myself, which helped me to tamp down my anxiety to focus on our next steps.

"You said my father gave you these?" Glory asked, gesturing to the black cloak and leather gloves that I had set out on the bed.

"Among other gifts," I said. "Why?"

"Black was always his favorite color," she smiled.

"Mine, too," I said. It was stark and somber, it was the color of night, neutrality and mortality. The hue seemed especially appropriate for my role. Wrapping myself in the cloak, it didn't feel like hiding under a cover, but rather like brandishing a banner. "I noticed your mother wears white often."

"She says it's the color of purity, light and goodness," Glory said.

I brushed back a platinum lock from my cream-pale forehead. "It is also the color of me, and I am none of those things." I tugged on the gloves and faced the mirror.

I barely recognized myself, but I had the effect I wanted. I was a dramatic, monochromatic figure, severe and unyielding but undeniably female in form. I gave myself a last, critical glance in the mirror and nodded. "This will work. We'll save the last of it for tomorrow when we depart."

"You look … unearthly," Glory swallowed, undoing the clasp of the cloak at my throat. "I feel nervous around you, and I helped you look this way."

"I'm still the same Snowfleece," I said, shedding the gloves and cloak. "I just look more intimidating. It's merely theatrics, like war paint."

I had just finished reversing my transformation and changed into a tailored dark blue velvet gown when a knock sounded at the door. When Jeysen entered, he gestured to Hephaestus to leave a package on my chair and ushered the golems out.

He was garbed in his dress uniform from when he served in his sister's Imperial Guard. He was sleek and elegant in the dark grey, and I imagined that he hadn't changed much in the decades since he wore the uniform last. He wore his hair tied back, his beard trimmed. He exchanged a quick glance with Glory before he said, "It's dusk. The first arrivals are ready for you, *Keeronae*."

I nodded slightly at the title, knowing that he was not using it ironically. "Thank you, *Keeron* Jeysen. Let's not keep them waiting, then."

"Good luck," Glory said. "I'll join you later."

Jeysen peered at me, offering his arm. "Nervous?"

I took a deep breath, slipping my hand around his elbow, and I felt strangely at peace. "Oddly, no. Should I be?"

He patted my hand. "We'll find out soon enough."

Jeysen accompanied me to the former ballroom where we had trained for the past few weeks and opened the doors for me. He did not announce my entrance, but all eyes turned to me as soon as I stepped into the gleaming chamber. In the intervening hours after our last session, Jeysen had restored and refinished the ballroom to its former splendor, and it showed no trace of the brutal violence and mayhem that had transpired there recently.

Dispersed throughout the ballroom was the assembly that I had requested of Jeysen, save a few who were expected by morning, all dressed in the dark Imperial grey of Adella's Guard. Moving as one, without prompting, they genuflected to me. The room was utterly soundless, and I felt as though all the air had been forced out of my chest.

I looked over to Jeysen and saw that he had done the same, with his eyes to the floor and his fist to his heart in earnest salute. I was awed and humbled to be shown such respect, but I took a deep, calming breath and counted to five in my head, skimming my gaze across the room. Now was not the time to appear flustered or giddy.

Gathered before me were forty of Junus's elite chosen, some seeming older than others, but all in their prime, all of them mages. There were to be fifty-one altogether, counting Jeysen. I recognized Mareos, Flyn and a handful of others from my days of traveling with Sarc. *Dear, clever Sarc.* I was starting to think that nothing he did was ever random or arbitrary. Inasmuch as he had been escorting me through the Realm, Sarc had also used the opportunity to reveal me to his fellow retired Guardsmen, to let them know it was almost time to act.

"Rise, Guardians," I addressed the room. Once I saw that they had returned to their feet and were focused on me, I continued. "Thank you for answering the summons. I will be brief and succinct, as I wish to be respectful of your time. I intend to reclaim the throne from Malya in the name of the true Empress, by whatever means necessary. The means are my concern, as Malya is my burden. I will need your assistance, however, to ensure that I reach her without having to kill every last man in her Guard."

I saw a flicker of uncertainty amidst the crowd of trained soldiers and warriors. They were trained for combat and tactical assault, magical and not, and my order was not entirely what they had expected. Even my appearance, soft and feminine, was not what many of them had anticipated.

"Every Guardsman has sworn an oath to serve the Empress, as you all once did," I reminded. "It is a noble calling, so if we are to enlighten those who have been deceived, we will do so with mercy," I said, my confidence growing as I saw their assenting nods. "The true Empress's path to her rightful throne should not be sodden with unnecessary blood."

As Glory coordinated the golems for dinner service, Jeysen handled the introductions of the men who had answered our call. Some names I recognized from the list of safe houses that Mareos and Rijena had given me months ago, and I recognized more faces than I had expected, but most of them were new.

Dinner was served in the main dining hall, which had been designed to accommodate up to two hundred guests, with room to spare for an orchestra, had Jeysen opted to engage one. Thankfully, he did not, but the room was still lively and raucous with the conversation of dozens of Guardsmen recalling old exploits or sharing more recent ones with one another.

Between introductions, I sat quietly and observed the members of my troop. I did not have a tightly-ordered, well-rehearsed team supporting me, but rather something that resembled a dysfunctional family at a long-overdue reunion. I noted which men were well-acquainted, and which ones were estranged. I noticed the hardened soldiers, and the practitioners of gentler magic. The braggarts and the wallflowers, my jesters and assassins, had all traveled distances to answer my summons, as delivered through Jeysen. Still dressed in my finery, it was easy to remain in my physical persona as the *Keeronae* — calm, commanding and regal — but Jeysen knew me too well.

"You're not eating," he noted at one point.

"I am nervous, after all," I admitted in the same hushed voice. "All of these men are depending on me to lead them safely through to the end."

Jeysen looked at me sternly. "They are expecting nothing of the kind. Guardsmen expect to sacrifice their lives for the greater good. They came because they wish to serve under your command, and to patronize them would only injure their pride and disparage their abilities."

I nodded, grateful for Jeysen's correction. Amid the gentle, respectful flattery that I had received from our guests all evening, I felt grounded by Jeysen's bluntness.

As Jeysen left my side to visit the other tables, Mareos approached, and I invited him to sit with me. It was heartening to see a familiar face, especially one as pleasant and good-natured as his, and his imposing physique reminded me that impressive strength did not have to represent aggression.

"Rijena and the girls send their regards," he said.

"Thank you," I said. "I hope not to keep you from home for long."

Mareos held up his hand dismissively. "Fringe women do not wait idly and pine, *Keeronae*. Delenn is busy with her ferry, and we have friends to keep her safe. Rijena may miss my cooking, but I've stored aside enough to keep her happy until I return. She and the other mages are busy overseeing the defenses for the villages, and have done such an excellent job of it that some of the Imperial troops now think the Fringe is haunted by angry spirits and refuse to cross it."

I stifled a laugh. "My compliments to Rijena and her fellow conspirators, then."

"You should come pay your compliments in person, after all this is over. A personal question, if I may," he said, more seriously. "When you visited our home, you told Rijena that you were bonded to a guardian," Mareos said, then tilted his head in Jeysen's direction and narrowed his eyes. "Did you mean him?"

This time, I did laugh, but quietly. "No, not Jeysen! Ajle forbid. I was bonded to Sarc, once." We were still bonded, now perhaps even more deeply, but that was probably more information than Mareos needed. I also didn't have to elaborate on who Sarc was, as I heard his name mentioned in conversations throughout the room. "Why do you ask?"

Mareos looked back and forth between Jeysen and me, and his dark eyes settled on me once more. "I see a connection between you, but I can't quite see the detail… It doesn't matter," he said with a shake of the head. "But I do see that you are fractured."

"How do you mean?"

"You have bonded to more than one mage," he said in a hushed whisper.

"Yes, that's true," I said, suddenly feeling like a cheap flask of wine that had been passed around.

"When you are bonded to one, your thoughts may not always feel like your own, but you can learn to distinguish them," he explained. "Because you are fractured, thoughts and emotions can seem more muddled, more conflicted, because there are more of them fighting for your attention."

"My head has been feeling crowded, as of late," I admitted. "I had hoped that when I took the other mage's blood, it would negate the bond between us." Certainly, I felt none of Jaryme's presence in my head since my return from the fortress.

Mareos bobbed his head uncertainly. "Possibly, or maybe make it even stronger. Your situation is a unique one, and it may be unimportant, but still something to note."

It was not until Mareos had returned to his seat that I did recall a crucial detail that I had overlooked, that I hoped would not be my undoing: Malya had also tasted my blood when I was presented to her in her throneroom, which meant that I was now bonded to her, as well.

I slept little, but remarkably, I felt energized when I awoke before dawn, in time to hear the din downstairs when the last of the fifty men arrived. We were scheduled to assemble in the yard to get ready for our departure, and before I joined the men, I repeated the dressing ritual from the day before. This time, I didn't have the golems or Glory to assist me, but I was able to recreate the effect I needed, and embellish it further. I pulled on my night-black leather gloves last, took a breath and turned to look in the mirror a last time.

My clothes were the dark hue of Adella's Guard, contrasting with the pallor of my hair and skin, and my torso was encased in the armor that I had asked Jeysen to craft for me. Not armor made from just any metal, but the same dark, gleaming Imperial steel used for weapons and Jeysen's golems. My eyes were ringed in black, and my mouth was painted scarlet, so that whoever saw me would never mistake me for just another soldier. I couldn't be bothered with taming my hair, so I contained what I could of my white locks behind my head with one of Sarc's black ribbons.

When I joined the assembly in the yard, Jeysen made no remark on my appearance, nor did the others. With my severe, dour façade, I was far removed from my genteel and ladylike guise from the night before. Likewise, my professional, stoic troops were very different from the merry, bawdy revelers who had only vacated the ballroom a few hours earlier. I imagined our true selves were some combination of the varied semblances we assumed.

Jeysen surprised me with one last detail, which he presented with little ceremony. He offered me a sword-belt, carrying a weapon so pristine and ornate that it seemed ornamental, and murmurs rippled through the group. "*Keeronae*, this was my grandfather's sword, and it would honor his memory if you carried it." *It's a sound blade, I reforged it with the same metal as mine.*

"The honor is mine, your Highness," I said, accepting it with both hands and a grateful bow. "Thank you."

"We were about to discuss the journey," Jeysen said, gesturing to the handful gathered around him. "We have intelligence that Malya's moved from the palace to the northern summer fortress."

"That's the one northeast from here, back on the mainland?" She had put the Inearan Sea, plus an additional thousand kilometers, between us. East also meant closer to the Dark Lands.

"Yes. It's too far for a single portal, but we can cast a series to get us closer. What do you think?"

"One portal to get us across the sea. Can we do that?"

Jeysen raised his brow. "Of course, it's no more than a couple of hundred kilometers across, at its narrowest point."

"Good, then we can start overland before we camp for the night. We shouldn't charge after her, without knowing what awaits us," I said. "Plus, there should be nothing of our arrival that appears underhanded or clandestine. We are delegates of the true Empress, and it's important that we appear legitimate and open, even ostentatious. A party of fifty on horseback should be showy enough, without having to appear out of thin air, or frightening citizens by brandishing weapons."

"The Empress will know we're coming then," said one of the mages. "She'll have several days to prepare her guards."

"She can prepare however she likes," Jeysen said, understanding my reasoning. "But our cause is just, so we will not hide from her. Very well, let's get the mounts ready."

Many of the Guardsmen had brought their own horses, and Jeysen supplied mounts for the rest of us from his extensive stable. I learned that Sarc's old companion, the jet-black Paol, had also been sired and raised in the Imperial stables, as were many of the mounts in our elite company.

For me, Jeysen chose a spirited black mare named Kali, whose non-fading coat looked almost blue in the sunlight. He told me that she was named for a dark and fierce goddess of time and change, which he thought was apt for me. Kali was also one of the horses from his stable who had bonded with me, and she took my direction easily. For himself, he selected his favored mount, a young black stallion named Ares, whose coat took on shades of blood-crimson in the light.

After we bid farewell to Glory and the golems, Jeysen and I led the procession from the courtyard, with the road leading from the manor wide enough to accommodate five riders traveling abreast. Surrounding the grounds were mountains that were unfamiliar to me, and I followed Jeysen's lead. The horses, however, were familiar with the terrain, and stayed together with little guidance from their riders.

Jeysen and I conferred mentally, unable to shout over the wind and galloping footfalls, once we reached flatter terrain, and the horses picked up their pace. *There's a site we can use for our portal up ahead,* Jeysen directed. *After we're through, we can probably cover another hundred kilometers before nightfall, if we keep our rest periods brief. For the remainder of the trip, I would recommend portals to shorten our travel.*

I agree, especially for the more challenging ground. I looked around at our retinue. *We also didn't pack enough provisions.* I answered Jeysen's withering glance with one of my own. *Mages or not, I don't want us having to waste energy conjuring needlessly. I'm trusting you to tell me if the group needs anything.*

I will tell you, he promised grudgingly. He noticed that I kept looking over my shoulder at the group assembled behind us. *What is it?*

Nothing, I said shortly. *I'd like you to coordinate the portal and lead the way through. I'll ride behind and make sure we stay together. It'll allow me a chance to get acquainted with the men.*

As I fell back, the group stayed in its formation, with all eyes fixed on

Jeysen's lead. Perhaps I was worthy of some of their deference because I was the *Keeronae*, but Jeysen was their commander and, more significantly, their prince. Without knowing the true Empress that they were serving, they saw in Jeysen the next closest to a rightful ruler, and I had a feeling that many of them would have supported him, if he decided to take the crown for himself.

I let the majority of the group ride behind Jeysen and circled around the back to herd any stragglers, but the soldiers in my company were skilled horsemen, who were able to stay together even at our hurtling speed.

One of the riders rode exceptionally well, despite the bulky woolen hooded cloak he wore, and his slight build was partially to account for the agility, but there was more to it than that. I didn't bother to shout over the hammering of hooves, only pulled alongside and projected my question: *Does he know you're here?*

I saw a shining gold curl peek from under the drawn hood, but Glory did not turn her head to answer me. *No, and I'd rather you didn't tell him.*

I won't have to. As soon as Jeysen gets a chance to count to fifty, he'll know we have an extra person.

I need to be here, I can feel it, she said, her pace never slowing. *Plus, Malya was my mother. I should be there for her passing. That is, her permanent one. You understand, don't you?*

I do, and I'll keep silent, I said, keeping my eyes on Jeysen to make sure he wasn't watching. *But you have to tell him yourself, before he finds out, or there will be hell for both of us.*

Hell arrived swiftly but from an unexpected source. Shortly after we had emerged from the portal and landed on the mainland, Jeysen dropped Ares back from the lead and approached Glory's mount. She dropped her hood, and he only slowed slightly to give her a chastising glower. In fact, he made some remark that caused her to laugh, even as he remained stone-faced, before he spurred Ares back to the lead.

I pulled alongside Glory, whose cheeks were turning rosy with windburn and mirth. *What did he say?*

That my parents didn't discipline me enough as a child, but that he would correct the situation later, in private, she said, then the smile vanished. Mareos and Bael, one of the other mages from the Fringe, raced to us, and Jeysen signaled a halt.

"*Keeronae*," Mareos said, "there is something coming."

"A storm?" Glory asked, glancing at the sky.

"No, my Lady," said Bael. "Not a storm, but something big."

I followed their line of sight towards the distant east and thought I heard something over the hooves which I could only describe as pounding,

343

almost like thunder but deeper and more rhythmic. "Stay with her, Mareos," I said, and gestured to Bael to accompany me to the fore.

"I hear it, too," Jeysen said, before I even spoke. "Sounds like battle drums. Bael, we need an assessment."

"Yes, Sir," he replied, then lobbed a fist-sized sphere of white light into the air that dulled to grey, then black, and shot ahead of us, assuming the shape of a crow. Bael spurred his mount and galloped ahead of us to follow his sentinel, and they both vanished.

By now, most of the men were on their guard, having noticed our heightened vigilance. While we waited for Bael's report, Jeysen led us to a small ridge where we could take up a defensive position, if necessary. It was the only defensible area on the otherwise open terrain, and had our group been any bigger, our cover would have been laughably inadequate. Some of the men gravitated around Glory, whether unconsciously or by prearrangement, and I was reminded of Grey-Eye's pack protecting its own.

"You think Malya knows we're coming?" I asked Jeysen.

"She should, unless her spies are completely inept," he replied, a wry smile tugging at the corner of his lips. *How many do you think we have in our company?*

I named the two that I suspected, and Jeysen nodded. *Not bad, for knowing them so briefly. There may be more.*

I sensed his disappointment at the betrayal. *It's unfortunate, but they're old enough to live with their decisions.*

Bael came tearing back, without his sentinel, as Jeysen finished checking his pistol. I looked over my shoulder to see that the men were ready and turned back around to hear Bael's report.

"Close to four hundred cavalry, six dozen archers and twenty catapults accompanied by infantry," came Bael's report. "They have mostly single-shot pistols, otherwise. They seem prepared, and they're advancing quickly to intercept us. It appears that they know exactly where we are."

"Thank you, Bael," I said, then turned to Jeysen. "Your pick."

"I'll go first," he said, then whistled sharply to his team. Immediately, a dozen of the mages came forth on their mounts. "We'll target the catapults and archers, but once they spot us, the sky will darken quickly," he warned.

"Understood," I said, gesturing to five of the mages to take position around the remainder of the party. As soon as Jeysen led Bael and the rest of his team of mages around the corner of the ridge and out of my line of sight, I signaled to my group, and together, we erected a canopy shield that floated just a few meters above our heads.

Within seconds, the air was strafed with a shower of arrows and cannonballs, and it didn't take me long to realize that there had to be mages in the attacking group in order for them to have closed on us so rapidly. The debris that crashed down on our shields fell to the side harmlessly, but the ground was quickly littered with spent arrows and missiles. Gradually, the shower lightened and eventually stopped altogether, to be replaced by the sound of erupting gunfire, some of it close enough to shake the air and ground.

"The ten of you stay here," I ordered the men closest to Glory, including Mareos. "Guard her with your life." Glory opened her mouth to protest, and I shot her a glare. "Not negotiable. Your father would expect nothing less from me," I said humorlessly. "The rest of you, come with me."

I snapped Kali's reins and steered her over the ridge, casting a broad, heavy shield ahead of me to catch any gunfire that was aimed at me and my group. Steady and smart like all of the horses in Jeysen's stable, my mount was unperturbed by the spectacle of battle that was spread before us, and charged down the slope without fear.

In the few minutes since the battle began, Jeysen and his team had managed to demolish all of the catapults and had incapacitated all but a few of the archers who were falling back. Jeysen was a fearsome dark spectre, perched atop the blood-red Ares with his katana in hand, giving chase with a handful of his men in tow, while the others of his team were directing their volleys towards our enemies who were further afield.

"Take out the guns!" I shouted to my group and charged ahead to join Jeysen in the chase. In hindsight, it was unwise strategically to have us both exposed, but I could not let Jeysen go alone. I ignored the jostle as Kali trampled the fallen to catch us up to her master. Jeysen's riders cut down our attackers with their individual spells of choice, composing a nightmarish mélange of fire, lava and shredding ice. Over my head flew additional fireballs and chains of lightning from my team that further diminished the enemies' firepower.

I had almost caught up to Jeysen, who was being surrounded by the enemy. It was his intention to draw their fire, and he accomplished it brilliantly, with dozens training their weapons on him. Sweeping up the soil, stones and anything else that was loose from the ground ahead of me, I amassed a maelstrom of debris that I unleashed on the soldiers who were distracted by Jeysen, knocking down and burying many of them under the crushing weight. The sight of an unstoppable wall of earth, pocked with the occasional body of a fallen compatriot, was enough to make the rest of them flee in terror.

Jeysen looked over to me, awaiting my call on whether to pursue. With Malya's forces splintered and demoralized, it would've been easy to kill or capture the last of them, but I shook my head and watched to ensure their retreat. I called over my shoulder: "I need three Collectors."

Bael and two others came forward to join me, and Jeysen turned to regroup with the others. The Collectors and I began our grim task of picking through the carnage, watching for signs of movement. More specifically, we were looking for signs of reanimation, as the fallen mages in Malya's troop began to transform into gemwraiths.

Bael spotted the first wraith, and he set upon it with frightening speed and accuracy, gouging its chest with a stiletto and popping the stone into his free hand with a flick of his wrist, as though he was shucking a clam. To his credit, he recognized that he was cutting into something that had been someone just moments ago, and he performed his task with the utmost sobriety. He even gestured a blessing over the body before he set it alight.

Out of the corner of my eye, I spotted another wraith gradually coming "awake." I dismounted and was at its side in seconds, plunging one of the discarded Guardsman's swords into its soft flesh before I set it ablaze with the hottest fire I could manage. It was a purple, almost invisible, flame, and it consumed the body ravenously, leaving only an amber magestone behind in the oily ash. By the time I picked the stone free, the remains had had all but disintegrated, leaving little behind to suggest that it had ever been humyn.

And so it continued, until we had searched every corner of the battlefield. Altogether, we found ten magestones, none of them capable of any great power, individually, but dangerous as a coordinated force. In silence, the Collectors brought the reclaimed stones to me and accompanied me back to the other side of the ridge.

From a distance, I saw the men of the company resting, while their horses grazed. This had likely been the first battle that many of them had joined in many years. Jeysen was tending to those who sustained enough injury to accept aid. Watching his interaction with his grateful patients, I was also reminded that the healing spells that I had taken for granted, were still unknown to most.

I slid off Kali to give my mount a rest, and went to join Jeysen as he finished the last of his healing spells. I clapped him on the shoulder, and he looked at me sharply. It was a brief touch, but it was enough for me to transfer some of the injuries that he had absorbed from the others, to myself.

I'm not a child, 'Fleece, he said. *I can stand some nicks and cuts.*

I know, and that's why I didn't take them all from you, I said. *Given the speed at which you heal, just the fact that there was anything left for me to take means there were a fair number of them. Just say 'thank you.'*

"Thank you, 'Fleece. Do you still want to let them go?" he asked, nodding his head in the direction of the retreating stragglers.

"Yes," I replied. "I want them to tell everyone that we are coming, and that we are not to be underestimated, so that Malya is forced to empty her fortress and send every Guardsman to confront us." I recalled the sight of the plain, littered with the fallen and their mortal treasures, and I was dispirited by the idea of having to repeat this encounter again and again, until Malya's forces were depleted.

"I don't want them underfoot to tax our limited store and energy. Let Malya decide their fate." I recalled Sarc's words, that disappointing the Empress sometimes meant a painful death. "In the end, some of them may wish they had died here today in battle."

Chapter 27: The Uninvited

With the altercation interrupting our journey, and the men and their horses fatigued by their efforts in battle, I did not want to push them to complete the hundred kilometers by dusk, and I recommended to Jeysen that we find a suitable campsite. While Jeysen felt that I was being soft-hearted in my treatment of the company, he also understood the advantage of having the men and horses fresh and rested for when we inevitably would meet Malya's forces next.

Near dusk, we arrived at a long-abandoned settlement, complete with derelict cottages and barns, some of them built of mortar and stone. The thatched roofs were in disrepair, but the walls were sound. While I assigned the shifts for the night watch, Jeysen arranged the bunk assignments, and I was only slightly surprised to find myself sharing a cottage with Glory.

"You should spend as much time with her as you can," I suggested.

"We're not hormonal young lovers," he remarked. "We don't need private moments to reaffirm our devotion to each other."

"That may be so, but this has been a stressful day, and she's not a trained soldier," I returned. "She may welcome your comfort."

"Let's walk while we discuss this," he said amiably, herding me towards our makeshift barracks, out of earshot of the others. *We may have three agents amongst us, perhaps more. If we are to draw out the traitors, we need to set the right trap, and for most, two women together would appear an easier situation to manage.*

We stopped at the door. *You mean to use her as bait?*

At this point, Glory is as much of a target as you and I are, so as bait, you're both enticing, he said. *Please stay with her, as a favor to me.*

At the earnest, searching look in his clear blue eyes, I could not deny him. *Bastard. All right, you win.*

He bowed his head, trying to fight the victorious grin forming on his lips. "At your service, *Keeronae*. Will you join us for dinner?"

"Of course," I nodded. "I wouldn't miss one of Mareos's meals for anything. I'll be out in a moment."

Inside, I was greeted by Glory's proud, willful glare, which softened once she saw that it was me. "What's the plan, then?"

"I will need you to stay close to me, Glory," I said. "You have a keen sense about the members in our group, and I'll need your help to ensure we identify all the infiltrators before we reach the fortress."

Glory nodded. "Jeysen's asked you to babysit me, hasn't he."

I stepped closer so that we could speak more privately. "He did, but I don't think you need that, unless you're planning to get yourself taken?"

"Again, you mean?" she said, with her father's knowing smile. "If I can be an effective distraction or an irresistible lure, to gain you an advantage, I'd play that role for you."

I could easily imagine Sarc thinking the same, months ago, when he knew that we needed to separate eventually. "That won't be necessary," I said. *I think you're more powerful than you let others believe, than even Jeysen realizes, and I'm not about to give up that advantage.*

She giggled. "What other value can I possibly have?"

"I'm not certain yet." I nodded my head towards the door. "Let's not keep the men waiting on us for dinner. We'll have time to speak later."

I saw Jeysen clearly, seated on one of the salvaged benches around the campfire, and it was more than simple recognition. My eyes were drawn to him in a way that felt strangely intimate, and there was something in his beauty that nearly blotted out my awareness of everyone else in the vicinity, including that of Jeysen's beloved less than a meter from my side. Rather than try to suppress it, I took a moment to analyze the feeling. As close as we had become, there was nothing in our relationship that would've encouraged such an attraction to him, but perhaps someone else's...

He stood, along with the rest of the men, and held his hand out to Glory to guide her to her seat next to his. The others in the group bowed to me, and I acknowledged them with a nod. As Mareos doted on Glory with his tantalizing treats, Jeysen took a side-step closer to me.

"You have an unnerving stare sometimes," he remarked, meeting my eyes directly. "It can be incisive and vacuous at once."

"Not unlike yours," I said. "Except for the vacuous component, thanks." It felt good to joke with him, even at my own expense. "It feels like we've known each other for ages, doesn't it?"

"Living together for the past few months might account for it." At a table where Mareos had set out an assortment of beverages, Jeysen poured me a cup of tea, brewed to my liking, nearly to the point of bitterness. He did, in fact, come to know me very well.

"I think it's more than that," I said, capturing a brief flash in the back of my mind of how he looked fifty years ago. It wasn't merely a figment, but an actual memory. *She loved you, Jeysen, as much as she knew how.*

Jeysen's eyes flashed to Glory, who gave us a curious but easy smile. He motioned that we would only be a moment more. *What are you talking about?*

Clyara, I said, warming my hands around the cup of steaming tea. *She wanted you but felt you deserved more, so she kept you at a distance.*

Jeysen's brow furrowed, and for a moment I was afraid that I had made a mistake in mentioning Clyara to him at all. *Your predecessors are still in your head?*

Like they're chatting in an adjoining room of a very cramped house, I said. *Clyara and Aron are the most recent, so their imprints are the strongest.*

Jeysen noticed that we were getting a few stares and cocked his head at me, subtly signaling that we should rejoin the others around the fire. "I only know Aron by reputation."

"You're lucky. He was a misogynist and a bigot who had no intentions of ever relinquishing or sharing his power, certainly not to his apprentices. If Junus and Clyara hadn't found their escapes, he would've eventually destroyed them. He hated everyone who wasn't of use to him. If you notice a cruelness about me, that may be Aron's essence lingering. I'd prefer to think so, anyway."

"You think Aron's the cause of all this, then?" Jeysen said, looking around. "Decades of conflict, the destruction of thousands?"

I shook my head. "He was perhaps the impetus, but the conflict existed long before. I have five hundred years' worth of memories in my head from ten different mages, and none of them involve a plan for peace," I said bitterly. "Domination, perhaps, but never peace."

"Maybe it's just who we are," Jeysen said. "Whether we already had the tendency for aggression, or our magestones make us this way, we seem unnaturally well-suited for warfare. There's even a theory that these gems of ours were created to be used by soldiers to enhance their skills."

We walked the last few steps to the fireside in silence, and I took a seat that Mareos held out for me. *Whatever the case, I'll be relieved when my work is done. I want to leave this magestone with some benevolence to pass onto my successor.*

Jeysen took his seat next to Glory and smiled. *If you lose to Malya, she may be your successor.*

I buried my head in a cloud of tea-scented steam. *Hilafra, Jeysen. You really are a bastard sometimes.*

After Glory and I returned to our quarters, I stayed awake long after she had retired to bed. I was due to relieve Jeysen in only a few hours for the latter shift but found my mind too busy and cluttered to rest. Knowing that there were agents in our midst, waiting for the right moment to act, did not help. I wasn't sure what possibility troubled me more: that Malya had sent her best agents into the Dark Lands to deal with Sarc, or that she had retained her best team to guard her interests in the Realm.

Either way, I did not foresee having to wait very long for someone to act. Rather than lie awake in bed, I extinguished the lights and sat on the floor, next to the door. I left my sword and armor neatly stacked near the bed, as it seemed unlikely that a metal suit would protect me more effectively than a magical shield. As my eyes adjusted to the pitch darkness, I cast a sentinel spell around the perimeter to warn me of intruders, and listened to the stillness.

The stillness lasted only a few minutes. A silhouette passed silently in front of me and stopped between the beds where Glory and my illusionary sleeping form lay. The figure didn't act right away but stood over our beds motionless, as if weighing the decision.

"I know I triggered your sentinel, and I know you're hiding," he spoke. I closed my eyes in disappointment that our suspicions about Bael had been right. "You can show yourself."

Once your stiletto is safely sheathed.

Bael looked about the space, still looking for where I was hidden, with his dagger in hand. "This can still end peacefully."

I agree. When the Empress recalls her troops, we can negotiate. There was no need for a preemptive strike against the Dark Lands.

"Why must they fight the Empress? Is it better for your people to suffer, than to live under her Majesty's merciful rule?" He took a step away from where I was, then turned abruptly and stepped closer, hoping to startle me into giving away my position. "The people in the Realm don't deserve to have their lives destroyed by this vendetta of yours, and the ridiculous prophecy of an old blind fool."

He struck out suddenly, inches from where I was, but I did not flinch. *You underestimate 'my people,' as you call them, as much as you overestimate the capacity and munificence of your putrefying false Empress.*

Bael kicked into my satchel, rattling the glass bottles held within, and waking Glory in the process. To her credit, she stirred but did not startle when she opened her eyes and saw Bael. I didn't want him acting rashly, and I had already made him anxious by being awake. I cast a spell around her, just as a precaution. *Be careful.*

"I am under orders to spare you," he said to Glory, stepping over to her. "But I would have done so, regardless. I was always fond of you, my Lady, and I hope to serve you when you inherit your mother's throne someday."

Glory rose too slowly to avoid Bael's grasp, but as soon as his free hand touched her shoulder, he jerked back with a pained snarl. His fingers gushed with blood where my protection spell for Glory had sliced him. Some of his blood even spurted onto her pristine white gown. As she retreated to the wall, he stared at his shaking, dripping hand until it healed. He knew better than to try to touch her again, probably deducing that he would experience more of the same. Interestingly, Glory did not sound an alarm, realizing that I was still in the room. She remained unmoving, back to the wall, peering at Bael with a calm curiosity.

I'm rather fond of Glory, too, I replied coolly. Tiring of the exchange, I rose silently to my feet. *You've insulted me, dishonored your uniform and betrayed your brethren, Bael. You can either surrender your magestone now, or allow me to pry it from your dead body.*

"My mother stole her throne," Glory said, "so it is not rightfully hers to give to me or anyone else. She was a deceitful murderess, who expected the same conduct from her followers. You've chosen a poor mistress, Bael, and I don't want your mercy."

He turned his head one way, then the other, sensing us on either side of him but not sure which of us posed the greater threat. He probably saw Glory, as the non-mage, to be the lesser opponent, so he directed his attention to seek me first, turning his back to her.

Glory moved with startling, almost supernatural, speed. Before I could stop her, she swung her arm in a graceful, almost dance-like gesture down Bael's back, rending his flesh with her fingertips, using the protection spell I has cast upon her as a weapon by forcing contact. Bael cried out and tried to turn around, only to be crippled by Glory's second swipe, which she dealt at a crouch across the backs of his legs, severing the ligaments behind his knees.

"I'm sorry," Glory said, raising her hand to deliver a killing blow.

I saw a glint of metal as Bael prepared to thrust the stiletto upward into Glory's side, and I redirected his hand easily, forcing the blade into his own jugular instead. As the blood streamed from Bael's throat, Glory dropped her hand and stepped back, knowing that I had interceded. I summoned Bael's stiletto into my hand and plunged the blade into his heart, killing him instantly. With a twist of the wrist, I heard a stomach-turning crack as I forced my way into his ribcage and gouged out the magestone.

"Are you all right, Glory?" I asked, my eyes fixed on Bael's corpse as I tried to figure out how best to dispose of him. I canceled my spell of invisibility and tossed the stiletto dagger onto the body.

"Me?" she replied. "I'm not the one with my hands covered in blood. Well, just my clothes," she said, looking down at herself self-consciously. She seemed more embarrassed by the awkwardness of the scenario than the actual killing itself, as though she was accustomed to slaughter.

I closed my sticky, crimson fist around Bael's magestone and finally let out my breath. The next breath was sweet, thick and metallic with the odor of fresh death, and I stood as I felt the sentinel trigger a second time.

"I heard a noise," Jeysen started, then stopped when he smelled blood and cast a torchlight for the room, illuminating the carnage on the floor, and Glory and me staring grimly back at him. "Glory," he called, reaching for her.

"Don't!" she and I said in unison, and I dispelled the protective shield around her before she could hurt anyone else. As she went to Jeysen, I returned my attention to Bael's twitching corpse and ignited it in an incinerating, blue-white flame, rendering it into ashes in seconds. Jeysen recognized the clothes and the form, but said nothing.

"She knows what I am," I heard her whisper to him.

"Not exactly, but I can make an educated guess," I said. "You may not have a gem inside you, but you know how to transmute the magical energy around you." She could manipulate spells to her will to use as her own, as she had done with my shield, which was no mean feat, even for experienced casters.

"My talent for being a child of two mages," Glory said, not altogether happily. She looked at the pile of disjointed, ash-coated bones in the middle of the room. "Did Bael have family?"

"No, but I will let Mareos know. He was the closest to him," Jeysen said. "We can announce it to the rest of the corps in the morning, There's no need to wake them now, nor do we need to alert the other spies that we're aware of them. 'Fleece?'"

I nodded in agreement, frowning. "I had hoped to convince at least one of them to return to our side, but out of reason rather than fear for their own lives."

"If they turned once, what is to guarantee that they wouldn't turn again?" Jeysen said.

We were interrupted in our conversation by a sentry's voice, announcing a visitor to the camp. Jeysen, Glory and I exchanged uncertain glances: a visitor, at this hour?

"I'll see what it's about," said Jeysen.

"I'll be there shortly," I said, then cast a quick spell to clean the drying blood from Glory and me and clear what remained of Bael from the floor. The odor of death and smoke still lingered in the room, but our clothes were pristine again. It seemed too easy to pretend that we hadn't just killed a man, whether it had been self-defense or not.

I jerked my head in the direction of the voices outside, coming closer. "*Hilafra*, what is he doing here?" It had been so long since I had heard the voice, and conflicting emotions simmered and clashed, with a sudden swell of belligerence emanating from my magestone mixed in for good measure. Glory needed no explanation; her green eyes widened in amazement, as well, and she rushed outside to meet the visitor. I stopped myself before I reached the door, remembering that I did not have the same liberty as Glory to act on impulse, and I reached for my clothing and armor.

When I emerged in my armor, Junus's eyes turned to me immediately, and it was no longer a vague, unfocused gaze but sharp and

353

deliberate like an eagle's. He was encircled by Jeysen, Glory and several of the others, and I took a moment to study the scene, and to quell the churning in my chest.

When I had met Junus in Ruvyna, my gem had been subdued and dulled by Jaryme's spells, and now that the memories of my predecessors were unlocked, I found that I strongly detested the sight of Junus because of Aron's recollection of him. I forced myself to try channeling my other predecessors' relative indifference instead and further tempered my distaste by giving my attention to Jeysen and Glory in turns.

"We were just commenting on *Keeron's* decision to reclaim his sight," Jeysen said. He was noticing my conflict, so he kept his voice neutral for the sake of the others watching us. It was important that we appeared to be united on all matters. "He's apparently grown weary of his blindness."

"It is good to see you, at last, *Keeronae*. I am your servant," Junus said, bowing as smoothly and properly as any courtier.

"I doubt you'll ever be anyone's servant, truly, *Keeron*, but your company is welcome, nonetheless," I said lightly.

"I'm glad to hear that." Junus raised his brow in inquiry. *I know Aron's thoughts are inside you somewhere. He felt very differently, did he not?*

I really don't care what Aron felt, the gem is no longer his to command. "How did you find us?"

"You have mages from Ruvyna amongst your number. One keeps an owl, who brought me a message and let me accompany it back," he said. I noticed that he carried no baggage. "Has my old command met your expectations and requirements, *Keeronae*?"

"The men have been exemplary," I replied. *Except for a handful.* "I could not have asked for a more committed legion. You must be weary from your journey, *Keeron*. Let us bring you some refreshment, perhaps some tea?" I let Glory take his arm to guide him to Jeysen's quarters, as I did not trust myself not to recoil from his touch.

Jeysen walked with me a few paces behind them. *What is it?*

I despise the sight of him, Jeysen. I didn't feel anything like this when I met him the first time in Ruvyna. I think it will do some good for the men to see him, but Ajle help me, I want to kill him. Aron must have been the most hateful, malicious being who ever lived, in order for this gem to be so imprinted with his loathing. I guess there was some good in Jaryme's hold over me, after all. I sensed Jeysen's disgust and managed a smile. *I'm kidding. About Jaryme, that is. A part of me really does want to see Junus Escan's ashes scattered to the wind.*

Jeysen shrugged as he held the door for me. *You're in good company here. All of us have felt that way about Keeron at some point or another.*

Word spread quickly through the camp that Junus Escan had arrived, and Jeysen's room saw a steady stream of visitors before we had any opportunity to discuss with Junus why he was there. By the time the last visitors left, we had only a couple of hours before dawn, Junus had said nothing of his intentions, and Jeysen's pale blue eyes were rimmed red with exhaustion.

"Go get some rest in our quarters," I suggested to Jeysen and Glory, who could barely keep her head aloft. "It won't be for long, but you need sleep more than I do. I'll keep *Keeron* company until daybreak."

"You won't try to kill him?" Jeysen said in semi-jest.

"I'll do my best not to provoke her," Junus returned from his seat at the small table, as he poured himself another cup of tea. He dismissed them with a wave and waited for me to return to his side. "Jeysen should keep the beard. He finally looks like an adult, almost like his father."

While he did not stare, Junus noted details easily. "The armor looks like one of his Highness's constructs."

"It is. I asked him to craft it for me from Tenn's remains."

He took a sip of tea. "Is there some symbolism in the fact that you are wearing your dead golem's skin?"

I looked down at my metal-encased limbs. "I didn't think it was all that subtle, really. If I am to be a weapon, there's no reason that I shouldn't look the part."

"To be used and forgotten once the battle is won. Is that what you see for yourself?"

"The purpose of a weapon is intrinsic to its being and immutable, *Keeron*. What else is there? Once my task is complete, I will leave the throne to the Empress and Jeysen, and their kind, and I will fade into obscurity." Junus did not look surprised by my stance, but nor did he look pleased. "You knew that would be the case all along, didn't you?"

"That you would not be Empress? That was never in doubt," he said.

"No, you knew what this gem would do to me, what's going on inside my head," I clarified. "It does not want me to feel, to be emotionally attached to anyone. Clyara felt it, too, and isolated herself until she could manage it. She told you that."

"She did," Junus admitted. "But you've done exceptionally well, given the circumstances," he said, almost smugly. "Better than I thought you would."

"I'd like to see your head on a pike," I blurted.

He raised his brow. "A bit of Aron slipping through?" he asked.

"No, that was Clyara's remnant, peeved that you doubted her," I said. "Aron's remnant is laughing nastily that even those whom you count among your friends don't like you very much."

He was fascinated by my veiled hostility. "It would be very interesting to study you when all this is over."

"I am thinking that when this is over, I should give up this magestone before I go insane," I said, trying not to raise my voice to hear myself over the remnants crowding my mind. "I cannot live the rest of my life like this, *Keeron*."

Junus set his cup down and looked at my squarely. "You don't have much of a choice, *Keeronae*. You would not survive an extraction at this point. The boys can verify that, with all the gemwraiths they've had to put down over the years, from mages bearing gems far weaker than yours. And while they have no desire to see you suffer, neither Jeysen nor Alessarc would be able to bring themselves to end you."

I closed my eyes, struggling to still my mind. "You could do it."

"I would have no choice," he snapped. "And if you disappoint my boys by taking the coward's way, I would put you down without shedding a tear."

I smiled warmly at his gruffness, admiring his fierce protectiveness of his favorite apprentices. "I was merely considering my options, *Keeron*. I have no intention of destroying myself, but I am very tired. Shall we get to the purpose of your visit?"

Junus turned his attention back to his tea. "I came to ensure that your victory is not only certain, but swift and bloodless. Aside from those traitors in your midst, that is. Those can be dispatched in whichever ghastly method you choose."

I laughed without mirth. It was easy to deal with Junus when my mindset was equally cold and practical. "And why would you waste your time coming all the way from Ruvyna to oversee this exercise?"

"Because I hand-picked those men out there who serve you, and I invested a great number of years in their training. I will not have them give their lives needlessly, if it can be helped."

"Agreed," I said. "I wanted your mages for a show of support, not because I actually needed their sheer strength, so I'll try not to imperil them more than absolutely necessary." I refilled his cup and poured some tea for myself. From his demeanor, it was clear that Junus was not done with me. "Why else did you come?"

"I had a vision," he said, his face drawn and white.

"So, I've heard you say," I simpered behind my teacup, then caught myself. *Hilafra, Aron, shut up.*

"Quiet, you wretched lich," Junus snarled, recognizing his old master's cadence. "This one was of Glory, cradled in your arms, bleeding to death. Your armor lying in pieces around you. I had hoped that I was mistaken, and that I wouldn't find her here." He did not sound accusatory, but his solemnity was telling.

I wasn't sure how to respond, and even the voices in my head decided to be silent. "I can send her back home. Jeysen would be relieved, if I did."

Junus shook his head. "The vision will not change; the events are fixed."

"But you said that you might be mistaken," I said. "There's a chance?"

"A fool's chance," he scoffed. "I healed myself and came to see with my own eyes, to disprove myself, but it is exact to the last detail, including your armor and her clothes. I saw my granddaughter's death."

"No, I will not accept that!" I said, slamming the earthenware cup onto the table, chipping both the cup and the table. "If I was in your vision with Glory, I will save her."

He shook his head again. "You won't. You let her go."

"I would never do that. You're wrong." *But Junus's visions are hardly ever wrong, are they?* "I'll find some way, even if I—"

"*Keeronae*," he said, straightening. "That is your title, and also your fate. You do not get to sacrifice yourself, unless it is for the good of all, even if it means that my Glory's life is forfeit. Believe me, she is the brightest star of my miserable life, so I do not speak carelessly."

A soft knock sounded at the door, and it was only then that I peered through the window and realized that dawn was breaking. Dearst, one of the mages from Altaier, entered with an anxious expression. His dark eyes moved between Junus and me, and he lowered himself to his knees, his eyes fixed on the floor. It was not the customary greeting that Junus had been receiving all night, so clearly something was different.

"Dearst," Junus greeted without concern. "It has been a long time."

The man's already pink face was red with nervousness, and a bead of perspiration dotted his greying hairline. "I have had a terrible lapse in judgment, *Keeron*, and I come to beg your forgiveness."

He was one of Malya's spies that we had spotted early in our journey, given away by his agitated manner. I did not bother to feign surprise, but Junus was feeling playfully cruel.

"What kind of lapse?" he asked softly.

Dearst shifted his weight, rattled further by Junus's calm. "The Empress ... that is, Malya, approached me with an offer. She said that all I needed to do was to report back once in a while with our location, and she would reward us ... me, generously."

"You took a risk coming to us," I said. "Aren't you afraid that she'll punish you for betraying her?"

"With all respect, *Keeronae*," he said, his eyes barely meeting mine, "I think I am much more afraid of you."

"Well, Dearst, I see a dilemma for you," Junus said lightly. "If you're surrendering, I suppose it would be ungracious to execute you now. So, your dilemma is: to whom do you concede?" The man raised his eyes uncertainly. "If you submit to me, you must forfeit your gem, which most likely means forfeiting your life. If you submit to her," he suggested, gesturing to me, "she may yet have another purpose for you."

Shortly after sunrise, we broke camp and started east. Bael's blue roan gelding took easily to Junus's firm hand, and the men were somber but not broken over news of Bael's betrayal and execution. Glory rode with Junus near the center, protected section of our pack, and Jeysen again led. At the first crest, he waited for me at the top.

"See that jagged ridge on the horizon," Jeysen pointed east, past the vast ocean of evergreen forest below us. "The forest stretches for about a hundred kilometers; there are mountains after that for another hundred fifty. How fast we get through will depend on a few things."

"There's a great deal of movement in the trees," I noted, seeing the occasional treetop sway with a jerk. "Is that normal?"

"Define normal," Jeysen said. "There are hunters stationed in the trees at intervals. Malya also has patrols and traps set throughout the border regions. Want to take a guess at how I know?" he said wearily.

"You've encountered them before," I said. "At least, you're still in one piece."

"Yes, because her best hunters are presently in the Dark Lands." Before I could comment, he said, "Your sister and Sarc can hold their own on their side of the Fringe, so keep your focus here."

"I'd feel better knowing where your brother is."

"So would I, but you won't see Jaryme leading any army, as he prefers to keep his own sword clean. He'd rather creep in after the blood spatter and dust has settled," Jeysen said. "So, 'Fleece, what is your order?"

I was conscious of Dearst's presence close behind us, and that he would send word to Malya of our plans, per my earlier instructions to him. He had a hawk perched on his arm, ready to take whatever message we wanted to send. "We'll lose too much time picking our way through the woods. How far can a portal take us?"

"However far you wish," he said. "We have the portal components to avoid the woods altogether. We would have to cast multiple portals, for the size of our group, but it's easily done. There are secure sites throughout the mountains, if you prefer to camp there tonight."

"Maybe," I said, tentatively. "If you had asked me yesterday, I would have said that I want to end this as quickly as possible, but now..." Junus's account of his latest vision repeated in my head, and I wanted to forestall the inevitable.

"Glory is at peace with whatever happens," Jeysen said. "She's glad that Junus told her. Not all of us have the luxury of knowing when we will die."

"What about you?" I said. "Are you ready to let her go?"

"That doesn't matter, 'Fleece." Jeysen peered over his shoulder, seeing her in the middle of the pack next to Junus, and I saw the answer in his expression. "If we had a thousand years together, I still would never be ready." He turned back to me. "So, how do you want to proceed?"

"Get us past the woods, Jeysen. I'm not in the mood for slaughtering this morning," I said, nodding to Dearst, as well. "Then we'll see if anything awaits us in the mountains. By tonight, we will be less than two days from the gates."

I watched from the crest, as Jeysen went to gather the casters for the portals, ensuring that Dearst heard the plan. Our newly-reformed turncoat knew that there was another agent, but he had no other details to share. He had even been unaware of Bael, so if there were multiple infiltrators, they were working individually to increase their odds of staying hidden.

As the mages prepared the portals, I watched Dearst's hawk hurtle skyward and eastward, ahead of us. As the portals bloomed and merged before us, it occurred to me that there had not been any instances of sabotage, yet. Surely, Malya's agents did not intend to assassinate each mage individually, nor was there any single mage within our number strong enough to threaten the entire group at once. So, what other possibilities existed?

Jeysen led the group through the portal, with Junus not too far behind, but Glory waited as I descended the crest, in no particular hurry, as I was lost in thought. The group was more than three-quarters through the portal, and Glory had just ridden through with Mareos, when it came to me, and I jerked Kali's reins so roughly that she almost reared. What better way to divide the group than through the portals!

Racing towards the opening, I noticed that one section was slightly different from the others, although all the portals should have originated from identical samples. I pivoted and rode in Glory's wake, into the segment that had been altered, steeling myself for the worst.

The tinny, high-pitched tones of distant screams reached me before the deeper, gut-wrenching sounds and visceral, animal odors of massacre washed over me. I emerged from the portal invisible, which gave me a few precious seconds to assess the trap that had been set for us.

We were being ambushed from above and at ground-level, and stranded when the portal dissipated behind us. Glory had been thrown from her horse and was entangled in rope, struggling to get free. Mareos had already freed himself and was keeping Glory shielded from fire. I followed the rain of flaming mortars up into the dense, shadowed canopy of evergreens, where archers and mages perched in the shade, almost invisible amidst the branches. Some of our company had already fallen, but most of us were still on our feet, focusing their retaliating strikes upward or at the surrounding hunters on the ground.

"Cover each other, and watch your heads!" I shouted to the group, dispelling my invisibility to divert attention back to me. I dismounted from Kali, pointed to two of the mages who met my eyes and said, "Shield yourselves, and follow me."

I drew my sword and ascended through the trees, firing off flares into the branches to expose our targets, and slicing down the ones who were within easy reach. I raced past them, tantalizingly close, and several of them shot their compatriots in the zealous cross-fire. I was grazed once or twice, but the temporary scratches were worth it, to trick the hidden targets into firing and revealing their position. Flyn and Enoch, a second behind me, caught on quickly to what I was doing and remained a beat behind, to pick off the attackers left exposed.

I reached the treetops and looked eastward to where Jeysen and the rest would have emerged. *See us, Jeysen. Look behind you!* A shot across my thigh snapped me back into the fight, and I turned to Flyn and Enoch. "Head back down, I'll give you two seconds."

One-Ajlekuun, Two-Ajlekuun…

I grabbed one of the top boughs of the nearest tree and set it ablaze. It was fresh, dense evergreen wood, so it didn't burn easily, but the smoke billowed beautifully. I didn't need it to burn hard, just long enough to be a beacon to the others. I let go of the branch and let myself drop, avoiding smoldering needles and fallen archers, making myself invisible before I reached the forest floor.

Mareos was keeping Glory shielded from the barrage of projectiles and debris. Glory, for her part, was using a revolver that looked identical to Jeysen's, and firing back into the trees with uncanny precision. I looked around at the rest of my group; there were eight of us still standing, and we were still outnumbered ten-fold. *Where are you, Wessel…* I spotted the traitor who had cast the portal that led us into ambush. He seemed panicked by the mayhem he had invited. *Was it worth it?*

He swung wildly, his eyes wide but unable to see through my spell. "It wasn't supposed to be this way! They were going to take us alive!"

Stupid, cowardly humyn! You're unworthy of the gift you've been given, just like all the other treasonous filth. Without hesitation, I slashed his throat, severing his head from his shoulders as easily as scooping a dollop of cream. I watched how the body teetered to aim the second swing, cleanly down his ribcage to where his gem was housed. *Still cleaning up after Uscari's mess, after all these years.* I wrinkled my nose, summoned the gem into my palm and considered shooting the traitor's flaming corpse above the tree line as a flare … then reasserted myself.

That's enough from you, Aron. I let Wessel's body burn without further desecration and returned to aiding the others. I peered into the trees at the shadows perched in the high branches, shooting at us, even occasionally shouting to one another. *What crude, uncivilized little monkeys. Ill-mannered, stinking beasts. Let me think, what do monkeys hate?*

I conjured illusions of snakes and large insects dropping from the higher boughs, creeping down along the trunks to where our enemies perched. It only took a few moments for startled cries to overwhelm logic and escalate into hysterical screams, driving our attackers out of the safety of the branches and into the open, where we cut them down with ease. I checked quickly to see that our group and our horses were out of range, then cast a wave of lightning that crackled and careened through the forest, striking anyone who remained standing. The forest fell quiet. *Stupid little monkeys.*

"By the Goddess," I heard Mareos gasp.

"The trees will be fine," I said casually, feeling Set's admiration for the majestic, soaring conifers around us. "These are strong redwoods, impervious to nearly everything. They will outlive all of us, most likely."

I turned around and saw the blank, stunned faces staring back. Glory understood my mindscape and gave me space, turning her attention to reloading and returning her gun to its holster under her skirt.

"The magestones won't collect themselves," I said. "Let's see if we can stop some gemwraiths from popping up, shall we?"

A portal opened, and Jeysen came through with some of the others, ready to assist. I blinked at meeting his eyes, and the rigidity went out of my spine and my thoughts. "Mareos, please check for injuries and find me if anyone needs healing," I said, more softly. "The mage corpses will start reanimating soon, and we can't afford to let them get far with their gems."

"Yes, *Keeronae.*"

"Perhaps my team can help," Jeysen suggested. "They're fresh, and it will give your men a chance to rest."

"Fine," I said, wiping the blade of my sword on the hem of my skirt before sheathing it. I found Kali standing with the other mounts, but she shied from my hand. She was sensing that I was different.

"To whom am I speaking?" Jeysen asked over my shoulder.

I forced myself to breathe. "I'm 'Fleece, for the moment." I relaxed enough for Kali to allow me to take her reins. Wessel's horse and two others waited in vain for their fallen masters, but they would find homes with those whose mounts had perished in the fight. "I should've been quicker, Jeysen."

"I was careless with the portals," he rejoined. "I hadn't suspected Wessel, but I should've watched our casters more closely."

I did a quick head count. "Where's the other half of our group?"

"I left them with Junus where we emerged, past the edge of the woods." Jeysen watched the salvage and reclamation with me in silence. As always, it was a grisly and solemn affair. "Which aspect of you decided to bifurcate Wessel and electrocute the forest?"

"Aron and Set, respectively. Aron hates people as much as Set loves trees, and Set enjoys setting things on fire."

"You think you can rein your remnants in a little, for the sake of our remaining party? You're scaring the ones who are just starting to know you."

"I'll try my best," I said. "But Clyara misses flirting with you."

After we reunited with the rest of the retinue at the forest's edge as we had originally planned, we prepared for the passage through the mountains. I addressed the men and shared with them what had happened to Wessel for his duplicity, but I did not call out Dearst, as he had played his double-agent role without fault. I hoped that it was the last time I would have to speak on the matter with the men, but I was feeling less optimistic.

Glory rode alongside me. *You think there may still be another agent?*

It would be foolhardy to assume otherwise. I'm glad that you have one of Jeysen's pistols, just in case. Of course, if we do discover another traitor, I'll be just as happy to have the opportunity to execute him myself.

To have him surrender would be less messy, she said, unperturbed by my sourness. *Another execution would be terrible for morale, a horror to clean up, and not at all what Snowfleece of Moonteyre would choose.*

Her use of my full name was like a slap — not an angry or punitive one, but a sharp tap to restore me to lucidity.

Glory smiled at my silence. *I'm not sure if you're aware, but Clyara and I spoke a lot about you the morning she took me to Jeysen's home. I told her that I thought you seemed too young and unseasoned for what she had planned for you. She said —*

'Snowfleece understands more than you realize', Clyara recalled through me. *'I told you that she was tough, but that she was not yet hardened by her life.' 'Fleece still felt compassion and empathy, which I could only feign.'*

Just so, Glory said. *But I reminded Clyara that, while you're not the youngest mage ever, you would be the youngest to ever bear* this *gem. Your identity is still forming, 'Fleece, and there are too many forces trying to shape it.*

I appreciated that Glory was still speaking to me, and not any of the facets I manifested. *Then maybe that's what needs to happen. I need to absorb all of these forces and make them a part of me.*

A part, yes, but not to replace you, she said. *You have to find a way to keep forgiveness in your heart. To show mercy, and be better than the ones who came before you. That is the only way this will end.*

Be better. Be kind. The words resounded. Clyara had said them to me, more than once. *I will, Glory. I am blessed in a way that none of my predecessors were, and I don't take my good fortune lightly. I have the most powerful army at*

362

my command, and I have you and Jeysen here to keep me grounded and sane.

I remind you of my father, don't I?

In some ways, but I see something of your mother, too, I said. *It's not an awful thing, it reminds me that she was humyn once, too.*

Chapter 28: Savages and Sages

The sky began to darken as we emerged from the mountains, and the winds coming down from the peaks blew colder. The days were getting shorter, and winter was upon us. Our group was quieter than usual, as the morning's battle and losses had taken a toll on our collective well-being. I asked Junus and Glory to speak with the men in the company, and the idle conversation distracted them and helped to keep them from sinking into utter despondence.

We took position just past the foothills, in a secure area with unobstructed views of the surrounding areas, to avoid camping in the exposed valley. Even though the clouds hadn't thickened much overhead, flurries began while we set up our tents, and a thin layer of snow blanketed our camp quickly. Although the area was new to me, I recognized the weather pattern, enough that I could anticipate the amount of snowfall by the moisture on my skin. I took the first watch, so that I could see the last light disappear behind the mountains.

Jeysen came to relieve me when the sky had turned to mottled slate. It was a poor night for star-gazing, but the brightest stars of the Silver River constellation managed to peek between the thickening clouds, oriented east-west. *This passage is Iavan's Crossing,* Jeysen said. *He apparently liked to visit often.*

He mapped it during one of his surveying missions for his Emperor, when he was still Advisor, I said. *I know, he wrote about it in his journal. He considered coming here when the Emperor hunted him, but he chose the Dark Lands instead.*

Jeysen settled on the boulder near me. *That was hundreds of years ago. Iavan was the first of our people to host this gem. He carried it for a long time, but he was still learning, so it didn't grow much under his care. His use was much more basic, more primitive.*

As I watched, Jeysen unholstered his pistol and emptied the chamber, exchanging the bullets for something I hadn't seen before. *New shells?*

New type of bullet, he said. *These contain an explosive core, that detonate only once they hit the target. If my aim is good, death should be instant, though there may be some bone and armor shrapnel for anyone in the vicinity.*

Hilafra. Considering the damage from conventional ammunition, I could only imagine the mutilation from an explosive round. *For mercy's sake, I hope your aim is excellent.* He reholstered his gun and secured it. *You're not planning to use them yet?*

Not yet, not while I have another choice. They haven't been tested, so I haven't crafted any for Glory's gun. Even if they work ... this is a coward's way.

It's not like you to be unsporting, I agreed. Then I realized, *You intend to use them with Jaryme.*

He looked weary, but determined. *A blade is too messy and intimate of a weapon, and his death should be quick and certain. I will hesitate if I see his eyes — he looks too much like our mother.*

You're certain that it has to be you, to end him?

It's been foretold, he said, resigned. *Jaryme will die by the hand of another mage in the House of Thorne. That would be me.*

I left Jeysen to his watch and checked briefly on Glory's tent, where we had posted two of the mages to guard her. I bid Glory good-night and returned to my appointed tent, where a paper-wrapped package waited for me on my cot. A simple note lay on top, reading: "A gift for you from your *keeron*. Regards, Junus."

From Clyara? It was thin, pliable, and looked very ordinary wrapped in the dull brown packaging. It felt as weightless as it appeared, and the paper parted to reveal a slash of jewel-bright silk underneath.

I unwrapped the paper and recognized the tailoring and cloth from Clyara's pastel-shaded healer's robes, only more vibrant in its sapphire and amethyst hues. *Mine were like that once, too, my girl. They only became faded and frayed after long years of wear.*

A note tucked inside the bodice bore Clyara's script: *"If you choose the Healer's life."*

I traded the golem-metal armor and rigid uniform for the feather-light robes, and the new clothes fit like a skin, both in their comfort and how they altered my mental state. For a moment, I put violence and warfare out of my head and recalled a simpler life, when I was alone in my own mind.

The others continued to prod and pace at the edges of my consciousness. I was no longer individually Clyara, or Iavan, or any of the others, in turn. I was all of them, while still myself, crowded into one body, and after living alone happily for years, in isolation even, I found this state of being stifling and claustrophobic.

I perched on the cot and closed my eyes. In spite of the closeness of the tents, the air was still and quiet at the late hour, further muffled by the snow. There were few hours until dawn, and while I was too restless to sleep, I could at least meditate, to help clear my thoughts. As much as my mind-guests would allow, anyway.

A signal interrupted my meditation. Flyn reported from his sentry post on the mountainside, *Keeronae, a group approaches from the north. One hundred sixty men, on foot. No mages, that I can sense. Shall I intercept them?*

No, let them pass, but stay hidden, I replied. It was too small to be a serious threat. *Report if there are others, in case this is a diversion.*

Yes, Keeronae.

People have a distinct odor, more so when they are tired and stressed, and certainly when they haven't had the opportunity to bathe in some time. Even through the snow, I caught their scents on the wind, dozens of individual odors, layered with leather, metal, gunpowder and smoke. The smells were getting stronger, and the sounds of approaching boots became less faint, but more tentative. Even their crunching footfalls on the snow were unsteady, uncoordinated and plodding.

I did not bother changing into my uniform, as I wove my way through the camp to meet the approaching group. Several of our mages cut short their rest to join me, as well as Jeysen, who had also received Flyn's report. Jeysen kept his weapons readied as a precaution, but he seemed calm and untroubled.

He noticed the new robes, of course. *That's … colorful. New gown?*

Healer's silks, I said. *They're warmer than your uniforms.*

It was a ragged bunch that presented itself, dressed in the modern Imperial grey of Malya's army, with faces dulled by haggard, beaten expressions. Facing our wall of unsmiling, suspicious mages, they did not dare advance past the border of our camp, although they outnumbered us nearly four-fold. One of them stepped forward, an older officer who seemed like a chosen representative rather than a commander, whose face blanched when he saw Jeysen.

"Your Highness, my Lord," he said, genuflecting at once. The others followed suit, although only some were close enough to the front to catch a glimpse of their prince. "My Lord, there were rumors that you were alive, but we didn't realize—"

Goddess take us all. Jeysen grunted his annoyance at being recognized. "State your business," he interrupted, more patiently than he felt.

"Of course, my Lord. We are here to pledge our allegiance to you," the officer said. Another bow of the head. "Once we were deployed into the wilderness, some of us heard that the heir of Empress Adella is still alive, and that you are helping her to take the throne. If that is true, we wish to join your army and follow your wisdom and leadership."

Jeysen and I looked at their insignia and noticed different markers. "You haven't even met us in battle, yet. Did you desert your posts?" Jeysen asked icily.

The man shook his head. "No, my Lord! Never. We have not fought you, Sir, but our regiments did try to fend off a force of…" He hesitated. "They called themselves the 'True Queen's Western Pack.'" He scratched nervously at his sleeve, stained with streaks of dried blood in the pattern of clawmarks.

"I see," Jeysen said. *The wolves still hold their territory on this bank of the*

Channel. "You managed to escape with your lives."

"Yes, Sir," he said. "We are all that remain of three regiments, of nine hundred men in total. They stalked us by day and attacked our camps at night, destroyed our supplies and armory. We were told that our lives would be spared if we continued southward, to here, and surrendered ourselves to 'the Protector.'"

The wolves herded them to us, like sheep, I said to Jeysen.

The corner of Jeysen's mouth twitched with an involuntary smile, as the man bowed his head to him again. "It is not my army, nor my decision," Jeysen said, gesturing to me. "*She* is the Protector, to whom you must make your plea. This is *Keeronae* Snowfleece of Moonteyre, Protector and Vanguard of the True Empress, and I will abide by her judgment."

Thanks a lot, I quipped. "How many are you?"

"One hundred sixty remain," the officer confirmed. "Your Ladyship," he added, with a hasty bow. "We are humble in number, but we will serve you bravely, and with honor."

They'll slow us down and drain our provisions, Jeysen said. *But if we turn them away, they will perish with the next frost. Some of them don't even look like they'll last the week.*

They are lucky that the wolves spared them at all, I said, recalling the ruthlessness of the packs. *But I agree, some of them are close to starvation and need immediate care.*

The surrendering Guardsmen watched our silent exchange with trepidation, knowing that we were conferring about their fate, and they were hesitant to interrupt our unspoken discussion. Neither of us had even asked for a name, demonstrating our suspicion or possible indifference.

"You are welcome to stay," Jeysen finally said, as I gestured to Mareos and Enoch, both close by. "We will take up the matter of your allegiance in the morning, but we have some basic rules of the camp, if you are to remain."

I let Jeysen detail the camp rules for our guests. I delegated the task of feeding and temporary shelter to Mareos, while I instructed Enoch to coordinate a sentry, both for the safety of our camp, as well as to monitor the welfare of our fostered Guardsmen. As the men selected their teams from their fellow mages who were present, I returned to Jeysen's briefing in time for the end, and I was acutely aware of the distrust and veiled hostility that permeated the crowd when our guests looked at me, in my vibrant new elfyn clothes.

"One last matter, before I entrust you to Mareos," Jeysen said. "I'm certain that by now, most of you have seen the propaganda produced by Malya's court; if I'm mentioned at all, I'm accused of treason for attempting to usurp the throne, and the *Keeronae* has been slandered and labeled as a foreign invader," he said, saying aloud in much more polite terms what had already been fomented. "They are lies, designed to deceive and frighten. Some of you are old enough to recall when my sister chose Leode as her consort, and that he was purported to be a descendent of the elfyn mage Set." A few nods appeared amongst the soldiers who remembered the golden years of Adella's reign. "So, the elfyn and humyn have always lived in peace, as one kind, yet Malya proposes to exterminate the elfyn in order to preserve the humyn? That distinction no longer exists."

Jeysen let that sink in for a moment. "Tonight, you owe your lives to the *Keeronae*'s mercy, and that of our allies. If you can't repay your debt in service to the True Empress, then you may leave at dawn, without obstruction. Afterwards, any hate or duplicity you harbor will be your undoing, as all of us," he said, nodding to the mages of our company, "treat one another as family, as one people."

Jeysen suggested that I return to my tent to rest, but sleep eluded me, so I returned to oversee the care of our guests. The soldiers were humble and respectful, docile even, when they realized that we would not mock, mistreat or humiliate them for their misfortunes. Uther was the name of their de-facto commander, who had spoken on their behalf, and his sober, disciplined manner served as an example to the rest of the men.

Mareos, how are our provisions? I asked, watching our stores of fresh water and bread being passed around to our guests.

He nodded his reassurance, with his broad smile unwavering. *We have encountered harsher winters in the Fringe. This is nothing more than a few extra mouths to feed.*

Thank you, Mareos. Rijena made a good provider out of you, I joked, setting my hand on his mountainous shoulder. *Carry on.*

Jeysen noticed my vigilance in monitoring our team. "I don't think our guests are in any condition to try to overtake the camp," he said.

"On the contrary, some of them seem awe-struck, especially of Mareos."

Jeysen smiled. "Mareos hasn't been seen within the borders of the Realm in over forty years; he's practically a legend among Guardsmen. Not many men would've dared to steal from Junus, let alone a magestone, and escape with their lives. Something else on your mind?"

He read me too well. "Just watching Aeneas getting overwhelmed," I said. The lanky, dark-haired Aeneas was one of the field medics on shift, and he was surrounded by patients. "Some of their wounds are infected. I don't smell the onset of wet gangrene, yet, but—"

Jeysen stayed me with his hand on my arm. "Let him handle it."

"Pasca is the other medic on shift, and he should be here," I said. "I saw him on watch with Razul, outside Glory's tent."

"He must have switched duties at some point. I'll relieve them and

368

check on Glory," Jeysen said. "Let Aeneas work, and don't hover. Oversee, but keep your hands to yourself," he warned, with a paternal scowl.

Yes, 'Uncle' Jeysen, I teased. *But I can heal them faster.*

So can I, but our mages need to play their roles, too, he tossed over his shoulder, jogging towards Glory's quarters.

Aeneas had a pleasant bedside manner, and he even attempted minor healing spells to accelerate the recovery for some of the patients, but he began to tire. Unlike Jeysen and me, he was unused to the constant healing and self-repair that was required for the number and extent of injuries that he treated. I became restless, waiting anxiously for Pasca's arrival, which seemed like it would never come.

With the recent flurry of activity around the camp, Junus arrived to see our visitors for himself. He observed without comment for a moment then, seeing Aeneas struggling, he barked: "Mages have specialties for a reason. You, Aeneas, have all the surgical finesse of a drunken blacksmith. Step aside, or better still, go make yourself useful and bring me more bandages."

Aeneas nodded with a relieved smile. Despite its biting tone, Junus's comment was also a compliment, as it indicated that Junus wanted Aeneas to return to assist him.

'Fleece, came Jeysen's brusque call. *Glory's tent. Now.*

I was afraid of what awaited me inside Glory's tent.

It wasn't Pasca's body, smoldering into ash with a gaping crimson pit in his chest, and an oozing hole in the center of his charred forehead. I recognized the mortal head wound from the times that I had witnessed Glory's accuracy with her revolver.

It wasn't even that Glory was gone. Her few furnishings were strewn, signifying a struggle before she was taken, but there was no other blood aside from Pasca's, so she hadn't been hurt. She did, however, dispatch Pasca with certainty, judging from the lethal aim of the single shot. Whatever had transpired had been quick and quiet, as to not draw attention from anyone passing outside.

What frightened me was Jeysen, seething but stone-still with murderous wrath. He stood over Pasca's remains, with a clenched fist dripping with blood; he hadn't needed or bothered with a blade to tear out the turncoat's magestone. In all the months that I had trained under him, his measured strikes had never been dealt in anger, and now he looked very close to losing control. He was furious and restive, as though he had been cheated of an opportunity to vent his rage to his satisfaction and was now looking for another.

I knew not to speak or to touch him, yet. I let Jeysen simmer, confident that he would not lash out at me, allowing him a moment to settle. Instead, I walked around him to examine the rest of the tent. His volatility served to force me to stay level-headed and remain his counter-balance.

Glory's revolver was missing, so I had to guess that she still had it with her. Razul, the other mage sharing guard duty with Pasca, was also gone. I saw the familiar pattern on the ground to mark where a portal had been cast, marked with only a few pinches of soil, too little to use for another portal to follow.

Swept to the side, however, was an additional streak of soil, embedded with Glory's shoeprint. Glory had left us crumbs to follow, literally.

"*Keeronae*," called Junus's voice from outside.

I looked at Jeysen. *Are you good?*

He took a deep breath and nodded.

I will speak with Junus. There's some soil trace over there that we may be able to use for a portal.

Junus was flanked by Mareos and Commander Uther, and none of them were oblivious to my solemnity. "Something's happened to Glory," Junus said. "She's been taken, hasn't she?"

"Yes," I admitted, "but we'll get her back."

"Where are the guards?" Junus asked, but he already suspected the worst.

"Pasca is inside, dead." He had seized the opportunity to act when the rest of us were distracted by the arrival of Uther and the others, but the guilt was mine, for underestimating the need for Glory's security. "And Razul is missing."

Mareos frowned at the mention of Razul's name, as he was one of his oldest friends from the Fringe. "Should I alert the others to break camp?"

Uther ventured, "My men will be ready to travel. We owe you our lives, and we are not mages, but we will fight for you, for the true Empress."

Junus watched me closely, his blue eyes sharp and cool. "*Keeronae*?"

Jeysen emerged from the tent, then, holding a vial of the recovered soil. "I know this mixture. It's unique to the fortress region. There wasn't much to recover," he said, shaking the vial. "We would only be able to cast a small, brief portal, but it will reach the gates. We can open more from there to bring the others."

"I will only need one," I said. "Everyone else will remain behind."

Both Mareos and Junus looked to interject, and I raised my hand. "That is my order." I addressed Uther, "I am honored by your offer. Anyone who wishes to remain with our group is welcome, but we will not conscript those who are unwilling to serve. They may leave at first light, as agreed."

370

Jeysen was silent, his mind shielded, but his expression conveyed his disapproval clearly enough. "Tell the men to assemble in ten minutes," I said to Junus, Mareos and Uther, then turned to Jeysen. "Walk with me, your Highness, please."

"It wasn't your fault," he said, once we were out of earshot.

"It wasn't yours, either," I said. "We were both preoccupied, and we let our guard down. I'll fix it, and I'll get her back."

"*We* will get her back," he said, stopping in front of my tent with me.

"I'd rather have you here. I need the men to help the Western Pack hold this region, to prevent any additional forces from reaching the Dark Lands. They've already helped to weaken Malya's forces, but they'll look to you for leadership to maintain their focus."

Jeysen scoffed. "That's just an excuse. Junus is more than capable and more than happy to be your surrogate here, but he doesn't know the fortress like I do." He looked at me directly. "My place is with you, 'Fleece."

You are always with me, Jeysen, I noted to myself. The dread of losing Glory was compounded by the awful prospect of losing Jeysen, also, and I wanted desperately to spare him the pain of witnessing Glory's death first-hand.

My hesitation was revealing, and he said, "You're wasting time on sentimental notions. You'd be stupid to go alone and ruin this chance, and Malya won't give you another."

Noble, unshakable, indefatigable Jeysen. "Frost and I could've used someone like you, after our parents were gone, instead of the ineffectual, spineless uncles we got."

"Does that mean I'm allowed to come along, 'Fleece?"

"'Uncle' Jeysen, I don't think I could stop you, if I wanted to."

I dressed for battle one last time, fixing the dark golem armor and swordbelt over my iridescent healer's silks. I reapplied the stark colors to my face, as they were as much a part of my ritual as my gloves, cloak and metal shell. Outside my tent, I fastened my packed satchel to Kali's saddle. Everything I brought with me to Jeysen's home, I was leaving behind. "Be a good girl," I whispered, stroking Kali's forehead a last time.

"I'll take her when you're ready, *Keeronae*," Flyn called behind me.

"I hope you're as good with Jeysen's field hunters as you are with your carriage horses, Mister Flyn. Kali can get a little nappy."

Flyn took Kali's rein with a sure, gentle hand. "I've spent most of my life around horses, and a good number of years working in the royal stables, my Lady. I think I can keep them out of trouble." Kali gave a little nicker in response.

As I walked to address the assembly in the clearing, Kali followed me on her own, and Flyn let her have her head. Her warm blow at the back of my head had a calming, therapeutic effect, and I stroked her velvety cheek, as I waited for everyone's attention. Our army had grown to nearly two hundred, literally overnight, and the camp was filled to the edges. The camp was utterly silent, the continuing snowfall muting even the slightest noises.

"I thank you all for your company, your time and your conviction. You have served your true Empress valiantly, and followed me into battle with as much faith as spirit, and I could not have asked for a stronger or braver host to stand with me." I peered into their faces, some somber, some concerned. "From here, *Keeron* Junus will lead you, to where your strength can better serve our allies, so that no more need die for this conflict," I said, looking at Uther and his men.

"And what about you?" called Enoch.

"As I said at the start, *aylonse*, I needed your help to ensure that I reach Malya without having to kill every last man in her Guard, and you've delivered. My path now leads directly to her, and I will follow it to its end before the day is over," I said. "We have already lost too much time, and too many lives, for this to go any longer."

"You mean to face her alone?" Mareos scowled.

"I will attend to the *Keeronae*, as her guardian," Jeysen said. "Just as we all are sworn to protect the true Empress, as her Guardsmen." It was a pointed reminder for the men, that they had served alongside me for the larger purpose, but they did not serve *me*.

Jeysen and I kept our parting instructions brief and departed with minimal fuss. It was safer for us to cast our portal some distance from the camp, in case Malya's troops managed to follow our portal back. Junus accompanied us and shared some wisdom and encouragement, as only he could.

"You are a miserable, dismal pair," he said. "Do either of you even expect to live through the day?"

"If I didn't have hope, I wouldn't bother going," I said.

"And I still have matters to discuss with my brother," Jeysen said.

"Good," Junus replied. "As long as you appreciate that there is still work to be done, after you finish this chore, so be quick about it. As soon as you see it, kill it. Without hesitation."

"I will be merciful with Malya's wraith, if I have any choice about it," I said. "Clyara expects nothing less from me." I met Junus's glower with my own, daring him to challenge my stance on Clyara's directive. "We will rejoin you in the Dark Lands, when our business is done."

"As you wish." Junus bowed his head. "Enoch and Uther will post a watch here until we break camp, in case you need us. May the stars guide you, both."

"May Ajle keep you safe, *Keeron*," we said in turn.

Jeysen and I were silent for the moments after Junus left. Jeysen found a suitable spot for the portal but did not start his trace, as we had seconds before the snow would turn our precious soil to unusable mud. "What couldn't you say in front of Junus, 'Fleece?"

"Same as you, Jeysen," I said. "If one of us survives, it will be a victory. Both of us would take a miracle."

Jeysen pulled a small, dirty stone out of a pocket. "I believe in the Goddess, and that she gives us the instruments to create our own miracles." He held it up for me to see.

What I thought was dirt was actually dried blood and ash, encrusted into the runes etched onto the surface. "*Hilafra*. Is that a portal key, to the fortress?"

"It is. Without one, the gate charms would keep the portal from opening inside the walls, but I had a feeling Pasca had a keystone, if his task was to take Glory back. When you left the tent to speak with the others, I sifted through the remains, and found it implanted between two ribs."

"Our first miracle," I said.

Jeysen turned away briefly to cast the portal, with barely a sound or discernible gesture, and the swirling egress yawned open before us, silently. He looked back at me and smiled reassuringly, holding his hand out to me. "Ready?"

I slipped my gloved hand into his and gripped it tightly. "I'm glad you insisted on coming with me."

He tugged at my hand and planted a kiss on my forehead for luck. "That was never in doubt. Let's go."

The cavernous room was still and cold, with one side exposed to the outside chill. Jeysen knew immediately where we were, and he drew his pistol, his eyes on the Guardsmen's bodies that peppered the snow-covered ground. I was unfamiliar with the layout of the fortress, and I took a quick glance around. Cobbled path, leading to a yard. The fading smell of horses and leather. *Carriage house.*

A weak, tremulous rasp drew our attention to the double-doors that led inside. I recognized Razul by his thick black braid and tan linen robes, and I blinked to his side, easing him gently onto his back. *Shh, don't try to talk.*

His eyes were closed, but he knew me. *Protector. I tried to stop Pasca, but he managed to push her through before he fell. I followed to guard her, but we were outnumbered here, and they took her inside.*

Razul was pale from shock, and he winced when he tried to move his arms to support himself before I nudged him to stay still. A dull, metallic click sounded behind me.

"I found Glory's revolver," Jeysen said. "It's emptied. How is he?"

I shook my head. "Possible internal bleeding. Multiple breaks in left radius and ulna, distal fracture in right clavicle." I followed a couple of holes in his robe to dark bruises in his side, and found the roughhewn bullets Razul had pried out on the stones next to us. "Some bruising on the ribs..."

My stone healed the worst of it, and I'll be fine in a few minutes, he assured us. *Don't waste your energy on me, go.*

I draped my cloak over Razul to protect him from the cold, and Jeysen left him a flask of water. "Find us inside, once you're feeling up to it," Jeysen said, and Razul managed a weak salute.

Jeysen and I phased through the double doors, into an arched corridor that stretched in both directions. Footsteps were fast approaching from one end. "They're coming from the throneroom. That's most likely where we would find Glory and Malya. Follow me," he said, sprinting in the opposite direction, and reloading Glory's revolver on the way.

"What? Where are we going?" I kept pace with him, but I was confused.

"Trust me. Oh, and switch your sword with me. You'll want something faster and lighter than Grandfather's sword when you face Malya." We stopped at the end of the corridor to swap our weapons, and I looked up at another set of heavy double doors.

"Why all the massive doors?"

"Easier for transporting some of the larger war machines in there," he said casually, unconcerned by the din of armed soldiers headed our way. "Looks more impressive, too."

"So, this is the armory? We already have weapons—" I looked down at the sweet-smelling biscuit he handed me. "I'm not hungry."

"Trust me," he reminded me. "Start eating, anyway." He waited until I tossed the biscuit in my mouth and started chewing, then he spoke, very fast: "Your stomach has been empty since yesterday morning, and you will be using a lot of magic, very soon. There is nothing within these cold, dead stone walls that will help restore you once you've depleted yourself, unless you want to resort to cannibalism." He conjured a cup of warm tea for me. "Now, swallow."

Jeysen passed me Glory's revolver, reloaded and cocked, and lay his hands on the doors. "Hold them off, try not to hurt anyone unless they try to kill you first. Keep your remnants under control, too."

Before I could rejoin, he phased through the door, leaving me in the corridor to face the guards alone. I braced myself, gripping the pommel of Jeysen's sword with one hand and holding the gun aloft with the other. I cringed at the sound of crashing metal in the closed room behind me but kept my eyes ahead.

The guards opted for a show of bravado rather than stealth, as their yells announced their presence well before their hulking forms filled the hallway, six abreast. There were about three dozen, armed with the finest weapons that the current technology afforded, their shots riddling my shield with a fair amount of force and precision.

Jeysen, however, did not limit himself to the current technology where his personal arsenal was concerned, and I reminded myself that my aim was to distract and intimidate, not to kill. I took careful aim with the revolver, at some stones over the guards' heads, and whispered under my breath. I only squeezed the trigger once, but my spell amplified and mimicked the sound, so it sounded like dozens of shots. It was enough to make the guards pause and take cover for a few seconds.

Before they completely recovered, I followed up with an illusion that had rats and scorpions emerging from between the stones, skittering across the floor towards them. Logically, the guards knew that I was the source of their discomfiture, but they were still affected enough to slow their advance.

The doors slammed open behind me, and I expected Jeysen. Instead, the guards shouted for retreat and fled the way they had come. Before I could turn around, an animated swarm of metal armor suits flowed around and past me and flooded the corridor in pursuit. I recognized the markings and sculpting of the limbs speeding past and turned around to Jeysen. "You kept golems in the armory?"

"Why, where would you keep them?" he quipped, emerging from the room. "I'm just glad they were still standing undisturbed in the back, just more forgotten relics from my father's time."

I eyed the sword that Jeysen held in his hand, as he resheathed it. "Your grandfather's sword was a beacon to trigger them."

"It seemed appropriate," he said, dashing past me after the golems. "Come on, the way to the throneroom should be clear now."

"You could've told me," I said, jogging to keep up with him.

"I wanted to see the look of surprise on your face. It's cute."

"You're actually enjoying this, aren't you?" I noted.

At the throneroom doors, Jeysen turned to me with a sober expression. "I haven't forgotten that Glory dies today, so I will savor my petty amusements while I can."

We were interrupted by a panicked yell coming from another hallway, and Jeysen rolled his eyes. "The golems can't kill anyone, but I guess the guards don't know that."

"How many did you awaken?" I asked.

"There are about two hundred in total. I only activated the half stored in the north armory."

"Do you think you can secure the fortress with the golems, so I can focus on Malya without interruptions from the guards?" I didn't want Jeysen in the room with me, potentially distracted by Glory's presence, and distracting me with his.

He realized it, and he nodded. "They're both in there, I can sense them. I'll wait for your call."

For a moment, he looked as fragile and brittle as I felt, and I embraced him impulsively, for both of us. With our armor and weapons in the way, it was comically awkward and uncomfortable, and we both stepped back with a chuckle.

He started away, in the direction of the scream. "Good luck, 'Fleece."

I set my hand on the throneroom doors and watched him disappear around the corner. *May your Goddess keep you safe, Jeysen.* With a shove, I pushed the doors open.

Chapter 29: Put Down the Weapon

Without fires to warm the chamber, the room was cold enough for me to see my breath. After all, Malya did not need the comfort of warmth anymore. As I stepped into the still, dimly lit throneroom, the doors closed quietly behind me, sealing out the ambient sounds and heat. The chamber was sparse, furnished only by the occupied raised throne, and the slightly smaller consort throne, also taken. The windows were darkened by heavy drapery, and the few tapestries looked threadbare and faded, even torn.

"You cannot win, little white witch," Malya called from her dais, enunciating her pejorative label for me with exquisite effort. Glory, seated on the lesser throne, was unbound but unmoving and silent.

"That depends on what happens to Glory," I said, stepping carefully on the marble squares, testing for potential traps.

"What is your concern with her?" Malya asked, her head tilted curiously. She glanced at me, from top to bottom, studying my peculiar mixture of healer and golem layers. "She is not yours."

"She's my guardian." Glory's eyes widened with surprise, and Malya seemed speechless. *Interesting.* "And we've come to take her home."

Can you move, Glory?

No, I'm trying, but I'm paralyzed.

Malya shook her head, finally. "You've come to face me alone."

I stepped closer. "We don't need an army for you, Malya. 'You were always too clever for your own good, even as an apprentice.'" My remnants were reemerging, whispering what they wanted me to say. "No one can evade death forever, not even mages. You shouldn't fear it."

Malya was confused, I could tell from her hesitation. "Who are you?"

"I am the White Witch," I said, peeling off my golem carapace and tossing aside my weapons. She could easily rend the metal into shards to shred my flesh, if I kept any of it on. "'And no fortress will shield you from me.'"

The last words made Malya straighten, and I pressed on. "Yes, I know what you said to Aelora when she was a child. I know what you said to Clyara, too, and to Sarc—"

That did it. I raised my shield just in time to deflect the gilded throne that Malya launched at me. I swept the debris aside and yanked the drapes off the windows, flooding the chamber with morning light. "'It is inevitable, that I will take what I want from you, by force, if I need to,'" I taunted Malya with her own words, even as my throat tightened with imagining what Sarc had felt when he heard them from her lips.

I continued to evade Malya's attacks, retreating slowly to draw her down from the platform. It was easier than I had envisioned, as she was lashing out without strategy or guile, but that also meant she was careless with her aim, so I had to act quickly.

I phased next to Glory for a moment, just long enough for a tap to free her from her paralysis, then blinked away before Malya's eyes tracked me back to the floor. With a sweep of her hand, Malya enveloped me in the fallen drapes, constricting and pulling, lifting me from the floor by a tightening loop to strangle me.

"Stop!" came Glory's voice, finally loosened. "Mother, put her down!"

"She would keep us apart," Malya said.

Glory shook her head sadly. "She's the only reason that I returned. I came to say good-bye."

In a fit, Malya slammed the drapes against the floor, hoping to crush me, but I had already freed myself, thanks to Glory's distraction. I summoned the closest weapon to my hand, Glory's pistol, and fired twice at Malya before she could deflect the bullets.

The rounds struck Malya squarely in the chest, as evidenced by how her robes rippled, but I lowered the gun. Malya wasn't bleeding, and she looked unaffected by the gunfire. *How can that be?*

I heard a gurgle, and smelled a whiff of blood, and I dropped the pistol. *By Ajle, no.* I went to Glory and caught her as she slumped to the floor, her bodice already soaked through, the bullet wounds still hemorrhaging.

This was Junus's vision coming true. I barely recalled what he had said to me that morning, only his imperious admonition that I was not to sacrifice myself. *To hell with you, Junus.* With Malya in my periphery, as she pulled Jeysen's sword from its scabbard, I whispered a quick spell to free the bullets from Glory's wounds. … *To you, unworthy and beyond Ajle's grace* … I tried to transfer Glory's injuries to Malya, but I felt Glory shaking her head.

"She's bound us together, 'Fleece," Glory managed. "Any harm you do to her will transfer to me. Just let me go, and you can end her."

"She doesn't get to decide your fate," I said, grasping Glory's hand firmly. As I began to take her wounds for myself, Glory balked and tried to pull free, but I held firm until Malya bore down on us and forced me back.

Malya had the advantage, recognizing that I would not hurt her, if Glory suffered for it. While I recovered my strength, Malya became bolder in her attack, both with the sword and her spells, knowing that I would not directly retaliate.

"You remember that I tasted your blood, don't you?" Malya said, swinging at me wildly, almost playfully. "I can read what you're thinking." She anticipated my dodge and caught me by surprise, slashing my wrist, almost severing my nerve.

Just as quickly, the cut started to heal, and I heard Glory's involuntary gasp, as she clutched her bleeding wrist. She was using the residual healing energy I had shared with her to turn the spell back on me, absorbing my injury back into herself.

"Glory, no!" I yelled. I jumped back quickly enough to only suffer a gouge on the cheek, as Malya resumed her attack, and that healed by itself rapidly enough that Glory only felt a scratch. "Stop it!" I cried, desperate for Glory to stay alive.

Stay alive. That's what Malya wants, to be alive again. She can't think for herself anymore ... so, give her what she wants.

"What are you offering, little witch?" Malya asked, intrigued by what she was picking from my mind.

"I can give you all the knowledge that Clyara kept from you," I said, keeping my thoughts simple for her. "It's all in my mind. You've already taken my blood, you can take anything you want from my head."

Malya lowered the sword, tempted by my offer. I seized her moment of hesitation and lunged, gripping her head between my hands. *Take it all.*

I shared everything — my fears, my horrors, and most of all, hundreds of years of voices and remnants inside me who wanted to be heard again. Malya had my blood inside her rotting core, so my gem latched onto her through our bond, identified her as another vessel, as an extension of me, and I flooded her mind with five hundred years of knowledge and madness. I even gave her some of my energy to restore part of her corporeal mind, so she could appreciate the scope and depth of what I felt, as I concentrated on my own deepest despair and dread: *I cannot let Glory die. She is my friend, and Sarc's daughter, and she is worth my life.*

I released Malya's putrefying skull when I heard Glory's cry. Malya's brain didn't function the same anymore, and it was incapable of processing everything that I had dumped into her, so that pain transferred to Glory, too. As Malya was gradually wasting away, so was Glory, forced to share her lifeforce to slow Malya's decline. I knelt at Glory's side, supporting her as she slipped into unconsciousness.

"Step away from her," Malya ordered. "She is not yours."

"Not by birth." I held Glory tighter, trying to break the spell that was keeping Glory linked to her mother. "But I love her as my own, and I would never let her suffer for me." A memory flickered before my eyes, Clyara's recollection of the last moments of her life, when she gave all she could spare to protect me from Malya. "'This was never Glory's battle to fight.'"

Malya stood, wavering for a moment, then knelt in front of Glory, looking at her with empty, dead eyes. "She was my daughter, my perfect child." She seemed to be struggling to remember. She touched Glory's pale face with her cold, doll-like hand, and a spark of clarity lit her face briefly. "What have I done? What did you do to me?" she asked, her eyes narrowed.

"I reminded you what it means to feel," I said. "To help you recall whom you used to be."

Malya slumped, the light in her face dimmed again, and I braced myself, ready to teleport Glory and me from the chamber, if necessary, but Malya stroked Glory's cheek tenderly. "She was the only perfect part of me."

As her fingers rested on Glory's cheek, the color started to return to Glory's face, and her body stopped wasting away. In contrast, Malya's figure became gaunter, and her flesh and skin became more brittle, almost papery, until it began to flake.

Glory began to stir, and she shrank back from the ghastly form that her mother had assumed. As if ashamed at her own appearance, Malya withdrew her hand and began to pick and tear into the drying flesh of her chest, exposing the lace-fine network of vessels that enmeshed her gem in her body, "I will not fight you. Take it, for Glory."

Glory shook her head, repulsed. "I don't want it."

"Glory's still too weak," I said. "It would kill her."

It won't, Malya said, her throat shriveling, no longer capable of producing sound. *Glory is a part of me, and it knows her and will heal her. Just as our mistress's gem did not reject you, because it recognized you and wanted you to be whole.*

I plucked the gem from Malya's chest cavity and held it out for Glory, but she was still shaking her head vehemently. "It's a cursed inheritance; I'd rather die."

Already, I could see the transformation in Malya. In seconds, she would become a mindless, animated shell, but with enough of the gem's residual magic coursing through her to make her lethal. "I can't take the gem myself, Glory. It will fight me; it is not meant for me. I can't put Malya to rest without you."

Glory glared at the stone, sparkling like a pale citrine, the source of so much suffering. "If I agree, will you extract it for me, when it is over?"

I nodded, with my teeth clenched. Depending on how her body reacted, there was a chance that Glory would never recover fully if the gem was removed, but I had to honor her request. "If that is what you wish."

Glory swallowed the gem, and I cast a shield around us both to protect us from Malya's first assault of conjured metal shards, shredding their way towards us. I expected Glory to struggle in the first moments of taking the gem, as I had with both of mine, but her reaction was entirely different, extraordinarily so.

Glory gasped audibly, and her eyes widened, as though she had just awoken or surfaced for air. "Get the sword," she said, getting back to her feet just as the shield was beginning to wear. I summoned the sword back to my hand and waved my hand to sweep Malya's shards out of Glory's path. She advanced carefully against Malya, but the gemwraith ignored her and flew towards me. Glory turned and grabbed Malya's robe. "I command you to stop."

The wraith flitted back to regard Glory, as if seeing her for the first time. It recognized the gem inside her and obeyed her, just as Aron and Set's decayed forms had eventually yielded to me.

"You need to rest now, Mother, and be at peace," Glory said, and the wraith bowed its head and dropped its shoulders. "Now, *Keeronae*."

The most merciful way to end Malya was to sever her head cleanly, and I took it with a single swing, letting the body fall bloodlessly to the ground. I looked for some sign of grief on Glory's face, but there was only a sense of relief. I said, gently, "I need to immolate the remains, to keep them from reanimating. You are welcome to help."

Glory nodded. "Thank you."

I took Glory's hand and let the knowledge of the spell flow telepathically to her, and together, we cast our fire to render Malya's gemwraith form to ash. We watched the flames in silence and leaned on one another for support. As the smoke began to billow, I was reminded of when I had destroyed my own gemwraiths, who weren't nearly as dear to me as Malya was to Glory. "The smoke contains a remnant of her, if you want to keep her with you."

Glory shook her head and released my hand. "I had her in my head long enough. For the first time in my life, I can be alone in my mind."

Still, I gave Glory a moment alone with the ashes, as I picked up my armor and weapons.

It is done, Jeysen. Join us.

Just as I had sheathed the sword, Jeysen arrived with Razul, now back on his feet. Jeysen's eyes widened with surprise and joy at seeing Glory, and I stepped aside to let him pull her into his restorative embrace. I rested my eyes for just a moment and considered Malya's final sacrifice for her daughter. I wondered if Malya knew that taking Glory from us would force me to act, or if she realized how much I was willing to risk to save her.

Even in her decayed instability, Malya had known that her gem would protect Glory and save her. *'Just as our mistress's gem did not reject you, because it recognized you and wanted you to be whole.'* How did it recognize me? I raced through the memories in my mind of all the gembearers before me. Who was my ancestor who linked me to my gem?

Not Clyara, nor Aron. '...descendant of the the elfyn mage Set.' What had Jeysen said, when he addressed Uther's men?

"Are you feeling well, Protector?" Razul asked.

My knees buckled, from exhaustion and shock, and he caught my arm. Distantly, I heard Glory's alarmed shout, and Jeysen caught me before I crashed. "'Fleece, what is it?"

I looked into Jeysen's clear blue eyes and wondered how I had ever missed it. My gem's prior bearers knew Jeysen's family and mine, before I was ever born. "I need to get home."

He nodded. "Of course. You're exhausted and need to rest."

"No, you don't understand," I said, drawing on the last of my strength to remain awake. "It's not over, our work isn't done."

It is not finished, my girl.
I know, Clyara. Malya has been laid to rest, but I must see to Frost.
You must see the Empress safely to the throne.

With that, the darkness yielded to light, and I eased my eyes open. I was no longer in the throne room, or even the fortress, but in a tent, with distant voices raised in plenty of loud conversation. I tried to remember the last people I had seen... "Glory. Jeysen."

Glory squeezed my hand. "I'm right here."

"Don't get up too fast," Jeysen said, his voice coming from somewhere behind me.

"Razul," I called. He was also there, before I fainted. "And golems."

"Razul's outside with Junus and the rest of the mages," Jeysen reported. "While you rested, we rejoined with the group, and we've combined our numbers with the western pack. I've taken the liberty of discharging Uther and his men, and most of the mages, from their service, but some of them have volunteered to stay behind, just in case we need them. As for the golems, I posted them around the fortress and relieved the Guardsmen of their duties until ... until all of this is resolved."

Empress. "We need to stop Jaryme, he's distracted us long enough."

"We were discussing where he could be," Glory said, holding a cup of water for me. "He's far, but I can still sense him. I seem to have inherited my mother's bond to him, and it is a strong one."

I mumbled into my water cup, "I hope the bond happened before she died."

Jeysen made a disgusted sound. "Anyway ... how far would he venture?"

"He would go wherever Frost is."

"She would be in the Sighing Fields, with Sarc," Jeysen said. "Once word reached the front lines that Malya was dead, the last of the Imperial supply lines dried up, and her army abandoned the objective. Your sister is moderating the negotiations with the generals for their surrender."

"By Ajle, how long was I unconscious?"

"Only a few hours," Glory said. "That kind of news travels quickly."

"You're too generous with time when it comes to letting me sleep," I chastised. I turned to Jeysen. "We'll start there, then, if you can coordinate a portal."

"I'll get the materials," Jeysen said, and left Glory and me.

"No adjustment, yet?" I asked Glory.

She shook her head. "Already finished," she said. "Jeysen stayed with me through the process. I may get a full calibration cycle later, but I think the gem wants to stay, for now."

"I'm sorry," I said. "You took it under duress, and I wanted you to have a choice about keeping it."

"Don't worry about it," she said blithely. "Mother was all about forcing situations on people without their consent."

Hilafra. Physically, Glory may have been fine, but Malya's imprint within the gem was weighing on her. "You have control over your life," I said. "Remember what you told me: these forces may try to shape you, but they don't replace you. The gem is yours to command now, there's no one else."

"She was never sorry, for any of it," Glory said. "I have all her memories of beating me, of raping my father, of poisoning Augus..."

Jeysen returned then, and he went immediately to Glory, and I knew that he was the anchor that would keep her stable. "You can't undo her damage," I said, "any more than I can undo the destruction that my gem's hosts have caused during our tenures, including mine. We can only offer restitution and seek forgiveness for ourselves, and strive to become better and wiser."

"There's a lot that requires forgiveness," Glory said. "There will be time to discuss this later. Right now, you have to go save your sister. In the meantime, I'll spend some overdue time with Junus. There was a lot left unsaid between him and my mother."

Emerging from Jeysen's portal, I took a second to get acclimated to the sharp, stinging air that whipped around us and across the Sighing Field. The plains were bleaker in winter than when Grey-Eye had led me there in autumn, but the grounds were no longer empty. The fertile land overtaken by wild grain and brush, was now a clear expanse overrun by tents, cooking fires and people, and Jeysen and I were not alone for long.

A familiar woman's called voice to me: "Protector!"

I greeted Rijena and Rija with an embrace, and smiled at Grey-Eye, close at their heels. "It is good to see all of you."

"Has my Mareos made himself useful to you?" Rijena teased, her brown eyes twinkling. "If not, we can use him here. These Imperials are decimating the winter stores, and my husband needs to make sure we don't starve."

Grey-Eye stopped in front of Jeysen and bowed his head. *Master.*

Jeysen bowed his head in turn to Grey-Eye. *I haven't been master to your kind in generations.*

Your Highness, then, Grey-Eye said. As always, he picked up my thoughts with ease. *I last saw Alessarc and the Queen by the ruins of the farmhouse.*

"The wolves call Frost the 'Queen'?" Jeysen said, making the connection at last. "So, he's after her for more than revenge against you."

"Details to come," I said, bolting after Grey-Eye in the direction of Aelora's former safehouse. Feeling encumbered, I held my sword in hand and tore the hem of my robe to free my legs, but the wolf still outpaced me.

I slowed once I saw that Frost was safe and in the company of many others: soldiers, Elders and Sarc. She looked surprised to see me, but no more than I was to see my ethereally-beautiful sister in a crisp, tailored Adella's-Guard uniform, her lustrous silver locks cinched into a practical top-knot.

It wasn't until I touched her that I realized how much I had missed Frost. I allowed myself a deep, shuddering breath when we hugged, then stepped back with my mask in place. "Have you seen Jaryme?"

"There's been no sign of him." Sarc shook his head, but a flash of alarm crossed his face. "You shouldn't have come, 'Fleece."

"The fight is here," I shot back, suddenly angry at Sarc for questioning my decision, and hurt that he wasn't as welcoming as I had hoped. "Is everyone safe? Are the children here?"

"Don't say another word," Sarc snapped.

Frost ignored him. "No, 'Fleece, I did not bring the children into battle with me," Frost said hotly. "I left them in Moonteyre, under the care of Sun-Catcher and the wolves."

Sarc swore under his breath, and pulled a vial from his pocket. Without a word, he emptied it on the ground, and a portal bloomed. "Let's go."

I stopped Sarc with my hand on his chest. "No, you stay and watch over Frost." *Hilafra, what's going on here?*

"Fine." Sarc stepped back. *You've led him straight to your family, Ajle'xon.* He looked at Jeysen. "Go, before it's too late."

Jeysen pulled me after him, while I was still processing Sarc's rebuke. Stepping onto the cobbled path leading up to the roots of the Ancient, I finally realized what Sarc meant, and I wanted to run back through the portal, but it was too late. *There's still a chance,* I hoped, as I saw the scores of children playing under the boughs of the Ancient, protected and distracted by their adult watchers and the silver-coated wolves, led by Grey-Eye's daughter, Sun-Catcher. A crowd of laughing, playing children at a playground, would have seemed care-free and heartwarming, but I wanted to hide.

Too late. A young boy and a younger girl broke free from the group and darted towards me. *No!* I recognized them immediately, and I knew in that terrifying instant I had betrayed them to Jaryme.

Thank you, 'Fleece. I heard Jaryme's voice in my head before I saw him appear behind Rigel and Kaylis, seizing them by their collars. I charged at him, straight towards the wall of blue flame that stood between Frost's children and me. Jeysen was just a beat faster than me and one step closer, and he pulled Rigel out of Jaryme's reach. With Kaylis thrashing in his arms, Jaryme challenged me with his grin. *You know where to find me.* He vanished, taking Kaylis with him.

"*Hilafra*, 'Fleece!" Jeysen yelled, dispelling the lethal blue fire before I touched it. He tucked my nephew to his chest, and shook me gently. "'Fleece!"

I stroked Rigel's downy brown hair and looked up at Jeysen with tearing eyes. "What have I done, Jeysen?"

"Focus, 'Fleece," Jeysen said sternly. "Where do we go?"

"I have to think," I murmured. Jeysen carried Rigel back to the group and exchanged a meaningful glance with the commanding and stoic Sun-Catcher, who herded the boy back with the others. Jaryme hadn't needed a portal, so he hadn't gone far. "Back to where we started," I said.

"Where's that?" Jeysen said.

"His camp in the woods, near the west bank of the Yirae," I said. "He had sheltered me before my adjustment to Clyara's gem, before Sarc took me to the Haven."

"He kept that a secret. I don't know where it is," Jeysen said.

"I'll never forget it," I said, grasping Jeysen's hand. "Ready."

I closed my eyes, envisioned the clearing and the surrounding trees and took us there. There was a quiet click, as Jeysen warned, *Don't move,* and I forced myself not to flinch as the triggered wires and blades sliced into me, for a few endless seconds. When the assault stopped, I cracked my eyes open, and spied the traps and weapons still untripped all around, still glinting with menace, with Jeysen and me at the center, cocooned within a protective shield. Jeysen blinked away a rivulet of blood trailing from a forehead cut, already dried.

It wasn't booby-trapped the last time I was here, I apologized.

It's all right, I've been through worse, Jeysen said. *But we don't have time lo disarm everything.*

I glanced around without moving my head. Aside from the traps surrounding us, Jaryme's tent looked exactly as I remembered: solid despite its fabric construction, its pitched roof made sheer to allow in the dappled sunlight. *I can't believe I ever felt safe here.*

"You were safe. I would never have hurt you," called Jaryme. "I still won't, unless you insist on fighting me." He looked at my hand, still gripping Jeysen's tightly. "Does Sarc know that he's been replaced?"

Don't respond, let him keep talking, Jeysen said.

"Let me save you the trouble, little brother," Jaryme said, disarming the traps with a wave of the hand. "I don't want to kill you, either, just slow you down, as you came charging in with your guns and swords."

Jeysen and I dropped our joined hands. "Where's Kaylis?" I demanded.

"Safe, for the moment," he said. "I've hidden her, for my own protection. If anything happens to me, then her fate is uncertain." I tried to peek into his mind for information, and he shut me out harshly. "I'll give her back once I get what I want," he growled.

"You can't stop Frost's ascension," I said. "And you can't use Kaylis as leverage to influence her."

"Not with your sister, no," Jaryme agreed, then looked at Jeysen. "But my brother is another matter. What do you say, Jeysen?"

Jeysen drew a deep breath, his jaw clenched.

Jaryme laughed, seeing my confusion. "Your compassion is endearing, 'Fleece. Given time, your sweetness might convince me to reclaim my humanity, but that was never in your guardians' plan." He opened his hands to Jeysen. "So, brother, do you fulfill your prophecy and cut me down today, or does our great-grandniece Kaylis get to live?"

"I can't let you walk away from this," Jeysen said.

Jaryme motioned subtly to cast a spell, then again, without success. He tried to escape, then tried to reactivate his traps, and it took him a second to realize that I was thwarting his attempts. "Kaylis will die, unless you let me go," he said.

"If I let you go, you'll just continue tormenting our family," Jeysen said evenly, drawing his pistol. There was no hesitation, barely enough time for Jaryme to throw up a defensive shield.

One bullet was deflected by the shield, but the second struck Jaryme squarely in the shoulder, and exploded in the bone, effectively shattering the joint. Almost instinctively, Jeysen cast a shield around me before Jaryme could turn the wound back. So, Jaryme pivoted and redirected the wound to Jeysen, instead.

"Go ahead, brother," Jeysen said, calmly switching the pistol to his other hand, and I saw his bones reknitting behind his torn flesh. "I could always heal faster than you could hurt me."

With Jaryme's attention on Jeysen, I stepped forward and swung my sword, slashing Jaryme's throat. His reflexes, however, saved him from a beheading, and he staggered backward, clutching at his spurting throat and preparing to pass that pain onto Jeysen next.

No, no, no! I snapped the sword to divert Jaryme's attention to me. When he did not waver, I lunged forward and ran my sword through him. As the metal pierced the layers of his bone and flesh, I grabbed Jaryme's shoulder to keep him from vanishing or casting any healing spells. "Jaryme, look at me," I whispered.

Shuddering with pain, impaled on his grandfather's sword and unable to escape, he looked at me with hate-filled eyes. *What?*

"The prophecy about your death, by a mage from the House of Thorne," I reminded. "That would be me, Uncle."

"'Fleece," Jeysen said. "You don't have to be the one to end him."

"Yes, I do," I answered, holding onto Jaryme until he was too weak to stand on his own. I let him slide to the ground, onto his knees, but I kept my hand on him and did not pull out my sword, as his eyes were still angry and defiant in his last moments of life.

"Kaylis will die," he said weakly, savoring his small victory.

"No, Sarc has already found her," Jeysen said. "You get nothing."

Jeysen cast a barrier between Jaryme and me, separating us, as Jaryme took his last labored breath. Before his brother's body slumped to the ground, Jeysen raised his pistol a last time and fired. With a direct hit to Jaryme's chest, the explosive bullet shattered his magestone, and the shrapnel sprayed the shield that protected me.

I remained kneeling next to Jaryme's mutilated corpse, nauseated by the horrific extent of damage, but also relieved that it was over. Jaryme was dead, his magestone destroyed. My mind was finally clear, silent and calm. I pulled the sword from what used to be Jaryme's torso and flinched when the body burst into flames.

"Jeysen." He stood frozen, his eyes on the blue-white fire that he had cast to consume his brother's remains. I touched his face, diverting his eyes to me, and I wrapped my arms around him. His rigidity yielded, and he allowed himself to grieve, if only for a moment.

"I had to be the one," I said. "Despite everything, he was still your brother, and you don't deserve to suffer the guilt of his death."

Jeysen nodded. "What about you? He was your family, too."

I held my tongue. I had been more humane and less vicious than Jaryme deserved, for Jeysen's benefit. Had he not been related to us, I would have given Jaryme a more painful and prolonged death, for all the suffering he had inflicted.

I will not tell him, either, Grey-Eye's voice entered my head. *We are glad to find you both well.*

Grey-Eye and Sarc entered the tent, with Kaylis cradled against Sarc's chest. I exchanged a relieved smile with Jeysen and went to my niece at once, showering her with caresses and kisses. "How did you find her?"

Jaryme knew to guard against another mage trying to read his mind, but our minds work differently, Grey-Eye said. *Once I caught a glimpse of where he had taken your niece, it was simply a matter of tracking her scent. She smells strongly of milk and apples. And wolf dander.*

"I was in a cocoon high up in a tree!" Kaylis squealed. "Like a butterfly."

"Let's not tell your mother that part right away, sweetheart," I cooed. *Or, ever.* "So, you both followed us from the Sighing Field? Did you know?" I asked Jeysen, and he shook his head.

"We couldn't let Jaryme suspect anything, so we couldn't tell you, either," Sarc said. "Sometimes, guardians have to do what's needed, even if it's not requested or known, even amongst ourselves."

Jeysen twisted his lips with annoyance. "Yes, about that."

Chapter 30: Want and Need

Frost was waiting beneath the bare boughs of the Ancient with Rigel, when we returned with Kaylis. Seeing both of her children safe again, she visibly relaxed, and she seemed even more tranquil and poised than she had been on the Sighing Field, negotiating peace terms from the victor's vantage. Even clad in the austere dark grey uniform of Adella's Guard, Frost was a charismatic, approachable figure, as much at home under the cover of the Ancient as she was on the battlefield.

"I told Sarc to stay with you," I began.

"I've told him many things, and he rarely listens," she replied.

Me, too. I felt a flicker of something like laughter from Grey-Eye, as he joined Sun-Catcher and the other wolves basking in the warming sunshine. They watched with casual interest, as the villagers who returned from the Sighing Field with Frost, reunited with their families, children and partners.

I was staring but didn't realize my distraction until I felt Frost's arms encircling my waist. She unfastened my sword belt and bumped her shoulder against mine. She pointed her chin at Jeysen and Sarc, walking away. *Go with them, you know you want to.*

We have some catching up to do, I replied. *And what do you need to get ready? Do you need help with packing?*

She set her hand on my arm. *If I need you, I'll know how to reach you. Go.*

I gave her a hug and dashed off, catching up in a few short steps.

"...So Aelora Mareni became Rija, and she remained in the Dark Lands," Jeysen said. "And the wolves continued to protect her, from a distance?"

Sarc nodded. "They watched over her for the rest of her days. When she passed, the wolves continued to watch Aelora's daughters."

Jeysen glanced at me. "One, who is the heir, and the other, her Protector."

"I think the titles are arbitrary, depending on the day," I shrugged, recalling all the instances during childhood when Frost had been my champion and defender. "If Frost's latent power was much stronger, I would be redundant."

Sarc smiled at Jeysen's confusion. "You'll understand once you've spent some time with her. 'Fleece is right, Frost is a natural empath, and her telepathy is getting stronger by the day."

"Frost and I have had a link since we were children, and we never knew the origin of that magic, but then, you mentioned once that Adella's consort Leode was a descendent of Set. Even though Leode wasn't a mage himself, there was enough trace passed down to us, that Clyara's gem recognized it and accepted me as its new host."

Jeysen looked astounded. "Aelora was here, alive, and I never knew." He frowned at Sarc. "You bastard, you let me believe that she had died. You convinced me to stop looking for her."

I took Jeysen's sleeve. "I know you feel cheated, but she had to be kept hidden from you and from Adella, to keep her safe. If not, Frost and I wouldn't exist. Please know that she lived a peaceful, happy life, and she was a wonderful mother."

"You're lousy at keeping secrets, Jey, especially from your siblings," Sarc remarked, then looked at me. "Probably runs in the family."

"You kept it from me as long as you could," I said. "You knew that my bond to Jaryme would reveal the truth to him, as soon as I figured it out."

"He made a lot of things more difficult," Sarc said. "No offense," he added with a nod to Jeysen.

"No, that's fair to say," Jeysen admitted. He looked at Sarc's hands for the first time since we arrived in the Dark Lands. "Your ring, Adella's signet. She had given it to you as a gift."

Sarc held out his bare hand, which had previously been adorned with the gold band set with a blue cabochon. "It lost its meaning for Adella once she thought that Aelora was gone, but it's always been intended for the first-born, for the heir, so Frost wears it now."

We had returned to the Ancient, where Flyn and Razul were paying their respects to Frost, who remained poised and gracious despite her exhaustion. While she exhibited no outward signs, I recognized a familiar pattern of breathing and stillness.

The men bowed their heads to me and Jeysen. "*Keeronae*, the men await your orders at the western camp," Flyn said. "*Keeron* Junus is ready to return to Ruvyna, and Lady Glory awaits his Highness's return. The horses are getting restless, too, especially with the wolves about."

I took a deep, restorative breath, and Frost held my swordbelt out to me. I gave her a last embrace and signaled to Jeysen. "Can I trouble you to stay here a little longer?"

"Of course," he said, stepping aside with me. "What is it?"

"Frost will need your guidance to coordinate her transition, and you know the protocols and nuances of Imperial politics better than anyone, at this point." The second part was harder to say. "Glory needs her father. She has inherited an immense burden with Malya's magestone, and only he can help her manage it." He began to interject, and I raised my hand.

"I've seen a glimpse from Clyara's memories, and it's not something that either you or Glory should have to endure. Not with everything that's happened today. Please, Jeysen, stay."

The rest of the day passed in a blur. As soon as Sarc and I returned to the Realm with Flyn and Razul, we hardly had a moment to speak. He accompanied Junus and Glory to Ruvyna, and I rejoined the mages who had remained behind, to officially discharge them from their duties. Much to my relief, Jeysen had made my task much easier by having the letters drafted and stashed in his saddlebag. He had also given instructions to Flyn for returning the remaining horses home.

"No horse for you, Mareos," I said, presenting his discharge orders. "You're to return to the Fringe immediately, per Rijena's order, before your people starve."

Mareos laughed, his chest proudly puffed under his massive black beard. "That's my girl, emptying our larder for every stray in the Fringe. Come on, Razul, we have days of restocking ahead of us," he said, nudging his friend with an amiable grin. "I hope you come to visit us soon, Protector, and that you bring your family along."

When the camp was emptied and broken finally, it was well past dusk, and I remained in the clearing to savor the tranquility and stillness of the forest. For the first time, in what felt like days, I was left alone with my thoughts, and I laughed as I sat on the cold, hard ground and looked up at the stars. I hadn't packed any portal ingredients in my satchel, so I was stranded in the wilderness, very literally.

Not a bad place to be, I mused. I closed my eyes and breathed in the frigid forest air, still tinged with the smell of spent kindling and crushed winter grass, warmed by the scents that lingered on my cloak from my months under Jeysen's roof. Though no trace of combat remained on my skin or under my nails, the memories of Malya and Jaryme's deaths still replayed in my mind, intangible but painfully vivid. *These are my memories, no one else's.*

With my next breath, I released all the pain and anguish that I had been suppressing, and I let myself cry. Once the tears started, the catharsis was so liberating that I couldn't stop myself. It was as though my psyche was trying to purge itself and reset. Back to where I began. Before I had adopted the title of *Keeronae.* Before I learned to tap into the cataclysmic potential that my magestone held. Before the practicality of warfare allowed me to justify the slaughter of dozens by the wave of my hand.

"Don't do that," Jeysen said quietly. He crouched in front of me, pulled my cloak closer against my shoulders, and took my quivering hands. "Don't second-guess your decisions, or it will never end."

I continued to sob, and Jeysen did not try to dissuade me. He simply stayed with me and continued to warm my hands with his. Finally, he said: "Did you know that your sister is not as stoic and dispassionate as she appears?"

I wiped my eyes. "How so?"

"I noticed when I spent time with her this afternoon," he said, taking a seat on the ground next to me. "Frost has had a long, long day, and given the strain, she could be forgiven for any misjudgment or show of temper. But there wasn't anything in her actions to fault her."

I smiled weakly. "She's flawless."

"She's flawless because she leans on you," he said. "Whether she realizes or not, she uses the link you share to manage her emotions." My reaction was underwhelming. "You're not surprised?"

I shook my head. "I'm not. She was doing that when I was in the Haven, and I'm not even sure she's aware of how she does it. If it helps her, especially now, I don't mind."

He looked stunned at my complacency, but happily so. "It would appear that you're still the Queen's Protector, indefinitely."

"It's what sisters do," I shrugged and got to my feet, and he followed.

"By the way, she says to let you know that you will always have a place under her roof, but that she doesn't expect that she'll see you often. What does she mean by that?"

I smiled. "Frost knows me, and she knows I can't stay in any one place for very long. I'll always be her Protector, regardless of where I roam." I looked at Jeysen. "What about you? Are you still my guardian?"

Jeysen laughed and pulled me into his arms. "I never had the chance to see your mother grow up, 'Fleece, so nothing will make me give this up. You girls are stuck with me, for the remainder of my days."

"*Hilafra*, Jeysen, that could be centuries."

"Possibly," he said, "but I think you can still use my help from time to time." He looked around at the fathomless darkness of the desolate woods surrounding us. "Like when you get stranded in the wilderness without a portal, or a horse."

I accompanied Jeysen to Ruvyna, to collect his things and bid farewell to Junus. After that, I had made no plans, despite the advice that Sarc had once given me. Crossing the portal into Junus's sitting room, I was welcomed by the familiar, soothing smells of tea and books, so much like Clyara's cottage. It was a warm, welcoming setting for a visit, but it would stifle me if I had to reside in such a place.

"See, Sarc, Jeysen managed to secure a portal amulet to get here," Junus's voice sliced through the momentary silence. He was seated in his wingchair, a cup of tea in hand. "But his aim is appalling. Two meters to the right, Jeysen, and you would be standing on my table."

"Only if I want to," Jeysen said confidently, flashing a smile at Glory, who was leaning against her grandfather's chair. Standing close by, filling the doorway to the back room, was Sarc. "Should I forge another key for you, *aylonse*?"

Sarc gave his friend a half-smile. "Between the new Empress and Glory, you won't have time. I'll just borrow yours, since you won't be traveling much, anyway."

Glory approached Jeysen and circled her arms around his neck. "You've finally come to collect *all* your belongings?"

With a cursory glance at Sarc and Junus, Jeysen answered, carefully: "My things *and* you, if you'd like to return with me."

"Good answer," she mouthed silently. Glory pivoted to face her father and grandfather. "So, am I free to go?"

Sarc nodded and said, "Remember what I told you, and you'll be fine."

"Good." Suddenly, she hooked her arm around mine and dragged me to the front door. "Give us a few minutes." She gave Sarc a pointed look. "Don't leave."

Outside, Glory pointed me to a bench that stood on Junus's porch. Just beyond the picket fence, the townspeople were stringing banners and hanging decorations by lamplight.

Preparing for a festival? I asked.

Glory sat next to me and pointed to the gregarious Mistress Belladonna across the road, directing the activities with great vigor and girlish glee.

"Bella and many of the others have been waiting for years to throw this party," Glory said. "They finally see a lasting peace, and they don't have to think of Ruvyna as a sanctuary or shelter, anymore. They can go home, if they want, but most of them will probably stay."

"It's good to have choices," I smiled.

"You can go anywhere, too," Glory said. "You would always have a place in the Imperial Court, but somehow, I don't think you'd be happy there. You're not one for cages, no matter how gilded."

The Haven had been well-gilded, but what had driven me to leave? "As long as I have company, I would be content."

"You deserve more than contentment," she said. She tilted her head towards the house. "Have you talked to him? My father?"

I laughed. "Seriously? I've barely had a moment alone with him."

"Good point," she said, getting to her feet. "We'll clear out and give you some privacy, then. Don't let him leave until there is a resolution. He needs closure, as much as you do."

"I'm not so sure. He's done fine without my disrupting his life."

"Trust me, I've known him longer," she said, rising to her feet and

393

pulling me to mine. "Some men, like Jeysen and my father, need disruption and chaos, or their idle minds and hands will cause havoc and pandemonium that we can't even imagine. They're wired to solve problems, to save the world."

Back inside, Jeysen and Sarc were both outfitted to depart. Jeysen held Glory's cloak for her, as she returned briefly to his side. Jeysen took my hand, as Glory said farewell to Sarc. "Thank you for not breaking my grandfather's sword," Jeysen said. "I can't promise that your armor will stay intact, though. I may need the parts to rebuild your golem."

"It's better that way," I said. "Although, Tenn was never mine to own or keep. She's more suited to be a nanny, maybe for Rigel and Kaylis."

Jeysen nodded his agreement. "Don't stay away too long, 'Fleece."

"I won't, Jeysen ... Uncle." The title made him smile.

"I reserve the right to visit unannounced," Junus proclaimed, as Jeysen opened the portal back to his home, the summer palace in Inear. "To ensure that nothing unseemly is transpiring in that house."

Glory gave him a defiant smile. "I will make no such promise, Grandfather, so you come at your own risk." With a laugh and a wink, she vanished through the portal, with Jeysen closely in her wake.

"Off with you, then," Junus said to Sarc, as a knock sounded at the door. Mistress Belladonna's keen voice was calling us outside to join the festivities. "Unless you want to stay and indulge before you go. No doubt many of my neighbors would relish the opportunity to speak at length, especially with you, *Keeronae*, about olden days."

A wisp of air, and Sarc was gone when I turned around. "Junus! I can't believe you let him leave like that!"

Junus was unapologetic. "He's seventy years old. I don't *let* him do anything."

"But you knew he would go without saying good-bye."

"He wasn't specific about his intention," Junus said smartly. "Really, *Keeronae*, you should take a moment to savor your youth and good fortune. There are plenty of eligible prospects to consider, instead of a secretive, shifty seventy —"

"Why do you keep mentioning his age?" I asked testily.

"To remind you that you're dealing with a grown man, not some callow, flighty, hormonal brat," Junus said. "I may tease him on occasion about his competence, but the truth is, he is deliberate and canny on many levels. Clyara and I would never have trusted him for so long, with so much, otherwise."

I spoke slowly, so there was no confusion. "Then you can understand why none of those 'eligible prospects' out there in the world, have anything to offer me. If I'm going to be a living archive for centuries of knowledge, then I'm going to need someone who can keep up."

Junus seemed to consider my words, then smiled. "That's fair. I want to be sure you're not after him for just his pretty face." He walked over to his windowsill tray of herbs and medicinals and waved Bella away through the window, and returned with a vial of pink sand. "I told Sarc I wouldn't stop him; I didn't promise to prevent you from tracking him."

I looked at the shell-pink sand in the vial. "He's gone to Mione."

"It's the closest he has remaining to a childhood home." He drizzled some of the sand into his palm. "This will leave you on the beach. I trust you'll figure out the rest on your own."

Junus emptied his handful onto the floor, muttering something about having to sweep afterwards, and stepped back. "May the stars guide you, *Keeronae.*"

"And may Ajle keep you safe, Junus. Thank you."

There were no stars to guide me where I emerged. I was on the beach in Mione, all right, with the beautiful, glistening pink sand pelting and scratching my exposed skin, and fierce storm winds churning sea foam and saltwater into caustic spray that doused me thoroughly. The heavy rain saturated me wherever the saltwater missed.

I looked up at the thick storm clouds, blotting out the stars and moonlight that would have lit my way. Over the howl of the wind and waves, I could barely hear my own voice, as I screamed my frustration into the darkness. *Ajle is not going to make this easy.*

I tried to pick up the sweet scent of the wild roses that grew around Sarc's house, but all I could smell was the saltspray burning my nostrils. I picked my way inland, trying to remember the path from the last time I had been there, and trying to compose something clever to say. I finally spied a bluish light, bright and steady, shining not too far away. *That would be a magical light; regular lamps and candles don't glow like that.*

I was shivering uncontrollably with icy damp and fatigue when I reached Sarc's door, still without a clue about what to say when—

The door opened, and Sarc looked surprised. "'Fleece?"

"Y-you d-d-didn't say good-bye," I managed, my teeth chattering. *Not my best moment.*

Sarc found a blanket and wrapped me in it, ushering me inside and shutting the door. "By Ajle, I told Junus I was coming back. See?" He showed me a tiny stone trinket he had tucked in his pocket. "Jeysen lent me his key to Ruvyna."

Junus, you frejyk bastard. "H-h-he didn't tell me that part."

"*Hilafra.* I wouldn't have left without saying anything to you," he said, guiding me to his black brocade chair in front of the fireplace, glowing hot with the magical blue flame that had guided me to his doorstep. "Let me get you some tea."

I shed my gloves and cloak to warm myself by the fire. "I think maybe

Junus was tired of playing host and wanted to reclaim his privacy and space."

"That sounds like Junus." Sarc brought me a steaming cup of fragrant tea and took a seat on the edge of the low table next to me. "You're soaked through," he noted, reaching for my hair to dry it.

I shied from his hand. "I reek of animals and saltwater. I need to wash."

He brushed my damp hair back from my face. "You're still beautiful," he said, and kissed me before I could react. "But I know what you mean. I was wearing the uniform for so long that it felt like it had fused to me. I'll get a bath ready for you."

As he got to his feet, I noticed that he was back in his civilian clothing: soft, smooth fabrics that closely draped his lean form. "That looks comfortable … and clean … dry, too."

Sarc laughed. "Come on upstairs. I'll draw the bath, and you can help yourself to anything in my closet."

In the corner of Sarc's room stood a large porcelain tub that had definitely not been there the last time. Sarc had asked Slither to check on the house while it stood vacant, and Slither had taken advantage of Sarc's absence to make some surprise renovations.

I rejoined Sarc downstairs after my bath, and he stopped in the middle of pouring tea to watch me cross the room to him, He nearly overfilled the cups in his distraction.

"Is something wrong?" I stood in front of him and looked down at the linen shirt that I borrowed from his closet. "Am I missing something?"

"No, nothing's wrong," he swallowed. "Well, there is something missing." He gestured for me to turn around, and when I did, he looped my silver locket around my neck. He swept my hair back from my nape to let the locket ribbon and the shirt collar lie flat, and he kissed me lightly where his fingers had grazed my skin.

"Yes, I was missing that." Already warmed and relaxed from the bath, I was ready to melt into a puddle, and I leaned back into him, letting him wrap his arms across my midriff. "What do we do now?"

The heat of his hands warmed my skin through the thin fabric, and as his lips brushed my ear, he broadcast all sorts of thoughts to me. "I have some ideas. You'd have to be more specific." He spun me around in his arms. "Or, just show me."

I kissed him, deeply, and locked my arms around him. He smelled of cypress, juniper and cedar, as always, and I wanted to lose myself in it, in him. "I've wanted you before I even realized who you were. I want you to stay with me, Sarc. I need you to stay in my life." I took a risk in saying it aloud, and I could feel that he savored hearing the words from me.

But while his embrace tightened, his breath was a melancholy sigh. *I must be out of my mind to say this, but…* "What if I told you that I can't stay? Would you still want this, with me?"

Yes, I wanted to cry. If all I had was this one night with him, I would take it, and let the memory keep me warm in the decades or centuries ahead. *No, I deserve an explanation.* "You fulfilled your obligation, so now you're leaving, and we go our separate ways after tonight?"

I started to push against him, so we could speak without his presence affecting me so profoundly, but he held firm. "No, it will never be like that! I've loved you since I was a boy, *Ajle'xon,* and my feelings won't change, ever. I am your guardian for life, and I will always come when you need me, but there are things happening that I can't change or fix, if I stay here."

Hilafra, Glory was right about him. He really does think he has to save the world. "Who said anything about staying in the New Realm, or the United Realm, or whatever this blasted kingdom is going to be called?" I grabbed his collar and resisted the urge to shake him. "If I had to bounce back and forth between Moonteyre, the Fringe, Altaier, Ruvyna, Adelleen, and so forth, I would lose my sanity in less than a year. Frost doesn't expect me to stay here, and neither does anyone else."

"So, what are you asking of me?"

"Stay with me," I repeated. "By my side, or with me at yours." I kissed him again, more ardently. "Or not. Think about it, and let me know in the morning. If you leave without giving me an answer, I'll have to hunt you down for it."

"Traveling the world with my vengeful and deadly princess, that is a tempting offer," he mused. "And this does feel very nice, too," he admitted, "but also very wrong. You feel so soft and warm, and it wouldn't take much for me to give in, but I can also tell you're exhausted to the point of delirium, and there's also more that you should know about me before we go any further."

"Are you actually rejecting me, Sarc?" I pouted. He was right; my recent trials had left me starving and sleep-deficient, but somehow his chivalrous rebuff pained me more.

"The offer to share your bed tonight, yes, for your own sake," he said. *By Ajle, I'll regret that.* He lifted me easily and carried me upstairs, letting me rest my head in the crook of his neck to inhale his scent. "I'll think about the rest of it."

Gingerly, he lay me down in the center of his bed, and I knitted my hands behind his neck to keep him with me. "'Fleece, you need to rest. I give you my word, you'll have your answer in the morning. *Hilafra,* you're strong!" he laughed, unable to free himself.

"Just stay a while," I said. "I've missed having you close and hearing your voice."

Sarc covered me with the blanket and stretched out on the bed next to me, keeping the quilted layers between us. "What kind of bedtime story can I tell you, to send you off to sleep?"

I leaned my head against his arm. "Tell me about my mother?"

"There's a lot to tell. She kept a journal, which I gave to Frost before I left Moonteyre today. For now, I'll start from the beginning." He tucked the blanket around my shoulders. "Once upon a time, there was a princess named Aelora," he began. "She was a miracle, in so many ways. The Empress had tried to conceive for so many years that she had almost given up hope, but then, Aelora arrived. She was kind and beautiful..."

"Was she smart?" I asked drowsily.

"The smartest child of her age, boy or girl. She was everything a future Empress should be, but she had a secret. She could read feelings in other people, and she knew that it scared them..."

I listened as long as I could until sleep finally overtook me.

That night, for the first time in my life, I dreamed of my mother.

###

Thank you for taking the journey with me!

If you enjoyed this story, won't you please take a moment to leave me a review or a note? There is more to tell, so please stay in touch.

Thanks again for reading!

Ande Li

Clyara's Map

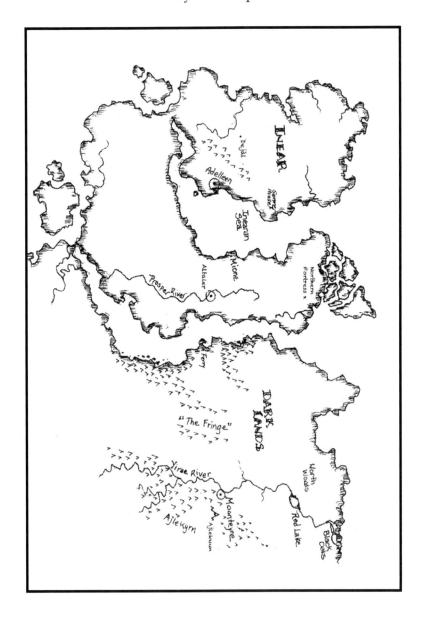

About the Author

Ande spent her childhood in Hong Kong, China, and the various boroughs of NYC, and has settled in the NJ suburbs with her husband and co-conspirator Maurice X. Alvarez, their children, their free-range budgie and exquisitely patient mix-breed dog.

She will not stop writing until all her imaginary friends have had a chance to tell their stories.

Discover other titles by Ande Li
    The Trouble with Thieves (co-written with Maurice X. Alvarez)

Connect with Me!
    Follow me on Twitter: https://twitter.com/andeliauthor
    Friend me on Facebook: https://www.facebook.com/ande1
    Subscribe to my blog: http://wearywondrous.wordpress.com
    Favorite me at
Smashwords: https://www.smashwords.com/profile/view/andeli

Made in the USA
Middletown, DE
26 September 2018